Vaccine: The Cull

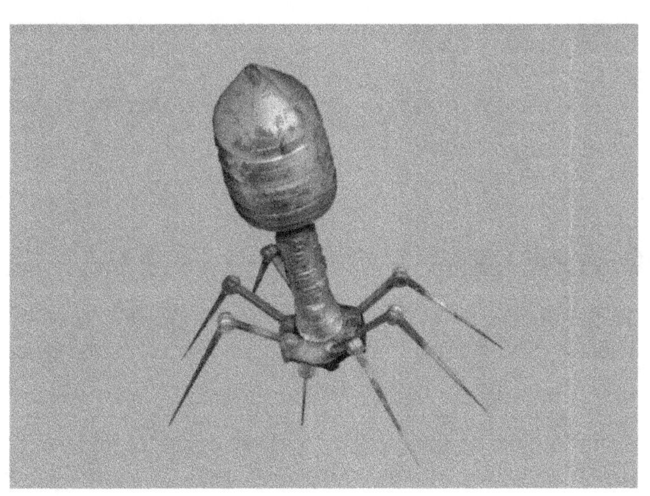

Vaccine: The Cull
Nae-Née Wasn't Enough
By Stephanie C. Fox, J.D.

Have you ever read a dystopian novel in which you wondered how the world as we know it collapsed?

Well…this novel explains that.

Most apocalypse stories begin sometime in the future, after the devastation has been wrought.

Not this one.

This one lets you watch the horror unfold.

After the U.N. population treaty implemented a policy of world-wide use of the birth control nanite, Nae-Née, human-caused stressors on the ecosystem literally heated up.

No longer was our planet on the brink of collapse due to biodiversity loss, rising sea levels, floods, droughts, overdependence on fossil fuels, and the climate changes that drive all that.

No – collapse was upon us at last.

The measures taken to handle resource shortages right in everyone's backyards are shown: a population cull hidden in a vaccine, and a militarized surveillance society to manage the overflow.

Vaccine: The Cull

Nae-Née Wasn't Enough

Stephanie C. Fox, J.D.

QueenBeeBooks

Bloomfield, Connecticut, U.S.A.

Library of Congress Cataloging-in-Publication Data
Name: Fox, Stephanie C., author.
Title: Vaccine: The Cull – Nae-Née Wasn't Enough / Stephanie C. Fox.
Description: Connecticut: QueenBeeBooks, [2015].
Identifiers: ISBN: 978-0-9996395-2-8 (paperback)
Subjects: FICTION / Science Fiction / Hard Science Fiction. NATURE / Environmental Conservation & Protection. LAW / Government / General.

www.queenbeeedit.com

Cover design by Stephanie C. Fox
Cover Illustration by Steve Palmerton

This is story is a work of fiction.

Any similarity to persons living or dead
is purely coincidental.

The names, characters, and incidents
have all been created to build an engaging plot.

Also by Stephanie C. Fox

Nae-Née
– Birth Control: Infallible,
With Nanites and Convenience for All

New World Order Underwater
The Nae-Née Inventors Strike Back

What the Small Gray Visitor Said

Intrigue On a Longship Cruise

Scheherazade Cat – The Story of a War Hero

An American Woman in Kuwait

Hawai'i – Stolen Paradise:
A Travelogue

Hawai'i – Stolen Paradise:
A Brief History

The Book of Thieves

The Bear Guarding the Beehive

The Slamming Door:
Bone Cancer, Asperger's, and Loss

Elephant's Kitchen
– An Aspergirl's Study in Difference

Almost a Meal – A True Tale of Horror

The Visitor Experience at the Mark Twain House

This story is dedicated to Earth's inhabitants,
both human and others.

I wish that human arrogance of species would cease.

If it did, we might actually survive.

*World population growth is widely recognized within
the Government as a current danger of the highest magnitude
calling for urgent measures...
There is a major risk of severe damage
[from continued rapid population growth]
to world economic, political, and ecological systems and,
as these systems begin to fail, to our humanitarian values.*
-    National Security Study Memorandum 200:
Implications of Worldwide Population Growth for U.S. Security and
Overseas Interests
The Kissinger Report
December 10, 1974 – Declassified December 31, 1980

In a time of universal deceit, telling the truth is a revolutionary act.
- George Orwell

*In order to stabilize world population, we must
eliminate 350,000 people a day.*
- Jacques Yves Cousteau

*Democracy cannot survive overpopulation.
Human dignity cannot survive it.
Convenience and decency cannot survive it.
As you put more and more people into the world,
the value of life not only declines, it disappears.
It doesn't matter if someone dies.
The more people there are, the less one individual matters.*
- Isaac Asimov

*Basically, then, there are only two kinds of solutions
to the population problem.
One is a "birth rate solution," in which we find ways
to lower the birth rate.
The other is a "death rate solution," in which ways to
raise the death rate – war, famine, pestilence – find us.*
-- _Paul Ehrlich_, *The Population Bomb*

Table of Contents

One person's utopia is everyone else's dystopia.

No one seems to have a viable solution to human overpopulation and the pressure that it puts on the planet's ecosystem.

We humans are an invasive species, using up the Earth's resources at a rate that it cannot keep pace with, and so we are currently experiencing an age in which other species are being depleted at a rate that qualifies as the sixth mass extinction ever detected on our planet.

In just half a millennium, we have lost 322 species, and another 20,000 are at risk.

So what, some say. Let's live for today. Let the next generation deal with it.

Others simply disbelieve the science, pointing to religion over logic, preferring the mythological fairy tale that some divine entity granted humans primacy over all other species, to do with as we please.

That selfish idea is at the root of it all.

Oh, but if only we humans would ALL do as we should, we would have a sustainable future for as many of us as we wish to procreate, others say. Since when have ALL humans EVER done that?!

Never, that's when.

This is why I say that no one, no matter how logical and carefully thought out their idea, has yet come up with a viable solution to this problem.

Hence the Orwellian solution that the United Nations pushed through on December 21, 2012, the date that conspiracy theorists had so loved to promote as a harbinger of doom. Why not? Might as well choose that date!

The solution was to co-opt the voluntary nanobotic birth control device that my husband and I had created (I thought of the idea, he made it a reality), called Nae-Née, whose name translates from the Scottish-French as "Not-Born." Now every woman on the planet had one, tracked by government computers. Constant surveillance of our fertility was the implemented "solution".

We had made a tremendous financial profit on it before that happened, paid back my father for his start-up funding in patent fees and legal assistance, advertising, and so on. After that, we had gone on to enjoy life for a while.

But...then the effects of anthropogenic – human-caused – climate change began to be felt. Life changed even more drastically as sea levels rose dramatically, with more people existing on less land.

Chapter 1

Nae-Née Wasn't Enough

In many ways, the world around me looked the same, but it felt different. It felt like it was…contracting.

That gave me a steady sense of anxiety, which came with a slight shortness of breath.

The best I could do when that feeling hit – which usually happened after reading, listening to, or watching the news – was to think of something else. Playing my violin helped. So did writing. The music let me escape into the movies, and books-in-progress let me concentrate on whatever topic I was researching. There were plenty; I was always curious about something.

Another option was to watch a movie, preferably a science fiction one that presented an optimistic view of humanity in the future, such as any movie in the *Star Trek* universe. That helped until I would remember that we were experiencing the sixth mass extinction of species that our planet has undergone. Good times!

Sea level had indeed contracted the amount of land on which Americans and people all over the rest of the planet had to live. Temperatures had gone up by four degrees and were rising. Growing seasons were fluctuating, which made it tough to know when to plant crops.

When the oceans had risen, my husband, Hamish James MacDonall, and I, Avril Antoinette Châtelet, had returned to my parents, and our two cats, Spock and Eowyn, who got along okay. Back to his wife's old room…a son-in-law's dream! It was now August of 2015.

We had plenty to do. Hamish was busy with other medical and nanobotic inventions. Some were aimed at improving human health, particularly in the immune, nervous, and cardiac systems. I was implementing our own sustainable living and farming practices, things that people with a bit of land to grow anything on could do on their own. The idea was not to have to rely on a huge, decaying infrastructure to move foods around, but rather to grow them closer to home.

Our greenhouse and the gardens in our yard were a good distraction as I learned how to make herbs, fruits, and flowers grow. The greenhouse was easier than the yard, but I was managing to produce my favorite, raspberries (very important!), some strawberries, avocadoes, and even some heirloom tomatoes in a bright, sunny patch of what was once our lawn, and those were particularly difficult to grow. Meanwhile, the greenhouse herbs were a steady, reliable crop.

Despite the fact that I absolutely refused to use any insecticides, we had a steady crop. Instead, I got my exercise by weeding the yard by hand, and Hamish helped me. He too was adamant that no insecticides be used. One remark from anyone about how using them would make our lives easier would set off a lecture from him about non-Hodgkin's lymphoma and other cancers, and with that, the fool would stop. As for me, I wanted to save the bees.

No insecticides were allowed on our lawn. It was no longer a monocrop of perfect green grass blades. That wasn't good for bees. They would starve on nothing but grass. Instead, little wildflowers grew all over it in hues of purple, blue, and yellow. There were dandelions and tiny, wild violets. On the perimeter of the yard and around the house I grew pastel pink peonies, raspberry pink peonies, and lavender and blue irises in the spring. Later in the summer, I had lavender and purple bee balm growing. The latter attracted hummingbirds, which was fun.

I had even experimented with a couple of beehives – the latest model, called top-frame, not Langstroth. It let the bees construct honeycomb themselves, thus varying the sizes of the individual cells. That was better for the hive, because the inner cells could be smaller, with graduated sizes in between, and the largest, most easily reachable in the outer areas of each panel. It enabled the bees to keep mites out, if nothing else. The honey that they produced tasted wonderful, with notes of wildflower and raspberry in it.

It was fascinating to go out into the garden and see the Italian honeybees foraging – those that hadn't taken advantage of the full range of our neighborhood. They were beautiful, tiny animals with fur coats to carry the pollen that they collected. Also in our yard were wild bumblebees, big and black with yellow stripes, and also furry. They never attacked us. We didn't bother them, and they went about their important business of making fruits and flowers grow.

When I was done with all that, I wrote a book about honey bee colony collapse disorder. It had cover art to match its metaphors, and described the problem of a broken government failing to protect the bees against the ultimate enemy: corporations with unbridled greed and leviathan bank accounts to fund ruthless, pressure-pointing lobbyists. These lobbyists were making sure that poison would be used to squeeze money out of every pore of society until the ecosystem finally collapsed, leaving us with no raspberries, flowers, or honey.

After realizing that I was shouting into cyberspace with the strangling sensation that no sound was coming out – this, despite going on Facebook and linking that account to Twitter – I was depressed. I hadn't gone anywhere for years since Hamish and I had driven out of a flooded Manhattan. Neither had he, nor had my parents. Our Greenwich Village firehouse and their Chelsea apartment were still there, watched by Blackout Security, for when we chose to return.

Whenever we went out, we were trailed by Blackout Security guys from a private company. Hamish had hired it Nae-Née first became a social and political issue rather than a merely voluntary birth control device. The United Nations had instituted a global population policy that was helped along by every nation's government except the Vatican's.

We stayed home in Connecticut and watched the world changing on the news. It wasn't pretty, it wasn't neat, and it wasn't reassuring. It was chaos. For now, we were holed up on Stoner Drive. Luckily for us, our converted firehouse was just above sea level, and a massive infrastructure project was changing Manhattan into a modern U.S. version of Venice.

That sounded great if one lived in the northern parts of the planet, away from the "tropics of chaos" where climate change was ruining any chance of farming. Drought and floods were constant, and they either scorched or washed away any human efforts at growing food.

I wish I could say that this was science fiction, but the fact was, I just couldn't.

No one could – not even the naysayers who denied that climate change was real and human-caused for the simple, insupportable reason that they didn't want anything to change. Denial didn't change any fact, but conservatives who wanted big business that made huge profits would say and convince themselves of anything in order to keep those businesses going indefinitely.

Schools and hospitals reported statistics to support that, yet many op-ed writers insisted that the data was skewed, or not reported accurately, or somehow not true. The fact remained that the Nae-Née treaty was achieving its purpose: fewer people were being born everywhere.

But every day, letters and e-mails came to us, imploring us to contact the Birth License Committee of whatever region of the United States and even of other nations on behalf of aspiring parents. They were filing their birth license applications, worried about their chances, and begging us to plead for exceptions for them. We wouldn't do it.

We also got hate mail from angry people who wished that we had never invented the Nae-Née device. The letters and e-mails railed against us, and some contained powders of dubious makeup. That kept Blackout busy, at least.

We had been forced to employ a specially trained letter and package opener to handle these. Blackout Security found him for us; he was an eccentric type with covert ops experience, chemical weapons training, and a bomb-sniffing pet beagle. He worked in a run-down-looking, small house that was covered with vines, located near the intersection of Mountain Road and Farmington Avenue. We had bought it just for the hate mail.

I didn't worry about it anymore.

The past didn't seem so bad; it was the future that scared me.

That was because I had already survived the past.

That was my world now, for the most part, except when I drove out to the health club in Avon, or to Blue Back Square in West Hartford, our home town, to buy whatever I couldn't grow. I also visited the Stop & Shop and Big Y stores.

Yes, our world had contracted, and it was still contracting.

I wanted to go out and see more of it before it contracted any further.

What was going on out there, really?

The news only showed so much, and I suspected that that was partly by design, not merely a by-product of the viewpoint of the newscasters. Liberal, conservative, Libertarian, radical, fringe, whatever…being there would always show more than the confines of a television or computer screen could ever hope to present.

What I needed was a good old-fashioned road trip with my husband, just like the kind that I used to go on with my parents when I was a tween and a teen, and on into my college days. On summer vacations, we used to drive into upstate New York, across Pennsylvania, then on down through the Blue Ridge Mountains and into the South to see places like Thomas Jefferson's Monticello, Colonial Williamsburg, and the monuments in Washington, D.C. There was one other place that I had not seen before, however, and was determined to check out this time. It was the Stonehenge of America, and it was in Georgia. More on that later.

A trip like that ought to reveal something of what was different about America, something more than what I was seeing in the news. I decided to plan and it and to insist that Hamish stop working in his lab at Blue Black Square and come with me.

If he didn't want to go, I would just tell him I was going on my own. That would get him to come with me. Insert evil grin here – no way would he let me go on a long trip by car alone. Once on the road, he would start to enjoy the experience. We would listen to music and notice things, and trade stories that we hadn't shared yet. There was always something new to discuss.

Yes, this would be great – Hamish would see those places for the first time, I would see them again, we would eat in the Trellis Restaurant and enjoy some of the recipes of Chef Marcel Desaulniers, the author of the *Death by Chocolate* cookbook, and tour historic America while seeing how it had changed up close.

We wouldn't spend the whole trip close to the shore, but we would spend some of it there, and thus see how the land had changed, and see how people were managing. We would go as far as Florida, or…what used to be the northern part of it. At that point, we would have to turn back.

Damn humans. We are an invasive species.

We just suck up and use up every resource we come across, with reckless abandon and little or no thought for the future. We are foolish, short-term thinkers rather than careful, long-term planners. There were too many of us on the planet now, with no natural checks on our numbers.

We had defeated so many of the diseases that used to keep our species numbers down via sanitation, vaccines, and personal hygiene. As a result, we resorted to unnatural checks on our population. Well, one check: Nae-Née, the birth control nanite that contained a life-time supply of the French abortion drug RU486. It contained a sensor that detected hormone levels in a woman's body, gauging whether or not there was a pregnancy in her uterus. If so, it released a dose. A doctor monitored the device.

Now the government monitored it, too, via a network of Operators who sat at remotely located facilities in undisclosed locations around the nation. The United Nations, with its concerns about sustainability, watching as ever-expanding numbers of resource-devouring humans stamped our carbon footprint on the Earth, saw to that.

It seemed like a decent solution, one that would not involve genocide to bring our numbers down – just crushing disappointment to many who wanted children. Governments would control the Nae-Née nanites. Birth licenses would be granted to less than forty percent of couples who passed the psychological and economic review portions of the applications.

It seemed a lot better than a resource war to me. Any artificial effort to bring down our numbers without murder seemed better to me. A resource war would be Nature correcting itself for over-reproduction of our species. It would also involve mass deaths by murder. No thanks.

That treaty seemed like a good solution to the problem of feeding ourselves.

News and opinion pieces were routinely laced with words and phrases like "sustainability" and "smart growth". If we would just manage our land and resources properly, the thinking went, there ought to be enough of them for everyone.

That was quite the opposite from political cartoons and social commentary in the funny papers. It was routine to see strips about how our species is the one that needs to be culled rather than deer, bears, and other species deemed "invasive" simply because we humans had invaded their territory to build more houses for our own.

That may be true, but how to change that situation other than legally sanctioned murder? It was an ethical conundrum with no moral solution. There could be no compromise on that. People had to have their lives to live once born. The only acceptable answer was to birth fewer humans.

My interest in – no, my morbid fascination with – this topic had led me to gather collect and save virtual political cartoons and comic strips to my computers, plus articles, and to buy many books. I was a data junkie on human overpopulation and on the areas that it affected: ecosystem collapse; fossil fuel and nuclear fission use with their consequences and dangers; insecticides and fungicides; and of course rising sea levels, floods, and drought now that New York City and the rest of the planet's coastlines had become inundated and permanently sunken underwater.

I knew the problem well by now.

It was still a problem, despite the fact that Nae-Née was now a global policy. The damage had been done, our species still existed in vastly higher numbers than our planet could comfortably or even reasonably support, even with this humane reduction measure in place.

It was mid-morning, and I had walked around the house and garden, checking everything. I had played my violin for a while. Breakfast eaten, coffee drunk, cats fed and petted. Like a fly drawn to a spider's web, I felt drawn back to my computer to surf the World Wide Web.

There were various websites that one could visit to look at population "clocks" in one format or another, and I visited them all to study the numbers, and then again to stare in fascination. Despite Nae-Née, death rates were not outpacing birth rates as yet. We could thank medical technology and nutritional education for that.

Hurray for the miracles of modern medicine and all that, but I and plenty of other people did not want to live like sardines, stacked high in skyscrapers in an urban environment to accommodate us all. That was natural enough, and I didn't feel guilty for seeking that sense of independence.

Once again, I took a tour of those population clocks on the Internet.

The one maintained by the U.S. Census Bureau provided a large display that focused on U.S. population on the left, and world population on the left: http://www.census.gov/popclock/. It said that the U.S. currently had over 324 million people living in it, with the precise number at 324,256,942 and counting. Wow. It broke that down to list births, deaths, and increases due to border crossings. Immigration was pushing our numbers up also.

Hamish had sent me a link via e-mail that led to a conspiracy site, and I clicked it. It said that massive depopulation was in store, though it didn't say how, by 2025. That wasn't all that far off. It got specific for the U.S., kind of: by that year, the U.S. would have EITHER 69 million people in it OR 69 million less people in it. That seemed a bit vague, but 69 million was still a huge number. It was just a link, though, with no measurable or verifiable proof to consider.

I went back to the world population clocks, looking next at the one for Worldometers: http://www.worldometers.info/population/. It presented various options, and I clicked on the one to see the planet's total on one page. When I did that, I saw a seemingly endless backdrop of human stick figures, like wallpaper, below the ever-increasing numerical one: 7,352,655,984. That was a bit disappointing by having such succinct and limited information. I wanted more.

The third site I visited was the best one. It was maintained by the Education and Health Development Foundation: http://www.eahdfoundation.org/world_live_clock.php. This one was highly detailed, and unless one clicked on a particular category, it continuously rotated from one to the next to the next. It started off with the planet's total human population, which was always whatever it was and counting, and since several minutes had passed since I had looked at the previous one, this number was higher: 7,363,890,306. Odd…the 3 sites were not in sync.

This clock's categories were as follows: 1. Intro, with a total plus births and deaths listed below that; 2. Population, both by Demographic, which meant the above-listed categories plus a breakdown by age groups, and by Region, with listings for North America (U.S. and Canada), Europe (United Kingdom and Russian Federation included here), Asia (highlighting China and India), Africa, Latin America, and Oceania (to cover all Pacific Island nations plus Australia and New Zealand); Mortality by Injury, Infectious Disease, Non-Communicable Illnesses, and Other Causes (such as nutritional deficiencies and childbirth); Illness, both by Disease and Injury, complete with a list of them. I love data – the more the better! I was a data junkie, in fact.

Interestingly, this same clock had categories about other things, factors that led to ecosystem collapse, which was why this was the clock that I preferred to the others. The categories were: Environment, with an IPCC (Intergovernmental Panel on Climate Change) Global Warming Projected Anomaly section at the top that dealt with expected overall planetary temperature increases, and under that other listings for CO_2 emissions and concentration, overall sea level rise since 2000, extinctions, deforestation, and desertification; Energy by Fuels and Electricity with fossil fuel and renewable sources listed in each section; Food by type; Economy, complete with Gross World Product (GWP), Global Public Debt (GPD), Global Taxes, Military Expenditures, and right at the top, U.S. National Debt – all in the quadrillions, not the trillions; and Crime, broken down by type and the costs it incurred to societies.

After all that, probably just to cheer up visitors to the site, it actually included a category entitled ☺ Smile – it isn't all bad news! The listing for Divorces in the U.S. belied that title, but several were cheerful enough: First Kisses; Marriages in the U.S.; Beer Produced; and Wine Production. Some inclusions were dubious: Servings of Coca Cola Consumed (that stuff was corrosive – it could clean battery acid off of car parts, and I had always been revolted by it even before I knew that);

and Cars Produced (like we needed to consume more metals and glass, and generate more plastics!). Google Searches…that was interesting…and Google Searches for the "World Clock" rounded it out, with that last number at a rather pitifully disinterested 11,761,618.

Clearly Nae-Née wasn't shrinking our species' numbers at any great pace, I concluded.

What else would get the job done but such an evil act as a species cull?

No…that was too crazy. No one would do that, I told myself, and moved on.

I foresaw more research in my immediate future. Foresight wasn't much help just now as to what topics to delve into, but I would talk to Hamish and keep track of changing conditions to figure that out. Whatever I had to learn about in order to understand the plans of the proverbial powers-that-be, I knew it wouldn't be pleasant. I'd better have fun on adventures with Hamish now while I still could, I realized.

With these disturbing thoughts, I got up from my computer, went downstairs, paused to pet each cat on the way, walked out the back door, and paced around the garden for a few minutes.

Hamish was in his basement laboratory here at home for the day, or so I thought. I decided to go down there and see what he was doing, and announce our travel plan. I did, and he was out. Damn…just when I had an exciting announcement to make! Oh well. I had forgotten that Dad had dropped him off at his lab in Blue Back Square.

Now what? Back upstairs. I paced around a bit. What was I going to do next? Drive over to the lab and talk to Hamish? No. I could tell him all this later. We could go out to dinner, just the two of us. This could wait until then. It was Monday morning, and I was done with my entire routine, including reading the newspaper. Everything that might delay me from moving on to the next item on my agenda was done. I paused and spaced out for a moment, needing to relax.

There was no point in being in such a rush to do each and every single thing that came to mind as soon as it came to mind. It would all get done; I wouldn't forget any of it. A nagging feeling that I had to be doing useful, meaningful research and writing at all times was spoiling my ability to relax and think calmly. It was ridiculous. I did myself no favors by living like this.

I still had to plan the whole trip on the Internet, looking up every last detail, and book hotels and bed-and-breakfast rooms anyway. Meanwhile, I had other things that had already been scheduled to do later on in the afternoon. But that was later.

It was mid-morning, and time to do…nothing. Time to breathe and relax, not sit in front of the Internet, waiting for it to show me something a little more soothing, a thing it most certainly would not do.

So, what next? A movie: I put on *Star Trek: Into Darkness*, the one with the terrorism theme, and settled in to enjoy the hilarious chase scene that it opened with. Soon I was laughing at Dr. McCoy's complaints, and talking to the screen, telling Spock to stop being such an Aspie.

The Spock in my own world, my gray Chartreux cat, walked in as he heard his name. He was followed by Eowyn, the tortie female that Hamish and I had adopted. She looked almost completely black in the dimmed living room, lit only by the flickering movie. Eowyn mrrowed at me; Spock looked like he was saying, "What? Why were you calling me?"

I grinned and said, "Not you, feline Spock – I'm talking to Spock the Vulcan, for whom you are named. Let me watch," I said, turning back in time to see the volcanic charge go off. The cats leaped onto their favorite spots on the poufy back of the sofa and curled up, losing interest. Good. The music turned up and I felt more cheerful already, as its uplifting tune rang out louder and more triumphant with each note.

Some time went by like this, all the way to the part where Kirk and Khan were in space suits going over Earth's orbit, across to the dreadnaught ship, when my mother came home, accompanied by Aunt Zoe and her younger sister Mindy.

Great.

Mindy always treated me like a kid, even though we were the same age, and in our forties. It was irritating. At least now I knew what it was about: neurotypical (NT) snobbery. That obnoxious attitude of some but not all NTs was that their way of perceiving and relating to others was the correct way. They thought so simply because the NT brainstem was the majority model of human brainstem.

Not all NTs had this attitude, but Mindy did, and I had no use for it. At least Aunt Zoe didn't share it. Aunt Zoe had never treated me like that. Too bad a few spoiled the image of the rest. The fact was that we Aspies were mentally enabled in ways that NTs were disabled, and vice versa, so there was no reason for either of us to be snobby toward the other.

Now that I had finally researched and read and watched enough to understand that – plus thought a great deal about it and chatted on Facebook with other Aspies – I was having none of it. We on the autism spectrum with Asperger's could express ourselves quite well, thank you very much. We had more connectors on our brainstems than NTs did, and those connectors went in many more directions.

I was happy to pay with the disability aspect of being an Aspie that manifests as difficulty navigating social interactions in exchange for a mental super-power of intense focus and highly detailed interests. It had certainly served me well as an editor, researcher, author, and inventor. Also, as an Asperwoman in my forties, I had plenty of data stored in my brain from past social interactions, so those were getting easier, and mortifying gaffes were fewer and farther between.

At least Mindy didn't have any of her many kids with her. They were unhappy kids, always vying for her attention, and not very successfully. Mindy loved babies and toddlers, and had reproduced several times in order to prolong her time with that age group rather than get a job with preschoolers, which would have accomplished that.

Only the Nae-Née policy had stopped her. It was like a tax penalty on reproduction, with its hefty application fees. Without it, Mindy would have gone on having kids. Her husband, Jack, had a lucrative insurance job and could afford to fund this predilection. He was the executive vice president of corporate counsel to one of Hartford's many insurance groups.

She was Mrs. Jack Long, and I had had a bit of fun telling her not to sign credit slips that way – because that's forgery. "Sign Mindy Long," I had told her.

She did. It was one memory of many interactions with her in which she didn't act like I was a silly kid. Those were getting fewer, thankfully. Staring steadily at her while saying little was an Aspie trait that put a damper on that, and I enjoyed knowing that my quiet observation could make her a bit nervous.

Hey, whatever it took to shut that down was fine by me, even if she found me creepy. That assessment was, I had found out when I pressed her on the subject, due to my steady gaze. When I was listening and observing, I stared, and we Aspies don't blink nearly as much as NTs do. The whole idea made me laugh whenever I thought about it. Why should I care how someone who patronized me felt about my demeanor?!

I put the movie on pause and said "hi" to everyone.

"What are you watching?" my mother asked.

I told her.

"How many times have you seen that one?" Aunt Zoe asked.

I grinned. "Maybe fifteen, maybe more." Why should I apologize for it?! I loved it.

Mindy rolled her eyes. "I thought that science fiction was for guys."

"You would think so," I said, rolling mine and grinning at her. Come on, snobby NT, I thought, push it and I'll push back. At last, I know what to say. "I've got news for you: Aspie guys aren't the only ones who love *Star Trek*, *Star Wars*, *Dr. Who*, *The Lord of the Rings*, and other fun stuff. We Aspergirls and Asperwomen love it too. After all, it's not just guys who invent and create and discover things. Marie Curie won the Nobel Prize in both Physics and Chemistry, and she showed many of the markers of being on the autism spectrum."

Mindy looked at me, exasperated. This was fun! She was playing right into it. She said, "But all that stuff is so immature. When are you going to grow up and like more adult things?"

"Never," I said with a grin. "Well...I suppose I could stop enjoying it, act like a robot, let that part of me that feels intense thrills of enjoyment die, and stop losing myself in the world of whatever story, but why should I? You make growing to adulthood sound like death. No thanks."

She had no suitable answer to that, and my mother and aunt looked sold on what I was saying, so she didn't push it.

I grinned again and added, "Maturity is grossly overrated. I also love the Asperwoman author Jane Austen's books made into movies: *Pride & Prejudice*...any version has its attractions...*Sense & Sensibility* with its opening scene that reminds me of my trusts and estates class in law school, *Mansfield Park* showing an author of fiction as she gets her writing career going and gets married to her best friend. They're all favorites of mine, and I'm sure any neurotypical would approve. I also love the E.M. Forester story, *A Room with a View*, which is billed as the most romantic movie ever made, complete with opera diva Dame Kiri Te Kanawa singing in it, don't you?"

"I don't know that one," Mindy said.

"It's right here," I replied, pulling it out of the bookcase. "Aren't you free for hours, with all of your kids at day care or school?" What was I doing, offering to watch this with her? She was usually so condescending. Oh yeah…she was a relative, Aunt Zoe's sister.

"Why not?" she said, sitting down on the sofa next to me, careful not to disturb Eowyn.

My mother and Aunt Zoe headed into the kitchen. My mother actually smiled at me.

Mindy was not someone with whom I would ever have been great friends, but I could manage when necessary. The problem was not entirely about Mindy herself, thought that was certainly part of it.

No, it was with parents in general. I just didn't trust them. They would insist that people not say certain things around their little darlings, but it was like a game with the deck stacked against everyone else. What that meant was simply that you never knew what was not to be said until after it was said. Then the parents would give you scathingly nasty, censorious looks. That was why, whenever someone had announced a pregnancy, I had always pulled away from them emotionally and socially. So did Hamish, for that matter. No wonder we were soul mates.

The movie started, and Mindy did indeed get quite caught up in it, as did I, yet again. We watched the whole thing, and ate lunch on the sofa. My mother brought it to us, and went back to the kitchen to eat and chat with Aunt Zoe.

When it was over, Mindy commented that the story was a very nice one and said that she had enjoyed it.

"Good! I'm glad you liked it."

"When did it take place?"

"1910. Just before the world went to hell in the First Great War, also known as World War I. Movies and stories tend to be about nothing heavy or alarming in such times – the calm before the storm. We're about due for another big one, though who knows exactly how or what it will be like, or how soon. I'm thinking soon, though."

She stared at me, horrified. "Such a nice movie, and then that thought."

"Indeed. I'm always thinking that things can't stay nice if they are nice. I don't like to be startled by the change when it comes."

With one last look at me, she went to get her sister.

After Mindy and Aunt Zoe left, my mother actually complimented me on how I had handled the encounter with Mindy. I rather enjoyed that. "You know who you are, and you don't let any NT clique-type intimidate you. I'm proud of you," she told me. I hugged her.

Then I said, "Let's see if you're still saying that later. A reporter from *The Hartford Courant* wants to ask me some questions about Nae-Née. She's meeting me in West Hartford Center later this afternoon."

My mother just grinned.

"What?"

"Oh, I know you'll say something shocking and enjoy doing so. Have fun."

I stared at her for a moment, then got my handbag and headed out. We were due to meet in a half hour at La Petite France, on Farmington Avenue. The place was never crowded, and it offered French pastries and good coffee.

After parking and seeing the Blackout guys who had followed me from home to the Center settle into a spot not far behind me (somehow, they managed to find an empty space to parallel park in, never an easy feat there), I got out and walked over to the café.

I liked it in there. La Petite France had a bookcase full of French books and a French dictionary (not that I needed it much), and comfortable chairs to sit in by the window. Flouting Blackout's admonition not to sit close to the window, I chose a spot in the corner next to the bookcase where I could watch when the reporter walked in. I put my sweater where I wanted to sit and got in line at the counter.

The reporter had described herself as a fortysomething woman with a dishwater-blonde ponytail whose name was Deanna Holland. I was early, so I got myself a café au lait and a raspberry madeleine cookie while I waited for her.

Two of the Blackout guys were hot on my heels, and bought coffee.

I tried to act as though I wasn't with them, which, technically, I wasn't. No need to freak out the reporter by drawing attention to the private security detail that Hamish insisted I have each and every time I left the house.

Halfway through the treats, she showed up, wearing a lavender running suit with a large, black bag slung over her shoulder. It looked big enough for a laptop, and sure enough, it was. Well, this was fun! I would see how she worked. Stuff like that always fascinated me. I loved to find out how people in different professions worked. Granted, she was just one journalist, but the laptop didn't seem like a unique tool. Now to be careful what I said to her…

…while still saying what I really thought. That laptop had a camera. Every word I said would be recorded and saved for analysis and edits later. Perhaps some unfair edits would be part of those edits, I mused.

She got right to it after getting a café au lait and a lemon madeleine cookie. I guess she wanted to seem friendly and relaxing, but I knew she would do her best to induce me to say something controversial and eminently quote-worthy.

Oddly enough, I looked forward to it. What fun is life when it is bland and without any controversy? I was already the bitch who had co-invented the world's birth control nanite, so why not own it? Well…own it figuratively as well as literally…without apology. Why should I feel apologetic?! It wasn't my idea to make its use compulsory. I had intended it as a safe, voluntary, device of convenience, not the reverse.

Deanna was amiable enough, and one of the most glaring questions she had for me turned out to be about the Catholic Church and the Pope. Huh…I didn't care if the clerics didn't like me. I was an atheist, annoyed by patriarchal religions. Wicca was more my speed. It had a goddess and cared about Nature and the ecosystem rather than about using up whatever Nature had to offer, as if we humans were entitled to it. Keep that up and we'd have nothing and die horribly in a resource conflict! I told her so when she asked.

"But what were your thoughts when the Vatican refused to sign on to the Nae-Née treaty? And about the comments that the Pope and the Cardinals at U.S. dioceses made about how Nae-Née can be equated with voluntary sterilization? The Catholic Church is against that. What do you have to say about that?"

I smiled. "Of course the Catholic Church is against that. I have no fear of excommunication by a bunch of aging male virgins, as I never went through with confirmation rituals. Once I realized that they were all about controlling people, and that women are edited out of any real power or say over policy within that organization, and that enjoyment of sex is considered sinful, I refused to do anything more about it. My parents didn't push it, either. We aren't religious. I married someone who agrees with me on that, too."

Deanna did a good job of concealing whatever emotional reaction she had to that.

She pressed on. "So are you an atheist?"

Yes. I don't care what a bunch of men who want to control others think. I will not go to a church and listen to them talk, either. I'm like my father: a heretic who goes to church for the music," I summed up with a grin.

She looked nonplussed, then asked about my parents. "My mother was raised Catholic, but it seems to be more about culture than belief with her. My father joined St. John's Episcopal Church when he moved here, because he likes the music. It has a pipe organ and a talented choir. I only go when he goes, actually."

"What about Hamish?"

"Hamish was raised Scottish Presbyterian, but he's like the rest of us – not religious. He won't let any pastor, vicar, priest, whatever, tell him what to think or how to feel. We're all independent like that."

"What do you believe in, if not a higher power?"

I grinned. "I believe in the Higgs-Boson particle...and in the U.S. Constitution. It grants us both freedom OF religion and freedom FROM religion."

"Why are you so down on religion?" she asked me. "I mean, don't get me wrong, I'm not asking this because of some philosophical objection to that type of freedom, but I get the sense that there is something more to it with you."

I smiled. "It's about obedience and the duty to question authority. Religions don't like that."

She typed that into her laptop.

I watched her do so and waited for the next volley of questioning.

"If you are an atheist, are you also a transhumanist?" Deanna wanted to know.

"Oh. Julian Huxley came up with that word – Aldous Huxley's brother. No," I said. "We shall not become Borg, resistance to technocracy is not futile, and we humans are not endowed with the power to transcend Nature and evolution and thus direct it ourselves. A lot of people accuse atheists of being technocrats who wish to do just that, but I'm not one of them."

"You're not?" Deanna queried. She was just drawing me out, I knew. I didn't mind.

I smiled. "You're drawing me out. That's fine. Technology is a fun adventure for what it enables us to do, but it is no substitute for the natural world. I am depressed to sense a great die-off of Nature. That's why I did that book on bees and colony collapse disorder. I want honey and bees and flowers and raspberries."

After a pause for a sip of my coffee, I continued. "I don't want technology INSTEAD of Nature, and I am afraid that we may be heading for that. We should all be afraid of that. If we were, we might be more careful, and perhaps scream and cry less about not being able to abuse technology until that is all that is left to us, and all that still lives."

That wasn't it yet. I was full of thoughts to share on this topic. "Religion got us into this mess by encouraging humans to multiply. That led to a determination to eliminate checks on our population – checks from disease, accidents, wild animals, whatever – and thus fewer deaths. More and more healthy humans living full lifespans and wanting things…and conveniences…led to technology and technocracy, and now here we are, with too much of both."

At last, I summed up: "We need balance. Our society and our ecosystem is way out of balance. Religion is not going to solve that. Technocracy won't solve it. Transhumanism won't. We need a balance that brings us closer to Nature, to save as much of it as we can. Some technology is good, but it should not dominate, nor should religion. And transhumanism will just swing us wildly in another wrong direction, yet again with reckless abandon of independent and critical thought. It seems like just another way to avoid thinking, and I don't like that."

That must have scared her a little, because she paused and gaped at me before typing my answer in. I waited while she did so. At last, taking a deep breath and moving on, she asked me, "What do you have to say to all of the women who are angry about having missed their chance to have children?"

"The same thing that I have to say on my website and on Facebook, which is that no amount of calling me a bitch who seriously needs to die will change the reality of overpopulation with all of its horrid consequences. As much as it may comfort many of them to blame me for not being able to pile on to that problem, I had no role in creating it. Neither did they. None of us asked to be born, after all. The planet's carrying capacity for humans is 2 billion. Before Nae-Née came along it threatened to reach 10 billion, yet with it, we are still way above carrying capacity."

"Tell me about your website, and about what you do on Facebook."

"Okay." I smiled. It was nice that she was asking about that. It's always good to promote one's own work. "I have a personal Facebook page, which I am judicious about accepting Friends with. I have taken advantage of its option to create other pages, and have made two more. One is my author page, entitled Avril Antoinette Châtelet Author Page, on which I post articles that relate to my writing and editing career. The other is for Nae-Née."

"What do you post on your Nae-Née page?"

"Anything that pertains to population issues and growth: birth control, abortion, religious views on freedom of speech and reproduction, other views and articles on reproduction, either natural or via fertility drugs despite the fact that they are now a thing of the past, stuff about honey bee colony collapse disorder, economic and ecosystem collapse, SmartTechnology and its health and privacy hazards, vaccines, Asperger's, autism…quite a laundry list of topics."

"And on your website?"

"On my website, I combine all of that, plus I include some random other issues that pique my interest, and I advertise my books there, with hyperlinks to Amazon and Barnes & Noble sales pages. My books deal with history, herstory, Asperger's, travel, honey bee colony collapse, birth control herstory, and more. I might as well just use the word "herstory" for that last topic, since it is women who have used it most throughout time. The website also functions as a blog."

Deanna smiled. "You keep yourself very busy."

"It is certainly the best cure for boredom or worry about the future."

Deanna suddenly looked a bit sober. She asked, "Are you sure you want me to write about all this? Aren't you going to ask me to not publish some or any of this?"

I looked at her. In what universe would a journalist agree to that, I wondered? "Why would you do that once you've heard an interviewee say anything?" More likely than not, she was just trying to draw me out some more. Fine.

She smiled, then said, "I'm just asking because you are telling me some things that may threaten your safety. Some lunatic could read what you've said to me and come after you."

"Oh, I see. You think that there was ever some chance of safety for me once I co-invented Nae-Née, don't you? Well, there never was. Because I am the one who thought of the concept of Nae-Née – and probably because I am female and thus a convenient target of anger – I am blamed for the world Nae-Née use policy far more than Hamish is, even though he is the one who made it a reality."

I added, "I gave up on the idea of fairness and safety long ago. It doesn't matter that I meant it as a voluntary use product. Few rational thinkers will even care, so I might as well enjoy life on my own terms for as long as I can. Hmm…I fully expect to be misquoted sooner rather than later on that last bit about enjoyment."

Deanna looked alarmed (for show, or for real?) and said, "You won't be misquoted by me."

I gave her a steely smile. "Really? That part about enjoyment? It's not merely enjoying life, but enjoying it on my own terms that I care about. Don't gloss over the fine points if you are really serious about that. At least show me that it will be some reporter who comes after you – someone you don't know – who twists my words."

"I promise," she said.

"Thank you," I replied, wondering how this interview would really look when published. To myself, I thought, we shall see.

Deanna had one other important question for me, which I was happy to answer, because it was often on my mind: "But what about charges that people such as yourself are denying others the chance to have children and denying future generations the chance to enjoy all that your generation was able to enjoy? What do you have to say to them?"

To that one, I replied: "It's not those of us that don't want kids or who invent birth control devices who are doing the denying. It's people who won't study what's happening to our planet and stay informed on those issues. That's how our species and our planet got into this situation, by insisting upon having as many kids as they either wanted or carelessly produced, so that there isn't enough of everything for all."

"This means spots in colleges and universities, fresh fruits and vegetables, and sufficient space to lie in within without being crammed in like sardines in high-rise apartments with a gazillion regulations. It's selfish to want kids at this point. Under those conditions, and it will be under THOSE conditions, they won't have the same life that we ourselves have had access to."

"They will miss out on far too much, and they will know it, feel it, and be emotionally and otherwise crushed by that. I hate the idea of that happening to them. People have no say over whether or not they are born and have to deal with such problems. Aspiring parents ought to think their potential offspring's chance over VERY carefully before reproducing."

She wondered about my direct, articulate, and intractable viewpoint. "You are quite adept at expressing yourself. Clearly, you think a lot. Yet when you interact with people who are new to you, you tend to be quiet and watchful, or so I have been told. Why? Does this have anything to do with being on the autism spectrum, with Asperger's? Do you find that you have difficulty connecting with most people? How do you think you are perceived by most other people?"

Wow. This was getting fun.

"Okay…so you want to know about life as an Aspie. Good." I smiled, ate the last bite of my raspberry madeleine cookie, washed it down with a long sip of café au lait, and stretched. "What sorts of things are you wondering about?"

Deanna gazed at me for a moment, then asked, "Can you read nonverbal cues? Facial expressions? Can you empathize with others? What about eye contact?"

"Oh…this feels very familiar. Nonverbal and social cues are a time-consuming game, and an obnoxious waste of time. Too much of social interaction has been on NT terms. That's why I won't hide or expend enormous amounts of emotional energy on them. I'm busy! I have books to create and a life to live. I won't let people who aren't accepting of Aspies steal that from me. I've been the lonely 20something who wanted friends. Now I'm the unyielding 40something who has a few good friends and I have no time to waste on those who demand nonsense of me."

I wasn't done yet.

"We Aspies have loud voices, steady, nearly unblinking gazes, we don't do up-talk (that thing where a sentence sounds like it ends with a question mark even though it's a sentence), and our personalities tend to grate on some people. As we age and get into our work, we have less and less use for emotional baggage. Maybe neurotypicals – NTs – do too, but I don't speak for them. We are a normal, minority model of normal human, and NTs are a normal majority model. We and they have always existed. Isaac Newton was likely an Aspie, and he had few friends. Thomas Jefferson was likely an Aspie and he did have friends. We are all different. If you've met an Aspie, you've met ONE Aspie. We're all unique."

It was never a quick explanation so I continued.

"Women on the spectrum manifest the condition differently than men do. We tend to make eye contact more, to answer that question. Hamish can just bury himself in work, speak in a confident tone and drone on and on about his work without interruption, and people expect that. For me, a female Aspie, when I do that, I get called rude things such as selfish, loud, bossy, aggressive, and more. I have to tell myself not to care too much because if I do, I will be anxious and accomplish little. That's no way to live. I am not responsible for the happiness of every stranger I encounter. I follow basic polite social niceties, then move on."

"Also, we are not obedient, we do not like what most people like, and we question authority."

"One last point: we Aspies can suffer from too much empathy, not too little. We have heightened sensory awareness, and when we find out all about a particular form of suffering, we think about every detail of it until we suddenly find ourselves feeling very, very upset. But what is it that sets this off? Usually points that the majority do not notice. That's probably what leads us to invent, create, and write things that stands out to humanity. That makes me feel very good about the way that we are. Aspie and proud of it," I summed up.

Deanna actually looked both impressed and intrigued. With that, she thanked me, we gulped the last of our café au lait drinks, and were done. I decided I liked her, as far as journalists went.

I let her walk out first, watching as she headed down Farmington Avenue toward LaSalle, wondering how soon I would read whatever she published. It could be tomorrow, or it could be in a few days. When it happened, I was sure that no matter how fairly she meant to present my words, someone, somewhere, would somehow twist them to their own ends.

After that, I thought, I want a vacation – one that is about exploring and seeing what's changed. I want to take off and look around outside of Connecticut in my car before things get much different…before it's too late to move freely about the nation.

I didn't want to just do this as an armchair tourist from the safety of my computer. I wanted to take my husband with me and see whatever I wanted at my own pace, and trade in the mental geographical layout of the United States that I used to have for the new reality. That new map included sunken beaches, and a whole state, with certain treasures from those areas having been relocated in a mad dash of activity before it was too late.

It was the result of the sea changes that I wanted to see.

I hoped Hamish would agree, and that we would go soon. I was getting less afraid of travel now that a couple of years had passed since it happened, and more and more curious to see it all.

Time to go pick up my husband. I pulled out into traffic and drove down the street to the intersection, turning south on Main Street. This area was home, and I didn't want to move away from it permanently, even if we could return to our Manhattan home.

Passing Kaoud's Oriental Rugs store, I grinned as I thought of my father's response to their family business TV ad. Ten Percent Charlie was one of the two sons, always featured at the end of each ad, after his father and brother. My father liked to joke that he was going to go in there and ask for Sixty Percent Freddie. "Oh, we fire him!" Mr. Kaoud had said when I went in there to buy rugs. Fun, even if it was pure silliness.

Life should have more of that in it.

I could have walked from La Petite France to Jerome Street, but Hamish and the Blackout Security guys would never have gone for that, so I drove around the shops, looking for another parallel parking space. No parking garages; too easy to corner me, they kept warning.

There was an empty space across from Munson's Chocolates, near The Cheesecake Factory. That would do for an impromptu dinner date. I didn't like being told what I could and could not do, so I didn't give Blackout any indication of my plans. Hamish would be the first to know about it. His lab was upstairs in one of the brick buildings of offices in Blue Back Square, just above that restaurant.

The office spaces there were attractive enough in their institutional/corporate décor, and had a nice view of the square that overlooked the library, a Barnes & Noble store, stores. If it wasn't a Thursday, Friday or Saturday, Hamish and I would eat there sometimes.

Hamish had set up his laboratory there, and although he saw some patients, he preferred to work on his nanites and other projects. He was still miffed at having to start almost from scratch on the neuro-nanite project after the initial phase had yielded a weapon and the government had demanded that he sell it for use by N.S.A., the C.I.A., and other agencies.

At last, Hamish was onto the next phase and seeing some tangible results that might do patients some good, such as spinal cord injuries. If he could get the nanites to mimic the functions of normal, healthy nerves, those people might be able to walk and live independently again. His lab was full of visitors who came and went – graduate students, colleagues, and N.I.H. administrators – after seeing whatever of his patented efforts he was ready to show.

I had forbidden him to show anyone anything that wasn't patented.

At first, he had protested, saying that we were now so well off that we would never have to worry again, but that wasn't the point, and I made him sit down and listen. The point was a legal and logistical one. A patent would give him full control over who did what with his work. It would give him some hope of preventing abuses and misuses.

Dad had just sat there, silently watching and listening, waiting for me to do my worst.

I summed up by reminding him that Einstein had been horrified that his $E=mc^2$ equation had been perverted into a nuclear bomb and used as the ultimate weapon in Japan.

That did it; Hamish was sold on the idea. He let Dad patent everything ever after without a murmur. We still trusted Attorney Dad with all of our patents. He was semi-retired, only working on what he liked at this point.

As I parked and got out of the car, I knew that once again, some Blackout guys would watch the car while others trailed me at what they hoped was a not-too-obvious distance. It was hard to ignore them, but I did my best. These guys weren't strangers to me; I had met them all.

Today it was Ed and Aaron walking with me. Once we were inside the building, they stopped pretending not to be with me. "Hi guys," I said. "How did you like La Petite France?"

Aaron was a tall, lanky, dark-haired and grey-eyed guy with a habitual grin and a past with secret, covert military ops. He liked to try any food that came along, and the healthier the better. He also enjoyed gourmet cuisines. He said, "Good lattes."

Ed rolled his eyes and said, "Too fancy. I can live off the land if I have to." Ed was from Kansas, and didn't care about farm fresh or food adventures. Ed had also worked in covert ops, and with Aaron. They had been working together since they graduated from college, and were best friends. I was used to the way they teased each other about everything.

Aaron was from Chicago, and more flexible. He grinned and said, "Philistine! We can both eat whatever comes our way and be tough, but I appreciate the difference between fine dining and junk foods!"

I pressed the elevator button, and it opened right away, so we all got in. I hit the button for the third floor and we rode up there. It was after 6 p.m. and the offices had that early evening, almost-deserted look that comes from a lack of visitors and most of the staff being gone for the day. Hamish was likely in there alone, except for a stray Blackout guy in the waiting area.

The sign on the door looked benign, despite whose office this was and what he worked on.

"MacDonall Laboratories" was all it said. No mention of Nae-Née or nanites. Sometimes, it paid to be low-key, and not to advertise. I opened the door and walked in, trailed by my entourage.

"Hi Jack," I said. Blackout Jack sat in the one corner of the waiting area that provided a view of all entries and exits, just past the door and somewhat out of sight. You had to walk in a few feet to see him.

"Hi Avril." He gave me a polite smile and a nod. He was one of our longest-serving security companions, having followed us around since Hamish first hired them to watch out for us in Manhattan.

Blackout Rick had to be somewhere nearby, mostly likely at the back service door.

I went on into the back, with Ed and Aaron fanning out to case the joint. There were quick and silent about it, as ex-Navy Seals would be. I didn't even see them go back out, and they didn't hover around as I found Hamish working in his back room, tinkering with his nanites. We had ample privacy.

"Hi Hamish!" I said, walking up behind him and hugging him.

"Hey Avril!" he replied, yanking off his magnifying glasses and hugging back.

"I'm taking you out to The Cheesecake Factory for dinner, and plotting a getaway with you," I informed him. "I'm going to kidnap you, and interrupt your work for weeks!"

"Okay. Wait, what? What do you mean?"

"I'll tell you on the way."

"Fine. Let's go." He didn't look happy about what I had just said.

I just grinned and headed for the elevator. "Come on, Hamish. I've got cabin fever. You can't actually have expected me to stay put forever. Let's have a nice dinner together and I'll tell you what I have in mind."

"Fine," he said, following me. "I guess a chat about a getaway is nothing to overreact to."

Over crispy crab bites, fried zucchini, a shared kale and quinoa salad, and half each of herb crusted and miso salmon (we liked to switch plates halfway through), followed by a shared Kahlua Cocoa Coffee Cheesecake slice, I told him what I had been thinking about.

It was nice to be out with my husband.

After all of the news I had stuffed myself with, it was also a pleasant surprise to find that it was still possible to stuff ourselves with the same foods that we enjoyed most. "I wonder how much longer our favorite foods will be available," I said, "and I want to do some exploring in person to get a sense of that and many other things."

Hamish stopped shoveling kale into his mouth and looked at me. "For a price, probably as long as we want."

"Oh, I know, but that won't be true for other people, and that's what I hope to find out, even if only from a distance in a moving car. I want to see what's changed since the last time I was on an East Coast, hotel, bed-and-breakfast, orange grove, museum and museum town, road trip. The landscape and coastlines are different, the people are relocated, and that's just the start. I want to see it from a less controlled perspective than television news presents."

He looked at me for a long moment. "I knew you would want this eventually," he sighed.

"And you were wishing that you could put off 'eventually' indefinitely."

"Well, yeah."

"Of course you were. But you can't. So...are you coming with me, or not?"

He smiled grimly. "Oh, of course I'm coming with you. Did you think I'd let you go alone?"

"Hell, no." I grinned. "I know I'm suggesting something that's a bit questionable and possibly dangerous, but we have Blackout guys to follow us, and I'll bet they would like to see what's going on closer up than they can around here, too."

"Oh, I know for a fact that they would," my husband said, glancing around at our shadows, who were eating at the table across the aisle from us.

"Okay...I want to have some romantic fun as well as some exploratory fun," I said. "We should drive down through New York State to see the dams and dikes being installed, cross into Pennsylvania, see the sugar beet farms around Hershey, and smell the chocolate in the air. On the way back we can see Maryland, Delaware, and New Jersey.

"Meanwhile, moving south, let's check out Washington, D.C., see how the Potomac River is doing...and how the capital city is faring. Next, we can go to Virginia, where we can see Thomas Jefferson's Monticello. I know we've seen it before, but with climate change, the gardens may have changed. I know you thought his inventions were the coolest part, like the copy machine, but Jefferson designed the gardens, not just the building, and they will have changed. Besides, going through that whole area, retracing old steps, will show us things I'm looking for."

"Maybe we can see Colonial Williamsburg, and eat at the Trellis Restaurant."

"Why is that of interest?" Hamish wanted to know.

"A French-American dessert chef, Marcel Desaulniers, who wrote a great recipe book called *Death by Chocolate*, set it up. If it's still there and still run by him, it would be great to spoil you by taking you there. It's just a few steps across the street from the museum town. Also, that museum town has at least four restaurants in it with historically accurate cuisine, which is fun."

Hamish grinned. "Tell me more."

"After we see the museum town – or before, it doesn't matter which – we can drive farther south. I want to see Florida's relocated orange groves and the Georgia Guidestones."

"The what stones?"

"They're like another Stonehenge, but in North America, with writing in several languages on them, saying the same thing in each one. They're aligned with the stars for some cool astronomy trick, and were paid for and designed by some secretive, anonymous guy who wanted to warn visitors about the dangers of human overpopulation. They were finished around 1980, and they're on some farmland, out in the middle of nowhere."

He was staring at me now. "Really? That's fascinating. And Blackout will love protecting us on that leg of the trip." He looked skeptical, but I knew he was sufficiently intrigued to go there.

"Blackout will just have to figure that out, because that is high on my list of sites to see."

"I'm sure it is." He paused. "Now it's on mine. Whoever thought of that must have been farsighted indeed."

"Definitely."

We looked at each other for a long moment, and then Hamish asked, "You do realize that there are displaced people all over the nation now, and that we will likely see them in random places as we go along? They could be desperate and a bit dangerous."

"Yes. I'm counting on that. It will get me out of my sheltered view of the world for at least the duration of the trip, and give us information that the news doesn't."

"Okay then. Just checking."

With that, our slice of chocoholic cheesecake arrived, complete with two forks, and we settled in to focus on that.

Not bad for an impromptu date and dangerous vacation proposal!

Chapter 2

The Hartford Courant *Reports Record College Rejections*

For the rest of the week, I wondered what to expect while trying not to think about it.

There was plenty else to keep me occupied: a garden and conservatory to run, books to read and research, cats to play with, and food to prepare. Oh, and television shows. I liked to watch television in the evenings, but never during the day. Daytime programming was dreadful, in my opinion, but at night there were plenty of dramas and comedies that featured Aspies, murders, neurotypicals, history, science, and whatever else. No talk shows!

Thursday evening, for Dad's birthday, we all went out to eat, in Glastonbury, at Max Fish.

To get there, Dad drove us up Mountain Road to Albany Avenue, turned right, then left to go north on Main Street, which ran to Cottage Grove Road in Bloomfield. From there, we took the highway south toward Hartford, diverting just north of it to I-84, then Route 2. This path took us past the Hartford city dump, which was east of the highway and nearly full, then close enough to the river that we could see it part of the way.

The Connecticut River had never looked so high. In fact, there wasn't much of a drop from the bridges to the surface. We had read and watched the news reports for over two years about the dikes that were being built at the mouth of the river, where it opened into Long Island Sound, and the dams north, where it met the Saint Lawrence Seaway.

That project was nearly completed. When it went online, the reports kept promising, the level of the river would drop by perhaps ten feet or more. It would never be as low as it was before, but it would be lower than it was now. That was something.

A vaguely foul smell assaulted us as we headed toward Hartford on I-91.

"Is that the dump?" my mother asked.

"No," Hamish and my father and I all chorused.

She looked around the car at us all, craning around at me and my husband from the front seat.

"It's the river, which is carrying corpses of wildlife, inundated sanitation systems from all the way up the river to Canada, and runoff from farms and old insecticide applications that date from before Rachel Carson's writings and testimony stopped a lot of that…and who knows what else," I summed up.

"I forgot that the author of the bee book was in the car," she said with a grin. "Why haven't we smelled more of this before?"

"Oh, we have," Dad said. "You just put it out of your mind every time, and I usually pick a route that doesn't take us this way. It's been getting better as the sanitation facilities along the river have been remediated and updated anyway."

"Oh."

We rode along in silence until we got to the restaurant, not thinking of much else to say until we were seated and poring over the menus. Dad chose a bottle of

Merlot for us to share, and we waited for the server to come back and tell us about the specials. This was fun; we hadn't gone out like this in a long time.

My mind wandered. I would have to tell my writer friends, two nice women whom I had met at the West Hartford Public Library, about our travel plans. Sophia liked to write science fiction-fantasy, and Ginger liked to write…smut. That was also the only genre she liked to read.

Sophia was a single mother with a teenage daughter who studied like her life depended upon it and aced everything. Sophia's writing was wonderful – wonderfully full of vivid colors and garden imagery. It drew the reader into scenes of vibrant beauty, right up to sudden danger.

Ginger was a widow in her sixties. I had borrowed a couple of her novels in order to get the feel of the genre when she asked for my feedback. It was pure fun to read whatever either of them wrote, and a nice break from my heavy, detailed, densely-researched stuff.

The waiter appeared and reeled off his expertly memorized specials choices, in tones that made it all sound quite enticing: reduction sauces, compotes, purées, fresh-caught this and that, truffle and saffron embellishments, and so on and on. Ginger's genre came back to mind; this was food porn at its best. Thus teased with anticipation, we placed our orders and waited.

My mother ordered last, as usual, wanting to hear what everyone else was having. My father ordered the seared tuna special. Hamish ordered the monkfish. I ordered the scallops, and with that, so did my mother. I knew it! We also got some appetizers to share: crab cakes with smoked chili aioli, Rhode Island mussels with caramelized onions and vermouth, fried calamari with pepper-almond romesco for Dad, and New England clam chowder for my husband. He hadn't had that lately, and he liked it.

Yes, definitely food porn.

I thought glumly of all of the news I had been reading about fisheries migrating to colder waters or simply dying off, and wondered how much longer it would all last. Dinner was delectable, meanwhile, and ended nicely with key lime tart, crème brulée, and chocolate mousse cake. Really, I ought to focus more on enjoying life rather than on overthinking it.

It was a lovely evening, and the staff sang *Happy Birthday* to Dad when his tart arrived.

We went home, happily sated, and gave him his gifts: more music for his collection from me and Hamish (I had found some medieval French stuff that he didn't already have), and a gift card to his favorite Manhattan camera store, B&H, from my mother. The gifts were rounded out with a few funny cards, some of which were signed on behalf of the cats.

The next, day, and the day after that, I spent wondering about and dreading the publication of that interview, and reading a lot. None of it cheered me up, but I kept it to myself, madly reading as if that would prevent the anxiety from surfacing. It helped until I read the next article on population and birth control.

Op-eds about the pope and the Vatican were always annoyingly unrealistic on the topic.

So were people who simply wanted what they wanted regardless of the Earth's capacity to accommodate it. I watched a movie called *The Age of Stupid* that explained that if people on every continent consumed resources in the quantities that Americans did, we would need six more Earths. Terrific!

The talk shows my mother tuned in to watch on Friday featured unhappy people whose birth license applications had been turned down. Adoption was discussed and dismissed as insufficiently satisfying. How fast could I brew, pour, and add milk to my coffee so I could leave the kitchen, I found myself wondering?!

It seemed that people did not understand that the population policy had not magically solved the problem of homeless, parentless children. These people still wanted children who shared their own DNA, and thought that it would just be easier to have them, if only their nanites could be disabled. A heated session of fantasizing and wishful thinking ensued.

In short, too many people preferred to engage in genetic narcissism than adopt.

Sunday's issue of *The Hartford Courant* attested to that.

Hamish had gotten up hours ago to go down to the basement, where he still had several of his original nanite testing machines, and seen it first. When I came downstairs a few hours later, the cats had raced in with me and leaped onto the kitchen table, but didn't stop there.

My mother was a pretty good deterrent, but she wasn't in the kitchen. She would make sure that they saw her, and then face them with a forbidding look in her eyes as she said, "Noooo…." in a low, steady tone. I told them "NO" on my own, so they both got onto the wide bay window that jutted out over the back yard and settled into their ring pillow beds. After a moment, they had turned around to watch birds and chipmunks, ignoring the human disciplinarian.

I set up the coffee machine; I always made enough for me and Hamish, even though he had a cup at 6:30 every day, and my mother sometimes drank the last bit, just to taste the toasted almond or hazelnut flavor. She liked to get up at eight o'clock. My father typically got up at seven. We women were night owls. Hamish appeared as the coffee brewed.

I knew something was up when he tried to hide the paper from me.

"Where's the paper?" I asked, looking around for it.

"I don't know," he lied. "Maybe your parents took it out in the car with them."

"They're home," I said. "My mother is intent on rearranging her entire wardrobe, going back and forth between the basement cedar closet and the closet in her room. What are you hiding? Is that interview in today's edition?"

Hamish looked at me unhappily, said "yes," and produced the paper from under the stack of magazines that my mother kept on the windowsill by the kitchen table.

"Why hide this from me? We knew what the interview was about…did the reporter turn out to be sneaky and write a vicious attack of me? I mean, what's the big deal? We already know people out there hate me just for thinking of the idea for Nae-Née."

"And we know how much you hate that," Hamish replied.

"Why shouldn't I hate that and resent the hell out of it?!" I shot back.

"Because it's pointless," he said.

"That changes nothing about my attitude," I groused, grabbing the paper and opening it.

Let's see…cover section, complete with world news, with stories on topics such as Ebola epidemics in West Africa and cancer research efforts, a *Dilbert* cartoon, a Bob Englehart political cartoon, and some editorials…I barely glanced at that. I would come back to the specifics later. For now, I was looking at the layout. Connecticut section…full of the usual green initiatives, land trust takeover stories, utilities stories, local crimes, and then pages of obituaries. Living section…with some fun arts stuff, an Amy Dickinson *Ask Amy* advice column, horoscopes, and best of all, the funny pages with three puzzles.

So what? Where's my alleged interview?

Oh…in a *Special to The Courant* section. This special section contained not only my interview, which was actually fine and did not twist my words, but many other related items. These items included the expected story on angry women who wanted to reproduce and blamed me for being barred from that opportunity. They specifically stated that they viewed it as their right to do so regardless of population pressures.

I was disgusted. They weren't at all concerned about the future of the environment, about whether or not it would even be habitable to their offspring. It was all about them and their current wishes, just as I had charged in my interview. Idiots – they didn't even bother to think about who was really to blame for the policy. It was the policymakers, not the inventors!

Contrasting with that was a huge story with individual testimony from teenaged kids around the state with stellar academic and extracurricular records who had not been accepted to college. They were devastated. Backing up that story was a slew of graphs and charts that illustrated how human overpopulation was the reason behind this. That felt sickeningly, horrifyingly, familiar.

It reminded me of the graphs that I saw every time I read about the limits to growth, the finite resources and growing capacity of our planet, graphs with the same line pattern. There were 3 of them: a graph of wealth distribution that illustrated how one percent of the world's population owned almost all of the wealth on the entire planet; a graph of temperature that went from millennia ago to the present; a graph of human population on the Earth from millennia ago to the present. All showed a long line that stayed close to the bottom, and then spiked sky high.

I laid out my breakfast – strawberries and plain Greek yoghurt with honey, some cereal, and orange juice – and poured our cups of coffee with milk. Hamish looked up from his laptop and kissed me as I put the cup down next to him. Then he asked, "Did your mother tell you what was in the paper? Did you see it?"

"No," I said. "What is it?"

"Some kid killed himself, and it's a big deal because he left his rejection letters in front of himself, neatly laid out on his desk in his room," Hamish told me. "He was from this town."

The Hartford Courant *Reports Record College Rejections*

I stared at him for a moment, and then found the story. This was the sort of thing that I had expected to hear about sooner or later: college-age kids who were well qualified not getting accepted due to overpopulation. With nearly 8 billion people, there just weren't enough places for them in the schools. I thought of the kid with the college rejection letters whom we had met at the mall a few years ago; at least he was on his way to medical school now.

There it was: *Class Valedictorian Commits Suicide Surrounded By Rejection Letters*. A high school photo of the kid, no doubt from the Conard yearbook, was under the title next to a shot of his home and another of a group of his friends crying.

"Did you read the article?" I couldn't help asking, even though I was about to do so.

"Yeah, of course I did. But I won't spoil it for you. It reads like a recipe for Nae-Née and an indictment of RE and other crazies, and there is no satisfaction in being right about that. Go on, read it, and maybe you will have another epiphany about how to help other kids. You've already been a golden goose once."

A golden goose indeed; I had done the opposite of laying eggs when I had conceived of the idea of nanobotic birth control, safe and convenient though it was. It had been great until governments all over the planet had made it mandatory for every woman on the planet.

RE stood for Reproduction Entitlement, an extremist group that the government had busted a couple of years ago. But just because its members had been stopped from assassinating anyone didn't mean that there would be no others, or no other groups like RE.

Thanks to computer capability and infrastructure along with military and medical assistance, the Nae-Née policy had been in force for over two years now. The nation's mysterious Operator, whose identity and location were undisclosed, made sure that each device continued to release a dose of RU486 each time a pregnancy was detected…unless a birth license had been granted.

Each country had an Operator. Some were more cryptic than others, but the end result was the same: the government was now able to prevent people from having children without the express consent of its own biostatisticians.

Developing countries found this particularly incomprehensible because couples there tended to have children as insurance policies. Children there were insurance against the deaths of some of the many that a couple would choose to have, thus ensuring that at least some would survive to adulthood where there was limited access to clean water, sufficient and nutritious food, and health care. It assured that the parents would have help farming and elder care someday.

In developed countries, it was less upsetting unless a couple who wanted children got no license at all. Of course, many wanted multiple children and were outraged at government control, and heedless of the fact that a college education for a single child currently cost approximately \$200,000 at a competitive university.

With multiple children, this became a pie in the sky rather than something that could be acquired when the kids came of age. Costs used to be a lot lower.

Long ago, in the 1960s, attending Cornell University cost $5,000 per year, tuition and all, and that was not much of a parent's income.

The problem was that middle-class parents could not borrow the entire sum of one child's college education, let alone another's. The child could not do that either. Even combined, the loans would not be enough to cover the cost, and that was where the parents' income had to either fill the gap or the student would have to withdraw from school. If the student was so lucky as to make it all the way through and come out with a college diploma, the loans that he or she would have to carry would be crippling for decades. The graduate could forget about home ownership, a nice wedding with friends, vacations, or perhaps even an apartment.

In fact, jobs were now so scarce that college graduates even now couldn't start to pay loans.

Despite valiant struggles with Congress session after session, the President had barely been able to push a budget through for the past few fiscal years. The U.S. national debt had ballooned to what felt like oxygen-starved altitudes, and many financial analysts now wondered when it would hit the quadrillions. The college tuition bills would only get harder to afford.

Forget retirement, Medicare, social security, veterans' benefits and a plethora of other things, the Congress seemed to imply every time it was time to prepare the next budget. What about growth? The only choices were service jobs, health care, and energy industries.

But little or no effort, thought or resources were being expended on alternative energy sources, which offered hope for jobs and thus a way to pay down the national debt, reduce costs, and give the next generation a sense of hope about being able to pursue any kind of happiness.

As for the older generation, it didn't include enough people who understood just how difficult things had become. The focus hadn't really shifted from controlling costs – such as by trimming both the budget and overall birth rates – to planning for a sustainable, enjoyable future. The benefits of Nae-Née would take a while to be felt anyway.

Now I was in a really glum mood.

A quick glance over the story about college applicants indicated that a huge part of this problem, new since overpopulation had exploded the numbers of applicants, was flooding. Many colleges and universities that were located in flooded areas were shut down, either temporarily or permanently while their officials and administrators scrambled to relocate all premises inland. It could take years, and meanwhile, these kids were going to lose out.

Another story went into detail about the displaced Americans from Florida and coastal areas. These were people who had lost their homes to flooding, and had fled inland. They were crowding the southern states, the states on the west coast, and the states on the east coast. They lived in homeless encampments, in hastily assembled trailer parks, and in hotels and motels. Travel was becoming prohibitively expensive due to the high demand for rooms, leaving most people stranded where they were.

I flipped back to the editorials page, suspicious now.

Sure enough, there were two on the Nae-Née policy and both brought me and Hamish into the discussion. One was in favor of the policy, and the other against. The one in favor of it treated us quite reasonably by pointing out, yet again, as I wished more writers would do, that the policy was not our idea and that we had merely invented what was offered as a voluntary, effective device. The other blamed us for carelessly creating it, because of the opportunity it presented for twisting it as a police state device that took away civil liberties. Oh, yay…

People still thought only of their present comfort, desires, and instant gratification.

That was why Hamish and I were so isolated.

We had invented the very thing that thwarted a great deal of that, profited from it to point of becoming wealthy, and didn't miss what we couldn't have – several children – because we had never wanted even one child to begin with.

We were happy with our situation, and that just galled those who weren't.

It galled them because they wanted what most people wanted, and now they couldn't have it because the lawmakers of this planet had finally realized that if people weren't forced to go without having everything that they wanted, soon – very, very soon – the comfort and security of most of the developed world would be threatened, and that of the undeveloped world would be utterly and irrevocably gone for generations.

No one wanted to face that.

"Okay, Hamish. Got it. Now I know. And I'm going to read this stuff in its entirety."

He looked at me. "I already did. I knew you would. And I've been dreading it."

"Well, first I'm going to enjoy my breakfast and coffee – and the funnies and puzzles too."

"So, you're not going to let this ruin your morning?" he asked, looking hopeful.

"I make no promises. But I'll damned well enjoy the fun part first now that I know what else is there. How did you find my interview?"

"That was the best part. That reporter was true to her word to you, at least. Fair and balanced, and didn't make any snide, judgmental remarks in her summation at the end."

"Wow. And I thought that that would have been way too much to hope for."

"Indeed. As you saw, that part is in the other segments."

He got up and hugged me, then sat down to keep me company while I ate. Oddly, he stuck around to watch and make sure that I really did read the funnies, the advice column, go over what we liked to jokingly call the horror-scopes, and do the puzzles before leaving the table.

"You stayed just to make sure that I relaxed!" I said, happily.

He kissed me, said, "aye," and headed to his basement laboratory.

"Hey, don't you want a ride to your office lab? It ought to be nice and quiet there today." My workaholic husband usually liked going to his office on a weekend. No clients or patients going in and out of the other offices meant that he didn't run into people who recognized him.

"Not today. Not with that out. I'll work at home. We should lay low today, if possible."

"Hmm…" That was just perfect. We were shut in by the mere thought of angry people, whoever they might be, wherever we might run into them. And yet…I did not wish to go out unless and until I had read and made copies of every word on this topic that today's paper contained. That would take me the rest of the morning, and it was half past ten now.

Oh well. Fine.

"Wait…come with me while I tell my parents why they can't – well, shouldn't – go out in their car for a nice long drive this afternoon. There's a significant possibility of that once my mother finishes going through her closet. She will want to visit thrift shops, dump bags of clothing off to be sold on consignment, and root through the racks for more."

He did, but they were smart, with enough sense to have already decided to stay home.

They were sitting in the living room, reading and watching the news. My father was looking at his camera equipment, a favorite hobby of his, while my mother read spy novels.

"You're not rearranging your clothes after all?" I asked her.

She smiled at me, glancing at the news occasionally. "Oh, I will in a few minutes; I just wanted to see what was on the news first. I suppose you are going to read the whole paper before looking at the news?" she asked.

"Of course. Why?"

"They're rehashing people's interviews, including yours."

"Then I definitely don't want to hear any of it unless and until I've read this stuff."

"Sounds reasonable," she replied. "I'm going to get back to organizing my closets. It's almost September, and maybe tomorrow Dad and I can go to the thrift shops. The uproar ought to have subsided by then, with people back at their offices." She stood and headed for the staircase, going up.

Hamish went down to the basement, and I took the paper upstairs to my desk and read it all. I went heavily up the steps, realizing how lightly I had gone down them. After I had read everything, I saved it all to Word files. It was my usual daily routine, but it felt different.

I thought about it some more. It was tempting to post comments online, but as the subject of one of the articles, I decided it would be the better part of valor not to say anything else. The urge to respond drove me crazy for a while.

The common theme to all of these stories was a mix of bitter unhappiness, crushing disappointment, and blame. The blame went to the government, the wealthy, and to me and Hamish for inventing a stop-gap to the flood of humans.

None of the blame went where it was deserved: to religious doctrines for their vitriol against abortion and birth control…or to themselves, for being asleep to the inevitable outcome, for their blind obedience to that authority, or to their own stubborn desire to perpetuate their own DNA and have babies and little kids around them.

The Hartford Courant *Reports Record College Rejections*

It seemed that the desire to reproduce was so strong in most people that they simply did not care or give any thought to the probable future of any children of theirs until that future was upon them. It was far easier to scream and cry that they found their children's future – no, make that their children's present – completely unacceptable and to rail helplessly against it.

What next? Complaints that their kids weren't moving out of the house and supporting themselves with nonexistent jobs? Accusations that their kids were lazy, good-for-nothing sponges on their parents and on society, suckling at their retirement funds (such as those were)?

What choices did any of these kids have in this time of contracting resources and opportunities?! I saw no point in making everyone more miserable by blaming the wrong people. It was after noon when I looked up from all this, exasperated and angry at everyone.

I needed some chocolate.

Oh wait…soon chocolate would cost an absurd amount of money. Growers of cacao beans and sugar were having difficulties with their crops thanks to rising temperatures, droughts, floods, and social unrest. Soon that panacea would be hard to access.

Well, it wasn't impossible just yet, but I should eat lunch first. I folded up the paper and went downstairs to find Hamish. My parents were already in the kitchen, eating sandwiches. No point in telling them that sandwich ingredients were soon to be scarce…

…I had to stop depressing myself by thinking so much.

The people I had just angrily read about clearly didn't think enough, while I did that too much. It did me plenty of good, but only to a point. I had to force myself to relax.

Without more than a perfunctory nod and smile to my parents, I continued on down the stairs to the basement, walked past the cedar closet area (all organized by now, I noticed), and into Hamish's laboratory.

He was sitting at his metal table, alternating between leaning over his magnifying lens and manipulating microscopic nano-parts via remote computer control, as shown on the screen next to the scope. He also wore glasses that made him look like a cartoon character, and with them on, he could see nothing around him.

"Boo," I said, to snap him out of his intense concentration and back to our macro-level.

He looked up at me from across the table, unseeing, and I would have laughed at the googly-eyed mien he presented if I weren't so fed up with everything. Realizing that he couldn't see me, he yanked the glasses off, blinked, and grinned.

I didn't.

He stopped grinning. "So…you've read everything, saved it, and gotten angry?" He asked, just to confirm the obvious and expected.

"Yes. Let's have lunch. I'll make us something."

He groaned. "Fine. This can wait at least long enough for that," he said, shoving his stool back and getting up.

I started to turn around and leave, but Hamish came up behind and put his hand on my shoulder, so I turned back to look up at him. "What?"

He grabbed me and hugged me. "This isn't our fault, you know. Things were going to get like this whether we invented Nae-Née or not," he said. "Someone else would have found a way to enforce a population policy, with some other device."

"I know. But I hate feeling shut in, and I'm disgusted with almost everyone out there. I want to go on that road trip with you and see what's happening in the country with my own eyes, not a news screen on television."

He let go and looked at me. "You still want to do that? Don't you realize how difficult and dangerous that is likely to be?"

"Yes – in theory. I want to see how it is in reality. Information is limited to what gets piped, wired, delivered, and otherwise transmitted into one's home. Who knows what's being held back, either deliberately or simply because it's too much work to show it all to everyone?"

"You aren't going to let go of this idea, are you?"

"No."

"Great. Fantastic. I'm really going to have to stop work and come with you."

At last, I grinned.

Hamish started to smile.

We went into the kitchen and I took out some food.

I started dishing out curried butternut squash soup that I had made while watching *Hawaii Five-O* and *Blue Bloods* on Friday evening. Next, I made sandwiches in the panini press, including basil leaves from our little conservatory, heirloom tomatoes from Whole Foods, and some sliced gouda cheese. My parents had had cold cuts in theirs. They only ate vegetarian when I made soup, or when my mother made salads.

Hamish was glad to eat vegetarian food as often as possible. He had confided in me when we met that he hated haggis and hoped to never see it again, let alone eat it. That was good news to me, and one of the reasons I was happy to start dating him. Organs – yuck! Foie gras was the French equivalent, and there was no way would even try a pâté made by burying a duck alive so it could never pee just to make its liver taste…however that made it taste. Sick!

My father was such a fast eater that he was done by the time I put our lunches on the table, but my mother was so slow that she had started eating when my parents sat down, and finished when I was finished.

In no hurry to leave the kitchen, I got some lavender refrigerator cookies out and passed them around. We all ate a few, and I cleaned up. I felt like I was stalling.

My mother turned the television on.

I really didn't like to watch television during the day, and this was why: talk shows.

A talk show with several people at a round sofa pontificating about the population policy was on, and my mother turned the sound up. It was just more of the same: a heated argument thinly disguised as a debate, hashing out the same points I had just read over and over and over again.

"I'm not watching this," I said. "It's the newspaper all over again, the same stuff."

Dad looked bored too. "Nothing original. Just people with nothing new to talk about."

"I like it," my mother said, and made herself a cup of tea.

Hamish and I left the kitchen.

"I'm going to research our trip," I said to him.

"I'm coming with you to hang out and pet the cats, if they follow us," he said.

"You don't want to go back to work? This might get boring," I warned.

"I can take a break. I need to wind the projects down anyway if we're going on the road. The solar power nanite program is done, and I have a couple of other things brewing that can be paused for a trip. How long of a trip are you thinking of us taking?"

"Three to four weeks."

"That sounds fine," he said. "I can stop for at least that long."

I smiled. This wasn't going to be difficult – at least, not the part about having him with me.

Spock and Eowyn were playing pounce in the front hall, running at each other from the living and dining rooms, meeting in the middle. They saw us heading upstairs and stopped in mid-grapple, broke apart, and then raced to the top of the stairs. When we got to the upstairs landing, they ran into our room.

Hamish found some cat toys, sat on the bed, and started entertaining them.

I settled in at my computer and to start researching our crazy adventure.

One distraction delayed me, if only for a moment.

It was a Facebook post on a page about overpopulation, shared from the page for Population Matters. There were several, and it was reassuring to see that at least some people agreed that overpopulation was an issue that mattered. Many of the chat page members just used it to vent, which was fine but liked this post.

It showed the actress Ashley Judd, looking absolutely gorgeous, in a portrait. The caption quoted her as saying: "It's unconscionable to breed, with the number of children who are starving to death in impoverished countries."

That was perfect. I shared it to my page for Nae-Née with this comment: "☺ Why can't more celebrities say this?! The masses listen to celebrities. They don't listen to professors. They listen to those who are popular first, and those who are right...maybe. We need those who are popular to say what is right."

It took me all afternoon, but I had our entire itinerary laid out by the time *Jeopardy!* was about to start. Hamish enjoyed alternately looking at websites with me and dozing off on the bed with the cats. Men and naps...I preferred to get all of my sleeping done at once.

The planning went smoothly: I made hotel, bed-and-breakfast, museum, and dinner reservations, with only one disappointment. The Trellis Restaurant still existed, but chef and founder Marcel Desaulniers had sold it and retired. The chocoholic desserts and menu were not as they once were. Scratch that off the agenda, except perhaps for a nice lunch.

Now to break the news to my parents, and make sure that they didn't do anything foolish while we were away. I doubted that they would want to go traveling at the same time. They would likely stay home and want us to check in periodically.

My mother wasn't going to want us to go, I suspected.

We went downstairs, armed with printouts of the itinerary, complete with websites, addresses, phone numbers, confirmation numbers, dates, check-in and check-out times, and whatever else might be worth sharing. One was for each of my parents, plus another for the Blackout Security company. Hamish called Ed in from the gatehouse out front to get it.

Ed came up, took it, and said, "I figured she would be quick on the draw with this."

Hamish grinned. "I'll get you a memory stick with this stuff on it, so you guys can plan."

These guys were good. I knew that they would be able to keep up with us while getting enough sleep and food along the way. Our very own posse, and it moved with stealth and precision.

Back in the kitchen, my mother was serving up a recipe that she had gotten off of the Internet after watching Chef Giada de Laurentiis on the Food Network. She liked to cook that way. I preferred to work from my favorite cookbooks, or invent something. Either way, we ate well.

Tonight's selection was a wild mushroom and shrimp risotto, followed by strawberries with zabaglione. I took out salad ingredients and started cutting up tomatoes, basil, mozzarella, lettuce, scallions, and sweet orange and yellow peppers. No more avocadoes; California had been forced to cut us off a few months ago due to drought. That state was being fracked to within an inch of its water table as well.

Water use was intensely regulated, and ocean water was seeping in to replace its drained water tables. They just couldn't be replenished by Nature under the onslaught of relentless demand for water by its population, which was double what the area's capacity could cater to. It was a classic, glaring example of how the Earth simply wouldn't do what it couldn't, no matter how much humans wanted it to. The fracking suggested that the state's government had given up on the population's welfare as a lost cause, and was now simply out for profit.

No wonder they had finally had a huge earthquake.

Congress was under pressure from lobbyists hired by huge agribusiness corporations that produced and transported food. They were big campaign contributors. What remained of California was regulating water use: no more lawns! And no growing one's own food or enjoying a garden of any kind there. There was water-shaming of wealthy lawn-growers, and heavy fines for filling swimming pools. It was misery there, and people were migrating out.

My mother started to throw the stems from the tomatoes, basil, and strawberries in the garbage. "No, Mommy – put those in the compost bin. I need to keep us supplied with all of the things we like to eat that the stores don't stock anymore," I said. She rolled her eyes and did it.

Hamish handed my father his copy of the itinerary. My father took out his glasses, read through it all, and then said, "At least you have a good pair of bodyguards to tail you everywhere you go. Otherwise, I'd be worried."

My mother looked up from the stove. "What's this?" She put her spoonula down and walked over to her computer, where Hamish had put her copy. She grabbed it, scanned it, and then looked at us. "Whose idea was this?"

"Mine," I said. "I want to see some very specific things, and whatever else the news isn't showing us. And I want to get Hamish out of his lab for weeks, just for long drives in the car with music playing. And I want to visit and revisit historic sites and museums with him – things that we have talked about seeing for years and never gotten around to doing, and whatever has changed thanks to sea level rise."

She looked at me, then said, "And you will be checking in with us as you go along? There are all kinds of dangerous people out there now, people who have lost everything, who are desperate and who might recognize you."

"Of course. We'll call you almost every day. Maybe every day, and more than once."

"Good." My mother looked less than thrilled, but she wasn't about to insist that I drop this idea. She sat down to go over the list, and we settled into our dinner. It was very good, and seemed to improve everyone's mood as we went over the specifics.

We would spend at least 2 nights in each place, so that we could enjoy the sites, and not hurry through the area. That would leave time to calmly drive to the next stop. I liked to see where I was going and enjoy the drive – and stop at rest rooms whenever I wished – so this plan ought to do nicely.

I had looked up bed-and-breakfast inns anywhere and everywhere I could find them, though a hotel wouldn't be unwanted. It was just that bed-and-breakfast places had the most imaginative breakfast menus, unique décor, and non-commercial ambience that they seemed nicer.

Hamish warned me that we should go nowhere without a hotel reservation, or we would find no place to sleep. I realized that this meant that the inland diaspora of displaced humans was part of the problem.

Here is the trip that the itinerary described:

1. Home in Connecticut to Hyde Park, New York. See the Roosevelt home, which was a National Historic Site, and the Culinary Institute of America, also known as the other C.I.A. Tour each place, and eat at the C.I.A. To get there, we would drive on Route 44.
2. Hyde Park to Hershey, Pennsylvania, and then on to Bear Run, Pennsylvania. See the sugar beet farms around the chocolate factory and smell the candy in the air. Visit Frank Lloyd Wright's work of architectural genius, Fallingwater, at Bear Run.
3. Head for Washington, D.C. from there to see the infrastructure projects there, and how that affected access to the monuments, museums, and whatever else.
4. Go to Thomas Jefferson's Monticello next. Hamish would love the inventions in it. I would love that and the gardens and the library, and the violin...

5. …drive to the eastern Blue Ridge Mountains of Appalachia to enjoy the scenery, see some black bears, white-tailed deer, songbirds, and whatever other wildlife inhabited that area. See what was different about it since driving that route with my parents in college.
6. Cross through North Carolina, South Carolina, and into Georgia after seeing all this.
7. Look for orange groves, which had been relocated from Florida to Georgia. Hamish wanted to show me something there. I was hoping to see honey bees…and hoping that the bees were doing okay.
8. We would visit the Georgia Guidestones next, then turn around and head home.
9. Heading back, we would visit Colonial Williamsburg and tour the area. I had used a topographical website to check on this place, and amazingly, it was still well above current sea levels, by over thirty feet, despite being close to the coast.
10. Drive through Maryland, Philadelphia, and New Jersey at a leisurely pace to see how those coastal states looked, and how much of their land area remained. Also, see the Benjamin Franklin House in Philadelphia. I just couldn't resist historic sites.
11. One the way home, we would stop in Manhattan to see what was going on there.

One of the major questions I wanted to answer on this trip was: what difference would a sea level rise of 20 feet and counting plus a global temperature increase of 4°Fahrenheit make? Obviously, it would make quiet a difference, but I wanted to see it for myself in order to fully appreciate and understand it.

Chapter 3

Awful Offal and Engineering Projects

"Let's get this trip on the road!" I said to Hamish as I packed our bags.

He grinned. "You're packing for me? I feel spoiled."

"Is there anything in particular you want me to put in your bag?"

"No. It looks like you've got it covered. I take it the most formal situation we'll be in will be business casual, whatever that means?"

"That's the idea. For you, it means khaki pants in navy blue, dark olive green, or black with nice shirts. For me, it means…hmm…what the hell does it mean? Dark blue or black linen pants for this time of year, thanks to rising temperatures, and pretty shirts. I'm just trying not to pack too much stuff. We don't want to have to lug it around."

"One small suitcase on wheels apiece, plus our laptops and your camera bag. Nope…we can handle that, and keep it all in the trunk, out of sight, as we drive through the country. It should be no problem."

"No problem, until we go somewhere that doesn't allow photographs," I commented. "I'll just buy DVDs and books about the museums, and take photographs outside and wherever it is allowed. What I wonder about it is whether or not I can photograph infrastructure, MRAPs in action, and displaced people. The only thing I have qualms about photographing is the people. Doing that feels like invading their privacy and focusing on their misery. Or is it noticing them and taking them seriously?

"Probably both," Hamish said. "Let's see how it goes and worry about it as it comes up."

"Okay. But I'm keeping that camera bag just behind my seat. I can pull over and photograph things from inside the car without getting up and opening the trunk that way."

We left in mid-September, heading up Route 44. It was mid-morning, and I expected to get us to Hyde Park, New York by lunchtime. We drove past our familiar stomping grounds first. Crossing the now dammed-up and thus not flooded Farmington River, things looked oddly unchanged. There was Max a Mia, a restaurant; the Secret Garden shop, which sold the prettiest and funniest cards, and The Grist Mill overlooking its parking lot; the turn-off to Route 202 North that led to a health club where I took yoga classes; and Avon's police department, which was in a converted mill (no MRAPs visible).

The U.S. military had been donating its old MRAP vehicles to police departments all over the nation and buying new ones. An MRAP was a mine-resistant ambush-protected armored vehicle. It looked like a cross between a tank and an oversized Humvee. Once received, the police had them repainted to show their own shields and town names. I wanted to see some without asking to do so, from a distance, outside.

What were the cops doing with this stuff? It was overkill, pun intended. They didn't need their enforcement capabilities amped up to the extent that they were almost on a par with a military unit. They liked to play with them like toys; numerous YouTube videos attested to that.

Cops lacked the training and discipline to wield this stuff calmly. They were too thrilled by it, too emotional, and having way too much fun with it. No good could possibly come of it, especially since they had been sufficiently effective with police cruisers, mace, night-sticks, and pistols. The general public wasn't enough of a threat to justify this. We weren't at war.

As we passed the Avon police station, Hamish asked, "What makes you think you will see any MRAPs today?"

"Nothing. I think we are too close to the calmer areas of the nation to see them. It's only the first few minutes of the trip, and we haven't really left home yet. Give it time. But when we do see some, I'm looking for signs of something called Jade Helm 15."

"Ah…the training exercise for martial law. That's been in the news a lot lately."

Jade Helm was a training exercise for the military in civilian areas that we had actually seen in action last year. It had run from July to September, on the 15th of each month, in the year 2015, hence its name. It was a multi-state exercise, and it had involved multiple branches of the military, including the U.S. Army Special Operations Command (SOC). It was bigger than all previous such exercises in that it involved more troops and more geographic space.

Anyone who objected to it was immediately labeled a conspiracy theorist. "What a great defense mechanism, pun intended on the Defense Department," I said wryly as Hamish outlined it. He nodded and went on. Jade Helm involved troops sneaking through private property with night vision and full battle gear, stopping, arresting, and detaining private citizens, and behaving as though the U.S. Constitution had been suspended.

I lapsed into thought again. Another thought, a disturbing one, came back to mind. As much as I hated guns, and didn't want one, I didn't want the Second Amendment to be neutered, either. Get rid of that, and the people would be disarmed. Thanks to a few lunatics in schools and movie theaters, there had been a lot of noise about that in the past couple of decades, increasing in frequency in the past few years.

"Hamish, has it ever occurred to you that disarming the public entirely and letting militarized police have ALL of the weapons, is as idiotic as women entrusting the vote entirely to men? I mean, since when would a group that is entirely in control or either security or politics or both ever put the wishes of the other group ahead of its own, even though it is supposed to protect that group? It would always put its own interests ahead of that disadvantaged group. That's why women fought for the vote, and that's why citizens should be very concerned about efforts to restrict gun ownership while militarizing the nation's cops!"

"Who are you and what have you done with my wife?" Hamish asked. But he looked like he admired me for what I was saying as I glanced at him, not like he was actually worried.

"I don't want a gun, I just don't want to wake up and find that no private citizen has the right to own one, and that we are all expected to just surrender them to whatever authority wants them. I hate guns! They blow flesh, bone, and blood every which way. I don't like the idea of even handling one. Guns freak me out. But the idea of having no legal access to one worries me even more. That's why I want to know all about the MRAPs and see them in person. I'm not joining the damned NRA, though," I added.

Hamish just grinned. I knew he was thinking and plotting plenty on his own. He always was. This was the man who had invented a nanite gun that caused instant nerve torture to its target, and no one had known what he was up to until the deed was done. Cool! He had even saved my life with it, which was hot, and I had told him so. "Now I've lapsed into neurotypical metaphors and applied them to you. But I can't help it. You were awesome when you did that."

Hamish leaned over and tried to kiss me at that point, but I kept my eyes on the road.

Not long after the Greenland ice sheet had mostly melted away, the President had said that we would have to allocate funding to ensure that our continent didn't turn into one big Superfund site. A Superfund site was one designed by the Environmental Protection Agency as being so contaminated by pollutants as to require immediate and costly remediation.

Remediation meant a major cleanup. That meant big money. The EPA had always kept a grossly inadequate fund to handle such things, relying heavily on lawsuits for the rest. But you couldn't take Mother Nature to court and sue her for what your own species had done, so that fund was necessary, and so were the lawsuits.

Our species had recklessly burned and emitted fossil fuels since the Industrial Age. The atmosphere was hotter by at least four degrees and rising. Granted, the Earth went through cycles of climate change on its own, and it was likely that our emissions had coincided with one of the warmer cycles, but human activity had added massively to the effect.

Anthropogenic climate change was upon us, and I wanted to go see some of it.

This was morbid curiosity on my part – blatant and reckless – but irresistible.

What was it like out there? I was too accustomed to how it was in Connecticut.

Yes, the shoreline had receded, pushing wealthy people's homes, the historic Mystic Seaport area, and whatever else on the coastline inward or simply obliterating it. Yes, there was a dike nearly in place for damage control, and water would be continuously pumped out to sea.

But what else was out there to observe? Hamish admitted to being just as curious.

A long time ago, it now seemed, before these changes had been wrought, when I was working as a historic interpreter at the Mark Twain House in Hartford, I had read *The Prince and the Pauper*. It was a fun book in which Prince Edward, the future King Edward VI, had secretly traded places with a pauper named Tom Canty.

Tom Canty lived in London with his family on a street called Offal Court.

Offal? What was that, I had immediately wondered, reaching for the dictionary. It was sewage, garbage, and whatever other waste that humans had cast off, and the place was named for it due to a general lack of sanitation systems. Gross! Tom Canty lived on Shit Court, I had thought in disgust.

Well, now awful offal was overflowing everywhere, inundating North America as badly as those revolting photographs I used to find of polluted places in China as I surfed the Internet. There had been a mad rush in the past couple of years to clean it up before our part of the planet also had puke-blue sludge with dead fish floating in it, yellow rivers, red algae, and who knew what else every which way we looked.

The U.S. and Canada were suddenly joined in a big fight with water…and noxious gas.

I hated the smell of methane. I doubted I could find anyone else who liked it, either.

That's why it seemed so odd that the human species had taken the easy way out of dealing with fossil fuel dependence until the stench of methane that bubbled up and out of melting arctic ice was now wafting with unwelcome regularity down from Alaska and northern Canada.

We drove over the next mountain into Canton, and I suddenly decided to stop at the Canton Village Shoppes. "Let's visit the nice lady at The Spirited Hand and pet her greyhound dog," I said. We can get coffee for the car ride at Sur La Table, too."

"Okay."

We liked that lady, Nora, and her dog, who was a rescue and retiree from the greyhound racetrack, wherever that was. The dog was female, very quiet, and she liked to sleep on her bed behind the counter. Her name was Ruby. I like to go around the back and kiss and pet her…and admire the beautiful embroidered collars that Nora put on her. Today she wore a lavender satin one with red roses.

Ruby had cancer in her shoulder muscles, but was doing great on a spice treatment that Hamish had developed. She took capsules of turmeric and capsicum (cayenne), and needed less pain medication as a result. Those spices kept inflammation, the root cause of pain, down to such an extent that she could go into a deep, relaxing sleep any time she wished. She was a sweet dog.

Ruby's human Nora, who owned the shop, was a very nice lady. We bought gifts for business associates from her, and she always wrapped them prettily for us. I had a routine of getting coffee at Sur La Table, across the parking lot from The Spirited Hand, and then going over to see Nora and Ruby.

Hamish and I did that today, and found that everything was fine. I told Nora about our trip, and that we were heading out on the first leg of it as we spoke. Was I silly, telling people all of my business, or was I cautious, telling people so that people would know we were out of town?

We were being followed by Blackout guys, not that I informed her of that fact, but I liked to cover other angles. I always wondered whether or not anything might "happen" to us at any time. We were not the sort of quiet, obedient people who would be protected. We questioned things.

After that visit, we were on our way again. It wasn't until we passed the sign that said Satan's Kingdom that I felt that we had left our usual haunts. Satan's Kingdom was where people went in the summer to enjoy swimming, boating, and freshwater fishing in the Farmington River.

On and on we drove up Route 44, through Ralph Nader's hometown of Winsted, up to Canaan, and on past the turnoff to Massachusetts, which was another country route. That way would take us to Tanglewood, in Lenox, Massachusetts. Maybe next summer, if the world wasn't falling completely apart, Hamish and I could go on an overnight trip to hear the Boston Symphony Orchestra perform there.

I drove and drove until we got to New York State, and before we knew it, we were in Hyde Park, along the Hudson River, checking into our bed-and-breakfast inn. It occurred to me then that getting the first set of photographs that I wanted wouldn't be as difficult as I had thought. I could just go to the campus of the Culinary Institute of America and look out over the river to get a good view of its level. It was a bit early in the trip for anxiety, I decided.

Would I have any trouble from militarized police if I wanted to photograph a river rising high enough to touch a bridge? Or a dam or a dike? I wanted those images as souvenirs. I wanted to study them, and show my parents what I had seen. Maybe I would show my friends these things, too. I should have the freedom to gather this data. Maybe, when it was time to drive across the Newburgh-Beacon Bridge, it would be a problem. We would know in a couple of days.

We knew that Blackout guys were following us all the way, but they were trying to be inconspicuous. That was difficult once we got to the inn. I tried to act like I didn't know them as Ed and Aaron signed into a room, posing as an utterly unconvincing gay couple. At least gay rights gave them a good idea for a cover story, but I was forcing myself not to laugh.

Hamish and I went up to our room, put our stuff down and shut the door. With that, I started laughing. So did he. "They are not perky, they are not happy, and they do not seem gay at all. Maybe they need a different cover story…and more room reservations. Don't they have girlfriends they could invite on this trip? I wouldn't mind paying. They should have a life, too."

Hamish was still grinning from ear to ear; Aaron had nearly fainted when Ed had winked at him and replied "Yes, dear," to his suggestion that he not forget the other bag. Ed had grabbed the one that, presumably, contained their computer. Both were packing guns, of course.

"No," Hamish said. "They'd never do that. Too unprofessional, and to distracting."

"Do they have girlfriends?"

"Yeah…Ed has one who is in the F.B.I. She's in D.C. Her name is Allison. Aaron's girlfriend is an engineer with the U.S. Air Force. They see each other a couple of times a year."

"So they won't be joining us on this trip, then."

"No."

At last I could keep a straight face. "That's cheerful. They don't see each other much. I guess they will continue to provide amusement on this trip, pretending to be what they're not. They should watch our local weatherman deliver the Connecticut reports if they're going to keep this up. He's a real gay person, not a fictional character, so it might be helpful to observe his mannerisms."

Hamish started laughing again.

"Oh, forget it. Let's go eat lunch and see the Roosevelt estate," I said. I went into the bathroom to get ready. All that meant was a quick hair brushing and touch-up of my makeup. Hamish was even faster.

As soon as I had decided to go on this trip, I had gone online and booked lunch and dinner for the first two days of it…at 4 of the C.I.A. restaurants. Hamish was very excited, as was I. More food porn coming right up! Lunch today was to be at the Apple Pie Bakery Café (online at http://www.ciarestaurantgroup.com/apple-pie-bakery-cafe/), no reservation required. I had deliberately chosen this place for that reason, so that our arrival time would be flexible with our plans to eat and then go touring.

We weren't in any great hurry. Tours went out until 4 p.m. at the Roosevelt estate. The café was worth the delay. We stuffed ourselves with goat cheese, avocado, and watercress sandwiches and a side each of grilled shrimp and truffle potato fries, followed by a raspberry tart with this description: "Raspberry & pistachio diplomat cream inside a crisp Breton tart shell" (me) and an Opera Pop made with "Layers of chocolate ganache, espresso mousse & jaconde cake soaked in espresso, glazed with dark chocolate" (Hamish). We had bites of each other's desserts, of course.

Thus happily sated, it was off to the museum estate to (hopefully) walk off those calories while absorbing some history. At least I was sure about the history part of that plan! All my worries about the state of the nation and the environment were happily on hold.

The estate was, as expected, the ultimate handicapped-accessible historic site. We saw Franklin Delano Roosevelt's self-designed wheelchair, made of a kitchen chair that had large wheels in front instead in back, and small ones in back. No wonder he could pull himself upright; he got a constant workout by propelling himself around, and he was a very determined person.

Dinner was at place called Pangea (http://www.ciarestaurantgroup.com/pangea/), after the supercontinent of the late Paleozoic and early Mesozoic Eras. The menu was paid for by buying a ticket rather than by making a reservation, and featured vegetarian and carnivorous fare, plus desserts. Its webpage advertised:

"Expect the unexpected when you enter the Hudson Valley's new, pop-up restaurant Pangea. As the world's population explodes and earth's resources labor to keep up with demand, the need for conscious dining has become a culinary imperative. We must engage in intense conversations about how we produce and harvest the food we eat, and the effect that has on the health of our planet and ourselves."

We had a fun dinner there, sharing every dish, with an order of each menu to taste.

The next day, after lunch at the Ristorante Caterina de' Medici, we took the full tour of the Culinary Institute of America. High school students and their parents came on it also, as prospective college students in the running for careers as chefs, bakers, hoteliers, and restaurateurs. I don't think anyone recognized us, and that made it easy to focus on the tour.

We saw students hard at work in kitchen after kitchen from behind the glass, or taking copious notes in classrooms. They looked just like other college students, except for their attire: chef jackets. The 4-day, several-thousand-dollar master chef test was described, and we were told that the famous Parisian chef, Paul Bocuse, had sent his son here. High praise indeed!

The Conrad N. Hilton Library was a feast of books, audio-visual aids, and other ways for students to virtually study every food preparation and recipe creation method developed thus far in human history. The bookstore was full of temptations as well, and I succumbed to a couple of books, including *The Culinary Institute of America Cookbook: A Collection of Our Favorite Recipes for the Home Chef*. My mother and I would have fun with that.

After the tour, we went out to the car. Time to view the river! I put the bag from the bookstore in and took my camera out. Then it was back to the campus, which was a good walk from the parking lot. We didn't care. We had taken in enough calories here that we felt obligated to find as many excuses to walk and move as possible.

We got up to the front of the main administration building looked out. It was a beautiful view. This, even though the surface of the river seemed awfully close – much closer than I remembered it from when my father and I had driven through this area in the 1990s. I had ridden with him on a day-long excursion to see a client's 1960 Porsche where it was recovering from a crash (the subject matter in a case). We had been unable to get seats in the French restaurant for lunch, but the American one was, well…awesome. Dad had been happy with it, and so had I.

So…the river was extraordinarily high in its bed. That was it?! I took the photographs I wanted, and then took some of the C.I.A. just for good measure. "You'll have to go on more of this trip to see anything really Earth-shattering," Hamish remarked.

"Very funny," I said. "Let's go back to the inn.

"Why?"

"To put on something really nice for dinner. I packed a jacket for you, and skirt and nice shoes for me. We're eating at The Bocuse Restaurant tonight."

"What's wrong with what we're wearing?" he asked.

"Are you doing this on purpose?"

"What?"

"Being a typical guy. You know damned well we have to dress up to eat there."

He just laughed, chortled, cackled, and got into the car. He wasn't going to resist, but neither would he desist. "I'm going to wear my undershorts on my head to this place."

"Shut up, Hamish." I drove us back to the inn, we changed, and went back. Hamish did not dress oddly. He looked handsome in his dark blue pants, navy dinner jacket, and oxford shirt in a medium blue hue with white, green, and gold grid lines. I wore a pink blouse, matching sweater, pearls that he had given me, and comfortable, flat, rubber-soled dress shoes. At least I could either run or sneak about dressed like this, I thought with a grin, and I didn't look funny.

This dinner was so worth it that it wasn't funny. The Bocuse Restaurant (http://www.bocuserestaurant.com/menus/) was the most delectable, decadent experience that we could have hoped for. Graduates who had studied here ought to be well-prepared for the next stop in their careers. We shared black truffle soup, chestnut soup, and another appetizer (yes, 3 of them!) advertised as: **Warm Goat Cheese** – *Fromage de Chevre Croustillant*: Baby Kale, Asian Pears, Pomegranate, Spiced Pumpkin Seeds.

This couldn't count as food porn because we actually got to eat the food, I commented to Hamish. He liked that. When the server walked away, he leaned over and said, "We can enjoy something else later." I grinned. The entrées were as good as the menu promised, and we switched plates halfway through as usual. We ate: **Textures of Squash** – *Assortiment de Courge*: Coach Farms Goat's Milk Consommé, Mixed Mushrooms, Alfalfa Sprouts and **Roasted Fluke** - *Flet Rôti*: Braised Savoy Cabbage, Bacon Lardons, Root Vegetables, Orange-Fennel Broth.

Dessert could not be skipped here. Even though we were feeling a bit full, we shared **The Mocha** – *Le Petit Déjeuner au Dessert*: Mocha and Toasted Baguette Gâteaux, Sweet Butter Brioche, Tangerine and a **Pomegranate-Caramelized Apple Galette** – *Galette de Pomme Caraméliseé à la Grenade*: Sable Cookie, Sweet Miso Butter, Pandan Ice Cream.

"I can't finish it," I finally said, after we had made it through half of each one, which meant a quarter of each dessert per person. "Do you think our shadows might want this?"

"No…" Hamish said. "They're stuffing themselves at the table across the room. It's up to us. Let's take it back to the inn, put it in the fridge, and finish it just before breakfast."

"Deal." I grinned. "So…are you glad you dressed up as my eye candy for this?"

"No comment," my husband said, but he was grinning at me.

We paid, left, and went back to our nice room at the inn. I felt a bit guilty for not fully appreciating its breakfast offerings each morning, but with competition like that down the road, what could its owners expect? Their food was actually really good, though, and I suspected that their breakfast cook was a chef-graduate of the C.I.A.

Time to take off into the unknown wilderness of our drowning continent again! We packed the car and took off, camera bag ready. Now I got a really good photo-op as we approached the bridge. Looking furtively around for a passing MRAP (or at the very least, a police cruiser), I found a spot where we could pull over and view the bridge. Incredible! No cops, no problem whatsoever, and I took the photographs. The water was just a couple of feet away from the bottom of the bridge. With that, I put the equipment away and drove across.

Hamish stared out the window and down in amazement. "It's one thing to know about this, and quite another to actually see it," he remarked. "No wonder you wanted to do this." Even out the window, the water looked close…very close. "Suicidal bridge-jumpers may have to come up with another plan from now on," he added dryly.

I gave him a sideways glance, but said nothing and lapsed into thought again as I drove toward Pennsylvania. There was a long stretch ahead before we would make it to Hershey. It was just highway – boring, standard, interstate highway for miles. Maybe I could get us off the highway here and there to look around. How else would we see anything amiss?

There had to be some signs of displaced people around here somewhere, I thought. People had moved inland in droves from some of the boroughs of New York City, from New Jersey, and from the suburban areas of Philadelphia. It wasn't just around here, either, but here was where we might see some evidence of that.

Mass migrations were underway in staggering numbers. People had been moving north (or south, depending upon the latitude) from the flood-and-drought zones between the Tropics of Capricorn and Cancer for decades. They wanted to be where things still grew without either drying and frying or being washed away before harvest time. It was perfectly understandable.

But now they were moving south, too. Canadians didn't like that methane stench – which was caused by the exposure of thawing plants that dated from 30,000 years ago. It smelled like a cow farm. If you have ever driven past a dairy barn on a summer day with your car windows open, you knew the smell.

Methane wasn't the only thing that was driving Canadians south; the polar icecaps had melted, leaving polar bears no option but to stay on land year-round, looking for food. Hunting areas had changed, but the laws protecting the polar bears hadn't. They were endangered, and so were the humans who came in contact with them.

And yet humans were legally barred from shooting them, even in self-defense. That left lots of dead bears with unexplained gunshot wounds thanks to an unenforceable piece of legislation. Canada's parliament was debating a change, but meanwhile, people kept quiet about encounters with polar bears.

With a population of almost 36 million people, Canadians had enough room to cope with this, but it still wasn't pleasant. People who had thought that they could enjoy rural, wide-open spaces were losing that lifestyle as others crowded in. Yes, they didn't feel the need to leave Canada and push into the United States – not like Mexicans did – but they did have to relocate.

Land values in Canada were responding to the situation by going down in the far, arctic north and up in the south, near the U.S. border. The U.S. was experiencing something similar. Even areas with high crime, areas where subprime loans had devastated neighborhoods with decaying, abandoned homes filled with squatters and gangs were suddenly desirable again.

Detroit, an area that had been largely abandoned and left to rot when the auto industry suffered a downturn, was reviving due to climate change. Seeing it on the news with bankers and home improvement reality shows and new residents was something that we were getting used to. Some Americans had moved away from the Great Lakes and the Saint Lawrence Seaway areas.

Maybe we would see greater numbers of people from there in Pennsylvania. They would have signs saying where they used to live, I scolded myself. This was the research talking, not the view in front of me.

Jobs were not following people. The auto industry had yet to catch up and get reliable electric cars on the road. One problem was a lack of recharging stations around the nation. Another was the lack of political will in Washington, D.C. America needed a government that would invest in clean energy transportation, bypassing the need for Congressional votes, and it didn't have it. The economy was as stagnant as the air.

The air that hung over even cities as small as Hartford now visibly demonstrated the climate crisis with a steady haze. The color of the haze went from green to brown to clear as the weather went through cycles of rain, clear skies, more clear skies, and finally, after a long wait, more rain to clear the haze, which then started right back up again.

It wasn't even our haze; it was haze that had wafted across the planet from developing nations. As it was, the damage that had been done was now being felt, and worse was on its way because nothing had been changed for too long. It was just easier to keep going with fossil fuels. What would it take for panic to set in? Or at least anxiety about the future? Something to induce long-term planning was needed.

Why was it that we could get a population control treaty signed and ratified but not a climate change treaty? The U.S., after all, had over 324 million people, and as a developed nation, that meant that we were gluttons for resources, plastic use, and trash output. We were world leaders in awful offal production, and we were working hard at becoming leaders in coping with it rather than letting it overwhelm our ecosystems altogether. That was why the treaty had been signed in the first place: what people wanted and what the planet could realistically provide were two entirely different things.

I wanted democracy and personal liberties, but that wasn't going to make space and resources infinite in their capacity to accommodate that. I hated it, but there it was. Unhappiness was inevitable, and could no longer be postponed. Thomas Malthus had been hated for saying so, and here I was, agreeing with him.

But it seemed that because this fact wasn't yet painfully obvious, because the pain of insufficiency wasn't yet being felt yet in developed nations, it wasn't understood. Only experience could demonstrate a thing that people would not study and plan for. Painful, bitter, terrifying experience was coming for many, while for others it was already a reality.

Mexicans and other Latin Americans were pressing north in greater numbers than ever before. They crossed scorching deserts, many getting raped, tortured, and murdered along the way, only to get trapped in converted industrial parks and other old properties that the U.S. government had bought up and left there, in legal limbo, for months and even years on end. But I shouldn't get ahead of myself, I thought. If we were going to see even those American climate refugees, it would likely be in the southern part of this trip.

As if all of these changes were dramatic enough, the north was inheriting the climate that the south had in the past. The reason was simple, appalling scientific fact: after the planet's temperature had in fact risen the four degrees that climatologists had warned about, it was still rising. In less than another decade, it would probably be six degrees higher than it had been when the treaty was signed.

This was happening fast.

Where could people go with less land on the planet to visit and more humans scrambling for space to exist on it? And how could we get there? There was a huge portion of the planet's infrastructure – airports, railroads, bridges, and roads – that needed rerouting and rebuilding.

No wonder the budget was such a mammoth undertaking each year. It had to include replacements and raising of many of these bridges, from little ones like the concrete miniatures that connected back country roads to the major ones over rivers like the Hudson. Those little ones had always fascinated me. They had the year that they were built etched into them, always in the 1930s, during the Great Depression. Train tracks had to be rerouted and replaced, too.

We would see some of this era's massive infrastructure construction while it was underway, and after a lot of it had already been done. It made sense to go and see this now that there had been time to implement many of the proposed changes. The President had had to keep on allocating and spending money to do all of that. At least it had created jobs.

But those jobs wouldn't last forever. It was like a new WPA program, one that came during a terrible economic crisis to begin with, and one that had new problems. Like the Great Depression of the 1930s, the Great Recession of the 2010s had an economy in shambles after a decade or more of unchecked greed with the controls on banking and investment switched off. Added to that was a catastrophe of erosion in the Midwest, which meant that the Dust Bowl had made a horrific comeback. Water tables were lower than ever thanks to the increased demand on them. That translated to no relief in sight and more heat exhaustion-induced deaths.

Scientists – climatologists, biologists, environmentalists, ecologists, conservationists, engineers and others – had tried without success to explain the need for this for over forty years, but they had all been put off. There was plenty of time to agree on a plan of austerity, going green, and preservation of the planet's rainforests later, they were always told.

Big businesses had undermined the efforts of the United Nations and countless non-governmental organizations (NGOs) for decades, always concerned with present profits and comforts, oblivious to the collapse that they were enticing with their greed.

At one climate conference after another, nothing constructive had been accomplished: the Kyoto conference, the one at Rio de Janeiro, and at another in Indonesia, let alone at U.N. headquarters in New York City. Now New York City was partially underwater, the polar icecaps had melted like so many cubes in a glass of water, and the oceans were turning to acid as coral reefs died off.

Building and rebuilding and rerouting the nation's infrastructure was expensive, but the President had managed to convince Congress to fund it when the nation's landmass shrank. The evidence of pressing need was just incontrovertible. Added to that was the selling point that once accomplished, all this work would come with a wonderful payoff: ease of transport and a long warranty on completed bridges, roads, and railroads. However, no longer would the government insist that flood insurers pay for land permanently lost to the rising oceans.

The greenest aspect of it all had been a bit of a letdown: loading the goods-filled holds of tractor trailer trucks onto trains and moving them around the nation via railroads rather than burning fossil fuels and filling roads with huge trucks. Truck drivers had protested this move en masse, but the idea had gone through; a new federal statute requiring that goods be transported this way had been passed last year. The truck drivers had calmed down when they realized that they would be living closer to their families and driving shorter distances in the future. Roads would also be safer with fewer tired drivers operating huge vehicles.

We used to drive everywhere, and my father still enjoyed driving for hours on end.

We had driven to Cape Cod, Massachusetts almost every summer and stayed for a week or two. There were shops, beaches, The Sundae School ice cream parlor, and restaurants that we visited each year. No more; most of the Cape was underwater, and the scientific research facilities at Woods Hole had been relocated inland.

The government called what it was doing eminent domain, a term I had studied in law school. I called it Nature's eminent removal. Same difference: Nature was forcing things to be either forsaken or relocated, and the government was acquiescing to that as it chose to save whatever it could.

That meant that people who were perfectly happy where they were, with property safely inland, were not safe after all. They were forced to sell it to the government for a pittance and find another place to live. Those too close to the water were out of luck, however, and displaced.

This situation was why I was on edge constantly, alert to the possibility of being forced to move. So far, so good: I checked topographical maps and our surroundings as I attempted to gauge the chances that the government might come knocking on our door, demanding to buy us out and relocate us.

If that happened, we would have little or no time to plan our next move, and limited options. This was to be avoided. What would those options be? Could we stay in central Connecticut, where sea level didn't imminently threaten our way of life? Could we avoid being in close quarters with lots of other people? What other intrusions into our daily lives threatened then?

Better not to find out via direct, up-close-and-personal experience, I warned my parents and Hamish, and they agreed. This wasn't a vacation; it was a covert reconnaissance mission. Overtly, Hamish and I would try to have a romantic time of it in each bed-and-breakfast inn or spa, and we would enjoy the historic and cultural sites.

But I was determined to find and see people who had been displaced everywhere we went. That was what scared me, but there was no point in wishing it away. It was real, it was happening now, and I intended to see it and see it until the fear wore off. When I realized that, I had told Hamish so.

He smiled. "That is what I had not been able to put into words, but it's what everyone needs to do now that it is part of real life everywhere. Fear makes it all that much tougher to deal with. Take away the fear, and people can think clearly again."

"Indeed. That's why I research and plan so much, and look at topographical maps. I don't want that fear to take hold of me and stop me from thinking clearly. I want to know the enemy. Police should not be militarized. It will help me to write about that if I see it. Theory is just a baby step. It's just an ivory tower idea. We have to see blatant signs of the police state creeping up on us in order to have a clear response to them."

"What would you say?"

"I don't know. I have to see it first," I said with a wry grin.

"Fair enough," my husband replied. I think he was both pleased and worried by my plans.

Now I was executing those plans, and I realized how much Hamish had done to enable them. He had to have stopped working and met extensively with his friends and colleagues in Blackout Security to make my plans a reasonably safe reality. The Blackout SUV was following us by a couple of car-lengths back all the way into Pennsylvania.

We took I-84 into Pennsylvania, and with that, I pulled off the highway. Time for a bathroom break, and time to look at the road map. I didn't believe in GPS devices. They kept a record of wherever you drove that could be referred to by some remote surveillance hacker…forever. Besides, I loved maps. You could turn the pages, get lost and found, and really memorize the terrain and understand where you had been, see where you were, and know where you were going. It was just better that way.

We drove south, just as I used to do every few years with my parents while I was growing up, taking scenic routes through national parks and visiting historic sites. When I saw a Dunkin' Donuts (those usually had much cleaner rest rooms than fast food burger joints, with the added dividend of not smelling like burgers!), we used the facilities, bought coffees with milk, and got back into the car.

I leafed through my road atlas and decided to head for Route 209. That would take us close to Hershey, and we ought to see more there than on some stupid, sanitized interstate highway. I left the atlas opened to that page, checked that Ed and Aaron were settled and ready to take off again, and pulled out.

A few minutes later, once I had found Route 209 and looked like I was sticking with it, Hamish's cell phone rang. He checked the number on it, answered it, and then turned to me. "Where are you going?" he asked me.

"NOT on the stupid interstate highway. We'll never see any displaced people there," I replied, staying my course. I started up the CD player with some Beethoven music.

He grinned and spoke into his phone. "Did you hear all that? It looks like she's going to make you earn your pay on this trip after all. The relaxing stretch of it just ended," he quipped.

I glanced in the rearview mirror. Ed was driving, and Aaron was on his cell phone. As Hamish spoke, Aaron's expression changed from one of inquisitiveness to full alert. Yes! This was going to show us something. I felt a slight thrill of fear as I realized that Aaron's next move was to his gun; I recognized the motions of someone who was checking his weapon.

Damn. I didn't want him to shoot anyone! I just wanted to see what was going on.

For the next forty minutes, nothing went on. The music played, Hamish and I drank our coffee, and we even stopped the cars for another bathroom break and refueling. Ed and Aaron switched places, sharing the driving. Hamish, with no driver's license, stayed in the passenger seat of our car. Route 209 was a pretty one, and thick with trees on either side. It looked like undeveloped, untouched forest of deciduous trees going far back into the distance.

Another ten minutes on Route 209 and I finally saw it: trailer after trailer, RVs, campers, and other recreational vehicles. They were all parked along the roadside – on both sides – and weeds had grown up around the edges of some. A few had tires that needed replacing, or at least re-inflating. I slowed down slightly to peer at license plates. "Can you see their license plates, Hamish? I want to know what states they are from," I explained.

"Michigan, New York, Indiana, Ohio…and Pennsylvania," he read slowly.

Families occupied these vehicles, and they included people of all ages. Some were visibly armed. I sped up slightly, trying to look less interested in what were clearly no longer recreational vehicles. I had read about efforts to criminalize homelessness in all forms, and many were in state where displaced Americans were most heavily concentrated.

Hamish's phone rang again. He answered it, and I could hear Aaron's voice as he practically yelled across to Ed, who I could see in my rearview mirror was the one making the call. "Go faster! These people look angry. If they recognize you too, we don't have enough bullets to defend you, and it might not even be about who you are. You look like people who haven't been displaced, and that may be all it takes to piss them off."

I drove at fifty miles an hour when I heard that, and glanced at a speed limit sign: 45 MPH, it said. I pushed it up another five. The view didn't change for another fifteen minutes, until we came to an intersection with lots of shops and big-box stores.

"Happy now?" Hamish asked.

I thought about that. "Somewhat, but that's just a little taste of what I expect to experience."

He looked around at the area. It was a rural, but busy, town center in the middle of Pennsylvania. Displaced people had to be all around here, too, and we were in a dark blue Mercedes. We stood out.

"I don't have to use the bathroom, and I don't plan to loiter about," I said.

"Okay."

"Are you angry?"

"No! I just want to make sure that you are aware of possibilities and our situation. I'm glad we're seeing what's going on too."

"Okay." I drove on through the intersection, and out of the built-up area. Soon we were passing through another settlement just like the first one. I couldn't go fast this time, though, because a huge vehicle loomed up ahead.

It wasn't a tractor trailer truck. It was an MRAP. Damn! I couldn't get the camera out. It wasn't as though I could claim to be a member of the media. Taking photographs would only make things awkward. Well, it was still early in the trip.

The occupants of the MRAP suddenly pulled off to the side of the road and waved us on. I drove past slowly. This was not a wide road. As we passed, I saw that the MRAP said Leighton Police Department on its side. There it was, a local, militarized police vehicle. Was that really necessary as a deterrent to attacks on anyone? Wouldn't a cruiser do the job better if the cops needed to go on a chase though narrower openings than this main road?

Whatever…I picked up speed and drove on. More displaced people filled the roadsides for miles. Occasionally, I would see pets with them, usually dogs sitting on laps or on the grass next to people in lawn chairs. What were they all doing for food and income, I wondered, using their savings? Did the government help? A cat stared out the top window of a camper at me.

"These people definitely look as though they fled their homes in these vehicles with everything that they could take with them from those homes," I said to Hamish. The music was turned way down low, and we weren't paying any attention to it. I think I had left it on just to prevent anxiety and for no other reason.

"Yes, they do," was all that he said.

I drove through Pottsville, and kept going until I saw a sign for I-81, then got on it. Hamish looked surprised. "Seen enough?"

"Well, that and the fact that this route connects with 78, then goes to Harrisburg and on to an easy way to reach Hershey. It just seems simpler, and I feel as though we've seen this leg of the displaced situation. We'll see more of it, maybe, on the way to Bear Run, won't we?"

"Probably."

We picked up some speed and got to Hershey an hour or so later, and could smell the chocolate in the air. Actually, their recipe wasn't really chocolate. No wonder I sought out other options most of the time. But, this was classic American junk, and even my discerning mother ate a few bars of it every year. We had to see this. So, we spent one night at a nearby inn and ate at the hokey restaurant (not right next to the squealing kids, Hamish told the server as she attempted to seat us that close in a huge and almost empty room).

The place offered a tour of the factory and a chance to wander around its shop. The shop sold tons and tons of candy, and a few tee shirts. I bought (big spender!) a red tee shirt each for Dad and Aunt Charlie, and a few large bars of chocolate, including Special Dark and Milk Chocolate Almond. With our proverbial ticket on this thus punched, we left.

The next morning, we ate a nice breakfast at the inn and took off. Ed and Aaron hadn't even cared about appearances this time. The gay act actually got scrapped after ten minutes inside the place, because another guest recognized us. It was suddenly clear that we were not traveling without protection. That was just as well, because a real gay couple was staying there, too.

Those guests were a professor and his husband who were on their way to give a guest lecture. They didn't make our Blackout escort nervous, though. It was the passersby – the owners and other guests – who concerned them. The professor and his husband (also a professor, just without a lecture assignment on this trip) taught sociology and anthropology. We traded business cards.

The other guests turned out to be benign enough when Ed chatted with them. More worry over nothing! They were doing a survey of bed-and-breakfast inns. Fascinating (sarcasm!).

The next morning, it was on to Bear Run, in southwestern Pennsylvania. We would be staying at a hotel nearby. Aaron looked concerned about appearances again, I noticed, but there was no point in saying anything about separate rooms for him and Ed. They had insisted, for security reasons, on booking one room as close to ours as possible.

I knew what they would do: sleep in shifts to watch us. That was why I had booked 2 nights there, with no plans off the premises other than to see Fallingwater. That ought to enable them to sleep enough and watch us.

How did I go this time? Routes 76 and 70 to Somerset, then roads. The roads around Somerset looked old. It was a small town, neatly laid out, and it looked like it needed all new paving on the roads, new lighting, and whatever else. The roads were good enough for supplies to get in and out, though.

"Ed and Aaron are going to love this," I said to Hamish as I looked at the road atlas in yet another Dunkin' Donuts parking lot. I showed him the problem. No main highways to use to get there unless we took a major detour. I was not going to do that.

"Okay," Hamish said, and called them to break the news. "Aaron, we're taking Routes 281, 653, and 381 in that order." It sounded as though that was no great surprise.

This stretch of the trip took us a mere 45 minutes.

They were not uneventful minutes.

A few miles out from Somerset, we saw tents, cars, campers, and people. Another encampment of American climate refugees was spread out before us, and then thick on either side of us. The license plates were from many of the same places that Hamish had read off of the vehicles the day before.

These refugees didn't look as well off as the ones we had seen upstate. Most of them didn't have vehicles that they could live in comfortably, for one thing. For another, not all of them seemed to possess vehicles at all. Had some of them hiked here?

Soon we saw a sign for Laurel Ridge State Park. That wasn't all. Up ahead, moving slowly, was another MRAP vehicle. We slowed down, and saw that cops with assault rifles were pacing up and down outside the entrance, and on inside the park as well.

More armed men were walking around on the road, and as we passed the MRAP, we could see that it was just the first of three. Only one of them claimed to be from a nearby town. The others were clearly still covered with military camouflage paint. Some of the men wore police uniforms, and some military fatigues.

They saw us coming, nodded, and waved us on. I drove carefully, not wanting to scare someone on foot by breezing by too fast…especially an armed someone.

Well, isn't this fun, I thought sarcastically. I felt sorry for these people, being displaced and policed to the nth degree. They couldn't go home, and a cold winter was coming, to be spent outdoors, homeless due to no particular fault of their own. It was just becoming clear to me that many Americans were suddenly homeless…many more than had ever been homeless, and that it had happened rather suddenly.

Just how safe were these people, from the elements, from each other, and from these guards? The news didn't provide any enlightenment on this issue. I drove on past them in silence, and Hamish had no jokes to crack.

I pulled into the hotel parking lot at what seemed to be not that great a distance from this disturbing scene. Ed and Aaron pulled in next to us, got out, looked over at us, and took out their overnight bags. Hamish and I got out and did the same.

We were all so subdued as we approached the building that we forgot all about cover stories, appearances, and any other nonsense. We were safe and comfortable, with places to go. Our problems seemed nonexistent after the past couple of days' worth of disaster tourism.

The hotel was 25 minutes away from Fallingwater, and as close a place to stay as any near it. It was really nice, and a completely different world from the park we had passed. Some park. I hated camping, and that version of the idea seemed like a travesty of it. That wasn't recreation. It was a hell of constant fear for one's safety, with one's own species as the primary threat.

This place was a huge, gorgeous, rambling, country home of a mansion-turned-hotel. A golf course surrounded it. Hamish, despite hailing from the nation that had invented that game, did not play it. Mark Twain said, "Golf is a good walk spoiled." Like that author-humorist, we agreed, preferring to walk at a fast pace and actually go somewhere, or explore.

After getting settled into our room, Hamish and I wanted to go out walking. Ed and Aaron said okay and followed us out. I took out my camera and hung it around my neck. We headed for the back, right out onto the golf course. It wasn't time for lunch yet. A couple of golf carts were in use. It was green and beautiful, like a dream world separated from harsh reality.

For a price, anyone could separate themselves from reality, I mused.

Hamish and I walked and walked. We saw the grounds, the huge expanse of green, and the first traces of leaves changing color. It was a beautiful place. We walked some more until we got to the edge of the golf course. Through the trees, I could see the road.

That wasn't all I could see. There were more MRAPs. They seemed to be on surveillance. They didn't see us through the trees and, as I had been photographing the beauty around me, my lens cap was off, the camera was on, and I was ready this time. I shot a few images, then turned the camera up to get some of the songbirds that kept landing on branches above me. I didn't care what species they were; I just wanted to make sure that if the cops or soldiers out there noticed me, they wouldn't think twice about what I was doing.

Apparently that worked, because no one paid any attention to us as we continued to walk around the perimeter, avoiding the golfers. When we had completed the circuit of the place, it was lunchtime, so we went inside to eat. A history of the place in the front hall told us that it was founded by coal tycoons. Great…fossil fuel use that had led us to this sorry state of being barricaded in and out of whatever place, depending upon one's circumstances in life.

We ate lunch. Crab cakes, vegetable sandwich wrap, lemonade. That was it. We wanted to scale back a bit after gorging ourselves at the C.I.A., so we did. Next, we went to our room to check our e-mail with the wi-fi service, read novels, and just relax until dinnertime.

Dinner was nice, quiet, and uneventful. I brought my camera with me. Ed ate alone across the room, watching us, while Aaron got room service and watched our rooms and our stuff. I took a few photographs, as a tourist might be expected to do, and we went back upstairs. I downloaded all photographs, labeled them, and backed them up to a remote server and a memory stick. Hamish did some work on his own laptop.

The bathroom was nice, so I filled the tub and took a long bath. The tub was big enough for two, so I got out and dragged Hamish away from his computer to sit in it with me. Soon it began to feel like a vacation again.

The next day, after lolling around all morning, we toured Fallingwater, the house designed by Frank Lloyd Wright. The architect had designed it and its guest house in 1935, and it was commissioned by the Kaufmanns of Pittsburgh, who owned a department store there. They lived in Fallingwater with their adult son, Edgar Jr. The place was amazing.

Outside, it was levels of sand-hued, horizontal walls, held up by tall, vertical stacks of flat, gray stones, and with windows that had dark-red painted metal frames. It was set over a waterfall on the Bear Run section of the Youghiogheny River, and used a huge boulder as the main foundation and support for the whole structure.

It had a huge cauldron, a ball-shaped thing that swung over the fireplace or away from it, which had been used for hot cider, or some such treat. That was in the living room. The living room was a huge expanse of place with a stone floor, made of many stones that were laid in a perfectly smooth arrangement. The far end of the living room, which overlooked the waterfall, opened smoothly into a staircase that went down into a swimming pool.

Edgar Jr.'s room had intriguing windows; they opened in the corner by pushing the panes outward, leaving no metal frame blocking the view. It looked clear out to the woods – clever. A door-like window curved inward, and the wooden desk had a curving cut to accommodate it.

Walking up to the guest house, there was nice place to sit outside under a trellis that had wisteria vines growing up over it. I loved wisteria, and could imagine Mrs. Liliane Kaufmann reading under it while smelling the flowers' perfume around her. Hamish and I walked back down the path after seeing it all, and paused abruptly. A long, maroon on top, white on its belly milk snake was crossing in front of us. We waited for it to pass.

Ed and Aaron came running up behind us, but Hamish just stood there with his arm around me, waiting and watching. He told them to do nothing but the same. I did, while pressing up against him. I hated snakes. But what would Ed and Aaron have done, shot it?! That would achieve nothing useful. The snake slithered into the woods and was gone, and we were on our way. No use calling attention to ourselves.

We returned to the hotel. Dinner was again uneventful. This time, I asked Hamish if he would like to try an interesting alcoholic drink after dinner…just one. Okay. We went to the bar and sat down.

I never did stuff like this! But…we had all night to sleep off the effects of one drink, and breakfast with coffee the next morning. And I wasn't drinking on an empty stomach. Armed with a meal of baked brie with brown sugar, almonds, and raspberry sauce, Norwegian salmon with citrus glaze and rice pilaf, and a dish of vanilla bean ice cream, I felt up for this.

One raspberry blackberry rum vermouth something-or-other later and I was feeling happily buzzed. Without food, I would have felt ill. Hamish had a straightforward glass of Scotch whiskey. A Scottish guy drinking Scotch…that's it! I was officially silly. Time for bed.

We went upstairs. All was well. Buzzed, we checked our computers, the camera, and whatever else. Nothing amiss. Silently thanking Ed and Aaron for that, we went to bed.

The next morning, it was time to face reality again.

Most people did that by driving or taking public transportation to a cubicle hell.

Well, they used to. Now many of them faced it by wandering lost in the woods, trying to stake out a place to pass the time, wondering what would happen next and thinking that it would be nothing good.

We packed the car and headed out, toward Washington, D.C.

Chapter 4

Coastlines and Sea Changes – The Garden Uneven

The view from the International Space Station of the Earth's land masses had changed to the point that maps and globes were being redrawn and remade. Websites with the new data were competing with NASA's, and I had looked at all of them. They were just too morbidly fascinating to forget about. Day after day, I had stared at them, memorizing the new and comparing it with the old.

The shape of every land mass and continent had changed. The map of the United States that I had always seen in advertisements was completely different, and I could not get used to it. I was slowly memorizing it, but it brought an emotional reaction every time I saw it. It was disturbing, and sometimes it induced anxiety just to look at it.

Now we were starting to see it from the ground level, in real time.

As we headed toward Washington, D.C., we wondered how it would look.

This wasn't our first visit. We had gone there to attend academic conferences, tour the monuments, and view the art in the Smithsonian Museum. We had seen the United States Holocaust Memorial Museum. We had not toured the White House, but we had wandered around the Rotunda of the Capitol, seen the Frieze of American History in it, the John Trumbull paintings, and so on. In short, we had been there and done much of that, but not all.

As an art and history junkie, there was always, always more to see. I had never had the chance to watch a case being argued in the U.S. Supreme Court. Now that I stood a decent chance of being recognized by the media, I wasn't so keen on going in there, to be perfectly honest. But it would be great to see the Library of Congress. Let's face it: books turned me on more than oral arguments.

I really believed that I could make more of a difference with my books than with individual law cases. Attorneys who were newly admitted to the bar could expect to wait years – and maybe even decades – before their mentors ever allowed them to argue even a piece of a case in court. There was that, and the Aspie impediment of not having the ideal retort ready until hours later, by which time it would be useless. No…books were far more thrilling, and they were almost forever. A judge-made law could be negated by legislative law, and vice versa. Depressing!

We drove on highways this time, straight for the nation's capital. I wanted to just get there already, and see what was different and what wasn't. We had watched the transformation of that beautiful city over the past couple of years with morbid fascination.

One of the first things that the government had done was to relocate all of the art that was in the city to secret locations on higher ground…outside the city. A topographic map revealed that elevations varied all over the city, with the lowest points being, of course, where the majority of the museums, monuments, and other most famous sites were situated. Why was that? Well, they were closest to the Potomac River, which the city's designers had considered to be the most picturesque spots. Funny how such conditions didn't remain constant…

Humans loved to expend enormous amounts of resources and efforts on projects that they simply expected to enjoy the indefinite use of because, well, they had paid for them. Nature was showing them in one unpleasant way after another that life didn't work that way.

I thought of the cherry trees that ringed the Tidal Basin, a gift from Japan in 1912. They had been relocated along with the artwork and other precious artifacts. If they hadn't been moved, the influx of the floodwaters would have overwhelmed the inlet and outlet gates of the Tidal Basin. There was only so much that the U.S. Army Corps of Engineers could be expected to do to control all that water. But I knew that they were back now, along with a lot of the art.

The seat of government moved fast when its own premises were threatened by Nature. A series of dikes that had been commissioned by an elite team of Dutch engineers – the same one that was mentoring engineers in New York City, southern Connecticut, and Boston – had saved the day. The dikes were in place. They looked like something out of a Marvel Comics movie, which was cool, and pumps were in use to remove the excess water.

Washington, D.C. was nearly restored. We were about to enjoy the delusion of normalcy. I had suggested kicking off this delusion by visiting the lowest-lying presidential memorial, the one which honored the creator of the word "normalcy," Franklin Delano Roosevelt, and Eleanor too (the monument included a statue of her).

We could check into our hotel later. It was bizarre to be able to drive into the city within just a couple of hours of leaving southwestern Pennsylvania and see it looking almost as it had the last time we had been here. We had just seen hordes of displaced people and MRAPs. Now we were seeing what felt like an alternate reality: a beautiful, marble city on a beautiful day.

I pulled into the parking area by the Roosevelt Memorial and shut off the car. Hamish and I got out, stretched, and headed for the rest rooms. They were in perfect order. How nice! But when I went over to the water fountain outside, Hamish stopped me. He was using a gadget of his own devising that resembled a Starfleet-issue tricorder to analyze a stream of water from it.

"Don't drink this," he warned. "It might give you a water-borne illness."

"Really? Like what, cholera? Is it also contaminated by red algae and low in oxygen from being out in the ocean? Does it need desalinating?"

He grinned. "Wow. You do read a lot of environmental news. Yes, maybe, probably, and yes. But sanitation engineers are working on all that. In a few more months, it likely won't matter. Meanwhile, did you bring any bottled water?"

Typical guy – typical husband! – he expected me to have thought of such things. And…I had brought something, but it was only because my mother had put it into the trunk just before we drove away. We had twelve small bottles of water. I got 2 of them out.

The memorial was fun to see, with a bronze replica of FDR's wheelchair, lots of FDR quotes on the granite walls, and two particularly memorable bronze icons. One was the expected statue of Eleanor Roosevelt, a founding member of the United Nations, and the other was of Franklin himself, sitting with his pet dog,

Fala, at his side. The memorial was divided into four sections, one for each term that he had been elected to serve.

It opened out at the end onto the Tidal Basin among the Japanese cherry trees which, to my surprise, were in bloom. "Hey look, Hamish, I guess there's only so much that the government can do to keep up the appearance of normalcy. These trees shouldn't be in bloom until spring!"

He looked grimly up at the blossoms, but said nothing. The view across the Tidal Basin of the Jefferson Memorial looked as pretty as it ever had. Where were the stains of high water marks? Oh yeah…scrubbed away. Where had the budget money for that been found?

I could see the point in doing all this preservation work. Keeping up appearances was only a part of the motive. The rest of it was preservation of our culture and way of life. I didn't disagree with that. In fact, I approved of it. What was the point of surviving if we had no art and culture to study and appreciate? It would be boring and meaningless.

But was this going to actually work? Temperatures were higher, and the cherry trees might or might not thrive, along with honey bees, other bees, other insects, and countless other species. We needed them all. They all mattered, and were interdependent. Some meant food, some meant beauty, some meant both, and all supported each other's continued existence.

I wondered whether or not our legislators, located directly to our immediate east, fully understood and appreciated that. Would they only do that when they were out of time to make decisions that showed it?!

We got back into the car and drove to the Jefferson Memorial, walked around, and then moved on to the Mall to see how that looked. It looked okay. Trucks were busy going in and out of the museums that lined it, and Hamish shut off Aaron Copeland's *Lincoln Portrait* to tune into National Public Radio.

We were in luck; a discussion group was talking about historic preservation, art, architecture, and gardens around the capital city. Much of the Smithsonian's art collection was being put back into the museums now. That was what all the trucks were there for. The scientific collection would follow more slowly. Julia Child's kitchen, which was situated in the basement level of the National Museum of American History, would be back in place within the afternoon.

Interesting. We put the music back on and found a parking place, and went into the U.S. Capitol to listen to some debates. The politicians were hard at work doing little, as was to be expected. The heavy lifting was done, after all. They worked for their lobbyists, not for We the People. It was more like We the Cloutless and too often We the Clueless.

Some of us were just waking up, and when I considered how big of a shock had been required to achieve that, I was angry at Americans in general. We had the education and the legal freedom to educate ourselves about almost anything that piqued our interest. Yet the vast majority of us had cared too much about football and other team sports, online gaming, and reality shows to notice that we could not depend on grocery stores forever as a bottomless trough to enable us to continue that way.

From the gallery above the Senate chamber, my eyes glazed over as the politicians below argued about freedom to live as we always had, with liberty and justice for all. Nice fairy tale!

Freedom is not free. It costs money. It also requires room.

I recalled the Schoolhouse Rock cartoon segments of my childhood, watched over and over again on Saturday mornings, and thought of the one about elbow room. Thanks to human overpopulation, that was all gone now.

The Pilgrims had come here for elbow room so that they could determine their own government and have greater freedoms (ignoring the fact that people already lived here), and then they were followed by more and more immigrants, all émigrés who had tired of constrained conditions at home. That brain drain and skill drain had made them very comfortable here…until now, when it didn't.

Now, brains and skill still came here, but only after a green card lottery or a very expensive application – expensive due to attorneys' fees and other legal fees. But it didn't stop there. Climate refugees who were not acknowledged as such kept coming in also.

Climate change made floods and droughts, squeezing food supplies and other resources. Conflicts in the South and Central American nations had been pushing them here for decades before the floods affected the United States.

To make matters worse, huge corporations funded by Wall Street's fiat money schemes had established huge agribusinesses, which grew food for our sprawling empire – not for the immigrants who worked to grow it. Yet people still wanted to come here, and with good reason. Even if there were problems here, they were worse farther south.

Things kept getting more and more desperate at home, so they would save up their money to leave. When they were at last ready to go, they faced a perilous journey that could far more easily than not get them raped, maimed, and even killed. This was how people immigrated illegally, and the irony of it was that the cost could be even higher than for legal immigrants, both in money and physical danger and penalties.

Women had been taking birth control pills long before the advent of Nae-Née, some just for the walk across the border into the U.S., avoiding checkpoints. They walked with insufficient food and water through huge desert areas that spanned both Mexico and the side they so badly wanted to get to. Rapists preyed on them along the way. If they managed to avoid the rapists, they could still die of dehydration in the middle of nowhere.

Men and women and children made this trek. There were train rides, and many failed to survive them unscathed. People who couldn't pay enough to satisfy extortionists who, en route, kept raising the price of being smuggled across the continent, were often shoved off of moving trains. If they lived, they had broken legs that shut down their ability to work for months.

Trucks with no windows or ventilation were another way in. Border guards on either side could be bribed to overlook this with invitations to come on in and rape the female passengers. This was also the case with human traffickers.

Added to all of that was a loose end that most immigrants were inextricably tied to: their children. Children were a motivation to get here, to go back there, and to risk all this in the first place. There were just too many people even after Nae-Née was put into the mix, so this continued to be the case.

Children were often left behind with relatives – aunts and uncles, grandparents, cousins, whomever was available – to be brought later, perhaps by plane or boat, or more likely by human smugglers. More danger to face! It was either that or go back for them and pay for the whole perilous trek again, complete with all of the risks.

If children were old enough, they made the trek and got it over with, growing up in the U.S. Some were even able to go to school all the way through college only to find that they were not legal residents, and expected to go back to a culture and way of life that was not only far harsher than they could ever imagine while living here in the U.S., but alien to them. Simply being fluent in Spanish did not make it familiar.

Still other children were either born here immediately after their parents' arrival or were born later, thus making them automatic citizens, but at risk of having their parents deported at any time. What good did that do them?! They could end up in the proverbial system as foster kids, abused, neglected, and miserable. Granted, some foster parents were awesome people, but entering the system still meant being forced to play Russian roulette with one's future and sanity.

As if all these problems weren't enough, there was the commercial prison system that lined the borders. That was what an illegal immigrant who got caught could look forward to. These prisons were nothing but a big business to distant owners. They were overcrowded, which meant that they were uncomfortable and bred hostility between inmates and between inmates and guards. There was some risk of fire in many of them.

And, if that didn't make it miserable enough, there was the fact that the American legal system was glutted with cases, thus slowing the whole process down. Anyone caught by Immigration and Customs Enforcement (ICE) would be put on proverbial ice for years on end, waiting in a for-profit hellhole of a prison to be sent home while watching their lives and time waste away.

It was a terrible way of delaying people from restarting the whole process. These climate refugees lived a life of perpetual risk and misery, with instability at ever phase. They had no choice in the matter and no real hope of anything better.

The whole thing was just one odyssey of misery with a small chance of success. And what was success in this endeavor? It was the chance to work as a farm laborer or a dishwasher or a lawn crew member. Farm laborers had no days off, were sprayed with insecticides without warning, sexually harassed in the fields, and paid subsistence wages. Dishwashers worked in restaurants all over the U.S. for a pittance, living on a pittance in tenements that merely served as a place to eat and sleep.

The same was true of lawn crew members, with the added insult of having to groom the yards and edges the flower and vegetable gardens of people who, unlike themselves, had a yard with room to grow their own food. They had to eat cheap food that included processed junk, and what few fruits and vegetables they could afford were treated with fungicides and insecticides, coated with wax, and had genetically modified organisms (GMOs) bred into them.

The immigrants spent their entire lives working for and right next to people who had far better choices, choices which were unobtainable to them. Higher sea levels had pushed those of us who were already here into smaller land areas, and smaller, and smaller. Displaced Americans were now everywhere, joining the immigrants as refugees, crowding motels, hotels, and campgrounds.

Trailer parks had sprung up here and there, but they were insufficient to meet the needs of the U.S. climate refugees, hence, the impromptu congregations of yet more trailers along roadsides. Homelessness had exploded, both with and without trailers. It was a nightmare for everyone, with the only winners being the sort of cops who enjoyed being professional bullies.

All the while, stupid debates about climate change and anthropogenic (human-caused) global warming raged on. Which term was better, climate change or global warming? Was it human caused or not? Was it part of a natural cycle for the Earth to go through, or human caused?

It seemed to be both. Yes, we could very well be experiencing a cycle of warming all over the planet. But let's face it, since the Industrial Age of the mid-1800s, we humans had emitted so many fossil fuels into the atmosphere that we had amped it up. We watched the Senators waste time arguing over this as we sat in the gallery, and I was getting angry with them. Who cared?! Just talk about what you were going to do help people deal with the consequences, I thought.

Hamish was on the side of insisting upon having absolute proof that it was anthropogenic before he would accept that as the cause of climate change. I didn't feel the need for such an extreme amount of evidence. Over ninety percent seemed like enough for me. After all, since when did one hundred percent of ANY group agree on anything? To my recollection: never.

Global warming did not seem like the ideal term to describe this phenomenon.

No, climate change was better, because winter still happened. We had summer, we had winter, and both were being felt more intensely, with hotter summers and colder winters. We also had more intense superstorms: hurricanes, typhoons, tornadoes, haboobs (dust storms – an Arab word that fit the conditions of the North American southwest), and more.

Arguing over what to call everything was eating up way too much taxpayer time and money. Damn those senators! They lived in comfort. They were as silly as ivory tower twits in academia who spent their careers publishing papers, intent on nothing more than a reason to be granted tenure. Just focus on the needs of those who don't have comfort and security to fall back on, I thought from my seat, shouting it mentally.

But they didn't. I nudged Hamish. It was time to go – time to see more of what was wrong. There was nothing more to be observed here. It was too much like a bad daytime talk show. We walked out, got into our car, and went to our hotel room. We had forgotten to eat lunch, so as we ate dinner at a place called Le Diplomate on 14th Street. It was good, and it was quiet. Despite its name, we did not see any obvious politicking transpiring.

We ate quietly, not really interested in much more than a nice meal, avoiding social interactions and notice, and returning to our hotel to sleep. Luckily, no one noticed us. Our Blackout guys were doing a good job of preventing that. Did I mention that more than one pair of them were following and watching out for us? Well, another pair, even stealthier than Ed and Aaron, was on this trip. It was working. No one bothered us in D.C.

The next morning, after breakfast at the hotel, we took off for Virginia. The Library of Congress could wait for another time. Time to see more climate refugees and whatever else revealed itself.

Hamish and I were quiet as we listened to *Appalachian Spring*, not caring how much of a cliché that selection was for a couple who were heading toward that very mountain range. We were lost in thought, and when I checked, it turned out to be about the same thing: how lucky we were. We had the very comfort and safety that was blinding our politicians to their duty.

We did not have the insurmountable problem that so many others did – of relocation.

Relocation to where? Nowhere else welcomed climate refugees.

All over the globe, in every nation – some of which were now completely underwater – there were climate refugees. No country was immune to this, and what had happened with Florida was a horrific case in point.

Florida was no longer the same shape, size, and area that it once was.

Where it used to resemble a long tail hanging off of the east coast of the United States, dangling southwards and pointing to the Caribbean island nations, now it only reached half as far, and many of those islands had ceased to exist.

That was why my parents had stopped their trips to Florida.

Well, that was one of the reasons.

There were many, many more that explained it.

Each of them was more disturbing than the last, and all were associated with climate change, or global warming – or whichever term one preferred to call the phenomenon by.

Why disturbing? Maybe horrifying was more like it…

As sea levels rose, the most obvious thing happened: water covered land.

That meant that the expected consequences followed:

Coastlines receded, causing losses of what had been prime beachfront property. Cities on that beachfront property were inundated with water. Motor vehicles were swept away, drifting out with the tide to rust, leaking fossil fuels and worse, which included transmission and air conditioning fluids. This added to the pollution of the Atlantic Ocean, the Gulf of Mexico, and the Caribbean Sea.

Already riddled with sinkholes, those that were threatening to swallow up homes did so as the water covered the coast and continued inland, taking down homes before salvage attempts could be made.

Residents crowded the highways of Florida, these newly made climate refugees of America, as families and others who had denied the coming change, staying on and rebuilding after every hurricane, were finally flooded out for good. Traffic was at a maddening standstill.

This was what I had always sought to avoid, and why we had driven out of Manhattan in the early stages of this process up north, before it would be too perilous and slow to get safely and quickly back to Connecticut. Anxiety drove me to think and plan ahead. That anxiety was like a white haze in front of my eyes if I had too much of it and couldn't think clearly, so I did my best to keep on top of it. That was life with Asperger's, and it was a good thing. Not planning ahead was what most people did, and it was harder, slower, and far more stressful.

Most people had to crawl out of Florida, pushing their cars as they idled on the highways, in what my mother liked to call the dead-sea crawl, but running out of fuel. Suddenly that term that she had coined long ago had a literal meaning.

Road rage incidents soared of course, as people in bumper-to-bumper traffic lost patience with the slowness of their exit from a shrinking land area. Police could not keep up with the problem; there were murders, rapes, and thefts every few miles.

Eventually, people managed to drive or limp with their vehicle in neutral, pushing and panting all the way, into Georgia and Alabama and on north to higher ground. Once there, they found that they could not stop and rest, for the land was already spoken for.

People who had spent their entire lives living happily in homes spread out among few others suddenly found themselves moving to overcrowded cities, unhappy in their new circumstances.

It didn't stop there.

The real horror came from the Everglades.

The Everglades was a huge national park, but not one to be wandered heedless of the dangers within. A huge portion of it was tropical wetlands, which extended over the southern part of mainland Florida, south of Lake Okeechobee. Part of it had wooden walkways, with warnings not to put one's hand or foot in the waters below. The same warning went for air-boaters.

Always home to alligators, the Everglades were first joined by ever-so-slightly more vicious crocodiles, for Florida had always been home to a very few of those at its southernmost tip.

These Jurassic creatures already dwelled in the waters of just about every gated community, golf course, and suburban housing development in Florida. Puppies and toddlers could never be left unattended even before sea level rose, because an alligator could just as easily rise from a pond and snap them up. Animal controllers in every town in the state all had experience with routing them off of the front doorsteps of homes with metal nooses on long metal sticks, too.

But there was another horror brewing in the Everglades as well.

During the last few decades of the twentieth century, when humans thought that the Earth was a stable home that would not change significantly during their own lifetimes or even that of the next generation, they had been careless with pets.

All it took was a few people who thought it would be fun to have pythons and boa constrictors for pets, and a few others who thought it would be a profitable business enterprise to import them from other nations for that purpose. The problem with doing so is that a pet snake would grow, and grow, and grow…until it couldn't be kept. Zoos couldn't take every cast-off snake from a growing human population of fools, and so thousands of cast-off pet snakes had been dumped into the swamp of the Everglades.

They had joined the alligators.

There, they had grown to enormous lengths and widths, becoming the unwitting stars of reality and news shows. Sometimes a report would include a rather amazing photograph of a snake and an alligator, dead by attempting to swallow each other. These curiosities were then forgotten for a while.

The area also contained indigenous rattlesnakes, which were equally fast-moving death-delivery mechanisms. It was better to simply avoid this area altogether. But then sea level rose, swallowing the Everglades. The area was not going to avoid humans.

There were crocodiles at Florida's southernmost point, and they joined the alligators and pythons and boa constrictors, and then…they were borne out of their park and off to the north while they could still move independently. This was before the water level was so high that they would have simply been swept off with the tide.

No, it wasn't that simple, or that easy. The human population would have been happy to see them gone in that way. But no…no, these Jurassic and reptilian menaces infiltrated the land that was higher in central Florida.

Then, as the mass exodus of motor vehicles and humans headed north, there were incidents along the highways that became fodder for both movies and documentaries as Jurassic creatures came out of the wooded areas as people raged and argued about fender benders. They attacked without warning, adding to the carnage caused by road rage and criminal proclivities.

When the worse of it was over, little of the fun parts of Florida remained intact aside from Disney World, because Orlando sat on the highest ground still and so was not destroyed. But coastal cities were lost, and several insurance companies were bankrupted by claims.

NASA's Cape Canaveral was submerged. Whatever resources could be relocated elsewhere were moved, and eminent domain was invoked after a careful government survey to find a new location, one that was on the newly formed coast. What was once well inland was now the coast.

The famous Ringling School of Art and Design in Sarasota was hastily moved along with the nearby art museum. The beautiful pink marble mansion that housed the collection was sacrificed to the flood.

This story repeated itself in the Florida Keys and all around the state's coastline.

The long highway that led out to the farthest Key ended up as an underwater reef, and the Ernest Hemingway House museum was lost. The staff at last had to capture the resident cats and move them away. I think they moved to Louisiana, where people also lost their coastal areas. At least the cats were adopted out safely.

This was what the people we now saw had fled from. They were the few survivors who had made it out and avoided the carnage that Florida's dying ecosystem unleashed on them. That carnage was Nature's revenge, wielded as indifferently as our species had harvested its gifts for as long as we had been able to do so.

Nature was great as long as we were in control and able to take care of ourselves.

It was an instrument of terror and horror when we weren't. And now, we weren't.

We could postpone it with infrastructure, but one look at the newly defined land masses made it patently obvious that humans could not draw on Nature's bank account indefinitely. Eventually…and eventually was starting already…the account would be nearly empty.

As we drove through Virginia, we saw more hastily assembled human encampments, and many had Florida license plates. Some also had Louisiana plates. Not many had fancy recreational vehicles. Instead we saw tents and people living out of their cars.

Louisiana was another disaster area, with the delta of the Mississippi River now far inland. No more New Orleans, no more of the culture and restaurants that had distinguished it; all that was now consigned to memory, literature, and old movies.

We were headed for Thomas Jefferson's Monticello, and in order to see these things, I skipped the interstate highway system again. There was no better way to look for American climate refugees than to get off of that fast-moving, sanitized roadway system.

It would take us just 11 minutes more driving time, Google Maps had told me, though I expected that other variables would add to that. Those computer models never account for rest room breaks or slow-moving drivers. (Snarky of me to say that, but true!)

Actually, we had to use an interstate highway to leave the D.C. area, which meant using I-66, but once we were away from it, we took Routes 29, 15, and 231. Once on Route 29, we were back on my crazy plan, this time seeing U.S. Army MRAPs and soldiers.

It was getting less alarming as we got used to navigating it, but no less appalling.

I wondered what these people had gone through in order to get just to this spot. Was it as those horrific helicopter news reports had shown? How did these people survive it? Or were they lucky enough to simply drive out safely in time, only to get stuck here? But we couldn't just stop and interview them. "I doubt that these soldiers would allow that," Hamish commented wryly.

"Yeah, me too," I said. "I was just wondering about it out loud – I know that!"

We drove carefully through it all, stopped for fuel once in a town called Orange, and made it to the Charlottesville area in about 3 hours. I took us directly to our next bed-and-breakfast inn, which was called The Inn at Monticello. We were staying in the Lilac Room, which had a nice queen-sized bed in it, just like ours at home. It was very nice, and the place had a cat and dog living there. Both animals were friendly.

The breakfast the next morning was terrific, and Hamish and I both ate some of everything. The eggs had smoked Gouda cheese and chives in them, which was a treat, plus there was plenty of bacon, and lemon blueberry buttermilk pancakes. Coffee from a local beanery, orange juice, and fresh berries completed the sense of perfection. I wondered, though, how all this was available at all, even though the prices seemed slightly higher than up north.

Aaron and Ed had given up their gay couple act and all pretense of not knowing us. There was no hope of concealing our identities. A tourist couple who liked to read history had come across a book I had written about Hawai'i and spotted me. Oh well…that's what Hamish and I got for traveling. It was fine; the wife just loved to read, and had bought my book to prepare for the trip. Her name was Lisbeth, and she was a history buff like me so we got along great.

She recognized us over breakfast, and we ended up chatting about the Hawaiian royal family, the Bernice Pauahi Bishop Museum, and the botanical gardens. Her husband, Allan, worked in insurance, and this was just a romantic weekend getaway for them. They didn't live very far from here, and seemed to have no clue about the problems we had seen on the road.

"How did you get here from Woodbridge?" I asked.

"We took the Interstate most of the way," Allan replied. "It's just easier."

Hamish asked, "Easier than what?"

"Easier than slowing down for all of the squatters from Florida or wherever they came here from," he said. "I'll be glad when the authorities get them out of the area. It'll be a lot safer."

I glanced at Lisbeth. She seemed utterly unconcerned as she sat there eating, forking eggs into her mouth with her wrists decked out in David Yurman bracelets tipped with diamonds and amethysts. Her earrings matched, too.

Wow. So this was how one side of America – the safe and lucky side – viewed the unlucky, displaced population. Hamish and I looked at each other, appalled, but managed to keep our facial expressions neutral. No point in telling these people what we thought of their attitude. Was ours much better? We would try to make it so, I knew.

I was also wondering how it could be that we had heard of no food riots anywhere.

Breakfast over, we headed for Monticello. It was everything that I had hoped to show to Hamish, and he enjoyed it all. The only thing that was off was the climate, but the museum's curators could do nothing about that. The bulb flowers in the gardens were in bloom in September, which was strange to say the least.

Children on the grounds did not know anything different, and I wondered how it would feel to have no memory of nature as it was before it went so far out of balance as this. "It won't even feel weird to them," Hamish said. "They'll only find it weird when our generation tells them how it used to be."

The tour of the garden showed the tiny building, about the size of a telephone booth (another anachronism since the advent of cell phones!). It was made of brick with windows all around, and this was where Thomas Jefferson sat to plan what he would grow there. He liked to experiment and try new things – not surprising for someone who may have been an Aspie.

Hamish got a kick out of hearing me tell that last detail about our third U.S. president.

For dinner, we ate at the Michie Tavern, which featured a buffet of high-calorie Southern cuisine. It was inexpensive but very good. One more night and morning at that lovely inn, and we were on the road again, this time heading for the Blue Ridge Mountains. This was where I hoped to see some wildlife, and to be able to stop the car from time to time and use my camera.

At least, that was the story we were going with. If we ran into any MRAPs, that was what we would say. We didn't actually think that this National Park was going to be in the same low-occupancy, bucolic state that it had been before the events of the past few years.

This was more reconnaissance, and to do it, we expected to have to play dumb, at least a little bit. If any military personnel met us and realized who we were, however, the jig might very well be up, and we would have to fall back on our museum tour story. Hopefully, that would do.

The Blue Ridge Parkway was described on its website in great detail, and gave absolutely no indication that we would see any displaced Americans on it. I held no such delusions. They had to be there. What an irony! Native American tribespeople (Iroquois) had been forced out of these mountains almost three centuries earlier. Now I fully expected that to happen to any displaced people who tried to settle here for any length of time, however short.

There was a total of 15 visitor centers along the Parkway, 4 in Virginia and the rest in North Carolina. They were all at "mileposts" with distance markers on each one. In between them, pulling over was allowed as long as one got off the pavement. The road wasn't very wide. At least there were plenty of rest rooms, I joked to Hamish. One might as well be comfortable while trying to see a reality horror show. He agreed.

We were not disappointed, though I really, really wish we had been.

"I can see why this place has the word 'blue' in its name," Hamish commented. "There's a blue-gray tinge to it all. It's beautiful."

From there on, it wasn't. We got from one milepost to the next, and stopped because he wanted to get something from the trunk: 2 pairs of high-quality binoculars. "This is the one thing you didn't think of bringing, isn't it?" Hamish said with a grin. I admitted to it.

With these and my camera ready, we resumed the drive, Hamish training his all around. It wasn't long before he told me to pull over. I did, and we both stared through our binoculars into the distance, down into the west.

I felt like my breath had been sucked out at first. Tents and tarps littered the landscape. They were in bright, primary colors and in dull ones that blended in with the natural world around them. Camouflage was impossible, though. People were moving among the trees everywhere.

"There are all sorts of creatures that are indigenous to this area. I wonder how they are doing with all of these humans here," I commented. "There are birds, of course. Frogs, snakes – how are they dealing with those? Grouse, coyotes, deer, boars, turkeys…maybe these people are eating them. What else would displaced people with dwindling financial resources do for food?"

Hamish looked at me. "Yeah, that sounds about right. How long do you think they will be allowed to stay here and do that?" he asked me.

"I don't know. There are a lot of variables here. How long have these people been here? When did they get here and what is it like? What resistance are they facing to remaining here? Without safe places to rest, humans are vulnerable to all sorts of problems."

He gave me a grim smile. "Okay, just checking. I know you're not naïve."

"Thanks a lot. Do you think I would have planned this spy trip without you, Blackout guys, and a lot of reservations for safe places to stay and eat along the way? Definitely not. I may be curious and determined to find out the truth, with the resources to do so, but I'd like to think that I'm not stupid."

Hamish leaned across the car and kissed me. "I know you're not stupid, genius."

Mollified, I smiled and pulled out my camera. I shot several images with the telephoto lens, taking in the natural wonders as well as the human encampment. "If we meet some evil MRAP guys, I can show them my nature images…and hopefully delete the other ones before that."

"Wait." Hamish hopped out, opened the trunk, took out my laptop, closed it, and climbed back in. "Download it all each time, and delete it from the camera."

"Really?"

"Yes. Don't take any chances. And back it all up, too."

I got out the memory stick and did as he said.

We repeated this process the rest of the way through Virginia, moving slowly. We saw some areas with no human encampments. There were some turkeys and deer, and once I got lucky enough to photograph a grouse. Nevertheless, between each one, Hamish insisted that I save it all to my computer and another memory stick before we got to the next visitor center. I did that.

We started noticing something else at each visitor center: signs announcing that Jade Helm 15 exercises were being conducted. The notices explained that they were nothing but a training exercise, and that tourists should not be alarmed by the presence of military vehicles. I wasn't convinced that I ought to be complacent, but the people around us seemed that way.

There were lots of things to look at, including the Humpback Rocks, where one could go hiking or to see some nineteenth-century farm buildings, some mills, and other attractions. We stopped for lunch at Peaks of Otter Lodge because it had a restaurant. The place offered sweet potato fries, quesadillas and, best of all, fried green tomatoes. I explained about that movie to Hamish, and then he and I ate 2 orders of them. We were convincing tourists, I hoped.

After that, we looked around in the visitor center nearby. There was store for campers, so we went in and glanced around. And there they were: some displaced people. At first, I just thought that there were people who liked to camp, but Hamish dragged me away.

That was when I realized what was going on. No wonder they were keeping to themselves and not making much eye contact. Some of them had blank eyes that seemed shell-shocked and hopeless. Their clothes were ragged, but I had overlooked that detail, thinking that it was the normal wear and tear of camping. Hamish assured me that it was not.

We had just crossed into North Carolina when he commented that we weren't going to reach the end until tomorrow, at this rate.

"That's true," I said. "But not to worry; we have another reservation."

He started laughing. "Of course we do. Where is it?"

"In a town called Boone – well, near it. It's the Lovill House Inn, and it's yet another —"

"Bed-and-breakfast," Hamish interrupted.

"Are you tired of them? Should I have signed us up for a truck stop motel?"

"No, no, I love these romantic getaways. I'm just teasing you."

"Hmm…"

"Stop that! The food and the rooms are great, and Ed and Aaron are funnier at each one we stay at," he laughed. "Mostly it's Ed; he doesn't appreciate good food."

"Okay, fine. Maybe we'll meet another nice cat at tonight's inn," I said.

I pulled over yet again to take photographs. Binoculars first, though…

It was a good thing that lunch had settled.

"Holy shit!" Hamish said quietly.

There were MRAPs, jeeps, and trucks with long backs covered in army green canvas in the distance, off the trail down the mountain, and soldiers fanned out here and there among tents. They were U.S. Army, heavily armed, with rifles, and pointing them at the people in the tents. People were showing I.D. to them. "Do you think those soldiers are checking to see if they're meeting campers with homes elsewhere or displaced persons with no other place to go?"

"Definitely," Hamish said. "Oh no…"

"What?" I felt a sickening drop in my stomach.

"Look to the right past that pair of rocks."

"Where? How far…oh!" I almost dropped the binoculars. I had never seen a rape in real time before. It was the worst feeling I had ever had, because it was a combination of horror, revulsion, panic, and helplessness. How could I do anything to help this woman? I couldn't. I couldn't even let on that I knew that this crime was taking place. The soldier was holding his pistol against her side as he moved. There was no way I was going to believe that this was consensual.

Then I grabbed my camera. "Hang on…" I shot several images, framing it to get the monster's face, which wasn't easy because he kept moving, and to include what he was doing. I hated to include the woman's face, but if I could ever supply her with evidence – such a longshot! – she would need this.

The rapist was a bullet-headed bald guy with a tattoo of a flail on his butt. A flail is a medieval weapon, a spiked ball on a chain on a stick. The chain arced over his butt, and the stick went down his thigh.

The woman looked like she was my age, with her hair up in a messy ponytail, a tee shirt that was appallingly and unsurprisingly up around her shoulders, and jeans and sneakers. The tree bark had to be scratching her back and butt. No way was this something she wanted to do.

I sat back in my seat, heart pounding. I was panting just from the shock, and from the rush of activity. "That's it – our government is at war with us. It wants us dead, starting with the displaced of us. America is ruined." I looked at my camera, and at its case, disoriented.

Hamish had the laptop down by his feet. "No – just drive away."

I passed the camera to him. "Where are they taking those people? Homelessness has been made illegal in this state, and camping in the mountains is illegal, but these people had nowhere else to be. The law is just completely unreasonable…on purpose!" I drove along, ranting.

"Probably to a FEMA camp at some 'undisclosed location'," he replied.

"We can't help her. I don't know how I understand that, but I do."

"If we tried, we would disappear. If you were to check certain websites, you would find that this sort of thing gets discussed. But…one of the hosts, an independent guy from California who ran his own show, got 'suicided' a few months ago," Hamish told me.

"What does that mean?"

"It means that the government killed him and called it a suicide. It was obviously a murder; the guy had plenty to live for. He was happy enough to stay alive. He just wouldn't stay silent about what he knew. He was a journalist, though, so that is understandable. To deflect any serious attention from anything he has to say, the government calls these people 'conspiracy theorists'. That's what anyone who reports the truth about anything like what we just witnessed can expect: to be discredited that way."

"Having information but not being able to save someone with it is galling," I said.

"You may not be able to save those particular people, but there will be other chances later, and we'll be ready to help then. I'll figure something out, or you will, or we will. We just have to keep looking for information."

"Promise?" I asked, desperate to feel a sense of hope where there seemed to be none.

"Promise." Hamish smiled at me as he said that. It was both comforting and dangerous.

On to the next visitor center. I paused once to photograph some birds, anything so that if we were stopped, I could show that, but no one appeared. A minivan with a family of four and a Golden Retriever went by, headphones on the kids, map in the wife's lap. Incredible.

Hamish handed me the laptop this time, and I saved the crime images to a new folder. "Label that folder 'Woodwork' and put it separate from the park images," he told me.

I did. "Woodwork?" I asked, wanting to know his logic.

"Aye; an appalling metaphor, but it sounds like we went antiquing or something innocuous."

"I see." Stunned, I pulled into the next visitor center and we looked around, trying to seem calm, like tourists out for a good time together. Hamish bought me a chocolate bar and made me eat some of it. That helped. He sat down with me on a bench outside and put his arm around me.

"Some tour," he said.

"Yeah. Some tour. But at least we know that what we thought was going on is going on." I looked at the wrapper for the chocolate bar and noticed it said "fair trade" and "organic" on the back. All this advertising about making the world better for others, and this was happening here.

We drove some more, then realized that we were close to Boone and left the Parkway. The Lovill House Inn was very nice, and there was a cat to meet, which put us in a calm mood. But what would we see tomorrow on the rest of the trail?

Ed and Aaron seemed to pick up on our sober, stunned mood. Maybe they had looked down that mountain, too. They had binoculars or, for all I knew, sniper scopes. They and our other Blackout shadows probably knew everything that we knew and more. I wouldn't have been surprised if they had known it before we ever left on this trip.

I would have to ask Hamish about that at some point…like how they knew it.

The next day was much like the first. This time, we saw people being forced to leave their encampments, and without any of their things. It happened fast. Everyone was taken away to some trucks that waited near the MRAPs. Some looked back at their things and tried to ask questions, but were brusquely shoved along. The rest looked too shocked and scared to do that.

The military swept in once everyone was out, removing tents, tarps, lawn chairs, you name it – anything that gave any trace of people having staying in the park. It was obvious, as this was done, that the spots where this was done had not been official campgrounds.

The way that they cleaned up those spots looked like something I had seen in 1994, in a movie long ago, back when I was enjoying a hobby about U.F.O.s, called *Roswell*. The soldiers moved in one very long, tight line, picking up absolutely everything that was not part of the natural world. Not a trace of human litter would remain, even if had been dropped years ago, by some backpacking hiker carrying a package of granola around.

We drove as far as Ashville. Then we left the Parkway.

Chapter 5

The Guidestones

We drove into Georgia by going down I-26 in North Carolina to Route 25 in South Carolina. Nothing dramatic seemed to be happening around us, which felt surreal after what we had just seen from the Blue Ridge Parkway.

We just drove along, with our binoculars, camera, and my laptop in the back seat, until we stopped for rest rooms and to refuel. Then I put all that in the trunk. Highway driving was as dull, safe, and bland as that couple from Woodbridge, Virginia had represented it to be.

I had made reservations for the next three nights at yet another bed-and-breakfast inn near Elberton, Georgia. There was more than one thing that I wanted to accomplish here, so we needed the extra time.

This place was called the Rainbow Manor. We stayed in a room with a double bed (a bit small for a big guy like Hamish). It was called In Stitches, because everything in it was embroidered prettily. I hoped we would sleep well here, so that I could be a fully alert and safe driver.

The place had cinnamon sticks as its signature recipe and plenty of good Southern fare for breakfast. Hamish and I did sleep well enough, and so were ready the next morning to explore the area. I wasn't looking for military-run terrorism of our country's displaced citizens this time. We might find some of it anyway, but I had something else, something quite specific, in mind.

We wanted to find orange groves and beehives – displaced ones.

The idea that as the climate changed, with areas just to the north inheriting the former climates of the ones just to the south, and thus, presumably, the ability to grow the crops that had previously thrived elsewhere, intrigued us.

Would that actually work?

Gambling on the idea that it would, and desperate to make sure that we would not lose such wonderful crops as oranges and orange blossom honey, farmers and big agribusinesses and apiaries had decided to give it a try. Over the past couple of years, the news had been full of this massive undertaking.

It had been so full, in fact, that such stories had crowded out stories of displaced Americans. Certainly, the idea of saving the orange crop and the logistics of doing so was a more cheerful topic to follow while eating dinner every evening.

But what was happening to those people? What had been going on with them?

We had been shown the chaos of that panicked exodus from Florida, Louisiana, and the Mississippi delta area, then seen a few weeks' worth of news stories on people getting out and going elsewhere, and then…the news networks had moved on.

Was something being concealed from us? It couldn't be all about ratings. After what Hamish and I had just witnessed, we could draw no other conclusion. The soldiers and MRAPs weren't obvious about any future plans for the people they policed. It took someone with a military background like Hamish, and his former colleagues-turned-security detail, to know what was up.

Well…let's see the stuff that was shown to us up close, we said to each other. Who would care if we did that? No one, we thought. It was just orange groves. That plan seemed benign enough not to attract any notice. I imagined that if we were exploring the western part of the country, we would be doing a similar self-guided tour of almond and apricot orchards, which had been relocated from California due to the intense drought to Utah and Colorado.

By the time we were tooling through Georgia, it was blatantly obvious that the black SUV that was following our blue Mercedes was our security detail. It stuck to us like glue, and between the cell phone calls back and forth with Ed and Aaron, and our coordinated stops for fuel, rest rooms, lunch, dinner, and sightseeing, there was no chance of representing it as being otherwise. I even caught a glimpse once of another black SUV. Hamish admitted that it was with us.

That one was our shadow detail, and although I likely knew the guys in it, procedure dictated that we have no contact with them. They oversaw the safety of our reconnaissance trip, and we would not talk to them until we got home.

At least we were able to see things and move about with our Blackout team. The military units that moved about the areas of northern Georgia either knew about us or sized us up as big-shot elites who were not to be harassed. Either way, it felt weird.

"Damn. I should have realized that if agribusinesses and orange groves would buy land in Georgia and relocate here due to climate displacement, so too would military installations take land due via eminent domain." I was looking at the fourth Humvee with Army camouflage paint as it pulled out in front of our car and blocked our entire view of the road ahead.

"Yeah. You hate big vehicles," Hamish agreed. "You hate driving them, driving behind them, and the fact that they take up so much space."

"Indeed." I crawled along behind the stupid thing for a mile or so before it left the road.

A few miles after that, which were scenic ones, we did indeed find orange groves.

There were even shops in which to buy boxes of dark chocolate-covered coconut candies and bags of fresh oranges, which could be shipped home rather than carried. We bought both oranges and this candy and shipped a few boxes to my parents and to Aunt Zoe and Uncle Charlie. Grandmère would enjoy that, I hoped.

After that, we bought a small jug of freshly squeezed orange juice and drank some. It tasted as amazing as the juice that I remembered drinking as a kid on other road trips with my parents in Florida. We also found some orange blossom honey and orange blossom perfume, sold in little plastic ball-shaped orange bottles. I loved those, and didn't care that they were cheap, hokey, touristy things. I bought several.

Next, we asked about apiaries.

Yes, there were some, but they were not relied upon heavily for the pollination of orange blossoms. They were kept to maintain the species of honey bees, to produce orange blossom honey, and that was all. I knew from my research that oranges self-pollinated, so this did not surprise me, but something in the tone of the orange farmer caught my attention.

Hamish shifted a bit as I asked, "What about other crops around here? Don't they need bees?"

The man glanced at Hamish, and then said, "I recognize your husband from *Nanobot*." That was a journal that Hamish published in from time to time, a high-impact-factor one that specialized in nanobotic engineering.

I looked at Hamish. "What have you been working on?"

"Nanobotic pollination," he replied. "Surprise! Nanites are helping bees in many farms now. I've been consulting on it," he said with a grin. "Your honey bee colony collapse book made me curious to see whether or not I could help the situation with a nanobotic back-up."

"Cool! I found some articles about hand pollination in China and maybe India, but I didn't know our fruit supply was being preserved this way."

"It's just starting. I didn't want to mention it until we got here."

I turned back to the orange farmer. "Where can we see these nanobotic pollination efforts in progress, if anywhere?"

"There are some cherry, peach, apricot, and nectarine farms around here where it's being tested. I'll give you their brochures," he told me.

"Thanks!" I took them and announced a change of itinerary – to some of those farms.

Hamish didn't mind. We found a peach farm half an hour away, and were shown around. The trees were doing fine, and had bloomed in the spring. The farmer and nanobotic engineer, a brother and sister team, showed us their operation.

That meant that nanobotic pollinators were only shown in action on DVD at this time of year, but Hamish was really excited to see them in use. We saw the solar-powered bee simulacrums in action, looking like metallic versions of the endangered insects that were so crucial to crops and nutrition. "It works just as I designed it to," he said, delighted.

We were walking back to the car at that point. I was delighted that his invention worked so well and that it could do what bees did, but also scared by the decline of the species and upset. Also, the only job this had created was a part-time one for an engineer from CalTech University. "So this is what you have been working on in the basement and while I labored in the backyard with the honey bees?" I asked.

"Aye," he said, lapsing into brogue because he was in such a good mood. "I got curious to see if I could make it work. Don't worry; I didn't upset the live bees. They just kept working. I watched them. You sold your book, and I sold my skill with these nano-bees."

No wonder we had had no money problems even after the government had taken over Nae-Née. That invention still made money, but I didn't expect that golden goose to lay eggs forever. Eventually, humans would be all caught up with that and each woman would have a Nae-Née nanobot. We had to be almost there. Clearly, Hamish had thought ahead as I fretted about the future of the bees.

"This is terrific, Hamish," I said, "but I don't see nano-bees taking over entirely for all of the bee species that Nature created over eons of evolution. It can only help a little, here and there, in orchards and on farms. Meanwhile, the rest of the ecosystem may yet still collapse."

"I know," he said, "but I had to try and help with the food supply, and do something. I'm not imagining that science can transcend Nature. I know it can't. Science is great…to a point. After that, Nature on its own is just…better."

I smiled, feeling slightly better. Looking into the future at the state of the ecosystem was grim.

We drove back toward Elberton after that and found a diner with fried green tomatoes, chicken gumbo soup, blackberry pie, and other treats. Then it was back to the Rainbow Manor for the night.

After a second morning of touring the northern areas of Georgia, we paused. We had seen a few more military units. They seemed to be protecting the farms. No encampments of any kind were evident anywhere we went. It was just miles and miles of calm farmland, mostly orange groves and peach and apricot orchards. It was actually rather pleasant.

It was time to see that something that I had read about online that intrigued me, which I was determined to see: the Georgia Guidestones.

Hamish wondered where I was going as I suddenly tossed the road atlas aside and scrutinized printout from Google Maps. Then he remembered what was on the list. I was glad to be old-fashioned and low-tech about this, using paper maps, but still, the surveillance monkeys of the government's secret lairs could have noticed me looking this up as I had planned the trip.

I couldn't worry about that now. There were limits to how much covert behavior anyone could manage without being unable to go anywhere or do anything, I reasoned. At last I found it after wending my way through the countryside to this address:

The Georgia Guidestones
Hartwell Highway
Elberton, Georgia 30635
U.S.A.

The site was on a hill surrounded by farmland in a remote area. As we got out of our car and looked around, we saw no other human settlement or structure. After the online research I had done about this place, I suspected that this was by design.

The Georgia Guidestones were commissioned in 1979 by an anonymous donor who had given a fake name, and were completed in 1980. The guy had introduced himself to the head of a company called Elberton Granite Finishing, and explained what he wanted. All was done as he requested.

A local banker who handled the necessary funds had stayed in contact with this mysterious person until long after that. In 2012, he burned all correspondence associated with the Guidestones in a metal barrel. These documents were pre-computer, pre-Internet, so there were no other copies. That data was gone forever.

The structure consisted of 5 monolithic slabs of granite capped with another. Each upright slab was almost twenty feet high. The center piece and the top one were rough, and had no decoration or inscriptions. The other four were wider, and had writing on both sides, in eight languages. Walking around them clockwise, they appeared in this order: English, Spanish, Swahili, Hindi, Hebrew, Arabic, Chinese, and Russian. No French – oh well.

On each side, the same list of instructions was written:

1. Maintain humanity under 500,000,000 in perpetual balance with nature.
2. Guide reproduction wisely — improving fitness and diversity.
3. Unite humanity with a living new language.
4. Rule passion — faith — tradition — and all things with tempered reason.
5. Protect people and nations with fair laws and just courts.
6. Let all nations rule internally resolving external disputes in a world court.
7. Avoid petty laws and useless officials.
8. Balance personal rights with social duties.
9. Prize truth — beauty — love — seeking harmony with the infinite.
10. Be not a cancer on the earth — Leave room for nature — Leave room for nature.

Under half a billion? Wasn't that a bit low? And a world court? We already had one in The Hague, in the Netherlands. There was both a civil and criminal one. The criminal one was called the International Court of Justice (ICJ). A 2011 climate change convention held by the U.N. in Durban, South Africa advocated establishing an International Climate Court of Justice (ICCJ). However, the United States had never been willing to cede any authority to any judicial body outside of its own, and had been known to walk out of the World Court.

To have a world government – just one – for the entire planet would require something that we now have: the Internet. It could be done. The question that seemed to be before us was, is that really a good idea? There are arguments both for and against it.

One the plus side, the world of *Star Trek*, a peaceful one, had only one government, with lots of local governments in nations, counties, provinces, departments, cities, towns, and villages all over the planet. With such a government, the role of the United Nations would become administrative…IF there was peace. Peace required money, because peace meant security. With money, there could be democracy. However, without a population policy, money would dwindle, and peace would not last. Thus, to preserve democracy, the first item on the list was crucial.

Suppose that that whole fairy tale was to come true. What a lovely dream: we could have the United Federation of Planets and Starfleet and science and space exploration missions with no worries from within our own species and societies. Wouldn't that be great!

On the negative side, such a system presented its own opportunities and loopholes for abuse. Also, transitions are messy. What was I saying? I was saying that we could find ourselves trapped in a police surveillance state of our own making, and one of epic proportions. Who knew how long such a transition would take? During that time, lots of people would die. They would never get to enjoy the end result, the utopian society that the transition aimed for.

These Guidestones were describing how things ought to be after that time, if and when the awful period of transition ended. How would those in power, the ruling elites who orchestrated it, know when the deed was done? And how would they ever be willing to let go and restore democracy? The whole idea meant placing a lot of trust in them to relinquish control.

They might not be willing to do that.

This entire idea could go badly wrong, and any such transition would look like it already was going badly wrong. As I thought about what Hamish and I had seen over the past couple of days, I realized that we were already in the midst of that, and that it was just getting started.

The planet's population was still, as far as anyone was aware, over 8.4 billion humans.

And the author of this list thought that half a billion would be good?! How would we ever get there without a bloodbath? Who would be chosen? Would anyone be chosen, or would the collapse be one of the planet's ecosystem rather than a war-based apocalypse?

After seeing all those MRAPs and the rapist officer in action, a bit of both must be the answer.

I stopped thinking and saw that the list on the Guidestones wasn't the only thing to look at.

The center stone had two precisely calibrated features. One was a hole through which the North Star was visible at all times of the year, a thing that we would not be back to see (coming back at night seemed foolish considering that we were in the midst of an alarming transition). The other was a slot that that aligned with the position of the rising sun during the winter and summer solstices and the fall and spring equinoxes.

The capstone had a 7/8-inch aperture for sunlight to pass through at noon each day. It shone on the center stone to indicate the day of the year – a calendar. The whole idea was ingenious, to say that least. It was different from England's Stonehenge, but just as cool.

Off to the side of the site was another slab. On it was a complete description of the site, with a claim that a time capsule is buried underneath it. No one was certain that this was actually so, but it was interesting to consider. Also on this last granite slab was a carved square containing the words: "Let these be Guidestones to an Age of Reason." Around each side of that square were the names of the ancient languages of Babylonian (in cuneiform), Classical Greek, Sanskrit, and ancient Egyptian Pharaonic hieroglyphics.

Above the site, off to one side, high on a pole, was a surveillance camera. Its purpose was to deter vandals. Vandals had spray-painted their objections to the messages carved here, citing an evil New World Order and Satanic worship, among other complaints. All that had been cleaned, but the result was that our presence here would be recorded and noted. Anonymity was a fantasy.

After that sightseeing stop, we drove into the nearby town for some lunch.

It was then that things got weird – disturbing, even.

We had barely been out of the car for five minutes – just long enough to use the rest rooms and refuel the car – when a young guy, perhaps in his mid-twenties, appeared. He was walking toward the gas station.

He had shaggy, somewhat curly brown hair, and wore jeans, sneakers, a tee shirt, and an old, army-green jacket. He seemed overtired, and walked as if drunk. As he got closer, I saw him sneeze, and noticed that his cheeks were flushed. Then he paused and doubled over into a coughing fit, and I saw blood hit the sidewalk.

Hamish rushed up to me. "Are you done refueling yet?"

I looked at him. Hamish, despite being a doctor, showed no inclination to approach this guy. That couldn't be good. The pump made that contracting sound that they all make when a car's fuel tank is full, so I replaced the nozzle in the cradle, put the cap back on the fuel tank, and swung the door shut – fast.

I reached for the paper receipt, but Hamish grabbed it and stuffed it into his pocket, which was uncharacteristic. He usually let me put it into just the right pocket of my handbag. Something was up, so I didn't ask him for it.

Hamish rushed me to the driver's seat, urging me to shut the door. "Don't open the window," he added, running around to jump into the passenger seat. "Let's go – NOW."

I drove off, feeling conflicted about breaking the Good Samaritan Law mixed with a panicky foreboding sense about what I had just seen. Ed and Aaron had noticed the kid and also avoided him like the plague, which he literally seemed to have. They were hot on our tail, and looking back more than ahead.

"What was wrong with that kid, Hamish?" I asked as I pulled onto the road, going left and away from the kid instead right, which was where I had planned.

Hamish was staring back at the gas station as people approached the kid.

I looked in my rearview mirror and was momentarily shocked to see the motorcyclist who had been buying coffee in the convenience store as I exited the bathroom approach the kid, get coughed on, and immediately start to cough exactly as the kid was doing.

I quickly looked at the road ahead of me and corrected to avoid a mailbox. Whatever was going on, I had to drive normally and wait to hear about later, when we were calm, away from this, and not concerned with getting wherever we had to go.

Because I was married to a scientist and because I read and watched science fiction, I had a pretty good idea of what was going down back there. That contracting, anxious feeling came back. I had better get us to an area that Hamish approved and fast, I thought, so that we could rest, get lunch, and discuss this. Only then, when my suspicions were confirmed and worse, would I consider the full implications of what we had just seen.

That white haze of anxiety that I used to experience was getting more and more infrequent, though I still thought it could return to haunt me if things got awful enough. Perhaps I was getting older and more used to disturbing experiences. Maybe that was why I hadn't felt it so intensely that the world in front of me would cloud over again – not since I had realized that we would have to leave Manhattan and fast.

Hamish insisted that I drive without pausing to rest anywhere until we got back to Elberton, so I did. I drove us back to the same diner that we had eaten in the night before. Hamish didn't even seem to notice that it was the same. He just looked around like he half expected to see another sick person staggering around, but all was well.

We went inside, ate fried okra and more gumbo soup, and said very little.

It wasn't until we were back in our car that Hamish told me what he made of that scene.

"That kid near the Georgia Guidestones looked as though he had come in contact with a disease that is as contagious as they come. Any contact with it can lead to a fast and painful death. If he or any of the people at that gas station are still alive by tomorrow night, I would be very surprised. He may have escaped from some laboratory, or he may have illegally handled some lab animal. Or it may be caused by another factor. We may not find out about it."

"So it won't be on the news, I take it."

"Don't expect it to be," Hamish said.

"If I didn't think it could be an accidental release of a pathogen," I remarked, "I might say it's the start of a population cull initiative – a deliberate escape to see what happens in a small, rural situation, with few people for him to meet."

Hamish gave me a double-take of a look, then shook it off. "Let's just enjoy our trip and not jump to any conclusions as yet."

"Agreed."

One more night in Georgia and we were ready to head north again. Next stop, Colonial Williamsburg – and I took the highways to get the drive over with. I didn't want to spend a lot of time on getting there. Driving endlessly was getting tedious as well as stressful and alarming.

Hamish opened the glove compartment and took out the soundtrack to *The Monuments Men* by Alexandre Desplat. We listened to that for mile after mile, until we got there. The drive took all day – seven and a half hours – so we stopped for lunch in High Point, North Carolina. That place's claim to fame was as the disputed furniture capital of the world, and it even had a giant chest of drawers. We drove past it, doubled back, and I photographed it. Then we found a diner.

Back on the road, Hamish put on another CD. This time it was *Tron: Legacy*, of all things. A virtual computer world was the theme. That fit, except that I didn't see how Flynn Senior could have stayed alive and eaten meals inside his video game for two decades. Whatever.

At last we made it to Williamsburg and checked into our hotel. Not a bed-and-breakfast inn – we were actually staying at a hotel. "Ed and Aaron ought to be happy about this," I said in a wry tone as we got out, got our bags from the trunk, and headed inside to check in. It was the Williamsburg Inn, and it was very nice.

Hamish just grinned. The Blackout guys were relaxed and silly again, saying "yes, dear."

The next day, we set out to enjoy the historic museum town. Hamish bought me a pink ribbon hat in pastel and raspberry pink hues. It was a beautiful, wide, straw hat with a shallow dome for my head and a brim that stretched several inches away from my head. I bought a tiny one to put on Eowyn. It was in the other style that the vendors offered: flat-topped, with the ribbons shaped like small roses. We laughed at the idea of our tortie-coated pet in this pastel blue-and-white beribboned thing.

In Colonial Williamsburg, we visited the courthouse and listened to a historic interpreter who was simultaneously playing the role of court clerk and addressing the museum town visitors. He informed us that it was the court clerk who was actually a lawyer, not the elected officials who sat in the seats of authority conducting business. They would ask him questions, then do whatever they chose to do. That sounded a lot like how things were run in America today, I thought to myself in bemused disgust.

There were all sorts of historic tours to take. One focused on the women of Williamsburg, and we took it. A woman ran the newspaper, which was fun to hear about. We learned about maids, female slaves, milliners, and life in the governor's mansion, complete with balls that included minuet dancing.

Another presentation, one that we went back after dark for, reenacted some murder trials. This one was not held at the courthouse, but at another building. It had wooden seats that curved on either side toward a center one, which we were told not to sit in. No one else sat there; we had to imagine a judge in that seat.

Historic interpreters were everywhere, in full late eighteenth century costume. They never broke character, and it was clear that they had studied the history of Williamsburg, its people, its crafts, its cuisine, you name it. I was impressed, and having a wonderful time. So was Hamish.

We stayed for four days and tried each historic restaurant. Our car was completely unnecessary, left parked at the hotel, but we knew it was being watched by Blackout guys at all times. Our room was watched, too. I took my camera with me each day, and with no worries, downloaded all images each evening.

We felt calm and safe, and so called my parents only once on this leg of the trip. Assured that we were in a safe location and staying put for a while, they didn't insist on daily check-ins. Until this point in the trip, we had been calling each night upon check-in at the next inn.

After four days, we called to say that we were heading north again, and checked out.

Chapter 6

A Visit to the Manhattan Canals

We drove and drove, back into Virginia, through Maryland, and finally to a coastal area of New Jersey that hadn't been cleaned up yet. Signs said "Off Limits – No Trespassing" here and there. No one was around to stop us, so we got out of the car to look around. I was amazed that we could do this. Where were the MRAPs and cops or soldiers?

I had packed some old boots that we didn't care about. "Hamish, put these on first," I said, taking our footwear out of the trunk. Sludge, mud, fragments of building materials, upturned boats and vehicles, debris that had once been household possessions, and more littered the landscape. This was the result of flooding, Nature's version of eminent domain, which I called eminent removal. It was messy and nasty, and made quick work of destroying the efforts of humans to build comfortable existences for themselves.

In the debris, we were seeing the results of consumerism. The typical American consumed fifty times what the typical Kenyan did. Crap was produced in China, shipped in cargo containers to the U.S. (and to Europe and Japan), used briefly, and broken because it was so shoddy. Then the pieces got sent back to China, to languish for tens of thousands of millennia in some landfill. It would take the plastic components of these commodities-turned-rubbish that long to decompose.

Hamish and I walked around in this mess, taking in the scene.

Shells of houses remained. We had no intention of climbing through them. We may have been curious, but we weren't stupid. The Blackout Security entourage fanned out, checking for signs of other people. They didn't find any right away, so we walked a bit farther into the muck.

We saw mud-stained novels, plastic containers, broken dishes, family photographs in their frames with the glass smashed…and a baby doll. The face stared vacantly up at me through broken wood, its mouth permanently opened, waiting forever for a bottle.

How grotesque. "Feed me more," it seemed to say, heedless of the fact that doing so meant endless consumption of resources. Its mere existence was meant to perpetuate a mindset of doing so at an early age. No wonder so many women were so angry about the Nae-Née policy. They had been raised to expect to have babies and houses full of junk from childhood, but couldn't.

I had been given a doll like that as a child, and I had hated it. The stupid thing was nothing but an input-output device. Pour liquid in one end, and it came out the other end, making a mess to clean up. It said, "Mama!" too. Could a more irritating and useless toy have been created?!

Fortunately, I had a nice mother who was not concerned that I didn't like or want what most people liked and wanted. Instead, she had watched me and guided me toward what did interest and excite me, and enabled me to develop skills from those things. She was a clever and good parent. Making me miserable would have achieved nothing anyway.

We looked around for a few more minutes, saw only more ruins of what had been a functioning beach community just a few years before, and decided to go. Superstorms had destroyed all this. These storms were like a combination of hurricanes and floods that laid waste to these homes once too often. Insurance companies refused to fund any more rebuilding efforts. After that, the government had stepped in.

Coastline boundaries were officially redrawn on our nation's maps. Any development beyond these lines was made illegal with an Act of Congress, and the president had signed that bill, making it law. It was called the Coastal Limits Law, and it meant that Nature would be allowed to reclaim land that was underwater without any more resistance from humans.

There was only so much that humans could do to control Nature, the politicians said. The geoscientists, oceanographers, cartographers, and other experts who had been consulted had said the same thing. Insurers called this land recession an Act of God, and no lawyer or court of law could force them to cover those losses. This was not a new concept, but it was really an Act of Anthropogenics. This change was human-caused, not just a cycle of Nature.

So what happened to all of those homeowners? Obviously, they had to relocate elsewhere, but where, and what about their financial situations? Well, they lost their property and never got the value of it back in any form. They were simply out of luck.

Where they went depended on the individual circumstances of their lives – who they knew elsewhere, what opportunities they could find elsewhere, and what other financial resources they already possessed. If they had some money in the bank, they had hope. Otherwise, they had to completely start over, from scratch, and work at jobs or reestablish their businesses inland – far inland – to recover.

Doesn't that just sound so simple? Of course it wasn't.

Many of them hung around in big cities and coastal towns for a while, but this was not for long. There was nothing there for them. Soon they were gone, spread out inland to places unknown. Those of us who already lived inland watched the news and saw almost none of these people. Where did they go? After seeing those MRAPs and soldiers, I now had some idea.

I had asked a few people at the bed-and-breakfast inns that Hamish and I had stayed at if they had seen these displaced people walking or driving among them in the past couple of years. None of them had. Several of them had simply assumed that these hapless individuals and families had gone elsewhere, not to their area. I thought about this. It sounded absurd.

The displaced ones couldn't have avoided every area. They had to have gone somewhere, and the few people we saw along the roads did not account for the massive numbers of people who had lost their homes. Something was being concealed from the general public.

Were the few people we had seen along those country routes there just for show? Were they there to make it look as though displaced people had been left free and somewhat safe to fend for themselves and seek out new livings? And if that was true, what were we to conclude after seeing what was happening down the mountain from the Blue Ridge Parkway last week?

No. Something was rotten. Something was going on.

How was it that it was happening right under our noses? Were the vast majority of the safely settled, non-displaced people so incapable of basic observation and analysis that they kept missing it? Did most people not care, so long as they themselves were safe, and life went on as before for them and their own families? Or was this being concealed from the settled public?

Most likely, the answer was, all of that. I asked Hamish what he thought, and he agreed.

"Yes, that has to be it, but I'm glad we're awake. Just promise me you won't talk about what we saw to anyone for quite a while. We need time to think about it and figure out how to handle this information," he told me.

I looked at him. "There must be more data than just this to gather. We really shouldn't talk unless and until we have the rest anyway. And even then…the shock of understanding it may be huge. We should wait to calm down, get used to the new thoughts, and then think about what to do. Shocks make it hard to think clearly. We need to watch out for that."

Hamish reached over and held my hand when I said that. We were sitting at in traffic, about to cross the Hudson Bridge into northern Manhattan. This was the same way that we had left the city a couple of years ago, and now it was one of the only ways back in. The dike system that had been installed at the mouth of the Hudson River and also around all of Long Island covered the East River and blocked off the influx of the Atlantic Ocean. At a cost of 12.4 trillion dollars, it was at last complete, and water had been pumped out of the city.

Amazingly, the boroughs of New York City were mostly recovered. Some of it was gone, including much of Staten Island, but driving down the Hudson Parkway and down along the western perimeter of Manhattan was now possible.

The only thing that looked different – the only surprise – should have come as no surprise. Some of the streets of Manhattan were now canals, with bridges over them and wide sidewalks with granite fencing along the water. Our car could still move through the city, but I would need to buy a new map to guide me, both for driving and for walking. I was actually excited to try it.

We talked about how we remembered our exit ride, nearly hydroplaning along the pavement. Not anymore! Thanks to modern engineering and the demands of the ruthless one-percenters who ran Wall Street, the wheels held the pavement with no problem. They had wanted their city back, and they had gotten it. I wondered what else they had gotten with this deal.

We would see. It was almost eight o'clock at night when we arrived in Greenwich Village. Our street looked oddly the same, but a bit…cleaner and quieter. The little garden area in front of our firehouse had even been weeded, and the leaves of the pastel blue iris plants remained.

We drove up to the garage door, and I pressed the button to open it. It worked! I pulled in, waited as Ed and Aaron pulled into the spot next to us, and pressed it again. Hamish hopped out to turn on the light switch. That worked, too. You could ruin the water pipes in a house by turning them off, so we hadn't shut off the utilities since we had left.

Because I needed to use the bathroom, I dragged in only the electronic items from the backseat and my handbag and ran inside. All was well, and dusty. Yuck. I wanted to clean it up. First things first, though; I used the downstairs bathroom. The guys went in as soon as I was out. We hadn't stopped in over 3 hours.

The place still had basic supplies such as soap, toilet paper, paper towels, and shampoos. It was just the food that was missing, because we had taken it all away when we left. Hamish brought in the rest of our stuff. Ed and Aaron brought theirs in too. Were they staying here?

Hamish said that they were staying in one of our guest rooms until further notice. That was fine with me; I was still feeling sufficiently spooked by everything that we had seen and learned on our trip that I didn't want them far away.

I called my parents and told them where we were. My mother asked about the condition of the place, so I described the garden, the dust, and the lack of any other discernible changes. Satisfied, she said good-night and we ended the call.

"Hamish, do NOT invite ANYONE over until I can remove this layer of dust and scrub all bathrooms and the kitchen," I said once I was off the phone. It would be just like a guy to do that if not forbidden to do so in advance.

"Yes, dear. I mean, I won't," he said.

We had hardly gotten settled into our firehouse for the night when Hamish's phone rang.

Dr. Nurse was coming to see us.

"Not right now, I hope!" I said to Hamish.

"No! He's not rude. Tomorrow night for dinner."

"I'm not cooking. We just got here. I'll pick a restaurant."

"Okay. He can probably tell us anything he wants to discuss wherever we eat."

"I hope so."

I wondered what Jeffrey Nurse wanted, and seriously doubted that he wanted me back working at the Rockefeller Institute. It had been years since I had co-invented anything. Since then, I had just written books. Hamish had been mentoring graduate students and doing the actual inventing. Who cared about a wife who thought of the items for him to invent? They could get that for free. I came with the package. Besides, he could do plenty of that on his own.

All I had done there was research, write, publish, and hide from and then fire my crazy secretary after I refused to help her circumvent the population control policy. Oh, and foist my input on the government about a kinder, gentler way of implanting it. The Institute didn't make money from my work. Academic institutions were about money, as an episode of *The Big Bang Theory* had illustrated; Dr. Gablehauser told Sheldon that once.

My books didn't produce much money. My fame and Hamish's as associated with the Nae-Née invention could only take us so far. Hamish had produced another use for the Nae-Née delivery device that had made the Institute a good chunk of change when he defended me from one of the Clyde brothers. The nanite spray that tortured whoever got shot with that gun – with no physical after-effects – had been promptly coopted by the government.

The Institute was able to claim, as American institutions (academic or corporate) always do, that because the nanites spray was developed on its premises, most of the profits were due and payable to it. Hamish, as the inventor, was only due 5 percent of the profits, at the very most.

This is a typical deal. In Europe, it's just the opposite. So what did Dr. Nurse want from us? Well, we would find out soon.

I called to see if any of our favorite restaurants were still in business, and found that several were, so I called one and made a reservation. Might as well be nice and welcoming, whatever it was that he had to say to us, I told Hamish.

Hamish had said to choose a loud place, just in case Dr. Nurse didn't want us to be overheard, so I called the place called Max Brenner's Chocolate by the Bald Man, near The Strand bookstore. "That's perfect," Hamish said with a smile. "We can wander around the bookstore after the meeting."

"My thought exactly," I said.

With that, we hauled our stuff upstairs, Ed and Aaron following. They had waited in the living room until we were ready to go up rather than claim a room. On the level with the guest rooms, I paused and told them that they did not have to share a room. "We have 2 guest rooms, and we don't have to pay extra, so enjoy sleeping in your own space," I said with a grin.

Hamish and I continued on up to our room on the top floor, let go of our bags, and he said, "Home, sweet home."

We flopped on the bed. I sneezed. So did Hamish. I picked up the Kleenex box, blew the dust off of it, then rubbed it off on the carpet. We each took one and blew our noses. "I'm cleaning the house tomorrow," I said. "No exploring until that's done!"

"I'll help you," my husband promised.

"You will?"

"Aye. I'd be a cad if I didn't."

I grinned. "Let's get our guards and go out for dinner…and get milk, orange juice, and something to eat for breakfast tomorrow."

We found an Indian restaurant on 10th Street – which, happily, still had most of its Indian restaurants in business despite all of the changes the area had seen – and ate a great dinner. We filled up on naan with garlic and cilantro, curries, tandoori, dal, basmati rice, mango lassi, carrot kulfi…the works.

Aaron tried phaal, just to see how much spice he could handle, and Ed and Hamish laughed at him as he forced it down. I tried to tell him that it wasn't authentic Indian food, just a New York trick for the amusement of Americans, but he had to learn the hard way. Oh well. He ate extra bread with the stuff to mitigate the spiciness of it.

On the way back, we found a grocery store that was open and bought juice, milk, and croissants. "What about coffee?" Hamish asked. "You can go out and buy us some and bring it back," I said. "I'm going to clean right away – no getting sidetracked."

"Fine. Now let's go home and get some sleep."

We went home, put the food away, and went upstairs to unpack, shower, and sleep. Still, I couldn't resist a little cleaning in our bedroom before bed. I dusted while Hamish showered, then I scrubbed down the bathroom before using it, leaving no surface untouched. At least our upstairs suite was comfortable. The hall and stairwell could wait until tomorrow. Then I took a nice, long shower and went to bed.

The next morning, Hamish surprised me by going out with Ed to Christopher Street to see if McNulty's was still there. It was, so he came back with two bags of freshly ground coffee. I was thrilled! We had Toasted Praline and Mandheling Sumatra coffee. I brewed some of each and we drank too much coffee, but Ed and Aaron seemed as delighted as we were, so it didn't matter.

In fine form now, thoroughly hyped up, Hamish and I went to work on the house, waging war with the neglect of the past couple of years. Ed and Aaron watched, bemused at being our employees but not having to do this. "This is not *Downton Abbey*," I joked. That got a chuckle.

Hamish vacuumed the entire house. I dusted with rags, almond-scented furniture polish, and one of those dust-mop reaching gadgets for short people who want to get cobwebs out of high-up places. I also scrubbed the bathrooms, the kitchen, and mopped the floor. Satisfied at last, I announced that I was taking another shower. It was early afternoon.

That done, I was ready for lunch and in no mood to see a grocery store, no matter how much I liked to cook and bake. We intended to go back to Connecticut soon, so why stock up, regardless of what Dr. Nurse had to say to us? Hamish agreed. One week here, and it was over.

We found that Le Pain Quotidien was where it had been before. The white marble tables and chalkboard menu were the same, as was the hazelnut spread. I bought some, happy to see it again. Ed muttered something to Aaron about the nonstop gourmet food, and I said all that meant was that the ingredients were not processed, only fresh, really good food. Ed smiled politely.

"We can stop by a fast food joint if you want. We're going to be walking around."

Aaron rolled his eyes.

"No, this is fine, I'll eat lunch here," Ed said.

Huh. Okay. Far be it for me to stop a guy from eating well instead of rubbish.

We all ate, then walked outside.

"What next?" Hamish asked me. I was still the leader of this trip, it seemed. I'd better enjoy it while it lasted, I realized.

"Let's see the new canals," I said.

To get there, we had to double back the way we had come, and Hamish insisted on running into our house to get rid of the bag with the hazelnut spread. I went in and got a recycled Whole Foods bag, folded it up small, and stuffed it into my handbag in case I bought anything else. Then it was off to the north, to see what 14th Street looked like.

The place was no longer called 14th Street. It was now 14th Waterway. This made no logical sense in that it was not really the 14th in a series of waterways, but it made plenty of navigational sense to anyone who was used to the grid of

Manhattan. Renaming of everything would be idiotic. Confusion as part of an urban renewal project would just cause chaos.

We walked up and down on the newly reinforced sidewalks until we came to a subway entrance. It was still marked, but now it had a special cover over the top. The staircase that led below was capped by a pair of metal trap-doors. A sign and a wide, padlocked slide-bar across them said NO ENTRY.

We walked east to 5th Avenue, and that too was a canal. The sign there proclaimed that it was the 5th Avenue Canal. "Huh," I said. "Just like Venice. That city has a Grand Canal running through it and calls individual streets Rio de Whatever. Now we have Canals and Waterways."

We marched over a small bridge that arched just high enough to accommodate…a water taxi. Wow. Manhattan already had a fleet of yellow water taxis! Like cabs, they held about five people or so, and were covered and piloted by a driver with a steering wheel. Blue water busses also moved up and down, and were also low enough for bridge clearance.

Meanwhile, on 6th Avenue, cars continued to move up and down the pavement. The traffic now went both ways on any remaining avenue rather than just one way, but the smaller streets were still one-way streets.

We doubled back, crossed the 6th Avenue bridge, and walked over to see what Union Square looked like. More doubling back, but we didn't care. We were having too much fun seeing the changes all around us. Union Square had been a regular, fun hangout for us, along with several other spots around the island.

Now, it was surrounded by waterways and the 5th Avenue Canal. There was no Broadway Canal. Instead, the city had gone to the great expense of making it a pedestrian-only roadway with new cobblestones and granite curbing to match the granite fencing along the canals and waterways. We went up that way to the north side of Union Square.

The huge bookstore remained, as did the pet store with the cats that were up for adoption. The fun Fishs Eddy store with its themed dishes and glassware was not far north, a couple of blocks up Broadway. We stared around and around at it all, transfixed, but still moving along.

We walked and walked until we got to Times Square, which had been a pedestrian zone before the flood. Musicals and shows were advertised everywhere we looked on billboards. It was as though nothing had changed in this area, except for the fact that we had just passed a few more Waterways and seen Canals in each direction. There was the 8th Avenue Canal also.

I stared up at the billboards, and did a double-take. The Discovery Times Square was offering an exhibit about U.N. Agenda 21 – the agenda for the 21st century. "Come see model cities and towns, farms and factories, all with sustainable and renewable resource practices," it said. Images of green pastures and town squares with mixed use development illustrated it.

"Let's go see that right now," I said.

Hamish looked at me for a moment, then just said, "Okay." He knew something was up.

"This is how the floods are being handled, and used," I told him. "I just know it."

Sure enough, the museum was filled with exhibits that even EPCOT Center at Disneyworld could not have rivaled. The basement area was closed, I noticed, and roped off. A staff member explained that it was being pumped out, with reinforcement and waterproofing underway.

The entire exhibit on Agenda 21 painted a glowingly rosy picture of life under its policies, which made me wonder what we weren't seeing. The impression that the curators seemed to be going for was one of a beautiful utopia in which no one wanted for anything and everything was easily livable, walkable, and accessible to bikes. Green this and that, SmartTech, and "sustainability" were terms seen on every poster board, placard, and exhibit label.

Hamish and I read everything very carefully, saying little. Ed and Aaron paced up and down, looking at some of it, watching people around us, and just waiting for us to be done. At last we had seen it all, from the miniature models and video presentation to the SmartTech displays.

Time to go home and get ready to meet Dr. Nurse, we decided, so we deliberately headed for the 5th Avenue Canal to get a water taxi. Why not try one out? A Sikh man with a bright blue turban picked us up and chatted on and on about we knew not what into his cell phone as he piloted the little yellow boat south. It had power windows that could be used to keep out rain or snow, running boards to step on or off of quay-stops from, and seemed just like a car inside.

Ed sat in the front seat, and Hamish sat in the middle with Aaron and me in the back. Everything looked different from this perspective. I was on the far side of the car, watching other water taxis go by, and then I noticed some privately owned water-cars as well. They had the logos of cars that I knew well, but were clearly not amphibious. Oh well.

We rode as far as Washington Square and got out. Washington Square was like Union and Madison Squares, surrounded by a mix of pavement and water. The iconic arch was still in place. It was almost six o'clock, and we were expecting Dr. Nurse in half an hour.

There was still plenty of time. We walked home in about five minutes. I ran upstairs, made sure I looked presentable, checked Hamish for random stains and told him to comb his hair, and then sat in the living room, waiting.

Aaron and Ed sat there too. I knew that they must have checked the house and the general area for any credible threats and found none, but I was feeling a bit overstimulated by their constant presence. I needed to space out and really relax. Hamish seemed fine with them around, but that meant nothing. We Aspies don't emote enough to make that clear.

"I'm going upstairs to wait," I said.

A few minutes after I had flopped on the bed to space out, Hamish appeared.

"What? Is Dr. Nurse here yet?"

"No. I just wondered what you were doing." He came over and flopped on the bed next to me, kicking off his shoes as he did so.

"I'm tired and needed some time alone, or at least away from non-family humans so that I could space out and not sit alert, making sure that my every facial expression and tone is socially acceptable. That is what's making me tired. Do we have to have our Blackout guys with us this much? I need a break. Why aren't they staying in that apartment that we got across the street?"

Hamish signed and rolled over onto my shoulder. "I'm tired of their constant presence too, but we're paying them to hang around. After everything we've seen on this trip, there must be a threat worth guarding against. And don't forget that you've been a target before," he added.

"Oh, I haven't forgotten, but I can't stay on edge about it. That threat is gone anyway – you, my hero husband, took care of that." I hugged him. "But…if we were to stay here in our firehouse again, I don't want our security detail to live under this roof with us and be staring back at us for hours each day. We're private citizens, not politicians. We ought to be okay."

"We'll see. If and when we come back here, we'll see about that. It's close, at least."

The doorbell rang, so I hopped up and slipped back into my sandals – my nice leather ones. L.L. Bean occasionally made something that worked well with dressy outfits on my terms. If we weren't meeting a business associate, and in an area where nice shoes wouldn't fare well, I would have just worn my Teva sandals, the canvas ones, and not cared.

Hamish started rushing to put his sneakers back on. I went ahead without him, not wanting Ed and Aaron to greet our guest. But…they were checking on him before letting me answer the door. Aaron had even gone outside to watch Dr. Nurse approach. Ed looked out the peep-hole of our front door before, waving me back from it. A moment later, he stepped back and let me open it. Hamish was right behind me.

"Hi, Dr. Nurse!" I opened the door wide. "Come on in. How are you?"

Dr. Nurse looked as though he had aged slightly in the past two years since we had seen him. His hair had a lot more gray in it, but at least he hadn't lost any. He had grown a beard, too, which was neatly trimmed. He wore a bow tie and a tweed jacket, just as he always had. His gray eyes looked friendly, but I couldn't read facial expressions, and I knew he wanted something.

"Good, good, and you?" he asked, pulling me into a hug. He shook hands with Hamish. We stepped into the kitchen, walked past the dining room table, and sat down in the living room. Ed and Aaron stood by the kitchen counter, wanting to stay available but not interfere with the visit.

We assured him that we were fine, and Hamish said that we were on our way back from a trip south, where we had toured various historic museums and enjoyed long drives together.

"Sounds nice," Dr. Nurse said. "How was the weather?"

"Warmer than I remember Septembers being," I replied. "Let's go. I made us a reservation at a great chocoholic restaurant, with plenty of background noise so that eavesdroppers won't have an easy time listening to whatever you want to say to us."

He looked at me. "You're as blunt as ever. That's rare in a woman. I love it."

"Me too," my husband chimed in.

"Thanks," I said. "It's a classic Aspie trait, but it tends to stand out in women." I grinned.

Moving on, Dr. Nurse glanced at Ed and Aaron. I introduced them by name and as our shadows. "Don't worry; they won't share anything you say to us with anyone. They're just here to make sure no one kills us."

Dr. Nurse gave me a startled look, then said, "Oh, yes…we all remember that ugly incident on the Rockefeller campus. But, of course, your devoted husband wouldn't let anything happen to you." He smiled.

"Indeed. Hamish is a clever, stealthy hero."

"Should we go? The restaurant isn't far. We can chat on the way," Hamish said.

"Yes, let's get going." Our guest stood up, and we all filed out. I checked the lock, and we were off, with Hamish and Dr. Nurse chatting about science as we walked along. I tended to walk fast, so I was leading the way.

After we had walked about halfway there, I realized that my husband had spent the entire time talking shop, and said not a word about anything else. Aspie! I decided to interrupt at the next intersection, which was at a crossing of canals that we hadn't seen yet. Wow! A bridge that accepted pedestrians only arched over the 5th Avenue Canal and the 9th Street Waterway. It had a slight X-shape to it in order to accommodate the water taxis and busses.

Dr. Nurse had obviously gotten used to it, because he saw me taking in every detail and said, "So, Professor Châtelet, what do you think of the city's makeover?"

"So far, so cool," I replied. "We're planning to do some exploring for a week or so before we go back to Connecticut. How have you been during all this? How is your family? How did all this change your life? And Hamish, you haven't asked him ANY social questions – just work, work, work! That's not polite."

Jeffrey Nurse smiled, and Hamish just grinned. "I figured you'd do all that for me," he said.

Dr. Nurse laughed and said, "My wife would scold me too if she were with us. "Annabel is fine, doing well and still happy in our apartment on the Upper East Side. She still works at the Frick Museum. Our kids are okay, away at college. Dan is studying nuclear engineering at NYIT, and Elena is at Fordham Law School."

"Both at home in Manhattan rather than away during all these changes," I commented.

"Yes. It seemed safer and less expensive, what with Nature in flux and the economy too."

"Do they like school, and what they are studying?"

"Oh yes, very much. Dan is looking forward to continuing his studies, and Elena can't wait to practice law."

"What year is she in?" The traffic light changed, and we started to walk across the bridge, wending our way northeast.

"Her second."

"Does she have any idea what area she will practice?"

"Nope. Too early for that. We'll see what she can find. It's very competitive, as you must know, being a law graduate yourself. She likes city administration, though. She'll do an internship with City Hall next summer, if that works out."

Something told me that it would. Dr. Nurse was well-connected. We kept moving, walking over to University Place, which did not look different, and then up several blocks until we reached the chocolate restaurant. Social niceties and personal news exchanged, I let Hamish and our boss lapse back into talking about work.

The place was as loud as I remembered it, and Dr. Nurse had not been there before. He said he liked the food at lot, though, and would come back with his family. Good. I got the avocado B.L.T. with waffle fries. I had been looking forward to these fries because they were dusted with chili powder and cocoa powder. Dr. Nurse was intrigued.

"I thought a food adventure would be nice," I said, grinning at him. "Are you having fun?"

He smiled back and said he was. I didn't know whether to believe him or not, but decided not to worry about it. Ed and Aaron had tipped the hostess and gotten seated near us and within sight of all exits. I wondered idly what Ed made of the fries.

At last, as Hamish and I each ordered a Mexican hot chocolate for dessert, the conversation got to the point. Dr. Nurse hesitated, ordered a Swiss whipped one, and spoke. "So, Dr. MacDonall, now that the city has stabilized, would you want to come back?"

Hamish and I looked at each other. Hamish paused, then said, "That depends." I grinned for a second. I had taught him that classic lawyer response. Things do depend on many factors. You can't just make a decision without lots of data.

"On what?" Dr. Nurse probed.

Hamish looked at me, and went on, "It would depend on a tour of the Rockefeller Institute, on our reconnaissance trip around our old haunts in Manhattan, and on what you have in mind for us. I know you want me back in my old lab. But what about Avril?"

"We want her back too," he said. "And your old lab might need some new toys."

So it was that easy. He must know about Hamish's work with pollinator nanites, and who knew what else. I knew that there was always something else with Hamish. As for myself, my curiosity and directness was what drove my work. I let nothing in social conventions or taboos guide my curiosity. Academia with a legal angle was where I belonged.

"Come visit. Call my secretary and set up a time for whatever afternoon works for you before you go back to Connecticut. I'll make myself available. We've missed having the two of you around, and we'll see what we can set up that works for everyone."

"Okay," we said in unison.

Dr. Nurse drained his hot chocolate and took off alone, leaving us sitting there to talk.

"Hamish, I want to look around and see everything, and maybe visit Andrew Warne and Cassie, but I don't know about just abruptly coming back here. Something freaky is going on with the ecosystem and with our country, and maybe other ones as well. I need to understand it, and I worry about the wisdom of just moving back in here without having figured that out, especially after our latest trip."

He listened to me very steadily, then said, to my great surprise, "I agree."

"You do?"

"Yes, I do."

"Why? Don't you want to get out of a house that you share with your in-laws and live as a yuppie, alone in a big city with your wife again?"

He smiled at me, then took another sip of his spiced hot chocolate. "Yes, but as we both know, I am not a typical son-in-law, and this trip has made me a bit worried about them. I know you are too. Let's take Dr. Nurse up on his offer, look around, and see what he has in mind. Then we can tell him we will discuss it and get back to him later. He will understand that we can't just uproot everything in Connecticut and move everything back here."

"We might be able to do part of our time here and part there, but it's too soon to even choose that," I said, thinking about it.

"Yes, it is. Let's try to relax tonight, and we can call back tomorrow."

"Okay."

Thus full of dinner and chocolate, we headed across the street to another place that we had missed, myself in particular: the famous bookshop called The Strand. It had several levels to it, with discounted books, some old, some new, some used, some antique. The shelves looked like old library stacks. The basement was closed, I noticed, but a sign proclaimed the store's thanks to the volunteer customers who had helped move all of the books upstairs. Hardly any had been damaged when the flooding had started. Good.

I still had that large, recycled plastic bag with me, and I had a plan. It came as no surprise that a huge environmental section now took up much of the second floor. Up I went, moving with speed and enthusiasm. Hamish saw me go up the stairs, glanced at what that area offered, and followed me.

"Are you after what I think you're after?" he asked, watching as I found a copy of U.N. Agenda 21, and several other related books, both pro and con. Interesting: this was not a treaty. It was a plan of action. I tucked it under my arm and peered at the related books. The Strand was not pushing any particular point of view, just general knowledge. That was why I wanted to buy these books here – I knew I would find what I was looking for all in one place.

In my element and in a good mood, I grabbed a few more books: *Behind the Green Mask: U.N. Agenda 21*; *U.N. Agenda 21 – Sustainable Development in the U.S.A.*; *U.N. Agenda 21: Environmental Piracy*. Might as well read both points of view in order to make up my mind!

Human overpopulation had to be linked to climate change, environmental problems, and initiatives to deal with them. Better find some books on that, too. I had already read Paul and Anne Ehrlich's *The Population Bomb*. What else was there? Aha…*The Dominant Animal: Human Evolution and the Environment*, by Paul R. Ehrlich and Anne H. Ehrlich. Yes – there was no way that human activities didn't impact the environment. I also found a book entitled *10 Billion* by Stephen

Emmott, a British professor. This was both a manifesto and a warning, very accessible. It was like a coffee table book, a quick read, but in a small paperback.

"Professor Châtelet," Hamish said to me, calling around from one of the stacks.

"What?"

He came up to me and took some of the books I was lugging around. "You are your own think tank. I just know you're going to become the family expert on this topic in no time."

I grinned. "At least give me a few months to read all this stuff."

He kissed me. "Okay."

I gathered a few more on economic and ecological collapse, germ warfare, and one on life in Europe in the Middle Ages. I wondered what life would be like without technology to make it easier and less work, and seeing how it used to be ought to help with that.

Done shopping, I turned toward the stairs. Hamish grabbed all but the one I was still flipping through and started walking. "Don't you want to shop?" I asked him.

"I found one novel on nanites by Michael Crichton, called *Micro*," he said.

"We have that one!" It was really good. I read it on the way home from Hawai'i," I told him.

"Is it in Connecticut?"

"No. It's here, in our firehouse. I'll get it out for you when we get home."

"Perfect!" He tossed *Micro* aside and we got in line.

I found that book when we got home, and he and I sat in the living room for the next couple of hours, enjoying our books. We forgot to turn on the television or call anyone, but my parents knew we were okay, so we just keep reading until midnight, then went upstairs to bed. Ed and Aaron had checked on us a couple of times, realized we were in for the night, and gone up to bed with books of their own. They too had each gotten something to read at The Strand.

We called Dr. Nurse the next morning and set up an afternoon tour at the end of the week. After that, we decided to play for a few days, and to temporarily forget about all that.

Now that we were back in Manhattan, Hamish and I took a tour of our old haunts, or at least as many of them as we could find that still existed. We were really curious to see everything and get a sense of what was and was not different. We also wanted to revisit some favorite restaurants, if they were still in business.

One of them was called Marseille-NYC. The next evening, we went there. It was as delectable and iconic as ever, as was the food. We ordered moules et frites with Belgian Lambic framboise beer and settled in.

A few minutes later, the bread arrived, and we began to notice the other diners as we took in the ambiance of the place. By notice, I don't mean that we stared around at people's faces at first. No…something else caught our attention.

The man at the next table was eating alone, and enjoying his meal immensely. He was eating lamb with saffron couscous, carrots, and a myriad of other wonderfully aromatic flavors, and making long, drawn out sounds of enjoyment. Oh, let's face it – he was moaning in pleasure…in ecstasy. It went on and on.

I was torn between irritation and amusement. Pretty soon, amusement won out. I started to giggle and look at my bread plate, wrestling with my facial muscles. It was a losing battle.

"What?" Hamish asked. He wanted to be in on the joke, whatever it was.

Keeping my voice low, I replied, "The food porn going on at the next table."

Hamish's eyes lit up like it was Christmas. "Really?"

"Don't look at him!" I said.

He looked anyway, then turned back to me and grinned. The man was middle-aged, thin and balding, with round, wire-rimmed glasses, and impeccably dressed. He was entirely absorbed in what he was doing.

The moans of ecstasy continued.

I took another gulp of raspberry beer and ate some more French bread.

Hamish downed half his glass of the stuff – always an ominous sign – and turned to look at the moaner again. "What did you order?" he asked the man.

Startled, the man looked up, then replied, "Lamb in a tagine – a Moroccan-French fusion meal. A specialty of this place."

"It smells good from all the way over here," I said, hoping that this conversation would go okay, with no appalling incidents. One never knew with Hamish in the mix.

My hopes were soon dashed, but I tried to remember that we always enjoyed the stories later. Hamish told him, "You and your dinner ought to get a room. We can hear how much you are enjoying it, and it feels as though we are intruding on a deeply private experience of yours."

The man gave him an outraged, gaping-mouthed glare.

I couldn't help it. I collapsed with laughter, leaning over our table and coughing a bit on breadcrumbs. "Damn it, Hamish, if I choke on this bread because of you, you had better be ready to rescue me with the Heimlich maneuver!" But I managed to recover with a huge gulp of water.

The man shook his head and resumed eating – in offended silence.

So much for chatting with strangers, a thing that I enjoyed doing in restaurants – this guy certainly wouldn't want to chat with either one of us now. Oh well…maybe when he left, we would meet other interesting people. Our food arrived a few minutes later, and just as we got most of the shells off of our mussels, that was exactly what happened.

We soon met a nice couple from uptown who were happy to chat. Their names were Rachel and Joel, and they loved movies. She was a manager of a department of Macy's. He was an accountant for a theater on Broadway. That gave us some fun topics. But I wanted to know about the transformation of New York City.

After discussing several movies, I asked them about it. They had stuck it out and stayed here, and so were full of tales about life in Manhattan since the deluge of sea level rise, the huge, now-trillion-dollar infrastructure projects that it had spawned, and other tales of change and upheaval.

They told us all about it.

"First," Joel began, "the dikes had to be finished. But once that was accomplished, the rest happened with frightening speed. By last November, the water was pumped out, bringing the surface down to manageable levels. It seems that the engineers, architects, and granite preparers had everything prefabricated, all designed, measured, whatever, to just drop into place."

"Don't forget the creation of the waterways and canals, Joel," Rachel chimed in. "They had to do that before anything new could be installed."

"Right! My wife never lets me tell a story without remembering something I've forgotten," he said with a grin."

"Neither does mine," Hamish said, grinning back.

Rachel rolled her eyes, and I smiled.

Rachel picked up the tale at this point. "Actually, the pumping out was nearly done by October, and the Army Corps of Engineers swooped right in to gouge out parts of Manhattan for the canals. After that, the beautiful granite bridges and walkways were installed, and a fleet each of water busses and taxis just moved on it. The idea was to make New York as attractive as Venice, except that it would all be new rather than old."

"It worked, I said. "I like the effect. Hamish and I have been to Venice."

"So you can compare the two!" Rachel observed. "I'd love to go there."

We smiled, and then I said, "One thing that I have not noticed – but I have noticed its absence – is homeless people. Where are the veterans and other homeless people? I used to give them either money or coffee or meals when I went out walking. We've been here for two days, and I haven't seen any of them."

Joel and Rachel paled suddenly, exchanged glances, and then looked back at us. After a moment, Rachel said, "The homeless of New York City have become like the Jews, Romani, and others whom the established order deemed undesirable during the 1930s in Europe."

I gazed at her for a long moment, then asked, "You mean they have been forcibly removed? You saw that? What happened? Please tell us."

Rachel took a deep breath, and then began. "It was a lot like what my grandparents, who survived in Amsterdam and then Dachau, told me. Except, this time it's not about being a Jew or a member of any particular culture or ethnicity. It's about not having money or a place to live."

So I can relax a bit about my Aunt Zoe, I thought to myself. She was Jewish, but no one would be coming to cart her away from us over that. Still, I wanted to learn all other reasons why any of us might get carted away well in advance so as to avoid that!

Rachel continued, "At first, the homeless were invited to choose between staying in the city at shelters on the condition that they attend community college, or that working in various service jobs that had been left vacant when a lot of people moved out, so that they kids could go to school. The idea was clearly to make sure that everyone either worked or studied."

"What about those who didn't choose that?"

"They were taken elsewhere, to other jobs."

"What jobs, and where? We have been driving around rural areas to see historic sites, and we have seen displaced people whose vehicles have license plates from areas that are now underwater. We have seen the absence of opportunity, not the increase of it."

"You've hit the nail on the head," Joel said. "Military jeeps came in, and trucks with canvas covers, trucks that had room in the back for people to sit down. This went on for over a month. Then it was just over."

"They've been taken to nowhere," I said, looking blankly at the remains of our frites.

"Yes."

After that sobering dinner conversation, we exchanged business cards with our new friends, ordered dessert, and tried to cheer up. We and they wanted to keep in touch. Why not? It would be nice to have some new friends. Their last name was Greenberg, and they knew exactly who we were. They had no kids, were our age, and did not want any.

I was amazed that people like us – infamous over the use that Nae-Née had been put to – could have any such chance at making friends. We said good-bye and left after a while, and I was in a really good mood.

That is, until Hamish decided to have their backgrounds checked. "Why are you asking Blackout to do that?" I asked, shocked.

"To make sure that they are who they say they are, of course. If they are spying on us, a thing which is always possible, we won't contact them again. If not, great."

"How long will this background check take?"

It took a few hours. By midnight, Blackout came back with good news: we could be friends. What a fearful new world we were living in.

I sat on the sofa, looking at a new Manhattan map I had bought on the way back from dinner, at Barnes & Noble. Hamish had laughed when I said I wanted to go there. "Of course you do. Can't keep you out of a bookstore for long."

The map showed where each canal or waterway was, plus footbridges, vehicle bridges, bike paths, and more. I could see what was old and what was new. The Army Corps of Engineers had rushed to complete the project, fully funded by an act of Congress. Wow…when money talked (Wall Street's banksters' lobbyists doing the talking), things happened fast.

"Transhumanism…what bullshit," I muttered, looking through it all.

"What's that?" Hamish asked, sitting next to me, reading *Nanobot* magazine.

"Huh?" I looked up, startled. "Oh. Transhumanism is bullshit, just as religion is. Technocracy is real enough, but so is the relentlessness of Nature. The Army Corps of Engineers has fought and beaten Nature back for now, keeping the water from overwhelming Manhattan, but nothing works forever. This new world is both brave and scary."

"Aye, that it is."

We went back to reading for a while. Aaron came in once to get a cup of herbal tea, but other than that, all was quiet and comfortingly dull until we went to bed. There would be more to see and study – much more – before we went back to Connecticut.

I wanted to see old friends, so we called Andrew Warne and his girlfriend Cassie. Our friend, a social worker and a horse whisperer-artist, were still around, and had been able to settle back into their old apartment thanks to the dikes. They were fine, and happy to see us.

We met for dinner at a Japanese restaurant called Monster Sushi and caught up on news.

Andrew was retired now, so we could not find out any more about what had happened with the city's homeless. Sigh. He knew very little about that. Instead, he was having a fine time teaching at the Henry George School, which taught adults about social economics. His other interest was following the news of the economy. He wanted to see how it all turned out.

The economy had collapsed a few years before the Nae-Née treaty, and never really bounced back, despite claims to the contrary by the nation's banksters and hedge fundsters. The population far exceeded the number of jobs that paid a living wage, and big businesses were more concerned with huge profits than workers' rights. Andrew understood it all perfectly, and it fascinated him. He complimented me on my book, a fairy tale retelling of the problem.

His daughter was still working as a secretary and hating it, but wasn't running into any more trouble. She had even found a boyfriend, a guy who worked for Con Edison, the electric company that serviced Manhattan. It was going solar, and he was full of news about efforts to install glass panes all over the city that absorbed energy, stored it, and added it to the grid.

Cool! Hamish and I listened to this for half of the meal before I insisted that Cassie get to talk. She smiled and told us that the horses of the New York City Police Department were still fine, and still enjoying their stables and rides with officers. She loved to take care of them.

The next day was our tour of the Rockefeller Institute.

It was the same and yet different. The library had undergone a major renovation, and was beautiful. New carpeting in a pastel blue was everywhere, and wood paneling that complemented the Gothic architecture completed the décor. The basement was off limits. Everything had been moved upstairs to a new wing.

Small canals wended their way through the campus, but Dr. Nurse no longer needed to take a gondola around it. Pretty footbridges of granite arched over these canals also. The lawns had been salvaged, and the gardens looked much as they had before. It was quite lovely. Hamish's lab and our shared office was the same. Had Dr. Nurse been hoping we would come back for the past couple of years? I asked him this.

"Well, to be honest, yes. But I should tell you that I've been hoping that of several professors. We've had to cut the curriculum because of what we hope is temporary brain drain. I've spent the past several months working to reconstitute the faculty here."

"Any success as yet?" I asked.

"One person has come back. One. And I understand that this is a big decision for you both, so I am prepared to let you think about this for as long as you need to. If you want to split your time between New York City and Connecticut, I'm willing to work something out."

We thanked him very much for his honesty and flexibility.

And then we left it at that, because we really did need to think it over, go home to Connecticut, and assess our situation there. It was time to go back there and think about many things, not just this.

Chapter 7

Hamish's Nanites in The New York Times

Hamish's nanites were in the news again.

But it was okay, because they had been patented first. After that, they were published in high-impact, peer-reviewed journals. When that was done, Hamish's ideas were put on the market. Except...he swore that a lot of those ideas were mine.

What was he talking about? A mere suggestion wasn't much.

"Yes, it is," Hamish insisted over coffee. We were upstairs in our room because he had something to show me on the Internet. "Get onto the website for *The New York Times* and you'll see...something." He grinned.

We had come back from Manhattan a few days ago, by way of the Hudson Bridge and by avoiding southern Connecticut, which now lacked a tail. That was still taking some getting used to. So much for wealthy Greenwich, I had thought as I drove us back up to the area of Kent and Litchfield, and home from there.

"Come on, Hamish. You are the nanobotic engineer. I may have come up with the concept for Nae-Née, but so what? It would never have happened without your expertise."

"Look in the Technology section and you should see it."

There it was. I clicked the link and started reading through it.

Hamish wasn't done saying nice things to me, but I was getting curious about this new stuff.

"It would never have happened without you. Never in a thousand years would I have thought of such a clever use for a nanite. It takes a woman to come up with that, and I'm sure that being an Aspie had a something to do with it, too. But as they say, if you've met one Aspie, you've met ONE Aspie, because this Aspie wasn't doing anything but solar panel cleaner and maintenance nanobots, and you know how well that idea sells," he summed up.

"Great, wonderful, thanks, now let's see what they wrote about you," I said, impatiently scrolling through the link on *The New York Times* website. Already, I was set up to save a virtual copy, with full color and all images. It was like a compulsion now. When I had that, I was going to print up multiple copies to hand out to my whole family. "And don't say it doesn't sell. Once the tedious permitting process was over, you finished the whole solar panel project here. People will buy that – just wait and see." With that, I started reading the story off my computer screen.

"Nanobotic Engineer Develops Another Brilliant, Useful Idea – Pollen-Bots," the article's title proclaimed. The authors, Mai-Lin Ching and Arun Chandra, had published it under the "Bits" section (Bits – The Business of Technology). The article ran for over 2 pages, and included photographs of Hamish's nanites, including Nae-Née and the pollen-bots.

The Pollen-bots looked a lot like nano-bees, with tiny wings, six legs, and even stripes. Nano-fur with static-cling helped to attract and carry the pollen.

These nanobots looked just like the ones that we had seen at the orchards in Georgia. Cool! I said so to Hamish.

"Read on," he said.

There it was. "Hamish!"

He just grinned from ear to ear. "'I get roughly sixty percent of my ideas just from interacting with my lovely wife,' Dr. MacDonall said. 'In about half of those cases, she suggests things to me. Nae-Née was a case in point in which she outright came up with the idea. It was the most viable use of a nanite that I had yet considered, so I dropped what I was working on and followed through on it.'"

I looked up at him and gaped.

"Keep reading," he insisted.

"When asked how he came up with the idea for the pollen-bots, Dr. MacDonall replied, 'Avril turned the entire backyard into a garden for our family, plus she had a conservatory built for herbs and berries, then fretted over being able to keep the stuff growing. So, as she typically does, she decided to go all the way with it and keep honey bees. She took a class in that, set it all up, and then worried about colony collapse disorder…and then she wrote a book about it. While she was busy with all of that, I was reading her research and sending my nanobots out to observe the bees, with nano-biomimicry in mind. This is the result.' Thus, he explains how he gets his ideas from interacting with his wife."

"Good grief, Hamish! Keep some credit for yourself!"

"Well, I did take credit for doing the actual product development and testing," he said.

"I should hope so," I said, indignant.

"I also told them that you edit everything I write. That's in there, too. And stop objecting! I want your career to go well too. I love you," he added, coming over to hug me as I sat staring at the computer screen.

Sigh. "I love you too, but I want more fuss and fête on you."

The doorbell rang.

"Too bad," he said, and took off down the stairs.

"Huh?" Be he had left the room. I saved the article and hit "print", then took off after him.

A delivery guy was handing him a box from a florist, and he was signing for it.

"Thank you," Hamish said and shut the door. He turned to me, handed me the box, and said, "Let's celebrate. We'll start with this, and go out to dinner tonight. Do you think your parents would like to go to the Indian place in Avon?"

I looked at him and said, "Do bears hibernate in cold weather and wander through human overdevelopments?" and I grinned.

"Great. It's a plan. Now open that box."

The box held pastel pink roses, raspberry pink peonies, pink-streaked white lilies, purple irises, purple caspia, blue delphiniums, a few small sunflowers, and quite a few other flowers in hues that my husband knew I liked best. "Wow! I love it. What's the occasion?"

Hamish said, "I feel like celebrating while we can. Pretty soon we're going to know or learn a lot more about what we saw on our trip. I know this because you won't stop reading, and you'll get me to look into it, and I'll help you because I can't leave anything alone either."

"You're right – about all of that. I love you."

"I love you too."

"We're going to get ourselves in big trouble soon, aren't we?"

"I think so."

I thought about that kid near the Georgia Guidestones again.

Despite a search of the Internet, I had been unable to find out anything about that incident. It wasn't in the news, it wasn't anywhere. It was as if it had never happened. I continued to check from time to time until Hamish told me to stop, because searches of the Internet were monitored.

Finally, he just told me what he thought we had witnessed: a military test of a bioweapon. No wonder he thought we were going to get into trouble soon. People had died for that test, and it was being concealed. Did the government know that we had witnessed anything?

If so, why were we being left alone? Was it our fame, knowledge, expertise, what?

I wondered how soon we would find out.

Now that we were back, Aunt Zoe, Uncle Charlie, Grandmère, and my cousins wanted to hear all about our trip and what we had seen. My mother also hinted that they had some news. She said to be prepared to meet some new people at their house.

I got the photographs ready – of the Georgia Guidestones, Colonial Williamsburg, Monticello and its gardens – and then went to Whole Foods to buy some groceries with which to make a dessert to bring. When I drove over there, I wasn't really sure what I was going to make yet, only that it would involve fruit, and maybe some chocolate. I would see what looked good.

Ed was with me, which meant I could annoy him in good fun by describing how healthy and organic and otherwise good the ingredients were as I shopped for them. I picked out some black figs, a hunk of fair-trade dark chocolate, and mascarpone cheese. I would make a tart, I decided.

Ed rolled his eyes when I pointed out what was what, but agreed to taste one fig on the way home. To his surprise, his first taste ever of a fresh fig was good. I laughed. "You've been eating figs as Fig Newtons all your life, haven't you, and never fresh!" He admitted it.

"Those packaged produced are full of lecithin and other weird chemicals," I told him.

He just looked at me, then went back to watching the traffic around us as I drove.

When I got home, I made the tart crust, laughing to myself briefly as I thought of what Ed would say about the from-scratch, know-what's-in-it approach I had to cooking and baking, filled it with mascarpone cheese, washed and cut off the tips of the stems on the figs, sliced them in half, laid them over the cheese sliced-side-up, and drizzled them with a little orange blossom honey. There: done. It looked like food art. Pretty!

The world may have been overcrowded with strained resources, I thought to myself, but this was the sort of thing that made life worth living. This, and having my family to share it with. Those things, and having a fascinating career to pursue with cats to keep me company. Without all that, I didn't see what I would care about. Life would be pointless otherwise, like walking around to postpone funeral expenses.

Next, I decided to lay out the Agenda 21 books and other research materials to show the family, and included the things I had acquired from the gift shop at the Discovery Times Square Museum. Even if it felt like it was the wrong time to talk about what Hamish and I had seen in the Blue Ridge Mountains…especially since we were meeting strangers this evening…I could still show the family this stuff.

As I dragged a heavy canvas bag full of the books downstairs – and my laptop, with the photographs from our trip all organized and labeled – my mother met me, coming out of the kitchen. "Let's go; I have your tart packed. I made some mushroom caps with chèvre and dill."

"Great," I said, smiling.

"Are you bringing all that with you? People will get bored if you try to make them look through those books!"

"I won't do that. I'll just run through them with a quick show-and-tell, as I explain the trip photographs," I promised her.

"Fine. Dad's waiting with the car running, Let's go. Where's Hamish?"

"Here," my husband said, coming up from the cellar and taking the bag I was carrying.

When we got to Aunt Zoe and Uncle Charlie's place, I felt a brief pang of anxiety, then shoved it aside. So what if there were new people to meet? But I did hate surprises, especially social ones. Hamish knew that. At least I wouldn't have to endure some stupid surprise party for my birthday…ever.

We got out of the car in the driveway, which now had vehicles for each of my cousins. Jacques had just graduated in the spring from Wesleyan University with a degree in Earth and environmental sciences. That made all three of my cousins college graduates. They were lucky to have gotten past the admissions process, I thought, thanks to overpopulation.

None of them had asked for my help with that. Granted, Nae-Née wasn't a reality until after the youngest one had been accepted to college (that was Jacques) but Edgar and Fabian had been out for a while, struggling to find work with no success, and now Jacques had been out of school all summer and into the fall. Still, no jobs – only internships, which meant they worked for free.

And still, they had not asked me for help. I would love to help them, I thought. I just needed to figure out a way. Maybe if Hamish needed more office help…if he were seeing patients. But he wasn't doing that yet. He was still testing something that he was being very secretive about. He was probably using himself as a guinea pig. Scientists often did that, and the history of science had plenty of weird stories about that, many of which I had read.

Grandmère lived here too, and she was now 95 years old. We had held a party for her over the summer. Her birthday was August 3rd, and we had outdone ourselves spoiling her, with chocolat gateau. I had used the Marcel Desaulniers recipe with hazelnut butter, and she had loved it. My mother had gotten 95 butterflies to release, and we had been careful not to touch their wings as we did so; that would have made them unable to fly. Aunt Zoe had given her packages of 95 raspberries, 95 walnuts, 95 almonds, 95 you name it. Fun!

Grandmère lived in a tiny mother-in-law addition that Uncle Charlie had included in the design of this one McMansion. As the real estate developer for the area, he had been able to control such things. But with the economic meltdown several years earlier, his business had collapsed along with the housing market. He was retired now, at 60 years of age, earlier than he had planned. Aunt Zoe, ten years younger, was casting about for a way to occupy her time also.

No luck with that yet; she was volunteering at the local Jewish Community Center for now.

Dad helped my mother get the food out of the trunk, and they carried both items. Hamish and I carried the books and my laptop. We didn't have to knock because Uncle Charlie opened the door and waved us in. He said, "We've got a full house! Come on in and make it worse!" He was grinning, though.

We walked up the front steps and inside, glancing around. The living room was full of people. Grandmère sat in her usual spot on the sofa by an end table, close to the fireplace and the flatscreen TV. The boys were all in there with her. All three boys were dark-haired and with dark brown eyes, like their mother. Uncle Charlie's features showed on their faces, though, even if his shock of thick, graying black hair and blue eyes did not.

Aunt Zoe was in the kitchen with…two girls we had never met before. One of them looked familiar, though. I had seen photographs of her on Fabian's phone when he came home from Union College for visits. Fabian had known her for about two years now.

He got up when we walked in and said, "This is Claire, my girlfriend. We met in college. You've seen her picture on my phone, and now you can meet her. She's visiting from Philadelphia. We're hoping to find jobs around here together."

Oh! Good…Fabian had gone to Philadelphia (Claire's family actually lived in a suburb of that city) to try to find a job, but had come home empty-handed. Claire had hoped to leave that area anyway, so this was not a surprise. Claire was staying on Grandmère's day bed, in her part of the house. Apparently, they had hit it off beautifully, which was great to hear.

Her parents ran a fancy pastry business, one that did wedding cakes and other showcase desserts. I had found the website once and looked at the cakes for what seemed like a couple of hours. They looked fabulous, complete with ribbons, both of satin and of marzipan, roses sculpted from buttercream, butterflies, and more.

Edgar went next. "This is Ellie, Ellie Spinoza. She's an elementary school teacher now."

I looked at her. "You seem like someone I've met before," I said, "maybe at another family party years ago. Did you go to school around here with Edgar?"

Ellie smiled and shook my hand. "Good memory! Yes, we graduated from Conard together. I was at his high school graduation party here several years ago." Ellie lived with her parents nearby, but was looking for an apartment. So far, no luck; prices around here were too high.

I grinned and shook her hand. She was teaching at a school in Simsbury now. Lucky her! She had found a job. Of course, working with kids and service jobs were the best chances Americans currently had at employment in this economy. Too many industries had shipped their operations abroad. Unless and until that was brought back, my cousins, who were educated to do other things, would have trouble. I really had to help them figure that out, but I would not talk about it until I had done so.

Edgar had graduated from Penn State, majored in business, and gone back for an M.B.A. after that. It took one year. There had to be something I could suggest…a job I could conjure into existence for him. Fabian, Charlie and Zoe's middle son, who had gone to Union College, had majored in political science and minored in history. Law school seemed like a good next step, but he wasn't ready for it just yet.

"Hi Grandmère!" I said, dumping my stuff by one of the sofas and going over to her. I leaned over to kiss her thin cheek, and she smiled back at me, but she seemed lethargic and glum. "How are you?" I asked anyway, because it was polite.

"Oh, achy, cranky, creaky, and like I'm living too long," she replied.

"If Hamish can improve your situation, he will," I said.

Grandmère actually laughed. "I believe that," she told me.

I turned to help with the food, but all I ended up doing was hugging Aunt Zoe and getting thanked for the pretty fig tart. She was pretty much done with producing dinner, and she said that with Ellie and Claire, she had plenty of help.

Ellie called out to the guys at one point, asking for help. She called them all by name, and messed up the pronunciation of Fabian's name. No…she murdered the pronunciation of it. Claire patiently corrected her: "It's Fah-bee-ahn, Ellie. French. Not Fay-bee-an." Ellie gave her a smile like one that a nanny would give a loud and assertive child. Indulgent and not a thrilling impression, I thought.

When I glanced back at Grandmère, she looked pleased with everything that was going on around her. Interesting to live so long, see so much, and still be even as comfortable as she was. She got a bit out of breath whenever she walked from the car into our house, but she ate some of everything and chatted, showing that her memory wasn't fading.

Dinner progressed nicely, and I found out more about Claire. Fabian's girlfriend was a very nice person, I decided after interacting with her for a few hours. She liked to listen, she liked to talk about politics and art and culture, and she and Fabian seemed quite compatible. She had double majored in psychology and political science, and minored in French.

"Psychology?" I said over the salad course. "What sorts of things did you study, profiling for criminologists? Autism, Asperger's, neurotypicals? Id, ego, superego? The personalities of famous and infamous political figures throughout history?"

Claire laughed. "That's terrific! I did study some of those things, and once I even wrote a paper about Hitler's psychological makeup in a bidisciplinary class. There was one that cross-listed psychology and political science, of all things. Later, I got to do one about Churchill. I would have liked to research another about Iran's Mossadegh, but there wasn't enough time…or material. But I did learn about Asperger's and NTs, so I understood your interview, the one you gave before you went on your trip."

Wow. I just stared at her for a moment. "You're terrific! I know about Mossadegh."

We smiled. I would have to invite her over to look at my books on Iran.

Uncle Charlie spoke up. "So, are you going to give us a detailed lecture about your trip after dinner, Avril?"

Hamish grinned. "She's planning on it."

"We saw that you brought lots of exhibits to show us," Edgar said. "This should be good."

We ate dessert in the living room so that I could show everything, and Jacques wired my laptop into the huge flatscreen TV so that I could project the photographs onto it. When I got to the Georgia Guidestones, I deliberately left the image of the list of 10 ideas up while I showed the Agenda 21 books around.

Everyone flipped through the books, saw the stuff from the Discovery Times Square exhibit, and handed them back. Ellie said she thought that the link I saw between U.N. Agenda 21 and the issue of human overpopulation was a conspiracy theory, not to be taken seriously. "I wouldn't get worked up about this," she said.

"Interesting," was all I said. It was interesting to see how people who did not know what I knew responded to such concepts. I wondered what I would have to say after reading these books. The one about the Green Mask caught her attention, though. She flipped through it twice before passing it on to Edgar.

Edgar disagreed with her. He thought that it was intriguing and worth further study that a liberal Democrat and real estate expert had doubts – grave enough to write the Green Mask book – about a liberal agenda, an environmentalist plan for saving the planet from the damage done by human growth and resource consumption. That alone made him want to read that book, and I said I would share it with him. (Actually, I ordered him a copy online when I got home.)

After all images had been shown and all that Hamish and I had to share about our trip had been shared (skipping the escaped, dying guy near the Guidestones, the rape in the Blue Ridge Mountains, but not the sinister feel to the sight of MRAPs and displaced people along the country roads), conversations developed in clusters around the room.

Ellie came over to chat with me. "So how does an adult with autism fit into the world and make things work positively for you?" she asked. Claire sat with us, listening.

I didn't trust Ellie thus far. She seemed like a judgmental type, not a nice neurotypical, but I kept this to myself. I hoped I was wrong and that getting to know her would show me otherwise. Besides, I had just met her.

With a steely smile, I turned to speak to her. "The trick is to arrange one's life as an adult with Asperger's so that one is not in a position to have to constantly accede to neurotypical preferences," I told her. "For me, that has meant getting advanced degrees in academic areas that fascinate me, and then writing books and working as a professor. That makes the neurotypicals I meet elements of my life, but not the dominant social element. Allowing that to happen is what ruins it for us."

Claire said, "That sounds like a very good plan, and it seems to be working for you. I love it." She smiled at me, and I saw no judgment, only acceptance. It was weird to find someone I could like after such a brief encounter, and I was glad. She and Fabian seemed really compatible. That meant that getting used to her might actually be an emotionally sensible thing to do.

I smiled back. "Thanks! It is working, and quite well."

Ellie said, "I don't know. It seems sort of like you're avoiding most of the world."

"That's exactly what I'm doing. Since most of the world has no intention of offering acceptance – only the insult of tolerance, as if something is wrong with being different from the majority, when we Aspies are in fact a minority of normal people – I reject any who do that."

She smiled politely and said, "Yes, I read your interview."

Well, that confirmed it. She was part of the tolerance mindset.

I sat there on one of the sofas, facing them, looking at them steadily as we conversed with my unblinking stare. People had been known to call me creepy for that, but I could care less. I was just observing and taking in details.

As for the details I was taking in now, it was mostly sizing these two girls up. As girlfriends of my cousins, there was always the possibility that they could end up being adopted into the family…as wives. Then they would be with us long-term, which would make this worthwhile.

What did I see? I saw two attractive, neurotypical girls who differed from one another.

Both had long, wavy, styled hair. Claire's was a honey brown, parted on the side, with slight bangs brushed back from her face. Her eyes were a pale blue with flecks of green in them. She had a kind smile, and she seemed intelligent. She met my steady gaze calmly, and smiled back at me in a friendly manner.

Ellie's hair was darker, partied almost in the middle, and came just to her shoulders, whereas Claire's fell to her upper arms and chest. Ellie had gray-green eyes with a rather condescending gaze as she looked me up and down. Whenever she spoke, she closed her eyes at the start of her sentences, which drove me crazy, but I kept my facial expressions neutral. She smiled at me in a restrained but deliberately respectful manner. It didn't feel sincere, but then, I always had trouble reading people at first. I would have to spend more time with her to understand her.

Ellie talked about how worried she and her colleagues were about their futures as teachers due to the population policy and Nae-Née use. "Now that people can't have as many kids as they want, there may not be enough for all of us to teach in a few years." She looked at me, stopping there, but not saying more. Clearly, there was more on her mind.

I would have none of that. "Say or ask it, whatever it is, Ellie," I said to her, staring her in the eyes with a slight smile and a steady calm. I didn't care whether or not she objected to Nae-Née. What I wanted was an opening in which to tell her that the policy wasn't my idea…if on point.

Ellie paused, took a deep breath (so dramatic!), and then said, "Is it true that you dislike children? And did you have anything to do with the Nae-Née population policy? Because reading about that in the media is meaningless compared with asking you in person," she summed up.

I smiled now, mirthless though it was. "I had no say in the population policy. I thought of the Nae-Née birth control nanite – and its name – on my own, and Hamish made it a reality. I do not like babies. They tend to be funny-looking to me and some are downright ugly – hairless, messy, shrieking things that ruin the peace and quiet. They are slavery to those who are responsible for them, taking over one's entire life and thoughts. No thank you. I never wanted one."

I continued, "As for children, I like the quiet, introspective ones who would never bully anyone. For teenagers, I like the ones who would never, ever behave as though someone died and made them the final arbiter of what is and is not cool. But when reproducing, you have to gamble. You can't cherry-pick your offspring's personality. You have to take what you get. So, I'm not parent material."

There were a few more points to make. "We wouldn't be so grossly overpopulated and pressuring our planet's ecosystem so much if all existing parents had asked themselves just how accepting they would be of whatever sort of child they got, why they wanted kids, whether it was about perpetuating their own genetic code and surname or more than that, and whether or not it was about social expectations from their family and/or others…before reproducing."

Ellie and Claire listened to this explication carefully, and then Ellie said, "Wow. That was…honest."

Now I grinned. "I don't do insincere. No, I'm not the one controlling things, but that's what really goes on inside my mind. I want to work in peace and quiet and enjoy my husband, not give that up for a kid. I'm not evil, just not like 'most people'. The hell with what the majority of humans might expect and require me to like. I like what I like. If it coincides with that, great. If not, too bad."

Claire had a question. "How did you choose the name for Nae-Née? I'm curious."

"Oh, that's a fun one," I said. "I actually came up with that later in the same day that I thought of the nanite itself. 'Née' is French for 'born' but the idea was to prevent births with this invention. I was in the kitchen with Hamish and my parents, racking my brain for a cool, catchy name, when my mother told him to think of something. He said, 'Nae – I shall not,' and that was it! I had the idea."

"That's clever!" Claire and Ellie said in unison.

I gave them a big smile. It was fun to recount that tale. It was also time to change the subject.

Claire asked Ellie, "When you were studying to become a teacher, did you learn how to approach students on the autism spectrum? If so, what did you learn?"

Ellie said, "We learned to make Individual Education Plans for them, to address their special needs. Most of them end up being taught in special classes, apart from the majority now. IEPs seem to be the way it's going for them. They don't fit in socially with the other kids, so that makes it easier for everyone else."

Really. "Easier for everyone else and worse for the Aspie and autistic kids, it sounds like," I said. "Aspies belong in with the majority. They can study with intense focus and do very well. They will never fit in, and the best thing to do is to teach them that they are designed to stand out, not fit in, and that they should not care. They should own it. I was in with the others. I did very well, I knew I was different, and I just observed quietly. If I had an occasional meltdown, crying over being left out, it would blow over in a day or so and I would just go on."

Ellie smiled indulgently at me. "That's no longer seen as what's best for the others. Also, we don't want to expose the others to meltdowns, or waste time on bullying. That happens when the different kids sit quietly by themselves."

"So it's all about them now, and not at all about us. That's the wrong way to go. No wonder Einstein, another Aspie, said that he failed school – he was talking about high school in Germany – and that school failed him. Our schools are now poised to fail many Asperkids. This sucks."

Claire said, "Yes, it does. Didn't you study Aspies in college, Ellie?"

"No," she said. "I focused on the – what did you call them? Neurotypical kids? I concentrated on the majority. The special education teachers can handle the different kids."

"Ridiculous," I said, utterly disgusted. "When we Aspies are silent, wide-eyed, staring, withdrawn, and quiet – or having a meltdown – it is because we are overstimulated and stressed. This new policy of separation does a disservice to all of the kids. It teaches the neurotypicals – the NTs – to ostracize different kids, and it deprives Aspies of academic rigor."

Edgar wasn't listening to any of this, I realized. He and his brothers were busy chatting with Hamish about nanites. Fabian was closest; he glanced over and seemed to have heard this exchange, and he and Claire exchanged glances.

A little while later, it was time to go home.

Chapter 8

Packing Nanites

A loaded gun is just a machine until someone picks it up.

The NRA can and will tell you that, thinking that it is persuading people that guns are okay. That is the agenda of the National Rifle Association: to push the Second Amendment right to bear arms as far as it possibly can.

But there is more to the possession and control of a gun that just that.

It's all about who is holding that gun and what their intent is. Is it a good guy or a bad guy, a law-enforcement officer or a criminal, a moral person or an amoral one? And how do we know which is which?

People hate and fear what they don't know, and sometimes, when they do know something or someone but are horrified by what they have found out, they still do.

Villains have a lot to teach us. The intelligent ones excel at being bad, and the ones with experience behind them, those who have gone unnoticed, are the most dangerous. They aren't always the ones with actual guns. There are all sorts of ways to do harm, and all sorts of weapons to wield. Whenever a villain talks to much, they reveal a lot. It's better to silently take it in than to duplicate that error.

Where are these successful villains? Everywhere.

They are lawyers, of course, because lawyers learn to play both sides of any game, just like a chess match. They can prosecute or defend. They are changeable, which is why they are called hired guns.

As I said, there are many kinds of guns, not just the ones with physical ammunition.

Mental ammunition is very dangerous too.

My husband could offer both: mental acuity and nanite guns.

He wasn't thrilled over having invented those on the way to creating a neuro-monitoring system, but that was what he had done, and it had become known to the United States government the day that he saved my life with it.

Hamish didn't regret the fact that I was still alive or that it was because of his actions. He only regretted that the government now possessed yet another devastating weapon, and being the source of it. He would have preferred not to have been forced to keep its existence a secret.

It would have been useless to attempt to conceal it after discharging it in full view of a team of covert operatives dispatched by the National Security Agency – or No Such Agency, as it was known in the running joke among ordinary citizens who knew it existed, thanks to Hollywood movies, and thanks to puzzle and chase novels.

That team had been charged with protecting us both, and instead, Hamish had usurped their mission with his nanite gun, hitting not only the would-be assassin but also one of the N.S.A. operatives with its contents.

So the secret was out, if only to a select few in the government, and shared by us.

Now my husband wanted me armed…with my own secret nanite gun.

It looked like something issued by Starfleet. Points for coolness to Hamish.

It was made of plastic, not metal. It was small, fit neatly in my hand, and easy to operate, just as I would expect. It was lightweight, pale gray, and had a firing and reverse-firing switch, rocker-style. The nanites were inside, and would cause nerve pain, spasms, tics, and generally incapacitate anyone I fired upon. Great. Just what I always wanted: a weapon.

I didn't like guns.

Hamish didn't care.

"Every Swiss citizen is required to own and be qualified to operate a weapon," he informed me. "That's why the Nazi soldiers wanted no part of Switzerland during World War II, and why they hoped and prayed that Hitler wouldn't send them in there. They would have been mown down in short order."

I just looked at it glumly as he carried on, thought I was memorizing the new information.

We were upstairs in our bedroom at home, so we could talk freely and do whatever we wished. I had had no idea that this what my husband had in mind when he smiled and pulled me in here this evening.

"Now let's practice with this," he said, putting the nanite gun in my palm. "Shoot me."

I raised one eyebrow and regarded him skeptically. Hadn't the first people who had been shot with one of these things lost bladder control? "Go pee first," I replied.

Hamish looked at me for a moment, laughed, and then went into the bathroom.

I sat down on the cushioned bench at the foot of our bed, holding the gun and looking at it. It didn't seem hard to operate, but this was the first time that I ever held one. Odd, considering the fact that my husband had invented the thing years ago, and for peaceful, medical purposes.

Considering its design, it was no great mental leap to understand that it was not just a medical delivery device, but also a weapon. How appropriate in this age of weaponized molecules, both organic and cybernetic.

The toilet flushed, and Hamish came back in. "Shoot me," he ordered, again.

I raised the gun at him and said, deciding to have a little fun with this, "Move slowly with your hands up, over to the bed." I jerked the gun in that direction as I said this, staring him down.

If this was his idea of a sex game, I wasn't turned on. But I would act like a movie actress with it in a crime scene. Why not keep this as light-hearted as possible?

Hamish moved warily across the room, not understanding why I wanted this.

"Sit down on the edge of the bed," I said.

He did it, but asked why.

"So you have a comfortable place to collapse and don't hit your head or otherwise injure yourself," I said irritably. "I hate this, and I'm just practicing because you insisted on it. Now stay there so I can shoot you!'

"Yes dear," he said, grinning.

I was really annoyed at him now. Time to wipe that stupid, bossy grin off his face. I fired.

What happened next was sickening. My husband writhed and jerked on the bed, but fell safely backwards onto the mattress.

I rushed over, pressed the muzzle of the nanite gun to his neck, and hit the reverse switch.

Instantly, he relaxed.

"Are you okay?" I asked, crouching over him on the mattress, staring at him. I didn't feel guilty, but I hated this game.

Hamish grinned at me, pulled me close, and kissed me.

"You're smart!" he said. "You made sure I wouldn't pee the bed or worse."

I rolled my eyes. "Don't you EVER ask me to shoot you again!" I said, disgusted.

"Yes, dear," he said.

"Okay, me next," I said. I should understand what I was doing to people, and since it didn't involve getting injured with a bullet hole and scarred for life, the idea seemed reasonable.

Hamish stopped grinning and looked at me. "Are you sure?"

"Just wait for me to use the bathroom first," I said. "I'm not interested in making any messes." I was still holding the gun, too.

"Okay. Are you planning to shoot yourself? Because I don't want to shoot you."

"Oh really?! Now you get gun-shy. Yeah, I'm going to shoot myself. Just a minute."

I went in the bathroom and spent a while, deciding to brush and floss my teeth, too. What was I thinking, going along with this?! Oh well… I came back out to the bedroom, sat down on the bed, held the gun to my left hand, and moved my finger toward the rocker switch.

"WAIT."

I looked at Hamish.

"Don't just give yourself a full dose. Look, you can control how much to release, and either push the switch all the way, and release enough nanites to spread over an entire human body, or do it in 10 percent increments. Look at the marks on the switch and you'll see your options."

I had noticed that feature, but was planning to be fair, I explained to him.

"Trust me," Hamish insisted, "try it like this and you'll see. This was my idea anyway, not yours, and I know what I'm saying."

Okay. Might as well heed the advice of the inventor.

I held the gun back up to my left hand, pressed the muzzle into the fleshy area of the thumb, and pushed the rocker-trigger switch to just one mark ahead of zero.

Instantly, I felt like miniature knives were infesting and slicing the inside of my left hand. Abstractly, I understood that no actual damage was being done, but it sure didn't feel that way. I watch the clock on the wall, second-hand moving, and waited ten seconds. Before they were up, the little stabbers began to rush up my wrist and into my lower arm.

Hamish watched me. As I looked at my elbow, teeth gritted, letting the nanites travel to my upper arm, he said, "Put the gun back on your hand and retract. Now!"

It was harder than I thought it would be with the distraction of the pain, but I did my best to ignore it and comply. The nerve pain was definitely dulling my reactions significantly. Imagine how tough that would be with a higher setting and no warning, I thought to myself.

I felt the nanites race out of my arm and hand with amazing speed. One moment I was in terrible pain and the next I wasn't. "Wow," I said, offering the gun back to Hamish.

"No, it's yours," he told me. "Keep it. You insist on having pockets in everything you wear, so carry it everywhere from now on, in your pocket."

I looked at him coolly, then decided I might as well acquiesce. He had been pushing me to get a gun for years, and I had been resisting. This was as good as it was ever going to get. "Fine," I said, "but we're in for the night, you're supposed to be totally trustworthy around me, and I'm going to put it under the folded tissues and keys in this bowl with the rest of the contents of my pocket and take a bath and shampoo.

We each had a place on our respective bedside tables for such things, on either side of the bed. It was something I had learned from my mother as a kid. She kept a basket on the bow windowsill in the kitchen for my father's things, and I had watched him all my life when he came home, dumping his keys, watch, wallet, and coins into it.

So…when I got married, I put a small basket out for Hamish and explained what it was for. He had always simply tossed his keys and wallet onto a table, or thrown his pants into a corner without emptying the pockets.

Married life could be tough on a guy. He had to be neat and at least a little bit orderly. No more calling me from a business trip, frantic that he had lost his wallet when it was on the floor or a chair, inside the pockets of his other pair of pants! He had actually done that once, on a trip to L.A. last year. No basket there.

But back to the present. I had a painted porcelain bowl for my stuff, a family heirloom from my great-great-grandmother, who had liked to occupy her time with such crafts a century ago. So many lost arts…

I carefully buried my new nanite weapon under the tissues and keys, draped a lace doily tatted by the same ancestor over the lot of it, and headed for the bathroom. Hmm…something to add to my daily routine when I got dressed: armed and packing…nanites. I guessed that this ought to fit into my habits neatly. Hamish must have wanted me to have this weapon for a while now, and seeing what we saw on our drive through the Blue Ridge Mountains had clinched it.

"Are you coming?" I said to my husband. "I'm going to fill up OUR tub with lavender water and sit in it. I want company."

He jumped up, put his wallet and keys in his basket, and started stripping off his jeans and tee shirt. "Coming, Avril – be right there!" He was grinning.

So was I.

Chapter 9

Overshoot: The Consequences Begin

As I started to read through the pile of books on U.N. Agenda 21 that I had acquired in Manhattan, I kept some things in mind. These things were information that I had read previously on human overpopulation. That the trouble with having someone like me find a stack of books on a utopian plan for making it work to have more and more humans on the planet: I could see clearly that it just wouldn't work.

Our planet was operating way above its carrying capacity for human beings.

Back in 1968, when Paul and Anne Ehrlich first published their warning about the consequences of human overpopulation, they were vilified just for discussing the idea. They broke the taboo of doing so, as had Thomas Malthus in 1798. So what? Break it. Never declare a topic taboo! Population policies are not popular. Popular means that people like whatever it is that is popular, and the similarity of the words "population" and "popular" is no accident.

The Ehrlichs showed an equation from their research: $I = P \times A \times T$. In it, I, the impact of a population, is equal to its size *(P)*, multiplied by the per-capita consumption *(A)*, multiplied by the energy use *(T)* for the technologies to drive that consumption.

But it didn't matter how many scientists said so or how often they said it or how they said it or when or where they said it. It was just not what the majority wanted to hear, so it went ignored while the situation got worse and worse.

No wonder the Nae-Née treaty had only produced shrieks of rage and protest.

Our species had overshot what the planet had to offer a long time ago, but the same methods of producing income were still prevalent, and in the same areas of the world. The rich were getting exponentially richer while the poor continued to get exponentially poorer.

When I was in college, and still, whenever I met and talked with college students, I would hear the same tired truism that it was possible to provide for all of the people on the planet if the goods were distributed equitably.

Sure…just move economic opportunities and food supplies around, and don't allow a deprived majority to eat higher on the food chain than an elite minority of the human population. Pure fantasy was what that was. I doubted that the United Nations could push a mandate like that one through any time soon. The vision of *Star Trek* was a long, long way off still.

Overshoot was defined as a combination of three things:

1. Rapid change;
2. Limits to that change; and
3. Errors or delays in perceiving those limits and controlling the resulting change.

Humanity was showing all of these symptoms and thus losing its humanity.

There were a couple of different potential outcomes to overshoot: oscillation, or collapse.

Oscillation was infinitely preferable to collapse. With oscillation, growth would be slowed to ease the pain of lowered expectations and living with less in the way of material goods. When things slowed down, it might look like a collapse at first, but conditions would level off later and things would improve, although there would be less growth than in the past. This pattern would repeat until finally growth stopped and levels of population and production – both natural and manufacturing – held steady. The Nae-Née treaty was an effort at bringing this about.

But it was perceived as an opaque, controlling effort at oscillation rather than a consensus method with transparency. Hence the screaming and outrage associated with not being able to conceive as many children as a particular adult female and/or her partner wished. Of course, that wasn't all; there was also the basic instinct to have whatever one wanted, and as much of it as one could get, regardless of whatever those around one were doing, or needed, or wanted.

Some people believed in allowing for such selfishness regardless of the difficulties that this placed on others, citing survival of the fittest as justification. Others disagreed and expected humanity to think ahead and act with consideration for others, especially succeeding generations.

In the United States, we called the former Republicans and the latter Democrats, or Tea Party members and Liberals, or Libertarians and Communitarians, or one-percenter capitalists and everyone else. Perhaps frustration with the fact that collapse was imminent and a belief that nothing would ever be done to deal with or prevent it in a democratic, civil society was why the Nae-Née policy had gone through. There was that, and the fact that the Electoral College had been eliminated by a Constitutional Amendment a few years earlier.

That had happened when laws prohibiting excessive donations to campaign funds had conflicted with good old boys' club efforts to use money and influence to both elect and control members of both the House and Senate in Congress. When special interests could no longer buy their way into controlling the makeup of Congress, things had changed.

That at least partly explained how Senators LaRosse and Boenher, two people who held such opposite views as to how humanity's future should proceed, had found themselves arguing for and against population controls.

When Hamish was a little kid, twenty percent of the world's population controlled thirty percent of its wealth. Now that same group controlled over eighty percent of it. The descendants of the twenty percent of the 1960s made up the group who now controlled over eighty percent. In America, a top one percent controlled most of the wealth. It was folly to think that they would willingly loosen their grip in enough numbers to make a difference. We as a species were like France in 1789, with too much wealth concentrated among too few people.

When the Nae-Née treaty came along, the wealthy minority put up a huge fuss over the treaty, not wanting to give up any advantage or luxury. They didn't see why they ought to make any accommodations for others, yet the treaty demanded that they be included in a democratic application of its principles. The rich wanted checks on others but none on themselves; it was the same old story.

They wanted what they wanted, they felt entitled to it, and they weren't interested in the plight of others. Of course, listening to ordinary Americans complain about the policy and insist that there was no need to apply it to them – only to people in overcrowded, developing nations – showed the same mindset. It was ridiculous, because people in wealthy nations had much larger carbon footprints than people in poorer ones, and this was with fewer people overall.

When people in poor countries lacked checks on population growth, things only got worse for them. Each generation in the developing world not only become poorer as success was rewarded with more success and poverty was rewarded with less opportunity for success, but the smaller share of resources and goods (which includes food) was spread thinner and thinner among more and more poor people.

That just made it even less likely that women in poor countries would turn their attention to education and seek greater economic and legal freedoms. Instead, they would end up having more children, either due to a lack of birth control, a lack of hope, or both. With fewer children to occupy their time and attention, the Nae-Née policy aimed at turning their efforts to self-improvement, legal advancement for women, and eventually more equal distribution of health care, education and economic opportunity.

But most of what was heard on the news and around the world was outcry.

People were disappointed, and angry at a loss of control over their fertility. They didn't see that they were being directed toward a future of more control over more crucial things. These people were everywhere, but the loudest voices came, oddly enough, from the wealthiest, in the most developed countries. Sure enough, the comfortable felt entitled to control their fertility.

Journalists traveled to rural India, Africa, and Southeast Asia to interview women in less glorified economic circumstances about the treaty. How did they feel about it? Were they angry or sad about having to apply for a birth license? The answers came as a surprise: many women felt relieved by the conditions of the treaty. Relieved?! The journalists asked in disbelief. Why?

The replies explained the matter succinctly. The pressure from in-laws and society was off thanks to the treaty. Worry over aborting female fetuses was down too, thanks to the difficulty in having any children at all under the new laws and with the Nae-Née devices in operation. Licenses would still be granted, but not until a woman was at least nineteen years old in India and eighteen in most African nations. Not only that, but gone was the condition that a Nigerian woman have 11 children before being allowed to participate in the political process at all. It would all work out, the women who were interviewed told the journalists.

It was the interviews with the couples in Europe, Japan, Australia, Canada, the United States, and elsewhere in the developed world that got angry responses. Statisticians had a field day analyzing them, drawing correlations between those who railed the loudest against the treaty and their income level. The higher the income, it seemed, the greater the outrage.

There were exceptions, of course: people with health problems were left out, unable to get a birth license and upset about it. But the tone of their complaints was usually different, because their complaints were about a different thing:

disappointment tempered with acceptance. One ought to be healthy before starting a pregnancy. Others were outraged over being rejected for their age, or for economic reasons, or for psychological instability. They too complained bitterly, but it did them no good.

The religious right of America still held protests and made impassioned speeches about "God's will," but their events were heavily covered by police, who kept them from advancing too closely to anyone else. It was as if those in charge of law enforcement were convinced that they were hearing myth and self-destructiveness, and humoring the crowds of creationists without being impressed by their message.

Still, it seemed as though there was still an awfully large percentage of the human population, particularly in my own country, that wasn't thinking long-term and wanting to change its behavior to protect the future. They were too wrapped up in present comforts.

Was I one of the few people who realized this and got more upset about that aspect of the situation than facing its consequences? I couldn't seem to stop myself from thinking so. I thought about this some more. What I didn't mind facing was not having children.

What I did mind facing was experiencing a decline in my own quality of life because of the determined selfishness and gluttony of others who wanted multiple children and whose children also wanted multiple children and so on and on exponentially, along with the resulting carbon footprints that each resulting child would leave on the earth until there was no more room to enjoy a decent level of comfort in the present, let alone in the future.

But most human beings still wanted and expected the earth to accommodate growth, although when they talked about it, they focused on the specific things that they wanted: kids, cars, houses, vacations on beaches, and more.

Their parents' generation had been raised to expect all that, and had enjoyed it. Naturally, they expected to have the same thing. But there wasn't room for their generation to have that. We had reached the limits of growth on our planet. The three children of a set of parents could not have as much as what their parents had enjoyed.

This wasn't a new concept.

Long ago, when places like England had been divided up into huge estates, there had been a problem: should land be divided among the two or three sons of the landowner, or should the oldest son get it all? The answer had been to give it all to the oldest son and let the younger ones fend for themselves. That left the younger ones to either live as celibate priests or to make their fortunes with military careers while the oldest son enjoyed the estate in safety and comfort.

Daughters only inherited property if there were no sons – another inequality, one from an abomination that dated back to the days of Charlemagne, who instituted it. It was called Salic Law, and it was now crumbling everywhere. Good.

With this elite system now obsolete, anyone could buy a plot of land.

For several generations, while there had been more room for growth, there had been more room in which to spread out. Successive generations found that land existed in sufficient quantities for each son – and later each daughter, if she chose to do so – to buy some land.

But that only worked for a while.

With all of us allegedly equal, human beings in many nations had proceeded to inhabit every bit of land that they could acquire title to, and not always excluding low-lying wetlands, deserts, tornado alleys, or national parks. When a storm, flood or drought chased them out, there was usually outrage over the loss of life and property along with an expectation of rebuilding in the same places or reimbursement from an insurer.

They ought to just relocate, but to where?

Where else were people supposed to move to now, with much of Manhattan underwater, with Florida gone and the snakes and alligators of the Everglades encroaching upon the areas that weren't submerged, and the same thing happening in Pakistan, Bangladesh, Venice, the Netherlands, England, and elsewhere?

There was nowhere else to go, no more room in which to grow, and still people wanted children, and more than one per couple. Add to that the couples who divorced and remarried and then wanted to reproduce again, and the simple arithmetic became appalling.

It reminded me of upsetting stories such as the *Tecora*, which was just one of many true ones. The *Tecora*, a Portuguese slave ship renamed the *Amistad* in order to commit a treaty violation and thus continue the crime of human slavery, had routinely gone to west Africa, loaded way more kidnap victims into its hold than it could reasonably expect to feed for the three-month trip across the Atlantic Ocean, and headed for the Caribbean Sea.

The solution to this problem was as disturbing as one might expect: partway across the ocean, when some of the captives were sick, they were thrown overboard in chains so that they would sink like stones and drown. The 1997 movie *Amistad* showed this – graphically. A side panel was removed from the ship's deck, and screaming, protesting, terrified African kidnap victims were pushed out, slipping, sliding, and scratching frantically at the sides as they fell.

So, what did our planet's leaders do less than two centuries later when it became clear that it could not provide the necessities of life to all who would be born if growth continued unchecked?

They mandated putting the brakes on growth. It didn't seem all that bad; it wasn't a cancelling of the future, after all. It was a controlled continuation of what had gone on before. People could still have families, but the concept had been revised.

No more families of any size that a particular couple desired; no longer could anyone just have ten or even four kids just because they wanted them. That also put a damper on having multiple spouses, either consecutive due to death or divorce, or concurrent if one's religion allowed or encouraged that.

Women everywhere, it seemed, were deaf to cries of outrage from men anywhere about that. At last, an end to polygamy! Or so we all hoped… The point was that there would be no more multiple wives so that a man could have as many children as possible in as short a time as possible, or try for as many sons as possible.

I certainly found it entertaining to hear and read reports of unhappy, outraged polygamists whining and objecting pointlessly that this was unfair or unjust. It was absolutely fair and just! Women and girls were sick and tired of their quest for patriarchal dominance.

This quest had added exponentially to the population explosions in third world nations that struggled to provide sufficient food everyone. The list went on: India, China, Sudan, Yemen, Indonesia, the Philippines, Haiti, Brazil, Bolivia, North Korea, Guatemala…and so on.

But here in the Western world, there were plenty of wealthy, upper-middle-class couples who couldn't understand why they couldn't have as many children as they could afford to raise. That certainly made explanations more complicated, but at least the governments of the planet remained unyielding. Why should the citizens of the wealthy nations continue to live off the backs of the others indefinitely?

But the response was: So what if time was up? We don't care; we want what we want.

It was a good thing that the governments were finally, at long last, after much hemming and hawing and debating and saying that we had more time to delay and consider, facing the fact that we didn't have time anymore. I was fine with that. No one was being deprived of life and liberty.

Added to that was the fact that wealthy nations weren't entirely without a valid argument against continued growth: there was the simple mathematical certainty that when the children of parents who could afford college for each of their offspring came of age, a rude surprise was already waiting to confront them.

The colleges and universities that were considered to be competitive, more competitive, ivy league and otherwise selective enough to challenge their well-qualified, talented, hard-working and intellectually aspiring teenagers would not have room for them all.

Many of them were going to be left with no place to study but less competitive schools, or even community colleges. Those who had fondly nurtured hopes of graduate and professional school were going to have to forget about that and get low-level jobs that yielded slim economic rewards and prestige. Even starting up a small business was getting harder thanks to difficulties with a depressed economy and fewer banks that could or would offer loans.

But parents didn't want to hear such things; the future was unknown, full of hope and possibilities, and the choices were limitless while they stared adoringly at their darling little newborn babies or toddling kids. Even as I was fully aware of all this, I still looked at such people and thought that they were all crazy, thoughtless, and astonishingly selfish.

Overpopulation caused crowded conditions, which meant less individual attention, more unnoticed bullying, and fewer chances to interact one-on-one with teachers, all of which led to poorer academic performance. If a kid was lucky enough to transcend all that, college might very well be out of reach through no fault of her or his own, simply due to a lack of space.

I looked at the teenagers who were alive now and ready for college, teenagers with high grade point averages, a lifetime of violin, bassoon, or French horn lessons behind them plus the practice that went with that, with a slew of extra-curricular activities such as plays, singing groups and even sports, but still couldn't gain admission to a good college, and I got upset.

It was true that I didn't like babies and little kids, but when I saw older ones who were disappointed, I felt anger and outrage and frustration on their behalf. It was as though, thanks to the lack of a single maternal bone in my body, I saved all of my affection for older teenagers.

Many other famous and accomplished women had wonderfully successful careers in their fields, and had been happily married or happily single depending upon their luck and choices. I had been lucky enough to find and choose Hamish, and my career had at last worked out beautifully, even if I had to retreat from the floodwaters in Manhattan and return to Connecticut.

With the floods and tornadoes that were wreaking havoc on the nation's infrastructure, keeping Internet and telephone signals active was proving to be a challenge for governments and corporations. NASA had run out of money, but satellites still needed to be maintained. Our national debt was like a maxed out credit card. No one knew how this would all turn out; people worried that sooner rather than later, the satellites that we had grown so dependent on would begin to drop out of operation.

That would certainly change everyone's life in a big way.

Imagine all those people with iPhones and Blackberries, people who kept them on 24/7, people whose thumbs never seemed to stop moving as they texted and Tweeted and e-mailed one another; how would they cope when they suddenly found themselves abruptly and unceremoniously booted offline?

It wouldn't be pretty. As it was, things weren't pretty.

There wasn't enough food sometimes, and at other times, there was enough but the infrastructure necessary to get it to people who needed it wasn't in place. Trains and trucks were required to move food from one location to another. But train-tracks and bridges were decaying around the nation. They needed to be either repaired or completely rebuilt – now.

The president had turned his attention to this problem in his re-election campaign, and now he was well into his second term, working on it. Even Congress was interested in making a deal. But it wasn't a done deal, as the saying went, and so American citizens were left in our current predicament, often hungry until the food could get where it had to go. Next year was an election year; it looked as though banksters from both parties would run. I wasn't thrilled. Banksters wouldn't work hard at making sure that all citizens were comfortable, only a few.

Connecticut stores were comparatively well off; it was those living in more spread out areas that were in trouble, and those in devastated areas that had suffered destruction from storms and floods and drought that needed help most urgently.

Whole Foods had raspberries most of the time, and halibut for the outrageous price of $34.99 per pound, plus plenty of other options. Other grocery stores had somewhat lower prices, but also fewer items regularly in stock. Sometimes I would have to revise my cooking plans after a trip to the stores – all of them –

when certain things weren't available. At least I could get organic ingredients at Whole Foods, as Hamish insisted. Other stores were less reliable that way.

But if something I needed didn't come in a package – if it was fresh – I couldn't just buy it ahead of time and save it for later. Scarcity was taking planning ahead off of the list of options sometimes. It was also making any road trip, however local and however routine and necessary, a minor adventure.

While I studied and analyzed all this, and read my new books, our cousins from Paris had come to visit us for a couple of weeks. They were chic, slightly aloof, sophisticated, and I did not know them very well. They were a basic nightmare to an Aspie...except when I was showing them the local sights and giving a running commentary. During those times, they were impressed and pleasant. They stayed at the West Hartford Inn.

Each couple was in their late twenties or early thirties, had delayed reproducing, and now suddenly found that they had to wait until the French government granted dispensation to do so. At least they didn't blame us, and at least they weren't feeling a great sense of urgency about it just yet. They had come to see Grandmère, and to enjoy themselves for a week or so.

I led them each in succession around the Wadsworth Atheneum, the Mark Twain and Harriet Beecher Stowe Houses, the Hill-Stead Museum, and the Noah Webster House, surprised at how my old tour speeches came back to me in the Twain and Stowe historic houses.

Hamish and I took them out to dinner a couple of times, once with my parents and another time without them. Aside from that, we ate at home with my parents, moving from the small kitchen table to the larger one in the dining room, or over at Uncle Charlie and Aunt Zoe's place with Grandmère and my other three cousins and Claire. Everyone liked Claire.

Each of these situations was ripe for discussions about food.

Gourmet food, food cooked at home, restaurant food, fast food, and the effects of each kind on an individual's physique and on the environment – all these were discussed with intense interest. It was inevitable. France was rationing water use and food, and the U.S. was about to. Choices about food were not what they once were even in developed nations.

Grandmère observed it all with slight confusion, but her astonishment had long since faded with the regularity of news reports about famine in Africa (not just in Somalia) and elsewhere, plus persistent outstripping of water supplies in order to grow more and more food for a still-growing human population.

Growth seemed to have ceased at last, but too late. People around the world were dying because of disease and famine, not just because of human population controls. Food choices changed with rising incomes, land uses changed with industrialization, and water tables sank as people pumped it into homes and croplands faster than nature could replenish it.

My cousins were at their most entertaining when we ate out in a local sit-down chain restaurant such as Red Lobster or Ruby Tuesday. Once we were seated, they would look around surreptitiously at the other patrons, quietly observing them for the first ten minutes or so.

Hamish and I would look at each other and just wait for it.

It would come right after we had placed our orders and returned from the salad bar.

"There are so many fat Americans," they would say.

I would just smile and say, "Yes, there certainly are."

Then a debate would ensue over the causes for this: fatty diet, insufficient or total lack of exercise, a sedentary, suburban lifestyle…the usual. After all, French people went for regular walks, drank a mixture of red wine and water with dinner, and built exercise into their daily routines at every opportunity, including taking the stairs rather than an elevator.

One of the things I made sure to point out was the fact that many Americans were unable to afford a more nutritious diet, and so had become morbidly obese. Some were paid too little to afford regular helpings of fresh fruits and vegetables. Others were unable to eat a healthy diet because all they could afford on government assistance (food stamps were now called Supplemental Nutrition Assistance Program, or SNAP, benefits) was processed foods. Another root cause of obesity was advertising by the corporations that made and sold processed foods. The final nail in people's coffins, both literally and figuratively, was a general lack of nutritional education, both in diet content and in building healthy foods into their routines.

But what really fascinated us all was the lack of sustainability for fat Americans. When the bubble burst, would they change their lifestyles and get some exercise growing their own food at last, and with low-tech, somewhat labor-intensive methods? They would starve, and painfully. I described this problem to my cousins, and they stopped short. It was a disturbing thought, imagining a famine in what was a developed nation. It could not be far off.

Frustrated, I said that it seemed to me that we could all learn a lot from the Amish.

When I said that, my cousins demanded detailed explanation of Amish culture.

It was too bad that the Amish lived so far away, or I would have taken them out on a drive past their farms. But upstate New York, rural Pennsylvania and other areas with Amish communities were a bit farther away than we were about to drive and burn fossil fuels.

My cousins didn't expect any tours of those areas. But they were fascinated to hear how the Amish drew water from wells, lived with the irrigation that precipitation provided, and ran their homes and their farms entirely without electricity. The Amish made a great case in point for ways to save the planet.

Yet the Amish had also experienced population growth, and when the government went to inject the women with Nae-Née, the scenes hadn't been pretty, even from those peaceful people. The planners who had sent the injection teams had been wise enough to precede them with town hall meetings to explain the procedure and the policy, complete with the reasons behind it, in great detail. In the end, the reactions were fairly calm and accepting; the Amish would still have a fair chance at maintaining their pre-1990s numbers, which satisfied the elders.

At Uncle Charlie and Aunt Zoe's house, the situation was a bit uncomfortable.

The problem had nothing directly to do with Nae-Née, so Hamish and I felt okay when we went there to visit. But the problem was directly related to the consequences of human overpopulation in our developed, first-world, middle-class-minded nation.

Uncle Charlie had led all of his sons to expect that they would follow him into the real estate market after college and develop subdivision after subdivision. But with the housing market in a state of collapse, plus balloon mortgages that had popped all around the nation, both sales and new construction, the cornerstone of Uncle Charlie's business, had ground to a screeching halt.

He and my aunt were living off of their savings in addition to the trickle that he was able to keep flowing, and had been forced to tell all of their sons that they would have to search for jobs after college. Uncle Charlie and Aunt Zoe had had enough money to pay for all three sons' college degrees and then to continue to enjoy their current standard of living, but they doubted that there would be much of an inheritance for them after that.

None of this surprised me.

Edgar wanted to move out and get a place with Ellie, but that required an independent income. He was stuck visiting her at her place and then coming home at night. She had finally found an apartment in Elmwood, the old working-class neighborhood of West Hartford.

He had completed his education and could not find work. He had been home for a couple of years now, searching for work that he could drive to. He wasn't about to relocate and incur huge expenses that a job might not pay for, and no one blamed him.

Most of the jobs out there now had no benefits and were only temporary and part-time. There were no bites, and the stories of companies which made a living by gathering information from the Internet about job applicants for potential employers just kept cropping up.

It didn't help that Grandmère read them all out loud from *The New York Times* in her corner of the living room. She didn't seem to realize how upsetting it was when she harped on how grim the job market was, and her grandsons were a captive audience, unless they holed themselves up in their rooms.

Fabian was watching the conversations – and recriminations and arguments – with visible anxiety. Like his brother, he had no college loans, but now he was looking at graduate school and unpaid internships, hoping to put off the inevitable: seeking nonexistent employment that drew on his liberal arts education.

UConn Law School was within just a little more than 10 minutes' driving distance from his parents' house. Even with loans for that program, he would have a financial advantage over most others, thanks to the in-state, living-with-parents cost of attending that top-tier law school. Both Claire and Fabian had visited that school, hoping to attend. They were certainly well-prepared for it, but not ready to make the leap of debt it would involve just yet.

I didn't blame them, and was secretly plotting to pay their tuition if they chose to do that.

As for Jacques, he was leaning towards becoming a social worker, and the West Hartford branch of UConn had a one-year graduate program for that. He was the one of the three boys who followed my Agenda 21 studies with the most interest and understanding, thanks to his background in environmental studies. Talking about what we read was fun each week.

My cousins were really nice guys who were luckier than most, yet I still found that I felt sorry for them, and wondered if we could help, and how. Never mind more school just yet – they weren't actually planning to go. What I wanted to do was create jobs for them if none could be found. It really did seem that none were out there, and every day there were news reports of jobs being eliminated in favor of machines – computers and robots.

Edgar was now experiencing what Hamish and I had gone through a few years earlier. The fact that finding a place of his own, getting married, and having his own life might not happen for him due to a lack of an income to fuel it was devastating.

My mother warned me to keep out of it, and to say nothing at their house. My father and I exchanged glances whenever she did that. Could Hamish and I help, with his lab? He might need an office manager soon.

Edgar was trained in sales after a series of summer jobs, internships, and working with his father. Weren't people who had made as much money as we had supposed to take care of their families with their financial success and considerable resources?

My mother loved to watch the Food Network, and she would often point out a southern woman chef with beautiful, long white hair who had done just that after struggling to make ends meet for years and then suddenly made a fortune as a cookbook author and chef. She had seen to it that all of her relatives had jobs on her cooking show.

When all of these visits with our Paris cousins were over, I planned to go back to see the lawyer and financial planner that we had hired to oversee our finances. I had deliberately chosen a shark for the lawyer, one with some work experience but still young enough to continue working for many more years, and a famous author who had started her career as a counselor to people with debt management issues.

The lawyer was a Yale Law School graduate who had expected to land a lucrative job on Wall Street, perhaps with our national casino – also known as the New York Stock Exchange – and manage revenues while minimizing tax payments for the rich for the bulk of his career. His name was Jonas Strom, and he was from Greenwich, but after growing up in a gated community there, he had gone on to become a Bear Stearns casualty. He was delighted to work for us.

The financial planner was Sharianne Ormonde, and she had briefly been a television personality who had taken her counseling talents to the next level, speaking on talk shows and giving television interviews, sometimes with a live audience and sometimes in a closed newsroom. Keith Olbermann had even had her on his show, and spoken to her with respect. In fact, that was why I had hired her. She was all about sustainable futures and income sources.

I decided that I would have them create and manage some new positions for my cousins. The hell with waiting for the economy to improve, and for more jobs to magically come into existence! We would make those jobs exist. That's what family was for, as I saw it.

That was it. I was going to use nepotism to help my family survive all this in comfort for as long as I possibly could. Hamish agreed with my plan. He was already supporting his sister, Fiona, in comfort back in Scotland with our financial resources. Now we would apply them to Edgar, while giving him something useful to do so that he would feel just fine about it.

The hell with what anyone thought about nepotism. I felt forced to choose between that and watching my cousin's lives disintegrate into black depression and hopelessness. I remembered how it was when I thought that I would never be solvent and able to take care of myself.

I also remembered that no one becomes a success – however you choose to define that – without help from others.

So I would help others now that I was a success, starting with my family and friends.

Maybe that helpfulness could be expanded after a while. I hoped so.

Once I had made up my mind about this, I brought the subject up with Hamish.

He agreed to my plan immediately, without waiting for me to lay out the details.

However, he did want to hear what I had in mind, and he liked it once he had.

Edgar was trained in sales and business management, and could become Hamish's agent and career manager. His duties would be to promote Hamish's work with nanites and medicine, perhaps with some travel, and to liaise with people so that Hamish could keep working. He would also serve as office manager for much of the time while we were all together and at home.

Fabian could work part-time for now, so as to encourage him to go to law school. I was sure I could think of two part-time positions with flexible hours for him and Claire, perhaps keeping track of patient records and protecting patient confidentiality. In this digital age, too much personal data was out there, unguarded. People were entirely too casual with it. Both Fabian and Claire had expressed interest in this issue, and working with it would be good practice for aspiring attorneys.

As for Jacques, I needed help of my own, and he seemed like just the sort of person who could supply it. His skills were both with social networking and understanding environmental and population issues. I had written extensively about different aspects of the environment, economic collapse, and overpopulation, but had no clue as to how to promote myself. Nor did I have much of an inclination to spend time on this. I wanted to hire him as my agent.

Now all I had to do was broach the subject with my cousins.

The next time our family gathered together for its weekly dinner, they all listened as I outlined my blatant intent to practice nepotism. At first, they looked skeptical. But when I added that this was a blatant effort at nepotism that would be contingent upon a good attitude and diligent effort on my cousins' part, my aunt and uncle warmed up to the idea. Soon everyone was discussing the idea with enthusiasm, filling out details of this plan that I had needed help with.

The visit ended with everyone in a much more cheerful frame of mind than we had seen in months. No more searching pointlessly for jobs that weren't there while feeling undeserved sense of failure. Grandmère looked pleased, too.

Hours later, I reviewed the pile of research I had been accumulating. It covered several topics, and I could see that they were connected to each other: ecosystem collapse due to biodiversity loss and species depletion, rising sea levels and flooding of coastlines, land pollution, air pollution, dire consequences of fossil fuel and nuclear energy use, food shortages, natural insecurity (shortages of scarce resources).

One of them was the underlying cause of the problems covered by the others: human overpopulation. We were already in overshoot. In fact, we were so far past overshoot that it was frightening, and the signs were blatantly obvious every which way we looked.

The most incredible and alarming document I had come across was one that had been classified for a mere six years, then declassified. The document was: *National Security Study Memorandum - NSSM 200: Implications of Worldwide Population Growth for U.S. Security and Overseas Interests* (The Kissinger Report), December 10, 1974. Classified by Harry C. Blaney, III, Subject to General Declassification Schedule of Executive Order 11652. Automatically Downgraded at Two Year Intervals and Declassified on December 31, 1980.

It amazed me that it was ever declassified, so I thought about that for a while.

Why would it be declassified? It outlined a clear plan of population control, a thing that was necessary if our species was to avoid a self-inflicted bloodbath and a reign of terror. Implementing it would mean suspending civil liberties, a thing that would surely lead to mass protests and even a few riots. Of course, this depended upon the plan actually being implemented, or at the very least upon the general public noticing its existence.

There it was. The public had not noticed, and the plan had not been implemented. Well, it was not implemented in 1974, nor was it implemented in 1980. But now…now there was U.N. Agenda 21. THAT was being implemented.

Agenda 21 – the agenda for the 21st century – was slowly being implemented administratively to circumvent a little problem known as our vote. It was not a treaty, which made it unofficial. Instead, it was a policy that had been agreed to when it was first presented at Rio de Janeiro in Brazil, which was in 1992.

No wonder no one had raised a peep of protest in public.

Granted, academics and other experts had written about it in books, and I had several in my pile of research material, but that was about it. Now, as the consequences were starting to be felt, and as I was an adult in the middle of my career as yet another book-writing, degreed professional, I could see the pattern and trajectory of this situation.

It wasn't pretty.

Neither were the statistics I was learning about:

In 6,000 B.C.E., the Earth had 5 million humans living on it.

It took nearly 8 millennia for there to be 500 million humans, which was how many there were by the year 1650 C.E. That's half a billion.

Then, just 200 years later, it had a full billion humans, in 1850.

By 1930, a mere 80 years later, the planet had reached what scientists have determined to be the Earth's carrying capacity for humans, doubling to 2 billion. One would expect that once that happened, people (oh, but which people?) would realize that a threshold had been reached and should not be passed, but no one was watching carefully enough to notice that until much later.

It got worse. By the time I was born, there were well over 3 billion people on the planet.

Paul R. Ehrlich wrote his controversial book, *The Population Bomb*, in 1968, breaking a taboo against even hinting that humans should not be allowed to reproduce as much as they wish to reproduce. That act remained to be thought of as an inalienable right and liberty, regardless of the consequences.

Ehrlich went on to team up with his wife Anne and write a lot more on this topic, drawing in a lot of hate. So did the people who wrote *The Limits to Growth*, as they said things that people didn't want to hear. They said that the Earth cannot accommodate the needs and wants of any more humans than its carrying capacity, and so it simply won't.

Wow. That sounded familiar! It was something that I had been saying to myself for the past few years as I considered the reasons behind and consequences of the Nae-Née policy. No wonder I was so hated for my role in inventing that birth control nanite. I had given the Kissinger plan the means it had lacked for implementation.

The thing was, I didn't feel guilty. I just resented being blamed for what was not my decision, and not my original intention. I didn't set out to control anyone.

I had set out to help women who didn't want to reproduce to circumvent efforts to deny them control of their own fertility. The hell with anyone who raged at me for the fact that that effort had swung the pendulum so dramatically in the opposite direction!

The world was clearly far more crowded than it had been when I was a child, and as I had entered my twenties and gotten stuck in heavy traffic day after day, I really felt it. That had been a significant factor in my decision to go to graduate school twice. I was trying to escape that traffic by qualifying myself out of the running for a cubicle job with a daily commute through masses of my own slow-moving species. Traffic was such a waste of one's time anyway!

I didn't like crowds. With 8 billion people on the planet, crowds were everywhere.

And with sea levels abruptly raised by the Arctic and Antarctic ice melts, those 8 billion were pressed in closer together. Everyone could feel it, whether we lived in a developed nation or an undeveloped one. Life was already unpleasant, and it was going to get worse.

It was already hotter, with growing cycles thrown off of the seasonal schedule that we had lived with since before our species had begun to record its own history. Honey bees and other bees, plus many other insects that were crucial to the pollination that made fruits and nuts and vegetables grow, were dying.

Nanite pollination methods were being developed out of desperation, not because inventors thought it was an impressive application of their talents. Necessary as it was, I hated it. Hamish may have developed the nano-bees, but I knew he hated the need for them too. It was unnatural and disturbing. Technology was only cool and fascinating when it was separate from desperation, and while Nature was still functioning normally. Take that away, and it included a most unwelcome element of fear.

Chapter 10

Collapse – War Paint, Conflict, and Reckoning Time

Most people tend to think of collapse in terms of a cataclysmic series of events that happen over the course of just a few days. Death comes quickly as the Earth goes through various upheavals, usually involving earthquakes, volcanic eruptions, and superstorms – all at once.

In real time, a collapse is much slower. So slow, in fact, that people typically don't notice or realize what is happening right away. They don't notice that more intense storms each season mean that something in Nature is out of balance. They don't understand that they ought not to simply build homes wherever the land looks on its surface like a hospitable place, because there can be sinkholes underneath it. They don't see why crops won't grow as they used to, or at all.

They don't notice, understand, see, or appreciate any of this until it is glaringly obvious.

By then, it's usually too late to avoid the consequences.

One of my college professors once called the United States an empire in decline.

I still remember how I felt when I heard that: angry.

It's not that I didn't believe him or trust his judgment. No, I accepted what he was saying as true, even though I still had most of my college career ahead of me and lot more history to learn. No, belief was not why I felt angry. I was angry because it was a bitter truth that I didn't want to accept or deal with. I wanted what the previous generations had enjoyed: peace and prosperity.

I felt angry because I knew he was right, because I loved being a citizen of an empire with all that that entails. Being part of an empire means safety, security, and calling the shots in life. Who in their right mind would want that to fade away and cease to be so? No one, that's who.

Americans, at the time I heard that, which was the late 1980s, could go almost anywhere on the planet and enjoy respect, security, mobility, and reasonable safety. That is what empire meant to me, and it still did.

Later, in law school, I took a seminar on international environmental law and learned a word that summed that up: hegemony. Hegemony means world dominance and the ability to call the shots at a negotiating table with other world leaders, not being bound by the dictates of others.

That sounded great, too, except that hegemony was over for the United States by then.

American politicians had abused that privilege many times by walking out of the World Court and of the United Nations, and American banksters on Wall Street had been allowed to buy out politicians, corrupt the political and economic systems, and thus crash both our economy and the security that a healthy economy had bought for us for so long.

That summed up briefly why we were an empire in decline.

Damn them all! The previous, careless generations had enjoyed those benefits while asleep at the switch, allowing this to happen. The law that had kept the commercial and investment bank separate – divorced from one another since the economic collapse of the Great Depression – had been overridden, overwritten, and obliterated. While people were distracted with other issues, that was done, and a new Age of Excess, like the previous one of eighty years earlier, ensued.

I wanted those benefits too! But no…our economy and our ecosystem were collapsing together. Liberty and security are not free. Freedom is not free. It all costs money. That was why we were an empire in decline. We had allowed greed to rule, corruption to take over, and our system of protection to collapse. That collapse would now bring much more unwanted change.

As I had studied history, I had wondered what it felt like to live during a collapse.

Now I was finding out how the Mesopotamians felt when desertification took over, how the Persians felt when the Greeks ran through and burned Persepolis, how the Romans felt when they lost their security to greed and corruption, how the French aristocracy felt when they allowed such a skewed imbalance of access to resources with the general populace, and so on.

It was like the entire planet Earth was Rapa Nui – Easter Island – after consuming everything. Rapa Nui was now barren, a remotely situated microcosm of the future of the rest of the planet. Once we had used up everything with reckless abandon, we would starve and regress.

Too many stories, both in history and in fiction, don't deal with the process of collapse. Instead, as if that is too painful and terrifying to contemplate, they just show you how society looks decades or even centuries after collapse has occurred. But to those who live through it, there is no escape from that pain and terror.

It started with the crash of the economy.

That could be explained by the deal-with-it-later attitude that had allowed the gold standard to be abandoned back in 1972. When that was done, money backed up by gold was replaced by money by fiat – declaration. In other words, the U.S. dollar had been nothing but fictitious money ever since that year.

You can only go so long fueling the world economy on imaginary money before it goes "poof" and the whole illusion ends. It didn't help that the branches of investment and commercial banking had been allowed, via an act to repeal the old, sensible one that had separated them, to reunite. With that, the banksters engaged in the same pattern of greed and excess that had preceded the economic collapse of the early 20th century.

Economic collapse then ensued, to the abrupt shock and horror of people everywhere.

So, economic plus environmental collapse was happening all over the planet, faster and faster. I watched it, read about it, and focused a lot on my own continent. I couldn't help it. Trouble at home tends to grab one's attention and not let go of it.

I kept reading, and worrying that I did too much research while taking too little action. But uninformed action could so some serious damage, so the reading ground on. When reading induced me to look something up, I would go to my computer. It seemed that I was always online, researching everything, looking for answers to every question that popped into my mind. I didn't always find them, but I kept looking.

This could cause me to run to the computer at random times throughout the day, which I kept in sleep mode just to enable myself to get at answers faster. Late at night, I would sit in front of it after doing hours of research and writing, staring at the screen, willing it to tell me what to look up that might help.

What did I want from my computer? It had done everything I had asked it to. Maybe the answers weren't always on that screen. Maybe I could find them elsewhere and input the data. How was I going to see evidence of what I was reading up on locally, I wondered?

Also, how was I going to see it without being noticed? It would be stupid to just go around asking people about what I wanted to find out. Despite the fact that we Aspies tend to be socially uninhibited about who we will ask what, that does not make us foolish enough to forget about our own security. Hamish and I had demonstrated that in the Blue Ridge Mountains.

Reading is one kind of research, but I wanted to do more field research. But what would that involve? I couldn't just drive around police stations looking for MRAPs, or poke around the neighborhood looking to see which houses had SmartMeters on them.

"Let me get back to you on that," Hamish said to me. "I'm finishing up this solar panel project, and what you're asking will take some serious stealth."

I thanked him and got back to my reading list. There were lots of questions to face.

What was wrong with human policies and practices, and what could be done about them?

Our species labored under delusions of unrealistic hopes and expectations. As I read the news and editorials, a recurring theme emerged: one of asininity. It was maddening. It showed that people did not want to wake up and face any harsh reality, even though facing it and dealing with it would feel better than helpless stagnation. (Well, that and minimization of the Ebola plague.)

Each writer put forth the same idea, which was that if people would simply adopt a responsible careful, sustainable, conservationist, environmentally responsible way of life, all would be well. There would be enough resources for all, no matter how many human beings our species produced.

What nonsense! Since when has the human species done that? Never.

What, exactly, was the damage that our delusional species was inflicting upon the only planet we had, and what were the consequences? What areas had we lost, probably for the foreseeable future? How? Could we do anything to mitigate the damage, or not?

California had once been the domain of Hollywood and produce farms, plus the place where wild salmon was spawned and caught. Avocadoes and almonds, apricots and vineyards, had dotted its landscape. Not anymore.

Unregulated drilling for water had at last taken its toll on the world almond-growing capital. California suffered a massive earthquake that ripped through the San Joaquim Valley last year. That in turn had destroyed the dams that had been built to increase the amount of water available for farming upstate even as lakes and rivers downstate dried up. No more avocadoes or almonds from California now – the water wasn't available to grow them. Other crops were drying up also.

This begged the question: How would people be fed? There were far more humans than water to grow food for them. I just didn't see it adding up to a balanced answer. Starvation was likely near. The government was not going to admit that, however, because it would cause panic.

The salmon had suffered from this, and had not bounced back. They could not find their way back to a place that had changed in their 3-year lifespan, so they simply didn't. Ichthyologists were hard at work, searching the Pacific Ocean for them, assessing where they had gone and how they were faring, but for now, commercial salmon fishing was suspended, along with the livelihoods of fishing families.

That earthquake had reshaped California in many ways. When water was relentlessly sucked up to the surface of the Earth for showers, toilets flushing, dishwashers, laundry, and irrigation, and not replenished via rainfall, pockets formed deep below the surface. Those spaces would not stay empty forever. Their presence would only aggravate existing fault lines when they caved in. That had already happened.

The rate of water use by humans had far exceeded Nature's capacity to keep up with it. More than half of the planet's aquifers were already depleted. Conservation measures could only help a tiny bit, which meant that nothing was going to prevent a massive earthquake – nothing. An area over twice the size of Los Angeles in Central Valley was sinking at a rate of 11 inches per year.

When it came, it was a 9 on the Richter scale. California was partially prepared with the sort of architecture that would enable greater human survival rates, but objects do fall inside houses and onto humans. For homes that were not designed and built to consider earthquake stress, running outside was one's best bet. That didn't help much with a level 9 quake, though. People fell into fissures, which opened and closed just as they did in Hollywood's most terrifying motion pictures. The special effects industry had never produced anything so graphic.

When it stopped – days later, with lots of aftershocks – the state was laid waste. Roads, railroad tracks, bridges, and pipelines were all broken. The U.S. Army Corps of Engineers and FEMA went in and salvaged whatever they could. The Corps even assisted Hollywood in removing everything to a hastily-taken-over location far inland, thanks to the government power of eminent domain. The government knew what its taxpayers would sanction, that was clear.

Perhaps it was fortunate that this happened before the floods had inundated Hollywood and Pasadena, because they managed to move CalTech University, U.C.L.A., and the movie industry ahead of the onrushing tides. Hollywood ended up in southwestern Kansas and southeastern Colorado. The schools moved into the Sierra Nevada Mountains, changing their character drastically; so much for sunshine and beach appeal.

When I say it was a good thing that this cataclysmic event had taken place before the floods, it is because those floods brought more than water. They brought radiation. The groundwater along the West Coast of the United States had already been contaminated since the early part of 2013, when the radiation from the ruined Daiichi Power Plant in Fukushima, Japan, had at last reached the U.S.

Starfish turning to purple jelly and disintegrating had been our first, misunderstood clue. It was only misunderstood due to false reporting in the mainstream media. Fringe media, complete with interviews by radiation experts, engineers, and physicians, had tried to warn people, but they had been branded alarmists, conspiracy theorists, lunatics, and worse.

That was in 2014, and the west coast had been forced to face up to the truth.

There were millions of displaced people suddenly on the move, and they poured into the mountains. Most were just regular people, suddenly desperate after a lifetime of the comfort and convenience of going to grocery and other stores for whatever they needed. They soon panicked and lost all sense of humanity or decency, attacking one another for the smallest thing.

Some people were from Native American tribes, such as the Makah and the Quileute of the vampire novels of pop fiction, or the Sioux, or the Oglala, or the Cherokee. They fared better than most, because they were given amnesty on the reservations of other tribes inland.

This irony was not lost on the U.S. government. The tribes were now worried that they would lose even what little territory they had managed to retain from the U.S. government in the past couple of centuries. It wasn't long before conflict wars started up in the central United States between tribespeople and other Americans. The U.S. Army was called in to help.

But what help would they offer, and to whom? Some help went to each side in a random, disorganized fashion. It was as if the U.S. Department of the Interior and the Bureau for Indian Affairs was more concerned about its image than in restoring order. Perhaps restoring perfect order immediately was a fantasy, but the idea that image was being protected was no delusion.

Regardless, the tribes were now in full war paint every time any of their officials appeared on television. Tribal councils and inter-tribal councils met repeatedly to plan their responses to crises that arose daily. Why should they yield any more land to the descendants of what were, essentially, invaders and illegal immigrants?!

The Saudis and other Arab nations weren't selling it anymore; they were keeping it to power sealed, indoor cities that were perpetually climate-controlled. This was folly, but it was far from the U.S., and there was little point in explaining that, in the words of Agenda 21's proponents, such cities were unsustainable. Without fuel, people would just be roasted inside them.

Peak oil had clearly been reached and breached in the U.S., and now that there was less land for people to live on, fracking was bitterly opposed. People didn't want to spare a drop of water – used or not – for that. Fracking, the process of drilling deep into the Earth's crust to extract fossil fuels from shale rock by forcing water down into the holes drilled, killed the land above. It turned the grass brown, killed the nutrients in the soil, and made the water from house faucets detonate if a lighted match were held to it.

As if all that weren't enough, there simply wasn't enough freshwater – drinking water – for all of the people who needed it. Low precipitation, drought, and overuse of groundwater by a human population that was far higher than water tables could accommodate were the reasons why. Tariffs on water use by wealthy homes, golf courses, and big agribusiness were considered. The agribusinesses were deemed not to be overusing the water, but the homes and golf courses that wanted green lawns were fined. It was too little too late, though.

People needed fresh, clean water for drinking, bathing, cooking, and washing clothes. They also needed it to grow their own crops in small, home gardens, which cut down on the use of fossil fuels to move food around from monocrop agribusinesses to grocery stores. This logic was often lost with talk of mixed used, centralized housing for all under Agenda 21's plan, however. No yards were allotted to the people in those so-called green and eco-friendly high-rises. I knew I was looking for logic where it was lacking, but I wouldn't stop wanting it.

And Native People were being asked for help?! What was left to give, anyway?! Nothing.

It wasn't just those of the United States. Canada's native tribespeople were angry, too.

Despite the fact that two huge nations controlled their territory, they were under no obligation to respect or acknowledge that. And why should they? It was their land, and it had been stolen from them by a culture of wastrels who didn't respect the land.

And so the native tribes of both Canada and the United States combined to prepare and to put into action their own strategy to protect North America's forests – the ancient forests, the ones with ecosystems more ancient than any of the human cultures now fighting for control of them – and to stop big oil and coal companies from stripping them down to get at what was far beneath.

The Sioux, the Quileute, the Mohicans, the Seminoles, the Cree, the Inuits, and the rest of the native people of North America didn't give a damn that some wealthy corporations would not be able to remain wealthy without that oil, or that their customers would be inconvenienced by the lack of it. They could just go without, and work harder on developing alternative energy.

No, they were not entitled to just use up all fossil fuels that the earth had to offer first and then do that – they could damn well do it NOW. If that meant going without the energy needed to tote supplies around and for people to travel at the speeds that they had long become accustomed to, so be it. Let the pale faces learn what it was like to live at the whims of the planet rather than the other way around.

Let them learn it before the Earth decided that it simply would not support humans at all.

To emphasize their point, the tribal elders showed up for a powwow in what remained of Vancouver wearing full traditional war paint, some in traditional native dress and some not, but all with handmade cosmetics that emblazoned the absolute sincerity of their position.

The event was called The Powwow for Tree Whisperers, and was held at the Vancouver Convention Centre. When asked about the irony of this, Chief Alice Windtalker said that there was no irony in it at all. The tribes met in an urban environment deliberately, to attract as much media attention as possible while not doing any further damage to forests. Meeting in a forest would only threaten the wildlife, she added. This big-box convention center already existed.

News channels and online publications carried the story with full-blown press coverage, video, photographs and text. Interviews were given freely by the elders before and after each meeting for the entire four days that the conference met.

When questioned as to where alternative energy forms were supposed to come from, elders repeated their response in acid tones until journalists had collected a series of sound bites that all had the same answer.

This was one of the more polite replies: "That thing that many of us call the sky god – that star that you call the sun – that is where you will find more energy."

Another elder put it another way: "When Ronald Reagan removed the solar panels that Jimmy Carter had installed on the roof of the White House, we knew that the pale faces' government would destroy much more than it would protect."

But by far the most entertaining moment of all came when Chief Lynn Dancing Fox announced that the tribes had gotten together, found the best computer hackers among themselves, and seized control of the Nae-Née devices of every last Native woman on the continent, at which point they had set up their own control center and Operator.

It was good to see that no computer fortress was hack-proof. It also raised the respect for the tribes all over the planet. For centuries, they had been manipulated and pushed around by invaders. Now, they had thrown off the yoke of control and retaken control over their bodies.

And what had they done with it? They had independently gone to the United Nations to sign onto the birth control treaty! When members of the media heard this, they were amazed, showing that they did not understand Native People at all.

It was funny because any objective look at Native culture and philosophy would have told them that the idea of not overpopulating the Earth and not taking more than it could give was the most basic part of their way of life. This wasn't about doing something else; it was about tribal autonomy and respect.

All the tribes wanted was to control their own Nae-Née operations. "Thank you very much for the devices; we'll take it from here," they said. When offered free Nae-Née nanobots in perpetuity by the U.S. and Canadian governments, they had accepted on one condition: that the codes to said nanobotic devices would be handed over to their own Operator.

It was hilarious that it had come as a mild shock to the pale faces that Native People could hack government computers. But Keith Olbermann's *Countdown* soon put that into perspective: computer hacking is an innate skill, one that cannot simply be taught by anyone, learned by anyone, or bought at an ivy league institution such as MIT. Hacking was a talent that knew no race, gender, or culture.

"Take that, invaders and controllers," jeered Craig Ferguson on his show.

The Powwow ended with the formation of the tribes' own nation, called the Native Tribes of North America. Each reservation would be a member state or province. A capital was constructed along the border of Montana and Saskatchewan. It had a huge, sprawling complex for the politicians and their aides, most of whom were lawyers who had studied in schools around the United States and Canada. The design was cool; it combined elements of various tribal housing construction: mostly longhouses, teepees, and wigwams.

At least the news was entertaining. But then it got riveting.

When the Powwow broke up, the tribes did something else: they surrounded and camped out at the forests that they were so concerned about, armed not only with their convictions but also with traditional weapons – flint knives, spears, tomahawks, and even bows and arrows.

What were they thinking? What were they planning to do, get killed? It was like the Navi people of *Avatar* had come to the North American wilderness. I hoped they wouldn't get killed, but felt certain that many would be summarily murdered by angry corporate mercenaries. Hamish agreed; he suddenly wished that he could supply them all with his nanite guns. But they were okay. The Tribes had some modern weapons also, and they held intruders back.

On occasion, I needed to remind myself that I lived in an empire. As such, it would do terrible things to maintain itself, things that it will never, ever admit to.

It would make airplanes full of passengers seem to disappear just to prevent certain individuals with highly sought-after skills from traveling to certain places on the planet.

It would conduct torture outside of its borders in order to extract information, reasoning on mere technicalities that doing so is legal under its own laws because this was not done within its own borders. Never mind the laws of the entire planet...

Now I was getting the unsettling feeling that something far more widespread, something with a much, much greater reach, was in the works. This was because, as I continued to watch the war painted elders and the arguments and treaty signings, I noticed that something was not being reported upon anymore. It was all about this, and nothing about the climate refugees. We, the general public, had been distracted by headline news stories into forgetting other ones...again.

Where were the climate refugees going? Sure, they had fled flooded areas and drought-ridden ones, both inside and outside of U.S. borders. What had really happened to the U.S. citizens who had fled one area and gone to the other areas where Hamish and I had seen, well, some of them?

Where had they been taken? Why were some out in the open, left alone, while others were not? There had to be a lot more of them. When I looked up the total population of Florida from 2012, well aware that it was now zero, I had to wonder where 19.32 million people had gone. That many people do not simply vanish into thin air. So where were they?

Where, for that matter, were so many other Americans? Over half of them (163.8 million people) had lived in what were known as coastal watershed communities, which meant that the floods had inundated them. This figure came out of the total population for the United States. I could not account for them now based on my current research.

But as I searched the news for stories of their arrival, Googling the names of individuals whom I had seen in news clips as they left their points of origin, I found none. The longer it persisted, the more that the absence of data leapt out at me.

It was like the questions of the historic-sites-and-landmarks-tour with the covert-snooping-trip built in that Hamish and I had gone on all over again. We had looked into missing data there, too. (How much research would Hamish expect me to do before he would be ready to discuss this discrepancy with me? How much more time did he need to finish his solar panel work?)

The longer we waited to curb our carbon emissions, the closer the tipping point would get.

Our procrastination culture was to blame for what cultures around the planet were suffering from. We used fossil fuels with reckless abandon rather than making the switch to green alternatives well before supplies run out, so now our atmosphere was choked with fumes. As we in the developed part of the world did so, poorer nations suffered the consequences of land lost to floods and droughts. Now it was finally happening to us.

Methane was an even more potent gas than the fossil fuels that we kept emitting. If that melted and was released, things would get even more difficult. Unfortunately, it had started to melt, and the air quality up north was terrible. It was hotter and it stank. People in Alaska and northern Canada were already complaining bitterly about it. Between the methane and the polar bears, they were hemmed in.

Ten years ago, scientists had warned us that if we were to just add 2 degrees Celsius to the Earth's temperature, by 2036, we could be seeing even higher sea levels, hotter temperatures, very limited growing seasons, and resource wars. Well, we had already added 4 degrees.

No wonder Hamish kept at it with the solar array. He wanted us independent of all that.

His goal was to get our house off the grid with an independent power source, and preferably one that did not add yet more carbon emissions to the atmosphere. He insisted that it was possible, and swore that the only reason it had not yet been made standard practice all over the planet was the stranglehold that the fossil fuel industry had over the energy market.

Yeah, well, he was preaching to the choir on that one.

After all that research, I needed a break. I found Hamish outside, tinkering with – you guessed it – the sensor for the solar array. He was holding his own version of a tricorder/remote controller for a set of nanites that worked as a tiny robot army on the roof, adjusting settings and checking and repairing any weather-induced flaws in the panels.

"Hi Hamish," I said as I approached.

He looked up, blankly, like someone does when an interruption has abruptly brought them back to real life while watching a great movie by suddenly turning on a bright, disorienting light. A moment later he adjusted and smiled. "Hi Avril."

"So…I finished reading my pile of research on Agenda 21, individual disarmament, surveillance, radiation from that and from nuclear irresponsibility – power plants that use fission energy and melt down – irresponsibility that makes people sick, SmartTech, Quick Response Codes, militarized police, Readiness Exercises, poisons and GMOs in foods every which way one looks…it's like I just read through a huge conspiracy theory. But that's what government-sanctioned debunkers want, so I have an unpleasant suspicion that it's all horridly real."

Hamish stared at me with a solemn but pleased smile. Then he said, "It IS horridly real, and I'm glad you found and read all that stuff on your own. I encountered a lot of it in the military and in government medical laboratories, and was forced to sign release forms swearing me to secrecy forever. But…you told me about the spousal communications privilege, and I want to tell you everything, so yes, it's all horridly real."

"Wonderful. Perfect. Awesome. And so on." I was not happy. I sat down on a lawn chair with an annoyed and heavy feeling, and slumped in it.

I did not want any more changes or upheavals in my life. It was depressing to watch those ruining other people's lives also. Now, I fully expected to see even worse things than that happen to those other people, the ones that I saw moving about the country with dejected displacement, homeless and hopeless. Could I help them at all? And would it spread to our lives in some direct way? I couldn't help wishing and wondering about all that.

"What's next, water rationing in Connecticut? We can't just drill our own well."

Hamish looked frustrated at that. No doubt he was already plotting a workaround.

Chapter 11

Sustainable Growth: An Oxymoronic Term

"Maple trees migrating north?" Dad repeated, nonplussed. "Sounds like a science fiction story. Are they Ents?" He grinned, but waited for me to say more. Dad knew that I was referring to something real; he was just kidding.

We were eating dinner in the kitchen, and I had just added maple syrup to the grocery list as I sat down. I wanted to make pancake batter and put it in the fridge later.

"Yes, maple trees are letting their seeds move north, to cooler regions. They like a certain climate, and so as it changes slowly enough for them to keep up, they migrate, gradually building up their populations farther and farther north, until they find an area where they can thrive, and enjoy the climate there."

"You read about this?" Dad asked.

"Yeah – I can show you the article later. It has maps in Wisconsin, showing that state's maple trees as just one instance of this. No wonder the orange groves of Florida were hastily moved. No way were those trees going to have time to migrate anywhere without help."

My mother and Hamish kept eating their salads, listening to this exchange.

After that course, I ran upstairs and printed off the article with the color printer. It was rare that I printed anything at all. I would have my books printed and shipped here when they were done, but computer software made printing unnecessary. Still, my parents weren't going to come in here and peer at my screen, so occasionally I would print something.

Back in the kitchen, everyone passed the article around, more fascinated by the map of maple migration than anything else. An image is worth more than words for a lasting impression, it seems. I wasn't immune to this; I was the one who had insisted upon a road trip to the Georgia Guidestones, after all.

I never did find out what had happened with that odd incident after we saw them. Despite repeated searches of the Internet, there was nothing about that sick kid or the police or any of the other people who had been there that day, nor was there anything about that woman in the camp.

Later that evening, after my parents had gone to bed, Hamish went back to his basement lab to tinker with the solar panel nanite system, so I resumed my research and reading. There had to be some Internet sites that I just didn't know how to find, but I would worry about them after I had read through all of what I already had.

The term "sustainable growth" seemed to infest it. So did "eco-friendly" and "green."

We were working with several models of growth and resource use simultaneously.

That sounded like a sexy movie plot.

The reality of it was anything but; the models were not beautiful people showing off cosmetics or the latest creations of the fashion industry. Instead, they were the stuff that made our modern, industrialized lifestyle both possible and on a collision course:

1.   Our food system of agriculture and production;
2.   The industrial system of manufacturing goods;
3.   The population system, which continued to reproduce even with Nae-Née;
4.   The system of non-renewable resources, such as the Amazon Rainforest;
5.   The pollution system, generated by human activity.

They all existed concurrently, and they all contributed to an unfolding collapse. We were seeing a scenario of imploding models and food insecurity play out.

It seemed to me that focusing on climate change to the exclusion of the plastics, sewage, toxins, and fossil fuels that we human spewed into the ecosystem was folly. Not only that, but we were using up everything that the planet had to offer. We were repeating the errors of the population of Rapa Nui (a.k.a. Easter Island) on a planetary scale. After that, we would truly be out of renewable resources. No wonder Agenda 21 was riddled with the word "sustainable".

Just look at Sao Paulo, Brazil: over 11 million people using water until the government just shut it off for 5 days out of the week, without warning them. Being high above sea level didn't help if you didn't have enough water for everyone to wash themselves, their clothes, and dishes.

Hamish said that I was getting better and better at scaring myself all the time, and that he was worried about me. He may have been busy with his nanites in the basement, but now that we were safely solvent, my husband also took the time to check on me. He was interested in my state of mind, which meant checking to see what I was working on, thinking about, and experiencing on a day-to-day basis. Hamish wanted to make sure that I was still enjoying life and not driving myself crazy.

That was sweet of him.

But now it was time to go see Edgar, Fabian, and Jacques about applying for grants. If they could write them, it would save Hamish an enormous amount of time. Edgar was good at sales, Fabian at the legal angles, and Jacques was well-versed in the jargon of Agenda 21 – sustainability, eco-friendly, and all that. Claire would probably want in on this, too. Fine!

So, why not apply that to selling the idea of human survival with a decent quality of life? We might as well use that silly terminology. Since Agenda 21 used it with such enthusiasm, it had become fashionable and a necessity for anyone applying for grant money or hoping to garner enough positive publicity to make any project a success.

They could use some of the ideas in Agenda 21 in the business model, such as:

We could build exercise back into everyone's lives by growing our own food, or at least some of it. We could stop using so much fossil fuel to power our activities. We could capture more rainwater rather than simply sucking the groundwater wells dry, and plant more trees around our fields and gardens to save the topsoil. Why not? Hamish was full of idea for his nanites, and so was I.

Many great ideas came from the Earth Policy Institute and other environmental NGOs, yet they were all produced in dull, dry academic form. No wonder most of the nation's population didn't absorb a word that they said! Unless and until the intelligentsia of American learned how to connect with the popular culture-obsessed public, nothing would change.

My idea was really quite an outrageous one: pitch the idea of a sustainable future in many ways, so as to cover many of its fine points, and in a tone and medium that was so easy to absorb as to be almost effortless…like TV commercials, viral web videos, popular shows and movies, and so on, but not the same way that we saw it being done by the U.N. toadies. Our presentations would subtly go after Agenda 21 money and funnel it into environmentalist initiatives that did not take away personal property, liberty, or choices.

No land trusts in which the use of one's own property was regulated to the nth degree, no pushing people to only ride bikes and public transportation, no forcing them to give up their cars or switch to little ones with SmartTech that were so flimsy as to be death-traps on wheels. No. None of that nonsense.

Forget SmartTech altogether. Live off the grid as much as possible, and learn how to make independent power generators for each home, preferably with solar and wind energy. That's why Hamish kept at it with the solar nanites. Also, wind generators could be a lot smaller than the huge, towering white ones we saw off coastlines and in rural areas, on mountains and farms.

Cars ought to be like the ones in *Gattaca*, the movie about tailored DNA. Those cars were all old ones to that future society – attractive, well-built classics with the strength and reinforced construction of tanks, comfortable seating, and yet well-maintained. They ran on electricity without being death-traps on wheels. Electrical recharging stations substituted for gas stations, and they were spaced at sufficiently regular intervals for this to work. It was time to push for science fiction to become science fact, and to reuse a perfectly good resource: existing cars.

Already, I was directing Sharianne and Jonas to hire some Hollywood script writers for the task. They had looked at me strangely when I first brought that up, but after they thought about it some more, they got really excited. "This should have been done a long time ago," Jonas commented, as Sharianne grinned from ear to ear. She had caught on the quickest, thanks to her background as a TV personality. But they needed help, and my cousins could supply it.

I had included a tour of Hamish's lab and their office – which were both housed in in Blue Back Square – in the rounds for my Parisian cousins. It was just a small operation now, but I anticipated that it would get bigger. Dad, Hamish, and I were on the lab's board of directors.

My parents hadn't wanted us to move out when we drove away from the floods of Manhattan, which had surprised us both. We could have bought a condominium at Blue Back Square by now, but they wanted our help maintaining the huge food garden that we had built and set up in the Stoner Drive house. They also liked seeing us, eating the food that I made, and enjoyed seeing me haul my husband out of his laboratory for a bit of normal human social interaction. I needed that too; if it weren't for them, I would hardly have looked up from my own research studies.

But I was distracted. It didn't feel right to have my cousins growing up to face the exact same brick walls that I railed against in general, the ones caused by human overpopulation, while I enjoyed the results of the success that Hamish and I had. We were very, very lucky.

Getting them involved with the lab had been the best move we could have made. The whole family was much happier now, and Claire and Fabian seemed a lot more hopeful about their future together. To show it, they had gotten formally engage to marry each other.

This had happened over Christmas.

When Grandmère had heard that Fabian was about to propose, she was delighted. She called Fabian into her room, shut the door, and took off her own 4-carat, pear-shaped diamond engagement ring that our grandfather had given her. She told Fabian, "I have been planning to pass this on through the first of my grandsons to get engaged, and it's you. I know Claire won't disappoint us, and I want you to give this to her. I hope she likes it."

Fabian was thrilled, of course; he told us about this scene later. Claire did in fact love the ring. It was a plain setting on white gold with six prongs, and Grandmère insisted that she and Fabian take it over to Lux, Bond & Green for sizing and reinforcement of those prongs. They had, and now Claire was beaming with happiness.

She had called her parents, and they had driven up from the Philadelphia area for the New Year to spend a week visiting and getting to know everyone. Workaholics, they had actually left their business, Cake Artisans (with a website gallery of images to drool over), in the hands of a budding apprentice. This recent graduate of the Culinary Institute of America could be trusted to run things smoothly while they stayed at a bed-and-breakfast place that I had discovered on Simsbury Road, just over the mountain. It was a lovely, happy week.

John and Emily Charbonneau had no other children, so this was a big deal to them. Their only child was engaged, they knew Fabian and liked him, and they wanted to see the area where she was living and working.

It was a great relief to all of the parents to see that things were working out well. With the market so choked with applicants for so few jobs, there had been tremendous worry that no good future awaited. Emily had confided to me that she had actually thought that Claire would miss out on a nice life thanks to the collapse of overpopulation. Weddings and parties were fewer too, which had made it easier to get away for this visit.

Aunt Zoe and Uncle Charlie were bewildered by the developments of the past few years: Nae-Née, the recognition that human overpopulation was killing off many people already and would continue to threaten more of us all over the planet, the massive numbers of species die-offs, the shocking rise in sea level that had flooded Manhattan, Florida, and many other places, and the lack of opportunity for their sons.

How could this have happened, they had asked at dinner each week? We have educated our kids and provided every opportunity to prepare them. How could there be nothing out there for them if they were so well-prepared?

They just didn't see the lack of connection between the two phases of life, education and career. Just because one is ready, willing and able to move on to a middle-class career, that doesn't mean that the employment opportunities that constitute one of those actually exists. I told them why they didn't see it – it was because they didn't want it to be so. That got me glum looks.

Aunt Zoe was just 52 years old, and Uncle Charlie was 61. They had grown up in a different era, when the economy just kept on growing and they could expect to enjoy the middle-class American dream. They had seen no limits to growth. It was maddening to see Aunt Zoe admire little babies and say that everyone should have one if they could afford it.

What if a couple could afford kids?! The kids couldn't afford to grow up and exist!

There had to be something to grow up to other than overcrowding, a lack of opportunity, and an inability to move out of one's childhood home and progress onward and upward. Dad just looked at me when the two of them railed about all this after hearing me explain this logic. Later, he would tell me that their wishful thinking indeed hadn't yet caught up with harsh reality. Dad was the oldest of the three kids that Grandmère had; my aunt was the middle child, and those cousins from Paris were her children.

Uncle Charlie was the youngest, the one who had married late, after meeting an American woman that he had met when he visited my parents. That was when he decided to take advantage of the booming real estate market and settle in Connecticut. He took citizenship classes, following my parents' instructions and letting Aunt Zoe tutor him in things like the national anthem and basic American history, and with that, he was all set.

Life had been good for years, with restaurant dinners a couple of times a week and nights out at Hall High School and Conard to watch his sons play lacrosse, basketball, and baseball. They didn't like football, and I was glad because I got dragged along to a few of the other games, and they were dull. Football would have been worse. I hated watching team sports.

Uncle Charlie was frankly puzzled by me, but he was also impressed. I liked to watch figure skating events when the Olympics were on television every few years, and that was about it. I had married a guy who jogged alone for exercise, and now Hamish was trailed by some men from Blackout Security whenever he went out.

What could I say? I just didn't like what most people liked. If I had, the world would probably never have gotten Nae-Née, and it would never have had much hope of coping with the effects of human overpopulation.

In New York City, barriers were going up at a monumental cost to the government. Getting in and out of the city was no longer a simple matter of paying a bridge toll. Now, I.D.s had to be checked coming and going. No one could even walk into Manhattan anymore without it being noticed, noted, and recorded.

Taxes all over the nation had gone up, corresponding to infrastructure collapse due to the floods.

Meanwhile, with the world's economy a wreck, I wondered – and I was not alone in that – how the U.S. government would pay for it all. The U.S. wasn't the only nation that was both struggling financially and suddenly burdened with an environmental catastrophe. The Netherlands, Italy, Canada, Japan, China, Bangladesh, and many others needed to shore up the land that they had so that their people wouldn't lose it to the rising sea level. Many would not.

Of course, many already had, but the point of all these levy-building efforts was to reclaim the lost property, lost shorelines, and lost living spaces. Airports were the first priority so that goods and services would continue to be available, with those other land uses behind.

Equatorial nations were in the throes of horrific collapse. Bangladesh simply could not shore up anything; the nation was nothing but a huge river delta now, a mosquito-ridden, polluted wreck from all of the outsourced clothing factories that had polluted its waters. People were swarming the Indian border, which hemmed them in, desperate to get past the huge wall that that nation had erected to keep them out. The Indian Army guards simply mowed them down, refusing to let any of them in. The news showed Bangladesh as a river of human blood now.

There were other horrific examples, but that was the most shocking. Hong Kong had experienced a scorching summer, as had Singapore. The people who lived there, like sardines in the high-rise apartment buildings, had to endure soaring temperatures, and most of the elderly residents died as air conditioning units burned out. The next burn-outs were cremation fires.

My mother seemed to have found the ultimate in reality TV as the news suddenly captured her interest 24/7. She had always kept herself well-informed on national and international news, not the detailed extent that I did, but she did it nonetheless. Now, she was noticing the Ebola plague and commenting whenever there was a story about a patient who managed to travel out of the clumsily-enforced quarantine zones there. Some of these patients got to the U.S., and others got to Europe.

Hamish told us that no hospital in the developed part of the world could hope to successful treat more than one or two Ebola patients at a time. He added that those media assurances that the ones with special isolation units were nonsense, and the units would be overwhelmed and failures with any more patients.

That was disturbing, but he certainly knew what he was talking about. As both a doctor and as someone who had been all over the world in the military before going to graduate school, Hamish knew how to read between the lines and spot lies in the news.

When we had taken that in, we needed a distraction. The main, favorite area of my mother's news-following attention was celebrity stories. To relax, I had my favorite television shows and movies – *Bones*, *The Big Bang Theory*, *Scorpion*, *The Monuments Men*, *Star Trek*, *Pride & Prejudice* – but beyond noticing the actors who starred in them and reading their backgrounds on the Internet Movie Data Base, I lost interest. It was my mother who filled me in on the details of them by following celebrity news. We had fun filling each other in on all sorts of topics, though, and pretty soon we were focused on real news again.

For the past couple of years, she had watched the economic reports on the cost of the levies that would reclaim Manhattan with rapt attention, plus the construction efforts. There were endless interviews with the engineers, the construction workers, the mayor of New York City, and the public. She couldn't get enough of it, and I was sure it was because she missed going to Manhattan. The playground was closed until further notice, I would tell her, as she watched it all.

And now it was open. She could go back whenever she wished, but she had doubts about doing so after hearing how it had been for me and Hamish. It was a police state checkpoint experience, and that unnerved her, as well it should. Only the elite could come and go unchallenged, but we were all being watched as we did so. No doubt traffic cameras here and there in the city filled in the gaps once we were inside.

It was almost dinnertime, so I dragged my husband out of his laboratory. That took some effort; with the Parisian cousins gone, Hamish thought that he could spend extra time on his nanites. No such luck; I required him to get in the car with me and go home at a reasonable hour, plus accompany me through the Whole Foods store to get a few things before we drove away.

Grumbling, he programmed the nanobots to go into their holding cells for the night, put his lab coat aside, and followed me out.

It was a lovely evening, and oddly warm out for late February. Our plan was to go to Aunt Zoe's house and see Grandmère. I also needed a half-hour to get our food ready before we actually went there.

It was going to be an evening of grilled steaks. Uncle Charlie liked to cook them with fresh herbs – rosemary, thyme and a bit of salt – and then serve them up with whatever salad Aunt Zoe made. Dad had bought several six-pack bottles of Blue Moon and Leffe beer, and my mother had picked and mixed up and lovely fruit salad of blackberries and strawberries from the garden. I had helped by squeezing some orange juice for it, mixing in cinnamon and a small amount of sugar-in-the-raw, and tossing it all together.

But that wasn't all; Hamish and I wouldn't eat beef. No steaks for us. Last night, I had made a huge dish of barley, spinach, eggplant, plum tomato, basil, and chèvre (goat cheese). It was soft and easy to eat, and had taken a while, but I didn't mind that one bit as I watched movies on TNT and AMC. I could always enjoy cooking with another round of *The Mummy* or *Erin Brockovich* playing on the television.

Aunt Zoe had said she had lavender refrigerator cookies.

We loaded the car with our food, got in, and drove off down Stoner Drive, out the gate, and up Mountain Road to Beacon Hill. Soon we were helping Aunt Zoe set everything up as Uncle Charlie grilled the fillets of beef on the stove. It probably smelled good to everyone but me and Hamish. At least the local bears would stay away. It was still winter, even if it felt like spring.

Grandmère showed me her latest painting; her eyesight was fading somewhat despite two successful cataract surgeries that I had nursed her through, but her efforts impressed us all nonetheless. Grandmère herself seemed proud of her own results. This one was from a photograph that Dad had shot of Spock and Eowyn sleeping together on our living room sofa. They looked cute against the pale blue background, and Grandmère had expertly illustrated the weave of the fabric with delicate brush strokes, hinting at the floral design that was interwoven.

"I love it!" I found myself saying with great enthusiasm. I went on and on about how perfectly she had drawn the cats, and how expertly she had represented the sofa upholstery before I realized that she would probably have it framed as a Christmas gift for me. My mother was smiling a little as I carried on and on.

With that, dinner was announced, and we all walked away from the artist's corner of the living room and congregated around the table. Edgar was sitting next to his father, across from me and down a bit, and as I headed for my usual spot, I paused to ask him if we could talk after dinner. He looked a bit surprised, but nodded yes. His brothers didn't notice; they were still bantering about something and laughing as they approached. But Edgar looked serious; Aunt Zoe said that he hardly ever smiled anymore.

We sat down and passed the food around, and everyone politely took some of the barley.

As I watched my family eating higher and higher up the food chain, and as I thought about how much strain on resources and other human beings that caused, I felt no qualms about being "finicky" or for my increasingly vegetarian food choices. It wasn't just that beef disgusted me; it always had. The more I learned about how beef was produced, and the amount of resources it took to enable that, the more Grandmère's comments just rolled off me like water off a duck.

Fed up with the nonsense, I explained it all to her over dinner.

Usually, when one makes the effort to explain anything to an older person, there is some sort of punishment in store. It may come from the older person herself, who can't handle it and thus see it as being corrected or chastised. The punishment may also come from those around the two of you, who see age as a license to misbehave. I disagreed; age is not a license to be obnoxious, and I didn't mean anything condescending by sharing what I knew or what I was thinking about a political or social or environmental issue with anyone, regardless of their age.

And I particularly didn't appreciate any hint that I shouldn't be able to have a real conversation about things that matter with my own grandmother. So I told her why I was doing what I was doing. I also told her about wanting to have real conversations with her.

"Beef has always disgusted me, Grandmère; you know that. And there's more to it than that. I've learned some things that conveniently validate my refusal to eat it, and none of it is about bleeding heart pity for the cows and bulls. Hamish has told me that beef contains a cancer-inducing molecule, so right there I have the perfect reason not to eat it."

I continued, "But an enormous amount of grain goes into raising cattle for butchering, and that grain is grown on farmland that could be producing food for humans. If people in wealthy nations weren't so determined to eat higher and higher up the food chain, we wouldn't be facing such problems as poor health and rising costs to treat conditions caused by unhealthy diets, and there would also be a lot more food to go around."

"That's what you research, isn't it?" Grandmère said. "No wonder you know all this. You have found evidence that backs up the eating proclivities that you have had all your life." She smiled as she said this. It was true; I had been a very fussy, difficult eater as a child. Texture and flavor drove that, but now that I could cook, life was so much easier. I could hide that often.

"It's just that that food wouldn't be as high up on the food chain – it would be whole grains, which promote a thinner physique, and more fruits and vegetables. Look at your plates," I said, indicating most of the other ones on the table. "You all have way more meat on your plates than vegetables. And how many of you are taking pills to regulate your cholesterol and blood pressure? Don't answer that; just think it over. This is not an interrogation."

With that, I was satisfied…until the recriminations started from Aunt Zoe and Uncle Charlie for "chastising" my grandmother. I had been expecting this, so I hadn't put much more food into my mouth yet. Without missing a beat, I swallowed the last bit and spoke up again.

"Grandmère," I said, "is that how you see it? Do you assume that I mean to scold, lecture and chastise when in fact I am explaining and defending myself? Or do you realize that nothing nasty is meant when I won't just roll over and be silent?"

She smiled at me and said that she didn't feel scolded or talked down to, and told my aunt and uncle to stay out of it. "If Avril wants to talk to me about what matters to her and explain why she does what she does, she should be able to do so. I can't really know her if she doesn't."

My aunt and uncle looked at each other with surprised expressions, then ate quietly.

The rest of the meal was more fun, as were the lavender cookies.

They should have remembered that Grandmère was an imp.

After dinner, I rounded up my cousins, Claire, Hamish, and Dad, leaving my mother and Aunt Zoe to clean up. My mother knew that this was the plan. Grandmère didn't, but caught on fast as we all settled into the sofas and started brainstorming again. She listened with interest, smiling indulgently at my mother from time to time, and then at Uncle Charlie.

Edgar still seemed stunned to be included in all this. "Shouldn't I have to prove myself first? You don't know how I work, how I get along with people, how well I can attract business interests, and so on. Why did you really offer me this?" Fabian and the other seconded the query.

Uncle Charlie looked a bit worried as his son asked us this, but said nothing.

I had an answer for that. "No new hire is a truly known entity right away. New work environment, new duties, new people to work with…it all makes for unknowns. I've watched you study and interact with people since you finished school and before that. Fabian, I know you want to attend UConn Law School. You can do all of these things. You are neurotypical, so you can intuit your way through any social interaction, which is what a business negotiation is. I can't do that. Hamish can't do that. Besides, our careers are established, and we want to do other things than what we are asking you to do, and this is a great learning opportunity for you."

Fabian said, "You would have me work for you while attending law school? I know they have an evening program, but my experience consisted of a few summer internships and a lot of unanswered job applications."

Claire added, "We are very grateful to have this chance, but worried that we aren't giving you what someone with more experience could. We keep questioning what we churn out, wondering whether or not it is useful to you at all."

Hamish spoke up. "I have seen your grant-writing efforts – all of yours. They are coming along nicely, and I expect that soon you will have caught up. I showed you what I wrote in the past that reaped results, and I have it on good authority that the solar panel nano-bot grant you put together will be funded. Hopefully, homes and businesses everywhere will benefit."

Jacques looked quite pleased at this. As the youngest, he hadn't had as much time to search for jobs that weren't out there. He understood more in theory than in practice how bad the market was, so he was just delighted with the praise.

But Edgar still felt bad at being "rescued" as he saw it.

Grandmère chimed in at this point. "What were those endless job applications doing for you? Nothing. Try this for a while. Just because it's family offering it to you is no reason to feel bad about accepting. You can't live without a job forever. I saw you looking dejected around the house after you filed all those applications and made all those unanswered phone calls."

Edgar looked at her, open-mouthed. "I thought you thought I wasn't trying."

"No," she said. "But I see that it's a different world now, with a different economy, worse in many ways than at the start of the Great Depression of the 1920s. I was lucky; I lived in Paris and my husband was doing well. Now it's worse for young people. Women as well as men are expected to find jobs and live away from their parents even though that's no longer realistic. Families should be like ours, with multiple generations together. This American Dream of nuclear families is a failed experiment of the 20th century. That time is over. It worked briefly, in the most recent age of excess. Now we have to adapt by going back to older ways."

Uncle Charlie stared at his mother. "That's the last thing I ever thought you would say."

She smiled sweetly and knowingly. "You've been seduced by the American Dream. But not entirely; you do have me here. After your Papa died, I could have gone with either you or Henri, but I wanted the fun of watching my grandsons grow, and Avril was grown by then."

Dad grinned. "It's okay, Maman. I knew that."

She grinned back. "I had my fun living in the same building as your sister for decades. Now I feel as though I live with both of my sons, because I see you often enough. It all works out perfectly in the end."

I smiled and went back to my pitch for Edgar's benefit, addressing them all. "You see how the old model works. We need your help developing one for people to follow based on both the old and the new. This U.N. Agenda 21 model that is being promulgated every which way we look has flaws. It is communism dressed up with a new word to disguise it: communitarianism. Some of its ideas are good, and others are terrible."

"What sorts of things do you want to do differently?" Fabian asked.

"We need help, and we don't trust very many people. You can both keep a secret and you are family. That makes you trustworthy to us. With our background, you must realize why we have Blackout Security details following us everywhere. We would arrange things to fit law school or whatever graduate school into your schedule."

"But what ideas do you have that differ from those of Agenda 21?"

"Great question. I knew you were the right person to ask," I said with a grin, and outlined the electric car conversion idea from the *Gattaca* movie. We chatted about this for another hour or so, planning their schedules and ours. The Law School Admission Test (LSAT) was coming right up, and Fabian and Claire were prepping for that.

"Also," I continued, "as nice as Ellie is, she isn't careful with secrets. We have a lot of trade secrets to discuss tonight. They are not to be shared with anyone outside the family or the lab. Hamish is always working on another cool, secret project, and not a word about any of it can get out before it is patented. Only then can he publish. My books are less of a risk; I can chat with people about them while I write, and then release them. But we need you to understand that soon, he will share a significant one with you." Hamish had indeed been hinting at that.

When we went home, it was nice to see that Hamish was smiling, and looking relaxed at last. My husband no longer looked depressed or hopeless. He looked how most middle-class guys his age used to look decades ago, but rarely did now. He looked confident and happy.

If only I had known what he was plotting next, and why. I would have freaked out.

No wonder I had trouble shopping for groceries. I couldn't grow everything at home. Sometimes I had trouble growing certain crops because of soil conditions and temperature, which was more in flux than any gardening website seemed to account for.

I had thought that my parents weren't all that interested in such issues, but the frustration of spending hours shopping for supplies that used to be readily available and coming home with a fraction of the grocery list accounted for had changed that. They had raised no objection to my personal infrastructure project in our yard.

That was another thing: it was our yard now. Hamish and I had bought my parents out. We owned the house, and they were content to keep living in it. We felt safer, all together. We also had come to the realization that finding another house for me and Hamish to live in nearby was impossible. Nothing was available…except for some of the condominiums at Blue Back Square, and we had not wanted to move into them.

They were certainly attractive enough on the outside, but inside, let's face it, they were just more units in mixed use development. On the outside, the buildings were decorated with a façade of white paint and brick in tastefully chosen hues (red, dark red), plus white marble tile veneers. But that was really what they were: veneers. Inside, it simulated a city environment of closeness and the sounds of one's neighbors moving about, with not-so-solid construction.

I thought back to last year, when Hamish and I had toured a couple of them, which were among the last few that hadn't yet been bought and occupied. It was mixed use development, just like in Manhattan, but not in Manhattan. What was the point of leaving a big city if one found more of the same thing elsewhere, we thought?! I didn't want to live in an Agenda 21 home.

The real estate agent seemed to think that this was wonderful. Of course, how else would she pitch her sales spiel, but still…it was irritating. "Whole Foods is within walking distance, as are parking garages and the town hall. The area has a movie theater, a bookstore, chic clothing stores, and lots of restaurants. Even the public library is close by." She sounded like she had drunk lots of some super-spiked Kool-Aid.

As I mentioned earlier, I hated fashion, so this did not impress or entice me. Those stores thus held no appeal for me. I would still be wearing thrift shop treasures found by my mother, and buying from L.L. Bean and Lands' End for Hamish.

We walked around in one of the apartments that remained on the real estate market, and I paced the floors. Creak, tap, creak. "I can hear my own footsteps without much effort," I told Ms. Feldman. "I don't like it. That means that other people in other units can hear me, and I can hear them."

"That's normal in apartment living," she replied, looking concerned. Maybe she wasn't going to make a sale. Technically, this was a condominium.

"What about parking? Would we have assigned spaces, or would we have trouble parking each time we came back?" Hamish asked.

"You would have an assigned spot, plus bicycle parking. The town is trying to guide people toward using bicycles instead of cars."

"Really? I don't ride a bike. I can't balance. And I want my car, so that I can use it at any time, to go to any place I choose, not wait for public transportation to take me there." Looking back at this interaction, I was now suspicious that this had been a sales pitch for U.N. Agenda 21 as much as it was for the unit.

Ms. Feldman looked less than confident after that.

"I don't like what most people like, and I don't appreciate being guided toward someone else's agenda," I went on. This interaction was annoying me now. Hamish stood by the window, looking down at the street below, which afford a lovely view of…Crate & Barrel. No thanks!

Next, I heard some whooping and hollering above me. It was a Sunday afternoon. "What is that horrible noise?" I asked.

She looked up, then said, "It's someone getting excited over a football game." Footsteps danced and stomped, and the hooting noises got worse. It could have been one guy or many; it was impossible to tell.

"That's it. I'm not living here. I hate football, and I hate the sound of anyone enjoying it. Hamish doesn't like team sports, which is one of many reasons why I found him attractive enough to marry him. I don't want to look out my windows and see a big box store, much less Crate & Barrel with its travesty of aesthetics. I won't waste your time with wondering about the outcome of this interaction. Thank you for your time, but no thanks on the sale."

I hoped she would tell people what I had said.

Hamish looked pleased that the interaction was over. He hated shopping.

We all rode the elevator silently to the street level, said our good-byes, and parted company.

As Hamish and I walked toward the bookstore, I asked, "Did you particularly want to live here, or not? Please tell me."

"I did not want to live here. I don't like a faux-urban setting. Real urban is one thing, and we have a house in the real city, but this is contrived and authoritarian. I'm glad you saw that."

"What a relief," I said, putting my arm around his waist. He did the same, and kissed me on the cheek…twice.

With that, we had gone into Barnes & Noble, chose piles of history, biography, travel, and political books to look at, bought lattes, and sat down in poufy armchairs for a few hours. It was nice. That was when I had not understood the significance of the planning scheme of the area.

One of the books I had found described communitarian life in detail. It was still in the planning phases, the authors explained, but proposals were in the process of approval. Construction would likely begin soon in urban areas around the nation. The beneficiaries would be displaced persons from flooded areas and the existing urban poor. Really? Like those lost people we later saw on the country roads of Pennsylvania? Like the ones getting arrested for homelessness in a National Park?!

The book was full of charts on demographics that would be served by this plan, drawings of imagined buildings both inside and out, and photographs of model homes and apartments. The emphasis was on apartments. They looked like the hideous block-buildings of the Soviet Era, a communist nightmare of depressing, blah hues and gloom. Green indeed…it was gray.

I had since returned to that store, found that book, and bought it. It was full of details about future housing and mixed-use schemes that filled out what *Behind the Green Mask* described. Low-income apartments were being proposed that seemed like something straight out of a George Orwell novel. Everything in them seemed to contain Smart devices – everything! Added to that deficit was the lack of privacy and a décor scheme that screamed cell block hell.

A dark, cheap, cement finish was on the walls and floors. Bathrooms and cooking areas were communal. Water use in sinks and showers was timed, and there were no bathtubs. Only bedrooms were individual. Windows weren't a priority, though there were some, and lighting was controlled. It dimmed to a level just high enough to see safely by after 9 p.m.

How could a low-income resident with academic aspirations enjoy enough light to study by? Or read by in the night-time? Where could they sit together to visit? What would they do for comfortable living room furniture? There were common rooms with cushions on concrete that we so thin as to afford no long-term comfort. It was like a college dormitory, with none of the perks. No comfort to the sofas, not enough light to live happily by, and no studying or reading.

What about laundry? Oh, the communitarians had thought that one through! Low-water-use washing machines were provided on the ground floors or basements, and residents were expected to then laboriously hang up their wet clothing in their rooms. No dryers were available. Hooks and clothes lines were, however, thoughtfully part of the décor in each room. This would at least prevent theft of laundry as it dried.

How nice. No; how appalling. No thank you!

It was a nice, quiet afternoon at home.

Well, sort of. It was an election year. Thus far, the primaries were moving along with both parties offering up very similar choices: men who had worked on Wall Street as banksters or nearby as hedge fundsters. In short, the choices on the menu promised to offer no real selection.

The television news droned on and on tediously about this until I decided to stop watching.

I would keep track of it all and vote carefully, but that didn't mean being glued to it.

Hamish was out at his laboratory; I would pick him up later.

My parents were out driving around every back road in the state and perusing the contents of every high-end thrift shop my mother could identify. They wouldn't be back for hours. They were being followed by a Blackout Security car with two guys in it, and they knew it. It had taken some getting used to when Hamish first hired them, but my mother no longer freaked out about it or made comments about feeling like she was in some spy movie.

They were starting to notice what I had been reading and asking them about for months: that the state's rural roads were in a state of terrible disrepair, and so were some state and federal highways. For a couple who liked long car rides, it seemed as though it had taken them an inordinately long time to see this. I had noticed some of this on our road trip.

Meanwhile, our politicians in both state and federal government continued to say that there was no money in the budget for road infrastructure. If people wanted new roads (actually, redone roads) money would have to be found from social security and healthcare. Wow. The nerve of them! Due to having studied U.N. Agenda 21, I knew that it was more than that: it was part of a larger plan to get people to give up their cars, not travel far, and use local, public transportation.

No thank you! I would keep my car and go wherever I wanted, whenever I wanted.

The cats were flopped on the cat perch in my and Hamish's room that overlooked the street (Spock) and across the foot of our bed (Eowyn). Both regarded me sleepily, having worn themselves out within the past forty minutes by racing back and forth in the upstairs hallway.

To make sure that they would fall asleep and let me write, I had dangled a toy for each of them in turn. It was a rodent-on-a-fishing-line-on-a-stick. We would buy new ones from Amazon when they finally broke just to keep the cats happy; it was a major feline crisis every time.

Confident that the cats would not get up for a while, I turned to my computer, opened a blank Word file, and began to type what I couldn't stop thinking about. As for what I would do with all of this, I had no idea as yet. I would figure that out later.

We needed less growth, not more, to sustain our species. More growth would kill us. It would mean more resource use, more conflict over that, and more chaos. Everything I found about environmental initiatives – initiatives aimed at preserving our environment – talked about growth. Growth of the economy, growth of corporations, growth of this, growth of that…too much growth.

What were these writers thinking, if anything? Were they thinking that once Nae-Née had served its purpose, our species could go back to reproducing again with the reckless abandon for finite resources and space on Earth that it had displayed for all of recorded history?

Anthropocene impact – the impact of human-generated industrialized change – on the Earth's ecosystems was now irreversible and pronounced. Were these writers and policy-makers planning to bring it to a halt, or were they hoping that it could be avoided if only humans would all conserve resources and abstain from practices and behaviors that further degraded the planet?

It really seemed as though they lived in a state of delusional, wishful thinking.

No wonder the planet was still in such bad condition, mirroring the fate of dead civilizations long past – the Mayans, the Romans, Rapa Nui – whose ecosystems had collapsed. Granted, climate change had worked in combination with overpopulation and resource depletion to swallow them, and it wasn't always anthropogenic (human-induced), but the resource consumption that transformed the once-Fertile Crescent and Easter Island certainly was. Now the problem was planet-wide.

The fact of the matter is that it seemed as though two options were all we had:

1. Respect everyone's wishes to reproduce as they chose until there were so many humans on the Earth that its ecosystem could not support them all. At that point, continue to respect human autonomy and the right to fight for one's own existence, leaving everyone to their own devices. They would then show their worst, most selfish instincts in order to survive as they snatched food from one another and killed in order to remain alive. Quality of life would be nonexistent.
2. Regulate reproduction until humans numbered well below the planet's carrying capacity, which was, as mentioned before, 2 billion people. While our numbers decreased, an outcome which should be possible without bloodshed, control resource use carefully. Quality of life wouldn't be ideal, but we would still have some.

Of course, I was only contemplating a way to accomplish population reduction that wouldn't deprive people who were already alive of their lives. I wasn't interested in any other ideas. Don't get me wrong; I was well aware that there were faster ways, but they were evil, so I wasn't interested. I also had a hard time even imagining that such things would actually happen.

No, upping the use of Nae-Née seemed to be the only acceptable method of saving humanity and hopefully salvaging as many of the other species we still had…before the Earth's temperature rose much higher. Not that we could stop it from doing so…damn it. Once fossil fuels had emitted carbons, they could not, as yet, be taken back.

Unfortunately, humans had been emitting them since the nineteenth century, when the Industrial Age had kicked off. Levels of them in the planet's atmosphere were such that, no matter what we did, the temperature was going up by a few degrees, threatening our ability to grow fruits and vegetables, and threatening countless plant's, insects', and animal species' ability to survive at all.

Who knew what technological advances our species might come up with to solve such problems if we had enough time? That was the key: prolonging our survival enough to heal the planet. As it was, far fewer humans could reach the comforts afforded by a developed nation.

Why?

Well…development damages ecosystems. Development was a self-defeating endeavor if carried to too great an extreme. The whole planet could not be developed. *Star Trek*-level technology did not yet exist.

No, happiness was rapidly becoming a commodity that was both logistically and economically out of reach for most people. It had already been precariously perched on a very high shelf for a high percentage of our species, as shown by the existence of underdeveloped nations experiencing ecosystem collapse and exploding population. Nae-Née could only hit the brakes on the population expansion. Their ecosystems were still collapsed.

Sustainable growth. What an idiotic concept. What an oxymoronic term!

It had to be about marketing, a ploy to postpone the inevitable by hedge fundsters!

I stopped researching and reading for some really good tea. It was almost March, and I decided to have some Darjeeling tea with sugar-in-the-raw (granulated brown sugar) and milk, a handful of raspberries, and couple of lavender butter cookies. How long would it be before these foods would be impossible to acquire, I wondered irritably?!

Oh, yeah, surely mine is the saddest story, I jeered at myself mentally. Others have it worse! Not that such thoughts improved my mood… As I stood in the kitchen, leaning by the counter with my tea and cookies, the doorbell rang.

Damnit! An interruption…I went over to the window and looked out. It was a man in a business suit, smiling and holding some brochures. Aaron stood nearby, watching. Okay – it must be safe enough to open the front door and talk to him.

"Hello. What is the reason for your visit?" I asked, hoping I sounded polite.

"My name is Bob Reinhold, and I'm here to talk to you about land trusts."

"Land trusts. Why would I want to sell you one of those? And who do you represent?"

"I represent the town of West Hartford. The reason you might want to buy a land trust is to reduce the possibility of a foreclosure on your mortgage, and to give you a little extra money. It would make the land around your home permanently off limits to development, and lower your taxes on the property."

"Well, we don't have a mortgage, and this sounds as though it would put a plethora of restrictions upon the use of what has been our land and property. No thanks. We own this land outright, and we like it that way. I'm not going to sell anyone a conservation easement and thus have to worry about every little thing I do here."

"But wait," Mr. Reinhold started to protest. "There are lots of advantages and benefits, if not to you, then to the community. Don't you want to give back to your community?"

"Sure, but not that way. I shall decide the manner in which I give to my community. I don't like suggestions about that. I already give to public education for the arts, music, and drama departments of several area schools. That is what I like to do. I have no interest in what you are suggesting. Thank you for your visit, do NOT come back with this again, and good-bye."

He looked affronted, which was kind of fun to see, left some literature in the mailbox, and took off. Aaron watched him go, then yanked the lot of it out of the box to look at it. With the guy gone, I came outside with a couple of cookies for Aaron and took the literature. "Thanks, Aaron. This stuff will be interesting to add to my pile of research. What a creep. Oh well."

Aaron grinned, took the cookies with a thank-you, and walked off. I went back inside.

So what now? I took the food back to my desk and thought about it some more.

It was one thing to see that there were far too many of us humans for the Earth to support, to know that this many were unnecessary to the point of being destructive to our planet. It was quite another to just decide to get rid of most of us. There could be no compromise about that, and no discussion. This point was non-negotiable. There was no cull, I reminded myself, only the Nae-Née policy, but anyone awake to the problem I was contemplating ought to protect themselves. They ought to prepare a way to escape and outlast it so as to live to fight and tell about it later.

Maybe I could write a letter to the public with my thoughts on this matter. I wouldn't talk about a cull at all – why suggest it? It wasn't real anyway. No sense in putting that idea in anyone's mind. No. I wanted to talk about the fact that there was far too much talk about what people should do rather than what one could realistically expect our collective species to do.

Getting it published by a major newspaper such as *The New York Times* wouldn't be difficult. We still lived in a free society, one that protected freedom of speech and of the press, right? I hoped so, and I wondered about that, but until such time as we lived in a police surveillance state like the one in *Nineteen-Eighty-Four*, I intended to go on as if we lived in a free society.

Damn! I sounded like Colonel Nick Fury, I thought with a grin, looking at what I had already written. I decided to touch it up a bit more first, dressing it up as a neatly flowing letter to the public, and save before calling anyone.

A half-hour later, I saved the document, backed it up, and went onto the Internet. Who would I contact? Thomas L. Friedman? No…he didn't feel comfortable telling people how many children to have. He said so in *Hot, Flat, and Crowded*. Ehrlich? No…he was a professor emeritus, not a journalist with the kind of access I was after.

Got it! Johannes Ronan would do nicely. He was on the editorial board at that newspaper.

I looked up his phone number, which was not published, but he had given it to me and Hamish when we had left Manhattan for Connecticut. When we decided to wait out the massive infrastructure projects that would restore the island city to a significant extent, he had wanted our perspective on it all. The result was that I had published a short series on everything our family had done to make ourselves as self-sufficient as possible.

A moment later, I decided to just e-mail him and avoid the phone altogether. I hated phone interactions. Too risky! It usually took me a while to decide to actually call someone on the phone unless they were Hamish, my parents, or a close friend. I hated the sound of phones, the interruptions they caused, the startling distraction their noise caused, and most of all, I dreaded the social interaction of a phone call. It was classic Aspie angst.

Ronan had enjoyed my pieces, which included one on the conservatory garden I had set up with its herbs and berries, another on the fruit trees around our yard, and still another on our garden, which had replaced the huge, empty expanse of lawn.

Water use had been another issue that intrigued him. I had written about that, detailing how much work it had been first to rip up the whole lawn so that we could put a thick layer of clay underneath and then put it back. The purpose of this was to make the soil retain as much water as possible, thus reducing the need to use as much as we might otherwise have taken.

I e-mailed the piece to Ronan and waited to see if he would write back. To my surprise, Ronan wrote back after about 20 minutes. Then my cell phone rang. Disgusted with my wavering, I greeted him, and exchanged pleasantries, nervous or not. He had indeed received what I had written, so I asked him: Would his newspaper want to publish it?

"That would certainly be interesting to find out," he said, "but the only way to do that is to ask and see. Let me talk to the other editors and I'll get back to you. It would be nice to have another piece from you to run. We haven't heard from you in a while."

I paused. This felt all too real, just as the abrupt fame of Nae-Née had when it first started. It felt like I had just swallowed a stone. It was not good. Maybe I needed time to get used to this. Ronan's answer was ideal, I realized. I could talk to Hamish tonight and get his opinion.

"Okay, well…thank you very much. Can you e-mail me when you have decided?" I asked.

"Certainly! No problem. It was great to hear from you. Take care," he said.

"You too," I replied, and rang off without another word. That social interaction went well, I thought.

A week later, the piece ran, and the comments were interesting.

People did indeed seem to think about the fact that the Earth couldn't possibly accommodate us all in the manner to which we had become accustomed, and sure enough, no one wanted to make changes. Long, hot showers, any fruits we wanted at any time of the year, not merely in season, and lights on at night were part of a lifestyle that used a lot of energy and resources.

I got some hateful comments, of course, furious about the birth control nanite policy and blaming me as usual, but I didn't care. That policy hadn't been my idea, and they were missing the point. The question was: what was next? No one who already existed should have to die to enable the Earth to accommodate us all, and no one should be allowed to gamble with the futures of innocent lives – gamble that they would have enough space and food to enjoy their lives.

We were in for some careful adjustments to keep those of us who did exist in existence.

It might not work, but I doubted that most people were aware of that or tracking it.

Chapter 12

Communitarian Constraints

Something nagged at me…something that I had run across that had to do with land ownership, and the continuation of that possibility for small, family-business farmers, which lead to this: *Behind the Green Mask*. I went back and checked the details in it about land trusts. I had read it all once, but now I read the parts that I had seen crop up in everyday life around me.

I read on…and on and on and on. She listed the reasons provided for these efforts: temperatures are rising, icecaps are melting, biodiversity is dwindling, humans are overpopulated, we emit too many fossil fuels into the atmosphere, and on and on and on. The solutions offered were full of holes, and the author talked about them: communitarianism, the International Council on Local Environmental Initiatives (ICLEI), Local Governments for Sustainability, and the Delphi Technique.

She was right; something was off about all of this. None of them sounded like a pleasant way to live. Instead, they suggested regulation of every facet of our lives. Communitarianism, as I had said to my cousins (and I was starting to think of Claire as a cousin), was basically communism with a fancy new name to mask its own stench of usurped autonomy and choice.

On an afternoon in the summertime of last year, I had been out with Hamish, getting groceries, visiting the farmers' market, and looking around in plant nurseries. It was a fun, sunny day, and I had bought some iris bulbs to plant, and some more raspberry bushes. I drove down Flagg Road in West Hartford, past the array of beehives in a farm called Westmoor Park. They were easily visible from the road.

There was no particular need to drive this way; I just wanted to see the hives from the road. One of them was a top-frame hive, like the one I had, which allowed the bees to build their own honeycomb, thus making each cell a different size. That enabled the bees to keep mites out.

"Have you heard from that doctor who keeps those bees?" Hamish asked as we drove by.

"Yes, he's still at it, but he had to buy a few more hives from a bigger apiary operation. That happens every year, thanks to all the neonicotinoid crap that the suburban homeowners who surround the farm spray all over their yards," I replied.

We had driven north, almost to the end of the road. There was a small community garden on the left, not associated with any farmers' market, as far as we knew. An older, Asian woman with shorts, sneakers, tee shirt, and a hat on was poking around in one area. I pulled into the parking area and got out. So did Hamish.

"I want to talk to her and find out about this garden," I told him. He nodded. Ed was following us, so he pulled in next to our car and waited.

I went over to her and chatted with her for a few minutes. She had been growing some food here for a few years, and pointed out her rows. Anyone who wanted to grow some food here was welcome to try; they just had to sign up and agree to certain responsibilities, such as keeping the place weeded, and telling other gardeners if they noticed any problems with their rows. The idea was to warn of wild animals eating up the crops. No insecticides were allowed.

"This is probably the last year I'll do this," the woman told me. "Too many bugs, too much work," she said. She would buy her vegetables at a market and relax, she said, getting into her car. "It was nice chatting with you." I had told her about my own herb and berry crops.

Hamish and I got back into our car. "That was interesting," I said. "Community gardens sound okay, as long as they are entirely voluntary. Some models for future societies suggest that we should all grow food, and not necessarily in our own gardens. Others suggest our own gardens. They're all different. That seems fine as long as it's not communitarian."

"What does 'communitarian' mean?" Hamish had asked.

"It's a dressed-up, fancy way of saying 'communist' – dressed up to conceal that fact."

"I don't like it," he had said.

"Neither do I," I had replied.

Local Governments for Sustainability was really just ICLEI with a different label. It was a regional application of U.N. Agenda 21 with a more palatable name, disguised after ICLEI, created in 1990, proved to be a means of social control. Many local government officials around the United States, in violation of their oaths of office to serve the interests of their citizens, also sat on the National Board of ICLEI. This was a conflict of interest, but reporting them had gone nowhere. Any objections were Delphied away and thus dismissed.

The Delphi Technique was used at town meetings routinely now. It was developed as a Cold War mind control method by the RAND Corporation. The RAND (Research ANd Development) Corporation wasn't even a corporation; it was a government global policy think tank that served the United States Armed Forces. The purpose of the Delphi Technique was to channel any given group of people into accepting the proffered point of view while convincing them that it was their own idea. In short, it was the Newspeak of George Orwell's Oceania, tailored for meetings instead of the news broadcasts.

People were lapping it up, unfortunately, and U.N. Agenda 21 was proceeding efficiently.

Water was being privatized, rationed, and policed. The Metropolitan District Commission had its own police. In times of an emergency, a situation which was left conveniently undefined, water could be cut off entirely, and access to reservoirs by joggers and walkers denied.

People who lived in condominiums were noticing groups of engineers snooping around their swimming pools. Sharianne lived in a development where this had happened, and a notice had gone around to the residents about it. The notice had said that the property management company was working with the MDC Police on this.

It was a shock to her when I told her what could happen during a drought or a terror attack – no water. I would be just miserable. What a clever way for the authorities to control the general population: just shut off the water.

Not only that, but it had become clear that a concerted effort – no, policy – was in play to make Americans stop being economically independent, meaning solvent, on an individual basis. Why? Because solvency meant the ability to own small pieces of land, and that conflicted with the goals of U.N. Agenda 21.

No…the idea was to change that by impoverishing us all (or as many as possible) so that we would thus be pushed into high-rise apartments and packed in like sardines, just like in Shanghai, Hong Kong, Singapore, and other such places. Megacities, as seen via satellite at night, showed lights that seemed, like any organic life form, to grow larger and larger and then into one another. It was disturbing just to contemplate.

People who lived in those cities and others paid exorbitant sums each month for the privilege of dwelling in every-smaller spaces. Some of these spaces had to be climbed into and crawled through – they were that small. These apartments were claustrophobia-inducing, yet people wanted their chance to have families. These families would then have even less space to live in.

For those of us who did not live in cities, a campaign was in force to convince as many of us as possible that the American Dream was no longer a realistic one, and that we should settle for less. "Less" meant a tiny house on wheels, just one room, with no personal space for the occupants. Families with children, convinced that they could not afford a house with a yard and much stuff to go inside it, were already buying these homes.

The descriptions of these tiny houses on wheels were a bit sketchy on the details. Details such as how water would be provided for a tiny kitchenette and bathroom were lacking. How would that be dealt with? Was there some sort of hook-up attached? If so, where would the house be parked to avail the residents of it? Americans were used to taking a bath or shower daily, and we found any bodily odors unacceptable and a sign of slovenliness and low self-esteem.

How would that problem be addressed, and where would these houses be allowed? Some land would still be required just to accommodate them. Who would own it? Would it be rented? Was this the trailer park of U.N. Agenda 21 planning? I would hate to be in a tornado zone in one of those things.

Towns were requiring foundations rather than wheels for the tiny houses, so perhaps tiny plots of land would become the norm. Either way, I imagined living in one and didn't feel at ease at all. People could come very close and peer in, and with such small houses, they would end up close together in a suburban version of the sardine-packed, high-rise urban apartments that I dreaded so much. Same difference, different setting – no thanks!

How else to make that work but to mandate that we humans all accept and be content with less and less of everything, until the necessities were scaled back? There could not possibly be enough fresh water to wash in, cook with, and drink for much longer. The only way to make overpopulation work for so many billions of human beings had to be a stealthy plan by governments to impoverish as many of us as possible, and thus to limit our choices.

Once that was accomplished, we would all be forced to accept sharply reduced access to utilities. Forget having a shower every day – stink instead! Forget washing a load of laundry and then using a dryer. Forget having enough light to read by at night. And certainly forget being able to run kitchen or other appliances without blowing a fuse and knocking the whole building out of power for who knew how long. The public didn't need to read and keep informed of all facets of an issue. If it did, it would be difficult to control. No…take the nighttime lights away!

A Romanian-American writer who had experienced that under communism, and then immigrated to the United States to get away from it, had written all about this. She was understandably furious and outraged by the mere prospect of U.N. Agenda 21. I didn't blame her. I loved long showers, running my food processor, mixer, and oven whenever I felt like doing so. The nerve of anyone trying to regulate my use of any of that!

As if that wasn't infuriating enough, I would read about what it was like for people with little or no income to access benefits, both in the U.S. and in Britain. This interested me because I could never forget how scared and depressed Hamish and I had been about our futures when we weren't making any money. We had even had SNAP benefits for a while to get food.

Every time I went to a grocery store, I had kept my hand over as much of the silver SNAP card as possible, and swiped it through the card reader as fast as I could to avoid having anyone notice. The cashiers were always very good about it, never calling attention to the fact that I had one. Hamish had had a tough time just getting me to use one, because I was ashamed to need it.

Because we stayed with my parents, I was able to buy fresh fruits and vegetables with that card, and make nutritious vegetable puree soups every week. I could even keep baking things like whole wheat honey bread and batches of holiday cookies using family recipes. But I knew that this was a luxury; huge numbers of SNAP recipients could only make ends meet with cheap, processed foods and sugary-tasting, GMO-laden, canned corn and other such products.

Thanks to that experience, I would never forget that fear, or the angry and furtive feeling of watching those around me at the moment of payment in the checkout lane. I would also look for any chance that arose to pay for food for someone else.

Just before Thanksgiving last fall, I had seen a woman in the line ahead of me at Big Y. She had to remove items from her bill in order to make the SNAP funds in her account cover what she bought. That left her with very little. The turkey was the last thing to go.

As I watched what was going on, I started grabbing her food before the cashier could move it out of reach, putting it behind the divider stick that went on the conveyor belt between orders. My heart was pounding; would this woman allow me to buy this stuff and give it her? I didn't want to embarrass her OR let her holiday be ruined. The cashier caught on and soon, so did this nervous woman.

"Please don't take off or be mad at me," I pleaded with her. "I want you have your Thanksgiving dinner, and I used to have a SNAP card too." I couldn't believe it, but my eyes actually started tearing up. Stupid Asperger's! I was getting overwhelmed with empathy.

The woman looked at me, startled. She was neat and clean, about my age, and she had a silent, defeated-looking boy and girl standing at the end of the aisle, watching. They looked like they were 11 and maybe 13 years old. The family was probably a mix of African-American and Hispanic. The boy had glasses and clutched an inhaler.

"I'm not mad," the mother said. "Thank you! I wish you would tell me your name so I could pay you back when I can, though."

I took a breath and said, "No, there's no point in that. I'm okay and don't need anything. I would rather you wait until you are comfortable and safe and then help a person you see who does need help, not me."

The cashier had rung up the rest of her order and mine during this exchange, and a bagger had appeared and packed our things up separately, loaded hers into her cart, and I paid as the woman now subjected me to a series of "bless yous and thank yous". Rather than mention atheism, I had just said "you're very welcome" and "Happy Thanksgiving" to her.

With that, I had thanked the cashier, folded up the receipt, stuffed it into my handbag, and pushed off, away from everyone, hoping not to have attracted any more attention. I didn't want anyone staring at me, either. I was no heroine for this. It was easy to give someone food when you had everything you needed and wanted in life. The woman I had just seen was lucky in a way that many other SNAP recipients weren't: she lived within reasonable distance of a grocery store that sold fresh fruits and vegetables. Inner city residents often didn't.

For the poor of any country, they might as well already be living under the depressive conditions of communism that I was contemplating, and even far worse ones. What I found as I looked at articles that people posted on Facebook (with far more variety of topics, situations, and news sources than any local newspaper), I found stories of veterans whose needs were ignored, and of other people living below the poverty level who were also ignored.

These unfortunate individuals had diabetes, physical disabilities, and so on. They could not simply go out and get a job. Some of them were in chronic pain and could barely care for themselves, yet they had no one to depend on. The benefits systems that these people relied upon for any food money at all might abruptly cancel or delay their benefits payments due to some convenient clerical errors or computer glitch. How could this be so? Benefits employees told the media about it after leaving their jobs for less dehumanizing duties.

I was feeling more and more convinced that Agenda 21 was both coming and going to suck.

This whole scenario was rapidly destroying the proverbial American dream that our generation and many previous ones had been raised with, which was that if one worked hard, was careful, and followed the rules, one could own property, live comfortably, and have a secure retirement. Before we had created Nae-Née, I had been convinced that our future, after my parents had aged and died, would be one of starvation on the streets.

Now, I began to wonder whether or not having benefitted from what is known as a chaos event might be made to go away via clever manipulation of the world economy…like a crash of it. This chaos event was the fabulous economic success we enjoyed due to our well-marketed invention, i.e. Nae-Née.

Hamish had more nanotechnology ready once those sales had dried up, which they pretty much had when the initial boom of Nae-Née implantation was complete. The nano-bees were doing well, but I didn't believe in sitting back and getting too complacent.

Would there be a crash of the U.S. Dollar, and perhaps the Euro, one that would make us broke again? Not if Hamish had anything to say about it, apparently. As soon as I had told him what was on my mind, and showed him all of my research, he said, "That's it. We're converting the bulk of our money to Swiss francs. They're backed by the gold standard, and that is safe. The Swiss never bought into the Euro."

I stared at him. Then I thought back to my research. "Oh yeah…the Dollar and the Euro are fiat money. That means money by declaration, which is fictitious, imaginary money. We all stupidly stopped backing it up with a gold standard in 1972, which made the banksters and hedge fundsters of Wall Street and wherever the European ones hang out very happy, damn them."

Hamish grinned. "Indeed," he said. This had been in January, after Claire's parents left.

I called Sharianne the next day and made an appointment for us to see her and get that done. She wouldn't be happy, but we didn't care. We weren't responsible for her happiness; we were responsible for our own fiscal security. Take that, thieves and communitarians, I thought, disgusted by the whole mess. We couldn't save everyone else, though. The Swiss required a high level of personal wealth to buy into their gold-backed currency.

As for our own money, here was what we could look forward to: U.S. taxes would still attach to whatever we owned, because Swiss secrecy was over, but at least we would be safe from any bail-ins on our bank accounts.

Why was that? Well, the U.S. bail-ins could only happen in U.S. banks to the accounts in those banks, not bank accounts held by U.S. citizens elsewhere. A bail-in is what a government does when its economy crashes: it takes a significant percentage of all account-holders' money from each account in each bank that under its jurisdiction.

Cyprus had gone through this recently. Both Cypriots and foreign account holders lost out.

If this happened in the U.S., the contents of any safety deposit box would cease to be safe from the federal government, which would seize it. Better not to have any of those… Thus warned, Hamish and I were taking measures to protect the bulk of our money.

In Cyprus, the amount taken in the bail-in had been twenty to twenty-five percent. Who knew how much the U.S. government would scoop out when our economy tanked? I really didn't want to find out, and I was awake to that possibility.

Most Americans not only would not want to know, but they were neither awake to this possibility nor did they possess enough funds to buy into Swiss francs. (Swiss banks typically required a minimum amount of money for an initial deposit. Also, the I.R.S. had to be informed.) They were basically screwed.

If banks started bricking up the windows on any branches, especially any in major urban areas, that would be a tip-off that bail-in was about to go down. They would do that to prepare for riots. What a horror show that would likely be! Low-level employees would likely be stuck in there until the rioters crashed through, at which point they would be maimed and/or killed over money that wasn't theirs. Meanwhile, the head banksters would be tucked away safe somewhere, guarded by high-priced mercenaries. Perfect. Just perfect.

One could hope and wish that such a thing wouldn't actually happen, but it wouldn't make a difference one way or the other. No wonder Hamish was so determined to stay a few steps ahead of all that. He was always thinking ahead of everyone else, I told him.

"So are you," he had replied.

Yeah…so was I. Watching people manage their fears of the unknown with prayer grated on me, and I saw it on television and in person. Secular humanism – atheism – made more sense to me. I had been like this all my life.

At least it provided some amusement to tell the family about in March. Something had happened on a Saturday morning, when Hamish was at his lab and my parents were out driving around, probably looking in shops. I told them about it later, and Dad said I had to share it with the whole family at dinner next time.

This is what happened: I was home alone with my hazelnut coffee, the cats, and the newspaper. I was about to go upstairs when I heard a knock at the door. I don't open the door when home alone, so I cranked the window next to the front door open.

When I looked outside, and saw that Ed was out there, watching. He had allowed strangers to approach our front door. There, out front in their Saturday best, were two Jehovah's Witnesses: one male, one female, both in white shirts with black pants on the man and a black skirt on the woman. Great…they were there to steal some of my time from me.

Without waiting for them to launch into any nonsense about how their beliefs are better than everyone else's, I took a deep breath and boomed my voice out at them (so glad I learned how to do that in high school drama classes!): "Are you selling religion?!"

They looked startled and unprepared for such a reception, which was my intent. Then they replied, in very small voices: "Yes."

"I don't want any," I said. Crank, crank, crank, crank, CLICK.

An hour or so later, my parents came home and I recounted the tale.

My father loved it. My mother arched her eyebrows and looked disapproving, but refrained from scolding me. She was raised Catholic, but had always viewed religion as an escape and a way to avoid independent thought and analysis.

That was fun.

Hamish was pleased with and proud of my response to this idiotic intrusion, but he had stomped out to the small guardhouse to find Ed and Aaron and told them not to allow any more solicitors to approach the house. No legal reason to be there, no entry, as simple as that!

When the rest of the family heard the tale a few days later, Grandmère had grinned at me. She had no use for such nonsense either. Aunt Zoe had said that she would have just listened politely and let them do their speech, then said "no thank you" and closed the door.

"That's several minutes – or more – of my life I would never get back!" I protested. "No way am I going to listen to any tedious nonsense. No way will I give anyone a moment to tell me that their philosophy of life is better than mine. And you know what? The same goes for U.N. Agenda 21, even if I find it prudent to avoid it by stealth rather than directly. Weird that I would say that, but I think stealth is necessary."

"Why do you think so?" Ellie asked. Claire leaned over from her seat next to Ellie's, listening. Clearly, they both found this puzzling.

"Haven't you been following the news and reading between the lines?" I asked in return. "It is loaded with government warnings, all broadcast on major news networks, that continually harp on the fact that warming temperatures, resource depletion, and human encroachment into woods, jungles, and other natural territories spread disease, and that we should all change our habits to be in line with those that I have been reading about…and now my cousins and Claire are reading about. The only thing they leave out is the phrase 'U.N. Agenda 21' when they say it. It's the perfect cover for social control, which is coming."

"You are full of portents and threats, it seems," Ellie said to me.

Claire looked skeptically at her, and back at me. "I'm not so sure."

"Oh, they're not threats. Not anymore. They're realities now," I said.

Ellie muttered something about conspiracy theories.

Hamish said, "It's no conspiracy. The trigger will be pulled soon."

That weekend, Hamish and I took a trip to Switzerland, to the city of Geneva, to relocate the bulk of our money there. You had to show up in person to do this, which meant that most people on the planet could just forget about doing this.

Travel to Switzerland was expensive. It meant hotels, food, airplanes, meetings, hanging around long enough to meet with bank managers, and so on. We did all that in four days, and then come home, feeling a bit better than we had before about having control over our lives and over our ability to protect our family.

Yes, Switzerland was a lovely place to visit, and we had a great time there (even though it had too many foie gras items on menus, but that could be avoided), but that was all beside the point. The point was that unless one was beyond wealthy, one's money was fair game to the government.

If the government wanted money, it could just stick its hand into anyone's bank account and scoop out most of it, with no recourse. Most people could not afford to bank with the Swiss, so what meager savings they possessed were not safe.

Damn our government for its gross mismanagement of the economy and of its finances.

Working at a job or a career and saving money in a bank for one's retirement, for an education, for a future expense, or whatever other purpose should actually be reliable, not an effort that one's government could short-circuit.

It made me angry to think that everyone else could not count on doing what Hamish and I were doing to protect our money. Everyone should be able to enjoy that sense of safety and reassurance, not just a few people!

"There isn't always something that you can do to solve the problems that you see coming, as they will affect other people," Hamish told me. "You can't fix everything."

"I know," I said. "But I will vent about it. Maybe I can think of something eventually."

I doubted it, though.

Chapter 13

The 10 Amendments Institute

There was an infamously wealthy pair of evil twin brothers whom I liked to rail against.

Hamish had thought that I was losing it when I first started carrying on about them, because they sounded good in theory, especially to a newly sworn-in American citizen like my husband. Then he heard the details and saw that it was just another green mask, except that this time, the green was the color of U.S. paper money.

They were the Coke twins. That was their surname, and it had nothing to do with the Coca-Cola drink. The Coke twins hated public schools, and since they had been born with silver spoons in their mouths, and sent to private ones from toddlerhood on, that was no surprise.

Their vast fortune came from fossil fuel interests. Interests…they had a stake in corporations that handled the fuels, moved them from place to place, stored them, drilled for them, and so on. They employed a team of highly-paid lobbyists – pressure-pointing extortionists in my mind – to see that the politicians of the United States Senate, the House of Representatives, and legislators in states around the nation would do their bidding.

That meant arranging all laws and regulations to accommodate their business interests.

The idea was to fight any effort to stop them from drilling for oil in the Atlantic Ocean, the Arctic Circle, and anywhere in the United States that they could possibly extract any more. If they could frack land to get more, they would, but that was getting difficult as people learned about the death it wrought to the land above fracking sites. Still, they hoped to influence kids.

Kids, after all, were future voters, and buying out political campaigns and then haranguing politicians once in office wouldn't entirely get the job of controlling everything done for them. No, some extra effort at brainwashing young minds would also be necessary.

It reminded me of my own efforts to reach kids with my books about the banksters and about the corporations that made the poisons behind honey bee colony collapse disorder. The difference between us was that they had a huge engine behind their effort, plus a totalitarian attitude to go with it, and I did not.

Accordingly, they established the Bill of Rights Foundation to infiltrate public schools everywhere with their Libertarian agenda for the curriculum. Pandering shamelessly to the younger generation's distaste for a learning system that relied heavily on reading, they promoted their agenda via videos, games, and interactive computer software.

Essays were also part of the plan. Students were encouraged to write on prescribed topics, which included cherry-picked slants on the Bill of Rights. The Libertarian point of view that the Coke twins subscribed to was that property owners ought to be free to do exactly as they pleased with what they had, and with no interference whatsoever from the government.

What they left out was the fact that few people could afford to own any property anymore, and it was getting worse as the economy and resources contracted drastically. The fairy tale they preached was only for the wealthy few.

Not only that, but they conveniently failed to present any other point of view than their own, and children were almost always unable to notice this. Any student who did was at the mercy of the grading system anyway and could be silenced with low scores.

Topping that was the fallacy of Libertarianism, which was that some of our actions have an effect on other people, and other people have a right not to be harmed by those actions. Therein lay the cherry-picking.

It reminded me of law cases I had read over the course of my education and since then.

There were cases about land use, some as extreme as environmental degradation by dumping toxins into waterways or burying them only to have them leach into water wells. There were also cases as benign but still infuriating in which a homeowner could lower a neighborhood's property values by either letting his or her own house and yard decay or by painting the house orange with turquoise stripes. That was just amusing.

Vaccine law came to mind, too.

The case of *Jacobson v. Massachusetts*, 197 U.S. 11 (1905) was the one that stuck in my mind. That was the legal citation for the United States Supreme Court case about a guy from Boston who had objected to being required to accept a smallpox vaccination.

He lost for the simple reason that his Libertarian attitude would put the general public of the large urban area in which he lived at grave risk of contracting that deadly and disfiguring disease. Jacobson could easily get sick and come in contact with many people just by going about his business, and that was not okay. Hence, the Justices said that he must comply with the State of Massachusetts requirement that he be inoculated.

The Coke twins represented any effort by the government to control the actions of private citizens concerning their persons and property as illegitimate. But what about the actions of property owners via-a-vis other people?

Never mind that – never mind the right to be secure in one's own person or property. The government should not, apparently, be permitted to take any action to protect one individual against another, stronger one. Wealth is just one kind of strength.

Another was weapons, and as police across the nation enjoyed their repainted military hand-me-downs, I noticed that the hypocritical Bill of Rights Foundation had nothing to say about it.

Every so often, a lunatic who shot up a movie theater or a school would cause outraged members of the general public to call for gun laws. These gun laws were to be restrictions on who could own a handgun or other weapon. The people who called for them wanted all private citizens to be disarmed.

As it was, when some lunatic bombed a large public event, such as the Boston Marathon, the police donned riot gear and went around confiscating privately owned weapons by force. They did this in the name of public safety, but it seemed suspiciously to be more like a social experiment, as if to see how easily people would give up their legally acquired weapons.

The bombers never snatched weapons from private homes. Residents would have been better off if they could have surprised an attacker by producing their own weapons, yet this act of terrorism served up a convenient opportunity for the police to test people.

This leaves us with the question if, after martial law were declared and all privately owned weapons successfully seized, of what then? With the populace disarmed, and all property possessed by a very few, people would be at the mercy of a militarized police force everywhere. No one seemed to think of that.

This was all very ominous.

What was next, being told that acquiescence would set us free?

Free for what, work for almost no pay and control over our lives and choices? No thanks.

We had to keep the lights on at night, and read whatever we saw fit – all of us.

Chapter 14

Smart Gadgets

Smart Meters. Smart Watches. Smart This. Smart That. Enough already with the rise of the damned machines! No machine should be so revered. The idea was as insidious as the gadgets.

Even though that was just a brand-name, and the meters often went by other names, they were still absolutely galling. The main reason was that once one was installed, electricity providers flatly refused to remove them and put analog meters in its place. Instead, they sent out infuriating statements to the effect that, "unfortunately, it is not possibly at this time to replace the remote reader with an analog one."

This was what had caught Hamish's attention to point of infuriating him.

This was why he was so determined to get our house off the grid and independent of it.

It seemed that my research was giving me a detailed education about all kinds of SmartTechnology. Apparently, there was a plethora of too-smart-for-humans'-own-good gadgets out there, both on the market and already bought and in use. It was no great surprise to me, but it was certainly an outrage to know the intimate details.

There were trackers in cars, located just behind the airbags in the steering wheel. It was part of an NSA program to track people's whereabouts, movements, and habits. When I mentioned this to Hamish, of course he already knew all about it.

"I had Blackout remove those from our car and your parents' cars a long time ago."

"Really. What about Aunt Zoe and Uncle Charlie's cars?"

"Them too. Our guys are sneaky. That's what we pay them for."

"And Edgar, Fabian, and Jacques? Their cars too?"

"Aye." He was looking rather pleased with himself.

"Oh. Huh. Cool." I kissed him and turned back to the computer screen.

Next up: stores – particular the big-box ones – had started a new system of transaction.

It was clearly aimed at tracking one's every move and vital statistic. One could pay ONLY in virtual money – via a debit or credit card. Whenever anyone made their first purchase at one of these stores, it would not go through unless until the customer signed a contract. This contract allowed the store to access, in perpetuity, all of that individual's vital statistics.

This went beyond mere market research. This was an invasion of personal privacy.

Welcome to the surveillance state!

SmartMeters were only the visible things among all this, it seemed.

The damned things caused house fires. They were unreliable threats to safety and property, and yet California had made itself the proving ground for forcing them on everyone. No opting out! Once installed, getting rid of one and going back to an analog meter was next to impossible. After consumers got wise to this scheme, utilities started installing some that looked like analog meters, but underneath contained all of the stuff that any SmartMeter had.

They also enabled utility companies to track when any appliance in your home was used. Want to run your blender at 2 a.m.? Well, now the N.S.A. knows you did it. It's not that the N.S.A. cared, but collections of data told them a lot about large groups of people and their habits.

That wasn't all that Smart Meters could do to bother people. They could interrupt power in an individual home, just as that Romanian woman who had described fuses blowing from overloads said. Except that Smart Meters did it to preempt electrical overloads, as determined by utility companies! Good luck getting your chores done when you want them done.

Still not convinced that these electronic monsters were a problem? Wait – there's more. Smart Meters emitted Radio Frequency (RF) waves. These waves enabled the utility company's meter reader to simply do a drive-by of your house or condominium or apartment, and see how much electricity to charge you for. The RF waves had a range of up to 125 miles.

This remote reading system was easy to commit fraud with. It enabled overcharging via manipulation of the readings. It also eliminated many jobs. Seriously, the economy needed to be organized around a more ecosystem-friendly and human health-friendly energy policy, NOT the other way around. Paying the $100 fee to keep one's analog meter seemed far cheaper in the end.

This setup was perfect for benefitting the huge corporations that were utility companies, but not the health, privacy, or finances of the individual customer, nor for the general human population, and certainly not the environment. Things were out of balance. Neither all private nor all public works was good for a society. Having either one invited abuse.

If that wasn't clear enough, the RF waves – which were really just radiation aimed every which way – caused cancer with prolonged, sustained exposure. Different people experienced different degrees of damage from the waves depending upon where in the home their beds were in relation to the Smart Meter, or how close they spent their waking hours to it and how much time that was.

When he was a post-doctoral lab worker, my husband informed me that he had used the same RF frequency range and intensity that Smart Meters used to promote cancerous transformation of cells in lab cultures.

"Cancer! That's a total deal-breaker!" I said to my husband, outraged by all this.

"Indeed. I can tell you that all of the health problems people have from these despicable devices. Sometimes, the damned things are on the outside of customers' bedroom walls, and then the misery really hits," Hamish replied.

"Do tell," I said.

"Okay…symptoms are: headaches that are severe to the point of being migraines, and they persist as long as the person remains near the RF waves. People get nauseated, but of course lots of headache suffers have that along with the head pain. Insomnia is another fun problem. Remember when we stayed in that inn in Pennsylvania, near Hershey? You didn't sleep well."

"Let me guess: you went outside and found a damned Smart Meter on the wall of the inn."

"Aye, that I did. Shall I go on with the list?" he asked.

"Yes – let's hear it ALL. This is fascinating." I was more annoyed than fascinated, though.

"Okay…people are irritable around these things, but what else would sleep-deprived people in constant head pain be like?! They have difficulty concentrating, again attributable to the same problems. In fact, the rest of the problems seem to be traceable back to the first few: depression, lethargy, forgetfulness, heart palpitations, constant fatigue…oh, and high-pitched ringing in the ears and humming or buzzing noises."

"And the corporations have the gall to dismiss cancer and other signs of illness?!" I roared.

"Of course they do. The lobbyists you wrote about are the most expensive ones that money can buy, and they hound the politicians who enable this to continue relentlessly, insisting that nothing be done unless and until harm is proven beyond a shadow of a doubt."

"So…without a deluge of peer-reviewed studies to point to, the corporations that market Smart Meters and other invasive, harmful gadgets shall continue to hide behind the 'innocent until proven guilty' defense. Perfect. At least I pointed that out in my bee book. I said that we should not apply that standard to things that affect the health of the honey bees or other bees…that we ought instead to make insecticides meet a guilty until proven innocent standard. Looks like the same thing applies to Smart Meters, and that they are, in their own way, as toxic to humans as insecticides are to bees."

"It should be the same legal standard as Europe's – guilty until proven innocent – for both," Hamish agreed with me.

Hamish told me that these RFID devices were built into everything, and that it was driving him crazy to keep up with them all, and to evict them from our home, our gadgets, and our lives as fast as they cropped up. "These evil devices could decide without warning to shut off the air conditioning on a horrendously hot day and give your Grandmère heat exhaustion. Elderly people and children are at risk from Smart Meters, and I won't let one get attached to our home."

"Good! I know we can count on you," I said to him, and kissed him.

He went back outside to finish working on the solar panel array.

No wonder he was working so hard to get our house off the electrical utilities grid and independent. His solar panel array was excellent and, unlike most, did not have the panels up against one another. The array was many small ones, spaced apart so as not to be one large fire hazard. If we were so unfortunate as to have a fire, firefighters would not find our roof impenetrable from flames and access due to that solar panel pattern.

A little while later, I was pleased to be able to present my husband with some legal research that applied to the unwanted, unsolicited, and unauthorized installation of Smart Meters on private property, due to the injuries that they caused. It was a federal statute.

"Hamish, check this out: Title 18 of the United States Code, Section 113. It deals with criminal assault in both maritime and territorial jurisdictions. It offers a way to sue any corporation that installs one of these monstrosities on a house or other residence. Evil grin here!"

He loved it, of course.

Next item: SmartWatches. What an abomination! I hated wrist-watches as it was, and after fights over them with my parents when I was 14, they had given up and gotten me a pretty pocket watch. I still used pocket-watches…hence one of the reasons why I wanted pockets in all of my clothes (keys, tissues, pocket watch). But…they had an added dividend: no surveillance!

But to think that someone would strap a little RFID device that tracked their entire lives and transmitted it to some remotely located database was insanity. You walked to the local coffee shop? Recorded and transmitted. Bought a caramel latte? Recorded and transmitted. Drove to the bank? Same, complete with the time and date. There was no privacy. It was a wonder that any private investigator was needed with all this surveillance crap.

I was so disgusted that I posted a sarcastic, tongue-in-cheek, advertisement line with the link to an article about this wonderful new product on my Facebook page: "Check out A****'s new surveillance device in a watch! Just strap it on, and a hacker can find out what your current heart rate is and send it to who know where. Your personal data can be accessed from this device without you even noticing as you rest your chin in your hand at a coffee shop on a warm day, read right off the screen. Brilliant!"

It was spreading to schools. A hideous device called a Geospatial Common Operating Picture (GEOCOP) had been created. This was a "Sensitive-But-Unclassified web-based voice, video, and data overlay technology that instantly connects people, geospatial applications, and knowledge with operational processes." It was used on students at middle schools and high schools in America.

All this surveillance made me very, very glad that my entire academic career was behind me. I didn't want to have to rack up my credits with overreliance on standardized tests and then contend with potential employers being able to look at my every score for the rest of my life. How was anyone supposed to earn a living without losing hope and wanting to kill themselves?!

Kids were being conditioned to accept constant surveillance. *Nineteen-Eighty-Four*, here we come, with more sophisticated surveillance technology, so that it will be even worse – more oppressive – than in that novel. Already, microchips were being implanted not only in pets, but also in human children. How were they supposed to get those removed – ever?! Would a doctor even be willing to do so, or would he or she fear reprisal of some sort? Parents of wandering autistic kids thought this was terrific, but what justification was there for universal use?!

I didn't see any.

An outraged writer of a story on these practices commented: "Nothing that any of the data-mining firms or the security-monitoring firms are doing is technically illegal. The problem is that our technology is, once again, outpacing our legal structure, making a Student Privacy Bill of Rights needed. Now."

Yes, this was definitely a pattern, one of rule by technocracy.

There was one other invasion of privacy issue to deal with: the human element of idiocy.

Not only was nothing private now, but everyone seemed to want to be a celebrity, a filmmaker, or both. Ellie was no exception. She had an iPhone, and was constantly photographing objects and people with it, and recording videos on it. It was beyond irritating. I did not wish to star in her productions, nor was I willing to have them shown to who knew who.

We were having a family dinner party at our house on Stoner Drive this week, and Ellie had come along with Edgar. It was fine that his girlfriend was here, no matter who he chose for a girlfriend, but her behavior was really pissing me off.

The food and the company were lovely...except for that.

Well, photographing the carrot-raisin-walnut cake with ginger cream cheese frosting that I had made was fine. But recording every human interaction and showing what the inside of my home looked like? Unacceptable! I did not want her taking it to her friends or students...or parents...or anyone else without my permission, which I would not give.

I was getting into a foul mood over this, and stare-glaring as I walked around.

Hamish stopped me as I walked back toward the kitchen to get the peas. "What's the matter? You seem absolutely furious."

Knowing that everyone else could hear me, I went right ahead and replied, "I don't want to be on candid camera. I don't want images of the inside of our home recorded on anyone's digital device and shared. For all we know, Ellie may have hit 'send' by now. I want it all, all erased."

Ellie looked shocked. I didn't give a damn. I just glared back.

Edgar elbowed her and told her to erase it, and watched her do so.

Wow. It was that easy. I felt myself relax significantly and said so.

"Thank you," I said to her. "I was having visions of you sharing whatever you had with friends, students, parents, and perhaps the N.S.A. hacking your phone to get that data and know more about us."

"The N.S.A.?!" Ellie said. "That seems a bit...paranoid."

"Just because you're paranoid it doesn't mean they're not out to spy on you," Hamish said, backing me up.

"Thank you, Hamish," I said. Then I addressed Ellie and room at large again as I sat down with the dish of peas. "If our government can impose a birth licensing treaty and policy on us all, there's no reason to trust it. We are now living in a surveillance state, and nothing on those iPhones is secure. It's all stored in a remote, corporate-controlled server anyway. There's a reason why I only turn my cell phone on to check its messages and make calls, then turn it off. I don't want to be tracked. That phone is for my convenience, not Big Brother's."

"That's true," Dad remarked. "All images and videos you take of Avril and Hamish ought to have releases signed for them anyway," he added.

Incredulous looks all around. My mother brushed her chin-length, wavy hair aside, leaned over to pass the garlic-mashed potatoes, and said, "Really, Henri, that seems a bit excessive."

"No, it doesn't," my father contradicted her. "They're famous, and you seem to have forgotten all that tabloid nonsense with that crazy, idiot secretary of theirs at the Rockefeller Institute that Avril had to fire."

"Oh, right," my mother said, "that's true."

With that, the conversation paused while we started eating our hake dinner, something that I had not seen for sale in a while. We had salad with herbs, thanks to the little conservatory, and we were looking forward to the cake later.

Later, in the living room, we decided to watch a movie. Captain America: The Winter Soldier was on and we settled in to see him fight against an evil surveillance state. At least he could make a dent in it, even if we felt that we couldn't, I thought unhappily to myself. As I started to lose myself in the movie and relax, Claire started playing with my long, dark hair.

"Avril, you have great hair. It's so thick and healthy."

True…I didn't dye it, curl it, spray it, or otherwise mutilate it. "All I do is wash and dry it," I told her. It fell in waves down past my shoulder blades, and I kept it brushed to one side. "Sometimes, I let my mother trim it, and I call Hamish when he's at his lab to tell him. When I do that, I let him think she has cut off a lot, so that he thinks it is as short as hers."

"Chin-length?! Really? Then what happens?" Claire and Ellie both asked at once.

"He shrieks in outrage, wails 'Noooooo,' which I find hilarious, and then I put him out of his misery by telling him that I'm just teasing him. He's a terrible tease himself, so I have to do something back to him." I grinned mischievously as I told this tale.

"You're so mean," Hamish said, laughing.

Claire was still looking at my hair and playing with it. "Let me do a braid!"

"What kind of braid? I don't want it parted in the middle, whatever you do. I hate that look. It reminds me of the 1970s, when I found the styles ugly. I like the 1980s styles better, the hair, the florals, the deep pockets in women's clothing… Hey, can you do a French braid, the kind that seems woven into the top of the hair?"

Claire gave a big smile and said she could. "I love doing those. I haven't done one in a while. I'm usually in too big of a hurry to bother, but we're just sitting here now, watching a movie."

"Okay, go ahead then." I paused for a moment, then said, "Ellie, you can photograph this if you want. The wall behind me is fairly nondescript, and I don't mind." I was trying to be nice.

"Really?" she seemed…I don't know…mollified, like I had made up for my earlier irascibility. Edgar looked pleased.

I nodded, and the evening ended on a pleasant note.

When I got home, I was disgusted with her for being so tiresomely asleep to everything because of what I saw online. As usual, I could not resist checking the news. The President of the United States had ordered the creation of something called an exascale supercomputer.

Perfect. Just perfect, I thought to myself. This confirmed the end of privacy and sanity.

Skynet would soon be online, self-aware, and watching us for the United States of Oceania.

Chapter 15

The Mark of the Beast

Religious fanatics, adherents, whatever talked from time to time of the Mark of the Beast.

They didn't know exactly what it would look like, only that it would come in the end times.

With a collapse of the ecosystem upon us, this certainly seemed like the end times.

Then it appeared in the newspapers and online: tattoos of a little square symbol that could be varied by item, whether that item was a person or a product. The square was always made up of tiny black-and-white squares in a variable pattern, which was unique to each item it was assigned to. It was called a Quick Response Code (QRC).

Personal inking jobs were so commonly accepted that few questioned this.

It was touted as the epitome of convenience. Forgot your iPhone at home or in the car? Can't be bothered to get out of line and lose any time? No problem! Just wave your tattooed wrist at the scanner and you can I.D. yourself, buy something, whatever.

The only people who seemed have the sense to object to this madness were the few elderly Jews in the area who had survived Auschwitz and had unwillingly had numbers permanently inked into their forearms. Well, people who knew history were appalled too, but these Holocaust survivors had the most visceral reaction to this madness, and frankly, I agreed with them.

I hated the idea of tattoos anyway, and with this surveillance method added to it, it was the most unpalatable marketing idea that I had yet come across. When I saw the girl who worked as a personal trainer at the health club where I went for yoga classes, I almost immediately launched into a tirade against the QRC marks of the beast that was our surveillance state.

Her name was Lori, and she was used to me, and she knew what Asperger's was, so she wasn't put off. In fact, she had gotten married the previous spring and invited me and Hamish, so we were friends at this point. The reason I talked to her with such fiery outrage about this particular topic was that she liked tattoos. She had many of them, and all were beautiful.

She had a small honeybee on the side of her neck, and she kept her wavy brown hair cut to a chin-length to keep it visible. On her right bicep, soon to be filled in with purple, yellow, and green, was a huge iris. Peacock feathers in shades of blue, gold, green, and purple swirled down from it. On her other arm was a pretty quote in Sanskrit from the Hindu Ramayana.

Lori was a graphic designer, and drew beautifully. She had illustrated the cover of my bee book, in fact. All of her tattoos were her own work, transferred onto her body by the tattoo artist. She was always working on more. I teased her that she resembled *The Girl with the Dragon Tattoo* somewhat, a favorite Aspergirl book and movie character of mine.

Anyway, Lori listened politely to my rant and promised to just use her iPhone for any such purposes and to never get a QRC tattoo. She assured me that she understood why not, and thanked me for constantly keeping her informed of dangers that she would otherwise not have been aware of.

I sincerely hoped that she was taking me seriously, and not as some mad professor. After all, lots of Aspies got really worked up over whatever we were studying. People saw that and took it as eccentricity rather than something to take seriously, and this was very serious business.

Make no mistake: despite the appearance of a police state, what we were experiencing was even worse than that. It was actually a covert resource war, albeit a controlled one. Overt resource wars, as seen in conflict zones, are uncontrolled. They were chaos, and thus the exact opposite.

There was one other variety of a Mark of the Beast that galled me just as much: a new marketing campaign put forth by medical insurers of microchipping humans. It would start with elderly Alzheimer's patients, mentally retarded people, children, and soon spread to anyone with a criminal record. From there, it would ultimately infest the entire population. What an evil, slippery slope to go down.

Both examples of the Mark of the Beast amounted to a breach of privacy that also threatened the personal security of anyone with such a device implanted inside them or tattooed on! A thief could just kidnap any individual with access to whatever was coveted: a house, a vault, whatever. Or worse – a thief could rip off a body part to get access. I imagined people bleeding out, cursing themselves for ever having acquiesced to such idiocy.

The modern, high-tech Marks of the Beast looked an awful lot like a covert operation to me. They looked exactly as though the government hoped that, through corporations, it could gain access to data on the habits and movements of our very persons.

People were giving up the security and privacy of their own bodies with these tattoos and microchips. Forget the Fourth Amendment right to that, they seemed to unconsciously say – just take it, government, I don't mind! Sheeple. That's what you call a large group of compliant, non-self-aware people.

With a covert op disguised as a police state, it was possible for a government to control its population, lie to it, and maneuver it wherever it wants people to be and into doing whatever it wanted them to do. Fewer components of a society's infrastructure would get broken this way.

The only question was how long that could last before people caught on and figured that they had nothing to lose by fighting, at which point all bets would be off. I didn't see it happening just yet, and with these asinine tattoos, I doubted that it would until it was too late for a lot of people.

That made me angry, at the government and big corporations, but also at the sheeple.

My editorial had in fact been published in *The New York Times*, and the comments it had induced from the general public had indicated that people were anything but awake. Many agreed with me, but no one had the slightest inkling that collectivism was what was behind the communitarian suggestions in U.N. Agenda 21. People thought I was an alarmist.

It was extremely frustrating, to say the least.

My family told me that the responses were to be expected and not to worry about it.

My cousins and Claire, however, had read the books I had shown them and agreed with me.

That was something.

Ellie, who had not read that material, seemed blissfully unconcerned as usual.

True, she wasn't going to run out and get tattooed with a Quick Response Code, but she loved the convenience of her iPhone, and she enjoyed many of the group activities that led to large gatherings of crowds. These included rallies, marches, protests, and vigils.

I didn't see the point of participating in those when one could sign a petition.

Why get lost in a crowd? What did that really accomplish? The government would still do whatever it wished after all the noise that people made. It was legal documents that they had to receive and refusals to buy products that corporations pushed that mattered.

After all, it was corporations that now ran the government. They had bought it out by funding politicians' political campaigns. Once an election was over, those politicians were never allowed to forget how they either got their jobs or kept them thanks to the lobbyists that the corporations sent to hound them until they voted on whatever it was that the corporations wished.

Ellie called that a crazy conspiracy theory also.

She was certain that crowds at huge gatherings mattered to decision-makers.

Edgar finally just quietly told me to let her do what she wanted, but that he agreed with me.

That was something, even if it depressed me about the prospects of…sheeple.

Damn! Too many people – too great a percentage of us – were sheeple!

Chapter 16

Surveillance! Not if Hamish Can Help It

Some guy in a technician's outfit was at our door. It was mid-April, and a sunny weekday.

He was a tall, well-built guy, and he wore his sunglasses on the back of his neck. Something about that set off a warning in the back of my mind, but I couldn't remember right away why that concerned me.

I opened the front door and talked to him through the screen, keeping it locked. Out on the lawn, Ed the Blackout guy stood, paced up and down, watched, and listened.

This visitor wanted to come inside and check our equipment. What?! What for – check what?

I wondered how he had gotten past our Blackout Security guys, then decided that his story must have checked out with them. It was either that, or they figured that certain things were simply our problem to assess and deal with. Fair enough.

The technician explained that he was from the utility company, and that he had been sent to check our meter. It could not be disabled without an order from the utility, he added, so the company's computers had flagged our house when it mysteriously went offline several days earlier. He had been sent to check it out, and to make sure that our service continued.

Hamish had at last completed his solar panel nanite system, and both our house the guardhouse were officially off the utility company's electrical grid. We didn't need them. Consequently, I had been expecting a visit like this one. The new solar panel nanite system was self-maintaining, self-cleaning, and self-clearing of any precipitation. It was great. We could soak up a lot of energy that way. And Hamish had configured the amperage flow to give us plenty of juice for each appliance, either separately or with several going at once.

There was one other thing that we had done, but it was last year: we had remodeled the kitchen and bathrooms – every last one in the house. The reason was partly to make them all new and beautiful, as they had been getting old, but that was not all. We wanted water-saver, water-efficient sinks, toilets, showers, and tubs. It was beautiful now, with granite counters on all sinks and in the kitchen in pinks, whites, and mixes of charcoal. My parents liked it, too.

We would have preferred to get the water off the grid, but a well was not an easy thing to get in a long-developed area, and we had decided not to deal with a permitting process. We were stuck with water that tasted heavily chlorinated, and that Hamish fretted was fluoridated also. You couldn't beat everything in the system, it seemed, but there were filters on all of our faucets.

Hamish wasn't home at the time of this visit. I explained to the guy that we had gone off the grid and were powering our home with solar panels. (I didn't bother to get into detail, such as that those panels were spaced out in case of fire, to allow access to firefighters and water streams from fire hoses.) Also, I told him that Hamish had in fact disconnected the RFID meter and had it returned by the Blackout Security organization to the company with paperwork from our attorneys. The equipment was gone. Why didn't this technician's paperwork reflect that?

He didn't know, but insisted that company policy required him to personally inspect the premises and confirm that the equipment was or was not there. At last I recalled what was wrong with this picture. Sunglasses backwards on his neck… This guy was ex-military, perhaps Special Forces, or a Navy Seal! Why the hell did he want a tour, guided or not, of our home?

That's it – I wasn't letting him in. I told him he was not coming in, and to leave.

As I stood there, refusing him entry, a thing that was my legal right to do, he glanced at my whole body, looking me up and down. It wasn't flirtation, and there was nothing lascivious in his gaze. He was assessing me as a potential adversary.

I was dressed as usual, in comfortable clothing, with a pretty, raspberry pink shirt on (nothing hidden under there but my Victoria's Secret bra!), and loose, baggy, linen pants. The pockets were, as always, loaded. They contained my keys in the left one, and in the right one, folded tissues, my pocket watch, and something else. It was my nanite gun. That gun was so small that I doubted it showed, but it gave me a confidence that Blackout Ed alone could not.

Still, I wondered how this would have gone without Ed there.

In any case, the guy decided not to push his luck. He did try to shove a business card and a notice requiring compliance under the storm door, but I told him to just mail it to us, said good-bye, and shut the door. I looked out the window and saw Ed walk him to his van, which did look legit. It was painted with the logo of the utility company that we had just fired.

The nerve! Why not just let Big Brother come on in and wire up our whole house, complete with a television that has no off switch, just like in the world of *Max Headroom*, so that we could be watched constantly and never enjoy silence again thanks to endless white noise?!

It occurred to me that, not only are those who do not read history condemned to repeat it, but those who do not read literature are condemned to endure the tools of oppression described in it.

In this age of technocracy and shrinking personal privacy, it was sad to say that few people possessed the technical expertise that Hamish did with which to fight back. Count that as yet another reason why I was glad to have him for a husband, and proud of him. Hamish was able to actively fight to protect our family's Fourth Amendment rights.

Few people could, or even knew enough to do so. Too many people were so used to having their privacy eroded, attacked, and otherwise invaded to be motivated to resist. They had accepted it, and traded convenience for it.

The Fourth Amendment of the U.S. Constitution guaranteed Americans the right "to be secure in our persons, houses, papers, and effects, against unreasonable searches and seizures." That many of those paper and effects were now digital, and thus located in the creative cloud as well as in our personal computers, mattered not at all. Those things were ours. They were not for the nanny state or its minions to peruse at will. They were for us to conceal at will.

The same went for our homes. It was not for the government to foist a SmartMeter or other SmartTech onto us, claiming it as "necessary" in order to measure our energy use for billing purposes. There were less invasive, healthier ways to use energy and to measure it, and we had the right to insist upon them.

We did not have to accept SmartMeters, which emitted harmful radiation that disrupted REM sleep and could even cause cancer, enable utility companies to read them remotely, to manipulate those readings and thus overcharge, and to know when we use which appliances and in which rooms of our homes…and even to control our ability to do so by turning off the energy.

Hamish was incensed when he heard about that technician's visit, of course. He was also alarmed by the details I recounted, and agreed with my assessment about Special Forces training, though my method of drawing that conclusion amused him. The only trouble with it, he added, was that I was probably right, and that the utility company would not have sent such a person to check up on us. It had to be government surveillance, an attempt to gain access to us.

Lovely.

Meanwhile, my parents loved to acquire the latest and greatest technology and to keep our entire home up to date with it all. Even I liked that, although I felt no need to have one of every gadget known to humankind. I had pointed that out years ago.

"That's a relief," Hamish had remarked dryly.

He had just taken apart a new toaster that my mother had come home with, removed its RFID chip, and smashed it to smithereens with the meat tenderizer. My mother had no idea because he had waited until she and Dad had gone out for a long car ride and then done it. He melted the parts in basement lab after that, separating the materials for reuse later.

My genius husband was nothing if not efficient and eco-friendly. I had watched him do this, then dragged out the cappuccino machine. "Are you going to rip this apart, or can I make us a couple of hot drinks with nice, frothy milk on top?"

"Oh, I did that one when we got it as a wedding gift. You don't know how many of these devices I've taken apart since we got married," he said. He wasn't smiling, either.

This was why Hamish had gone on a rampage in our house, tearing its innards and appliances apart and rebuilding them. As soon as we had bought it from my parents, he had attacked them all. After that, he had turned his attention to the energy sources that powered our home, so that we would not need the utility company.

I looked forward to any showdown with the utility company and regulators, whom I fully expected to charge us a fee for living off the grid. The audacity of this idea alone was enough to infuriate me. They would actually seek to punish anyone who refused their services, even though those fees were illegal.

But before that could happen, we had a showdown with my parents that evening. They had decided to replace all four televisions in the house with large flatscreen ones, and had hired a technician to install them. Mostly, he was doing carpentry, mounting them on the walls.

Hamish came home as the devices came out of the boxes and had a fit. I just poured myself a glass of Merlot and watched it all unfold. He called Aaron in from the guardhouse, let him in, and told the technician to wait while he dealt with each TV. Then he went down to the basement, got his tools, and came back up to the living room.

The moment he popped the first TV's plastic housing open, my parents started screaming. "Hey," my mother yelled. "We just paid a lot of money for all of these things! What are you doing?! You're going to break them – they'll never work and we won't be able to get our money back under any warranty!"

"Oui – I mean yeah – STOP!" Dad chimed in.

"Nae, I shall not," said Hamish without missing a beat or getting upset.

I managed to gulp down the sip of wine I had just taken before he said that, and then started laughing. That was exactly, precisely, what he had said when I had asked him for help coming up with a name for Nae-Née, which had caused the name to just come to me. Cool memory!

"Avril, do something about your husband," my mother said.

"I have told you before that I can't control his actions, and I'm through working myself up by even feeling obligated to try. If what he's doing wrecks this equipment, we'll just give you the money, but I don't think it will go that way. Somehow, you realize that, so just wait."

They sat down on the sofa, looking really aggravated.

Hamish suddenly found the RFID chip in the TV – it was the biggest one, meant for the living room – and detached it. He pocketed it. "Got it. Now I'll reassemble this boob tube so that you can see that it's okay."

"How will we know that until we turn it on?" my mother said peevishly.

"You won't," Hamish and I said in unison. Aaron just stood in a corner, saying nothing.

The technician took the TV, plugged it in, put it through its paces with all sorts of start-up tests, and surprise! It worked perfectly, surveillance-free.

Hamish calmly moved on to the other TVs, all of which were a smaller size, and repeated this process. No need to bother with the DVD machines; he had gotten to those long ago, and no replacements were planned, fortunately.

"Why are you doing this? What are those?" my mother wanted to know.

"We'll tell you over dinner, when they're all installed," Hamish said, heading into the kitchen to get the meat tenderizer and the thick wooden chopping board for another smash-up.

Too slow…the technician informed them that my husband had just removed the RFID chips. They wanted to know what this was all about right now. My parents dragged me into the kitchen to get me to explain it, wine glass and all.

"Fine," I said. "Hamish doesn't want our every word eavesdropped upon and recorded remotely. That's what those TVs do: they listen to people. The N.S.A. accesses them remotely. Any attorney attempting to maintain privileged communications, or any doctor-patient or spousal privilege, is threatened by these things."

"So," Dad said, pausing as Hamish smashed the last chip and watching him work, "we have been invaded for years by these devices?"

"No, I said. "Hamish has been keeping up with them, taking apart and rebuilding every electronic device with the exception of our computers for years. No RFID chip lasts long in this house or in this family. This is just the first time you've been home when he did it."

My parents stared at me, exchanged glances, watched Hamish shove the microchip fragments into a ziplock bag, and then shook their heads.

"Can you imagine how much trouble it would have been this time for him to wait until the big TV was mounted on the wall, or all the smaller ones as well? Too much trouble. Better to just be an Aspie and make a scene with you guys shrieking, not understanding, and have to explain it all." They had to agree with that. It was a lot simpler that way.

"What about the cable company, though?" my mother wanted to know.

"I took the RFID chips out of their equipment, except for the router device, which is in the kitchen," Hamish told her. Then I put a scrambler next to it. It can only tell the cable company about what shows we watch and when, which is normal. And we have Ethernet for the Internet, so there is no RFID microwave damage being done to us."

Ethernet had certain advantages: it did not emit harmful radio-frequency radiation, and it was faster than wi-fi. It allowed a user to maintain security within one's own home. Any communication or net activity outside that home would not be secure because it required contact elsewhere. However, overlaying Ethernet with home security could prevent the surveillers from snooping inside your home. The security that Ethernet would be overlaid with had to be a customized alteration of all of your software, including your computer's operating system. Again, this was something that few people knew how to do, and Hamish was one of them.

Ethernet also had the added benefit of speed. We used to have wi-fi, but it was so slow that I would be in a rage part of the way through my work, much of which was online. "Hurry up!" I would yell at the computer, the Internet, and whatever else, furious. Hamish said that it was a corporate agenda to eat up as much of my time as possible, and everyone else's, so that we would not be able to focus on sending out our own content and thus use our own voices. No kidding. It was still slow on some sites!

As for all other appliances, if they still possessed their RFID chips, you could not prevent Big Brother from snooping, either through SmartMeters or those tattle-tale appliances, if you had any of those. That was why Hamish was vigilant about finding, extracting, and smashing the chips to bits, and why he had removed the SmartMeter from the side of the house.

Computers were about to switch over to the ultimate surveillance system, and Hamish was very upset about it. He had described how it would work. No longer could a user buy a computer with the capability of data storage. In the future, everything would operate exclusively through the creative cloud.

No more holding and controlling one's own data. No more saving on it. Your computer would become nothing but a terminal. The surveillers would hold all of your data in the creative cloud – photographs, written materials, whatever. This was not good news for my books, I had said. How was I supposed to write my stuff and protect it if it was out in the cloud before I chose to put it there?!

With that, Hamish had told me about the EFF – Electronic Frontier Foundation (https://www.eff.org/). It offered specialized technical and legal advice for computer users who objected to surveillance. He had contacted them for assistance, and I could get help from them as well in order to ease my mind about future writing projects and control and security over them.

But back to the TV installations…

"Yeah, Mommy, Hamish has all the angles covered, I said, grinning."

Dad grinned too. "Camille, it looks as though we're at the mercy of a polymath professor and her mad nanotexpert scientist husband."

"Looks like it," she agreed.

They didn't know the half of it; Hamish had worked on my cousin's cars, my aunt's and uncle's cars, and many devices in their home also. And…he had taught the guys and Claire all about it, explaining the reasons why, and dealt with their cars also. Now that they had read through a lot of the stuff I had shown them – my books from our trip, plus other research – they understood and took it all seriously. So much the better!

I had shown the stuff to Ellie also, but she wasn't interested. She would attend protests if it came to that, she told me in an offhand way. The trouble was, I believed her. She was just the sort of person to get lost in a crowd after the sheeple woke up and panicked. Well, that was a problem for later. Stopping her advance looked impossible, unlike with Claire and the others.

Back in the present, Dad poured glasses of wine for himself and my mother. Might as well relax! We all went back out to the living room to supervise the big TV's installation.

As I sat there with my family, watching the technician work, I thought about how it would feel to know that I was constantly being surveilled – watched! – and judged for potential law-breaking in my own home, not knowing what was and was not okay to do…or not do.

It must feel like a constant state of tension, perhaps with a stress headache that could morph into a migraine, I mused. One could never relax in a surveillance state. One would always be concerned about being interrupted from one's life, bothered, and perhaps even worse.

No thanks.

We were living in a cowardly new world with a new verb: "surveil".

One could be "surveilled" at every turn if one did not watch out for the damned watchers.

I was so glad that Hamish could thwart those efforts.

We would keep on doing so for as long as we possibly could.

That was our legal and moral right, thanks to the founders of the United States.

Damn anyone who might try to change that.

Chapter 17

Another Moving Experience

Also in April, Hamish wanted my help with a big logistical endeavor: another moving experience. He wanted to move his office out of Blue Back Square. As much as I hated moving, I approved of this.

I wanted him and his operations out of that Agenda 21 mini-surveillance community.

Accordingly, we hired a moving company, one that handled medical and nanobotic equipment as well as office supplies, and let Blackout Security vet it and every employee who would be assisting with this moving to the nth degree.

Aaron assured me that no unauthorized nanotech spyware, be it hardware or software or any combination of the two, would get past this process. Nothing would stow away for the ride or set up camp in the new office.

Good.

What about the employees? We had three in addition to our cousins, and we had to make sure that they didn't know too much about how security-conscious we were. We didn't want to alarm them while taking care not to let any RFID or other spyware hitch a ride in their purses. They all had iPhones, Droids, or some brand of Smart, hand-held communications device. They even played games on them during breaks, and stored family photographs on them.

Hamish and I were low-tech about that. We kept wallet photographs in little plastic sleeves that could be flipped through. We could take them out, show people our family, cats, wedding photographs, and put them back with the N.S.A. none the wiser.

Hamish had three office workers. He needed the help; he was seeing a few patients for a study on aging. They were all very nice women, all neurotypical, and happy working in the office. There was Ellen, Hamish's office nurse practitioner, Cara, the receptionist, and Leanne, the practice's insurance handler (health insurance companies kept her buried under lots of work).

Ellen was about thirty years old, newly engaged, and rather proud of her pretty new ring. It was three round stones, a diamond with two blue sapphires on either side, on platinum. The wedding was planned for late April of next year. She would be a beautiful bride. She had long, straight brown hair, usually in a ponytail. She liked to wear scrubs in fun patterns, and had been a qualified nurse practitioner for about 5 years. Hamish was satisfied with her knowledge and willingness to listen to patients and to his quirky, cryptic instructions and follow them.

Cara was the receptionist. Her nails were always perfect, and the latest color she had gotten her manicure in was a deep purple. She was in her mid-thirties, married to a trucker, and they had a son in junior high school in Newington. Her hair was chin-length, wavy, and highlighted in blond and brunette. She knew the office routines perfectly, and kept everything running smoothly. She had worked in a huge corporate office at Hartford Hospital before Hamish and I had hired her, and was glad to get away from both the traffic of the capital city and the ruthless policies of corporate practice.

Leanne was my age, and had over two decades worth of experience dealing with health insurance claims. She was a magician with getting claims accepted, always knowing just how to pitch them in order to get them paid. It was all about the patients to her, and about not bankrupting them. Most of the time, she won those claims, and her attitude toward big corporations was what I loved about her.

Leanne had dyed, dark brown hair, cut in a cute, naturally poufy do with sideways bangs and arcing to her chin. I had trouble believing that we were both 45. If I hadn't seen her driver's license when we hired her, I wouldn't have believed it.

When she found out my age, she flat out asked me about why I didn't look like her, with deep lines from frowning and smiling on my brow and elsewhere. I thought about that, and then realized, after observing her emote with pointless facial expressions while listening to me talk what the answer was.

It was about Asperger's – again! Since I had read about Aspies several years earlier, I had figured out many things about our brain stem type that intrigued me, and Hamish had been just as fascinated when I shared it with him. We were just a normal, minority model of human brain stem, and each one of us was different. If you've met one Aspie, you've met one. We can't be measured against one another, and I loved that.

Trying to sound tactful as I answered Leanne, I said that it was a difference between Aspie and neurotypical people. "We have flat affects and deadpan facial expressions. We feel overloads of empathy sometimes, which is why I could not do what you do," I added. "I would feel so upset about the plight of the patients that I would cry at the wrong moment, or go off on some tangent as I talked to them. And there's a tangent right there!" I said with a grin. "Anyway…with our deadpan facial expressions, I guess our skin doesn't get anywhere near the workout that NTs' skin does, hence the difference in wrinkles and lines on our faces."

Leanne had listened with a lot of brow-knitting facial expressions, and she suddenly laughed as she saw herself in the bathroom mirror. I did too. We happened to be chatting in the office's rest room. "Well, at least I get it now. Too bad I can't go back and undo all that."

"Oh, that would just cause you too much distraction, because it wouldn't come naturally," I said with a slight laugh at the idea. "Too much work, being so careful! We Aspies do laugh and cry, but for crying, we don't want our contorted faces to be seen, so we bury them in hugs or pillows or just turn away if none is available. Otherwise, we're masks of feigned equanimity."

"Why is that?" Leanne had asked.

"Bullies from childhood, in part, and the rest is just innate to us. I've been called creepy, but learned to own it and just give an evil grin. Being older helps, too, because you get more confident and don't care so much," I summed up, grinning. "Also, we Aspies never grow up."

Leanne smiled. "Well, this move seems to be shaping up nicely. I guess I'll go home now." She called her live-in boyfriend on her cell phone for a ride; her car was in the shop. Joe had been with her for about twenty years, and they had a house in Avon together. Leanne had been married to an awful, abusive spendthrift of a guy right out of college, and left him. She met Joe a year later, and they soon moved in together, but she was afraid to commit again. I hoped she would change her mind; Hamish and I had met Joe, a land surveyor, and he was a sweet guy.

It was early evening, and Hamish and I were staying late just so that I could put sticky labels on each and every drawer, box, and filing cabinet. When I was done with all that, we would go eat dinner at Grant's. I was looking forward to some truffle fries and a huge salad, plus some crème brulée. "Those things might not be available so much after a while," Hamish remarked. I told him that I knew that, which was why I wanted to eat those foods. I was following the British climatologist James Lovelock's philosophy, which was to enjoy life now, while I could, because after an ecosystem collapse, that wouldn't be possible anymore.

But back to the move: taking an idea from a long-ago college experience (summer and winter break, actually), I engineered the entire move, labeling everything in the office. When I was 20 years old, I had worked in the library of Dad's law firm and helped move the library to another Hartford skyscraper. Everything shelf had received labels that coordinated the old location with the new, and as a result, the move went off seamlessly.

The whole firm had moved into the new CityPlace building, which was still the tallest one in Hartford. At Christmastime, a wreath of red and green lights decorated its slanted rooftop on 2 sides, and we could see it from Avon Mountain and other high-up places. It was a beautiful place to relocate to, and remained so.

The library still had its forest-green-hued carpet and cherry wood paneling and bookcases. Sometimes, I would visit Dad and do research there just to admire it. It was either that or go to the UConn Law Library, which was also beautiful, like a gray Gothic mansion from a Poe story.

For this office move, I had ordered the renovation of the new place first, inventoried Hamish's equipment, records, files, and general use of space, and then planned its relocation accordingly. The labels I had prepared were all doubles; I had already affixed them to the new office, which was conveniently located in Avon, Connecticut, just upstairs from the health club where I attended yoga classes.

I later remarked to Hamish that this had been the most low-stress move I had ever been involved with, and that was a wonderful feeling. He had replied that money helped. He also remembered how anxious and stressed I had always gotten over transitions, especially if they involved moving and packing and unpacking. I would hyperventilate and sit down a lot.

The new office was great.

Chapter 18

Monsters, Microbes, and Regenics

Hamish was adamant that none of us get vaccinated for ANYTHING. Imagine that, a doctor who didn't want his family vaccinated. What was up with that? He made a big fuss about it, right after the office and lab move was completed. "Fine," I told him, "I won't get any more vaccinations. Just tell me soon what's going on."

He promised to do so…he just needed a few more days to get everything in order.

The next afternoon, I was out doing errands for a few hours while Hamish worked in his lab. I had visited Grandmère, and bought groceries and birthday cards to save for the next time I needed them. I liked to plan ahead rather than panic-shop.

While I had been out, Hamish had left me some text on Skype.

When I got back, this was what greeted me:

;((Crying Emoticon)
CANCER NEWS
*** Missed call from Hamish J. MacDonnell, Ph.D. ***
*** Missed call from Hamish J. MacDonnell, Ph.D. ***

I called him, convinced that someone we knew was imminently doomed to suffer a long, drawn-out, miserable death from the cursed vaccine culling campaign, and he sounded delighted to hear from me! What the hell?!

In his frustration at not reaching me instantly, he had completely forgotten that I was not sitting 24/7 in front of my computer. What I was seeing was aggravation at my temporary absence, then a hint of what he was working on, followed by some missed calls and a complaint.

I chewed him out. "I don't sit here every second and you know it! I have things to do!"

He realized how that looked and cracked up…at himself.

So much for drama. False alarm. "Insert uproariously laughing emoticon here," I said to myself, sending him one on the Skype chat. BAD Hamish. I got a grinning devil face back, followed by several hearts, Teddy Bears, and a couple of cats. Skype would show a cat washing its paws if a user typed an "@" in between a pair of parentheses, and we liked that.

He was calling because he wanted me to eat foods that contained laetril or amygdalin, such as millet and all kernels of fruit seeds, such as raspberries, blackberries, and strawberries. Why? To prevent cancer from ever taking hold of me.

Well, I was certainly covered, then, because I could never get enough of those. If I could not have raspberries several times a week, I felt like I was being punished. I reminded my husband of this fact, and he approved.

All organic, he reminded me, no soy lecithin, no high-fructose corn syrup!

"Yes, yes," I said, getting annoyed. "You know I hate that fake crap! Even though my mother keeps saying, 'well, it's your money,' like I'm wasting it, even though I know I'm not!"

"Good!" Hamish said. "Don't eat any of that, and don't let the rest of the family eat it."

"Okay. Hamish, you do realize that I studied this stuff on my own to write my honey bee colony collapse book, don't you?!"

"Yes, dear. I'm just checking," he said. I could almost see him grinning, damn it.

"Damn it, Hamish! Don't you remember me carrying on about initium, that crap that was bred into plants that were grown in Eastern Europe and elsewhere?! It's a fungicide that promotes faster plant growth. People who eat those plants thus have faster tumor growth! Insecticides are bred into plants that kill bees, and sprayed all over them. These neonicotinoids coat everything, and when eaten put more poisons into us. We're all eating cigarette chemicals if we eat those things. Are you convinced that I know this yet? That I only want organic foods and that I know why I want them?!"

"Yes, dear. I'll eat anything you put in front of me dear."

"Hmm…BAD Hamish, forgetting that I know what you know and agree with you."

"Yes, dear. I love you."

"I love you too. Bye."

That evening, a Monday, Hamish asked me to come down to the basement after dinner, to his lab there. We were sitting on the sofa together, relaxed, but having a lively conversation about subversion. We always enjoyed the mere idea of such a thing, let alone the real deal.

While humans had computer code, with algorithms that could manipulate virtual data in the creative cloud, Nature had wetware – real genetic code that wouldn't cease to exist if the power got turned off. It went on and on, replicating and mutating independent of conscious actions.

Humans could be brave, arrogant, or even evil enough to think that we could manipulate wetware, depending upon our objectives and the reasons behind those objectives. We were brave when it was about curing a disease so that people could live healthy, happy, productive lives. That's when we created vaccines that did no harm, containing no poisons.

Some humans were arrogant when it was about making money for an elite few first and foremost, no matter how careless they were with science, thus allowing patients to be harmed by toxins. We were evil when we deliberately added those toxins, or any other substance, for purposes of social control, thus taking choices away from others and doing permanent physical damage – damage that weakened those others.

Nature had no agenda but to go on, and favored no species over any other.

We humans were always determined to favor our own above all others, at any cost. The problem with that agenda was that it could cost us our existence, because we needed Nature and all that it provided for us. We might have science, but we must temper our agenda to keep it brave, work hard to not take short-cuts with it, and not use it to hurt anyone or anything.

This might leave us waiting a while for good vaccines – vaccines that wouldn't harm us. This might mean that some humans wouldn't survive to old age. No one survived life, after all. My husband understood this, but he reminded me that he had a laboratory and the know-how to filter vaccines, removing the additives that the anti-vaxxers objected to. He was all for vaccination as long as they really did nothing other than what they claimed to do.

We humans and our intellect had nothing on Nature. No matter what Hamish came up with, Nature would still kill us in the end. Hamish acknowledged that, but he still intended to delay that by quite a lot, and thus gain more time in which to have fun and to observe everything. He used what he knew to make this happen. He had a plan that he called Regenics.

His reasoning – one that I couldn't help but agree with – was that usually, by the time a human has earned enough money and achieved enough professionally to be content and feel independent, that human has aged to the point that her or his most physically comfortable and productive time is up. By then, it was too late to enjoy any of that. That really was a raw deal.

"Fine, Hamish – if you can change that for us without giving us a debilitating or terminal illness, go for it!" That was what I had told him when he first mentioned Regenics. I said it again now as he laid out his plan again.

He was going to try to extend the human lifespan by several centuries. "8 or 9 decades just isn't long enough to see and do everything, and I want more time with you," he informed me. "I've wanted to do this since I was 9 years old, and whenever I mentioned it, I have gotten either one or the other of two reactions."

"Oh? What are they?" I asked. This really did sound rather far-fetched.

"One reaction is that this is a cool idea. The other is that it goes against God, Nature, and whatever other higher authority they can suggest. I've actually had scientists say this to me, but I just don't care. I'm going to do it. I'll make the cats and your parents last, too."

He had been watching me listen to this, and when he mentioned them, I perked up. "Okay."

"But before I can do that, I must first repair the damage that the Farmers did to us."

"How?"

With that, he pulled out a nanite gun and said to me, "What about this nano-gun looks different to you from the one that I gave you, and from the any of the others that you've seen me use?" and he handed it to me.

I took it and turned it over and over, getting anxious. I hated to fail a test of observation. But…I saw nothing different. Finally, I handed it back and said, "Nothing."

"Very good! Nothing. That should make it easy for me to remove the nanites that I'm after. I have studied a blood sample from you, and some from your parents, and identified the 'additives' that the government has persuaded pharmaceutical giants to include in vaccines of all sorts. I have also studied the vaccines that were sent to me to administer to patients. The same evil, DNA-mutating nanobots have been added to all of those vaccines, and I have programmed several of these nano-guns to recognize and withdraw them."

"There are nanites in the vaccines?! What do they do?"

"They shut off your P53 proteins, which are cancer-tumor suppressors in your DNA."

"I know what P53s are, Hamish. It's not like I just met you," I said with a grin. "But how do the nanites do that?"

"They travel to your brain cells and alter their messenger RNA to respond to triggers."

"Triggers?" I knew Hamish was going slowly to pause for dramatic effect and thus teach me about this with maximum emotional impact. That method does work best, and tends to prevent forgetfulness. I used it myself.

"A trigger is a factor that, when combined with that damage, sets it off. No reaction unless and until that is done."

"And what examples of triggers should we be on the lookout for?"

"High-fructose corn syrup; chemicals in food containers, particularly metal cans; and anything with GMOs – genetically modified organisms – in the food itself. You studied all this when you did your bee book, so you know what they are. Messenger RNA carries this stuff around the body once it's introduced, replicating the damage, destroying the person who was injected with the original nanobots. These are soft-kills."

"Soft-kills?" I repeated, as a question. This was a new term to me.

"Yes."

"What would be a hard-kill, then?"

"A bullet, a noose, a broken neck, crushing…anything that causes immediate death."

I looked at him, considering that. "So, a soft-kill causes death later, like a murder that won't show up in an autopsy?"

Hamish grinned at me. "You're so quick," he said. "That's exactly what it is. The best way to explain this is to tell you that, normal, healthy, cells with normal DNA in them include cancer tumor suppressor genes, called P53. Those other vaccines contain something that both vaccinates as promised and shuts off those genes. Only a few companies make vaccines now – four, I think – which no doubt makes them easier to control."

"Don't those vaccine work?! Don't they do what they promise, and protect against the flu and MMR and whatever other illnesses they are advertised as protecting against?"

"Oh yes, of course they do, but that's not all that they do. These monster nanobots damage cell DNA, wait around until the trigger foods are eaten, and then they make sure that anyone who received the vaccination that carried them develops cancer. It's a population cull."

"What do they look like, and how do they do this?" I just had to ask.

"They have a six-legged, six-sided design. They have a tall head on top of the legs. Like a six-tentacled octopus, a drill comes out from between those legs and bores into DNA, tinkers with it, and withdraws. It disconnects the P53 proteins. My nanobots reconnect them. This six-legged monster is in all vaccines now, and has been for a while. That's why I don't want you to get any of those, and why I'm working so hard to remove these nano-monsters. What I would really like to see is the software in the next version of these monsters, version 666, as I like to call it. You know – the Devil's number." He grinned wryly…and mirthlessly.

"Are you telling me that the only vaccination sera available to the general public is this monster nanobot crap?! You mean I was right to think that not only is it impossible to promulgate the U.N. Agenda 21 policy for our entire species, but that there is an actual plan to solve that problem by getting rid of what the policy-makers deem to be an 'excess' of us?!"

"Well…yes. There are other sera out there for an elite few, but not many, and often, politicians in the know will simply forego a vaccination rather than get injected with a serum that is…infested with monster nanobots. They know it will just kill them later, so they opt out."

"And only four pharmaceutical companies make vaccines now?" I asked, incredulous. "That does make it easy. Those corporations have cornered the market! They can add whatever they want, whatever the government wants, and keep it a secret."

"Indeed. The situation of vaccine manufacturers, the FDA, and how and why things have become so complex and difficult that few are around today is a scary story. Smaller companies couldn't prosper with all of the regulations that the FDA piled on, so even though over a dozen companies were manufacturing childhood vaccines in the 1950s, by the 1980s, just about all of them had given up on it. They surrendered their licenses. Vaccines with licenses became an endangered species, further narrowing the market for just an elite few. Approximately 380 vaccines had FDA licenses in the1960s. Then in the 1980s there were 88, and by 2004, only a few dozen. Look at it this way: we went from having 26 companies making five important vaccines to only four were making any vaccines at all in the United States. Today, those four companies dominate the market for the entire planet."

I stared at him for a long moment, and he watched me.

"So you think that I have these monster nanobots in my system, and that's what you're working on undoing…turning my cancer tumor suppressor genes back on?"

"You bet."

"And you actually have a plan in mind for getting them out now? Will you get them out of my family too? And out of our friends? What does this have to do with Regenics?"

"Yes, yes, and it's prep work for Regenics. I have to do that first for Regenics to work."

"Wow. You're a genius and a mad scientist. If the corporations that make the soft-kills find out, there will be trouble. What will we tell patients, just the vaccine story, and not a word about the soft-kill?"

"Exactly." He showed me the vaccines that he had laid out on the table. "There is a plan being shared with physicians now – not with the general public – to require the entire nation to be vaccinated against 40-plus diseases. No opt-outs for religious or vegan or other reasons. Other nations are doing this also. It's global. Nothing has been announced yet. That would be okay if the vaccines really were just vaccines, and if they were being spaced out rather than hitting the human immune system all at once. That just crashes it."

He paused a moment, then went on. "Patients are going to have to be registered in a national database after having the vaccines. It's going to cause a tremendous amount of work and logistics, so some doctors have been pushing their patients to come in early to get vaccinated now. The data can already be entered. The database is set up, just not in the news yet. There's still time to space the vaccines out. But…that won't solve the monster nanobot problem."

"Somehow, I don't think that that will prevent you from solving it."

"No, it won't," my husband said to me with a grin. "I have been 'de-lousing' every vial of serum for every disease on the list, and I have received some of everything. That's why I wanted to see patients: to participate in this vaccine campaign. While I'm at it, once I've immunized a patient, if they want to participate in my clinical trial, they can get Regenics. That's ready also."

He showed me the nanite gun again. "Are you ready to start my secret program? I have to get your monster nanites out first, then vaccinate you slowly over the next few months with all these sera. But – and this is the good part – there's no need to wait for all of those injections to be complete before you can have the Regenics formula. I can give you that now, and keep going with the vaccinations."

"You can really turn the P53 proteins back on and affect our messenger RNA – edit DNA?"

"Aye. Exactly. Granted, this is ex post facto editing, not editing at the embryonic level, but it offers the same benefit. I've also removed the mercury 'stabilizer' from the sera." Hamish gave me a grim grin.

I paused for a moment, then said, "Gattaca, here we come. If it exists and people know about it, they will want it, and they will do it. Hey! Guanine Adenine Thymine Thymine Adenine Cytosine Adenine – G.A.T.T.A.C.A.!"

Hamish grinned. "You noticed that! Of course, you're a genius, so no surprise there."

"I should have noticed it when the movie was new – I made a model of DNA in my ninth-grade biology class a decade before it came out," I replied.

"Good enough," he retorted.

"So you plan to remove the evil nanobots from my bloodstream and whatever cells are affected and infested, somehow repair that damage, start to vaccinate me properly, with sera that lack noxious ingredients such as mercury and more damned nanobots, register it in an as-yet secret database, and then add the Regenics treatment to my bloodstream?"

"Aye. I will have to extract the bad nanobots and use good ones to repair the damage. Regenics will finish the job by making your system repair itself for far longer than it would otherwise do so." He was standing closer to me than the doctor-patient relationship would normally allow, and smiling.

"Cool. Go for it."

With that, I pulled me over to him, held the nano-gun up to my temple, and hit the 'withdraw' button. I felt nothing, but of course something was happening. No one holds a device up to and presses buttons without something happening. After a moment of watching the display on its side, he turned it to neutral and lowered it to his lap to look at it.

"Come over here, Avril," he said, going to a machine on a counter at the back of the room. It was both a receptacle and analyzer, designed by Hamish himself. He held the gun to the aperture in the front, hit the firing button, and waited. A moment later, he put it back into neutral. The aperture closed automatically, with a suction mechanism keeping all of the nanites inside.

Next, he activated the view screen, which magnified the nanobots gazillions of times – with a high enough resolution to make them visible to the naked human eye. Sure enough, they had six sides and six legs, and seemed to be running around, like the evil aliens that had sought to parasitize the Earth in *The War of the Worlds*. But they had nothing to work with, and soon stopped. They weren't broken, though. They were just suddenly jobless.

"That's what was wrecking my DNA?" I asked, angry. "Some health system. Forget the Hippocratic Oath – it broke it deliberately. All that screaming and yelling over abortion and birth control, and this was going on. Delayed murder, that's what this is."

"Indeed. Now hold still; I'm not done with you yet. I still have to fix you." With that, my husband held another nano-gun to my temple. I was allowing my husband to shoot me in the head with nano-guns, feeling total trust in him, absolutely calm. He pulled the trigger, and presumably let other nanites into my body.

"Will you be showing me what these nanites are like, too?" I wanted to know.

Hamish smiled, gave me a long kiss and a hug, and then said, "Yes." He hugged me again.

"Is it already working? Is that why you're suddenly so happy?"

"Yes." He didn't let me go for a while.

This was fun. I hugged back. "I want more hugs later," I told him.

He pulled back and kissed me. "You don't have to wait," he said, and locked the door.

A little while later, we got up, and Hamish showed me the nanites that he had put into me. They were eight-sided, and thus easy to distinguish from the evil nano-bots. Instead of a needle, they had ends that hooked ever so slightly.

Hamish also wanted some of my blood. He extracted some as he explained what he was doing. Then he loaded up the computer with several things to show me. There were videos and still shots of my blood, both before and after the evil nanobots had been inside me, plus more of how it looked with the good ones in service.

"The reason I didn't show you this right away was that the nanobots need at least a half hour in your system to have a noticeable effect. There are tiny cameras that will transmit a view of the changes to your brain cells, and I have had those watching all along."

I tuned in to watch the show. Yes, my brain cells definitely looked different already. Hamish showed me an image of a normal P53 gene first, then the before and after views of my own. Actually, my 'before' was after the evil nanobot had messed with it, so my 'after' showed that the damage had begun to be repaired. That show wasn't even over yet, but Hamish told me that it was rapidly being repeated in each cell. Cool!

"My hero!" I said. "I'm not going to leave you alone when we go upstairs, you know."

My husband grinned at me, and then said, "Tomorrow, we will fix your parents. Dinner is at Aunt Zoe and Uncle Charlie's place, so we'll likely be able to fix everyone there, too. Meanwhile, I have one more thing to add."

With that, he picked up a small vial. It was large, it contained a pale violet fluid, and it had a long needle with a plunger looped on either side. Oh, great, I thought. Needles…I hate needles.

"Ugh," I said glumly.

My husband smiled, swabbed my arm, and then did it again. "This will numb the area."

"What's that, an injection? It has been years since I was vaccinated."

"Aye. This one is for Regenics. That's this thousand-year-plan of mine."

"How does it work? Is it more nanites?"

"Part nanites and part serum," Hamish answered. "What it does is it instructs and assists your cells – again via messenger RNA – to replicate better and longer. The human body replaces every cell in it at least 51 times over the course of its lifespan. This combination will make it work a thousand times more. It will cause the cell replacement process to be with youthful, healthy cells rather than slightly less-so ones for far longer than otherwise expected."

Hamish also held up another one. "You're going to inject me more than once?"

"No – one for each of us," he said. "I've had these ready since last night. I didn't take mine without you, because I wanted to do it with you. Are you ready to live a thousand years?"

I must have looked a bit skeptical. "I guess. Who knows for sure how long any of us will live, though? The exact number of years, barring death by accident, cannot be known, can it?"

"Well, no, but I want you with me, and this will increase our time exponentially."

"Okay then, go for it."

"Wow. You're going to put those anti-aging cream manufacturers out of business."

He laughed. "Well, you'll still want to avoid dry skin, so I won't tell you to stop buying creams from L'Occitane. The ones that are sold there have no soft-kills – I've checked the labels on them. You also just happen to dislike junk foods and GMOs, which is a relief, so you never did that much damage to your cells with food or cosmetics. The Farmers would have been waiting a long time for you to actually ingest any trigger soft-kill foods with your organic diet."

He looked rather pleased with me and with that situation.

"*Star Trek*, here we come. I just hope that the planet is in good enough shape to enjoy it."

He sobered up a bit at that. "We'll find out, won't we?"

I smiled. "I suppose we will. I totally trust you, anyway."

He kissed me. "Next up, your first untainted vaccine. Ready?" With that, he showed me another vial. It had green stuff in it, and after I had gotten a good look at it, he loaded it into the injection syringe, replacing the needle and tossing the first one into the sterilizer.

"So that pale green fluid protects against MMR?" I asked.

Hamish smiled. "Nae – this one is just for the measles. Whenever I vaccinate someone, I space the injections for each disease out, a week apart. It's not good to crash the immune system even with 3 vaccines. It's been long enough since you had the MMR formula that you can have another vaccine for any one of those, and I have prepared different formulations for each disease. Each formulation will both vaccinate against whatever disease it targets without tampering with your P53 proteins. This is the one part of the op that works without nanites."

"What colors are the other ones, and will you be injecting me with those at some point?"

Hamish smiled. "Yes, all forty on the list, but these are just the first few. Every few days for the next few months I will do this until you have them all. These are just a few, which I will show you now and inject over the next few weeks. I keep bringing them home, enough for the whole family, including the extended, nearby family that includes Grandmère and Claire."

He showed me a few more vials, which he was saving for later.

"There is pale blue for mumps, yellow for rubella, red for smallpox, clear with a tinge of gray for polio, and clear for the flu. The flu is the most common kill-shot; just look at all of the TV ads for it, encouraging elderly people to go to their local pharmacies for it without even having to wait for an office appointment."

"Why the pressure…" Never mind. I got it. Nae-Née wasn't enough to reduce human overpopulation, of course. "So all those people who won't get their kids vaccinated because they think something awful is in the vaccines produced by big pharmaceutical companies are right. But…it isn't what they think, is it? It was never autism, which is genetic anyway. It's a soft-kill hidden in what is advertised as a life-saving serum."

"Exactly."

"Perfect," I said, feeling angry and resentful at the treachery of the government and corporations. "Spike the vaccines with something that shuts off cancer tumor suppressor genes, wait for people to be unwilling to take these tainted sera, then blame them when they get the illness that the vaccines were supposed to target. Vaccines do not cause autism, but if tampered with, they are great delivery devices for other horrible problems that people just find completely unacceptable…cancer being at the top of the list for most of us."

"We have to be very careful with this," Hamish cautioned me.

"But how do we, as awkward Aspies, persuade our families and friends to let you inject them with your formulations? I want those people alive." I glared into space, angry.

Hamish just looked at me for a few moments.

"Well?! How?!"

"Covertly and quietly," he replied.

"But you're going straight to the human phase of this without further ado? It's so fast."

"Well…not quite."

"What do you mean? Have you been using yourself as a guinea pig?"

"Yes…and some Blackout Security people who were injected against their will with the tainted stuff and whatever else when they were still in the military. Their trust in their government is shot to hell, so they wanted to gamble. They figured that they were doomed if they didn't try it and had something to gain if they did, so they volunteered. One of the perks of working for us," he summed up.

"Great…so that means that we have likely already been injected with those evil nanobots when we got vaccinated at various times in the past. I had to get the MMR vaccine before I could matriculate in law school, so that must be how I got this kill-shot…this soft-kill."

"Definitely. I got them when I was in the military, plus some other mysterious rubbish, but I've managed to decode it since then and get it out. Military personnel have no choice in the matter of vaccinations. Soon no one else will. But, now whoever we can share this with need not fear it. I've found a way to get rid of those evil nanobots AND reverse that damage with my own nanobots. The Blackout guys have made enthusiastic volunteers, I can tell you that."

"Are your Blackout colleagues okay?" I hated to think that these human guinea pigs were doomed for certain, having come so close to saving themselves from whatever vile experiment that the government had inflicted on Gulf War troops.

Hamish smiled. "Aye, they're fine. One of them did show some signs of a trigger interaction, which was what got the Blackout guys started with this. I had to rush to get the monster nanobots out of him, but he's fine now. That's what led to him volunteering to be a guinea pig. I promised them all a treatment to counteract the cull nanites – which is what they really are – and the Regenics formula when it was sorted out. I've delivered on the first part of that promise already. So at least their health has been restored to what it should have been to begin with."

"Was it Ed? He eats a lot of junk – like fast food."

Hamish rolled his eyes. "Nothing gets past you. Yes, it was Ed. He ate the triggers, and the evil nanobots in his system were activated. He started to get sick, but I stopped it."

With that, he gave me my first, untainted vaccination – the green one, for measles – and accessed the government database to register it on his laptop. Right after that, he injected himself with a dose also, repeating the data entry routine on the website. It looked like any other government database, but then, I had seen a lot of these things. Not much that was in writing intimidated me. It was run by the Department of Demographics, I noticed, not the Department of Health and Human Services.

"Interesting, which governmental unit is running this," I remarked.

"Indeed," Hamish replied. "Most people will likely overlook that. Meanwhile, me giving you your vaccines at home will seem perfectly normal, even from a computer at home. Physicians inoculating their own family members is not a new idea."

"Cool. Now let's go upstairs. I'm not done with you. Tomorrow, you can repair and re-engineer everyone else in this family, and maybe the cats too. But for now, you're all mine," I said, tugging on my husband.

He followed me upstairs, grinning from ear to ear.

The next day, Hamish carried out his plan to fix my parents.

We had everyone come over to eat dinner at our house, and Hamish fixed Uncle Charlie, Aunt Zoe, Grandmère, Edgar, Ellie, Fabian, Claire, and Jacques. He removed the evil nanobots, injected his own, withdrew them, explained with his before-and-after presentation for each of them, and then added Regenics formula in yet more of his nanites. He carried this procedure out upstairs, in the living room, using the big flatscreen television to show each patient's repair.

It occurred to me to ask whether or not our physical appearances would change after being affected by Regenics, and if so, how and how much. Let's face it, I was hoping to get rid of the white hairs I was starting to sprout. Hair dyes were no good – full of poisonous chemicals. Plus, they made your hair all one color instead of the natural three colors that undyed, not-graying hair had. I had had some coppery highlights in mine, inherited from my mother, and hoped they would recover.

"Oh yeah," Hamish assured me. "They will be back. I remember those!" He grinned. "You'll feel better, your bone density will increase, your cartilage will get more padding, your skin more elasticity, and even the dentin in your teeth will build back up. Don't panic if you lose a filling. These nanobots will build the missing dentin back up."

"That's going to freak out my dentist," I commented. "Should I change dentists to conceal this, or let the one I go to know what's happening when it does?"

"Change dentists. We're circumventing a lot of things with Regenics: aging, disease, population culls, soft-kills, you name it. I don't think I can even publish and patent this stuff for a while, if ever in the foreseeable future."

The family was fascinated by all this, and even Ellie seemed to know enough to keep quiet about this. She thanked Hamish for including her in this rare opportunity to reverse the aging process, and for teaching her that the vaccines that the government wanted everyone to get really were dangerous.

"Now you know how it feels to know something without being able to explain it to other people in a way that they would find convincing. Seeing really is believing, but the people you talk to can't see all this. If you try to explain this without a video presentation by a nanobotic engineer and physician, they won't believe you," I cautioned her.

"I understand," Ellie told me. "I won't do anything other than send people to see Hamish."

"Good."

Ellie had been an anti-vaxxer before this, but Hamish had convinced her that vaccinations could be acceptable if untainted. As for my part of the presentation, it was the legal aspect of the problem that I presented. Everyone now understood that vaccinations were in their near futures, and that it was better with Hamish's method than with the government one.

They also understood the need for secrecy. It felt strange, having such a huge secret. The best way to keep it seemed to be to forget to talk about it most of the time. Out of sight, out of mind; with the deed done and the needles and nano-guns put away, I could do that. At least, I could until it was time to subtly invite friends and other people into Hamish's office as his patients.

The best way, we all decided, to do that would be to casually invite them to avoid long lines, a rush from people who had delayed dealing with this, and to participate in the clinical trial if they wished. Yes, that would work.

I knew that Hamish was just getting started. He planned to do this for our friends, any employees we had at his office, and any patients he could invite into it. Unfortunately, this would not protect very many people. If the government were to go ahead with its mass vaccination plan, a lot of what Hamish had just done would be undone.

Unconcerned – and I knew that that was because he had accepted that – my husband repeated his efforts that evening with Spock and Eowyn in the basement, after filing away all of the family's medical data. The most difficult part of that last process was catching both cats.

Once we had coaxed them into the lab, we shut the door. They weren't usually allowed in here, so they sat and stared until I picked one up, cuddling and sweet-talking. They just purred in my arms as Hamish worked on each one…until the Regenics injections. Oh well!

"Hamish, can we really share it with whatever people we can invite, to fight the cull?"

He looked at me. "Yes. We ought to fight and not just save our own hides."

I grinned. "Good. We may have to watch out for hard-kills and dodge a few, but we don't deserve Regenics without sharing. Selfishness is evil. It's what we're fighting even at this early phase, as we protect ourselves."

A few evenings later, I went down to the basement lab to see my husband again.

"So, you are going to edit more DNA?" I asked him.

He turned back to the counter and picked up a syringe. "Nae – that's all done. It's time to continue your vaccinations, so that I can report them all to the government database. I want to get yours and the family's all done while it's still a voluntary process. Right now, every citizen can get their vaccinations done in doctors' offices or pharmacies, but just wait. Soon it won't be voluntary, and I intend to get the jump on that process and preempt it."

He loaded a pale blue vial of serum into the injector. "Hold out your arm," he instructed.

After pulling up my left sleeve, I did.

He swabbed a spot on my bicep with an alcohol-soaked cotton ball, numbed it, and injected me with the syringe. It stung of course, but he was careful not to jab me, and he depressed the plunger slowly, so as not to overwhelm the tissue. Doing that would make it really hurt.

"So…what was that that you just gave me?"

"A mumps vaccine. One with no nanites, no P53 shut-off crap, and no poisons."

"I didn't ask you this before: how did you get it?"

"Actually, I got the same soft-kill version that all physicians are sent from big pharmaceutical corporations. But I have my equipment, so I just removed all that nano-crap." He was grinning, and looking quite pleased with himself to say the least.

"Cool. You're a genius. You're my hero. You're hot."

He looked up at me hopefully at that last comment.

"Yeah, Hamish. Brains are hot. Brawn…just somewhat hot. Hair helps too, of course, and you have a full head of that. Face it, you've just got everything going for you." I grinned. "What? I can flirt with my husband if I want!"

We both laughed.

Then Hamish sobered up. "That's just the second of forty shots I have to give you," he said. "I already have most of the vaccines, and have been spending my time here removing the 'crap' as we called it. The next one will be for rubella, then mumps, then a flu shot, and so on, until finally – get ready for it – Ebola. That one should arrive in 2 weeks, which will give me time to remove any questionable additives."

"How the hell are you going to get the crap out of the Ebola one safely?!" I asked, shocked.

"I will put the dose under a nanoscope before the fact to see whether or not the monster nanobots are even in there. Actually, I doubt any will be. Even the pharmaceutical corporations aren't stupid enough to fool around with that one. This is supposed to be a cull, not an automatic species extinction event."

"I see." We paused to think about all this, and then I spoke again. "What next?"

"The new national database that the Department of Demographics is requiring all physicians to use will soon be made public. Soon hospitals and other places will be vaccinating the entire human population of the United States, likely with an all-in-one shot."

"And all of those doses will include those monster nano-bots, especially for crowds."

"You bet." He looked grim.

"So…how long before the family is fully vaccinated your way, and thus gets the jump of this Final Solution process? I want it pre-empted yesterday, of course."

"Another couple of months, but my sources tell me that's enough time. It won't be long."

Chapter 19

Endemic, Epidemic, Pandemic

When I had explained the law and history of vaccines and plagues to my family, Claire, and Ellie, I could see them settle in for a mini-lecture by Professor Châtelet. But not doing that seemed dangerous – to them. Ignorance can hurt you. So, I tried to be as succinct as possible while also being comprehensive. When it was over, they assured me that the presentation was fine. They weren't bored by what I had to tell them, that was for sure. I think I scared them.

The only difficulty was with Uncle Charlie, who wanted to escape, but fortunately, my parents had heard and seen enough already when Hamish had treated them, and Dad spoke up. "Charles, you don't realize just how much trouble – how much danger – we are all in. Listen."

With that, he sat down and settled in for the lecture.

Everyone had listened both with some alarm and some fascination as I gave them a crash course in why Hamish was in such a hurry to vaccinate them himself. When they had heard the whole thing, a presentation that I supplemented by passing around more of my books from graduate and law school, they understood what was involved.

"It's like an in-depth look at the movies *Outbreak* and *Contagion*," my mother said.

This is what I told them:

To say that something in the ecosystem is endemic means that it is native to particular geographic location, usually a precisely defined one. This particular thing can be an island, a climate, a tropical zone, or habitat. This something can be a plant, animal, insect, or microbe. (Endemic is not the same thing as being indigenous. An organism that is found elsewhere can be indigenous to one or more places; endemic is just about one place.)

A virus that has evolved in one geographic habitat and one only is endemic.

It is common knowledge that a virus is a microbe that causes disease.

An epidemic is the rapid spread of an endemic virus or disease to large numbers of people in a very short time, typically two weeks or less. This starts at a Ground Zero, among a host population. A disruption of their ecosystem tends to be what sets it off. A change in what humans come into contact with, a last-straw of a stressor on their habitat, causes a Patient Zero to exist and to pass the virus on to others.

A pandemic is an epidemic that has spread to other geographic areas. It earns this name if the epidemic spreads to just one other area, which it does via human travel, shipping of goods, living creatures, or even plants with insects, to name just a few examples. A pandemic can spread to various towns, cities, nations, continents, and even go planetwide.

The news was full of stories about Ebola and its evil cousins, Marburg virus and Ravn virus. Both were grown in the jungles of Africa, and as humans encroached further and further into animal territory and ate whatever creatures they found there, they got sick.

Ever hear the term "bat-shit crazy"? This is where it came from. Egyptian fruit-bats were the carriers for these diseases. As they flew around from place to place, they shat, and the disease was in their excrement. When humans came along and bumped into cave walls or stepped on it barefoot, they picked it up. They would also catch, kill, and eat bats. Big mistake!

Other primates besides humans could contract these horrible viruses, too. Unfortunately, with the human population so dense in Africa (just like everywhere else), people were hungry without being too fussy about what they ate. Some would even take home, cook, and eat the bodies of dead primates that they found lying in the jungle, never bothering to consider how they had died. It turned out that they had died of Ebola or Marburg. That, of course, was a big mistake.

Soon a disease that was endemic to the area became an epidemic. Death rituals helped to spread Ebola around. Relatives and friends would touch the corpses of Ebola dead, washing and dressing them before burial, so that the bodies could be viewed by mourners in an open casket. The mourners would touch the bodies, adding to the contagion. After that, as foreign doctors tried to help, contracted the disease, and got shipped home to Europe and the United States for treatment in isolation, the disease became pandemic.

Plus, some African people with relatives living abroad traveled in violation of travel bans from their areas, heedless of the risk to others. It was all about them. They wanted a chance at recovery after certain exposure, so they lied and headed away from home, where hospitals offered nothing in the early phases of the plague but certain death. Some lived, but most died…whether they stayed home and followed the rules or left home, breaking them.

Bubonic plague was another monster waiting to resurface, still alive and well in Madagascar. In 1348, there had been a terrible outbreak of that plague in Europe. Giovanni Boccaccio's *The Decameron* took place during that outbreak, on the outskirts of Florence, Italy. A group of young people, 3 men and 7 women, waited the plague out in a secluded villa that afforded a lovely view of the city, telling stories until it was all over.

That plague killed approximately 75 million to 200 million humans over the course of just several years. The total human population of the planet was only 450 million at that time, so just think about that. Nature's very own population cull was inflicted on us by our own prejudices, ignorance, and sheer stupidity.

What did humans do to spread it around? They killed cats. The bubonic plague was carried in fleas on rats and gerbils. It had come to Europe from Asia via the Silk Road and on merchants' ships. Cats killed rats if left alone. But, the Catholic Church wanted to stamp out all traces of the Nature-worshipping, goddess-revering religion that had preceded it, now called Wicca.

Elderly Wiccan widows with pet cats talked of Mother Earth, gathered herbs, and brewed medicines from them, having been passed ancient knowledge from their foremothers. They were also midwives. The Burning Times ensued, during which traveling terrorists known as mendicant priests visited as much of Europe as they could reach, and left one woman alive in every village. Cats were killed too, as the "familiars" with whom the so-called witches conspired against the church, particularly black cats.

It was all nonsense, but it stamped out the religious competition. It also cut down on Nature's main check against the bubonic plague. Skulls and bones filled catacombs underground in European cities as huge urban areas became infested with plague, and children created a horrifying nursery rhyme to sing:

Ring around the rosy,
A pock a-full of posy,
Ashes! Ashes!
We all fall down!

A ring of swollen tissue around a reddish pustule which was a pocket full of infectious, disease-spreading crap was how the plague manifested itself. As the dead bodies were removed, people covered their faces and wore bunches of herbs tied in front of their masks to deal with the stench of the rotting corpses. But just touching or breathing anywhere near them could infect a person with plague. As the priest was administering last rites, people could fall deathly ill.

If anyone thought that those days were all over, they were wrong. This brings us back to Madagascar, a large island off the east coast of southern Africa. If anyone thought that Madagascar was just a distant place that the rest of the world had no contact with, they should think again. Madagascar grew vanilla, the third most expensive spice on the planet, and a highly sought-after one. It also had lots of rosewood which, though scarce, was a prized, beautiful kind.

People went all over the planet. Old diseases and new were not conquered.

Well, maybe smallpox was. The last naturally-occurring case had been chased down and dealt with in Bangladesh in 1975, with a little girl named Rahima Banu. That disease had been the one responsible for the law that the United States government would now use to force each and every citizen to accept its vaccines. Judge-made law was being revived and aired out. Just to review, it was *Jacobson v. Massachusetts*, 197 U.S. 11 (1905). Jacobson lost.

There were plenty of ways to share a disease. Shaking hands was an ancient way of showing strangers that you weren't carrying a weapon. Disease could spread in other ways than by eating the wrong food or touching bat shit. Coughing and sneezing all over the place, touching a sweating patient, being a caregiver without the proper environmental suit, such as the flimsy ones we saw on television that left parts of the face exposed, could do it too.

People have always tended to insist upon following their cultural death rituals even in times of plague. This only spread the disease further. Not only would mourners and morticians touch corpses, but burial had its own hazards, such as decay and leeching into groundwater through soil. Just think of cholera in China, where people used to insist upon burials close to waterways. Forget it. Just cremate.

History was full of examples of diseases that had decimated human populations.

In the Antonine Plague of 165-180 C.E., the Romans returning from the Near East had brought both smallpox and measles with them. 50 to 100 million people – 3 to 5 percent of the planet's population in 1918 – died of the Spanish Influenza.

Polio, Bird and Swine Flu, the H1N1 virus, the H2N3 virus, and others filled out the list, which went on and on, right up to the present, and it was a myth that it would ever just stop. Plague had been used in biological warfare, too, by tossing the corpses of plague victims over city walls.

Now Congress was preparing a vaccine bill make it a federal offense to refuse vaccination against any disease that the Department of Health and Human Services declared to be a threat to public health, and the president intended to sign it into law. It would be one of his last acts before his two terms were up. The Model State Emergency Health Powers Act of 2001 enabled all this, but it had never been signed into law. Now it would be. It would be the act of 2016, it seemed.

The American people were going to get the soft-kill vaccines, and be set up for a cull. They didn't even know yet that there really was something wrong with the vaccines that were being doled out. For years, they had been touting nonsense that vaccines caused autism, which it didn't. That was nothing but parents laboring under wishful thinking and blame assignments. But stabilizers such as mercury in the sera and nanites with P53 protein shut-off programming – that was real, and it was coming.

The United States government wasn't the one only with such plans. Nations all over the world also intended to use this crap to cull their human populations. This was the apocalypse: a combination of an ecosystem collapse as floods shrank available land, and a massive species die-off ensuing while a self-inflicted holocaust on our own species, one of epic proportion, one that eclipsed Hitler's efforts, reduced the numbers of humans on the Earth.

There were health and biological research agencies everywhere to assist with this, in the most covert and shocking violation of patient trust imaginable. I thought of them as health management agencies rather than research and disease control ones. This list included many of them, and though not comprehensive, it showed the scope of coverage around the globe:

1. United States Army Medical Research Institute of Infectious Diseases (USAMRIID)
2. Centers for Disease Control and Prevention (CDC) – United States
3. Médicins Sans Frontiers (MSF) – France
4. World Health Organization (WHO) – Switzerland
5. Institut de Veille Sanitaire (Sanitary Surveillance Institute) – France
6. European Centre for Disease Prevention and Control (ECDC) – Europe
7. Public Health Agency of Canada (PHAC)
8. Health Protection Agency (HPA) Britain
9. Agência Nacional de Vigilância Sanitária/National Health Surveillance Agency (ANVISA) – in Brazil
10. Chinese Center for Disease Control and Prevention (CCDC)
11. Centre for Health Protection (CHP) – Hong Kong
12. National Centre for Disease Control (NCDC) – India

That list reminded me that the world's elite had an infrastructure in place with which to control diseases, health, and antidotes. No system was foolproof, but the leaders had a plan, whereas the general public was at their mercy. Too few of us had any weapons of our own.

Mississippi and West Virginia vaccination law had already been cited by the United States Supreme Court in a special opinion, solicited by the U.S. Attorney General. In it, the Court said, "Religious exemptions to vaccination requirements violated the equal protection guarantees granted by the 14th Amendment of the U.S. Constitution. While some had freedom of religion, others had the right to freedom from it, and one could not be allowed to impinge upon the other. Thus, such exemptions were null and void."

When this explanation was complete, Hamish had proceeded to extract the monster nanobots from everyone's system and present his before-and-after show of bloodstreams and brain cells. It was a shock to see that they were really and truly there, but they were. It also changed my family's perception of us both. They took us seriously, with no more talk of conspiracy theories.

Sure enough, not long after Hamish had cleared the monster nanobots from my family's bloodstreams and brain cells and whatever else, the government began to show signs of prepping for a major change in its vaccine policy. State governors had the power to mandate vaccinations for the general public as well as for all healthcare workers during a public health emergency or disease outbreak. The President of the United States had called an emergency meeting of all governors at Camp David, and the media was not invited.

Protests were held around the nation, but they accomplished nothing. Ellie missed them.

When it was over, the governors returned to their home states and each called a press conference. They announced that compulsory vaccinations would take place as soon as the vaccine sera could be shipped to hospitals, schools, and other places. Anyone who refused the vaccine would be quarantined until either proof of vaccination by a physician was presented or state police could bring that individual to a vaccine center, at which time he or she would be forced to accept a shot.

Great. The government wanted those vaccines in our systems…badly.

Chapter 20

The Deep Dark Net

If the government was actually planning a cull, I wanted to do some cyber-snooping.

We needed a hacker. And a burner computer. And access to the Deep, Dark, Net.

The World Wide Web was not what it seemed to be to most users.

To understand what it actually was, it helped to know that the Internet, as known by most people, was only the surface of an ocean of websites and data. Using any one of several search engines commonly known to the general public meant that a user was accessing just a fraction of all that existed within it. They were accessing the Surface Net.

The Deep Net was quite possibly more than 550 times larger than the surface web, and constantly growing. It was growing so much that it could not be quantified. Most of it was nothing nefarious, but some of it was, and law enforcement agencies wanted it regulated. But the internet couldn't be regulated, so they had to content themselves with the fact that the deep net was inaccessible without special software to find those other websites.

The Dark Net was something different altogether. The Dark Net consisted of databases and network hosts that were separate from the internet. This sounded innocuous enough, because most of the entities which had such networks were universities, colleges, scientific institutions, think tanks, and others. They weren't criminal enterprises, just knowledge bases. Oh wait...there were also corporations, which often committed acts that were legal, but a simple look from an ethical point of view showed that they were really criminal ones.

The point of this exercise was to be able to see all of that, and to take a virtual tour of the world. We wanted to see what we were not being shown, find out how we were being lied to (either by omission or design), and about what.

With access to those combined, we would be able to see what the N.S.A. could see.

Hamish got that taken care of. Blackout and Hamish were their own surveillance team.

After that...I began to see things.

I began to see things that I had long had suspicions about, things that I could vaguely know were probably transpiring but could not confirm until we had this covert equipment set up. It was terrifying to finally know what I knew.

With Hamish's nanobotic spying systems linked to this burner laptop computer, we looked and we watched. We watched as MRAPs moved around the nation, from police departments and through back country roads, and as the ones controlled by the military moved where civilians could not go without an escort.

We looked at land masses and water lines to see what had changed. We saw places that were familiar because we had been there before the water rose, or familiar from movies and television. Either way, it felt both ethereal and funereal.

It was not a happy mindwalk, but it was irresistible. Once begun, we could not stop looking. We could not look away.

On the Deep Net, we found a website that showed video tours of flooded areas, with before-and-after comparisons. Visitors to the site could choose almost any place in the United States. I wondered why this wasn't available to surfers of the Surface Net, until it got scary.

I chose Provincetown, Cape Cod. It was where my mother and I had wandered the shops on the main street many a summer, and then met Dad at an oyster restaurant that overlooked a wide parking lot that sloped to the water. Comparing memories of drag queens advertising their night club acts out in the streets in the early evenings as gay and lesbian couples happily walked up and down the street enjoying the area just as we did, and of the most beautiful, imaginative, and unique arts and crafts with this sunken ghost town was jarring enough.

But seeing it all first above the water and then below freaked me out.

The water levels in Provincetown were now so high that many of the buildings were rotting off of their foundations. A time-lapse video, sped up to show waters rising to current levels and then with more seasons passing to show the rot both above and below the surface, demonstrated this. It started off with a dream-like waterscape. The familiar main drag where the shops had been, Commercial Street, was an eerie place to see even in daylight. Not a soul was anywhere to be seen, but the buildings, signage and all, were there, partially submerged.

On second glance, we noticed that they appeared to have been hastily emptied before being abandoned, and I hoped that the shopkeepers had been able to pack up all of their wares before leaving. I knew from reading the news stories of their departures that they had driven away before it was too late to do so. Only a few elderly residents had held out, and they had been rescued by the Coast Guard and taken into Boston, to be met by friends and relatives. They were okay, mourning the loss of their home, like many other displaced Americans.

The virtual tour showed us this completely abandoned Provincetown, and I thought sadly of the tiny pink roses and morning glory vines that had grown on the fences of the yards of houses there. The tour went down Commercial Street in broad daylight, and a canal of water stretched across it and between every shop. Commercial Street was a huge, long strip, parallel to the shore, and when we came to the spot where we used to walk down the parking lot and then up an outdoor staircase to that oyster restaurant, the tour went underwater and then up those stairs.

The view turned to face out into the deep, under water, facing into Cape Cod Bay. Looking down underwater had always scared me for some reason, and it still did. I forced myself to look, and saw cars and debris, and the beginnings of building foundation collapse. Then the time-lapse function began to pick up speed, and the restaurant building fell into the water. We rotated the viewer back to Commercial Street, pointing it upward, and saw those buildings floating toward us. This had only taken a few weeks once it started, so it was over quickly.

We reversed the time lapse on the viewer to make the buildings reconstitute themselves because we wanted to walk up the restaurant staircase. Once up there, we stared out at Provincetown. Each building had been unique; some were painted bright blue, some were weathered Cape Cod gray, and a few even had brown-and-beige stonework on the outside. Rainbow signage decorated some shops, and blue-on-white script with swirling serifs graced others. A giant ice cream cone and a huge lobster pot were on some corner ones.

The viewer function allowed us to move as if flying just above the water level, up and down the length of Commercial Street. It was like a travesty of Google Maps with the little stick person in Street View. At last, we let the time lapse function go, while staying in one spot, and we watched as the buildings slowly swayed and collapsed into the street and were swept away, polluting the ocean with yet more human debris.

We repeated this virtual tour with other places: Charleston, South Carolina; Hollywood, California; Key West, Florida; New Orleans, Louisiana; Galveston, Texas; parts of Boston, Massachusetts. Any major urban area that was not in a river that could be protected by a system of dikes was a lost cause. Long stretches of coastland were forfeit to Nature's process of eminent removal. It was both devastating and mesmerizing.

Somehow, seeing that San Francisco was ruined by the floods was particularly depressing. I knew that *Star Trek* was just a fictional universe, but I had long held out hope that it would be there a few centuries later when Starfleet Academy and the United Federation of Planets could exist. I wanted a positive future for humans, and C.E.R.N. in Switzerland was making progress with antimatter, which would enable warp drive and interstellar travel. But it was not to be, at least not there, and so I went back to our perusal of flood zones.

Of course, we couldn't look at this stuff all in one day. This kept us occupied for a few hours almost every afternoon for over a month before it got repetitive. We were able to surf the Deep Net without any more assistance than some software that Hamish had uploaded to our burner laptop, so we were not concerned about being watched as we did our own watching.

We had to take frequent breaks for everyday life as we did this, or we would have gone stir crazy. And I had to be careful not to chat about it with anyone and everyone, which made it difficult to go to my yoga classes and not tell the teacher when she asked how I was and what I had been working on lately. I just said I was reading a lot, which she believed, and then turned the conversation to her life. Better to get her talking about running her latest marathon.

It was spring, there was the election to follow on in the news, and plenty else to talk about. Hamish's vaccine regime continued with the family, which we all now felt included Claire, and with Ellie also. Claire joined me for yoga classes. She had done them for years, whereas I had only recently gotten hooked. They were actually pilates and yoga, a combination called centergy. We loved the stretches and crunches. Shayna, our teacher, showed Claire the websites for continuing it on her own, at home, and sometimes I did this with her, in the living room.

But when we wanted to snoop around the Dark Net, we needed a hacker. We could not be sure that we would not be noticed carrying out this next escapade without expert assistance, and even my husband couldn't do everything. But he could find just about anything and anyone that we wanted. He found and hired a kid who showed up in a Dr. Who tee shirt to help us with that.

The kid's name was Jason Woodward, and he had graduated from M.I.T. only to find no job. He was 25 years old, with a master's degree in computer programming. Despite a careful search, he was having as much trouble as Edgar had. It seemed that every pharmaceutical corporation, hedge fund, think tank, and whatever else he tried was all set. Jason's other problem was that he didn't fit in very well, and didn't care to try. Hamish and I liked him right away because of that.

Jason had short, messy, sandy hair and silver-rimmed, round glasses. He told me over lunch one afternoon that he had chosen them because he liked Harry Potter's glasses and hated what was in fashion. "No wonder I approve of you," I said with a grin. "I hate the fashion industry. It makes things I love, then stops just to justify the employment of the idiots who keep creating new designs. I want a continuous, reliable supply of the stuff I like, and I won't be told what to like, buy, and wear!" Jason and Hamish both grinned when I said that.

Jason had come home to stay with his parents while he figured things out, and he wanted to earn enough money to pay off his college loans and get a decent place to live…with a fast Internet connection. Hamish and I were more than happy to pay him a nice income for his expertise – one sufficient to live comfortably near us and send enough home to avoid land trusts. It was a symbiotic relationship from the start. We had needed a computer hacker of our own for a while, and we had found one who was sympathetic to our goals.

Our secrets and our contempt for communitarianism were safe with Jason…and shared.

One of the first things we asked Jason to help us look at was a government database. It was the one for the Department of Demographics. What, we wanted to know, was the plan for the people who had been displaced by rising sea levels, and for the homeless people that we no longer saw on our latest visit to Manhattan?

"No problem," he said, cracking his knuckles and leaning over the laptop.

It was like something out of a movie. He could access anything without being detected. He explained that he was using his own secret software, which would route and re-route through servers around the globe, bouncing off this or that satellite, until the original signal was so tangled up with the others out there as to be lost to any surveiller. As it moved through cyberspace, it changed its code, making it even tougher to track. He called it Metamorph.

Metamorph enabled us to find some terrifying plans, some of which were already in action, and others of which were still in the works. It was like finding out about the Final Solution to human overpopulation. When I wondered who the Anti-Christ might be, Hamish and Jason said that it was likely more than one who.

"Okay, then, who are the members of the Secret Anti-Christ Society?" I asked.

Hamish suggested, "Probably the banksters and hedge fundsters that you wrote about – whoever controls most of the assets. You've said it before: they learned their lesson from history, particularly 1789 in France." Some more searching proved that to be true, and provided a detailed Who's Who of Cullers.

It was sickening to be right. Mark Twain had said that it was better to be popular than right. I was right, not popular. But was it really better to be popular?! This plan was basically a declaration of war on the general populace. Its attitude was that the sheer numbers of the populace made them a threat to be subdued, and with stealth and death as the method.

The first plan dealt with the homeless. This was the one that was already in progress. Each homeless person had been implanted with a microchip, some willingly, as a means of being granted food benefits, and some forcibly, after they had turned the idea down. At last, the problem faced by census counts each decade was solved: homeless people had always been tough to count, because that system relied upon finding people in their homes to count them.

The homeless people who had agreed to receive microchips, each of which consisted of a carcinogenic, radio frequency-emitting RFID chip, had gotten them injected at government benefits offices when they showed up for their routine reviews.

The homeless people who had not agreed to receive microchips had immediately been flagged as recalcitrant and tagged in the system as mentally incompetent. With that, they had been swiftly surrounded by government agents who represented themselves to be social workers and health care professionals (nurses, mostly).

These individuals were not really social workers or nurses. They were Army medics who knew how to inject microchips, and strong-armed thugs who could also inject tranquilizers. Any homeless person who showed the slightest sign of making a fuss was spirited away to a remote location, which was euphemistically referred to as a hospital on the way out the door.

It was actually a government laboratory. These places were typically within a few hours' driving distance from whatever urban area a homeless population was relocated from. Unconscious, or at least feeling loopy and compliant, each major city's homeless people had been evacuated over the first ten months since the water had risen. It had been 18 months since that had happened, we realized, when we read that.

What happened to the homeless people once they arrived at these news places?

A team from the United States Army Medical Research Institute of Infectious Diseases (USAMRIID) took charge of them, assessed their general health and diet, and then locked them up in medical testing facilities. These facilities were well-hidden in remote areas, and gated. Escape was impossible thanks to guards, guard towers, barbed wire, electrical fences, surveillance cameras, and the fact that each inmate was kept sufficiently medicated as to make clarity of thought unattainable.

Once locked in and high on whatever drug, the tests began. The USAMRIID had all sorts of biological agents stored in its facilities. Along with its civilian counterpart, the CDC, the USAMRIID was supposed to keep each germ contained, frozen, in stasis, and not a threat to the general population. In addition, it was supposed to be developing cures to these microbial threats. But since when do they do governments do what they are supposed to do?

Only if it suited their agenda, that was when.

Instead, the homeless had become human guinea pigs. Each biological agent was tested on a cohort of captives. One facility focused on the effects of measles: a group of a thousand was exposed only to measles, another thousand was forced to experience flu with measles, another rubella with measles, and another mumps with measles. Studies that would have made Dr. Josef Mengele proud were conducted on each as the diseases each ran their course, to see how long before death came and how it did.

The final study was aimed at including the nanites that Hamish had extracted from us all in the vaccine serum, but with a nastier, speedier effect. People would develop cancer far sooner after having this new vaccine, which the four big pharmaceutical corporations in the U.S. began to manufacture at record speeds. That was another Dark Net spy mission yield: by late June 2016, enough of it would be ready for at least half of the population of the United States. The plan was to keep making it, to supply the rest of the planet's nations for their culls.

The bodies were cremated after the phage was harvested from their bloodstreams.

This scenario had been repeated with other diseases elsewhere.

The scariest one was at a remote facility in Georgia. It had conducted a field exercise to see what would happen if a patient with Marburg virus, which was related to but even worse than Ebola, went undetected. It was carefully controlled, of course, the database claimed, yet it had not gone entirely smoothly. There had been a glitch near Elberton, Georgia, when a patient tried to run for it. He had gotten as far as the perimeter of a gas station.

When we read that, Hamish and I turned away from the computer and stared at each other, stunned. This was what we had seen from a distance! We really had just barely escaped with our lives. It was one thing to have thought so, and to have suspected it while dismissing the idea as just too crazy, too much of a conspiracy tale to be taken seriously. Reading that it was what we had suspected it to be was quite another.

The case study, as it was diabolically labeled ("more like a travesty of a study," I remarked), said that several local people who had come within five feet of the escapee had quickly succumbed to the disease. Quickly meant 24 hours; the gas station owner and the 2 employees on duty had all been rushed to the same secret facility, which was not far from the orange groves and apricot orchards that we had visited and toured.

A couple in a blue Mercedes and two men in a black SUV were seen pulling away about 40 feet away from the escapee, but they were all out of range of potential contamination, and had not been affected. A notation in the record chastised the scientists and personnel who had recaptured the homeless, Ebola-infected, escapee for not getting our license plate numbers.

Wow! "Hamish, do you happen to know anything about that?" I couldn't help asking.

He gave me a knowing, smug smile. "Anything about what?"

"Anything about how they failed to identify us and our vehicles," I clarified.

"Indeed I do," he grinned. "Nanites can rearrange and blur license plate numbers when passing detectors, and scramble Easy-Pass scanners sometimes, too. I knew when you wanted to go on that road trip that we would need a reliable way to avoid detection."

Wow. I stared at him, impressed and awed, for a moment, then went back to the computer.

I wondered what had happened to the doctors who did not want to participate in this crime.

There it was: they had been interviewed by psychological profilers in advance. The thinking was that making them all just disappear would never work. Logistically, that would be noticed. So, to avoid that problem, data was presented to them back at USAMRIID headquarters in Fort Detrick, Maryland, with details such as time and testing location changed. Just blame the Nazis and say that it was all recently discovered, the memo advised. Thus far, it was working nicely.

Wow…again. This was a bit stunning to take in.

A real vaccine was being developed, and so was a hybrid vaccine-bioweapon.

Who was each one for, though? We read on.

It soon became clear that the plan of the Farmers, as I had gotten used to thinking of these elite monsters, the bankster and hedge fundsters who controlled the world's financial assets and thus access to all of its real assets (food, rare earth elements, you name it), was not merely to ruin our lives, but to end them. The people who comprised the vast majority of humanity were mere excess to them, in the way of their comfort and security merely by existing.

The Farmers couldn't risk their comfort, security, and access to all that in a resource war. So rather than allow this vast majority to fight for their own existence, they were to be eliminated before they were even aware of the threat. The Farmers were the Anti-Christ Hitler monsters of our time. It was hard to believe that football games and reality shows were still being produced while all this went on, but I knew that they were.

"Most people are asleep to all of this," Hamish told me. "They are sheeple: unaware of it, blissfully ignorant, and the government likes it that way. Keeping the general public as sheeple makes them easier to manipulate and control. Distractions are provided to take up their time in the form of online gaming and other video games, football, reality TV shows, game shows, soap operas, science fiction shows, cop chase shows, you name it. It's working, too."

"Not entirely," I replied.

"Well, no system is perfect," he said, adding, "wink, wink, nod, nod."

With that, Hamish and Jason continued the virtual tour of environmental devastation, showing place after place that had been inundated by floods, never to be reclaimed by humans. It was scary and shocking to look at. Next, Jason hacked into Army databases to see where the camps were.

Many were empty, waiting for more occupants. With all of the homeless removed – and the ones who had willingly accepted microchips had followed those who wouldn't – we wondered who else would be brought there, and how it would be done without awakening the nation's "sheeple" to this agenda.

When we checked, we realized something: the camps were not permanent. They were mobile. They could be dismantled and packed up in military vehicles, then unpacked and reassembled, over and over again, crematoria and all.

Jason was remarkably calm as he discovered this with us. He did say he felt sick, but who wouldn't, except a monster who felt safe from this diabolical agenda? "When we figure out how to avoid this atrocity, we shall include you in the escape plan," I said to Jason. "Who do you love that we should invite?"

"I'm an only child," Jason said, "so my parents. And thanks."

"Of course," I said, and Hamish seconded it. There was no other reasonable response.

There had to be a tipping point at which people would notice that some evil plan was being carried out, right? How long would it take, how far would it have to go, before that happened? Would there be any way to fight it, or not? Would anyone be able to fight it? Would we be able to protect ourselves?

Knowing in advance was a weapon in itself, but was it enough? I should have known that it might very well be with Hamish in the mix. As it was, I wasn't very quick to lose hope and panic. I knew him well enough to know that he would have more plans, and plans within plans.

Hamish was like a rock of calmness to me. Just having him to watch and talk to every day made me feel like I could cope with all this. Of course, knowing all that I did and how we both constantly worked to make ourselves and our families self-sufficient and armed against all sorts of threats also accomplished that goal, but it wouldn't have been enough.

No, having another person, a companion who was my best friend and soulmate, was what made all of these hideous revelations easier to face, and possible to contemplate. There had to be something good that we could do for some other people in all of this, some way to make a decent future for some good people. It couldn't be survival just for the damned Farmers.

Chapter 21

Idiot World Order: Another Treaty

It was U.N. Agenda 21 turned into a treaty, one called the Convention on Global Sustainability and Communitarian Government.

When the announcement came on the evening news, I thought, that was it! The world was going to hell, and we got to watch the journey. I wondered how soon it would feel as though we had reached the accursed place ourselves. With this police surveillance state document being promulgated, it couldn't be long. How could anyone be safe?!

The whole thing was cleverly hyped, promoted, and advertised as the most benign thing designed for our own good. It was nothing but Kool-Aid, manufactured, packaged, and stamped with a pretty green label. It was a travesty of environmentalism – a perversion of its own ideals.

The new treaty was an abortion. It was an abomination. It was a perversion of Mr. Spock's Axiom: "The good of the many must outweigh that of the few, or the one." It took his words and twisted their intent. This was pure evil.

The announcement came on June 21, 2016 – three and a half years to the day after the Nae-Née treaty had been announced. It was signed in short order, and this time, even the Vatican joined in. After all, it contained not a word about birth control, abortion, or population policy. One had to read between the lines to see that, and to do that, you had to actually bother to visit the United Nations website and download the document.

The announcement was followed by a speech by the President, a broadcast that put me in a foul mood. I sat in the living room with my whole family grouped around us – including Grandmère, Aunt Zoe, Uncle Charlie, Edgar, Fabian, Claire, and Jacques – and glowered through it all. They had come over for dinner and a show, and what a nasty show it was.

Edgar understood it quicker than most, thanks to having finished reading everything I had given him already. He was appalled, and he actually began to pace up and down, hyperventilating at bit. Another family member with anxiety problems, I thought, and with good reason for them! As soon as the speech ended, he took out his phone and called Ellie.

"Don't worry," Hamish told me quietly. "You're all vaccinated – properly – and registered." It had kept him very busy, fussing with the timing of each of the forty shots, but he had done it. Everyone had let him, knowing that he must know best about this. Now they were spooked. Here was the evidence that he had known in advance that this trouble was coming.

Agenda 21 had been kept separated and divorced from the reality of human overpopulation from the time of its convention in 1992 at Rio de Janeiro, Brazil. This was done covertly by the Vatican, which preaches "do as I say, not as I do," while maintaining a zero population growth policy within its own national borders.

The hypocrisy that was now being perpetrated had been enabled at that convention by the representatives of Argentina and the Philippines, who relentlessly suppressed any effort to so much as mention the link between human overpopulation and environmental degradation.

The Philippines! Those who have suffered the worst consequences of a lack of access to birth control – consequences that include dire poverty – yet who are delighted whenever the Pope visits them, did this. It is insane, yet true. Pope after pope has no answer beyond a hug for children who cry about being homeless and starving other than to say that birth control is unacceptable.

Popes, no matter how sweet their personality and no matter how likeable, need a hefty dose of reality. People liked to have sex, and they would do so regardless of the potential for their uncontrolled fertility to produce more humans.

The reason was no mystery, especially when one considered the quality of life that someone living in poverty could expect. Orgasms and the sense that another human cares about that person in particular were too compelling to turn down, and possibly one of the rare and all too few thrills that a poor person can ever hope to enjoy.

Why take that possibility away from them?! How could a pope be so narrow-minded? It just came across as selfish and cruel. (These were just some of the thoughts going through my mind as I watched the treaty announcement on what was also my 16th wedding anniversary. Hamish and I had exchanged cards hours ago, and he had given me a dozen pink roses. That was all of a celebration that we could manage in the uproar of this alarming Idiot World Order.)

While all this was secretly in the works, the rest of the world had had no idea…as usual. Few people were likely to have even looked at the text of the treaty. They were in for a rude awakening. The only question was how soon it would come. What exactly would it be like, and what part of this would come first? The Farmers – hedge fundsters and bankster a.k.a. the ruling elite and indifferent .01 percenters – had been busy plotting all this.

In a repeat of the Nae-Née treaty, the President of the United States was on television at the end of a long day of world leaders trouping through the assembly room of the U.N. headquarters building in Manhattan. That had been shown on TV all day, too. The text of the treaty was online for anyone who was interested in seeing it. I had looked, of course, and saved a copy, and now my mood continued to spiral downward. Everything I had feared was coming true.

With John Lassiter, the Secretary of Demographics, sat nearby, and the cameras panned to him every time he was referenced. The President spoke in the House of Representatives about what the world's governments had just signed on to. He made sure to emphasize that with population pressures being what they were, shrinking land masses, and water tables everywhere sinking below sustainable levels, he said, "Never again can we afford to be without a Department of Demographics."

From there, the President went on to detail how the Department of Demographics would be taking the lead in administering and documenting vaccinations of everyone in the nation on a national database. Hamish and I glanced at each other as he got to that part. It was eerily significant, this correlation between vaccinations, water tables, sustainability, and population statistics. This was a cull plot, no doubt about it. Why didn't most people see it?!

Suddenly, with an abrupt shock of outrage, I was glad that Hamish and I didn't want kids for an entirely unselfish reason. Never mind protecting our peace, quiet, and romance from the intrusion of annoying children. This was different. This was relief at not being in the situation of having to protect any children of our own from this governmental intrusion…from this cull.

A vaccine was supposed to contain antibodies against whatever disease it sought to protect the recipient from. It should not contain poisonous stabilizers (such as mercury) in its serum, and it certainly should not contain malicious nanites, programmed with malware. Yet that was what was being perpetrated upon the unsuspecting public.

Anyone who suggested such a thing would be instantly branded a conspiracy theorist.

It was the ideal cover for this monstrous, diabolical cull plan.

The President seemed utterly unconcerned about his image, as one would expect someone who had served most of two terms to be. He could pretty much do whatever he wished at this point in his career, and go out with this agenda in motion. It must be the agenda of many, though.

"The president's going to be out of office soon, and the bulls of Wall Street will be taking over the government when his term is up," I growled. "It's an election year, and there's nothing on the menu this time but Wall Street banksters and hedge fundsters."

Grandmère was sitting next to me on the sofa. "The 'bulls' of Wall Street? What does that mean?" she wanted to know. Grandmère had always been well-read, but in literature, and mostly French literature. She was keeping herself busy now with American literature. When something from another field cropped up in conversation, she was curious enough to ask about it, and I enjoyed that about her.

"In the American stock market, which is on Wall Street, a market that is doing badly is a bear market, and one that is doing well, making tons of money, is called a bull market. Hence the life-sized sculpture of a charging bronze bull that an artist donated. It's near Wall Street, at Bowling Green on Broadway. No one has made a statue of a bear. No one would want one."

"Interesting. It is always fascinating to hear about metaphors and symbols," she commented.

"I no longer wonder exactly how Anne Frank's family felt when the Nazis followed them into The Netherlands," Aunt Zoe said, her eyes wide with horror. So…my family was actually waking up.

"Oh," I said, "you mean that now that it's happening in real time, to us, it's no longer experienced vicariously. It's understood with empathy, because we are living it rather than merely reading about it decades after the fact."

"Exactly," my aunt replied.

My mood got blacker. It was one thing to have researched and understood it all in advance. It was quite another to see it happen. I was being proven right, and I hated it.

News channels and news talk shows raged on and on about whose fault this was. The conservatives blamed the liberals, berating them as secular humanists, shrieking incoherently that godlessness was the reason why this was happening.

As a secular humanist, I resented that. Hamish wasn't a secular humanist; he was a Libertarian who thought that we should all be free to live as we chose. On that, he and I could easily agree. Should and could, however, were two different realities.

One could moralize this issue until we dropped dead, but the deeply unpleasant fact remained that we as a species were overpopulated and using too much land and too many resources. I was disgusted by the way it was being handled. There were better and more courageous ways than a secret, stealthy, monstrous cull.

Water rationing was part of the policies in this travesty of a treaty in many countries, we noticed. Fortunately, it was not yet in our area. I pointed out the fact that it did allow for military and police takeovers of our water supplies in the event of an emergency. "Emergencies" were already being conjured out of thin airtime on the news in the southwestern United States, plus elsewhere in the world, so there was no reason to expect us to be okay for long.

Our local news station even mentioned a plan to check and maintain the fluoridation levels of water reservoirs. "Perfect!" Hamish roared, making us all jump. "Fluoride, when ingested, is a toxin. It's only good in toothpaste. It's not supposed to be in the water! It inhibits brain function." We all stared. I had known this for a while. Hamish had long lamented the fact that I had grown up with fluoride in the water. Now the government wanted more of that, presumably to keep us asleep.

Next, an ad for genetically modified apples and potatoes flashed images of food that wouldn't go brown when cut, as if that was a good thing. Why couldn't people live with a little brown as oxygen hit sliced food?! What was being marketed was a poison, not a convenience, and no one in the general public seemed to know the difference. Hamish wasted no time in pointing out that trigger foods were what those were, and more sugary crap was advertised after these GMO frankenfoods.

It was driving me crazy to listen to and watch all this. At least my family was awake!

"This idiot world order is pure laziness, selfishness, and greed all rolled into one. This wealthy few prefers to cower in safety while its minions carry out its orders, then come out when the dust settles. What they should be doing is toughing out the bitterness and disappointment over Nae-Née policies around the planet and figuring out some way for all these so-called excess people to live comfortably." I couldn't help but rant about it a bit.

Hamish smiled. "This feels familiar. It's sort of like when the previous treaty was announced, but you're angry this time. I love it. What do you have in mind, even if we can't get the world to cooperate?"

Happy to continue my rant, I said, "They should be rearranging the world economy to revolve around developing nuclear fusion energy – don't tell me that scientists can't figure it out with enough resources at their disposal and time to calmly focus on it! They should also be figuring out how to increase our access to wind and solar energy, and to build solar arrays out of materials that aren't toxic."

Unlike with the Nae-Née treaty, which had put forth a policy that didn't involve ruining basic quality of life or ending anyone's life, the Agenda 21 treaty did exactly that. It was so obviously controlling and stifling that I started to hyperventilate. A few minutes later, I was crying from the stress of it. My family, with the exception of Edgar and my husband, looked puzzled by this.

"Apparently, none of you" here I gestured at everyone else "have any idea what the U.N. Agenda for the 21st Century contains, or even what it is, despite the fact that I have mentioned it repeatedly and described parts of it. It is just amazing how little attention people pay to things that don't imminently affect them unless and until they do affect them!"

My mother calmly asked me to explain U.N. Agenda 21.

"Okay. I'll try again. Just a moment – I'm going up to my desk to get that book. The U.N. actually published it a long time ago. I'll bring it down, explain it, and pass it around. While I'm at it, I'll bring a printed copy of this abomination of a legal document that they just created, too. I downloaded, saved, and printed it this afternoon."

I raced upstairs, grabbed it, and returned to the living room. Of course they were all, except for Hamish and Edgar, chatting about the treaty and how they didn't see what it could do to change our lives that quickly. Then they saw me standing in front of them, holding the book out, cover facing them.

"Have a look. The Sustainability treaty was based on this monstrosity. It just promulgated the Agenda for the 21st Century. It uses the word 'sustainability' a lot, plus 'environmental' this and 'environmental' that, talks about energy policy, land use, protecting and managing ecosystems, protecting freshwater supplies, human development, and so on."

Uncle Charlie seemed more interested in learning something outside of business than he usually did, probably thanks to the fact that his wife was freaking out a bit, and over this. "How will this change our lives?" Clearly, he hadn't been paying attention to the details.

"Wait until you see this treaty! It promises to ration our access to water, to conduct constant surveillance on every aspect of our daily lives and routines, control and limit our access to financial resources, and force us to accept vaccines for who knows what, with whatever noxious additives they see fit to include in the sera!"

A chorus of "Whats?!" greeted this rant.

"Oh, now you're ready to pay attention. Good. Here…" I handed Dad the treaty and Grandmère the book with the Agenda in it. "…have a look at it all. Take your time. Edgar knows all this. He has read all of the materials I gathered. Fabian, Claire, and Jacques must be almost done, too." They all nodded unhappily. Yes, they understood what this meant.

My family settled into their perusal of the documents, and soon Dad was irate, too. Handing these documents to another lawyer had been a good idea. A psychologist would have approved. Now someone other than myself was advocating for my position on this, not that it was that huge a leap for him to see that an assault on capitalism and individual liberty was at work in the treaty.

"So much for the U.S. Constitution being the supreme law of the land here," Dad said, outraged. "That was what attracted me to it in the first place. No world court could tell the U.S. what to do. This treaty all sounds so reasonable, logical, and good for the planet, but it requires collectivism and the taking of wealth from us in order to accomplish its goals."

"Welcome to the damned New World Order," I growled.

My mother looked at me unhappily, catching on. She had that look that she got when she found something deeply unsettling. After everyone had had a chance to look through both the book and the treaty, I had more to say to them. "Do you see yet that the things spelled out in the treaty have gone farther than that agenda? That they had to in order to implement it?"

"Yes," Aunt Zoe said. She was staring, stunned, at them both. The book and the print-out of the treaty were on the coffee table in front of her.

Grandmère looked appalled, too. "This is like when the Nazis marched into Paris," she said.

My grandmother was a hundred years old. We had celebrated her birthday last May, and it had made the local papers. Looking at her, seeing how she regarded this assault on our liberty, I was reminded that she had seen and remembered many events of profound historical significance. She added, "I thought that all that would shock me in history was behind me."

"Nope. Here comes more," I said. "I want some chocolate. Oh no, wait…we can't get that locally. They may soon cut off access to it. Does anyone yet realize that Agenda 21 would never have been workable without a drastic reduction of the human population of the entire planet? By that, I mean much, much fewer people left than any Nae-Née policy would leave."

Aunt Zoe looked like she was going to be sick.

"Mommy, we had better make some kind of calming tea for Aunt Zoe, because I'm going to say a few more things. Clearly, the authors of this Sustainability treaty have thought of this. It brings me back to the Georgia Guidestones, which recommend maintaining the entire human population on Earth at half a billion."

My mother glanced at Aunt Zoe and went to put the kettle on. I could hear her rummaging through the cabinet where the tea was kept, looking for the chamomile tea bags.

Continuing, I said, "We may now, thanks to floods and violent refusals to admit climate refugees to other nations' territories, be down to something like 6.9 billion people, but they won't stop there. There is no way that the plans in this treaty will work without simply getting rid of most of us. We humans are in the way of this plan. Just try to imagine society all rearranged to accommodate the ideas in this treaty, and you will see that. Also, with militarized police forces all over the nation, the tools are already in place to make sure that we comply."

Uncle Charlie said, "You're scaring us."

"Good! I want you to get used to this deeply unpleasant shock now, and then start thinking of ways to fight back. Hamish has already been doing that with his nanites. In case you haven't understood what that has been about, I'll lay it out for you."

"He spaced out your vaccinations rather than hitting your immune systems with an overload of all of them at once, as the government will surely do in order to get them administered quickly and efficiently to the huge population that exists now, which would crash and burn your immune systems. Then he removed the nanites that they contained."

"As he explained, those nanites would shut off your P53 receptors. P53s are your cancer tumor suppressor mechanisms. The plan is to make people sick with illnesses that slowly and painfully drag out our deaths while draining us of whatever funds we have, leaving nothing for their heirs. Most of us are not supposed to have any heirs left anyway – they'll be getting sick too under this Final Solution to human overpopulation."

"As for the surveillance, few people possess the technical expertise to fight that, but Hamish does. He has been removing the RFID chips that flatscreen TVs and toasters and whatever else come with, and destroying them. Those things are meant to tattle to the utility company whenever you run your blender or washing machine or even take a shower! Watch out, because next people will be required to wear SmartTech in watches, get Quick Response Code tattoos, or just get microchips implanted. Privacy and the security of one's person and property are over."

Stunned and open-mouthed, my family sat there taking it all in. They looked at me as I ranted, laying it all out coherently and heatedly, and then stared at the television, listening to the pundits. Aunt Zoe's tea was ready now, and she leaned into Uncle Charlie, sipping it and trying to relax. He put his arm around her and rubbed her shoulders absently, mesmerized by the news.

My mother had made tea for all of us – herbal, relaxing tea – and we all sat, staring into it.

Uncle Charlie asked how wealth was going to be taken away from people.

"Bank bail-ins, in which the federal government scoops out a huge chunk of the contents of your accounts for its own use, plus whatever is in your safe deposit boxes. You'd better empty those tomorrow! Watch out for attempts to sell you land trusts and greenlining of land. Those land trusts are aimed at taking control over how you use your property and fining you if you park so much as a service truck outside. Your heirs will have nothing of value to inherit."

"Greenlining is rezoning for the Wildlands Map, so that suburban land is given back to Nature and wildlife and humans may not hike or fish or whatever on it. Suburban sprawl has been encroaching upon the habitats of bears, foxes, lynxes – you name it – which is why they appear in back yards. Unlimited, unchecked human growth has led to this. But stopping that means a police state. Look out for Smart Growth plans, and don't sell land trusts when they come knocking at your door."

"Look up ICLEI, which is the International Council for Local Environmental Initiatives. It's been renamed to cover it up a bit, so now it's known as Local Governments for Sustainability. Agenda 21 has been implemented for years – administratively, to circumvent our vote. Now the Farmers, as I have come to think of the "elite" who run all this, are in a hurry."

"Who are these Farmers?" Grandmère wanted to know.

"They are the banksters and hedge fundsters from Wall Street and other nations. They are the ones who control the wealth. Wealth has been transferred already into the hands of a very, very few. That's why the economy is the way it is, with so few full-time jobs with benefits and a decent income. Instead of those, you see part-time jobs with no benefits and just a minimum wage and no union protections to prevent long hours from abruptly being forced on workers. Then you see reports in the papers about how employment has grown...with only 257,000 jobs!"

Grandmère looked disgusted. "So that's why my grandsons couldn't find work."

The liberals on television seemed a bit stunned to have had what they thought was their own environmentalist agenda turned against them. It was far worse: the joke was on them. Environmentalist ideals had been perverted to serve the interests of a wealthy few.

Those wealthy few had been intent from the start on creating a new world order, one in which they controlled all wealth, land, resources, and opportunities. They were almost finished executing their diabolical travesty of a plan. It was clever, one had to admit: make it look as though their own Hitler-esque agenda was their opponents' idea.

They seriously needed unmasking. Either that, or a taste of their own frankenfoods.

But...would doing so merely get us killed, to no other effect? Would it be wiser to be stealthy and not let on that their intent was now obvious, at least to a few of us? We could put up some semblance of a fight if we avoided detection, and our line of defense would be camouflage.

Maybe we should just remind ourselves of what those so-called "conservatives" – who didn't conserve anything – really were, if only to arm ourselves mentally for the fight: plutocrats, privateers, monopolists, authoritarians, exploiters, and commodifiers. They had a policy of turning anything and everything into a commodity that had to be bought and paid for or foregone, from basic necessities to anything that enabled anyone to earn a living.

They wanted us dead, and they wanted our money before we died. It was that simple, and thoroughly appalling once understood. There had to be a way to fight back. I looked at Hamish and saw that he was thinking about the same thing.

I wondered how many people...or how few...actually did understand that. My family did, at least, and I was amazed that I had finally gotten their focused, serious attention. Usually, I was regarded and dismissed as a hyped-up Aspie, overly fascinated by whatever research I was currently delving into, and wildly strident about things that interested me intensely but were seen as remote from our everyday lives.

Not anymore.

Chapter 22

Nae-Née, Operators, and Anti-Christs

The Operators were ready.

The Operator and his staff sat in their underground computer fortress.

He fidgeted by pushing the wheels of his chair back and forth, back and forth, just an inch or so in each direction. He was thinking of how to introduce their next move. At last, he spoke.

"We are going to have to take steps – drastic steps – to avoid massive civil unrest."

The four people who sat with him regarded him with calm expectation. It was an unsettling sensation. They had come to know that such placidly toned preambles led to dramatic announcements of changes that affected the entire country.

The Operator said, "What will the computer hackers – and there are always hackers – find in their quest for governmental transparency?" He continued, "They will find that Operators' decisions are informed in part by agricultural data. Food security drives the decision to grant or deny a birth license as much as the ability of prospective parents to provide a good life and education for a potential child. Tracking aquifer levels, desertification, deforestation, and competition for food between cars that need ethanol fuel and people who need to food eat will show what resources are available."

"Operators must consider this when allocating license, and hackers will see the need to deny the vast majority of birth licenses almost immediately in order to bring population numbers down in time to avoid a collapse. That's not all that they will find. They will also find that, even with a birth licensing policy, under this sustainability treaty, and with shrinking land masses and dying ecosystems, the resources that are available are insufficient."

"Look at China; it has an easy fix coming to it. Due to extreme parental selfishness combined with decades of selective abortions, its population is largely male. Many unhappy males will spend their lives alone with no wife for companionship, and will take care of their parents in old age only to have nothing to look forward to after that. Their parents got what they wanted, regardless of the fact that their sons will miss out on that same thing: marriage, sex, and companionship. That's how the population policy cookie crumbles. Too bad. Every society has its losers, and that's how it goes there."

"China's Operators are counting on huge die-offs of its population due to aging. At that point, their government has a plan in place to deal with those huge numbers of angry sons with no future to look forward to. Our government is considering a similar policy."

"Wealth can be a factor in the denial of a birth license, the hackers will discover. Too many wealthy people wanting cars and homes and places at universities will create problems, so the Operators will deny licenses to them, too. Governments do not want colleges and universities to expand in order to accommodate increased demand, so Operators must act to ensure that there will be no increased demand."

"In fact, since a majority, rather than a minority, of Americans have been raised to expect access to this 'dream' of higher education, that expectation has been part of the problem. People in other developed nations – in Europe – don't expect that most of their offspring will go on to higher education, or that doing so will be necessary in order to access a good job. Our job is to decrease the number of those demanding, expecting, and otherwise seeking higher education to much more manageable levels."

"But those jobs don't exist, and they won't, at least not in sufficient numbers to accommodate current population levels. Efforts to keep the public dumbed down and distracted via television and gaming are clearly not enough. Apparently, people still expect to get jobs that offer a high enough income to afford to buy a home and maintain it, go on vacations, and send their children to college even after watching reality and celebrity shows and football games."

"In any case, these distractions were only ever stop-gaps. Eventually, the gaps must be closed. Any potential for objections to the fact that this cannot be available to all Americans – or even most Americans – due to human overpopulation must be dealt with before the fact."

"Our government is not going to wait around for civil unrest to take any form. It is ready with a plan to deal with our lack of resources – of food, clothing, and space for people to live in. It should be clear to all of you that, with what our planet can provide, and under the terms of this new sustainability treaty, far fewer people can be accommodated in any comfort."

With that, the Operator looked around and asked whether or not there were any questions.

There were none. The implications were perfectly clear to his deputies. They waited.

When he was certain that no one intended to interrupt him, the Operator continued. "Steps shall be taken to prevent any riots growing out of any protests that arise, and count on it, sooner or later there are always protests. Riots – and wars – make a mess. Our job is to prevent that."

No one said anything, so he continued, "A plan is already in place, one that was prepared in the 1980s, before the planners had any specific idea as to just what it would be used to control or suppress. That's what all those Jade Helm 15 exercises were about last year – training for this."

With that, the Operator reached down into his lap and lifted five identical sets of folders stamped TOP SECRET onto the table. He passed four sets of them out and kept one.

They were labeled REX 84 – Readiness Exercise 84.

The Operator summed up with this remark: "Nae-Née wasn't enough. Now we have the vaccine, tested in our favorite proving ground, Africa, ready for use. It's being mass produced as we speak, and huge quantities are ready. Now we can really make a dent."

Chapter 23

Ideas and Executions

There was a saying about how those who would sacrifice freedom for safety deserved neither, but what really interested me what the lack of realism involved in doing that. Anyone who would do that must be delusional.

Why would anyone who would sacrifice their freedom for safety believe that they would actually be protected?! Anyone without full freedom would be fair game to their alleged protectors. The lives of those who existed under that protection would not all be protected. Only those who were in line with the protectors could hope to stay alive.

It is common knowledge that governments do or know how to do terrible things.

Ever wonder just what those things are? Well, with Hamish around, I didn't have to.

He was telling me all about what he had trained to do, regardless of human rights prohibitions on such actions. He was telling me about REX 84. He had helped design it, and wished he hadn't. He was also explaining how Jade Helm was preparation for REX 84. Hamish was very upset now about all of this. He had thought it was just a random creative effort when he and his cohorts were ordered to write up their ideas so long ago, and now he saw that it wasn't.

The odd thing about them both was that they could be read about on Wikipedia, of all places. It was just that the actual intent to use it and for what was what we had to hack in order to see.

A "REX" was a Readiness Exercise, and this plan had been developed in 1984. Wow. The very year of that infamous dystopian novel about a police state by the same name (its proper title was in words, not digits: *Nineteen Eighty-Four*), written in 1948, hence the novel's title. In any case, REX 84 was the icing on the cake to Jade Helm because REX 84 was not about practice.

REX 84 was about putting the lessons of Jade Helm to use. It was a classified scenario and military drill (drill meaning it was real, not just practice, as with an exercise). The U.S. government had developed it for the purpose of suspending the United States Constitution with our rights, privileges, liberties, and whatever else in it – and declaring and instituting martial law.

All that would take would be for the President of the United States to declare a State of National Emergency. Under REX 84, any American citizen who was deemed a threat to national security could and would be detained. Who would decide who that would be?! Regardless, once that was decided, there would be no appeal and thus no recourse for such individuals.

The Federal Emergency Management Agency (FEMA) was in charge of dealing with natural and human-caused disasters. Floods, hurricanes, tornadoes, earthquakes, you name it – this was FEMA's department. FEMA was infamous for its gross mishandling of the aftermath of the 2005 hurricane Katrina in New Orleans, Louisiana and the misery, rapes, and false imprisonment that had ensued.

Now it had numerous other opportunities to cement that reputation, and it was taking full advantage of them…both with and without news coverage.

On the news, we saw FEMA and the U.S. Army working together to carry out the vaccination program all over the nation. Also, on the international news, we saw that other governments were carrying out vaccine programs of their own. The intriguing thing about those newscasts was the lack of coercion involved in other nations' vaccine programs. Those people seemed willing to go along with the injections.

It was eerie. I wondered what we might discover about those other nations off camera.

Meanwhile, on the news, the situation mimicked that of George Orwell's novel. Platitudes about how compliance with the vaccine program was for the public good accompanied newscasts of Americans lined up for their shots. Interviews were shown in which members of the general public extolled the virtues of what was essentially a nanny state, imposing what it decreed was beneficial for everyone. All reports of a growing plague were brushed off.

The problem with all this grandstanding was that I knew that it was a big lie.

The vaccination program was nothing more than a population cull.

"Damn!"

My mother jumped when I shouted that out. We were watching the news, appalled at what was happening. "*Nineteen Eighty-Four* was a warning, not a damned how-to guide!" I roared.

She looked at me, looked at the newscaster, and then nodded. Hamish and I had told her and my father what was in those vaccines, and shown them the whole thing in the basement lab. They would not tell anyone outside the family. They had, however, backed us up when my husband got those monster nanobots out of everyone at Aunt Zoe and Uncle Charlie's house, and that had been enough for them all.

Oddly – or perhaps not so oddly, now that we knew that much was being withheld from the general public – we had not heard or read a thing about the masses of immigrants being detained for months and years on end in border prisons. These privately-run, for-profit enterprises rivaled concentration camps for levels and methods of inflicting physical discomfort and abuse. That much had been reported upon before the stories abruptly and oddly ceased.

It was suspicious, to say the least. Gone were the accounts of toilets that were not maintained and rapes in the prisons. Gone were the tales of lives on hold while people who fled climate change and the strife it induced in their home nations. Where were these people now? Were they still there? Were they elsewhere? Had they been forced to go back? What was going on with those prisons?

Time to check in with Jason and see how much tougher that kid was getting when it came to discovering more authoritarian atrocities! We called him on another Saturday morning, and he was, as usual, available. It turned out that he was, like us, a bit asocial, and addicted to online gaming. He liked medieval quests with anthropomorphic, animalian avatars. Great. Bottom line: he was easy to schedule for more techno-telepathic sessions in our basement.

What we found this time was that FEMA had taken those prisons over.

It was more of REX 84.

Those camps looked appallingly familiar. Where had I seen such things before? Oh yeah…Auschwitz-Birkenau. That was the advantage of being a historian. I could just remember it rather than search the internet.

On our own, with our own news-gathering system, we saw what was going on.

We saw it all because of Jason, and because Hamish had created his own ultimate spyware: flying nanites. Taking the idea from what we had read in spy novels, Hamish had tinkered in his laboratory yet again. Now he could make his spy nanites fly long distances and show us things that we were not meant to see.

Always curious, I asked Hamish why a swarm of them was necessary rather than just one, and what they looked like. He said, "It's a fail-safe; any mechanical problems can be repaired in-flight by other swarm members. And they look like little robotic insects." With that, he showed me a still shot from his efforts in the laboratory. Each swarm nanobot was accounted for at all times by a code, and if one failed entirely, the others would rip it apart and drop the fragments far apart from one another.

This techno-telepathy enabled us to witness evil ideas and their executions. It was a holocaust of epic proportions, different from the last only in that the targets were not the same as in the previous one. In this holocaust, it was about shrinking the overall numbers of our entire species, eliminating those with the most unhealthy habits, genetics, and overall health, plus those with the least economic resources.

Don't like to exercise? Love to eat greasy fast food? Morbidly obese? Have a lot of cancer and genetic diseases in your family? Any physical deformities? Mentally unstable? Are you chronically poor, homeless, or otherwise down on your luck? Well, you're going to be Farmed.

Off to the Farm – the FEMA REX camps. Holocausts come with camps. Camps make mass murder, body dumps, and body and evidence disposal quicker and more efficient, after all.

Jason hacked into a dark net database run by the USAMRIID command and found confirmation and full details of this vaccine cull plan. This was what Hamish had discerned on his own, but finding that it was true and part of a concerted, deliberate plot to reduce the human population of the United States – plus that other nations had similar plans – was still a shock.

Camps had been built in rural areas all over the remaining land of our nation, and they included every feature that the Nazi death camps had been built with. There were barracks full of bunk beds, kitchens, showers, yards to congregate in, watch towers, administrative offices, barbed and razor-wire fences, search lights, sirens, and ovens. Stacks of biodegradable coffins – rows upon rows of them – stood at the back of the camps, behind the offices, which were conveniently situated right next to the crematoriums.

And they were mobile, capable of being dismantled and moved without a trace.

That puzzled me until Hamish and Jason pointed out a piece of the USAMRIID file that we had found. It said that patients who died would be immediately placed in one of these boxes, and then carried off to the crematorium to be incinerated inside it. Oh. That explained it.

So…the plan was to take people who were suffering from a mysterious illness – the one induced by the monster nanobots – to these camps, wait until they expired, and then dispose of them. Yeah…that was pure evil. There was no intention of curing anyone in this operation.

And how would people be getting to these camps?

MRAPs and canvas-covered trucks, just like the ones we had seen in the Blue Ridge Mountains, would remove people. They would pull up to whole neighborhoods of houses and shout at the residents through loudspeakers. Residents would be instructed to be outside in 5 minutes, stripping off their clothing as they walked out their front doors. As an inducement to get people moving along, promises of jumpsuits being provided at the vehicles out front would be made in those announcements.

The announcements were a lie. Upon arrival at the trucks, which looked just like the ones that took Jews away to concentration camps, including Anne Frank and her family, people would next be subjected to rape by cavity search. Anyone who resisted would be clubbed. Soldiers did carry heavy sticks, after all. With that, everyone would be forced to take seats in those wagons.

Stragglers who resisted coming out of their homes would be tear-gassed out. Windows would be shot out, and tear gas canisters lobbed inside. After that, people would be dragged outside. Once all residents were removed and driven off, the soldiers would be allowed into the homes to loot whatever they wanted.

Oh, and there was one other thing.

Those announcements over the loudspeakers would advise residents to kill their pets so that they would not starve once their caregivers were gone, because they would not be coming back. The announcement would claim that the area was being decontaminated due to disease to explain that peculiarity away.

I wondered whether or not, under this plan, people would actually be sick before this monstrous plan was put in motion. "Not necessarily," Hamish told me. "Most likely, they will be made sick at the camps with food that contains the triggers: high-fructose corn syrup, Frankenfruits, and whatever other GMO crap the military can serve up. A clean bill of health will be no deterrent. This vaccine cull is part reality and part smokescreen. Everyone who gets picked up and taken away will get sick, but the timing may have to be contrived to suit the plan later."

Awesome. The damned holocaust is back. We're being Terminated (yes, like in the movie series of that name) by evil corporations in concert with the government. "I wonder how many soldiers and corporate pukes will lose relatives that they want to keep alive in the confusion that all this creates?"

Jason and Hamish glanced away from the video of the REX 84 training exercise.

"Some, certainly," Hamish said. He and Jason turned back to the other screen.

We found actual examples of REX 84 use – that was the horror show that unfolded on Jason's screen. We saw suburban areas being cleared out after just a few low-income people started to get sick from eating too much fast food. They lived in cities, too, in subsidized housing. It was just a month and a half after the vaccines had been administered, and already some people were sick with cancer. They were really sick, not just being told that they were terminally ill by government-funded, Hippocratic Oath-breaking doctors.

"Do you think that people in Hartford might have been taken?" I asked Hamish. "I don't drive into the city much, and neither do you – that I know of – but if so, how would people in the city be taken without it being obvious?"

"They wouldn't," Hamish replied. "Most likely, according to this, police cruisers would take them away, to meet those trucks. The cops would be told that it was cancer, and that a special treatment was waiting for those patients. There would be so many each day, day after day, that the cops would not have time for crime. The public would be too sick anyway. As this picked up, the military would soon go in to help, but dressed as cops to avoid notice."

"Clever. Evil, and clever."

"Indeed. But we found a schedule. Hartford and Connecticut are far down the list. They're working in the south and southwest first, focusing on the border. Some of these mobile camps won't be packing up and moving for a while."

"How can people who live near the targeted areas not know what's happening there?"

"Signs get put up saying "Detour" and "Road Work" while the military crews deploy some officers in disguises – road crew getups, like people are used to seeing," Hamish told me. "Most people don't and won't question that. Those that do, who go in to check it out, won't come out."

I stared at him for a moment, considering the implications of that. Wow. The government was disposing of climate refugees in a horrifying way. No wonder the news had less and less to report on them. They weren't visible, they weren't here, and so the news didn't talk about the absence of people, only the presence of them. I wondered if that might be by design.

Finally, I was able to speak and said, "People are being treated as excess to be disposed of."

"Aye." Hamish sounded depressed, which was about right.

We found videos of REX 84 being carried out in many subdivisions, starting with those that were predominantly in foreclosure. There were lots of blighted areas in foreclosure that dated from before the floods, thanks to the economic meltdown of 2008. Both squatters and mortgagees were being dragged away, never to return. This pattern suggested anything but legitimate illness. This was a cleansing of human occupation.

It continued rapidly into the countryside, or so we thought until we checked the dates on the files. We recognized areas that Hamish and I had driven through on our road trip, now empty of people and their vehicles and camping equipment. This part was seen via Hamish's flying nanite cameras, in real time. Where were these people now? They had been swept away by a REX 84 in the late fall! It had probably happened even as we were driving on another route back north.

Next up: the flying nanite cameras headed for some suburban sprawl in New Jersey, of all places. In real time, we saw people being cleared out of subdivided housing there. That sickening punched-in-the-stomach feeling hit me again. Jason started crying.

"Do you have relatives there?" I asked.

"No."

"Neither do we, but I'm having a panic attack and I feel like throwing up," I told him.

He just nodded and kept the show going. This was the most disturbing reality show ever, and I usually had no interest in watching any of the ones on TV. How ironic that I suddenly felt the urge to watch them. It was all about context, I supposed.

Northeastern Washington, D.C. was cleared. Jason was switching to recorded videos again, too upset to watch another real time nanocast for now. Pittsburgh, Pennsylvania…Detroit, Michigan…Long Island, New York?! I noticed that it was the older, run-down, aging areas surrounded by ugly strip malls that were always being cleared out. It was never a mansion.

Did the Farmers think that skipping the mansions would keep them safe? Apparently.

It was all termed "Continuity of Government" as if to excuse this travesty.

I asked Hamish what the purpose behind it was.

"To clear land," was the reply.

Interesting. What for, I wondered? Then I thought about something in my earlier research called the Wildlands Map. It was still available online, but it didn't reflect the loss of land to the floods. It was aimed at removing humans from most of the land on this continent, and at giving it back to the wildlife altogether. Hikers and campers would not be allowed into these expanded national parks, which was what that reclaimed land would be called henceforth.

I looked at the Wildlands Map on my own laptop as Jason kept the horror videos running on the other one. The distraction of having something else to study while that monstrosity was laid out was a minor comfort. Next, I looked on Google Maps, hovering over rural and suburban Connecticut, wondering what housing developments would be targeted.

Anything post World War II might just be fair game. Suburban sprawl stretched into areas that had been rural even as I was growing up; I remembered Dad representing some real estate transactions on behalf of wealthy land developers. It had seemed insane even then, as if humans intended to "develop" – meaning build on – every last acre of land that they could acquire.

Now the government seemed to be backpedaling on that, forcing a reversal.

The government still had to finish up the vaccinations. It had to put on a full show, plus complete the set-up for the camps, I supposed. Hamish said that was exactly what they were up to. Without the soft-kill, hard-kills would be used, and those were too obvious. The government had an image of freedom and personal liberties to maintain.

It wasn't doing a very good job of that, though. Hamish found something online and pointed it out to me: Jade Palm 15. This was another military exercise, one that was being carried out in the Southwest. It was an eight-week training program for Navy SEALS and other elite, Special Forces. Its purpose was to train military units – the ones that would be carrying out REX 84s – to not care about civil liberties, human rights, or the rights guaranteed to U.S. citizens by our Constitution. So much for life, liberty, the pursuit of happiness, or anything else in it!

People were being attacked by military groups, arrested, and detained. "Psy-ops" were included, in which people were entrapped in camps until they took a positive view on being subjected to martial law. Wouldn't they just lie to their captors, saying anything they thought that they wanted to hear?

The soldiers who did this were expected to be rough and even brutal with private citizens, wielding night-sticks and electric cattle-prods against them. It was something that had been going on for a while. I noticed that the areas where Jade Palm 15s were being done were all in rural, spread-out areas. Some were in cities. Sure, people could shoot back, but that was about it…until the soldiers disarmed them, and then what?!

It was better to be mentally armed with knowledge of one's rights.

Upstairs in the kitchen with my parents, and on other stunned visits to Aunt Zoe and Uncle Charlie, we watched this being done. Turning on the news and not chatting was now a regular part of the visit, whether at our house or theirs. So much for normal social interaction; what we were watching was the opposite of normal. Grandmère told us how much this resembled what she had seen in Paris when she was 26 years old, particularly in the Marais, where the Jews had lived until the Nazis took them away.

People were herded into hastily erected enclosures in athletic fields, in a stadium on the edges of Manhattan and other major U.S. cities, and forced to remain there in crowds for days on end without sanitation. Bowls of what looked, at least from a distance as shown by news crews on television, to be gruel were the only things they were given to eat, easily drunk out of paper cups. No…as we watched, we saw packages of ready-to-eat, processed foods being handled out also. They had familiar labels on them, as they were sold in boxes and bags in grocery stores.

It was not difficult to see what these people looked like.

They were – at least, the majority of them – African-American and Hispanic.

They were chosen for their economic level of American society – the poverty level. It was common knowledge that that level included a huge percentage of this demographic. There were a few others in the mix – some white, some Asian, some Native Tribespeople – but not many.

What happened next was not pretty, nor was it surprising: beatings, rapes, filth, and misery.

What else could anyone have expected?

What was also not surprising was what Mindy said one night as we watched these events playing out on television from the comfort and relative safety of the living room in Connecticut: "These people are animals." She and her husband were visiting Aunt Zoe with their brood. It was a Tuesday evening, and I found myself glancing out the windows, worrying that this development that Uncle Charlie had built was new enough to be on the hit list.

But when she said that, I turned and stared steadily at her.

She noticed, and looked defensive.

I said it anyway: "Do you really think that if the majority of the people entrapped in that enclosure were white, like us, the outcome would be any different? Decent behavior requires money, safety, and comfort. Those people are terrified and in a lot of discomfort. They can't sleep because they have to stand upright with nothing to lean on. They have no place to go to the bathroom privately. They're hungry. You can count on them being terrified, outraged, and generally furious at what is happening to them with no real idea as to why it is happening."

No one had any rejoinder for that. Mindy turned red and said nothing more.

Those unfortunate people were kept there for days, trapped until the vaccines could be delivered to each and every one of them. After that, they would be let out, but not before.

We turned back to the television and watched as the military officer on a raised platform held a loudspeaker up and announced that vaccinations would start shortly, and to please line up near the entrance, and asked that each person move aside in an orderly fashion as soon as they received their shot.

It was sickening to know what was in that shot.

Claire and Ellie were sitting on a sofa together, watching this. Ellie wasn't paying rapt attention; she kept allowing herself to get distracted, talking to Mindy's kids. She was determined to shield them from the most disturbing bits of the report, as if they would stay oblivious. I knew it wouldn't. It didn't work for Anne Frank, and her family had tried that.

The kids were being undisciplined nuisances as usual, and as one of them ran into Claire, slamming her knee with a toy MRAP as he stumbled, she seemed really annoyed. I realized that maybe she wasn't fond of kids. I knew she had had little experience with them.

Claire spoke to me in detail about the report when it was over, while Ellie continued to play with the kids. I was impressed that Claire cared to take it all in and analyze it, and that she took its implications seriously. Whatever we discussed, she remembered.

Ellie, however, did not. She didn't care about details, only the big picture, and as a result, the picture she saw was incomplete. She was still talking about protests and getting the government to listen to her and anyone else who disagreed with this policy.

When I pointed out that all such civil liberties were suspended during martial law, the look in her eyes suggested that this did not compute. I had seen that look before in others when their assumptions were challenged. "The government protects our right to free speech and protest," Ellie said to me, glancing up just to say that, then back at the TV.

Damn she was dismissive and irritating! "No, Ellie, it only does that in the absence of martial law. With martial law in place, it treats citizens like so much annoying cattle. The militia will simply knock you around if you go to an area that is under martial law, and if you don't desist, they will arrest you, detain you, and they may just kill you," I said to her.

She said, "I don't believe that."

Edgar finally told me to just let her be, and I did, but it bothered me. "Well, I tried," I said.

It bothered me because someone like Ellie could easily get Farmed.

The visits with Jason in our secret basement nanocast sessions continued, and we were getting used to seeing these horrors. Lots of white people were also being carted away from suburban areas. As the REX 84s continued, it was obvious that race was not an issue in whether or not a neighborhood would be emptied. It was sheer numbers.

The United States had, if the population clock on the Internet was accurate, over 300 million people living in it. I clicked on the bookmarked link of my browser and checked it. Was it my imagination, or had that number gone down by roughly 19 million in the past few weeks?

I started keeping a note for myself on a small post-it pad with no label, just a number.

Sure enough, each day, that number was going down! So were the numbers of humans in other nations, other continents, other everything. In every category, the numbers were dropping. When I pointed this out to Hamish and Jason, they just nodded. None of us was very hungry anymore after our nanocast and cyber-snoop sessions.

We looked at those massive, for-profit prisons on the southern border of the U.S. There were still there, but now they were run by the military, and crematoriums had been added. Of course the vaccines had been administered there with no resistance. The would-be immigrants could not have put up any realistic fight. They were trapped like rats. The crematoriums there were always smoking, and we looked each week at each camp.

Why Jason kept showing up to do this was a question on my mind. I asked Hamish whether or not he was entirely trustworthy, and Hamish assured me that Jason was watched and kept safe, and that he was with us to the end.

How could we know this? What proof was there?

Hamish looked a bit uncomfortable, and then he told me why. Jason's cousins had lived in Hicksville, New York. That was a town on Long Island that had been erased. He had grown up playing with them, and seeing them every Thanksgiving in Elmwood of West Hartford, and had been to their homes for visits. Jason now lived in a small house near West Hartford Center, and was using his pay to buy one next door for his parents. Like us, he was trying to avoid REX 84.

Okay then – Jason was trustworthy. He hated the Farmers because their seeds had enabled the farming of his own family. Hamish had personally visited Jason and his parents to remove the evil nanobots from their systems. I had gone with him, and we had made it seem like a friendly dinner party...until we pulled the shades and went to the basement to do the deed.

While he was at it, Hamish told Jason's parents about how we had been right next to that couple in a similar car who had gotten killed by a speeding tractor trailer truck. He also confided our suspicions about it having been a Farming attempt on our lives.

Jason suddenly remembered that he was supposed to check on that crash and did some hacking on the laptop. Yes, it was a Farming attempt, but not on us, so it was considered a success. That couple had been a pair of physicians and engineers who understood nanotechnology. They had figured out what Hamish had and, unlike him, were planning to go public. They had been on their way to meet a reporter and tell what they knew.

That resolved 3 questions: who had been the target, why, and should we tell what we knew?

Answers: other people, because they were planning to tell, and NO.

Whistle-blowing was not the solution; stealth was.

So what happened with the Ebola virus and the plan to use it in the vaccine cull campaign?

Something must have been going on, I figured, or why bother to test it.

When I mentioned this idea to Hamish and Jason, they had immediately started clicking away on our secret laptop. We were definitely going to have to wipe and destroy that thing if we left home for any length of time, I thought to myself.

"Well? Anything?" I asked after several minutes.

"Oh yeah." Hamish's tone was flat and appalled.

"And?"

"It was a last resort. The cancer-with-trigger-Frankenfood plan failed to work fast enough."

"Well, I figured it was another murder weapon, but how does this fit in, exactly?"

"Cancer is just too slow. Granted, in the massive number of patients with it that are being generated thanks to this vaccine cull program, cancer gets people removed from large areas. The numbers are too high for hospital infrastructures to handle, or even visiting nurses. So that starts people on the road to death. But once they are in the camps, they die too slowly with cancer. Adding Ebola to the mix hurries the process up."

"Why don't they just shoot people or gas them to death, if they're in such a hurry to see them dead? Are they trying to conceal the evidence for future generations, so that when this holocaust hits the history books, it looks like an ecological catastrophe?!"

Hamish gave me a mirthless grin. "That is exactly what they are up to."

"But that just sounds like a conspiracy theory!" I protested, pacing around the room.

"Aye. And that's the beauty of it. It sounds so outrageous that no one will take the idea seriously. It's the perfect cover for this crime."

I sat down, breathless even though I hadn't been exerting myself.

I couldn't think of anything else to say. What was there to say? I felt as though I had said it many times, and that it would never matter, no matter what I tried to do about it. How was I supposed to prevent the deaths of billions? Here in my own country, this meant the deaths of hundreds of millions – far more than the

100 to 200 million who had died almost 8 centuries earlier in the bubonic plague. It was incredible to contemplate.

"So how do they do this?" I wanted to know.

Hamish explained, "The vaccine already includes Ebola. The REX guys wait until they get all of the kidnappees to the camps, feed them GMOs, wait a week or so, and then, when that doesn't cause death fast enough to suit them, they herd each kidnappee into what looks like a huge, empty room, claiming that it's a vapor treatment that will make them feel better. Then they just wait a couple of hours, pretending to give people hope, gassing them to sleep until they die. At that point, they turn on the flames in that room, which is actually one of those mobile crematorium ovens."

I gaped at him, listening to this, and then closed my mouth. No point in staring like a dope. Yes, it was appalling beyond acceptability, but emotion expended on this as a reaction did nothing for the victims. I should be studying this problem and thinking of a way to fight it.

"Does it say what happens to the ashes?"

"They get scattered on the fields of big agribusinesses."

"What?! That's like Soylent Green in the Frankenfoods that they grow!"

"Aye, that it is."

"Yuck. It's a faster soft-kill, force-fed to captives before they die."

"It is. Damn, Avril, you just keep analyzing and correlating the most disturbing aspects of this into the mix," Jason remarked.

"I can't seem to stop," I replied.

With that, we all lapsed back into what we were staring at on our computers.

How many people had lived in the United States in 1930, when the Earth's population of humans was at capacity, at 2 billion? And if the Georgia Guidestones were any clue, even that number might be a lot higher than the Farmers wanted it to be. Calming myself down enough to look things up again, I went back to my own laptop.

Found it: the population of the United States in 1930 was 122,775,046.

Today, we had 300,086,002. It was less than it had been a week ago. Not much, but less.

That had to be an indication of something strange going on. Did anyone else who watched the news – anyone not like myself, not researching this, not questioning this in any depth – realize that this was not normal?

I ran that idea by Hamish. He and Jason both weighed in on that. They thought that most people were too distracted by the mass illnesses to be anything more than puzzled and scared. They lacked the advantages we had, advantages which freed us to think and analyze this situation: 1. Hamish had taken out the evil nanobotic monsters; and 2. we knew what was going on. Most people were still fair game in this holocaust, and did not know how to avoid it.

After listening to that analysis, I went back to my population counts. What about other countries? What about the total number of humans on the planet? There were over 7.4 billion last year. I knew that because population statistics fascinated me, be it morbidly so or otherwise.

There were just over 6.4 billion now. What were other countries doing?!

"What ours is doing," Hamish said.

I realized I was whispering to myself as I read.

Moving on to look up Ebola, which was oddly capitalized, unlike polio, smallpox, mumps, measles, or any of the other diseases that the vaccine campaign targeted, I found plenty to read. The first thing I noticed was that the United Nations had given Ebola blood samples their own code when transporting them anywhere: UN 2814. It indicated "infectious substances, affecting humans" and required that the vials of samples be packed in three layers of protective and absorbent material. Lovely! That made me feel safe, I thought sarcastically.

Ebola was spread through direct contact with bodily fluids. I thought back to what I had read months earlier about this disease. Funeral preparations and the funerals themselves in African societies helped it to get from one human host to another. Once delivered, it drained the host of every type of fluid a mammal could release: blood, sweat, tears, bile, urine, feces, saliva, you name it, all liquefied and oozing. Death by biological torture did not leave a peaceful-looking corpse for the mourners, either. Why didn't people just cremate?!

Customs died hard, just like people, with Ebola.

"This site claims that Ebola isn't spread through air or water," I said.

Hamish didn't even look up from what he and Jason were watching. He just replied, "That's not true. The virus has mutated. It's airborne now. USAMRIID doesn't want that getting out, but we've been looking at their data and publicity decisions. They're lying to the public."

"Wonderful." I went back to reading.

Patients, most of whom were still in Africa, had little or no incentive to cooperate with health authorities and quarantines. It was a one-way ticket to death, do not pass "Go" but go straight to a medical jail, never to see your family alive again. The flow of information would not be both ways, either. Language barriers, health care protocols, and the relentless pace of patients falling deathly ill prevented communication. No one had time to talk to scared relatives.

There was some effort made to show the relatives how their sick family members were doing from a safe distance, but for the most part, the disease was too infectious. The temptation to cross those barriers was also too great a risk. Most hospitals chose enclosed designs.

It was tough to work in the intense heat and humidity of Africa in the suits that health care professionals had to wear. Each worker required help to put the suits on, which slowed down the process of getting dressed just to approach a patient. Once ready, the nurse or doctor could only spend a couple of hours at a time around the sick patients before it was too hot to work. Needle pricks from jerking, spasmodic patients could condemn a worker to death by Ebola.

As I watched the news reports on the quarantine measures and realized what was being demanded of people – that they just go into the FEMA camps and die, only to have their remains incinerated without fanfare and be forgotten – I remembered how awful it felt when Hamish and I had no money and felt a sense of hopelessness.

We felt worthless, like we counted for nothing, and that all of our efforts to develop skills and earn academic qualifications were pointless.

We felt quite certain, as we struggled with our autism spectrum condition, trying to earn a living income and failing time after time, that society, without consciously contemplating our situation, just wanted us to disappear. It felt as though society wanted us dead and out of the way, and that there was no room for us.

Why should there be? I knew that the planet was grossly overpopulated even then. Every living being was struggling to matter, to survive, to find a way to produce an income and occupy enough space – and desirable space at that – to make the effort enjoyable enough to feel worth that effort.

If we felt tacitly hated, how must the people trapped in these camps feel?!

I used to find myself looking at homeless people and worrying that that would be our fate. It was terrifying, demoralizing, and left me feeling like I had a broken heart and a somewhat dead sense of rage. Not outrage – just rage. Why should I have to disappear into the shadows? I had skills worth sharing. I worked hard. I cared about things.

Whenever I saw a homeless person, I would give them money, and not just a few coins, either. I would carefully, nicely, place some paper money into a homeless person's cup or hat or whatever they had laid out in front of them, look them in the eye like they mattered, and pause to chat with them and hear their story. I didn't care whether or not that story was the real one – it was real to that person, and it was what they could bear to share with me, a complete stranger. It was the least I could do.

As I had been lucky enough to get out of that awful feeling of dread and despair about my own future and ability to take care of myself, I had carried around more money to give away, making it 5s, 10s, and even 20s rather than one-dollar bills. I would even go back sometimes with a meal, bought nearby, after checking to make sure that she or he would be there when I returned with the food.

This might sound stupid, but it was something I had always wished I could do for homeless people when I didn't have money, when all I could spare was a quarter or two. I could do this after Hamish and I got rich, so I had. The homeless person still had the choice of going wherever and doing whatever she or he wished after we met.

When I couldn't see a future for myself and Hamish as being capable of paying our own way, it was all I could think about for much of my time. Hamish told me it weighed on him too, and he often felt like killing himself. We didn't do that, obviously, but we felt like failures with our advanced degrees. There were many of them, we knew, people who could study their way right through to the highest level, but couldn't function socially in any work environment.

That was us. We just got lucky with our Nae-Née invention, and after that, my books and Hamish's other work were in hot demand. Lucky, lucky, lucky. We didn't have to be the kind of Aspies whose work was only appreciated when we were dead, like Vincent Van Gogh, to name one example. (One could observe the markers of Asperger's in people long dead, since before those markers had been identified.)

It sounded whiny and pathetic, and yet that was the hidden disability aspect of being an Aspie, latched onto a mental superpower of intense focus and hard work. It was like this for Aspies everywhere.

Now I looked at the live video feed on the laptop that Hamish and Jason were working with, at the Americans who were disappearing from towns and cities all over the United States and into camps. We saw the remains of aspiring immigrants going up in smoke at the border prisons. We saw kidnappings by military units repeated over and over, in suburbs, slums, little housing subdivisions, subsidized housing, and roadsides.

Most roadsides were cleared of people by now. The selfish couple we had met at that bed-and-breakfast inn on our road trip, the one from Woodbridge, Virginia, could probably go out for a nice drive in the country soon and see no sign of American climate refugees. As long as they didn't venture into areas where those camps were – and those camps were being set up and then dismantled wherever the military units went – they would see nothing amiss.

That was part of the ruthless efficiency of it all: the camps were mobile. They could be fully operational within hours of a unit's arrival thanks to the planning of USAMRIID, and then gone without a trace after the fact. Unlike the previous human holocaust, no memorial museums would be created at the crime scenes of this one after the fact.

And why was that? Because it would be almost impossible to tell where those camps had been. They were like ghosts before they had even created ghosts. An angel of death was sweeping the nation, and it had its own forensic experts to cover its tracks.

Our past problems and feelings were nothing compared to what its victims were facing. These people were doomed, like so much extra stock in a storehouse of live wares. They all had feelings and hopes and needs and wants and dreams, just as we did.

As far as the Farmers of our society's secret policy-makers were concerned, none of that mattered. These people were excess, and the excess needed to be reduced. Waiting for human population levels to go down quietly via the Nae-Née policy was too slow for them. Too many resources would be consumed that way.

It was sickening to know that this was what we were watching in the news.

It was presented in so subtle a way that it was not immediately apparent.

In order to draw this conclusion, one had to not only watch and read the news, but do so via multiple sources with a variety of viewpoints. The Deep Dark Net was proving very useful in this regard.

Another question nagged at me: was it treason to do this right back to those who were themselves so evil as to be on a par with Dr. Josef Mengele, the Anti-Christ of the Nazis? I didn't think so. I was glad that Hamish and I had gone to such lengths to infest Wall Street Farmers with their own nano-monsters. They had laid the groundwork for what was happening. They deserved a taste of their own poison.

Too bad the implementers of REX 84s couldn't be infested also.

Treason tends to be gets labeled as such simply because of who is involved: a citizen giving a tyrant a taste of his or her own poison. Well, if it's poison, then the citizens who know about it have a duty to force-feed it back to them! Or to covertly trick-feed it back to them…

And why?!

I could tell you why any time: because there should be no mass murder to deal with human overpopulation! It should only be dealt with via a birth licensing policy, so that we all may have our lives to live. Let it be each individual's own responsibility what we make of our lives, not the police state's!

Let us take the risk and burden of getting old without enough human caregivers to ease us through that last, difficult phase of life. So what, we'll be overcrowded and it will get tough. It was already going to be that way. Old age always gets tough anyway!

People should still have their lives to live.

Chapter 24

Anti-Vax

The news had been a chore to wade through today, perhaps more so than usual.

Water shortages, water regulations, water overuse fines, vaccine announcements and injection sites with rosters to check online, enticements to get one's car either converted to electricity or to just buy a new electric car, and on and on and on.

Then there was that suspicious death.

It was presented in a blasé manner, as nothing remarkable, but it seemed rather odd.

A doctor had allegedly committed suicide after being discredited by the American Medical Association for claiming that vaccines – particularly the new vaccine that the world's governments were administering – were dangerous. He had given a lecture about it last week and published online about it. Not only were vaccines dangerous, he had insisted, but they were lethal, carcinogenic, and capable of altering DNA. Well, I thought, that sounded familiar!

That he was dead at all was suspicious. That he was dead after saying all that, and once the vaccine was in use was suspicious. That he was dead in the manner that he was dead was even more suspicious, because it did not look like a suicide.

Dr. Anthony Warburg (whose colleagues jokingly called him Dr. Warbucks) had been a physician from the Dana Farber Cancer Center in Boston, Massachusetts, an oncologist and immunologist with over twenty-five years of experience in his field. He had everything to live for: beautiful wife who worked as a curator at the Isabella Stewart Gardner Museum, teenage daughter who played the bassoon and had been accepted to Wellesley College, golfing buddies, and a Golden Retriever named Winnie who rode to his office with him.

He had published over forty articles about his research and his patients admired him.

Why then would he shoot himself in the chest and leap into the Charles River? And how did he manage to get into the river after shooting himself? Did he stand up against the bridge railing and aim the gun at himself, so as to fall into the water? Usually, suicidal men shot themselves in the head and made a horrid mess for people to find and clean up, doing the deed at home so that they could be found by family members, as if to upset them after feeling so upset themselves that they chose to commit suicide.

No. This didn't fit the pattern of a suicide at all. It seemed more like body dump.

Someone wanted this guy silenced.

At the end of the day, Hamish called me and asked me to visit him in his new lab.

"Okay," I said. "I'm right downstairs, about to go into Shayna's centergy class, though. Can you wait until after that, and let me clean up, or are you in a big hurry?"

"Go to your class and take your shower," he said. "I'll be here. You have the car keys. I'm your captive passenger." I could just hear the grin in his voice.

I laughed and said I'd see him later, and hung up my cell phone. Odd…service in here used to be non-existent, but now it worked everywhere I went. Must be some new cell phone towers, or more compact cell phone equipment around here, I mused.

Shayna's class was as fun as ever, with her smiling like the yoga stretches and pilates crunches that she was leading us through were just the best feeling in the world. The class always made me a sweaty mess, but it also made me stronger and my sense of balance, which was shaky for Aspies, steadier. I loved it. Claire wasn't there today. She had left with Fabian and Jacques, so I was on my own, but I felt great even without the company. I loved those stretches!

I also loved following Shayna through the routines – even when they changed – because she smiled so pleasantly and sincerely. No wonder it all felt good to her; this was a woman who, unlike myself, loved exercise. She was a triathlete.

When it was over, I rolled up my long and thick purple mat and headed for the showers, skipping my habit of pausing to exchange a few bits of news with Shayna. She probably had to get to the pool with her boyfriend or home to her kids anyway. I tended to chat with people at the wrong moments or for too long, but I like the social interaction.

It was a bit frustrating…I liked some social interaction, but not a lot. Aspies could be asocial, and that was me for the bulk of my time. However, after hours on end of solitary research and reading, I suddenly wanted to move about and chat nonstop with people. It never worked well enough. I couldn't tell when I was overdoing it. Oh well…

That was what I thought about as I got my stuff and headed for the showers, and I pushed it out of my mind to chat with some of the elderly ladies in the locker room. They were an interesting lot: one used to live on Kaua'i, and she got a kick out of the fact that I could pronounce that island's name with the glottal stop at the 'okina, the upside-down apostrophe between the last "a" and the "i" in it. Another lady was doing her Ph.D. in psychology.

After that, it was onto the scale to wish I were six pounds lighter, then into the showers.

A little while later, I was putting on purple eyeliner (purple was fun!) and drying my long hair. I packed up, grabbed my stuff, and headed for the elevator. The stairs were in a well, and I didn't like it in there. Unless the building was on fire, I would use the elevator, despite the fact that these medical offices were in plain sight of a health club, easily visible from all sides over the balcony that spanned the entire atrium. Never mind that I imagined the disapproving gaze of doctors watching me not take the stairs, I thought with a grin.

The staff had gone home, and I knew that Hamish was in one of the back examination rooms, waiting for me. In fact, he looked very serious. He was comfortably ensconced in his new digs, and ready to start offering safe vaccines.

Good to see him combining his clinical and research expertise, I thought, and out of that Agenda 21 development at Blue Back Square. Hopefully, he would find a way to share his nanobotic engineering talents with some more people…covertly.

"Hi!" I walked right in past the reception area, waving at Ellen and Cara as I did so.

My husband was in jeans and a plain tee shirt as usual, but with a white lab coat so that patients would see him dressed like a doctor wearing his lab coat. He looked more like a physician than a jokester to me, dressed like that. Funny how important that was to people…

I smiled and kissed him on the cheek. He smiled and kissed me back, in a hurry to get past pleasantries, took my hand, and pulled me to an exam room in the back of the suite. When we got to it, he shut the door, waved me over to the pink-upholstered exam table, and pointed out his setup to me.

"Looks great," I said, impressed.

Hamish smiled, kissed me again, and leaned over me. "I'm going to undo the damage that that MMR and that flu vaccine that did to as many other people as I can," he replied.

"Is this this going to be like what you did to fix me at home?" I asked.

"Yes."

Without further ado, he started to show me his setup.

"What is this, your own assembly line of monster nanobot extraction?" I asked.

He looked at me, then said, "Yes. It's a secret. I will tell you the whole story, but this is not what I tell patients. For them, I will just say that the ingredients that they have doubts about, thanks to all of the anti-vax groups, petitions, and other protests that have gone on for years are removed with this process."

"Well…?" I am not the patient sort.

He sat down on the stool by the counter, still holding the now-empty vial, and rolled over to a spot in front of me. "I will explain that the vaccines will not be removed, but that this does provide a sort of antidote to them. I won't tell them what was in those injections. I won't tell them about the nanites. If you tell a secret like that, you either attract the attention of the Farmers, get labeled a conspiracy theorist, or both."

"Won't people ask why we would need an antidote to an antidote?" I asked. "Because we can't tell them that those other vaccines have in them."

"Indeed. They are actually soft-kills. Any foods that contain high-fructose corn syrup, fast foods, and anything with GMOs, such as Frankenfruits, are triggers."

"Yuck. No wonder you're so adamant that I buy organic foods. But not everyone has access to them. It takes money to pay for them. They cost more than the other fruits and vegetables and grains. And not everyone lives close enough to a Whole Foods store, or has a car to drive."

"True. There will be limits to how much we can help. People will still end up eating some of these poisons for that reason. But without the first part – the soft-kill ingredients in those travesties of vaccines – the secondary part, the trigger, won't work."

"You are a subversive one, aren't you, Dr. MacDonall?" I grinned at him. "You are living up to your name again, usurping the government's agenda. THIS is the real anti-vax – you removing the soft-kill ingredients from the patients themselves. You are the consummate, pent-ultimate usurper."

"You bet I am," he said, kissing me. "Now let's go out to dinner."

"Not so fast." I pulled out my memory stick, inserted it into his laptop, and opened the article I had saved on Dr. Anthony Warburg. "I'm glad you aren't making any big announcements about how dangerous this vaccine is. There's nothing to be gained from doing that. This covert way of fighting is better. You get to live, and whomever you help gets to live. This guy won't be able to help anyone with his strategy, despite the fact that he figured out what's going on."

Hamish read through the story quickly, looking grim, and nodded. "I thought as much."

"I'm so glad you're stealthy and not foolishly impulsive about this, telling the world."

"Me too, Avril. I love you. I'm going to do my best to keep us all alive and safe."

"I know," I said, and kissed him. He hugged and kissed me, and held me for a minute.

We left the room, said good-night to Ellen and Cara, and headed out into the parking lot.

Some Indian curry at the place on Route 44 in Avon, Bombay Grill, was on our minds. Spices were another method of staying healthy and preventing all sorts of autoimmune system failures – cancer among them – and they tasted so good!

I drove us directly there, with Blackout Security in covert pursuit as usual, and we ordered garlic nan, eggplant curry purée, bindi masala (that's okra), basmati rice, mango lassi, and finally, carrot pudding with cashews and pistachio nuts. Hamish got a beer, and I had a couple of sips. He had some of my lassi. I even enjoyed some chai tea with cardamom and ginger in it at the end of the meal, but Hamish wanted another beer. He said he needed the buzz to relax after a long day of formulating sera in his lab.

I just grinned at him and ate some more carrot pudding.

Chapter 25

Trust the Government…No, Don't

"Soon, higher percentages of birth licenses will be granted, so don't lose hope," John Lassiter, the Secretary of the Department of Demographics was saying. "Trust the CDC and the government; we'll safeguard the public health and assure our future."

We were watching a press conference that was being given in Washington, D.C. at the National Press Club, live on CNN. The whole family was gathered around the TV in Aunt Zoe and Uncle Charlie's living room, including Claire, plus Ellie, and plus Ed and Aaron.

As Lassiter spoke, the Surgeon General, a man named Loren Wilson, sat in one of the seats in front of him, facing the cameras. They were broadcasting from some government offices that I didn't recognize, with a sign behind them that said "U.S. Department of Demographics" that showed its logo: a human footprint. It was a carbon footprint, just to remind everyone of the effect that humans had on the planet. The Agenda 21 people must have suggested it.

Dr. Wilson was in his mid-sixties, a man of medium height and build with gray eyes and graying dark hair. He had made his career by promoting healthy eating habits, exercise, and preventive medicine. He looked very uncomfortable with everything that Lassiter was saying. And why not? His authority had been pretty much usurped by Lassiter.

I looked at Hamish. "That makes no sense," I said.

He looked at me. "Think about it. Why would a government official say a thing like that?"

"With a population nearing eight billion humans, Nae-Née won't slow things down any too quickly. We'll likely have to wait for at least a generation to start seeing its effects and benefits. So why would it be enough so soon for him to be saying that?" I needed more data to process if I was to come to any meaningful conclusion on this, it seemed.

Hamish watched me, looking both glum and deadpan at the same time.

I watched him.

Finally, he said, "Think of something that is not nice. Think of something that the general public…and you…would not want to contemplate."

Oh. "Think of something evil?!" I said, appalled but catching on.

He nodded.

"They're going to speed up the population reduction process somehow. With a method that doesn't look like that's what they're doing…" I was pacing around the living room. It was mid-afternoon on a Sunday, and my parents were out driving around again.

"You got it."

I looked at my husband again. "They're using the vaccine policy and laws to do this!"

"Right again."

I sat down on the sofa with a thud and stared into space. Soon I was railing against it. "I don't like it. They're going to kill lots of good people who don't deserve to miss out on a full-length lifespan. They're going to kill people who are fascinating and talented and inventive, and they're going to kill people with great stories to tell and wisdom to share, and they're going to kill lots of other people with qualities that we don't and won't know about because they will be dead."

Ellie stared at me. "You really don't trust the government, do you?"

Hamish and I stared right back, and then I said, "Did you understand nothing about why Hamish was so careful with all of our vaccinations? The government wants as many of us dead as possible. There is no other planet for us – just this one – and this idiot new world order of a planetary government as an umbrella organization that manages each nation has decided to cull us, picking us off until our numbers match those suggested on the Georgia Guidestones."

This did not seem to compute with Ellie. "But we can protest, sign petitions, vote…"

"Oh sure, we can do all of those things, but there is more to the law than that. And don't confuse law with justice. We are all nations of laws. The new world order has been at work for a couple of decades, being implemented administratively, to circumvent our vote. Fabian and Claire want to go to law school. They will certainly come to understand this if they do."

Ellie was still not settled with any of this. She had something else on her mind as well. "You don't believe in the goodness of people or governments, do you? I mean, you're an atheist. You don't go to church."

With that, I laughed. "Deism might work for some scientists and Aspies, but if there really is any such entity, I have no use for thinking of it as male rather than female – or gendered at all – or as benevolently concerned with the affairs of our species. There is Nature. But Nature or a goddess is indifferent to human wishes."

"So you don't believe we can trust the government, or that God will help us?" Ellie asked.

"No. Our species labors under the delusions of wishful thinking combined with arrogance that we matter above all others. It's killing us and those others. It's amoral, but what's new about that? The Farmers – the banksters and hedge fundsters who are engineering this new world order don't care about anything but power, control, and a stealthy acquisition of resources with no resistance. It's completely up to us to see that, think independently, and act on it…quietly."

"Why don't you just speak out about what you know?" she asked.

"No one would believe me. I would be treated as a modern-day Cassandra and ignored."

Grandmère chimed in at this point. "There's little hope of stopping it. History shows it."

"Indeed," I said. "We're all in a lot of trouble now. We'll have to be stealthy and determined in order to survive, to live to tell about any of this, and to make changes later on. We can't enforce our will, our wisdom, or anything else during an upheaval such as the one that we are experiencing now. We must watch and wait no matter how great the urge to draw attention to ourselves, because doing so will simply be game over for us. No…it's stealth or nothing."

I don't think Ellie absorbed that part of the discussion, but the others nodded agreement.

Sure enough, compulsory vaccines started – as many as the government could arrange.

Children were required to receive any and every vaccine known to humanity. Their often six-month-old immune systems were hit with a veritable assault of vaccines: measles, mumps, rubella, diphtheria, tetanus, pertussis, polio, smallpox, influenza, hepatitis A, hepatitis B, meningococcal shots, and so on and on.

This was being done at an early age, before their immune systems were ready, threatening the health of their still-developing brains and nervous systems. No spacing out of vaccines was allowed by doctors, some of whom even published letters to the public in newspapers laying down the law of their practices. No exceptions, no arguments from parents.

Schools began administering vaccines while students were away from their parents, and records were kept of any absences. The next time those kids showed up at school, they were vaccinated with whatever they had missed. If parents thought that keeping their kids out for a day or two would enable them to control that situation, they were wrong. No need to threaten kids with expulsion anymore; there was simply no way to avoid the vaccines.

The weirdest part of all this was seeing advertisements for free vaccines with kiddie meals at fast food joints. These vaccines would, not surprisingly, hit the kids' immune systems with absolutely everything at once.

Two days after Lassiter and an ill-at-ease Wilson had appeared on our screens, the national news ran a breaking story. "At the home of the Surgeon General this morning, in his study, Dr. Wilson's wife made a gruesome discovery. She found her husband hanging from the chandelier by his necktie. Emergency services arrived and took her away, crying hysterically."

With that, the feed cut to a video recording of just that, and I turned up the volume. Anne Marie Wilson was shouting about having seen bruises around her husband's wrists. That was when the video stopped and the feed abruptly returned to the newscaster. He announced that Mrs. Wilson had been taken to a secure hospital to rest and recuperate.

I sat there with my mother, stunned, and glanced over at her. She was staring at the TV still. We were having tea and cookies and it was the middle of the afternoon. The show she had been watching, some soap opera, had been interrupted for this, which was why I had sat down. "Did you notice what his wife was trying to say?" My mother asked.

"I did," I said. "Did you notice the other night, when John Lassiter was announcing the vaccine policy and Dr. Wilson was sitting near him, how uncomfortable he looked? I wouldn't be surprised if it turns out that his computer has been wiped clean, probably of whatever statement he wanted to release about that, contradicting Lassiter about some of its points."

My mother gave me a long look, and then gazed into her tea. "Me neither."

Parents who sought to avoid the new policy by home-schooling their children were visited personally by representatives from their local boards of health. Police officers accompanied them. Despite assurances that noncompliance meant fines or jail, parents still objected. While those parents were locked up, their kids got vaccinated. When the parents were released, they found that their wishes had been circumvented by their government.

State and federal agencies had been tainted – no, contaminated – by money from pharmaceutical companies, parents thought. If only they had known that it was worse than that! It was a population policy at work, with an agenda of "managing" health to reduce numbers.

Boards of health, state agencies, federal agencies, the Center for Disease Control…all of these organizations, sanctioned by the government, were not seeking to preserve and protect the health of the citizens whom they governed, and whose tax revenue paid for them. No…they sought to manage their health, as if being healthy were the problem to be solved.

It was the ultimate lie – the ultimate soft-kill – in that the illusion that humans had no real checks from Nature on our population would be preserved. While this vaccination policy was being carried out, that lie, I knew from Hamish's nanobotic removal process, would be a murder weapon. It was the perfect cover.

That wasn't all.

Bank bail-ins started. I could tell they were about to happen when banks began to be bricked up, covering all windows. Any bank that had not yet blocked off tellers with thick plexiglass did so. Anyone with money in an American bank lost forty percent of it.

Lines formed outside of banks everywhere regardless, and people looked frantic.

The New York Stock Exchange froze up and was closed with no word on when it would reopen. The bubble from buying stocks has risen in China, and that had affected markets across the globe. China's entire loss exceeded the budget of individual European nations, which was something to fathom, and something mind-blowing to non-trading mavens.

Chinese peasants had ceased to farm during trading hours so that they could go online and engage in day trading. They had done this solely on the strength of hearsay and inflated estimates of their chances at making a profit reported by government news sources. When the bubble inevitably grew just as it had in the 1920s, it burst, just as it did on October 24, 1929.

Predictably, Twitter lit up with speculative nonsense from individuals, pundits, major television news sources, and whoever else cared to add their now worthless two cents to the mix. Various theories involved unrelated, unlikely tangent thoughts, conspiracy theories, and ideas that were not researched and not proven yet on point…and still labelled conspiracy theories.

As for the banksters in charge of the New York Stock Exchange, they dismissed the shutdown as a technical computer glitch, said it had been fixed, and that it was nothing to panic about. The market reopened after a lapse of a day and a half, and trading resumed.

Consumer confidence was muted, of course, but too many ordinary citizens involved in day trading in the United States were too involved to just back out. Accordingly, trading resumed with a tinge of fear and a faint note of desperation. As for hope, I guess it remained for those who didn't kill themselves, and there were a few of those in the news.

In response to all this, corporations all over the United States cut thousands more jobs.

People weren't needed to make a corporation profitable, and it was all about profit.

The corporations hid under the aegis of legal "personhood" – such contrived bunk, we all thought, but it would take another Supreme Court case, an Act of Congress, or even a Constitutional Amendment to fix that – and remained at war with everyone else.

Whatever the cause, we were in the throes of another shocking and debilitating economic meltdown worse than the one from 1929. Fear would make people easy to control, we knew that much. Fear did not grip us, however, because we were prepared for this.

Hamish had insisted upon transferring the bulk of our financial holdings to Swiss banks long before this, so we were covered. We had a Swiss attorney moving a monthly allowance from our accounts there to our accounts in the United States, so the U.S. government was disappointed when it tried to acquire our money. Too bad; it only got a trickle.

Meanwhile, we had a credit card linked to one of our accounts in Switzerland, so we were safely able to afford the basic necessities and whatever else. It felt surreal and monstrous to be comfortable while those around us were barely able to buy food. Prices on certain items had dropped to a bare minimum to encourage their distribution, while other items – natural ones – remained just out of reach so as to become "luxury" foods.

This was all over the news, with interviews of angry shoppers emerging from supermarkets.

This was disgusting; the economy had been artificially crashed to create a panic, and it had worked. There wasn't a famine going on in America! The government just wanted to tighten its grip on the population, to control as many people as possible so that they would be quicker and easier to vaccinate and cull.

Forget retrieving the contents of your safe deposit box – nothing was safe there anymore. The government was about to stick its hand inside and scoop out anything of value: money, stocks, bonds, rare coins, jewelry, you name it.

Clearly, the combination of these actions – compulsory vaccines and bank bail-ins – was no coincidence. Governments everywhere were doing this. The agenda behind these actions was obvious, at least to me and to Hamish. It was to loot as many assets as possible from citizens before their lives ended...or were ended for them.

As I watched the news and went about my daily business, I noticed that the prices of organic, healthy, non-GMO foods shot up, both in Whole Foods and other grocery stores like Big Y. I bought what I needed, then wondered about the cost of trigger foods.

"Come on," I said to Aaron as I paid the cashier in Whole Foods. "We're going sleuthing in Big Y next. I don't really need more food, but I'll figure something out. Maybe I can buy some broth just to explain the excursion."

Aaron looked at me like he understood what I was up to, and I'm sure he did.

I drove us over there and went into the store, grabbed a basket, and started making the rounds of the store. Produce cost as much in this store as it did in Whole Foods. No surprise there. I noticed Aaron glancing at the prices as well as watching for threats to my safety. He was getting curious and distracted, but was still about to keep an eye on me.

Next, fish, poultry, cheese, deli, and finally aisles and aisles of canned and packaged goods. Now we were going to see what was different, I thought, and we did. After grabbing the bouillon cubes I was after, I looked like I was shopping rather than sleuthing, or so I hoped. On to the packaged, processed products: Wow! They were so cheap that I could have filled a cart up with them and had the family live off of all of it, except that we all knew better.

Canned goods with artificial ingredients were sixty percent as much as plain ones. Boxed mixes were cheaper than ingredients…and their prices had dropped. News reports had tipped me off, and I was annoyed at myself for reading, filing, and moving on mentally. Come on, I was out in reality, shopping! I should have thought of this sooner. I knew this before I left the house!

After touring the aisles in depth without adding anything else to my basket, I realized I no longer seemed like a shopper. I got some orange juice just to keep up appearances, but Aaron gave me a smile that suggested the ruse was no good. I bought the food and we left.

Hamish laughed when I told him about that, but then got serious. Yes, he agreed, the prices of trigger foods were definitely being lowered to induce more people to eat them. The whole point was to get this plague show on the road as fast as possible. What he wondered was, how fast-acting would it be?

When I asked him for his guesstimate on that, he looked really grim. "Fast, I think. So fast that it will be obvious to us all, with or without any medical or scientific expertise."

Wonderful.

I told him about a word I had run across in my research: "obesogens". It meant chemicals in our foods and in other things that we came into regular contact with that made us gain weight. It meant anything that induced obesity. The trigger foods were full of those, I knew.

"Obesogens! I love it," Hamish said in disgust. "People will be terminally ill in no time flat."

The strategy at work here was just like a false diagnosis of cancer, or induced cancer: give a death sentence, seize all assets from the condemned, and then send in the MRAPs to deliver the final death blow. With that, the job is done. No mess, no heirs, no loose ends. It was the perfect crime, made legit via laws, treaties, and the police power of a police state.

We had no other planet to conveniently colonize, so Earth was it for us humans. Even if we could travel through space within just a few years at most, as luck would most likely have it, we would just find that some other sentient species already lived on whatever planet we found. We would thus find that this indigenous species viewed us as illegal immigrants.

Irony of ironies…just like the Native Tribes of the Americas, these hypothetical aliens would deem us to be the aliens and want us gone.

No…we had to make things work here, but genocide could only ever be the ultimate cop-out.

Chapter 26

Transportin and Exportin

"Whatever the transportin is bound to, it won't be found in a gene bank." Hamish was explaining how the vaccine worked. Not just his safe one, but the government's cull vaccine, or any vaccine. The only thing he was leaving out was the part about the secret ingredient in the government's formula: the monster nanobots.

"It attaches itself to messenger RNA – mRNA – and I know for DAMN sure that I wouldn't want to be injected with this cull formula," he continued. He was keeping it general, and being purposely vague so as not to give up the game being played by either the government or us. The government was playing cull; we were playing subversion.

"If mutation occurs in Ebola that results in a fluid-independent strain, capable of surviving desiccation, then humanity might as well begin getting its affairs in order," Hamish warned, with a disturbing touch of dry sarcasm…pun intended by the word "dry".

The vaccines that the government was forcing on the general population included a soft-kill mechanism involving micro-RNA that did precisely that, Hamish had explained to me. Exportin was a protein that complexed with micro-RNA. The very strong signal that he got when he experimented with the vaccine samples he managed to procure had frightened him, because it was then that it became very clear to him what the soft-killers were trying to do.

"Don't worry," I told Shayna. "He's just getting really into explaining how viruses work."

I had invited Shayna and her youngest child, an Aspie boy who played the oboe and read voraciously, into the lab after the yoga class. Zachary often came with his mother and read while she taught the class, so it had been a simple enough ruse to invite them upstairs.

Zachary wanted to hear this. He asked a lot of questions.

What had motivated me was the fact that Shayna had mentioned, as if it were no big deal, that a vaccine had been administered at Zachary's school that day. He was eleven, and in a summer orchestra. Any kid in a summer program – summer school, summer camp, summer arts and music – was fair game. The government wasn't waiting around for the summer to elapse and school to resume before injecting everyone and anyone with its formula. The kid looked tired already, and he had only had the formula in his system for a couple of hours.

Hamish took some of Zachary's blood and ran it through the large, box-like machine in a corner of his back room. Next, we all watched it churn and crunch data. Soon the computer display was ready. Somehow, Hamish was collecting the nanites that tainted the vaccine from the government, without showing that to our guests. All they would know was that damage was done to the human immune system by hitting it with too much at once, and that Hamish was going to repair that damage with his own nanites.

"Looks like the government formula hit him with everything at once. I guess they'll do the other kids in the fall, when school starts up again," Hamish said, reading it.

He turned around with a nanite gun and approached Zachary again. "I'm going to see if you have anything else in your system. I'm looking for things that could have been added years ago or recently, and that may or may not be apparent." With that, he hit the reverse switch.

I watched my husband's face, as did Shayna, and sure enough, he was noticing a change. That meant that the nanite gun was filling up with nanobots. He dumped them into another machine and stared through the magnifying scope at them.

"Is it what you thought?" I couldn't resist asking him.

"Aye. Good riddance to these."

"So my son will be completely rid of mercury and whatever else?" Shayna wanted to know.

"Yes," Hamish replied. With that, he approached Zachary again, put the nanite gun up to his neck, and let his own nanites loose in the kid's bloodstream. I knew that they were racing to his brain as we waited to undo the damage caused by the vaccine.

Hamish turned to Shayna next. "Now let's see about you. Have you had a vaccination recently?"

"Yes. I took my other kids and we went to the pharmacy for ours just before coming here. Might as well have this out of the way as soon as possible, I thought. My boyfriend came with us. Zachary came along for the ride, and Naomi and Benjamin got it done. Jack, my boyfriend, went first to show Ben that it was no big deal. The place was giving away candy and snacks with shots, but we didn't eat any."

Hamish glanced at me, one eyebrow raised. Today was Monday. With that, he approached Shayna, took blood, went through the whole routine again with the big box analyzer in the corner, and announced that it was the same story. He promptly extracted the nanites from her also. With that, he discharged them into the analyzer, which, invisible to the naked eye, interfaced with them and began reading their software. At last, Hamish was going to see that.

Great, I thought morosely, they're all doomed. Or not… "So," I said out loud to her, "when can you bring all of them here for this?"

"How about this Thursday?"

"Perfect," Hamish said. "Bring them all with you. We can meet after the yoga class. Make sure to be here," I said. And then I wondered, how would we explain all this? How would we deal with records of this? What would we be saying to people in order to get them in here for nanite extraction without telling them what this really was?

We needed a code, and a non-computerized record-keeping method, I realized.

Then we would have to destroy each record after the fact and rely on our memories.

It would be the ultimate covert operation, and worth it.

Shayna agreed to bring her children, but didn't know about her boyfriend.

"Get him here one way or the other," Hamish insisted, making eye contact and staring seriously back at her. That was rare for him.

Shayna was a high school English teacher who knew about Aspies and eye contact, particularly in males. After all, she had a son with Asperger's – Zachary. She did a double-take when my husband looked at her like that and seemed to realize that this was no joke. She knew that both Hamish and I were on the spectrum.

But we couldn't get everyone in here that easily.

However, as long as they were actually here…

Hamish brought out another nanite gun and shot some of his repairing nanobots into the mother as well. Those could remain for 20 minutes, and repair the damage to their cells. That was convenient; I had wondered how long was long enough, and Hamish had realized, after refining the Regenics process, that the repairs – a separate matter from Regenics – could be done either simultaneously with administration of that violet-hued serum or not. In this case, not.

For me, he had left them in overnight, but realized, after running the video on my cell-repair process the next day – sped up with the time-lapse clock running in the lower right corner of the screen – that the deed had been done in just 20 minutes. Perfect!

"Okay, please have a seat in the waiting area. I'll call you back in here in about 20 minutes," Hamish advised. "At that point, I shall extract my little video-bots and see how you are doing. Those things cannot stay in your systems, so don't take off."

They agreed to that and walked out. Zachary, totally and happily unconcerned, was already reaching for his copy of *The Hobbit*. Cool kid; he couldn't wait to get back to a book.

While Shayna and Zachary waited for the nanobots to do their thing, I asked Hamish, "What are we going to say to people for a code about this? It would be wise to have at least three different tales to tell, so that we won't be easily tracked."

"Damn," Hamish said. "You hate lying. You're not good at it. I'm better at it."

"I know," I agreed. "Mark Twain was right: 'If you tell the truth, you don't have to remember anything.' But I think this is a time to worry about remembering rather than to stupidly write everything down. Also, there is one thing that will make doing this procedure off the books easier: most people have day jobs. If we are inviting them in after hours, our staff won't see much, and keeping non-digital records won't be so weird."

"You're right." Hamish gave me a wry grin. "You could have a future in revolutionary espionage, did you know that?"

"Oh, great. Just what I always wanted."

"None of us wanted what's happening…except perhaps for Regenics."

"We're not doing that for everyone, though. We're just subverting the kill-shot here."

"Right. Regenics is going to be kept separate for now. Even though it's essentially worked out and ready for use, I'm going to play it as a project that is still in its developmental phases, because I have a plan for us. If we need an escape, this is it. We can go somewhere nice with it."

"Oh? Where? I don't want to leave my country and be a guest in someone else's."

"Switzerland – the French part."

"Are you trying to sell me on this? That is one of the few places on Earth I might be willing to go…as long as we can come home after a short stay. It's also one of the most expensive on the planet, but since we have parked a lot of our money there…"

Hamish just grinned. Then he checked the data in the nanite analyzer. He looked horrified.

"What? What do you see?" I asked.

He turned to look at me. "These nanites look the same as the earlier version, but they do a lot more damage. Trigger foods will bring on the damage a lot faster, but even without them, it will still be a fairly rapid onset. This version of the monster nanobots will induce multiple diseases."

"Wonderful." I glanced at the clock and realized it was time to get Shayna and Zachary.

"Wait," Hamish said. "We need to work out the code. Tell her that her family must come in to get rid of the mercury stabilizer in the vaccines. It's a partial truth and a lie that omits what we're really doing here."

"Just one excuse?"

"For now. I can't think of three off the top of my head, and all those parents who are health and organics enthusiasts will love it. So will any child-free enthusiast who just wants to be healthy and live a normal lifespan."

"Okay. We'll go with that, then." I smiled and went out to the waiting area.

Shayna and Zachary's blood showed the same thing, as did their time-lapse videos: full repairs completed. Take that, government cull operators!

"Do you prefer organic fruits and vegetables and other foods?" I couldn't resist asking her.

"Of course! Don't you?" she responded.

Hamish and I grinned. "Oh yeah," I said.

"I would expect nothing less," she laughed, and took her son out. "See you next week, and thank you very much! I really appreciate this."

"No problem. Bye!" I locked the door behind her with a wave, then returned to Hamish. "So she'll send her friends next, and it will be about mercury, right?"

"That's the plan."

"A yoga instructor who is also a triathlete isn't going to eat trigger foods. I doubt that we would have seen a lot of that damage this soon after the shot," I commented.

"No," he agreed, "but soon we ought to see something in others. Watch the news."

That Thursday, I raced through the locker room, barely on time as usual, changed, and rushed into the yoga class. The lights were dimly lit for the relaxation aspect of it. Good; Shayna was there. Now the other people in the class would hear us talking about this, I thought. Fine. Maybe we could get some of them into the lab also. This was a health club, after all. I hated to think of people who came here to maintain their health having it stolen from them.

"Hi Avril!" Shayna greeted me. "I've got them all here – even Jack."

"Oh – excellent! This can be a done deal all at once, then," I said happily.

"Yes. Thank you. I don't know what your husband did, but Zachary and I feel more energetic and just…better somehow. But everyone else is…wiped out. We're hoping Hamish can fix us."

"Well, he is a genius," I replied cryptically, hoping that, since medicine wasn't my field, that response would satisfy her. Apparently, it did, because she started the music and launched into the routine without another word, looking quite calm and content.

When we got them all upstairs for the appointment with Hamish, her boyfriend and other kids all had monster nanites to extract. They looked like they needed to sleep for a week, and they had rashes. Shayna's older son, Benjamin, had eaten some of the free trigger foods that were given out at his camp, so Hamish had to spend extra time on him, tinkering remotely with the nanites and gathering data. Fortunately, the family was out in the waiting area.

When they came back in, Shayna was concerned about the extra time that Hamish's nanites had remained inside her kids. Ironic! Those were the harmless, healing nanites! Hamish assured her that they were not a threat, and that he had just been studying the data. He spent some time explaining that he had left the nanites in himself and in me overnight, only to find that 20 minutes was enough, and that the rest of the time, the nanites had sat idle, with nothing to do once their mission was accomplished.

"Oh," Shayna said, breathing an amused sigh of relief. "That sounds okay, then." If she had only known what Hamish had found in her other son's system, I thought!

Hamish warned them all off of trigger foods, and explained why in some detail.

Naomi, Shayna's daughter, seemed to be an Aspergirl, like me. She was very particular about food, and said she could taste chemicals. "So can I," I told her with a grin.

Benjamin rolled his eyes, and Shayna scolded him for that. "If you could taste those things, you wouldn't have eaten that junk food that the vaccination team was giving away! Don't eat any more of it." She looked really annoyed over that. He said he wouldn't, but wasn't convincing.

Regardless, the trigger was disabled. Interesting…three days out, and Hamish was able to fix what the monster nanites had started to break. Without another injection of that tainted vaccine, he wouldn't get sick…unless he ate a steady diet of mostly junk. No chance of that with a nutritionally educated mother raising him. I was betting that he would grow up to be a healthy eater thanks to her, and that her lessons would stay with him.

Jack had a slight rash, but it seemed to be healing as we spoke. "Amazing," he said. "What was in what you gave us?"

"It's really about what was removed from what you already had in your system," I said.

"Indeed," Hamish added. "There was too much mercury in that vaccine."

That seemed to satisfy Jack and Shayna. They left, happy and healthy.

As for Hamish and I, now we could see what would happen if those nasty nanobots could be extracted quickly from people who exercised often and ate no trigger foods…or only a bite or two of them. When I said so, he warned me that variations in people's genetic makeups could vary the outcomes, plus there were other factors.

"What other factors?"

"I have received three different batches of the vaccine. Some have different nanites, which work more aggressively and faster, and which seek out fatty tissue to bind trigger molecules to."

"Wonderful."

The next afternoon, I was shopping in Whole Foods, minding my own business, with Aaron and Ed circling the produce aisles. Ed was a lot more interested in eating a healthy diet lately, I noticed, and would take cues from me about what foods to choose. It was gratifying after all of the scoffing he had done at the gourmet foods I liked on our road trip the previous fall.

I moved past the raspberries, heirloom tomatoes, and fresh herbs toward the apples and onions, pausing to get some Asian eggplants for a curry recipe. Glancing around me, I realized that the traffic around me had moved, and that other people were now nearby, and an annoying wannabe repeat mother was among them. I could see her eyeing me resentfully, but she pushed her cart off in the opposite direction, and I turned back to face the baby eggplants.

"Alicia!" I heard a woman say.

I glanced to my left, and saw her. She had glasses and a running suit on; she looked like she had been at a yoga class. A tween girl, about eleven years old, paced next her, pushing the cart and eyeing the apples and pears in it. Maybe she liked healthy foods, I thought. Good.

On to the onions; I got a plastic bag and chose four red onions, then took another bag and put two Vidalia ones in it. Then I glanced up again to see who Alicia was. Alicia was another mother who had a daughter with her, this one a few years younger than the other woman's kid. The mothers were chatting, paused in the middle of the potato aisle, off to one side so that they didn't block other people from moving past.

"Jessica," said the one called Alicia, who wore a pants suit and thumbed through her iPhone as she spoke, "Alix and I were just at the doctor's office for her check-up, and he insisted upon giving us each a huge combination vaccine shot of you name it: measles, mumps, rubella, meningitis, polio, smallpox…and more. Can you believe it?!"

The yoga woman did a double-take. "No way! I thought those were supposed to be spaced out over a few weeks, not given all at once. Are you going to go back to him again?"

Jessica looked annoyed. "I don't know. The doctor actually said that our health was good, and that it wasn't worth the inconvenience. He added that the new treaty requires this, and that he must enter it into a government database!"

Alicia looked like she was considering that. Then she said, "Wow. Did you hear that for people who don't have their own cars, and especially those who are even somewhat disabled or who live too far from public transportation routes, vaccination crews have been visiting them?"

Jessica turned to look at her. Now I was blatantly listening, having pulled my small cart aside. This was interesting. I had never heard of such a thing. Since when, other than to implement the Nae-Née nanite program, had the government done that?

"Yeah," Alicia continued, "my cleaning woman told me about it. There is a morbidly obese woman in her thirties living on the floor just below hers in Elmwood who got vaccinated that way. She doesn't even go out much, so she wondered why they bothered, but she let them give her the shot. They also gave her some free food, but it's all junk – nothing I would buy. And my parents don't drive anymore, so they got their shots in Newington right at home. I brought them groceries and they told me."

Jessica and Alicia saw me listening. As usual, my deadpan facial expression and steady, intent gaze revealed little beyond rapt concentration, but what did they really expect from me for a reaction to this? I didn't know what to make of this as yet either.

Not that that prevented them from asking. "You're Avril Châtelet, aren't you?" Alicia asked me. Not waiting for me to confirm this (why bother?!), she asked, "What do you make of this?"

Relieved to be addressed by total strangers who were not spewing vitriol at me for inventing the birth control nanite, I said, "This is the first I've heard of this, but it's intriguing. I'm going to ask my husband what he thinks." I smiled politely at the end of all that, hoping that I looked pleasant. They seemed satisfied with that, so I pressed on. "Have you seen that morbidly obese woman since she got her vaccine? And how long ago was it that it was done?"

"It was a couple of weeks ago. I just saw her walking her dog a couple days ago. She looked strange, now that you mention it. Different…out of breath from just walking to the corner and back, and her dog isn't a puller. He just walks by her side nicely. I asked her if she was all right, and she said she was still tired since the shot."

"How did she look?" Jessica asked.

Alicia thought a moment. "I don't see her often, so I was shocked to see her. She had a rash and looked like she hadn't slept well in a month or more. She smokes and doesn't exercise much, but that doesn't explain it. Aren't people supposed to recover their energy in a day or so after getting a vaccine?" Alicia and Jessica both looked at me, expecting a definitive answer. That was the trouble with being married to a doctor – what if I gave the wrong answer?!

I thought for a moment. "Well…this vaccine isn't the MMR one. That one does three diseases in one shot. This new one does forty in one shot. I guess being tired isn't odd."

They considered this for a moment. But I didn't wait for them to say anything else. I had another question for Alicia. "Did you say you just went to your doctor today and got that forty-plus vaccine shot?"

"Yes. Why?"

"Well, how do you feel? Are you tired yet?"

Alicia thought for a moment, then said, "It's starting to hit me now. I'm hoping to finish this grocery shopping in time to get home and collapse. At least my arm isn't sore. The doctor said that if you go to your physician, he or she won't be so rushed, which means that the shot can be administered slowly, so as not to inundate the tissue and make it hurt."

I stared at her as she said this. Then I spoke. "So he didn't press the plunger in a hurry and hurt you, but the end result is the same: too much at once. You're going to feel very tired soon." Alicia's daughter was already leaning heavily on the shopping cart, looking like she was going to collapse into it.

Alix was looking like she was asleep on her feet, actually. I felt both sorry for her and horrified. These people took care of themselves and were obviously educated about nutrition, but this vaccine/cull program simply deemed them "excess" humans and sought to eliminate them.

Suddenly I was angry. I had to get them all into Hamish's office.

The hell with the cull – I would thwart it if I possibly could, and I could!

I hoped that my hard expression wouldn't be misinterpreted as simple dislike for children as I looked at Alix, assessing her fatigue for what it was. This wasn't about that, and Alix was too exhausted to be a rude, irritating child. Damn it, she ought to be feeling well enough to be annoying, well enough to learn to behave well, not canceled out before the fact!

I looked at Alicia, and saw that Jessica was looking at them both with concern. She said, "Alicia, you look like it's hitting you now. Can you shop and drive home? Do you need help?"

Alicia smiled, looking tired, and said, "I think so. But I'll be glad to get home and sit down. I'm going to get something that I don't have to cook tonight. Whole Foods has soups and breads and other things that I could just heat up."

"Let us help you get that stuff. You and your daughter look too tired to shop all of sudden."

They all looked at me, nonplussed. "You just met us! That's very nice."

"Well, you need a little help, and it's not like I have to get back to my computer and complete a writing project immediately," I replied with a slight grin.

That did it. We walked around together, Jessica and I helping Alicia shop, with their daughters trailing along. We kept glancing at Alix, who said, "I'm okay," each time. I doubted it, and I could see that her mother wanted to finish up and get out of here. How was I going to get them into Hamish's office?!

Aaron and Ed followed along, watching this scene unfold with blatant curiosity, saying nothing. Jessica noticed them and asked me if they were private security. "Yes, they are like family now – our constant shadows. Not our only ones, but we know them best of all. They are very nice guys," I answered, smiling back at them.

Jessica smiled, and did a double-take as we both looked at them. The two of them had gaped at me for a moment. "What, you didn't realize that by now?" I said to them with a grin. They shook their heads, smiling.

We were almost at the check-out line now, and Jessica at last spoke to me about the vaccine. "Do you think we might run into you in Blue Back Square again?" Jessica asked. "I mean, do you come here regularly? Because I'd like to ask you about the vaccine in a few days, after you've had a chance to ask your husband about it," she summed up.

"So would I," Alicia said.

Uh-oh…what if these people were spies, not people who needed help? What would I say? Well, I would worry about that later. Or not…Ed looked up from his phone and nodded at me, glancing at both women. I realized that he had checked their backgrounds and found that they were just regular people. Excellent; I could help them if I wanted to.

"Yeah, I'll be back. Why don't you give me your phone number, and I can call you if and when I have a better answer than "this is the first I've heard of this"?" I offered, mocking my previous response with a slight smile.

"Okay – thanks!" Both women pulled out business cards and handed them to me.

I took them and said it was nice to meet them, and we chatted a bit longer as we waited in line. Alicia seemed more inclined to chat now that she had to wait, and with the urgent business of collecting purchases for a mysteriously exhausted family taken care of, I began to find out more about them.

Jessica Langerfeld worked as an attorney in Hartford, and Alicia Black did indeed take yoga at the health club that Hamish and I were members of. Great…she might just track me down in the locker room there! I didn't tell her that we were members there. Why rush things?

"How old are your daughters?" I asked, looking at the girls. "Are they enjoying school?"

Smiles. Parents love it when you ask about their kids, I know. Feigning interest and learning about other people's lives isn't nosy, it's polite, my mother had assured me long ago, so taking a chance on a social interaction and being friendly seemed to be working now.

Alicia answered first about her daughter. "Alix is eleven, she's in fifth grade at Sedgwick, and she's in some honors classes," the yoga teacher said proudly. "She just brought me a bumper sticker about that for my car."

I hated those bumper stickers, I thought to myself, but smiled politely. That meant that Alix got all As, a feat that had always eluded me. It wasn't until I learned what Asperger's was that I realized that that was normal for us Aspies that I had stopped worrying over it and caring. But growing up, I always felt that I wasn't measuring up, that I wasn't giving my mother enough bragging rights. I excelled in some but not all areas – classic Aspie.

At least it wasn't as extreme as what happened to Einstein, who said that he failed school and school failed him. I doubted that I could go on to do so fabulously well after that. Only the rarest of Aspies had an extra-developed frontal lobe to go with our Mercedes or Porsche or fill-in-your-favorite-over-the-top-model-of-car brainstems. Our wetware was just…differently wired, and more elaborately so. Aspie brainstems were cool.

I looked at Jessica next. Melanie was eight years old, and doing well at the King Phillip School, she told me. She took clarinet lessons. "Oh, really?" I said to the girl, interested. "I play the violin, and started when I was your age. Do you like the clarinet?"

Melanie looked at me, smiled slightly, and replied, "It's okay, even though I have to suck on the reeds. And I wish I could play the oboe instead; it sounds prettier," she added.

"Well, I think you can graduate to that from the clarinet. Ask you music teacher," I said.

"I will," Melanie said, sounding a bit shy but pleased. That went well, I thought.

"Are you working on any new books?" Jessica asked. It seemed like she asked to be friendly.

As a matter of fact, I was. I was drafting one on the history of vaccines, I told her, and some short stories about girls on the autism spectrum, girls with Asperger's. Both women paused at that, looking at me carefully. Jessica looked intrigued.

Alicia spoke first. "I had heard that you had that. Is it okay if I say that? Do you mind?"

"Not at all. Asperger's is a cool thing to have!" I replied. "Marie Curie, Jane Austen, Virginia Woolf, Thomas Jefferson, Nikola Tesla, Mozart, and many others were Aspies. Have you heard of Temple Grandin, Ph.D., the famous autistic expert in animal husbandry?"

They had. I told them that I had to promote the condition as a good thing, because kids and adults who have it needed to hear that from other people on the spectrum who were happy about it and who knew how it works and why it is good.

Melanie was watching me now. "I have that," she said.

I smiled at her. It was a long, comfortable smile, not the kind I had been giving to the mothers, which was a tense one that suggested that they would never, ever include me in anything unless they wanted to pick my brain. All my life, that had been the sort of interaction that most people would offer me. It was a self-esteem boost, but never enough. It was not friendship – it was use. Oh well.

To Melanie, I said, still smiling, "I thought you might." Then I went on, "The best thing you can do for yourself is to learn what it is and how it works, and to see a scan of an Aspie brainstem next to one that belongs to a neurotypical – the standard model of human. We're just different models of our species, and both necessary ones. Be glad you are in the minority and enjoy standing out. We're not built to fit in; we're designed to stand out. Own it and enjoy it."

She looked really pleased now. Jessica was looking at me thoughtfully. I hoped that I had done this mother-daughter relationship some good. I said to Jessica, "I grew up undiagnosed. Your daughter gets to know what she is dealing with. Don't let anyone cut her out of anything just because they don't understand it. She can go anywhere and do anything, just like the others – travel, participate in activities, study, get married or not, you name it."

Jessica smiled a real smile at me now.

"Thank you!" she said, straightening up a bit and breathing deeply. She asked me about my Aspergirl stories, so I told her some titles, and she said she was going to look them up. Alicia listened with interest. I guess they were surprised to hear that my entire career didn't revolve around dreaming up new and exciting uses for nanites.

What else did I like to write about?

I said I had made notes for a science fiction novel on life after sea levels rose, and I grinned as I added that they would never rise to the levels shown in Kevin Costner's *Waterworld*. There just wasn't enough ice on the planet for that to happen.

Alicia asked how I knew that, so I told her that *National Geographic* had done a story on that several years earlier, complete with hypothetical maps prepared using data provided by mathematically accurate software.

"Oh." That satisfied her. She said she would call before going to her doctor for a vaccine, giving her friend a worried look. "Maybe I can still get my vaccines without this effect," she said hopefully. "Our appointment is in a couple of days. Maybe I should see your husband after that."

"Maybe," I agreed. "Call me and I'll set that up for you." Jessica smiled and said she would…and I actually believed her. Alicia was dragging her feet, and I could swear she had suddenly developed dark circles under her eyes. We walked out to our cars, and Jessica and Melanie went over to help Alicia and Alix load their car up.

Maybe it would be okay to run into Alicia at the health club…if she recovered from this shot. Jessica was also a member. They seemed like nice people, but I was shocked to see how Alicia and Alix were reacting to that vaccine, even though I knew it was tainted.

When I got home, Jessica called me. I put Hamish on the phone with her, and he set up and appointment for her at his lab in Avon for the evening of the day of her vaccination appointment. She and Melanie would thus meet him almost immediately after she got that kill shot.

As for Alicia, I wondered how she was going to cope and whether or not she would make it to his lab at all. If she did, we would have to be very careful about what we said to explain why she was feeling better after the nanite extraction. It wasn't like we could talk about with the people we were helping. Well, that was something to talk about next time, if there was a next time, I mused.

A few days later, Alicia called Hamish. She wanted to know what he thought of the combo-vaccine, and whether or not he thought that any follow-up was necessary. Her doctor seemed to consider the matter closed, and had no interest in further questions.

He invited her to bring her daughter to his office after she got out of work.

She accepted, and they agreed on the next Wednesday evening at 6 o'clock.

"That doctor either knows exactly what he's doing or is inundated with work to comply with the new regulations," Hamish told me when he got off the phone.

Jessica and Melanie had appeared in the lab the evening before.

Within a couple of hours after getting their shots, they had looked as appalling as Alicia and Alix had, complete with the same haggard expressions, dark circles under their eyes, and feeling so exhausted that they could hardly drag themselves in to see him.

But Jessica was determined to do what she could to avoid whatever it was that had filled her with a sense of dread when she saw her friend, so she had come in.

Hamish had looked grim but not shocked when he saw them. He had greeted them nicely, invited them into his lab, and let me stay as he worked with Jessica and her daughter who, like Zachary, asked questions.

Hamish was ready for them, though. He had thought of the perfect cover story and gotten into the groove of using it. He extracted the tainted nanites, arresting their progress in shutting off the mother and daughters' P53 proteins, and dumped them into his collector. Explaining that he was just removing the mercury stabilizer, of which there was more than in most vaccines due to the ambitious nature of this formula, he smoothly moved on to introduce his own nanites, which went to work immediately to reactivate the P53s.

Melanie was fascinated. Jessica was delighted. "So removing that toxin will do the trick?"

Hamish told her, "Partly. You will still need this check-up and energy boost that I'm giving you now to mitigate the damage that that formula did, so that's why I'm keeping you here for another twenty minutes to a half an hour. Also, if you're interested, I can offer you a chance to participate in a clinical trial of my Regenics formula, which will go a long way toward boosting your body's ability to heal."

Jessica asked for some details, and when she heard that Hamish and I had taken that formula, she agreed. So, when he was through with them both, and his repairing nanites were pulled back from their bloodstreams and stashed in their container in the lab, he gave them each a dose of the lavender serum. Jessica wasted no time in calling her husband and signing him up for an appointment the next afternoon. "John had his shot yesterday, and I'm worried about him."

"Well, let's get him in here tomorrow, and he should be feeling much better soon," Hamish said with a smile.

Jessica and Melanie looked really happy when they heard that. "Dad's been sleeping nonstop at home. He could hardly make himself get up and go to work this morning," Melanie said.

Hamish looked very serious and told Jessica to get him in here tomorrow if she had to drive him herself. She said she would…that she definitely would.

We said good-bye to them, saw them out, and looked at each other, shocked.

"It's starting and it's getting going fast," I said.

"It's going as I thought it would," Hamish replied.

The feeling of having swallowed an ice cube had started up during this visit, and got worse.

That Friday evening, we were in our bedroom, about to go out to eat. I just wanted to get changed and wash my face; it was a hot day. If I could get Hamish to put on a different shirt, so much the better; he was wearing a tee shirt with the Periodic Table on it, and I wanted to go out to a nice place. He didn't put up a fight when I mentioned that.

John had come into the office that afternoon, Hamish told me, and Jessica had in fact driven him. It was a repeat of the evening before, only John looked somewhat worse. The beginnings of a rash had broken out on his arms, legs, and torso.

Hamish gave him the full treatment, complete with Regenics, and asked him to come back the next week for a check-up. When he left with his wife after an hour, he was feeling almost normal. I hoped we would be able to both help lots more people this way and avoid detection.

Hamish added, as he told me the tale, that the cull was certainly proceeding with alacrity and with great efficiency. "The method of hitting patients with all vaccines at once, laced with mercury and monster nanobots, is definitely the fastest they could have devised." He looked angry, and rightly so. It was awful to see the effects and how quickly they manifested.

"Yeah. Did you see the editorial in today's paper about that? A doctor wrote that there would be no spacing out of vaccinations in his office. They would just be done quickly and efficiently, with no nonsense from people who didn't believe in vaccinating kids. That's the law, and that's all there is to it, he wrote, and even cited *Jacobson v. Massachusetts*."

"No. Show me."

I called the file up on my computer and he sat down to read through it quickly. He was done in a couple of minutes. "That is exactly the party line that the government wants us all to toe," he said, sounding furious and getting loud and fast.

"Of course it is. Operation 'Vaccine: The Cull' is underway. I wonder what horrors we will see once that phase of the operation is complete," I said, distracted and disturbed by it.

"Probably mass illnesses – cancers, most likely," Hamish replied. "On that note, let's go out to dinner and continue to secretly and quietly stalk people to rescue from that grim fate."

Alicia and Alix arrived the next Monday. Liam, Alicia's husband, drove them.

By now, Hamish's lab was stocked with that pernicious vaccine. He had removed the tainted nanobots from every last vial, giving him quite the stockpile of them, invisible to the naked eye though they were. He would soon be adding to it.

I went to Hamish's office a couple of hours ahead of my yoga class to meet them, and was shocked by their appearance. They had lesions on their arms, legs, and torsos, which meant that the rash we had seen with John and progressed in just under a week to this point.

Worse, Alix was getting what looked like a hard pustule on the left side of her face. It was about the size of a dime. Alix was frantic. "I'm going to be scarred for life, aren't I?! This is worse than acne, and I'm not even fourteen yet," she wailed.

Ellen spoke soothingly to her and bandaged the spot, warning her to just leave it alone. "It will heal much better if you don't touch it," she said, covering it up. She looked doubtful, though. How could such a thing heal up with leaving a hideous scar?!

"If I didn't know better, I would think that she had a smallpox scab forming," I said to Hamish out in the hall.

He looked at me grimly and said, as quietly as he could, "She does."

Ellen looked shocked, horrified, and like her suspicions had been confirmed all at once. Fortunately, Hamish had protected his staff and their families with his nanites and sera, and they understood why they should not say anything. Still, the fewer people who knew what was going on, the better in terms of secrecy.

Hamish grimly went through the whole nanite removal routine, put his repairing ones in both the mother and daughter, leaving them there. The question on our minds was, would that arrest the progress of the disease or not? And would Regenics help?

Liam let Hamish do his vaccine then and there, and Hamish knew that at least he wouldn't get sick at all. "You'll sleep heavily tonight and tomorrow night, and be sluggish for a day or so, but that ought to be it. Call me and tell me how you're feeling, though, and I want to see all you back here in two days."

Two days later, I went back to see how they were. I wanted to know whether or not Hamish could do anything to save people from this kill-shot, and what the outcome of it all would be, whatever that was.

Liam was fine, which was no surprise. Hamish would not knowingly inject poison into anyone. How could those other doctors out there do it, though? Did they not know? Did they know and not care about anyone or anything but themselves and their own health?

Those questions were going to go unanswered, I knew. It was time to look at Alicia and Alix, who looked grateful for our interest. "I'm so glad we ran into you at Whole Foods," she kept saying to me.

I smiled, but said, "Hold that thought until your outcome is complete and positive," I said.

"Indeed," Hamish said.

The two of them looked better, but not great. Hamish took some blood and studied it. The results were encouraging, but not complete or even conclusive. He explained this to the parents, and checked the mess on Alix's face. It was definitely going to leave an ugly scar.

"I'll get a pretty tattoo over it," she said. "No way am I going through life with just a scar."

Her parents didn't even blink. I could hardly blame them. I didn't want a tattoo, but when presented with a scar, my answer would change. The question that interested them right now was health, not cosmetics.

In the end, Hamish gave them all a Regenics shot, and that settled the matter. He extracted his repairing nanites, and in a few days, the whole family was healthy again.

When we saw them again, the effect was as if they had never been sick, except for that damned scar that was forming. It was a huge, round, caved-in sort of impression in Alix's cheek. The scab was gone, and bandage no longer necessary, but it was bright pink. I t made me angry, and I could see that it made her angry too.

Alix was feeling so much better that she was actually frantic about it. She had no idea that her own murder had just been foiled, and that this was least of her problems, but if I were her and did know, I still wouldn't feel any differently. I would want my skin looking unchanged, regardless of everything. I even said at least that much.

Hamish referred the family to a plastic surgeon, and Alix begged her parents for an appointment as soon as possible – yesterday, if they could manage it. Her father started to say that it was too expensive, but Alicia cut him off with a scathing look. They called and set it up.

Still, I spent the rest of the night in a silent rage over that smallpox scar. It was right on her face! Alix should have her skin looking perfect, not marred by this cull shot. I was so upset that I had trouble calming down and going to sleep. No plastic surgery would fully restore that mess.

Chapter 27

Sheeple

Too many of us were asleep.

Americans and others, but particularly Americans, were maddeningly asleep to danger, and now it was catching up with us. It was catching up via that damned treaty, SmartTech, regulations everywhere, inspections, and so on.

It made me wish for a shock that would wake people up.

Right after the December 7, 1941 attack on Pearl Harbor in Honolulu, Hawai'i, the Japanese admiral who orchestrated it, Isoroku Yamamoto, commented, "I fear that all we have done is to awaken a sleeping giant."

Well, as a nation, we Americans were a giant, and we needed to wake the hell up…NOW.

Humans would fight back if we knew that our freedoms were being deliberately taken away.

Something sneakier was therefore required if the Farmers were actually going to succeed at taking them. Trickery was working nicely. They were busy persuading humans everywhere that surrendering their freedoms would preserve their security.

Nicely done, but…whose security would be preserved?

That was the undefined variable that had been slipped past most people.

The new world order had been revealed at last. Again, I ranted about it, but to myself.

How many of us recognized it for what it was?

How many of us saw that the ruling elite of the world's societies – those who controlled the wealth – were actually Farmers of everything that they touched? Because that's what they were: Farmers. They farmed the food, the shelter, the clothing, and even the people.

People were like sheep: asleep, obedient, oblivious, and clueless. Sheeple.

How was it that time and distractions made people forget?

How was it that greed made people forget?

One of the most wonderful stories I ever read, one that became a movie recently, was Lois Lowry's *The Giver*. In it, the Giver was asked to advise the elders about the wisdom of increasing the population so as to get more workers. He used his memory of starvation and misery due to insufficient resources to tell them not to do that. They heeded his advice.

But real life was not just some story which people could take wisdom from. In real life, people did what they wanted, not what they should. They forgot all that they were taught in childhood and in school, they forgot to appreciate their elders, and they made terrible choices.

The Olympics were a case in point. They were in Brazil this summer, and any athlete participating in a water sport was getting violently ill from the feces and dead fish in the water. The Brazilian population had increased for so long without upgrading its sewage system in Rio that things were thoroughly out of control now. Meanwhile, the vaccinations were being given.

Why couldn't people remember the mistakes of the past and learn from them? Why?! Things were all out of balance. Neither all private nor all public worked as an economic system. Having either one invited abuse.

Hamish may have been able to get the taint of P53 shut-off nanobots out of us, but we knew that it wouldn't be long before we would see it being forced on everyone around us. Granted, I didn't go out much, but sooner or later I would have errands to do. It was just a matter of time before I saw MRAPs right here at home, enforcing the vaccination policy right and left, and registering each injection on that Department of Demographics database.

As I drove to West Farms Mall, I realized I was preoccupied enough that I had no recollection of having actually driven part of the route. Apparently, I had driven distracted down Mountain Road to Ridgewood Road, curving around to the southeast as one connected with the other, turned right, and then stopped at Tunxis. Now I sat at a red light, waiting.

Better pay more attention to what's happening in real time and not go on autopilot, I scolded myself in disgust. This must be what it felt like to text and drive, and I had ordered it disabled on my phone! I breathed in and looked around.

It was a lovely summer day. The grass was green and tiger lilies were starting to bloom.

Warm weather was my favorite. I should have been admiring the plants and enjoying the fresh, warm air as I drove along, not spacing out. But I was anxious and my mind was racing.

Whatever. I would keep busy and try not to think about what I read in the news. If it wasn't about the elections, it was about potential water rationing, Ebola patients here and there on the planet (who had managed to leave West Africa and go to other continents), or the vaccines.

With a CD of *Schindler's List* by John Williams playing in the car, I drove the rest of the way to the mall, parked out in the sunshine in the middle of a row near the Lord & Taylor side entrance, locked the car, and walked in. People were looking among the nightgowns, moving items back and forth on the racks.

On to the center of that anchor store, through the men's department, and out into the hallway I walked, my mind on errands. It seemed like there was a huge crowd of people up ahead. How annoying! I had come on a Wednesday afternoon, at two-thirty, just to avoid crowds. Why hadn't it worked?!

The moment I had stepped into the hallway, a crash of human noise hit me like a shock. It was like an abrupt assault of sound, amplified as if at a rock concert, and it was harsh, shrill, and deafening. Talking, nattering, and shouting pervaded and echoed off every inch of space.

It was like it had punched me in the chest, but the sound went into my gut. What the hell?! Next time, I would go online and order my stuff, I told myself. Never mind, I thought. I would try to get my errand done and then see what was up.

I went all the way to the center court, annoyed, and didn't look into the middle. Sidling along past long lines of bored people – parents with children, late middle-aged people, teenagers, single people, couples, people in business attire, people in service uniforms – I moved to the left. Skirting around a few more people and past the elevators, I walked into L'Occitane.

"Hello," said a girl in one of the store's aprons, smiling.

"Hello," I said, stopping and relaxing slightly. At last, I was in here. It was always nice in this store, and the scents and people were pleasant.

"Can I help you find anything?" the girl asked.

"I think I can do it, but I'll let you know, thanks," I said, smiling politely.

"Okay. I'm Amy, in case you need me."

I smiled again, took a basket, found some soaps, lotions, and the face cream I was running out of, and met her at the counter. As she started ringing it all up and packing it, I noticed a bandage on her arm. The bandage consisted of a white gauze pad and a long strip of white surgical tape.

"What's that bandage for?" I asked, as I got a sickening, sinking feeling just looking at it.

"It's for the new vaccine," Amy said. "Haven't you gotten one yet? We all have to."

"My husband's a doctor. He already vaccinated me and filed it online."

"Oh. Lucky! You're all set, then. I had to come in early for this. Luckily, the lines weren't so long, or I would have had to do this after work."

"Did you just get that done today?"

"Yes – out there, in the center court of the mall."

Wow. I didn't ask her anything else about it. She had me choose free samples, packed the last of the items in my bag, had me sign the receipt, and then handed my bag over with a flourish and a smile as she stepped out from around the counter.

Then I had another thought. "How does your arm feel?"

"A bit numb at the injection spot, actually. And sore. I hope it goes away soon; it's making carrying stock around harder than usual. I'm tired, too."

"I hope your shift ends soon and you can get some rest," I said.

"Thanks!" she said, tilting her head slightly and dragging out that word as she smiled.

I gave her a small smile and walked out of the store, staring into the center court.

A surgical team from Hartford Hospital was set up directly across from me, facing us. There were four people in it, each wearing scrubs and lab coats. Something in my peripheral vision caught my attention. It was a sign for St. Francis Hospital with a similar group, just to the right of the information desk. Far off from the desk, in the middle, was a group from the New Britain hospital. Cops paced around with what looked like iPads, checking people's I.D.s.

As I watched, the team from St. Francis was about to inject a girl who was accompanied by her mother and baby brother. The mother was enormous – morbidly obese. Her bleached blond hair showed brown at the roots, and was pulled tightly back into a knot. The girl looked like she might have been 8 years old. She was wearing a tee shirt from the Disney movie *Frozen*. The mother kept moving the baby brother back and forth in his stroller to quiet him.

The guy who injected the girl could have been a nurse, a doctor, or a physician's assistant, for all I knew. I wasn't about to move any closer than where I was standing to check that detail. As he did the deed, what I noticed was the hurried manner in which he proceeded. Not surprisingly, when he depressed the plunger too fast for the tissue to absorb the serum at a manageable rate, the little girl screamed and started crying.

No wonder the girl in L'Occitane said her arm didn't feel well.

The mother looked outraged, but the guy just injected her fast also, and she gave him a nasty look. He was nastier; he didn't even bother to make eye contact. He just took up another one for the baby and injected him too, and of course screaming ensued.

"Next!" he called out, deliberately heedless of the misery he was inflicting. The assembly line of inoculations ground on as though an abusive factory line boss were cracking a whip. There had to be a supervisor somewhere, cracking a metaphorical one, pushing these health care workers to hurry up, to do these injections faster, faster, faster!

Oh…there they were. Damn them! Wearing a name badge that identified them each as being from whichever hospital their team represented, a business suit-clad individual was in fact stationed at the three points around the center court. Each one looked grim, corporate – and merciless – as she or he patrolled the tiny staging area of injections.

The surgical-scrubs-clad people glanced nervously at these corporate monsters from time to time, and they looked anxious. I got it: it was their jobs or the vaccinees. The public was doomed to painful arms and no time spent on bedside manner. Clearly, a government contract was in the mix, and these evil bosses were here to see that the money was used swiftly and efficiently.

I wondered what these hospital employees would have done if they had known about the taint of nanites in the serum they were injecting with such ruthless rapidity. Would they have quit? Would they have protested? But they did not know, so neither would I.

Off to the side was a sign that took the cake, both literally and figuratively. It was a giveaway, pitched as a consolation prize, for everyone who got vaccinated. The prize was a chocolate chip cookie. These cookies were made by a major trigger foods producer, one that I had researched. Palm oil, soy lecithin, beet sugar, high-fructose corn syrup, you name the trigger ingredient – all were in the mixture of these treats.

Clearly, the government wanted to make damned sure that the trigger foods that would set off a pernicious case of cancer got ingested immediately after the kill-shot was meted out. Yes, it was a very efficient mass murder op that I was witnessing, in progress right in front of me.

The news announcements had said that this was indeed the shot that took care of forty different diseases – measles, mumps, rubella, on up to Ebola – all in one injection. Hamish would never approve. No wonder he had done our family and friends' injections so carefully, spaced a week apart for every vaccine and patient.

My cell phone rang.

Damnit! I hated getting cell phone calls. I didn't even realize I had left the damned device turned on. I thought it was off when I drove over here, I thought to myself as I rushed to open my handbag, grab it, lift it out, and unfolded it. It was Hamish calling. Just before the fourth ring, when the phone would have gone to voice mail, I was able to answer it. Stupid thing! "Hi Hamish! What's up?" I said.

"Avril! Where are you?!" He sounded frantic.

"I'm at the mall. I just finished shopping."

"I know you're at the mall! Aaron told me that. Where at the mall are you?"

"Why, are you stalking me?" I asked.

"Just tell me where you are and stay there!"

"I'm in front of the L'Occitane store, but I was about to leave. I see a bunch of vaccination teams at work in the center court. And I got a pretty good look at the operation, too. Thanks for taking care of my shots; the girl in the store said her arm feels numb and sore. She's having a hard time working and lifting stuff."

A hand gripped my upper arm just then. For a moment, I panicked, convinced that a vaccination cop had done it, even with Aaron following me around, but it was Hamish.

"Hamish, you scared me!" I said, annoyed, but I hugged him.

He leaned over and kissed me, and tugged gently. "Let's go. Now."

"Okay. My car is out by Lord & Taylor."

He shifted his hand from my arm to my hand, staring around critically at everything. He gave a long glance to the left, took in the vaccination scene, and pulled me around past the information desk. Aaron and Ed, who had obviously brought Hamish here, stood near us.

A cop appeared in front of us. He was a bit overweight, with a crew-cut and an iPad.

"Good afternoon. Have you both been vaccinated?" he asked.

Perfect. Just perfect. Hamish was going to be mad at me, too.

"Hello officer," Hamish said, looking as calm and nonchalant as possible. "Yes, we're all set. Vaccinated and filed online."

"Really? What are your names? Let's see some I.D., please," he replied.

I looked at his badge. Officer Lynnwood, it said. Hamish and I produced our I.D.s and showed them.

"Dr. MacDonall? You must have been able to vaccinate your whole family early," he commented. "Convenient."

The horrifying, Orwellian system that our beloved government had created to manage and direct the enforcement of the new vaccine policy was fully operational. Everyone had to be registered with its new database. It was called the "Vaccine Tracking Database" – a part of a policy initiative called the "Draft National Adult Immunization Plan" – but there was also the "Draft National Child Immunization Plan" to cover the rest of the population.

Can't have anyone getting left out! The purpose was to make damned sure that all citizens, regardless of medical history, got all of the vaccines that the government wanted. With over 40 of them, the effort by physicians in their offices had gotten this process started. Because Hamish had done ours, slowly and carefully, for the entire family for months, we were all set, and no one could surprise him with more shots for us.

The cop looked us up in the system, and I still worried that he would find some problem. But after a moment, he said, "Yep – all set. Thanks a lot! Have a nice afternoon."

We put our I.D.s away, said thanks, wished him the same…and then kept walking.

Aaron had managed to nonchalantly walk past us during this encounter, but when he walked the other way, he found Ed being checked by another cop. We waited while the whole process was repeated, with Hamish's name coming up again as the vaccinating physician. That cop looked over at us as we watched.

Fortunately, I am capable of looking calm and curious while I take in a new experience, so we didn't attract any further notice from either officer and were soon walking through the nightgown area of Lord & Taylor. There were no cops in there.

Predictably, Ed had managed to park across the aisle from me. Hamish and I got into our car, and Aaron and Ed took off in theirs. Our little caravan went around and then out of the mall property, passing a security vehicle, but that didn't alarm Hamish. What did alarm him was my little tour and what it revealed at the front of the mall: a huge MRAP parked in front of the main entrance, plus several police cruisers in the handicapped spots closest to that door. Having seen what I had gone there to see, I drove out of the mall parking lot and off that property.

As we rounded the corner to wait for the traffic light that would let us back onto Ridgewood Road, Hamish spoke again. "Why did you come here today? I was terrified that they would grab you, ignore the fact that you already had the real vaccination, and inject you with that kill-shot!"

"I didn't know they were doing this today! The news said that only those without documentation would be notified about where to go and when. Those of us who were already covered weren't going to know," I protested. "You're mad at me. That's not fair!"

"No, I'm not mad at you. I was just scared. Let's get away from the mall," he said.

"Do we have to go right home or back to the lab?"

"Why?"

"Well, you're already out. Let's get ice cream at that farm in West Simsbury. There should be no vaccination teams, we can enjoy a visit out together and calm down."

"Okay. I don't feel like going back to my lab today anyway after that scare."

We went all the way up Ridgewood Road and turned left on Mountain Road, continuing right on past Stoner Drive. Lovely post-World-War II homes lined the street, and all of their lawns were neatly groomed with flowers in their gardens. No drought here, unlike in the Southwest. No…but we had other problems here, problems that had migrated here from there.

It looked idyllic until we got to the traffic lights, and then we saw lots of traffic. "Maybe people are trying to relax after being summoned out for the vaccines," I said, staring up ahead. "I don't see any police lights."

Hamish rolled his eyes. "That doesn't mean anything. I think you wanted to go exploring."

"Okay, fine. Guilty as charged. But the chance I just got to see things at the mall was a total accident. I had no idea or thought of that."

"Uh huh."

"You don't believe me?! You jerk!"

"I believe you. You're a terrible liar. It's just that you almost got injected with that crap."

"Oh."

The traffic moved along, and despite the amount of cars up ahead, it soon thinned out. No sign of danger anywhere. I drove all the way up through Bloomfield, up the over Simsbury Road to Hopmeadow, turned left to head for Tulmeadow Farm in West Simsbury, found a spot, and parked the car. Ed and Aaron parked next to us as we got out.

"Come on," Hamish called to them. "She wants to get some ice cream."

"I think they figured that out by now," I said to him wryly.

My husband just said "Yes dear," and headed for the ice cream window. I followed, admiring the flowering plants and herbs on the stands all around us. "One signature flavor dish of red raspberry chocolate chip ice cream, please," I said. It cost double what it had a year ago.

Hamish got pumpkin spice ice cream and sat down with me. We were on a bench along the front of the building. Ed and Aaron got vanilla peanut butter cup ice cream and sat eating it on a bale of hay that served as another bench. It looked the same as it had every summer, which was comforting.

My husband sat with his arm around my waist, and I realized that he was still trying to calm himself. Just being with him had calmed me, so I leaned against him and enjoyed it. "I love you," I said to him.

"I love you too," he said. "I wish I could get you to a safer place."

"Nowhere is safe anymore. Topographically and from a geoscientific standpoint, central Connecticut is one of the best places. As for human threats, it's still decent. I'd rather not try our luck elsewhere."

"I wish you were wrong, but I think you're right…again, damn it," he said.

Ed and Aaron sat silently listening to us. Ed saw me looking at them and said, "Hamish, you know she is."

"I don't care how much the Farmers think that thinning the herd of sheeple is good for the planet and better for those who don't get culled. From the point of view of the culled, it's pure evil and misery. Why should anyone have to yield their very existence just because there are too many humans living off the Earth and its resources?! And who died and granted them the right to decide who stays and who goes?!" I ranted, and it felt good to do so. There were no MRAPs in sight to record my malcontented remarks.

Hamish just looked and me and listened. He was a rare guy that way; he knew when I just wanted a listener and when I actually expected him to do something. He would know that when I came right out and asked for something.

"I won't stop being pleased when medicine, science, technology, and whatever other innovation solves someone's physical problems of disease or disability and enables them to live on and enjoy it. If I can help enable that, I will. I won't die for the damned Farmers, either. Fuck them and that idea."

They were all listening, and I wasn't being overly loud, despite the fact that Aspie voices tended to carry a bit. We were outside, and I knew that my topic should not be bellowed out. Only Hamish, Ed, and Aaron were hearing this. Besides, there weren't any other people nearby; it was still a bit early for the ice cream crowds to start gathering. It was midafternoon.

"Hamish, you know how my mother and I watch *Downton Abbey* every Sunday evening during the winter?"

"Aye." He wasn't sure where I was going with this.

"Well, at the end of it, an ad for a hospital always comes on. It shows a girl with long, wavy hair and braces talking about how she could have lost her leg to some debilitating medical condition, but thanks to her clever and determined doctor, she didn't. The Farmers might slate people like her for a cull. The hell with that! She and they ought to live and be happy, and I shall continue to very glad when I hear such stories. If I can help make more of them come true, I will. Please tell me you will too."

He grinned, leaned over, and kissed me. "I will." Little did I know that he was plotting our escape…and our way of striking back.

Chapter 28

Fighting the Soft-Kills

"Great. I'm not letting them shut off everyone's P53 proteins!" I said, getting really angry just from thinking about what was going on.

I thought about a conundrum that I had been pondering for a while.

It was this: in a struggle for survival, one could fight either openly with physical force, killing in chaos in a very obvious resource war, or one could fight covertly, by stealth, using intellect and cunning, in a not-so-blatant resource war.

Either way, one would kill others to achieve survival.

Either way, it would be a case of survival of the fittest, be it physical or intellectual.

Or perhaps both – life and death are not always black-and-white. There are gray areas.

One who killed covertly was just as bad as one who killed overtly, and vice versa.

It had taken me a while to realize that.

Yes, some people demanded chaos, no rules placed on their actions, and fought for that.

But others fought for order rather than chaos, even if that meant a police state.

Either way, they were using whatever methods they had access to in order to survive.

I didn't see a way to condemn them for it.

It looked as though it was time to stop philosophizing about it, pick a strategy, and fight.

"Let's call Jason," I said to Hamish over breakfast and coffee. "I want to do some more cyber-sleuthing, hacking, subversion, and otherwise fighting of soft-kills and cull-shots. I also want to expose that rapist we witnessed in the Blue Ridge Mountains. There has to be a way to ruin his life and not ours with techno-telepathy. Why should that woman he attacked be the only one who suffers?!"

My parents were out driving, tailed by Blackout guys, so I wasn't worried about them. They wouldn't overhear me; they wouldn't know anything about this. Meanwhile, no one would bother them, no matter how many MRAPs they encountered and told us about seeing later.

Lately, we had each been seeing them out and about at last. It was disturbing, to say the least.

The damned things were everywhere now. The police had given up all pretense of not using them without the sort of emergency that would normally warrant calling in a S.W.A.T. team, such as some nutjob with hostages. No...now cops were driving around town in these stupid things, ruining pavement everywhere they went due to the weight of the MRAPs.

At first, they just patrolled neighborhoods.

But, soon the militarized police were escorting vaccination teams to the homes of anyone on the government's database of citizens who was not also listed as having been vaccinated. Doctors' offices were no longer expected to take care of the vaccinations. Now it was being taken care of this way, to make sure that the anti-vaccination citizens who thought that they could hold out in rural areas were also injected.

No longer could people just claim that they didn't need to be vaccinated because they would not visit any major urban areas. The government wanted to go beyond *Jacobson v. Massachusetts*, and would not accept "no" for an answer.

Parents who thought that home-schooling kids would solve that dilemma were rudely awakened, both literally and figuratively, by intrusive, state-sponsored, taxpayer-funded, home invasions. Welcome to the new police state of Vaccine: The Cull. What an evil operation.

The government claimed it was protecting us against ever suffering from a known plague again via this diabolical vaccine program. Notice that this was the government's scientists, not independent ones, who were the ones promising this.

Scientists in general swore that no plague would decimate the human species, and that any death toll would only be a proverbial drop in the bucket of the overall human population. That meant, I realized, that no naturally occurring plague would make a significant enough dent in our numbers to save the ecosystem from the destruction that our species continued to wreak.

But…with an artificially created plague, the government could simply claim to have erred.

As it was, martial law was being declared here and there around the nation, as it was elsewhere. Wherever the vaccine campaign was tightest, martial law was declared. Once it was finished with an area, it was being lifted. All this was to make a show of good will to the people, to reassure us that no power-mad lunatic would take and hang on to totalitarian control.

I didn't believe it for an instant.

Hamish called Jason. Since it was a Saturday, he didn't have to go to his lab or office, and we were caught up, for the moment, on the subversion of the cull. That was not to say that we wouldn't find more people to help, just that we currently didn't have anyone scheduled to visit our secret operation. We would get back to it soon.

Jason met us in our house, and we took the precaution of going down to Hamish's basement lab again. Then I showed him the memory stick from our road trip – the one with the photographs of our exalted government's criminal activities. When he saw the rape images, he nearly fainted.

"Well, what did you expect to see, secretly and covertly in a basement?!" I asked.

"It's just more real and certain, that's all," he said.

I sighed. "I should give you a break. You are, after all, a twentysomething. But you might as well know that our government has ceased to live up to its high-minded ideals. Thomas Jefferson and George Washington would be aghast at this, but they are dead and gone. Our empire has curdled into a surveillance police state with its own secret terrorism to maintain itself. This is just proof of its plan to control the population by controlling health, movement, and space."

Jason sat there, stunned, staring at the computer screen.

I went on, "They want to get rid of what they now consider to be excess humans. If that woman is still alive, I would be amazed. It's the officer who raped her who is likely still around to face up to what he did…IF that can even be arranged. It's early in the game, but I would like to think about a way to make this go viral and not be traced or stopped."

Hamish chimed in, "This is the sort of thing that typically ends up on conspiracy websites, not mainstream media. It may take a lot of planning, research, hacking, and other ingenuity to track that bastard down and expose him. We don't expect to have this all figured out today."

Jason seemed to recover enough to function. He said, "You're right. I will need to spend some time. We will have to leave this laptop and data here. I hope you have a good hiding place for it. I can stay all day today and work, but when are your parents coming back?"

"Not until late afternoon. They'll call when they're on their way back. They drove to some outlet stores in Vermont," I said. "When they call, I'll tell you and you can pack up."

"Okay. Let's get started, then."

Hamish and I didn't tell him where our hiding place for this equipment was, and Jason didn't want to know…yet. It was in a secret compartment right in that room. We would put it back later, after Jason left, and we would make sure that he didn't forget something, turn back, and come in and see us doing so. Good thing I watched a lot of movies, I thought to myself.

Jason worked all day, stopping only to come upstairs and eat lunch with us. At the end of the day, he showed us that he had sent the data to some remote servers and through many others. There were some dark net places for data to be sent in various secure locations around the globe, and Jason had used four of them. They were programmed to release the data to every major news outlet plus the conspiracy ones…plus Wikileaks…in a month.

My parents called just as he was showing us all this, and he packed everything up.

We thanked him and let him out, saw him drive off, and then went back downstairs to hide the laptop and shut off the lights. After that, I started making dinner. Hamish was sitting in the kitchen, helping me pluck rosemary leaves off their stems, when my parents' car pulled into the garage. We were watching movies on the kitchen television, relaxed and ready to see what my mother had found at the shops.

Everything about us looked as normal as we could make it, and that was important.

It seemed that there was nothing for it but to break the Hippocratic Oath and give the elites of the planet a dose of their own poison.

I felt as evil as they were when I suggested the idea to Hamish.

"Don't feel too evil about it," he said to me. "I've been thinking of cooking something special up just for them. What were you thinking about?"

"Shutting off their P53 mechanisms – those cancer tumor suppressor proteins or genes or whatever they are – in such rapid succession that no oncologist could hope to keep up with it."

He nodded.

I wasn't finished. "I do see some flaws in this idea, if only because I'm not the mad scientist in this equation. I'm merely the psychopath on the opposing side of the fight who is suggesting a general plan of action."

Hamish smiled slightly, and said, "Go on."

"Okay. How can those cells really be shut off that fast? Is it even possible, or am I just writing science fiction? I mean, it's always easier to destroy than to create or heal, yet we have seen both going on for the past year or so. What would be involved? Wouldn't an oncologist have time to do something to interfere with this plan? Would it be necessary to keep doctors away, use false imprisonment just to give these anti-P53 nanites time to do their diabolical job?"

Hamish took a long breath, then said, "Actually, no. It would be a simple yet risky matter of ensuring that the Farmers get their evil nanobots back. They would have to think that they were safe just by getting vaccines that lack them, when in fact they would be getting them…airborne. And they would think so, because – count on it - they have been vaccinated as I vaccinated you and the rest of the family, slowly, spaced out, and with no tainted nanites in the sera."

"Oh."

"Yeah."

"So it's on. We're planning a reverse attach on the monsters who put this system into play."

"Aye…" Hamish was really thinking about the logistics in detail. I could see it.

"Am I evil?"

"Nae…you're a warrior woman, just for suggesting this. I must assume that you mean it."

"Oh yes. The only thing I don't see myself pulling off…and here is where I feel like I'm no different than Hitler or the bastards who gave smallpox-infested blankets to Native American people…is doing the deed. I'm just suggesting the idea, but I'm not a medical or nanobotic expert who could deliver this. And this means dose after dose. I'm an author and historian, not someone who could get that kind of access. Maybe I can help somehow…come with you to do this…but I don't know how to proceed. It all feels impossibly safe right now, like I'm just thinking of us clicking a few computer keystrokes and making this so."

"True. But it could be tricky and dangerous to deliver this stuff to the Farmers," Hamish said.

"How the hell are you going to avoid discovery while giving that Degenics shot over and over?" I wasn't interested in losing my husband. I knew that was terribly selfish, but if I was going to give them a taste of their own medicine, I might as well go all the way with it and insist on having my life and future to enjoy and that of my husband, too.

"Degenics," Hamish repeated. "I love it." He grinned. "Don't worry. It won't be a shot. I can't possibly deliver one on the scale required. I'll need help from my network."

"What, all over the planet?"

"Aye…all over it. They won't know what hit them, they'll think it's they're safe and that getting their precious secret vaccine will have protected them, end of story. It's all in the delivery. They're going to be taking delivery of something without knowing it. Thus, it won't just be the general population of our species that gets culled after all."

He paused a moment, thinking, and I watched him. He really could be as deliberately stealthy and deadly as I could plot to be, yet more so with his military experience and medical and technical expertise.

At last Hamish looked up and said, "There are still going to be far more hedge fundster and bankster Farmers and their mellifluous, self-entitled brats than there will be places at universities and in government. I was thinking it might be fun to watch them fight amongst themselves for those prizes, but even that is too good for them."

I took a long, satisfying breath and said, "That's one aspect of it. The other is that we wouldn't get to witness it anyway, even if we live to see it, because it would likely all happen behind closed doors and get hushed up. Yeah, better to take that control away from them. That's what they have been doing to everyone else that they could possibly reach: hitting them with a mysterious, rapid, and unstoppable death without warning, explanation, or hope of recovery."

"Indeed. Now I have to figure out how to do the deed – this covert method of delivery."

As Hamish and I continued to wage our own private war on the Farmers, it occurred to me that even though he hadn't worked that bit out yet, he was getting there. I thought about it some more. If my genius husband hadn't yet figured this out, he would soon, or he would just invent his way to a delivery method. If I could help him with do the deed, I would.

One night later that week, as we lay in bed in the darkness, I asked him something. "What have you done with all of those nasty nanobots that you have removed from people? Have you saved them up, destroyed them, studied them, what?"

"I saved them and studied them. Why? What do you have in mind?"

"Repurposing them."

He rolled over to look at me. Moonlight streamed in across our bed. "Repurposing them?"

"Yes. The only question is one of delivery without detection. Can you make them fly? And guide them into a particular individual's bloodstream? How long a distance can you get them to travel intact?"

Hamish stared at me for a while. He was thinking this through.

At last, he spoke. "I think I can do that. I would have to load a nanite gun with them first, then get reasonably close to Wall Street during business hours. Perhaps we could use a boat in New York Harbor…which we would have to buy and remove all surveillance devices from before this op is carried out. After that, we could conceivably infest several evil Farmers with their own nano-monsters."

"How many would it take per individual to do this, and how many have you got?"

He grinned. "It only takes 10 or so. That's how many I've extracted from each person thus far. I've just been saving them all together, but…there is a way to fire them now, with a guided trajectory. I have my own guidance and tracking software that can be ride with them, release, and return. The only limitation is that you can only infest one Farmer at a time. So you fire, guide, infest, and repeat."

"How fast do they travel?"

"Fast – they could get from the harbor to an investment bank's locker room in a little under a minute. After that, it slows down for the fussy part of the job, which is seeking out the intended target. We would have to have this planned down to the last bankster, complete with pattern or movement, schedule, you name it."

"I'll bet that Blackout Security could help with that. Isn't that one of their areas of expertise?"

"Aye. It is." Hamish grinned.

"Well then, let's make it so. It would be a shame to waste all those nano-monsters, wouldn't it? They ought to be put to good use, turned back on those who deployed them, tainting their P53 proteins. Otherwise, it's unfinished business, and we would be discovered in possession of them eventually. I'm worried about that. We must cover our tracks, get rid of this stuff, and not keep any around."

"You're right. Okay, then. Tomorrow, we start our offensive battle plan."

"Aye, Hamish, make it so." I grinned.

"What are you, the captain of a *Star Trek* op?"

"Indeed I am. You, my genius husband, are the chief science officer/engineer/weapons officer. I think of things to do, and you have the skills to make them so. Just pretend I've gone through some command training classes at Starfleet Academy when I think of stuff like this."

He started laughing at that point, climbed over to kiss me, and didn't stop. I laughed, too.

We drove down to Manhattan when we were ready, and bought a small yacht. (That only took us another week, after Hamish had contacted a yacht broker.) It was the smallest size we could get and still call it a yacht – no sails, just a motor and a comfortable sleeper cabin with a full bathroom er, head, below. We had to name it, so I suggested naming it the *Sarah Connor*, after the woman who fought the Terminator and Cyberdyne Systems.

I hung out in the cabin while Hamish and Jason and some Blackout guys who had assisted him with de-bugging our cars went over the yacht with a fine-toothed comb, looking for RFID chips and whatever other surveillance crap they could extract. While they worked, I served a feast from Dean & DeLuca, just to make it look like a pleasure outing rather than an op.

At last, the RFID junk was all gathered on the kitchen er, galley table. I had brought a cutting board and the metal meat tenderizer all the way from Connecticut, and Hamish smashed everything up then and there. After that, he swept it all into a box, just as he had at home, and added a few nanobotic scrap separators to salvage the parts for use in future projects.

With that, we were ready.

I sat there and watched as tiny cameras – built into the nanites – allowed us to watch our own movie being shot. The six-legged, six-sided nano-monsters were carried by Hamish's nanites. Together, they swarmed like a hive of stinging insects, moving like bullets across the water, over Battery Park, past Bowling Green and the bronze statue of a charging bull, onto Wall Street.

From there, they entered the first bank on our list. Banksters didn't actually hang out at the New York Stock Exchange. They stayed in their skyscrapers and enjoyed their corner offices, emerging every so often to yell at their armies of up-and-coming bankster minions as they drummed up stock sales on the acres of desks. We saw our first bankster doing just that, and the nano-monsters sailed undetected across a room full of desk with small, flatscreen computer monitors and phones.

The bankster was a short, bald twit with a very high opinion of himself. He had been written about extensively by the media, photographed, interviewed, and vilified in at least one ex-banker's memoir. Yes, this was definitely the right guy: he was abusive and self-entitled. Up his nose the nanobotic demons went, and soon we were looking at his blood cells.

Hamish took the controls from Jason at that point, guided them up to the bankster's brain, and released the lot of them, leaving them there. Within a minute or so, the nano-guidance swarm systems had returned to the *Sarah Connor*. "Okay, that's one down. Next lot, please."

I took a deep breath and sat back, stunned. We had done it – once. Now we were going to do it again. The enormity of this act began to hit me. This must have been how Hitler's assassins felt. I hoped we would fare better than Colonel Claus von Stauffenberg. Of course, we weren't even getting close enough to look like we were involved, and there was a significant time delay with this weapon.

That evening, in the privacy of our bedroom in the firehouse, with Ed and Aaron downstairs and Jason no doubt clicking away online with laptop open in the living room, Hamish explained to me how this op would play out.

"Avril, I want you to understand something. The banksters and hedge fundsters – Farmers – that we infested with those evil nanobots are not going to get sick anywhere near as rapidly as the general population. I want you to know that, and to understand why so that you will know what to expect."

I was a bit surprised, but then said, "I guess that shouldn't surprise me. There's always some out for them, some benefit that most other people don't have access to. What is it?"

My husband gave me a wry smile. "You're already on the right track. These Farmers don't eat GMOs, and they weren't given that culling vaccine. Like you and the rest of our family, they had the luxury of going to private physicians for properly spaced out vaccines, and those vaccines of course had no nanites, no mercury stabilizers, no nothing in terms of harmful additives. Their doctors were not pressured to get their vaccinations done and registered quick, quick, quick. Oh no…these patients were special, ahead of the line, and although they were no doubt registered with that national database of injections and injectees, they received nothing harmful and nothing but the very best."

I listened carefully, then summed up with, "In short, they got what you provided, but from someone else."

"Exactly."

"So…how soon will they get sick? And will they stay that way?"

"It should take months, not days, and that's as long as no one either realizes what has happened to them or gives them Regenics. I have to tell you that I'm worried that they may come to me for Regenics once it's commercialized. It's usually banksters who are investors."

"I see. And if that happens, and one of these monsters gets Regenics, then what? How long will he – or she – survive? That is, assuming that the monster nanobots aren't found."

"They could have a life span that is almost normal, but not quite, and they will still die of cancer. That won't affect my reputation though; I'm putting in a disclaimer that individual DNA can affect individual outcomes. I don't want to get sued over failing to deliver on a fountain of youth. It's going to be sold as a crap-shoot, not as a sure thing, just to protect our own futures."

"I can live with that," I told him.

We grinned, then went downstairs to get Jason and our Blackout shadows. It was time to go out for dinner and think of other things for a while.

We stayed in our firehouse for a week, making sure to do a few fun things in the city so as not to appear to be overly focused on this new yacht-toy. Each morning, we went out in the new boat and delivered the evil nanobots to the banksters and hedge fundsters. Each afternoon, we enjoyed Manhattan like normal people. We visited Madame Tussaud's wax museum, ate in some of our favorite restaurants, and dropped by the Rockefeller Institute to say hello to Dr. Nurse.

He was not ready to have us set up shop again just yet, so this was just a friendly visit.

The Institute was still in the middle of a major renovation and redesign of some of its key buildings due to the floods. With some urging from me, Hamish sat down with Dr. Nurse and discussed ways to exploit nanites to do a lot of the clean-up work once the heavy lifting was complete. This led to a plan for the future that involved environmental uses of nanites and a new application of Hamish's inventive skills as a researcher and professor.

Cool. I had just acted as my husband's agent, and he had a future position with a new direction to it at our old stomping ground. As for me, it was now clear to Dr. Nurse that I was the instigator and planner behind a lot of Hamish's creations. We were a team. As before, I had a shared office with Hamish and a place to do whatever research struck my fancy.

But not just yet; we had other things to do, and we weren't talking about that. Dr. Nurse had no interest in that, nor did he have the inclination to inquire about it. As far as he was concerned, his world revolved around the infrastructure project he was overseeing, plus getting the financing for it. Hamish and I did agree to come back in a month or so, get dressed up, and appear at a fundraiser function to help him with that. Professors have to do such things. That's just the way it is. Academic institutions ran on money, not just on ideas and executions of them.

A few days after that visit, we went home to Connecticut. Hamish had used up all of his nano-monsters, and our cell phones were full of messages from people we could help. Soon, Hamish would be re-supplied, and hopefully the Farmers would be none the wiser about it.

He knew some nanobotic experts in Europe, Japan, India, and Australia and New Zealand.

They had learned from Hamish how to extract the nanobots-from-hell from patients, and had since collected and stored quite a few. They would soon be dumping their stash into the Farmers located in the high-rent districts near them. Good.

Meanwhile, Hamish had let it slip that he was doing a study for a medical project that he had dreamed of carrying out since he was nine years old, one aimed at circumventing the aging process. This was not odd to the journalists who interviewed him from time to time; they were used to hearing revolutionary ideas from him. So, all of these patients trouping in and out of his lab past his staff seemed like business as usual. They wanted to find out more about Regenics.

Jeffrey Nurse called as soon as the first story broke, one that ran in *The Washington Post*. He wanted in on it, and he wanted a clinic for Regenics in Manhattan. We did a conference call about that, and soon had a tentative deal set up. Meanwhile, physicians and scientists at other places around the world also contacted Hamish, wanted in on it. He fielded the calls, reviewed it all, considered where these places were and the logistics involved, and showed me the list.

It was impressive, but would take time. I wondered how we would travel to all of these places, spend time there, get settled, and then leave, with constant change. The idea of constant change of environment unsettled me, to say the least. Singapore, Canberra, Kyoto, Johannesburg, Bruges, Lausanne, Vancouver, Lillehammer…cities all over the world beckoned. They sounded like nice places, and expensive. Odd that money no longer seemed like an obstacle. Now the problem was limited to the Aspie fear of change. Oh well…

We spent the next few weeks as we always had. I would drive Hamish out to his lab, do a few errands, maybe visit our friend at the gift shop with her dog, then go home and read all day. Or I would let the Blackout guys drive him and read all day. It didn't matter either way. At the end of the day, I would go and get Hamish myself, and if it was a yoga class day, so much the better. He could tinker with his Regenics formula and write up his patent for that much longer.

As usual, I had forbidden him to publish so much as one academic paper without first filing for a patent, and not just a flimsy, temporary one. We now had the financial resources to patent everything ourselves. It cost a couple million dollars, but it was worth it. Attorneys' fees, filing fees, you name it made it quite a production. It was a far cry from the U.S. Patent Office's early days, when it only cost a few dollars to file an idea. Now one had to be fabulously wealthy just to try to become…wealthy. It was ridiculous.

But…that really wasn't what concerned us now. We were just very glad to have something going on that would explain Hamish's laboratory and mask our efforts at fighting the soft-kills. We looked legitimately busy with something that the Farmers would not call illegal, and that was what counted.

It was a Thursday evening, just after yoga, and I didn't feel like cooking.

"Let's eat at Max a Mia tonight," I said to Hamish as I walked into the lab.

He looked up from his microscope. "You don't want to cook? I could cook."

"No you couldn't," I said, grinning.

"Kidding! You don't want to eat anything I would make, and neither do I." Hamish laughed.

He used to call me up when we were broke, asking how to cook things when he was away on business and visiting colleagues at their homes. He once called me from San Diego, California, back when it wasn't flooded and in ruins. He was trying to roast a chicken. I had to talk him through removal of the packaging, of all things, and explain how to peel and slice an onion.

No…I wanted to eat something decent without having to prepare it myself.

We ate at that restaurant, and it was good. The specials were always delectable works of art, and we filled up on olives, roasted garlic, tomato-garlic sauce and olive oil with bread, salad, fish and a shared dessert. It was a white chocolate torte with raspberry coulis sauce.

Relaxed and happy, we pulled out onto Route 44 and headed for Avon Mountain.

It was only eight o'clock in the evening, so there were still quite a few cars on the road. I got into the right-most lane and had to wait at a red light. A car driven by a man in business attire nudged his way in right behind me, cutting off Aaron and Ed, and leaving them behind him. He completely ignored the honk of their horn.

Hamish didn't notice. He turned on the CD player so we could hear *The Phantom of the Opera* and was clowning around with the deep, echoing voice of the Phantom's lines, singing along and booming out his voice.

"Stop it, Hamish! It's too close and loud in here for that." It was late July, and I opened the windows and turned the volume down just a little bit.

"Aw, you're no fun," he said, but he let me concentrate on the driving.

I wasn't doing any actual driving just yet; the light was still red. Cars were moving north and south in front of us, fast. Glancing to my right, far south, I saw a pair of headlights – big, high-set ones – approaching fast. It was a tractor trailer truck.

The light turned green. The man behind me honked his horn.

I didn't move.

Just because you have the right of way is no reason to go. The coast has to be clear first. The driver of the car behind me honked his horn loudly. Well, so what,

I thought? I muttered "fuck you" at my rearview mirror and stayed put. The huge truck was still coming.

The car next to me, however, pulled into the intersection as soon as the light turned green.

The impact made a deafening sound.

That car ended up in two pieces, one of which was on the grass of Avon Old Farms Inn, diagonally across from us. Shards of it were all over the intersection. I still didn't move my car, but the jerk behind me wasn't honking anymore. In fact, he looked like he had failed at something and drove off. He didn't even stay at the scene.

Despite the shock and roar of what had just happened, that wasn't all that had me feeling stunned and like someone had punched me in the stomach. Hamish had noticed it too.

The truck had been huge, all black, with no markings of any kind to identify it, and I could have sworn that its windows were tinted black. There was that, and the fact that it had shot on by at top speed, never slowing. It was just gone, into the night without stopping for the crash.

"Are you thinking what I'm thinking?" Hamish asked me.

"Oh yeah. We almost just got Farmed. Let's wait and see who was in that car. The newspapers will have that unfortunate person or those unfortunate people's names tomorrow."

Hamish's cell phone chimed. It was Aaron and Ed, two cars behind us, checking on us. Hamish said, "Avril won't cave in to peer pressure, so we're okay. She wouldn't pull out into the intersection. She saw those headlights coming fast." They chatted a minute more and rang off.

We dutifully pulled over and called emergency services, only to be told that they were already on their way. People around us were getting out to see what they could see or do. Pretty soon, an ambulance, a fire truck, a couple of police cruisers, and one MRAP appeared on the scene to take charge.

The engine segment of the car was partway up Route 44 on the other side of Route 10, in flames. The passenger or passengers were…where?

Oh…damn…crushed up in the other piece by the Inn, that was where.

It was difficult to look at that, but I looked for long enough to understand what I was seeing.

The cops took everyone's statements, and we headed home, taking a roundabout route. I would not go where that huge truck had gone. I wanted to steer our car away from wherever we thought it went. We ended up driving through Farmington and up Mountain Road from there.

As we drove along, everything seemed normal – dark, calm, and like usual.

But I didn't trust it anymore.

When I was almost ready to turn left off of Route 10 and onto Farmington Avenue, we saw some police lights up ahead. There was a line of cars, so we joined it. I felt like ice was in my stomach, and a lot of it. Hamish and I looked at each other, then glanced back to see our shadows, Ed and Aaron in the vehicle behind us.

Somehow, the fact that they were there failed to reassure me. If we had a problem, how could we get away? Sure, the nanite guns would help, but then we would be wanted, hunted, and on severely limited time. I resented it.

Hamish said, "I'm going to have Jason create and install software in a special, hand-held computer that spots police checkpoints and plots routes around them."

I looked over at him but said nothing. We had to get past the MRAPs up ahead first.

Our turn came, and the police looked at both of our I.D.s, asking Hamish why he had no driver's license. What dopes! "I don't drive," my husband replied. "I either ride with my wife, or with my driver. I don't want to drive. It's just another thing to worry about, and I'm busy working."

The cop looked nonplussed. "But why don't you want to drive? What happened?"

"I let my license lapse during graduate school, and since I was living in Boston, I just forgot all about it. Public transportation and killer, heavy traffic made it easier not to have a car. When I realized that I had let it lapse, I had my degree and didn't want to bother to get the license back."

I had just sat there the whole time, listening and watching as they talked across me.

The cop stared, but finally stopped asking stupid questions. He went back to his vehicle, which was parked by the MRAP up at the intersection, and handed it to another cop. We watched for five minutes as the other cop presumably checked his computer.

At last, he came back. "It looks as though everything is in order," he told us.

I couldn't resist asking him a question. "Are there a lot of drunks out tonight, or is there some event I paid no attention to and drove in the path of, like some sports thing?"

He smiled at that. "No, ma'am. We're just checking vaccination records. You're all set. Although…we are checking for drunks also. None yet, though. It's a weeknight."

I smiled back even though that giant ice cube in my stomach felt colder. "Thanks!" Then I had a thought. "What do you do when you find that someone isn't vaccinated, give them a ticket?"

He laughed. "No. We just make a notation in their record and a vaccination teams finds them, wherever they are – home, work, school, movies, you name it."

The cop gave us our I.D.s back and waved us on. We didn't bother to ask what this was about. We knew we would have just been told it was a "routine traffic check" or something about drunk driving…in the middle of the week.

I drove slowly, so that Aaron and Ed could catch up. Soon we saw them in our rearview mirrors, and Hamish's phone rang. Ed was irate over being unable to stay on our tail. The guy certainly had a strong sense of duty, that was for sure, but they both felt like family to us now. The feeling seemed to be mutual.

Hamish assured him that it was not his fault, and they hung up. Soon, we were at home.

The next morning, it turned out that the people in that smashed car had been a husband and wife, both professionals like us, and they had eaten at Max a Mia also. Their car was a lot like ours, a blue Mercedes sedan. We didn't know them. I tried to remember seeing them in there, but I couldn't. They must have sat in the other dining room. But that wasn't the eeriest part.

It seemed worth investigating further, and Hamish was sure Jason would find out what had made the Farmers want them gone. He called Jason and ordered the MRAP tracking software, and then we settled in to wait the day out until the visit. Hamish worked at home, and I was glad.

Did the Farmers know what we were up to, or did they just want us dead because of who we were and what we were capable of?

Hamish said that the latter was plenty of reason on its own. Perhaps they just didn't want Regenics competing with the cull vaccine program.

Jason came over in the evening and showed us his new police checkpoint tracker program. He had spent all day writing the code for it.

"You should be able to move about unimpeded, even if thoroughly inconvenienced and rerouted," he assured us with a smug expression. "The program is called Poliggy-Sniffer."

Hamish roared with laughter and shook his hand. I grinned from ear to ear.

Why be easy to catch, spot, or otherwise Farmed?!

We weren't planning to be easy to kill.

Chapter 29

The Grim Data Reapers

The world's elite were not willing to wait that long for the cull to do its work. They wanted to go faster. As I sifted through my research and continued to read the news, I had a growing and sickening sense that this cull of humans was going to speed up soon. The Farmers were grim data reapers, watching their dirty work as it progressed. Whether or not that reaping was even-handed was another matter.

It seemed to me that this cull had nothing to do with race, ethnicity, religion, sexual orientation, gender, or many other factors, and only a little to do with economic class. I discussed that with Hamish.

"So if we are overpopulated as a species, doesn't it follow that we are overpopulated in every country, every religion, every ethnic group, every culture, and every economic stratum? I mean, if there are too many poor people requiring too much housing to accommodate them, and too many middle-class people wanting college educations with not enough places for them, aren't there also too many wealthy people wanting to run corporations and hold political office? Granted, my question has lumped each stratum of people into stereotypes, because poor people go to college, middle class people get elected to Congress, and some rich people don't work in politics or corporations, but you see my question, don't you?"

He did. Hamish said, "You're right as usual. What of it?"

"Is this population cull being committed or perpetrated or whatever on only the poor and the middle class? Are the rich saving themselves, planning to be safely alive once the dust has settled to enjoy the spoils of life that remain?"

Hamish looked at me steadily and said, "Nothing gets past you. Yes. The rich are saving their own asses as usual."

"Aha. That was the confirmation I needed to hear."

People were starting to get sick from the tainted vaccine, and the government could not claim that anything else was the cause. It had to be obvious to any layperson that the vaccine was the variable in their experience that didn't add up. The CDC claimed that something was wrong, not going as planned, and that the government would take care of everyone who got sick.

Reports trickled out into the media, into conversations between citizens, and all over the Internet about the illness. It was nothing that we had seen before, yet it was many of the things that we had seen. The government's genocidal plan was in play, complete with its cover story.

It was all sorts of symptoms from all sorts of diseases, manifesting and killing…rapidly.

Chapter 30

What About Society's Elders?

Societies – at least, those that I had known or learned about – had become used to viewing everyone as important, as someone who mattered, and as worth saving, complete with a good quality of life as well as a long one.

And why not? That's a good, honorable, and ethical way to be. The elders of any society are the ones with a wealth of experience and, hopefully, wisdom. Without them, the whole society is worse off, with no one to consult in times of uncertainty.

What if all that was going to be taken away from us?

Life was going to feel the opposite of being worth living, that's what.

Damn it…the Farmers actually seemed to be planning on that outcome.

I preferred old people to young ones for company. But elderly people were among the ones most vulnerable to health threats, with the most depleted immune systems. Unlike other viruses, flu viruses constantly mutated, presenting endless motives for vaccinations.

Flu shot ads seemed to target elderly people specifically, demonstrating a determined effort on the part of the government to get elderly people injected with monster nanobot-infested sera. Now, on top of that effort, the vaccine cull serum was after them along with everyone else.

That nasty feeling of sickening anxiety, complete with a gray haze clouding my vision, threatened to return and fog up my thought processes. I would have to calm down and think some more. I would also have to accept that Hamish couldn't save everyone. That didn't help.

Regardless of what the Farmers deemed to be of value, there was no substitute for the comfort and wisdom of being able to discuss ones worries and questions with an elderly friend or relative. The mere idea of doing away with elders was idiotic. Would there be any left? Elderly people got sickest and did so fastest…and died first.

Granted, we were taking care of Grandmère, but what about all of the others?

Okay, all of the others were obviously not going to be left free to live their lives, nor would lots of younger people be left alive either. But would the demographic distribution of surviving humans include any elders? Who would teach emotional intelligence and common sense?!

We needed them! Everything was just better with older people.

I wanted nothing to do with a future in which elders weren't around, and valued.

Chapter 31

Democracy is Not Free

Freedom is not free, and neither is the brand of it called democracy.
It all costs something.
The problem was how to pay for it with no way to control anything.

The banksters had seen to that by stripping the majority of Americans of their purchasing power. The middle class was, for all intents and purposes, gone now. No one could earn enough from just one job to pay for a house, its utilities, food, clothing, and a college education. Jobs were either mechanized or shipped to nations that were just starting to join the industrialized world, stripping our workers of clout. There were too few jobs, which made them desperate.

It took three jobs to pay for the standard of living that Americans had become accustomed to now, and no benefits were part of the deal. The trick was to give each employee too few hours to qualify for those benefits. Never mind that health insurance was now required by law for all. The government had to foot the bill, which meant the ultimate in no-frills, no-options patient experiences.

People felt that they had little or no control over anything, and I actually heard conversations during this election year in which they said that they saw no point in voting. It was a disaster. The republic was really in collapse if they were going to just give up without the slightest fight.

We must vote if we are to have any voice, plus sign petitions, and write whatever we wish.

It felt like something had died – something monumental – to hear this surrender.

The economy had crashed at last, and the government had devalued the dollar and taken so much money from ordinary citizens – pensions and bank accounts – that the vaccine wasn't the only culling tool in use. Now there were suicides as people realized that they could not afford to pay for the necessities of living. You know, groceries, rent, that sort of thing.

Voltaire said, "I disagree entirely with everything you say, but I will defend to the death your right to say it." Lovely idea, isn't that? It is the essence of democracy.

Francois-Marie Arouet (Voltaire was a pen name) lived and died in France as a wealthy, comfortable, privileged member of his society from 1694 to 1778…before the excesses of the aristocracy imploded that society in revolution. He had it all, enjoyed life as a politician, ambassador, writer, philosopher, and philanderer. He did get locked up a few times for his writings, though. He dared to write whatever he thought, and damn the consequences.

Arouet also pushed against royal authority with his writings. He believed in a monarchy, but mixed that belief with wishful thinking. He wished for the monarch – Louis XV – to be a benevolent sort who would not abuse his position and exploit the people as a resource, or have a problem with the exercise of freedom of speech.

Wishful thinking combined with a poison pen can get one exiled, imprisoned, and otherwise fettered. That was what happened to Arouet several times in his life. Nevertheless, he wrote. One of the things he wrote was a little-known short story called *Micromégas*. It was the first known science fiction story, about aliens from a planet that revolves around the star Sirius who visit Earth. The aliens laughed uproariously when they heard Earth's philosophers tell them that everything in the universe revolved around their planet.

That was pretty funny. Creative people tend to push their luck as a way of life. Societies as a whole demand democracy. We all expect and require it. We insist upon living as if we have it, regardless of whether or not we actually do.

But...money and security are necessary to the continued existence of democracy. Space, resources, money...without them, you get social unrest. Social unrest is a nice, sanitized term for mob rule and riots.

Elites – the privileged ones who have a large share of resources – typically buffer themselves against mobs, riots, and similar such unpleasantness. The Farmers thought that they had.

We hoped to prove at least some of them wrong.

It was going to be difficult, and I wondered whether or not those tainted nanite deliveries would make enough of a dent in those monsters to make a difference.

As I wondered, the President of the United States did what we had been dreading and declared a State of National Emergency, and instituted martial law. This was an odd version of it, however, in that it was a mobile state of emergency, one that was in effect in different parts of the nation at different times.

It was early July, almost a year from when the Jade Helm exercises had begun, and now REX 84 was in play. Hamish and I called Jason over right away to test a theory. Hamish sent his flying nanite surveillance swarm out to Georgia, North Carolina, and South Carolina to take a look around, and sure enough, that entire area was changing rapidly as we watched.

Mobile REX 84 camps and crematoria were transforming the landscaping, treating human settlements as infestations, taking the land back from them. Whereas days before there had been vast expanses of suburbia, now they were suddenly erased, replaced by flat, soil-topped land. New trees had been planted, grass seeds strewn hastily over everything, and all blacktop, concrete, and electrical wiring removed.

Most of the areas that had been forcibly reclaimed corresponded to those in the Wildlands Map, but there were others. These others thinned out the size of cities, mitigating urban sprawl in a travesty of going green. This was not what the environmentalists had meant by that.

Chapter 32

Awakenings

Gone were the Nazis who would rob people of all of their worldly possessions and just herd them into labor camps or crematoriums. Now we had a much more painful and slower process of relieving people of their comfort and security: cancer with bills that were too high to cope with.

This wasn't survival of the fittest. It was slaughter by those who had defined the game of those who hadn't yet noticed that the game was afoot. It was deciding on their behalf that we as a species would see a privileged, murderous few – plus some oblivious and lucky others – survive in comfort and safety at the expense of others.

It brought back thoughts of 1789 France, when the aristocrats had held most of the wealth. Those aristocrats were so careless as to let the populace feel pain and know that they were feeling it and know why and who was to blame.

Today's ruling elite had learned from that and decided to cull the population before they ever had the chance to fight back. The Farmers were not going to let any of their "crops" take over and hurt them, not if they could help it, and they thought that they could.

They thought that they could control information and knowledge.

They thought that they could control people.

We would see just how true or untrue that was.

The information was right there for the taking.

It didn't have to be overt or even directly conveyed.

One could figure it out by reading between the lines.

One could also see what was happening with Hamish and Jason's help. Those flying nanite cameras had revealed something close to home: Claire's parents were dead.

Claire had moved out of Grandmère's suite of rooms and into Fabian's room shortly after he had proposed to her. She had been happily making regular phone calls home to her parents, planning the cake with them, until this weekend. Abruptly, after Sunday evening, she could not reach them. Their phone numbers went straight to voice mail, and when she called the bakery the next day, a phone company recording said that the number (a land line) was disconnected.

Frantic, she called us and told us all this, and we had gone over to see her.

She was sitting in her room with Fabian, teary and out of breath, and I noticed a box next to her. It was cardboard, and open. Claire saw me looking at it and said, "My mother sent that. It just arrived on Wednesday. I was busy working, so I didn't open it until Saturday. It has the family jewelry and photographs, and some lace that my grandmother tatted."

"Your mother just packed all that up and sent it here? Just last week?" I asked.

"Yes – on the same day as my parents' vaccinations. When I looked through it, I realized that it wasn't just the pieces she would want to pass on to me. It was ALL of her jewelry, including her own engagement ring, pearls that were my grandmother's, and the rose quartz beads she always wears. That's when I got scared and called her." Claire was hyperventilating a bit now.

She went on, "I spoke to her on Saturday, right after I opened it all, to ask why she would send all that, and if she was divorcing my father. I mean, who sends their engagement ring away like that?!"

Claire paused to breathe, and Fabian put his arm around her. Hamish and I were sitting on the love seat across from their bed, listening. Claire held up the rose quartz necklace, and I remembered seeing it on Emily when they had visited. The engagement ring had a one-carat oval diamond on yellow gold with six prongs – also familiar.

"Claire, you should take care of that ring for your mother. Maybe wear it if it fits."

She slid it onto her right ring finger absent-mindedly. "It does," she said, looking at her hand unhappily. "My mother said that she and my father were perfectly happy together, but that she wanted this stuff to be safely away from Philadelphia with me, and that she was going to give me this stuff anyway. I found that odd, though, and pushed for more detail."

Hamish and I exchanged glances with each other and with Fabian. Claire continued, "Finally, she told me that they got their vaccinations on Monday and weren't feeling well. She saw people coming back into the doctor's office – people who were vaccinated the week before – and they looked terrible. That's why she sent this stuff here. Now I can get either of them on the phone, and I'm scared. What could have happened?!"

"We'll find out. I don't know how or what that will be, but we'll find out," I said, getting up and hugging her. Hamish promised to help, of course. He kept the nature of that help vague, but I knew he would think of something later, and that it would be of some use to her.

"Thank you," Claire said, crying and trying to breathe more slowly. "I know you tried to get them to come here and let you take care of their shots. They're just workaholics. I don't know what for. It's not worth it if it kills you."

It wasn't exactly workaholism that had done it, though.

If Emily Charbonneau had said that she and John weren't feeling well enough to work, that was significant. Anyone with a showcase cake business almost never took any time off. Since they had been vaccinated early last week, we knew that they would not feel well for very long.

Hamish had called them and called them, asking them to please come for another visit and let him administer their shots, planning to add a dose of Regenics, but no, they were too busy. They could not leave their bakery. Too many clients wanted cakes for weddings, showers, birthdays, corporate events…you name it!

Before the Charbonneau parents knew it, they were out of time.

We didn't know what else to say or do for Claire at that point, so we went home and called Jason. He had just gotten home after a long day at Hamish's lab, but he heard the tone in our voices and agreed to come right over.

Soon he had the laptop going, and focused on the suburb of Philadelphia where the Charbonneau cake shop was located. The problem was that it, along with the rest of its downtown area, was not there anymore. It was all gone, replaced with an expanse of newly-laid sod, even where there had once been pavement.

Jason's program ran a before-and-after view of every area it scanned. He had downloaded and saved the images from Google Maps, having hacked into its Dark Net server. That was yet another thing that we didn't ask too many questions about.

He had video surveillance to show us in no time flat, thanks to a set of flying nanites that he and Hamish had deployed in a sickened anticipation of this scenario. They couldn't help themselves; they watched some places more than others. There were the ones where people whom they knew lived.

As a result, that evening, Hamish and I saw what had happened there: another mobile camp had taken Emily and John, killed them, and spewed them out as human soot. The area where they had lived was now covered over with new grass, trees, and other vegetation, and left to the wildlife. All traces of power lines, telephone poles, pavement, housing of any kind, malls, schools, offices, you name it, had been removed.

We saw Claire the next evening for dinner at our house, and had been unable to say that. But it didn't matter. She knew when she looked at us, and said she wasn't ready to hear more. We felt terrible. I settled for giving her a hug and saying, "We love you. You're part of this family."

She looked up, startled but pleased, said "Thank you," and hugged back.

She wandered, dazed, toward the stairwell, obviously thinking of going to her and Fabian's room. I followed her, not willing to leave her alone right now. Fabian was in the den with Jacques, looking at something on the computer.

"Do you need or want anything? Whatever it is, if I can do it, just tell me," I said.

Claire smiled weakly. She was trying not to cry. We had walked all the way into her room.

"Go ahead and cry if you need to," I said.

"I don't want to upset anyone," she said, but she looked terribly upset herself, like she was on the verge of losing it.

"That's ridiculous!" I said. "The mere idea that people around you would choose to shy away from any unpleasant feeling or upset that we might experience in some second-hand way, by being there for you and listening, is selfish and despicable. The least we can do is face up to it for the benefit of the person who is feeling it directly. If we can't make things better, at least we – or I, anyway – can give you that!"

Claire looked at me, a bit taken aback by this little speech, and then flung her arms around me and hugged me tight. I hugged back, and she suddenly began to sob. We stood next to the bed like that for a minute or two, and then I reached for the box of tissues on the nightstand.

She sat down and took the box from me, blowing her nose, but started crying again a moment later. I turned to the door, torn between calling for Fabian and just staying quiet, but he was coming up the stairs. I could hear him.

He took one look at Claire and asked me quietly, "Did you find out what happened to her parents?"

I nodded. "Yes."

He didn't ask for details. He just sat down next to her and held her. I stayed a few more minutes, then stood up, thinking I should leave them, but when I did, so did Claire.

"Thank you, Avril. I don't want to think about this now. I'll find out more soon enough, whether I like it or not. I know it won't be from the news. They lie. You and Hamish will tell me after a while, I'm sure."

I looked at her. She was quick on the uptake, like me. She knew when things were too terrible to show out in the open, without taking precautions against detection. "Okay," I said. "When conditions are right, and when it's not such a horridly new thought to you, we'll show you what we know and how we came to know it."

Of course she wasn't ready to see what we knew, which was that her parents had, essentially, been erased from existence. That was what the government here and governments elsewhere were doing to people all over the planet now.

She and Fabian regarded me levelly, and then we went downstairs to dinner.

A few hours later, at home, Aaron came to the front door of the house with a grim expression on his face. What now?

Hamish let him in and beckoned him to follow to the basement, pausing just long enough to get out his cell phone and call Jason. It was after 10 o'clock at night. What was up?

A minute later, he hung up and said, "Jason's on his way over here."

"I figured," I said. "Did you tell him to just stay overnight, or will I have to call back and do that? Whatever you're up to, think about how secret and dangerous it is to find out and know what we know, and how easy it would be to knock him off or kidnap him in the dark. I hope you've had some protection on him."

Hamish did a double-take, then called him again. There was a brief exchange, and he hung up again. "He's bringing his toothbrush and whatever else," Hamish told me. Then he told Aaron to arrange protection for Jason.

I rolled my eyes. "I can't believe that you of all people just did this now, after I suggested it."

"Aye...well...I've got blinders on with my family. If you're not family, I have to be told it's necessary," Hamish said with a hint of ruefulness and chagrin. "But you're right. Someone like Jason is as much of a target as you and I are."

I went upstairs, checked the guest room, put out clean towels in the bathroom, and came back. A couple of minutes later, Jason arrived.

Downstairs in our basement lair (Lair! It was a furnished den with some lab equipment, I thought with a grin), Hamish said to me, "I asked Blackout Security, via Aaron, to check out that fatal crash that we were almost a part of in the Routes 10 and 44 Avon intersection. They found something."

"Oh? Why am I not surprised?" I said. "Let's hear it, then."

Aaron leaned forward. "Blackout has found out that the dead couple's car was one of the newest, fanciest, top-of-the-line cars with all of the latest and greatest gadgetry in it – including SmartTech such as GPS and self-driving software." He paused to let that sink in.

I listened, then got it. "You mean that they didn't willingly drive themselves into that intersection just then, right into that oncoming tractor trailer truck? That they were driven into it?!" I asked, appalled.

Aaron nodded.

Hamish looked grim, and Jason looked wide-eyed. He started panting a bit and rocking back and forth. Aspie, I thought. Good to have another one here, I thought a moment later.

Jason said, "Most people my age are too caught up in the convenience and fun of SmartTech to recognize the potential for hacker murders and other abuses of the technology."

Hamish gave him an appraising look and said, clearly impressed, "I knew you weren't a sheeple."

"I knew that too," I said, "but are you okay? It's still a scare and a shock. Do you want anything to drink? Alcohol? Chocolate? Herbal tea? No restrictions on anything," I added, smiling slightly and hoping these ideas would calm him.

Jason took a deep breath, thanked me, and said he might like something later.

Meanwhile, he wanted to do one more thing connected with this terrifying news, which was what Hamish had summoned him for: he wanted to hack some government sites and see what other plans there had been for that night.

"You're awfully calm for someone who may also have been a target," he told me.

"Yeah, well, this isn't exactly a shock to hear that the Farmers may want us gone," I said.

He went to work on the laptop then, and we all sat there, waiting.

After about ten minutes of typing and reading, he looked up. He looked calmer, despite the news he was delivering. The activity had to have calmed him. Doing something rather than passively absorbing information can feel a hell of lot better, I knew.

"Here it is," Jason said. "I found a report in which it says that there were 2 teams from the proverbial "Company" (a.k.a. the C.I.A.) there that night. One team was there to clean up. The other was in a car right behind you, honking loudly at you to move forward the moment that the light changed. They weren't counting on you to be the type to not move forward."

Hamish glanced at me with an admiring grin, then said, "She just swears at jerks who do that, even though they can't hear her through the glass, and stays put. I've seen her do this many times."

"Yeah, well, they thought she would move, and would have slammed on the accelerator and pushed your car into that intersection if there hadn't been more cars in the vicinity. They just couldn't clean up after so many witnesses, so they didn't. This whole plan was in place, complete with an abort – in the form of simply not pushing you forward – because you don't have SmartTech in your car. They had an old-fashioned hit out on you instead."

I thought, 'Watch out, Farmers. Some of us are reading the data and are on to you.'

They couldn't control us all.

With that, I went upstairs to make a big cup of hot chocolate for Jason. I added a generous dollop of Kahlua to it, too.

Chapter 33

Escape Plans

When a government wants something done that is morally reprehensible, it may slap a law on that action to deem it legal and force social compliance with its agenda. It also seizes people's assets – money, property, whatever. Continuity of government is the most convenient excuse for suspending or even terminating civil liberties.

Our nation had lost its security when it lost the capacity to accommodate its population.

Libertarian reproduction policies had gotten us to this impasse.

Laissez-faire reproduction…why did no one understand how making it taboo to say that babies are not automatic blessings had gotten us where we were now?!

Wishful thinking…industrialization of creature comforts and medical technology…that attitude and tacit policy was now showing us what dystopia was like in real time. We weren't going to be able to just fast forward to a world as it would be after an apocalypse.

We were watching that apocalypse unfold, and my husband had been arranging for us to head for a safe distance from which to watch it do so.

"We're leaving for Switzerland soon," Hamish informed me. "I've made the travel arrangements. The cats, your family, my sister, and Jason and his parents – we're all going."

"Switzerland? How can anyone travel during all this? Isn't all international travel being restricted?"

"Not all…corporate business trips with family members are still allowed. And they aren't watching all avenues of escape as effectively as they think they are." Clearly, my husband had planned for every potential objection or concern I might possibly think of.

I looked at him steadily. He was presenting me with a fait accompli, and I wasn't even upset. "Switzerland sounds nice. How long will this trip be? Can we come home eventually?"

"Yes. After a stay of indeterminate duration, it should be okay to return."

"Wow…how are we getting there? And when did you plan this out?"

"Well, as you were looking back and forth between laptops in the basement laboratory, I was making arrangements, with Jason's assistance, for our escape. I've got it all figured out. The toughest part is now ahead of me."

"What is that?"

"Persuading your family to trust me and come with us when I tell them to."

"How will you go about that?"

"Well…Jason and I found something that should help."

"Which is…?"

"A schedule; it shows when each area of the United States will be cleared out by the mobile military culling camps. Connecticut is down on the list, not too far in the future. It is still deemed 'overcrowded' by the Farmers. USAMRIID is coming here, and we will all be gone before it gets here, on our way to Switzerland, and out of their reach."

"You seem to have covered all angles and avenues. You're a genius."

"I'm determined to do everything I can to keep you safe, comfortable, and happy."

I hugged him and said, "I love you. You're the best guy in the world."

He hugged me back and said, "No I'm not. I'm grabbing my wife and running away."

I lay back on my pillow and said, "You can't save everyone. I came across something about how to handle things if society collapsed on the Internet several years ago. One of the things it advised was not to try to save everyone. That would be like trying to save a drowning person in the middle of the ocean with no life jackets. They will just pull you under and drown you both. That's nasty, but that's how it is. I hate it, and have been looking to save everyone I know."

"I know. Me too, to some extent." He lay back, staring at the ceiling. "During my military training, when I saw some of the reprehensible scenarios that they cooked up, I would opt out rather than enable and obey evil orders. I just left…and told journalists about it. I did it in undisclosed locations, far from populated areas, on remote camping trips. It was easier to communicate back then, when the Internet was a couple of years from going live. Now it's a lot tougher to do that covertly."

I sidled over to him and snuggled up, pulling our pillows closer, and we stopped talking.

Hamish and I each had our own expertise.

Mine enabled me to make people around me comfortable. It also enabled me to think of ideas that covered as many angles as possible…as many contingencies as might impede us. Hamish had that in common with me. What he could do with his expertise was shield those around him from danger.

He had made arrangements to have something to do in Switzerland that the Swiss would actually want, and that would make money. We would be using our skills there to develop his Regenics treatment at a clinic in Lausanne, which was a town on the north side of Lake Geneva. Geneva itself wasn't far; it was just around to the southwest of that lake.

It would be nice once we got there. The director, a Dr. Thierry Chavannes, was coordinating with Dr. Jeffrey Nurse in Manhattan to set up identical clinics in both locations. A neuroscientist by the name of Dr. Albert Vallotton would be assisting with the setup on the Swiss end. Hamish would be indispensable, of course, but the Swiss could get things started until we joined them.

Unlike other nations in Europe, Switzerland was not in the mess that the rest of the planet was in, either ecologically or financially. Well, a little bit ecologically; it was experiencing some of the species die-offs that the rest of the planet had to deal with. But it was high above sea level, so it wasn't losing any territory at all. It had no immigration problems. No Romany nomads, no climate refugees from the equatorial regions, no Muslim terrorists, no nothing!

How was this possible?!

Part of the answer was about its financial system.

If you wanted to live in Switzerland, you had to have a huge bank account, or you could just forget it. That left most of the planet outside this historically neutral nation's borders, end of story, no ifs, ands, or buts about it. The Swiss had never adopted the Euro, and their own currency, the Swiss Franc, was backed by actual gold. No fictitious money by fiat there!

Where did that leave us? With the damned Farmers, unfortunately. We might very well see some of them riding out the population cull there. I hope Hamish wouldn't be forced to remove the monster nanobots from any of them if we met them at this clinic in Lausanne.

Of course, we still had to get to Switzerland, the neutral country. The Swiss were not overpopulated. That was no surprise. They were a landlocked, self-interested, insular society. With finite land and resources, they were always determined to cover their own needs and security in case of a siege from outside their borders.

That's why few foreigners were allowed to dwell inside them with the Swiss.

Those few were among the planet's wealthiest, of course.

I realized that we would be near many from among the one percent of our own country who held the most wealth. Only they could buy their way into the Swiss banks and enjoy safety and comfort during the coming storm.

These were nasty people…selfish in the extreme.

Did that describe me and Hamish, just for being able to join them?

I hoped not.

I would have to meet some to make up my mind as to just how much – beyond our financial resources – we had in common with them.

We would have to be very close-mouthed about our opinions for quite a while in order to stay alive. It all felt very un-American to someone who had been raised to think of her country in idealistic terms. My generation had been ingrained with the idea that Americans and America could solve any problem and rescue anyone from anything. It was a lovely fairy tale, but nothing more than a fairy tale. That was a very unhappy realization.

"I feel like you have been taking most of the risks without telling me. At last, at least during the escape, and perhaps at Lausanne, I might get to share in some of the risk. We will likely meet some Farmers in Switzerland. That just seems like a place where they too will hide out to ride out this storm that they have unleashed onto the rest of the human population."

"Indeed. But so what? You're still taking on the risk along with me. And you're right – the danger will continue even there, in Lausanne, because even once we're there, many of these hedge fund Farmer assholes will definitely be there, wanting Regenics. I'll have to give them this serum there, too."

I was suddenly looking at Hamish in outrage, about to object. But what did it matter? We would figure that out when we got there. There had to be a way to continue to give the Farmers their own soft-kill nanobots. Apparently, the danger would continue a bit longer, as Hamish worked to reduce the excess population of the world's elites. If I could help, I would.

They deserved to fail at their own game.

That game was progressing relentlessly, and starting to affect travelers.

It affected Edgar's girlfriend, Ellie, when she went to Atlanta to protest the vaccination policy. The serum being used was so obviously behind mass illnesses that this fact couldn't be concealed any longer. The problem was that the policy was firmly in place, backed by that damned treaty, and martial law was blocking civil liberties. The people who objected were preparing a large demonstration in front of City Hall. Why didn't any of these people understand how useless it was to exercise civil liberties that they had been stripped of?!

Were they knowing martyrs, or complete and utter fools?

Sadly, I suspected the latter. Ellie had never shown any sense of understanding the difference between a U.S. Constitution in times of peace and security and how it worked under martial law. Most people failed to consider that angle of it. It came with curfews and cold silences, not with the right to freedom of speech and peaceable assemblage.

I couldn't believe it. Ellie had gone without warning into an area that was under martial law, and right where the CDC was headquartered. Why?! I had warned her about the dangers of doing such a thing, and she had disregarded me. She had walked right into a noose, practically inviting the lynch mob that was the militia there to pull the loop tightly around her and lift her up.

When the group applied for their protest permit, they all got vaccinated.

Ellie showed her I.D. and told them that her vaccinations were all done and in the government's computer database. That did not impress them. They just ignored her and said that they were only checking their own database, and her shots were not listed in it. With that, they injected her with what we knew to be the cancer-induction nanobots.

It made no difference that Ellie had already been vaccinated. There was a vaccination team camped out in City Hall, backed by armed military personnel, who said that that was the rule: anyone in the areas under martial law would be vaccinated, and independent vaccinations, regardless of database entries, would not be recognized there.

What had she been thinking? It wasn't enough that she was already properly and safely vaccinated. This wasn't really about protecting human health, as we had explained to her. It was about managing human health as some burgeoning problem to be contained, as we had warned her repeatedly. It had fallen on deaf ears, apparently. It was maddening to be proven right.

Edgar was horrified. So were we. We and the rest of the family – and her parents – told her to come home immediately, not that we actually thought she would be able to leave that area.

Ellie said that she would get a flight back here as soon as the protest was over.

We waited and watched the protests on the news and on the Internet.

Oddly, they went off smoothly enough, but perhaps just for show. After all, we only saw video of the protest, no sound, and a newscaster at a desk doing a bland report on it. The spin was that these were crazed conspiracy theorists who were protesting the vaccines, that it was common, accepted knowledge that vaccines were beneficial, and that any negative symptoms from the serum were aberrations.

We were disgusted and alarmed. We tried to stay upbeat and positive about Ellie's return trip, sitting with Edgar and behaving calmly. After all, it would do no good to flip out and say upsetting things before it was even time for her to head home.

But when Ellie and her group tried to get on a plane, she and they were all detained at the airport. She texted Edgar: "We're being led to a hotel at the airport. Will call."

That was in the afternoon. She had called him the day after she had arrived in Atlanta, which had been Monday. Her group had spent the week making signs and publicizing their protest plan. The protest was going on all day, and the Ellie's friends – a group from her college that she had kept in touch with – planned to end it when City Hall closed for the day.

Edgar was frantic. He called me, he called Hamish, and he told his parents what was going on. Ellie's parents, who lived in Simsbury, met us at Uncle Charlie and Aunt Zoe's house. We waited all day, but she didn't call. It was a Thursday, not a usual night for dinner there.

Hamish and I kept looking at each other, assuming the worst. At 10 o'clock, he told me to drive us home. I did it, and asked, "Why couldn't we have stayed longer?"

"Jason and I saw something about possible curfews and water rationing."

"For where? When?"

"For here in a few weeks. We have to prepare to leave. Ellie is not getting out of there, but we are getting out of here."

I felt sick. The walls were closing in on us all.

Jason met us at the door, and he had an overnight bag. We went straight to the basement.

He fired up the laptop, its location no longer a secret from him. Hamish and I had stopped concealing the fact that we kept where it was. We just took it out and let him get to work.

Jason had found a USAMRIID webpage that showed whatever the mobile camps were currently doing, where, and for how long. It had become the go-to page for our Saturday web-surfing sessions.

There it was: live feed of the protestors. They were all being held in a hotel conference room. They even had photographs of each protestor, and had identified them all.

There was Ellie. She was sitting calmly with her colleagues, and there was something different about her and them. After watching it for a few minutes, I realized what it was. They had no cell phones to text with or surf the Internet with!

The military unit must have collected them all.

Seeing young people with electronic devices was now such an expected sight that not seeing it was an odd and ominous sign.

Edgar and Ellie had refused to acquire most SmartTech beyond cell phones and computers…except for those ubiquitous ones that recorded photographs, videos, e-mail, texts, and phone calls. We had tried to talk them out of using such things, but they were addicted to them. In the end, we had given up.

None of the protestors had those quick response code tattoos that would have made it easy for the military unit to I.D. them. They were young, in their twenties, and they lived on organic foods. Now they were under a sort of arrest.

What excuse, what pretense, had been offered? A quarantine!

Were the latest vaccination nanites any faster-acting than the ones that we had seen?

No…Hamish checked that. The idea that people who had gotten sick were contagious was a lie to imprison the protestors. It was being used on any protest in any region where the cull camps were present.

Why hadn't we seen this before, I cried?!

"They just started this on Tuesday," Jason answered.

Ellie had left on Monday. She must not have heard about this yet, busy planning the protest.

She had coordinated this protest with people from around Georgia, and they had visited the Guidestones before meeting up at Atlanta's City Hall to get their permit. Instead of being able to tie in their statements about SmartMeters, Agenda 21, and their suspicions about a cull policy to bring about the numbers on those stones, they had been cut off before they could speak.

The protest had been presented quietly on the news, with no statements – only placards.

They were being censored and silenced.

Edgar had noticed this earlier in the day, and he pointed it out again as we had waited for word from Ellie. The evening news carried no mention of any links between the vaccines and the treaty, or between the treaty and the Georgia Guidestones.

Ellie had been caught among this group, and was trapped in a maze with no exit.

Jason sent the flying nano-cameras that Hamish had developed into that hotel.

By this time, Hamish had deployed groups of five nano-spy-bots to every major city in the United States. No wonder he and Jason had been so riveted on that laptop every week! The nano-spy-bots lay in wait under the eaves of local buildings that would not be razed, such as historic sites. These were places that were not being watched by government agencies.

We saw the soldiers handing out processed foods to the protestors as they sat on the floor of an airport hotel conference room. Many people refused to accept them, but when they asked to go out and buy other foods, they were told that they could not go anywhere, and that no other food choices were available to them.

At midnight, Ellie and her colleagues were escorted out of the hotel – out a back door – and into a canvas-covered military truck. When I saw that, I had a fit. I couldn't see in front of me. I couldn't breathe normally. That gray haze of anxiety that I hated so much was back, and I couldn't make it go away.

Hamish grabbed me and held on. When I couldn't breathe at all, I realized that he was having a panic attack of his own. After a moment of me struggling and pushing, he realized that he was squeezing me too tightly and loosened his grip.

Jason sat there watching the horror show unfolding in utter disbelief.

He had seen this scenario play out countless times, and all we had been able to do before was, as now, watch helplessly, but this time, he was freaking out. "I went to high school with Ellie," he said. "And I think I saw a girl I went to college with in that group, too."

We pulled him into a group hug and cried.

The next day, we had the deeply unpleasant task of visiting Edgar and bringing him over to our house to see the video recording of what had happened. Jason helped us. Edgar had not seen any of the previous camp showings, so at first he did not understand what was happening, although he did realize that the vaccinations were an ominous sign.

After he had seen the satellite views of neighborhoods being emptied and left vacant, soldiers going in and looting, dead pets, and then the camps...plus a sped-up time-lapse video of what went on in those camps and their dismantling and moving on, he got it. Ellie was lost.

He slumped in his seat on the basement sofa, stunned. We were ready for that.

Hamish had a light sedative ready, which he injected into Edgar's arm. We walked him upstairs to a guest room, took off his shoes, pulled back the bedcovers, and laid him on the bed. Edgar stared at us, loopy and stunned. "Avril...thanks for not telling me how stupid Ellie is," he said to me.

I gaped at him for a moment. "Why would I do that?! It wouldn't do any good."

He looked at me, listless. "I told her to come back over and over." His eyes closed.

"Can we call Aunt Zoe and Uncle Charlie to sit with him?" I asked Hamish.

"Damn. I didn't want to tell them all this yet. I may need more sedatives," he said.

The doorbell rang.

"Who could that be?!" I said, jumping. After what we had just looked at, and after having Jason overnight, ever sound had me antsy and suspicious. I half-expected the MRAPs to appear and haul us away at every instant.

Rushing out into the hall, I looked down the staircase at the front door.

Jason wandered by, looking unsure as to whether or not he should be there. But we had told him to stick around, and so he did. As I watched, he sat down on a living room chair, looking from me to the front door.

Grandmère was there. My mother had let her in. Dad came out and stood there, too.

Grandmère had called and insisted that Aaron and Ed drive her over after seeing us greet Edgar at their house and persuade him to ride back with us over to our house. Our facial expressions must have given away the fact that something horrific was afoot. My parents had not known that she had our guardians' phone numbers until now.

"Take me upstairs to see him," she said to me. "Then take me wherever I have to go to see and hear whatever it is that is going on," she added.

Hamish and I glanced at each other.

Grandmère had been given her dose of Regenics a couple of months ago. For a 96-year-old woman, she had been acting as spry as she had when she was in her eighties, we had noticed lately. She had stopped huffing and puffing after walking up and down stairs, and her hair seemed to be getting thicker. She looked good, and she told us that she felt good, too.

But she did have a heart murmur, a side effect left over from having had diphtheria as a 4-year-old. "I'm not going to drop dead of a heart attack," Grandmère suddenly announced. "I've seen expressions like yours before. It's been several decades, but you seem to forget what part of history I've witnessed. I can take it, whatever it is. Now show me."

I went down the staircase and met my grandmother, and we walked back up together.

My parents followed. They had been in the kitchen, watching cooking shows, unaware of what was going on. The game was up; Hamish and I realized that full disclosure of the cull was imminent.

I said, "You are about to find out why Hamish has been taking nanobots out of you, putting his own in temporarily, taking them out after that, and insisting upon carrying out all of your vaccinations himself. And that's not all you're about to find out about," I concluded cryptically.

With that, we went in to check on Edgar. He was starting to fall asleep, and I was glad for him. No doubt, he had been unable to sleep all night. When he woke up later, however, he would probably be a total wreck. It was just as well that we were about to share the reasons for this with other relatives. We were going to be rather busy dealing with the emotional fall-out from this.

A person is an organic being full of memories, skills, talents, likes and dislikes, personality quirks, and emotions. It always amazed me to think…to realize…that all of that could just be turned off, shut down, deactivated, and suddenly over and done with. Whether the person died from old age, illness, or murder, it shocked me to think that all of that could just cease to be.

And what about Ellie's parents?! What the hell were we going to tell them, that we had our own personal secret nano-spyware that had told us the awful truth? We hardly knew them. We were going to have to think of some lie, such as that we did not know any more than they did.

Grandmère and my mother leaned over Edgar and looked at him, and my mother asked Hamish what he had given him for a sedative. He told her.

"So he will wake up in a few hours, right?" she asked.

"Probably more like four," he said. "which means that we had better get going on telling you everything. Let's get Jason and go down to the basement."

Dad stared at him, then at me. "What have you been doing down there this time?"

"You'll see," I said. "Come on."

Grandmère looked at us, kissed and hugged Edgar, and turned to go.

We went down to the living room, and Jason was sitting there, his eyes huge. "How is he?"

"Sleeping, for now," I said. "Jason, this is my grandmother, Vianne Châtelet, and she wants to know what we know…all of it. We're going to tell my parents, too. We may end up telling Edgar's parents next, and possibly his brothers. They're all adults."

"What about Fabian's fiancée, Claire?" Jason asked. Jason knew that Claire was not going home. Home was now with our family. "Does she know that she can't go home to Philadelphia?"

"No. Yes. Maybe. She didn't want us to tell her when we first figured it out. It was like she understood what we had found just by looking at us. We're going to have to tell her eventually, but we think she has figured most of it out already. Her mother packed up the family jewels and photographs, and she sent them all to Claire. It was like her mother knew or sensed something was wrong," I said.

"Has Claire talked about it at all?" Jason wanted to know.

No. We'll just have to see how it goes," I said. "We don't want to push her."

With that, Jason stood up, said hello to Grandmère and shook her hand, and walked down to the basement. At least this room was familiar to everyone. Hamish had de-culled us all down here, and done the Regenics injections here, too.

We settled in for a long and unpleasant home movie.

When it was over, Grandmère sat there for a moment, shocked, appalled, and yet not surprised. "It's happening again. The difference this time is that there seems to be no hate directed at any particular group. It's simply a general cull, isn't it?"

"Aye," Hamish said, looking like we were attending way more than just one funeral.

"We're never going to see Ellie again, I can understand that," Grandmère commented.

My parents looked like they were going to be sick.

"Henri, Camille, you must pull yourselves together," Grandmère said, unexpectedly taking charge. "We are going to have to act like we don't know any of this."

They stared at her.

She wasn't done yet. "You weren't born yet when the Nazis emptied out Le Marais and took all the Jews to the Vélodrome d'Hiver," Grandmère told them, "but I have told you about it. This is just another example of how such atrocities are carried out. You have to stay calm when they come, and help those whom you can help. We'll start with Edgar, and continue with ourselves, or we won't be helping anyone else."

She was referring to the kidnapping and deportation of the Paris Jews during the Nazi occupation in World War II. Le Marais was a beautiful area in the 3rd and 4th Arrondissements of Paris, where the Jewish community had lived until then. The poor Jews were dragged away to a roller rink across the city, in the shadow of Le Tour Eiffel, and kept there for four days before being sent off to die in concentration camps. Perhaps FEMA had learned it from them.

"You are making this much easier than we thought it would be to tell the rest of the family why we have to leave, when and how we have to leave, and how to behave as we do so," I told her. "I thought it was going to be a lot more difficult."

"You forget what I have lived through."

"No, I didn't. I just worried that you might actually have a heart attack. But apparently, you are not only benefitting quickly from Regenics, but are also just...tough. That's why I like older people much better than younger ones," I told her.

She gave me a mirthless smile for that.

"What is our escape plan?" she asked next.

Hamish was ready with that. He laid it all out for us.

"This plan is for us all, including Jason and his parents," he began.

"Naturally," Grandmère said. "He's in on everything, so he would have to be."

Hamish went on to explain that everyone in this room, plus everyone at Grandmère and Edgar's house, plus Claire, Jason, and Jason's parents, Anne and Peter, were going first to Manhattan to stay in our house there, and then on to Switzerland. He had the transportation all arranged. We would be leaving soon, taking little with us, and spending a week or two in Manhattan before starting the next part of the journey.

"What's in Switzerland?" Dad asked.

Hamish told them about the Lausanne clinic and his Regenics program.

I explained how the Swiss immigration system worked, and that it let in almost no one.

The only thing left to do was to tell the others and get going.

Chapter 34

Ellie

It had seemed like such a simple, routine, and reasonable thing to do, fly down to Atlanta, Georgia, meet up with old college friends, and protest the vaccination policy in front of CDC headquarters.

Ellie realized that she should have known that it wasn't simple at all. No one was going to be allowed to protest anything in front of CDC premises. That would obstruct traffic there even without a health crisis. One couldn't legally obstruct movement in and out of a hospital or a medical research facility under any circumstances, so they had relocated to another, much more public venue: City Hall in Atlanta, Georgia.

It was supposed to be a fun week away. It was summer, she had enjoyed going on these trips with her friends when she was in college, and she wasn't missing work to do this. What a great thing it would be to tell her students about in the fall, Ellie thought to herself as she boarded the plane at Bradley International Airport.

The flight was uneventful. It was only when she got off that she realized that her classmate, Leanne, had been on it with her. Leanne was working for a private school in Salisbury, Connecticut, so she too was off for the summer, free to do whatever she wished.

Free. What a laughable idea, they had said to each other, discussing how the vaccine had been forced on everyone. Leanne's family was well-connected to the healthcare industry; she had been vaccinated, but in advance, as Ellie had been. Both were protected against all forty diseases that the serum targeted, but without those monster nanites.

The group Ellie was going to protest with were all people in their twenties, young and idealistic, and determined to expose the truth to the world. They had brought their phones, making calls to remind each other to repeatedly check that they had not forgotten their recharging cords. Nothing was going to prevent them from broadcasting their activities over the Internet for the nation and the world to see.

Ellie and Leanne arrived on Monday afternoon, found another college friend who had an apartment in the city, and left their things there. Karen was delighted to see them again, and frustrated at having been offered internship with an organic foods corporation. She wanted a job with them, but had settled for this, hoping to get her foot in the door this way. Her family could afford for her to take this route to employment. That was all there was for many young people seeking careers in big cities. New York City was full of such stories too.

Karen walked her friends to another apartment two blocks away, one that was shared by four guys. It was packed with people, and a mini-reunion ensued as everyone reconnected, caught up on the past couple of years, and shared stories of job-hunting and vaccinations.

It was interesting to note that all of them (and there were twenty-six of them) had been lucky enough to get vaccinated by parents or relatives who were physicians or who had friends who owed them favors. No one was feeling ill, but everyone knew more than most people in the country did about the vaccines for just that reason.

"I mean, we see people around us dropping like flies, looking like death warmed over as they go about their business, right?" Jacob, a guy who had been a brother in a fraternity at Ellie's college was saying. She remembered him as the chief organizer of one beer fest after another. When he hadn't been doing that, he had been active in the student government, a leader. He was somewhat short with sandy, curly hair, and he had grown a beard. He wore a tee shirt that said "Boycott GMOs", cargo shorts, and Birkenstock sandals.

Alan, his roommate, nodded in agreement. "We're fine, we see people getting sick, yet we're all vaccinated. Something is up, man. Something's different about what we got and what they're getting. Malls aren't supposed to be for injections. They're for shopping and hanging out. Something is screwed up."

Ellie took a beer and a looked around. Karen showed her the hat that was being used to collect money for tonight's dinner. She had ordered it from the local Whole Foods store, and the guys were going over to pick it up in a few minutes. Ellie added twelve bucks and wandered out into the living room, mingling and chatting with people.

She had so much fun connecting with people that before she knew it, it was going to be dark soon. "Come on," Karen said. "We have to get back and sleep before the curfew starts. It starts at 9 o'clock. Let's go." Leanne was already with her.

Feeling slightly drunk, Ellie grabbed her handbag and followed them out.

On the walk back, they saw some MRAPs and uniformed police and militia moving through the area. It wasn't time to enforce the curfew yet, but Karen made them hurry along. Ellie asked, "Can either of you tell which ones are cops and which ones are military? They look so similar," she said, keeping her voice low.

Leanne wasn't sure, but Karen said, "Dark blue for cops, green camouflage for militia."

The guys with the tanks and assault rifles looked at the three of them like preys they moved along, Ellie thought. She wondered what was in store for them all here, and wondered whether she should have come here. Too late now! Might as well do this protest, she thought, and have a nice time seeing my old friends.

They went inside, took showers, and turned on the television. Reruns of *Dallas* were on. The three of them giggled and watch John Ross and Christopher Ewing spar over oil in Texas until they fell asleep on the sofa. As a result, Ellie completely forgot to call Edgar or her parents. No problem, she thought as she nodded off, she had texted them all when her plane landed.

The next morning, with the curfew lifted again, she forgot all about the danger she had felt walking back from Jacob and Alan's apartment the night before.

She and Leanne followed Karen out to a Starbucks, got lattes, and hurried over to meet everyone else. Jacob, back in his leadership role, was outlining the plan for the week: Today they would go on a day trip, and tomorrow, they would prepare by buying materials for placards at local art stores, assemble them, apply for their protest permit, and announce their plan on social media. Thursday would be the big day, when they held the event in front of Atlanta City Hall.

Tuesday was thus spent announcing the plan on social media as they carpooled out to Elberton to see the Georgia Guidestones. The trip took just under two hours each way, and they had all day to kill. Everyone was having a great time visiting, heedless of the fact that the city seemed like a war zone after dark. During daylight, all was forgotten.

On the way to the Georgia Guidestones, everyone who wasn't driving was kept busy posting to Facebook, Twitter, Instagram, and whatever else occurred to them. Some people had their own websites, and Ellie posted a link to the feed that Alan had set up to her school's message board. The other faculty members could see what she had been up to later.

The responses were a bit disappointing.

One of them texted her: "Ellie, are you crazy?!"

Another said: "It's not safe. How will you get out?"

She texted back: "Return plane ticket."

The reply scared her: "Those aren't being honored in places with martial law."

But she pushed that thought out of her mind.

Edgar called when the Tweeting was halfway through. "Are you out of your fucking mind?! You've got to get out of there. There's no way anyone is going to be allowed to exercise free speech in Atlanta – especially if it's about the CDC!"

"Don't be silly Edgar," Ellie said. "I've seen no incidents of anyone being bothered. Yes, there are some cops and soldiers walking around armed, but they don't do anything. They just nod at us and look away. They're not interested in us."

Fabian's voice was audible nearby. "Jacques is going to ride with Jason. They're going to play some online game later. Is that Ellie? How's she going to protest anything with all civil liberties suspended?!"

Ellie heard Claire say, "What?! Where is she?"

Edgar said, sounding exasperated, "Atlanta." Then he spoke into the phone to Ellie again. "See? Claire and Fabian want to go to law school. They already sound like Avril. This whole idea is nuts. Come home."

"No. And don't tell Avril or Hamish about this. Just let them see it on the news tomorrow. I can't wait to come home and see the looks on their faces when I get back having protested this policy. They don't do or say anything. They just quietly go about their business, safe and secure with their security posse, leaving it up to the rest of us to actually exercise our rights."

Fabian took the phone and said, "You don't get it, Ellie. Under martial law, we don't have those rights. They are suspended. Leave now while you still can."

"No, Fabian. I came here for a purpose, and I'm going to see it through. Put Edgar back on."

He did, and Ellie spoke to him soothingly for a couple more minutes before saying good-night. "I'll be back tomorrow evening to tell you all about it and show you the pictures I took of my friends. Maybe you can meet them next time, after I show you that we can do this."

"Okay, Ellie. Stay safe, please. I love you."

"Love you too. Bye!" and she ended the call.

They had arrived at Elberton. She got out and walked over to the stones, staring up at the eerie structure. A chilly breeze swept over them as they read the message. Jacob came over and said that his family liked to fund archaeological expeditions, but this place fascinated him above all others because it had been deliberately built to look like a sort of Stonehenge, but with a creepy, apocalyptic message, as if the world had ended or something.

Ellie agreed. "My boyfriend's cousin and her husband came to see this last year."

"What did they think of it?"

"I don't know. Mostly they just wanted to see historic sites and Hamish's nanites at the farms and orchards around here."

"Wait – did you say Hamish? As in Hamish MacDonall?"

"Yeah. He's Avril's husband."

"Your boyfriend's cousin and her husband are the birth control nanite inventors?"

"Yes."

"Holy shit! What do they say about the vaccinations?"

"They don't approve of the policy. Hamish vaccinated us all himself. Didn't your family have your vaccination done independently too?"

Jacob was barely listening, but he said, "Yeah, they did. Spaced out carefully over a few months…and I feel fine. Our doctor said that's the way to do it."

"Isn't your family connected to some hedge fund?"

"Yes. I don't know much about it though. My brother manages it mostly. He thinks I'm too idealistic and uninformed, but I guess I'll learn the family business in a few years and help."

Ellie nodded, and turned to read the extra slab of granite off to the side.

Wednesday was another lovely, bright, sunny day, and although some cops with assault rifles were seen out and about, watching everyone who came and went, the group attracted little notice. They went out in pairs or groups of three to buy the art supplies, and there was more than one store nearby. That made their comings and goings less conspicuous.

They went as a group to City Hall to get the permit for their public gathering in the morning. When Jacob asked for it, the clerk produced the necessary form, watched him fill it out, and then asked for a show of I.D. from everyone who would be attending it. The rules were different here thanks to martial law. People couldn't just show up and protest. They had to identify themselves in advance.

Everyone printed their names on the form and signed next to their names.

After that, they got a surprise. A vaccination team arrived. The clerk explained that everyone in Atlanta had to have the government's vaccine now, and that any visitor to the city was included in that rule. "What are you protesting about?" she asked as she filed the form.

"The vaccine policy," Jacob said. "I'll be calling my attorney about this. I already got vaccinated by my doctor. It's in the government database."

The clerk looked nonplussed, then said, "That won't make any difference after the fact."

Ellie was horrified. She showed her I.D. and insisted that her vaccination requirement had been met, but the team didn't care. "Those independent vaccines weren't done according to CDC and USAMRIID guidelines. We aren't recognizing those anymore." They refused to check the government database for her records.

Two MPs walked up to her without any further preamble, gripped her arms, and the nurse with the syringe injected her. And that was that; they let go of Ellie, entered her name into their own database, and moved on to the next person.

The vaccination team was clearly from the CDC and the military combined. "USAMRIID" was on some of the uniforms. In short order, everyone had been given an injection and was rubbing a very sore spot on their upper arms. The team had not been in too much of a hurry, so it didn't hurt much, but it hurt nonetheless.

The nurse with the team tried to get them all to accept some free food and drinks, but it was all junk. "No thank you," they all said. The nurse tried to insist, but the doctor in charge told her to stop. Ellie wasn't sure, but she could have sworn that she heard him say, "We'll see them again soon enough anyway, and then they'll accept it."

Ellie walked off to the side of the lobby of City Hall, rubbing her arm. She told herself that she could just go see Hamish when she got back to Connecticut to assure herself that everything was all right. If there was any problem, he could fix it.

She tried to put that cold sense of fear that she felt from knowing about monster nanites out of her mind and focus on the protest that she was there for. No point in doing anything else at this point, she told herself.

For lunch, everyone split up and into small groups and drove to a Whole Foods, where they all got something organic to eat and drink. No GMOs for this group.

Next, they went back to Jacob and Alan's place to finish the signs. By late afternoon, all placards had been created. They said things like, "The CDC is LYING to you!" or "The Vaccines are TAINTED."

Ellie remembered to call Edgar at some point late in the afternoon, when she knew that Hamish's office was winding down for the day. She got him on the phone as he was walking out to his car with Claire and Fabian.

"You're where?!" he said incredulously. "Come back right now – that city is under martial law. Why didn't you tell me you were going?"

"Because I knew what you would say, and I wanted to see all of my old college friends. We're having a blast. I wish you could be here too," she told him. "I'd love for you to meet everyone. You'd like them."

"I'm sure I would," Edgar said, "but not like this. It's not safe. I can't believe you went there – of all places to go – for a reunion. What's really going on?"

"It's a surprise. I think you'll be proud of me. I'll tell you when I see you."

He protested some more, demanding full disclosure, but she dismissed him and rang off.

Dinner that evening was less of a big deal in that it was held in Karen's apartment, and several people failed to leave before the curfew went into effect. That left one couple that had reconnected hooking up in Karen's bedroom, and two other guys sleeping on the living room floor. The women sprawled awkwardly on the sofas, but they were poufy enough to provide a decent night's sleep.

The next morning, she and Leanne packed their bags, which were just small backpacks with a few essentials. Ellie figured she could do her laundry when she got back to Connecticut. It would be nice to get fresh underwear and a change of clothing after washing it out in Karen's bathroom sink. She was all wrinkled, but it was worth it, and she was having fun.

She pushed all doubts and thoughts of difficulties carrying out the plan out of her mind.

They walked over to Jacob and Alan's place and picked up their placards, and the group took an electric-powered SmartBus downtown. The ride took half an hour. It would have taken ten minutes in a car, but that was public transportation – slow.

"At least we've had nice weather all week. Today is going to be another sunny day," Alan commented as they got off the bus. Everyone had organic snacks in their bags, bottles of water, and their phones fully charged.

As they got off the bus, Ellie noticed a pair of news crews in front of the building and many, many cops and soldiers armed with assault rifles. An Army officer spoke to the news crews briefly, pointing at the protesters. The newscasters looked over at them, nodded, and went on with their broadcast without turning the cameras away from the building.

Of course, this was City Hall, Ellie reminded herself. It was right across the street from the Georgia State Capitol building, which also had a nice big lawn around it. Of course the cops and militia would be here in larger numbers. Nothing would go wrong with the media here, she assured herself. She just wished they would turn their lenses to face her group.

Everyone settled into place in front of the building. There was plenty of grass to stand or sit on, and they were prepared to stay there all day. Rest rooms had been staked out down the street at a pizza joint.

As she chose her spot and held up her placard, Ellie looked around, disappointed, because the news teams didn't seem to notice their protest. They were talking in front of the building, using it as a backdrop for the newscaster, who was talking about city news, the curfew, and vaccinations.

Jacob walked out in front of the group, with the video camera engaged on his cell phone, and motioned to everyone to start the protest.

Karen wasted no time. She started chanting about the vaccines, shouting loudly that something was amiss with them. "Why are only some people sick?! Why are no public personalities or celebrities sick?! Why is it that all doctors, politicians, and broadcast journalists are fine?! What are they hiding?!"

Soon the group was shouting "What are they hiding?!" like an ear-splitting mantra.

The militia and police were watching them now, but that was all they seemed to be doing.

The slogans went on until noon, with everyone walking around in a long oval-shaped pattern, chanting a bit less loudly to save their voices. They broke for lunch and a rest room break.

Everyone held up their signs as they ate, propped against their shoulders as they sat on the ground. Someone was broadcasting with a cell phone from various angles at all times, usually five or six people at once.

They took turns. Ellie spent half an hour doing this when it was her turn, and commented, "I'm almost glad our phones weren't this sophisticated when we were doing this in college." Several people grinned ruefully at her when she said this.

After lunch, the protest went on for another couple of hours before the news crews reappeared. Everyone perked up, looking hopeful. Jacob said, "Now we're getting somewhere. I e-mailed both of these stations about our protest yesterday. I'm surprised they didn't come over to us earlier."

Both news crews were back now. But rather than being accompanied by the newscasters, the camera crews simply walked over, filmed the protest for a few minutes, and left.

Jacob was outraged. "Hey! Don't you want to talk to us? Did you even get a recording of our chants? What are you doing, just recording this for later? This is censorship!" He had taken a few steps out into the street as he said this. Fortunately, the traffic was light.

Unfortunately, that meant that no one was noticing the protest.

Alan and Karen went out and tapped him on the shoulders, coaxing him back to the grass.

A little while later, the newscasters did come out and talk to Jacob and Alan and Karen, so Jacob was mollified. After a few neatly measured statements about how things just didn't add up with this vaccination policy, the militia made another appearance.

It was a lieutenant. He gestured quietly at the building and motioned the crew inside. They all headed in with a terse "thank you" to Jacob, and that was all.

Jacob turned around in time to see a guy coming toward the group, yelling and waving.

Everyone turned to look. The guy wore a set of army-green scrubs and was barefoot. He was falling down as he ran, but he kept standing up and moving closer. His face was red and scabby. "Finally! Someone cares! Someone is actually here to do something about this!" he shouted.

Ellie looked at him, nonplussed, as he came closer. He seemed really sick. Why wasn't anyone coming over to help him? And where had he come from, she wondered?

When he was just five feet away from the group, he collapsed into a severe coughing fit. Lynn, who had been the girl who hooked up with her old boyfriend Darin, actually walked up to him and touched him, trying to help him to his feet. "Why isn't anyone taking care of you?" she asked, looking around.

Just then, someone did. Two guys in Army fatigues and sealed gas masks came around the corner, took the coughing man by his arms, stood him up, and marched him into a waiting truck. It took off down the street, and that was that.

"What was that all about?" Leanne wondered.

"I don't know," Ellie said.

The protest continued until half past four in the afternoon, at which point people were ready to pack it in and go to the airport. Flights were scheduled to depart, and the event was over, for whatever it was worth.

"Let's go home and see how much media attention we managed to get for this," Leanne said.

Everyone agreed, shook hands, hugged, traded phone numbers, e-mails, and whatever else they could think of, and carpooled to the airport. The entire group went to say their good-byes, not just the people who were flying out. They were having too much fun visiting to go home.

When they got there, however, there was an unpleasant surprise waiting for them: militia.

The U.S. Army was all over the airport, and so were wanted posters with all of their faces on them. USAMRIID physicians in full biocontainment gear waited with soldiers, who all wore special gloves and gas masks. The only difference between the doctors and the soldiers was the camouflage pattern on the soldiers' suits.

Ellie froze as she entered the lobby, staring in horror at them, and Leanne ran right into her.

"What's the matter…? Oh!" Leanne said, stunned. She didn't say anything else.

"Come with us, please," said a doctor in a biocontainment suit. "You've all been exposed."

"Excuse me? Exposed to what?" Ellie said, hoping this was a mistake.

The USAMRIID doctor said, "That patient who ran up to you this afternoon. He ran away from us and we had trouble recovering him. We now know that he met up with your group, and we have eyewitnesses that one of you touched him. We have to assume that you have all been in close proximity with one another since then, which means that you've all been exposed. Also, even if only one of you actually touched him, we don't know which one of you it was. It really doesn't matter, though. The contagion has gone airborne, and he was just too close to you."

Ellie thought she was going to be sick. "What happens now? I have to go home! My family is waiting for me!" she said.

The USAMRIID doctor was a man with salt-and-pepper hair and a pencil-thin mustache, and a cold expression. He was obviously thin and fit under that biocontainment suit, and he was all business. Ellie could perceive no bedside manner whatsoever in him. No wonder he worked in the military, she thought. He wouldn't have to deal with patients' emotions. He could just order compliance instead of bothering to soothe anyone's anxieties or fears.

"I'm afraid you won't be able to go right back to them. You're all going to have to come with us to be put in isolation. If you don't show any symptoms after a few weeks, you can go home. Otherwise, you will most likely die from a combination of Ebola and cancer. That's what we're finding with cases that the vaccine fails to protect."

"What?!" Ellie felt a rising sense of panic now. "Why wasn't this risk disclosed to us?"

"For public safety. It's called herd immunity. Those whom the vaccine protects will be fine, and those whom it doesn't won't be able to put the rest of the public at risk of infection."

"Because we would be dead..." Ellie finished for him, feeling weak.

That was it, she thought. He wouldn't be telling me this much if I were going to be leaving here. How could I have been so stupid?! I had the chance to listen to Avril and I didn't.

The doctor wasn't paying any further attention to her. He was announcing that everyone was to move off to a side area, which was sectioned off and wrapped in plastic. It looked like a large, square tunnel to walk through.

"They will be sending trucks for you shortly, but for now, please proceed calmly through this biocontainment tunnel. We will meet you at the other end," he said through a megaphone.

Some of the soldiers followed them, while others led the way. They all had assault rifles, and they stayed back from the protestors. Ellie and her friends were in shock, and walked breathlessly along through the length of the makeshift tunnel.

As she walked, she texted Edgar: "We're being led to a hotel at the airport. Will call."

It came out at a service door to another building, which proved to be one of the airport hotels. The group was led into an emptied hotel ballroom, which was lined in more plastic. Everyone sat down on the floor, staring around them.

This was a place for job fairs and corporate conferences, Ellie thought to herself in a dazed panic, not one for plastic and contamination suits.

Leanne started scratching at her arms.

"Leanne, don't do that! If they think you feel sick, we'll never get out of here," Karen said.

"Sorry. I'm just anxious," she said. "I'm scared, actually. This is like something out of a disaster movie. Out of every disaster movie I never paid enough attention to."

Ellie wished she had paid more attention to a lot of things.

A soldier held up a megaphone and demanded that everyone hand over their belongings and change into scrubs, which were produced and handed out.

Ellie thought vaguely that these items were suspiciously and conveniently available, and awfully fast, considering the fact that her group had been allowed to drive itself to the airport. Not that any of that mattered now. They were trapped.

The soldiers forced everyone to change clothes out in the middle of the room, with no privacy. Once that was done, Ellie took out her cell phone and tried to put it into her pocket.

Instantly, a soldier snatched it from her and stuffed it into a large bag. He and several others were tossing everyone's clothing, purses, backpacks, and electronic devices into opaque plastic bags, leaving the group with nothing of their own, not even their I.D.s. At least they seemed to be separating each person's things, with a bag for each one.

A female soldier came around with a smaller bag, which contained clear ziplock bags, and a small machine that printed sticky labels. She approached each woman, took her name, created a label for the bags, and demanded all jewelry, watches, and other personal effects. These went into the bags. Leanne had a navel piercing, and that went into her bag. The woman soldier checked everything. A similar procedure was carried out for the men in the group.

Ellie was really scared now. So were Karen, Leanne, Lynn, and everyone else. Some people were starting to cry, some to hyperventilate, and others kept demanding answers that were not forthcoming.

Jacob was raving about his father, asking if anyone knew who he was.

Like anyone would care, Ellie thought.

The female soldier came back with packages of GMO-ridden food, which they all refused.

A few more minutes went by, and some people wanted to use the rest rooms, but were told that they couldn't risk allowing anyone to contaminate the hotel facilities. People were getting really uncomfortable and some of the guys were getting angry. However, they didn't object very loudly because of the assault rifles and the cold stares.

The soldiers ceased replying or acknowledging anything that any of them said.

Another twenty minutes passed. Suddenly, there was a commotion off to the side, at the end of the room where the entrance was – the one that led out into the hotel lobby. Ellie caught a glimpse of the hallway, and it didn't look like any effort had been made to seal it off. Odd…

Meanwhile, a small group of men in business suits was out there, shouting at the USAMRIID doctor that Ellie had spoken with in the airport lobby. Badges were flashed, and some papers were presented. Then a small, flat, computer screen was held up with an image on it. She thought it looked like Jacob's face on it, but she wasn't entirely sure.

The doctor turned to two soldiers and quietly barked some orders at them.

Abruptly, they spun around, marched into the room, and stopped where Jacob sat glaring with his friend Alan. "Jacob Uberfein?" They said rather than asked. They had seen his photograph, she thought, no doubt about it.

"Yes?"

"Come with us."

"Why should I come with you? Do you know who my father is?!"

They didn't bother to converse with him. They just picked him up by his armpits and lifted him to his feet, then dragged him, angrily complaining about being mistreated, across the room.

The USAMRIID doctor walked up to him without a word, held a gun just like Hamish's nanite ones up to his temple, and hit a switch.

Leanne screamed. None of the military personnel reacted to that at all.

Ellie just stared. She realized that she was the only one who understood what was going on.

The monster nanites were being removed from his system.

That was when it felt sickeningly real to her. Before that, the monster nanobots had just been an idea to her, and a far-fetched one at that. She had listened with bemusement to Avril, humoring everyone by allowing Hamish to treat her with his own vaccines, smugly enjoying the convenience of avoiding long lines elsewhere to get them done.

Now, however, she at last believed that nanites were in her system, wreaking havoc with it.

Already she felt her energy levels fading a bit, and imagined, horrified, tiny nanobots going to work on her DNA, ripping apart the sequences that kept her strong and healthy. She couldn't get those images out of her mind suddenly.

With a shock, Ellie realized that she did not feel the same sense of vigor and quick-wittedness that she had this morning. The cull formula was working! It was some special formula to be so fast-, faster-, fastest-acting as to make her clumsy and confused so soon!

She breathed in and out rapidly as she understood this. Of course this was the fastest version.

Whoever Jacob was, he was very lucky. Next, Ellie watched as he was injected with a syringe that contained a pale blue liquid. He didn't understand that, but it made no difference, because the next thing any of them knew, he was pulled from the room, out that door, and brought face to face with the men in the business suits, with all pretense of biocontainment abandoned.

He seemed very confused, but the men just led him away as fast as they could. Ellie and the others could hear him shouting, "What about my friends?" but they ignored him. He was marched away, his voice and theirs fading into the distance, and then he was gone.

It was clear to her now what was happening. She and her friends were being disappeared without a trace, just as Avril had repeatedly tried to tell her, while Jacob would be taken home after being scared into keeping his mouth shut. How they would do that, she would not find out.

Ellie was panicking, shutting down in more ways than one. Her mouth was dry, and she realized it was from hyperventilating. She was sweating, she was itchy, she was shaking with fear, and she felt horribly overtired all at once.

She couldn't think clearly; all she could focus on was being horrified by the idea that mechanized spider-bots were crawling around inside her, and that she couldn't scratch them away. Glancing around her, she realized that the others were feeling as she did. She suddenly envied her friends their ignorance of the cause of it.

A few minutes later, the soldiers ordered everyone to their feet and back out the door that they came in. They had electric cattle-prods for night-sticks, Ellie saw in her hazy state.

The plastic tunnel had been redirected. It led into the middle of a parking lot, which was almost cleared of vehicles. They emerged from the tunnel to face two large Army trucks that were covered with dull green canvas on top. They had seats in the back, enough for several people on either side to face one another.

Everyone was roughly ordered and pushed in, the back was closed up, and the trucks took off. Ellie could see out the back, but she was feeling too weak to try to leap out. Not that she could have managed it; they were moving too fast and the opening was too high.

The trucks drove out to the suburbs of Atlanta and keep on going for another several miles.

In all, the trip took about forty minutes. Ellie had no idea which direction they had gone in.

At last, the truck stopped and the door was opened again. She practically fell out, followed by Karen and Leanne and Lynn. Lynn had had dry heaves for most of the ride, which made everyone very uncomfortable, and Leanne was scratching her arms again, and now her legs.

Ellie wanted to scratch now, but was afraid to do it. She thought of those nanobots again.

The soldiers directed everyone to a large tent with cots under it. The sides were open. Everyone sat down on a cot, looking around, stunned.

A tall soldier, one who had ignored every question, spoke through a megaphone and announced: "Latrines are at either end of this tent. Personnel will be by shortly with drinks and something to eat. We would advise you to eat it, because there is nothing else available. You may use the latrines at any time."

Ellie and Leanne got up immediately to use the latrine near their end of the tent. It was clean, but she didn't like the sheets of toilet paper in it. They were thin, and in a dispenser box on the wall, like Kleenex. Hand sanitizer was in a squirt bottle on the inside of the door. So much for getting really clean, she thought.

She practically fell when she got to her cot. Suddenly, her head ached and she felt a bit nauseated. Her eyes felt heavy, too. Everything felt heavy. A wave of nausea swept over her and she leaned over just in time to puke on the grass by her cot. Several cots down, Alan had done the same.

Hours passed. Personnel left potato chips, chocolate chip cookies, and ginger ale for her, and she tried to eat some, but she knew it was junk and could hardly keep anything down let along left herself up to ingest any of it.

Activity seemed to be going on all around the tent, but she felt too ill to observe any of it.

Morning came, and she was shocked out of a fitful sleep by another megaphone announcement: "Please get up and use the latrines within the next ten minutes. Juice will be distributed. Wait for further instructions after that."

Ellie dragged herself to her feet. Where was she? Oh. Panic gripped her.

Damn…she must be feeling really out of it to have forgotten.

She wished she could just call her mother.

Her skin was bright red, raw, and inflamed. She scratched it, expecting relief, but it oozed a nasty fluid that was part white pus and part clear, like sweat…and mixed with blood. Disgusting. Horrified, she forced herself through the steps that the announcement had mentioned, gulping down some sickeningly sweet grape juice just before the voice boomed through the tent again.

"Calmly proceed out of the tent – we will direct you – to the metal chamber across from the tent. We will be administering a treatment that will make you feel better."

She didn't really care what that might be. The mental image of nanobots had faded.

Their job was done.

Following her old college friends across the grass, she glanced around as she scratched her arms and reached down to scratch her legs also. Tall bales of hay lined the perimeter, and trees stood in the distance, leaves rippling in the breeze. Other than that, she saw nothing that gave the slightest indication as to where they were.

The metal chamber proved to be a cargo container, much like those things that carried freight on the backs of tractor trailer trucks on highways. This one was plain Army green, with no markings on it. Its doors were open at one end.

Once she saw the interior of the container, its similarity to those cargo ones ended.

"Please proceed into the chamber and take a seat," the soldier with the megaphone boomed.

Benches lined the sides. There were nozzles in the ceiling, lights, and some sort of cameras in the top corners, like one would see in an elevator. They were round, with dark lenses. Oddly, there appeared to be some large panels on the upper halves of the longer walls.

Ellie was too exhausted and miserable now to care much. She walked in, still barefoot after the evening before, and a mess.

Her friends joined her, but she hardly noticed because she was too sick to look up at them.

The doors were shut, and dim lights came on. They heard a lever outside swiveling around.

Why were they being sealed in for this treatment, she wondered?

Oh yeah…to keep it from leaking out and affecting anyone else.

A hissing sound came from those overhead nozzles, and a faint scent of almonds and apples filled the room. It would have smelled nice if she had been feeling well. As it was, she was too weak to puke, and her eyelids felt heavy.

That sleep she had gotten last night had been terrible.

The fumes that filled the room were starting to soothe her. She couldn't stay seated upright, and she slid onto the floor. At least the urge to scratch was going away. Everything was going away. She was drifting off into a nice, deep, welcome sleep.

She fell into a lovely sleep, and stopped breathing, but didn't notice.

Nothing bothered her anymore, which was just fine when the top panels came down and the flames fired out from under the benches.

Chapter 35

Back to Rockefeller for a Fundraiser

Dr. Nurse was ready for us to attend that fundraiser he had mentioned months ago.

When I heard that, I groaned, but Hamish cut me off right away with the announcement that this was the greatest timing ever for a social event.

"Oh, really?" I was going to be skeptical until I had the details.

"Indeed. We can attend that, and ship out right after we leave."

"Like the von Trapp family. How trite." I grinned, though. "When is it?"

"In three weeks. Let's get our act together and get everyone down to Manhattan before then." With that, we went to it, getting everyone quietly informed and ready to leave. We weren't going to warn anyone else. That would possibly have tipped off the Farmers.

What we would do instead would be to act like this was a brief trip to the city for some fun and academic planning at the Rockefeller Institute, and then just not come back. As I mentioned earlier, academic institutions run on money, and sometimes, its professors are required to attend functions and schmooze with wealthy donors. This one was going to be with formal attire.

Wonderful; Hamish and I were going to have to dress up a bit. I checked his best suit and tie, prepared a long, rose-pink gown that had pockets (always a requirement with me!), checked my pearl necklace with the rose-with-tiny-pearl clasp and matching earrings, and figured we were both good to go. Oh! Shoes…I hated shoe shopping. Fortunately, that was done. I put the shoes out for both outfits, and packed it all in a garment bag. There – out of sight, out of mind.

No…not quite. The next morning over breakfast, my husband informed me that word had gotten back to Dr. Nurse about his Regenics project and the clinic in Lausanne, Switzerland. He wanted in, and he wanted to see how we looked.

"How we look? That won't tell him much. This is more about feeling better," I replied. "The white hairs I hated so much are turning back to brown with coppery highlights, my skin is tighter and moister, and my joints feel better. I'll bet that the cartilage in them is building back up."

"You look like you've aged in reverse," Hamish told me. "You've always been my knockout, but your regenerative effects are showing. Jeffrey is going to want to see that, and show it off to the donors. I hope you're planning to dress up a bit."

I glared at him for a moment with a long, steady stare.

"What?" Hamish looked worried, like he realized that he had said something wrong.

"I just went over our outfits, shoes, and the beautiful pearl jewelry you gave me last night. For your information, we're BOTH dressing up beautifully, and I shall wear a long, gauzy, chiffon gown in rose pink. You shall wear your black tuxedo with the satin trim, a new white shirt, and a bright, sapphire-blue tie."

"I'm sorry," Hamish said sheepishly. "I should have known you would have planned all that out immediately and taken care of it. You love to do things immediately." He grinned.

"Yes. I packed it already, too."

"Thank you, Avril."

"You're welcome. You have been looking hotter and hotter, too. Less salt than pepper to your hair…we're taking you out for a haircut later this week…and your skin looks rosier and tighter, too. How do you feel?"

"Like exercise will actually work again in making me thin and fit," he answered.

"You're a genius. Thank you, Hamish. I love de-aging." I grinned at him.

He leaned over and kissed me. "There's one more thing," he added.

"Which is?"

"Jeffrey Nurse is no slouch. He assumed – correctly – that I would have given Regenics to our entire family, and he knows that you have a 100-year-old grandmother. He wants her to attend the party."

"Are you kidding?! She'll be exhausted. That's not fair to her. Does he want any others?"

"No, just her. That's the beauty of it; if the rest of our group lays low, it will be assumed that we have to bring her back to Connecticut not long after the party. No one will think otherwise of someone your Grandmère's age. They'll just expect our stay in Manhattan to be a short one. And it will be, but not in the way that they think. We'll leave all right, but not to come back here."

"Okay. We'll have to ask Grandmère what she is willing to do. You don't just inform an elderly grandmother that you've put an event on her social calendar and expect her to jump at the idea and go."

But when we explained this request and how it fit into everything, Grandmère was game. She even insisted that I take her out shopping for a new dress. I couldn't believe it. The last time we had done anything like this was when Hamish and I were getting married. She had worn a lavender gown of silk with a shrug jacket, and my mother had gotten a French blue one.

So, on a weekday, with Aaron and Ed in tow, we went to the mall for gown shopping and lunch. I called ahead to Nordstrom and Lord & Taylor for help with this. Grandmère may have been regenerating, but that was no reason not to have chairs for her to retreat to at every turn.

My mother and Aunt Zoe came along for the fun of it, and it wasn't long before Grandmère had chosen another lavender-hued gown. This one was part silk and part lace. It was a sheath style with a wrap, and it looked comfortable and easy to move and sit in. Grandmère assured us that it was. She found a purse and shoes to go with it – flats, which was smart. "I may be spry, but no sense wearing heels and going head over heels and looking foolish," she winked.

We took her home after that, and Aunt Zoe packed the gown and accessories in a garment bag. She too was already starting to get everything ready to go. It was a good thing that my parents had kept their apartment in Manhattan; it had 2 bedrooms, and our group would definitely need them. I realized that with Ed and Aaron, who would be coming with us, we would be 16 people.

It had been a couple of weeks since Ellie had been lost to the cull.

We were absolutely certain that she was gone, yet we had to act clueless to her parents.

It wasn't as difficult as I had expected it to be. They had hired a private investigator to go to Georgia, and were absorbed in communications with him. They had never really approved of Edgar (or perhaps it was our family), so it took a few days before they bothered to tell us all that they had lost contact with the investigator.

Hamish and I immediately knew what that must have meant: he had been picked up.

Edgar was no long catatonic, but he was still stunned and quiet. We were all worried about him, and no one would leave him alone for long. At first, he had seemed fine with that, but after a while, he seemed a bit annoyed. "I'm not going to kill myself or sneak off to do that," he told us. "I'm depressed, but I can't thwart the bastards by killing myself. I won't give them what they want. I have to survive and help you cull the Farmers."

Edgar had adopted the terminology that Hamish and I had used for so long.

We had to tell him and the rest of the family to cool it with that, and not let anyone outside our group – our family, our Blackout detail, and Jason – hear us saying that. Edgar nodded, and went back to watching the news. He couldn't stop now that he knew exactly how to interpret it all and to read between the lines.

Fabian and Claire were horrified by all of this. They both had attended protests and marches during and after college, and had been on the brink of participating in some climate change gatherings. After what had happened to Ellie, and after Hamish and I took the family to our basement room so that Jason could give them the full disclosure presentation, they weren't going to do that anymore.

That was a relief.

It was also a relief that Jacques had no girlfriend and was equally horrified and awakened.

No one was going anywhere to get grabbed and culled again.

Jason came over often now, moving back and forth between the office and our basement. He was a fixture to my parents now, and they had stopped going on long country drives. Anne and Peter Woodward came over for dinner to meet everyone, and Hamish persuaded them in one visit to get out of Elmwood, the southern section of West Hartford, and move in with their son.

No sense being a sitting duck. Elmwood was first on the list for when the MRAPs would show up in our town. Next up were the newest developments, wherever they were, which was why, when Grandmère got home from our shopping trip, she had abruptly pulled me aside and had me go to her room and then to the living room with her.

She took the portrait of herself and Grandpère off of her bedroom wall and handed it to me.

I took it, startled for a moment, and then I caught on.

If the MRAPs came here, this house would soon cease to exist.

For some reason, Stoner Drive and our neighborhood were not on the cull list.

She wanted this family portrait moved to our house, and another painting also.

It was a painting by Monet, one of his Giverny garden scenes, of standard size, about two-by-four, and a beautiful piece in pastels. The flowers were gorgeous: iris blossoms mostly, but some tulips also. It was very relaxing to look at the purples, blues, whites, and greens.

Aunt Zoe helped me to wrap them each up in discarded newspaper, and I put them in the car, a bit intimidated to be handling a priceless work of art and a family heirloom. It's not as if I were a curator with the training to handle them properly.

My mother and I drove straight home with the paintings and decided where to hang them up without delay. No doing anything like that later! Something could go wrong, we thought, so it was better to get everything in place right away.

We chose a spot in the living room for each painting, making sure to put the Monet in a corner where nothing ever happened – no one leaned there, no one ate anything there – and where no bright lights would shine on it. The portrait went across from it, over a wing chair near the fireplace. Dad liked the effect.

There wasn't much more to think about or do at home after that, and since it was Wednesday, I decided to go see Hamish at his lab in Avon. What could happen in the middle of the week? Nothing, I figured. Maybe I would go wandering around the mall in Canton later, just to seem unconcerned and oblivious to events on the news.

Just because you're paranoid, it doesn't mean that they're not watching us, I thought.

Hamish was in his back room, going over data from the machines there.

He looked up when I walked in, shut off the machine, and said, "It's starting in Vermont. Leanne and Joe went to see her sister in Burlington, and the MRAPs were there yesterday. They're all gone. Ellen and Cara think that she's just late getting back from the visit, and I let them think so. They were talking about her taking a long weekend."

I stumbled backwards and tried to sit on the stool behind me, but it had wheels. I almost fell over, but Hamish rushed forward, steadied me, and helped me sit down on it. "Should we leave sooner? Go to Manhattan tomorrow?"

"No. We'll go on Monday, when the traffic is less of a problem. I knew that Vermont was up this week, but I had no idea that Leanne would go there. I didn't even realize she had family there." Hamish looked really upset. "I don't chat with people enough. I could have stopped her."

"Could you really? What would you have said, 'Don't travel or the MRAPs will sweep you up'? I don't see how you could have played that one. And even if you did chat more, Leanne's a professional. She doesn't…didn't…like to tell her boss much about her personal life."

"I suppose."

"What can we do for the staff here? Those who are still here? Do they live in some new housing, historic housing, what?"

Hamish brightened up. "Cara lives in historic housing. She may be okay. Ellen could stay with her. I could have Blackout do something to make Ellen's home very unpleasant, and encourage her and Cara to stay together…and just let it drag on until after the MRAPs come through Connecticut."

"Do it. Ellen got married last month; she and her new husband can both avoid the cull."

"Take me out of here. I'm going to talk to Ed and Aaron. In fact, I'll ride with one of them, and you can ride with the other. Let's all go out to eat at the Canton mall next, so that it looks like just an ordinary day out together."

We walked out, found Ed and Aaron, told them we were headed for Feng's in Canton, and Aaron got into my car as Hamish hopped into the black SUV with Ed. No sense talking over a cell phone. I knew that they would shut them all off, check them, and check again to make sure that they were off before saying anything. Aaron and I did the same.

"How are the plans coming along?" Aaron asked as I pulled out of the parking lot.

"Okay, I guess. What about you and Ed? We're taking you away. What about your girlfriends?"

"Mine is more or less safe, working in Washington, D.C., and Ed broke up with his."

"So you're not going to be worried about her?"

"Well, maybe a little, but she knows what to watch out for, and she's got a badge."

I didn't ask any other questions. If our Blackout guys felt okay, then so be it.

We got to the mall, and Hamish seemed to have made all arrangements because he looked like he was ready to move on and relax. It was almost five o'clock, too early for dinner, so we walked around for a while. We visited our friend Nora and Ruby the greyhound. Her collar had a sand dollar and starfish design on it this time.

Nora lived in a luxury condominium development with a golf course. Would the MRAPs move through there a few weeks from now and get her too? I persuaded Hamish to sit in the car with me and asked him what he thought about her chances.

"Jason and I checked. Not good. But I think there may be a way to get her out of the area too. There's a convention in Manhattan she can go to, one for gift shop owners. Blackout has seen to it that she is invited, and that she will want to go. There is a pet spa as part of it, complete with gift shop products for dogs. The dog will go with Nora."

"Nora doesn't usually bring Ruby with her on those trips."

"She will this time." Hamish had done Nora's vaccinations before the treaty was signed.

"You're trying to leave me with no one to think about here, aren't you?"

"Aye."

"I don't know how to suggest an out for Sophia and her daughter, or for Ginger."

"Your writer friends. Well, guess what? They don't live in the areas that are listed for a cull. The center of town is going to stay, so they can stay put. You can e-mail them when we get to Switzerland."

"Really?" I was actually getting excited. "That sounds too good to be true."

"I know, but it's true, and reliable, and there will be some Blackout guys at our house. They will check on your friends. Any sign of MRAP activity, and they'll get them to leave before the cull teams arrive. But their houses aren't new enough or in any of the cull areas. Don't worry."

I hoped that was true. I couldn't tell anyone else anything about any of this. It was too dangerous. We'd never get out if I talked. This covert protectiveness would have to do the trick. I would e-mail and check on my friends once we got where we were going – all the way there. So be it. I kissed Hamish, and we got out of the car, found Ed and Aaron sitting on a bench across from us, watching us and the area as usual, and went into the restaurant to eat.

The following Monday, we were ready to go.

Over the weekend, with many trips back and forth, we had moved everything of value, interest, and that documented our family history – such as photographs – from Aunt Zoe and Uncle Charlie's house to ours. We had situated everything in the other bedrooms of the house, with a view toward having it all safe while we were gone, and put neatly in place for use.

Uncle Charlie was in a state of denial about it all. He just couldn't believe that his house wouldn't be there when he came back, but Aunt Zoe wasn't taking any chances. Their clothes, her favorite dishes, you name it, got moved. The boys and Claire didn't need any such convincing, but Uncle Charlie was just in a daze, watching as things got moved.

Better to be prepared than not, Dad told him, and made him help.

Monday morning, I drove out of our garage with Hamish and Eowyn in one car, and my parents drove out with Spock in the other. Both cats were going to have to endure this ride in cat carriers. We had our suitcases packed in the trunks, and cat supplies, laptops, cameras…and my violin, DVDs, and CDs. There was still room for some more luggage, too.

Followed by Aaron and Ed in their black SUV, we drove over to Aunt Zoe and Uncle Charlie's place. Jason met us there with his parents in his car. They had no pets, fortunately. We got out, used the bathrooms, and got organized. Grandmère was going ride with us.

My parents would take Fabian and Claire in their car. Claire was wearing her mother's rose quartz beads. She had put them on a week or so after she understood what had happened to them, and we had all adopted her as one of us. Fabian would make it a formal relationship soon enough, we knew.

Edgar and Jacques would ride with their parents. This was going to be a caravan of five cars.

It didn't take us long to pack Grandmère's bags into our trunk, and soon she was ensconced in the back seat with Eowyn, sweet-talking to our tortie-calico cat.

We took off, down Beacon Street and onto Mountain Road, heading south. Everyone followed us.

"I hope we don't look too obvious," I remarked, "or see any MRAPs."

Hamish had a laptop out, one that was just like the one that Jason used. They were synchronized for this trip. We would be pulling over periodically to check on everything and everyone, and since Jason's dad was doing the driving, he and Hamish could keep in constant contact, watching our path for threats.

Our route was the same as it had been almost a year earlier, up Route 44 to New York State, then south to enter the city over the Hudson Bridge. Hamish and Jason were using live satellites to look out for MRAP teams. If they detected any, we would detour.

But we didn't find any.

Instead, as we drove through towns that we had seen last year, we saw something even more unsettling: evidence that the MRAPs had been there and gone already. Where there had once been middle-class and working-class towns full of old buildings, there were no people around, and…no more buildings.

I had to pull over and check the road map a few times in disbelief. Was I on the correct route? Was I lost? Was this the same place I had driven us through many times before, and ridden through with my parents many times before that as I grew up?

Apparently, it was. It just didn't look the same.

"The military must have removed everything and scrapped it all for parts," Hamish said. "The copper pipes and high-quality stones will be saved, marble and granite salvaged, and the rest repurposed somehow."

All those lives, ground under to reduce human numbers. It was astonishing to look at.

Even Grandmère was stunned. "It was nothing like this in Paris," she commented. "Not even when my grand-grand Nana told me about the razing of whole neighborhoods for Baron Haussmann's urban renewal. She saw that as a young girl."

I stared at her in the rearview mirror. "You never told me about that!"

She grinned and turned to pet Eowyn through the holes in her cat carrier.

"Damn. These cull idiots would take away society's elders and leave us without your fascinating stories, and without you to talk to when we need wisdom and guidance. They think they're so clever, but they're really just morons," I fumed, looking at the emptied land around us as I drove along.

Grandmère agreed, silently. She nodded and smiled, and reached over to pet Eowyn again.

Grass had actually been seeded, and streets ripped out. A concerted effort was being made to rush along the process of Nature reclaiming land after humans had left it. It never mattered how humans departed land; once gone, Nature always grew right over whatever traces they had left behind. But this was different: the MRAP teams had been followed by others.

"Who did all this?" I wondered aloud.

"The U.S. Army Corps of Engineers," my husband informed me. "I can show you the plan and the videos later."

"When were you going to tell me about that?"

"When I had gotten you safely away from it all," he replied.

I continued the journey after that in silence, except to watch the others. Everyone was still with us.

I had forgotten that it would only take us four and a half hours to get where we were going at the very most, thanks to the circuitous route that the floods had induced us to adopt. We used to drive directly southwest before that. Now it was across to New York State and south from there.

We opted to skip lunch and just go directly to the city. It was better that way, because we were all too nervous about meeting up with trouble of some kind along the route. There was only so much that planning could do for us, we knew, and then we had to be lucky.

We were lucky.

At twenty minutes past two in the afternoon, we all drove over the Henry Hudson Bridge and into Manhattan. I led the way directly into Chelsea, down into the neighborhood where my parents' apartment was, and stopped. It was okay to park out front and unload our stuff.

Nothing was happening with MRAPs in Manhattan.

That had all been done months ago, cull and all. It was now a model city, with bike paths everywhere we looked, above-ground trolleys that had taken the place of busses and subways, and of course the water busses and water taxis for the canals and waterways that we had seen here previously.

"The city looks like a beautiful utopia, but the way it became like this is pure evil and just unconscionable," commented, breaking my tour-guide monologue as I pointed it all out to Grandmère. She made a wordless sound of agreement, taking it all in.

Dad would put his car in a garage nearby after we got settled. It was still there, and part of the deal for apartment owners of this building. Agenda 21 may have wanted people to drive less, but it wasn't making it impossible to actually possess a car as yet. Once people were in the city, it was common knowledge that they would park and leave their cars anyway.

My parents and Fabian and Claire put everything in the apartment, then came out to talk to us for a moment. "We'll come over in a couple of hours," my mother said. "I'm going to get milk and orange juice and few other things, and make sure we'll be comfortable here first."

"Great; see you later," I said. They would be fine here. I drove off toward our firehouse, with the rest of the caravan in tow. Ed and Aaron and the Woodward family would stay in our nearby Blackout Security apartment. It had 2 bedrooms, and we had made sure that there was an additional bed for Jason. The place even had parking facilities.

Aunt Zoe and Uncle Charlie could park their car with us; we had a two-car garage.

"Grandmère, I hope you're comfortable here. Your room is upstairs with us, on the top floor, but I know you can deal with stairs much better now. You have your own little bathroom with a small shower stall…and a seat in it in case you get tired at any time. Let me know if you feel like soaking in a tub, though, and I'll set you up in our bathroom."

She just smiled and said that it sounded fine, and would enjoy seeing it all.

In another minute, we were pulling into the garage and my uncle was parking next to us.

We shut off the cars and I closed the door. I didn't want anyone on the street to watch us.

Going upstairs and unpacking, plus making the cat comfortable, was the next order of business. Then lunch…once we were settled, we were all hungry. I called my parents. They agreed to meet us at Le Pain Quotidien for a feast. We were all tired from the stress of getting into the city unmolested.

Ed, Aaron, Jason, and his parents came, and we ended up monopolizing a long, oval, marble table in the place. We were careful not to chat much about anything. This was covert behavior, aimed at not letting any plans or any knowledge that wasn't on standard news outlets slip.

Grandmère seemed like the smoothest operator of us all…and then I remembered that this wasn't her first time doing this. She had survived the Nazi occupation of Paris, after all. She knew how to keep a low profile while going about one's business.

I made a mental note not to talk about her great age of 100 in public at all.

When we got back, I didn't see much cleaning to worry about. Hamish told me that it had been taken care of in advance by Blackout, a rare treat for me. "I didn't want you to worry about that this time." I kissed and thanked him.

Next, my husband accompanied me to the nearest grocery store for milk, orange juice, and a few other items. When that was done, we went out to a bakery and stocked up on breakfast treats, and then over to McNulty's for enough coffee to keep the family caffeinated the whole time we were here. I got some half-decaf coffee for Grandmère, and checked the French press.

"What are we going to do for the next week and a half?" I wondered.

Hamish smiled. "Visit Dr. Jeffrey Nurse, read, watch movies, listen to music, walk around the city a bit, keep apprised of the news, guard our family against whatever dangers occur to us, and maybe seeing a few sights ought to keep us busy. That, and I have a few arrangements to make before the end of next week."

"I see." Our final escape details were, no doubt, part of his plans.

Uncle Charlie leaned back on the sofa. "I'm tired from all the driving and activity and stress of today. I'd like to do something easy for dinner, something that doesn't involve worrying about getting dressed up."

"Me too," I said. "There's a fairly quiet brewery near here that has good food. They have beer of all sorts, with fruit, with spices, plain, with wheat or rye, you name it, and great fries. I just wonder about dragging Grandmère all over the place."

Grandmère spoke up. "Don't you worry about me. I can come with you, sit and eat and then come back here just fine. But I may take you up on that offer of a bath tonight – early."

I smiled. "No problem. I have lavender bath gel, too."

"Perfect," she said.

Jacques and Edgar were sorting through my collection of movies and music, and they had brought their own. It was going to be a shame to leave it all behind, for who knew how long, if not forever. Switzerland? Could we ever come home? Would it ever be okay here? Hamish said, "Don't stash that stuff away. We can bring it with us. I won't get into any details just now, but set aside whatever you won't be watching or listening to much. It'll get moved out soon."

We all looked at him, puzzled.

"You're just going to have to wait for more detail, so don't bother asking."

Grandmère said, "He's right to do it that way. The less we know, the fewer the slip-ups we might make that could ruin it all. Whatever the plans are, don't mess them up."

We laid our heads back onto the sofas and poufy chairs and spaced out at that.

After about a minute of that, I suddenly sat bolt upright, took out my cell phone, and dialed Bethany's number. Would she answer? Sometimes, when one called friends, you had to leave a message and wait to talk to them. This felt urgent. We had checked on her area, and it was still intact, but I had no delusions about its permanence; it was part of suburban sprawl, after all.

Fortunately, she answered on the third ring. "Hello?"

"Hi Bethany!"

"Avril! How are you?"

"Okay. How are you?"

"Okay. Do you still have that aunt and uncle in Amsterdam, in the Netherlands?"

"Um, yes…why do you ask?"

"If I told you to pack up your family and go to their place tomorrow, and to stay there until I contact you again, would you do it?"

"What?! Why?"

Hamish took the cell phone out of my hands. "Bethany, this is Hamish. Please do it, and do it now. I'll even get the tickets ready for you. We can't explain it all right now, but we will when you get safely out. Just please go, and go now. I'll get your tickets ready at Logan Airport immediately."

Silence for a moment on the other end of the line.

"Bethany? Are you listening?"

At last, she spoke again. "Yes, I'm here. If I know you and Avril, this is serious. Yes, I'll pack up now. Phil!" Hamish was leaning over the sofa, holding the cell phone, so I could hear Bethany calling to her husband. "Get the suitcases, get the kids, and let's hurry up. We're leaving." She spoke into the phone again. "Matt and Angelica are home. I won't let them go out much anymore. People in nearby towns seem to be disappearing, and I swear, I drove through one of the newer parts of Natick yesterday, and I got a shock."

"What do you mean by that? What was different?"

"It was just…gone. Like it had been not only razed but the landscape had been deliberately restored to its natural state, foundations removed, people gone, everything filled in and landscaped. I've never seen anything like it and it scared the hell out of me. So yes, thanks, we will leave as soon as those tickets are ready."

Aaron came in the front door and nodded at Hamish just then.

Hamish took the cell phone back. "The tickets are ready. It's British Airways." He read Bethany the flight numbers, had her print everything off of her computer, and made her promise to stay with her aunt and uncle even if it dragged on for a few months.

"Months?!" She paused. Then she said, "Okay. I'll wait to hear from you. I'll send you our address in Amsterdam. It's my Annika and Jan van der Waals, on the Prinsengracht. I don't speak Dutch, but they speak English, and we have a standing invitation."

"If you can't stay in their house that long, we'll pay for a hotel," I told her. "Just stay away from home for a while, please! This is not a joke, and not craziness. We'll explain later. Just be safe and do this."

"We will. Thank you, Avril." We ended the call so she could pack. Phil had been laid off from his computer programming job when his boss retired and sold the company. They lived in a suburb. They were prime candidates for a cull, and Bethany was my best friend from college.

"Thank you, Hamish," I said.

He hugged me. "No problem. We'll try to meet up with them before it becomes 3 months, but even then, I don't see them going back yet. You were smart not to tell her too much. Of course, it helped that she saw a missing residential area and freaked out over that."

The next week and half went fast. Hamish kept us busy buying extra coffee from McNulty's and making lists that were sent off to be filled. He brought me a deed to the *Sarah Connor*, our small nanobot-delivery boat. I signed it away to the Rockefeller Institute as a gift. It was Thursday, the day before we were to attend the fundraiser.

Then he had me sign another…for a huge yacht. "Say nothing to anyone about this." This yacht was enormous. The specs described the sort of boat that one saw in movies, or on travel shows about wealthy tycoons. I realized that we were in that category. This yacht was 346 feet long (105.46 meters).

I nodded. But I also asked, "Have you visited this yacht personally and done due diligence to make sure that it isn't leaking water into its hull, that its engine is sound, and that all over facilities on board are in perfect working order?"

Hamish grinned. "Aye, of course. I wouldn't dare come to you for a signature without doing all that. It's a thing of beauty, and trustworthy."

"Okay then. I'll sign. I never thought to own such a thing, but then we're not just playing with it. It's a tool. Just don't call it 'she' – I don't like that." And I signed the deed.

"One more thing," Hamish said. "This yacht needs a name. What do you suggest?"

"Oh! A fun aspect to this," I said. I thought about it for a moment, then said, "*Shadowcat*, for Kitty Pryde of the *X-Men*. She's stealthy, she can phase through solid objects, walk on air, and she knows all about computers."

"Done. I'll have that name registered and painted on for the title transfer," Hamish said.

"Thanks for letting me name the boats," I said. He smiled, kissed me, and left.

So that's where our supplies and CDs and DVDs had been going. Tomorrow, my violin and the rest of our clothing would be added. My parents and everyone else would be sent along with it to wait for Hamish, Grandmère, and me to join them at the end of the evening. None of us knew exactly where this would be, however, and that did not concern us.

Grandmère had enjoyed her visit to Manhattan. We had taken her to our favorite French restaurants, and regaled her with the food porn eater story from the previous fall. She loved it. She also loved the food at MarseilleNYC. Other than that, she had a few more lavender baths.

Friday came.

The fundraiser was to be in the newly refurbished academic hall of the Rockefeller Institute, and a gourmet catered dinner would be served. Grandmère would be seated with us, which was a good thing. I could make sure that she was comfortable, and take her to the rest room whenever she asked. She would have no trouble handling conversations with banksters and hedge fundsters – the wealthy donors that Jeffery Nurse was soliciting funding from.

This was going to be a bizarre, surreal experience. The very individuals who were Farming the nation of those whom they deemed to be excess humans would be schmoozing at this party. I had to remember to hang on to my appetite. Damn them.

Fine…just remember that Hamish flew their own monster nanobots up their own noses as you eat and chat, Avril, and you'll be able to calmly face these hateful, evil, selfish creatures. They're not people. If they won't think of everyone else as people, we won't do that about them!

Hamish caught me muttering this to myself as I got ready for the party.

He hugged me and dragged me to the bed to sit down, and said, "That's a good way to face them. I hate them too. Just try to relax and not let them bother you."

"Okay. They're monsters in human bodies. Genocidal maniacs. Hitler cloned exponentially."

"Indeed."

We finished getting ready, and I checked on Grandmère. She looked perfect. Her silver hair was beautiful coiffed and curled, and we had similar rosette pins to wear to hold it in place. Her hair was up, and mine was down. I had my pearls on, and the rose wedding ring Hamish had given me, and the pink diamond heart engagement ring. I was all set.

The doorbell rang.

My parents wanted to see us before taking off.

My mother had something for me, too. What was this about?

She gave me a small box and said that it was Nana's, and now it was mine.

It was Nana's pear-shaped, pendeloque, diamond engagement ring. There were 3 tiny round diamonds clustered on either side of the center stone, and it was on white gold. It was beautiful. My mother insisted that I enjoy it for the rest of my life. "Looking a bit prosperous won't hurt you among those banksters," she added. "And yes, Hamish, we're at home, so I can say it."

She added that I was to wear this on my right hand. I put it on. Wow.

"Okay…you're ready." My mother was actually excited that I was going to this event. "Tell me all about it later – every detail. And make sure that you meet us later, wherever we'll be."

Hamish smiled cryptically and called Ed and Aaron.

They drove us to the Rockefeller Institute, and then Ed left us to take care of transferring the family and our guests to the yacht. It was a nice, balmy, warm August evening…perfect for a party and a secret getaway. Grandmère was walking at a brisk pace, and looking around her with interest. She definitely wasn't acting her great age. The donors were going to notice. No, everyone was going to notice, I thought.

"Grandmère, do you have your I.D. with you? Not your passport, your U.S. I.D."

"Yes, I have it. It shows that I'm 100 years old. I knew you would need me to have that."

"Good." We all had our passports with us, too, but we weren't going to show them here.

When we arrived at the fundraiser, it was just getting started. A chamber ensemble was playing music quietly in the foyer. They were students hired from Juilliard, Dr. Nurse told us as he greeted us at the door and walked us in.

"Professor Châtelet, you look beautiful. Dr. MacDonall, you look suitably impressive. Madame Châtelet, what an honor it is to meet you!" Dr. Nurse gushed. "I can see where you granddaughter gets her looks and brains now." Our donors await us." With that, he led us forward into a decked-out lobby, transformed from its standard, institutional look to one fit for a grand ball.

Banners with the Rockefeller Institute name and logo festooned the place, the lighting was lowered, and posters of nanotech corporations and various charitable foundations covered the walls. So…these were the legal entities who wanted Hamish to share his intellectual property with them. Their representatives were going to get a kick out of seeing Grandmère.

Waitstaff in what Hamish called penguin uniforms walked around with little trays. There was champagne, and we each took one, even Grandmère. She sipped hers very slowly, hardly tasting it, though. I followed her example. Next came trays with some delectable gourmet hors d'oeuvres, and we tried some of everything: smoked salmon on blinis topped with caviar, avocado and shrimp in mini tacos, raspberries, pistachio, and goat cheese on crackers, and so on.

It was great, but I wondered if we would eat dinner when the time came.

Dr. Nurse knew that I would stare intently, smile politely at people when they approached, and make conversation. He knew me well enough not to expect that conversation to be of the neurotypical variety, so I wasn't worried. Hamish would be similar, talking mostly about work nonstop, with me occasionally interrupting to tell him to listen to the other party.

Grandmère was another story. She had been the neurotypical wife of an international business attorney, just like Dad, but in Paris. Her French accent would present an air of sophistication and allure that would help our presentation, and I realized that Dr. Nurse was looking forward to that, and likely planning to exploit it in any way he could.

Fine. I didn't really care. We just had to charm our way through one evening, show what Hamish had to offer, and let Dr. Nurse strike a deal with whomever to share Hamish's research. What Jeffrey Nurse had to work with was the fact that Hamish's Regenics and nanotech projects were already set up so that we would keep that magic number of the profits, 51 percent. The rest was fair game.

When that part of the deal was being struck, I had insisted upon that number, no lower. Dr. Nurse knew what it meant, and had looked a bit frustrated, but I had made eye contact and smiled politely, thinking, you want us, that's how it will be. We won't just sign over all of our future profits. After all, the world already had Nae-Née, and it didn't need us anymore. Who knew what would happen next? We had to protect ourselves in every way while it went to hell.

Dr. Nurse had to know how bad things were outside the city. He had insulated himself here, and kept his entire family close. Something he had mentioned on the phone a while back suggested that his college-age kids had wanted to go farther away to study, but he had insisted that they study in Manhattan.

I wondered how many people in the U.S. still did not understand the danger around them.

A lot of them must not have a real clue, if the fact that people were being taken from all walks of life in all regions, in increments. The sheeple had not yet awakened.

But back to the fundraiser…after about half an hour of standing around and eating gourmet goodies, meeting people who were dressed to the nines, the waitstaff started rearranging the room. In minutes, small round tables appeared. White cloths covered them, followed by cloth napkins, metal cutlery (it was nice, not the flimsy bent stuff from the cafeteria), plates, goblets, and floral centerpieces. The finishing touch was chairs that looked like they had come from a high-end wedding hall. They were wood, brushed with gold paint, and had white cloth seats.

There were even seating arrangements, we were told, when I wondered where we should sit. Hamish, Grandmère, and I were to sit with Dr. Nurse and a husband and wife whom we had not yet met. Dr. Nurse would only say that they were the biggest donors of them all.

"We want them to fund a large new laboratory devoted to promoting Regenics," he added.

Who were these people?

We turned to meet them and managed to do some fast and, we hoped, clever acting. It also helped that they turned to Grandmère first, studying her carefully. They had to know her age, I realized, taking a deep, not-too-audible breath.

It was that bankster that Hamish and I had guided the first set of monster nanobots into.

He didn't look sick. Neither did his wife, but we hadn't infested her. We hadn't known who she was or what she looked like anyway, and we weren't particularly concerned with her. But why wasn't he sick yet? I thought about that. Aha…no trigger foods! The guy probably lived on a totally non-GMO diet.

As we shook hands with them, at last their names registered with me. I had put this bankster's name out of my mind for a while to avoid talking about him. There had been no reason why I should know him or be focused on him in any way. But now…

…now that had changed. The bankster and his wife were Leo and Leah Uberfein.

Leo was shorter than his wife by perhaps three inches, and wearing lifts, so maybe it was more. I gave his tuxedo a quick glance and decided that Hamish's suit was formal enough. It was a tuxedo, but I hadn't bothered him with a box tie – he had a long, silk one. Leo's tie had a hideous hounds-tooth pattern in black and silver. I could see the top of his bald pate, and his hair was so short that it looked almost shaved around the sides and back of his head.

His eyes were light gray, and he talked fast, saying nothing much. I smiled politely and let him kiss my hand when he turned to me. Of course he gushed over Grandmère first, which gave me a chance to look him over and observe him.

Leah Uberfein stood next to her husband, watching and smiling, waiting for her husband to finish putting himself forward. She wore strappy heels with sequins, and her orangey-red-hued toenail polish showed in the open toes of those shoes. Her dress was as long as mine, but very straight, satiny, shiny, and silver. Her face looked like it had enriched the Botox company.

Her hair looked like it had been zapped out from her head in all directions, and then sculpted back to a helmet shape. It was frosted blond. Her lipstick matched her toes. She was smiling at me while looking me up and down. Did she see something to find fault with? I did.

I kept my expression neutral. I really didn't care what they thought about our aesthetic tastes or our demeanors. We would be polite and make engaging dinner conversation, and then get out of here, end of social interaction.

Dinner proceeded. I noticed that Dr. Nurse's wife, Annabel, was at the next table, chatting up another couple. Hedge fundster and his wife, perhaps? I smiled to her when she saw me looking in her direction, and she smiled back. Her hair was twisted up, and she was wearing a beautiful sea-foam green gown, and it looked easy to move in. I had only met her once before, at another fundraiser, but she had been very nice. She was a tax attorney for nonprofit organizations.

Dr. Nurse directed us to our seats. He put Hamish on my left, and Leo on his left, then Grandmère and himself. Leah Uberfein was sitting next to me, and I found myself feeling glad that it wasn't Leo. He was disgusting to me. However, I did manage to chat on a bit to him from across the table when I had to. It was something about my books.

"Professor Châtelet, when you aren't thinking of inventions for your husband to make a reality, I'm told that you write books," Leo said. "What are they about?"

Good thing he hadn't checked to see the ones I had written about social issues, such as banksters, lobbyists, corporations that made GMOs, and honey bee colony collapse disorder, I thought. Or had he? "Short stories and short books," I replied. "I've done travelogues about Kuwait, Hawai'i, Japan, the Maldives, and histories of those places. Also, I've written stories about teenage girls on the autism spectrum, with Asperger's. That's easy for me, though, since I was one of those girls."

Leah looked surprised. "I thought that was a disorder? You seem so high-functioning!"

I gave her a grin that didn't reach my eyes. "There is no high or low. We are simply another normal model of human. Our brain stems come with more connectors that go in more directions into our brains that those of the majority. The majority of humans are neurotypicals – NTs for short. We Aspies are just one of some of the other normal models. You want inventions and creativity amped up, this is how Nature pays for it. Basically, it shuts off the distractions that NTs thrive on, which are heavy on social interactions and the urge to spend more time on that. We're happy as we are – we love being who we are."

Grandmère actually looked pleased with me as I glanced over at her. She smiled at me and nodded. I was a bit…delighted by that. I smiled back. "You know who you are, Avril," she said. "I have read your stories, and for fun, looked up the biographies of some famous people in history…and, as you say, herstory…to see what they were like. They were like you."

Dr. Nurse actually looked intrigued. "I never knew that. How fascinating."

Wonderful…we Aspies were doing well socially this evening. But… "Enough about our brain stems," I said. "What else can we talk about?" Better not to drag this topic out, I decided. Better to get off it on a thoroughly positive note. Hamish and Grandmère seemed to agree.

Leah turned to me, picked up my right hand – hers was a bit larger than mine, with claw-like ovals in that same awful orangey-red color that looked pressed on – and asked about my pear-shaped diamond.

"That is gorgeous. How many carats is it? And where was it made?"

"Paris, three carats, and it was my grandmother's on my mother's side. I called her Nana."

"And your engagement ring? Is that a pink diamond?" This woman liked jewelry. She was wearing a lot of it, too. At least I knew what I would talk about for the next few minutes. For some reason, I found this topic entertaining. Wandering through Tiffany's was always fun, although I didn't want to acquire lots of stuff. Apparently, Leah did.

"Yes," I replied. "It's a pink heart, 3 carats, on yellow gold so that it goes nicely with my rose-and-yellow gold wedding ring. See the rose motif? I love anything that accurately represents the natural world."

"Oh, I see, yes. You didn't want more diamonds to go with your engagement ring?"

"No. I didn't want the distraction," I said. No sense telling her the history of our finances, that Hamish had saved that raw stone, that he himself had dug from a mine in Australia and saved for years until we met, and that it was all we had been able to have at that time. The chips had financed us a little when the stone was first cut. No, those details were none of her business.

"Less is more," I summed up. "This looks exactly as I want it to. I'm very fussy about aesthetics, and have little patience with the fashion industry, changing things and expecting women to like, buy, and wear whatever it dictates."

Leah smiled. "I tend to like a lot of modern styles, and change is fine with me."

I smiled. This evening was going to move along just fine if I could keep going with this. "Okay, your turn. Tell me about your jewelry. I love wedding stories and stories of gifts from husbands. It's like the fairy tale part of life continuing."

"Wait," Leah said. "You didn't say anything yet about your pearls. Are they Mikimoto?"

"Yes, and they were a Christmas gift from my wonderful husband a few years ago, right after Nae-Née went on the market. I think he was celebrating our success, weren't you, Hamish?"

Hamish and Leo had been listening while Grandmère and Jeffrey Nurse chatted. She was finding out all about his wife, kids, and how they had found the changes of Manhattan as they took place. "Yes, I was," Hamish replied with a smile.

"So, Leah…tell me about your right-hand ring, your wedding and engagement ring, and your earrings and necklace." She was wearing a matching set, it appeared. All of except the wedding stuff was a matching set of tanzanites and diamonds.

Smiling, she took her turn at last. "It's investment jewelry. We keep it in a vault when we're not attending a fundraiser or a ball. It's from Tiffany's. I love their designs." She was wearing the very designs that I found to be the most extravagant and, well, ugly. Emerald cuts were nothing I liked. She appeared to be encrusted with diamonds – small round ones – around large blue ones in square and rectangular shapes. Ugh. Not enough curves; too sharp and harsh.

It suited her. "And your wedding jewelry?" It was all white squares, with a trio of more princess-cuts that had a huge center stone. The wedding ring was an eternity band of smaller ones, but not much smaller.

"Tiffany's also."

I nodded. "I love Louis Comfort Tiffany's designs of dragonflies and flowers. I wish they would bring them back. You like more modern designs, I can see."

"I do. Next year, Leo is getting me some new ones."

I looked over at Leo. We all did. He said "I am?"

"Of course you are, dear," said Leah with a steely smile.

With that, he nodded and smiled back, and raised his glass to her.

Interesting…and appalling. Just how oblivious were these people to the economic crisis that others around them were enduring? Or were they simply and selfishly indifferent to that, as long as they were solvent?! But I had to act unperturbed and draw no undue attention to myself, so I turned to her and asked, "New wedding and engagement ones?"

"Yes. I like a change every now and then. Don't you? Oh, no you don't."

"No. I like my original things. No need for more stuff." I gave her a grin and a laugh. "So, Leah, what do you do with your time?" I didn't want to assume that she had a career or not.

"I attend fashion shows, fundraisers, and volunteer at the Met. I help the curator with the modern art collection." Of course she did, I thought.

"Are you a curator? Did you study for that?" I was just curious.

"No, dear, I'm a volunteer. I studied art, and met Leo in college, when he was a new banker and I was at the Tisch School. We had put on a modern art exhibit – student stuff – and he was attending."

I smiled. "You're lucky to have met your husband so early." Leah smiled happily at that. The dessert arrived. Mini mousse cakes in dark and white chocolate with raspberries on top. We turned our attention to it for a few minutes.

Then Leo turned to Grandmère and asked, "Madame Châtelet, is it really true that you are 96 years old, and that your grandson-in-law injected you with his Regenics formula?"

She smiled sweetly at him and said, "It is."

"How long ago was that?"

"About four months ago," she replied.

"You don't look your age," Leo observed.

"I no longer feel my age," Grandmère said.

"Have you been doing things that you had stopped doing?" he wanted to know.

"Such as?" Grandmère expected a more leading question than that one.

"Oh, I don't know. Baking, reading, hobbies that you might have lost interest in."

"I see. Yes. I have been reading again, my appetite has increased, and I can hear and follow television and movies again. No more can, and I feel stronger, which is nice, too. Life is more fun like this; I can certainly tell you."

"Have you been enjoying your visit to Manhattan?"

"Oh yes, immensely. Avril has shown me her favorite haunts, and the city has gone through a fascinating transformation in the past few years. She has helped me to make sense of it all. I must say the granite work on the canals and waterways is very attractive. It reminds me of Paris."

Leo looked pleased at that…so pleased that I realized he was flattered. He must have played a role in the revamping of the city. He smiled, said he was glad she approved, and then turned to Dr. Nurse.

"Well, Jeffrey, I've heard enough. We'll fund your new Regenics wing, and I shall be one of the first patients. I can't wait to start living forever!"

Oh, great. Just what the world needed, I thought. Leo Uberfein, in it forever. I smiled politely and tried to look convincingly pleased about this. There had to be a way to get some GMO foods into Leo. We would just have think about it.

When the party was over, Aaron appeared and drove us to a heliport on 34th Street. It was a canal now, but the heliport was still in service. We boarded a sleek helicopter, and he started the engine. Soon we were in the air over Manhattan at night. The land mass had been reclaimed with the Dutch dikes. The shape was oddly the same at night, all lit up as before. Lovely and eerie.

Chapter 36

Traveling

The helicopter moved east across Long Island, which did not have its familiar shape.

We got a good look at the dikes around JFK International Airport. It was the first time we had seen them in person, and they were enormous, and a bit terrifying to look at, even in the dark. They were so well-lit that seeing the details was not difficult. It was as if a huge wall of water were rising up over the tarmac and about to fall on it. That was just the initial, first-glance impression of it; the water was actually being held back by the strongest levees in history.

Grandmère and I stared out at it from either side of the back seat of the helicopter. Hamish, who had seen this awe-inspiring feat of engineering in daylight, was busy conferring with Aaron in the front seat through their headphones. Grandmère and I had headphones on too, but aside from a glance or two at one another to check that we were both staring at the sights below, we just looked and looked. We would ask Hamish and Aaron our questions later on.

The helicopter went over Long Island until it had passed the Hamptons, such as remained of that area, and kept on going. At that point, Grandmère and I sat up in our seats. There was no reason to crane our heads awkwardly so that we could stare into the darkness. We looked at each other, wondering how far we would have to go in this thing before we got to the yacht. She didn't know that it was a yacht, and neither had the rest of the family or Jason's family.

About 10 minutes later, Hamish spoke to us through the headphones. "There," he said, pointing down to the right.

We looked down, Grandmère leaning across my lap to do so.

Below us, anchored and moving lightly with the waves, was a huge yacht, lit up.

There was a place up top for a helicopter to land, too. This was our *Shadowcat*.

Aaron let us see that, and then began the descent carefully, positioning the helicopter to align with our landing spot. Funny…I had seen a mention on his résumé years ago about being a helicopter pilot and forgotten about it.

"Hamish, can Ed fly a helicopter too?" I asked through the headphones.

"Yes, he can, and they can both pilot a yacht."

Cool. They could alternate duties and still sleep.

We landed, Aaron shut down the helicopter, and we all took off the headphones and unfastened our seatbelts. Getting out of this machine was another question, however. How did we do that? Grandmère and I both wondered about that, looked at our long gowns, and decided to let the guys help us out. They did, Aaron on her side and Hamish on mine.

"We're here!" Hamish said with a grin. "This is our getaway boat. Flights out of the country are being restricted. We would have had to leave everyone behind, including the cats, plus our work materials." He hugged me, and then led us down metal staircase that hugged the side of the uppermost deck of the yacht.

Grandmère seemed perfectly calm. I kept looking up at her, checking to see if she needed help steadying herself, but she was okay. Hamish knew I was a bit uncertain going down staircases, so he went slowly ahead, watching us both. Aaron had gone down right away. At last we got down to the next level and went inside, with me holding Grandmère's hand at that point.

We were on the bridge with our 2 captains, who were bantering over who was the captain. I wasn't concerned by this, though. Ed and Aaron wouldn't endanger anyone by caring too much about that. We said "Hi" to Ed and looked around.

The bridge was wood-paneled and streamlined, just as any yacht in movies. After another quick glance around, Hamish led us to the room behind, and there was a lounge with built-in sofas and chairs. Everything was nailed down or otherwise attached, and every fixture had little brass railings to keep things from sliding off of tables and shelves.

My parents were waiting for us in that lounge, and they looked relieved when we appeared.

"We wondered if you would get here okay," my mother said, getting up and coming over to me as my father went to Grandmère to lead her to a seat. "It's almost midnight," she added. "How long did that fundraiser run? Did you have something nice to eat? Tell us all about it."

Dad said, "Let them get settled first, Camille. They're tired and will want to change."

"We're fine," Grandmère said. "It was fun, the food was delicious – very fancy, gourmet items – and we were seated with some wealthy donors. It was some Wall Street banker and his wife, and I sat between him and Dr. Nurse."

"I was between Hamish and the banker's wife, and Hamish was next to the banker. We were at a little round table," I added. "Now you know the whole seating arrangement. The wife wore some rather tasteless, over-the-top, Tiffany investment jewelry…a matching set. She informed her husband that he is buying her new wedding jewelry next year. Apparently, she has him pay huge amounts of money to change it every few years. I don't get it."

My mother and Grandmère laughed. "That's what the one-percenters can be like," they said.

After briefly describing our evening, it seemed that my parents were ready to describe theirs.

As soon as Aaron and Ed had gotten us to the party, Ed had left to start ferrying everyone to the yacht. We had gotten there at a little after 6:30 p.m., so he had about 5 hours to work with. He took my parents, Fabian, Claire, and both cats first, which meant a brief stop by our firehouse to pick up Eowyn, as Spock had been staying in Chelsea with my parents. Next, he took Aunt Zoe and Uncle Charlie and Edgar and Jacques. Finally, he took the Woodward family. I wondered how they had felt while waiting to go…like whether or not we were serious about taking them with us.

That was it; we were all aboard now.

When they arrived, my mother had found everyone's rooms and looked around, settled the cats into my parents' room and into mine and Hamish's room.

She put Claire and Fabian in separate rooms, but not out of judgmental prudishness; we didn't have enough room to fit everyone without rearranging people by marital status and gender.

Claire and Grandmère were to be roommates. I hoped they would get along, and that Grandmère wouldn't think a young person's euphemisms were rude. That had happened to me as a teenager when traveling with one of my maternal aunts, but when I had cried, she understood that I wasn't rude, and we had got along fine after that. We had been in Italy seeing the sights.

Thinking of the present again, I listened to my mother describe how much she liked the yacht. She had only ever seen such things on television before, watching a special channel that featured luxury vacations, yachts, resorts, and the like. The same was true of me.

After figuring out which room to put Claire and Grandmère in, my mother had gone into the galley to look around. What she found was amazing: Hamish had inventoried our pantry at home, listed it all, and arranged for duplicates to stock the yacht. There was a huge refrigerator, a spice drawer stocked with all herbs, spices, and salts, a baker's cabinet with drawers that pulled out, containing everything we could want to work with, and a huge freezer full of bags of fruits, vegetables, fish fillets, shrimp, crab, chicken, bacon…you name it. My mother had cooked up enough dinner for everyone as soon as she saw it all, with Claire's help.

Claire had turned out to be a good cook and a budding chef. We were all quite pleased and happy for Fabian. She was a nice girl, talented and curious about the world. We all felt bad about her parents, yet relieved that she had had the sense to stay safely with Fabian once she understood what had likely happened to them and what was definitely happening elsewhere.

The galley was astern; it led out into a big dining room, and on to a forward living room. Behind the galley, Hamish told me (he had just come into the galley to watch my mother give me the grand tour), was a lovely deck where would could sit and eat in nice weather. "Wow…just like in the movies," I remarked. "This is some getaway conveyance you've arranged for!"

He shrugged. "I like to be prepared. We're going to be out to sea for a while. I'll explain the plan to everyone tomorrow, if they are all asleep, or in a few minutes, if not."

Good. I didn't really want to wait until tomorrow, but it would be a good idea to finish looking around first. This time, Hamish led the way. I remembered suddenly that he had been here first, to see if he wanted to buy this yacht, tour it, and close the deal.

We had still been one level up from sea level. Now we were down at the same level as the water, and when we went into the room that Hamish and I were to share, I looked outside immediately. The moonlight on the ocean showed me that the water was lapping the yacht just a few feet below the porthole.

Eowyn was crouched on the bed, wide-eyed. "Good cat!" I said, petting her from head to tail. "Don't worry; you'll get used to being on a ship soon." I kissed her on the top of her head and turned to look around. Grandmère, oddly enough, was not sleepy despite the excitement of the evening, but I was starting to think that she would be shortly.

"Shouldn't we get you comfortably settled in for the night, Grandmère? It's after midnight. Even if you don't want to sleep yet, at least you would be ready to do that."

She was grinning, and seemed to be having a great time. "I'm fine, but I'll get out of this formal gown and into my nightgown and robe. I just wanted to see that the cats are okay. All right; I'll see the other one after I change."

We were in the prow of the ship for the main cabin – my mother had given me and Hamish the biggest suite. Nice, but what were the other ones like? No one would switch things around at this hour, though, I realized. They were probably all asleep by now.

But once we went out into the hallway, heads poked out of two of the six other cabins: Aunt Zoe and Uncle Charlie down on the right, and Anne and Peter Woodward just past them. Straight ahead, at the stern, was a lounge. Hamish said it had a television and DVD player, and lots of books. Perfect.

"Dad and I have the room across from your aunt and uncle's," my mother said, pointing at the one to the left. "Grandmère and Claire are in the cabin on your right." There was Claire, ready for bed but fully awake, looking out at us where my mother gestured. The one across from theirs was empty, but I knew Hamish had to have plans for it.

"Hi Claire," I said. "Looks like you and Grandmère will be roommates. You can get to know each other." I smiled, hoping that she felt calm and comfortable about it.

She smiled back. "Hi Avril! Yes. I hope you like having me for a roommate, Madame Châtelet," she said to Grandmère."

"I hope you like having an old lady like me for a roommate," Grandmère replied.

"Let's get you settled in now, Grandmère. If we stay up all night, so be it, but we should all get out of these formal clothes and learn where everything is, what there is, and get a little bit familiar with it before we fall asleep. I don't want anyone to fall in the night when we aren't alert, perhaps from forgetting where we are. Oh, and I hate to say this, but we probably shouldn't take any baths until we hear what the water situation is on board," I summed up.

We went into Grandmère and Claire's cabin, and it was all lavender. French lavender flowers patterned the bedding, the curtains, and the chairs. Pretty! There was even some dried lavender out. The scent was calming. I hoped that it would continue to calm everyone in here. We would need to be calm; I suspected that we would soon find plenty to feel anxious about.

Hamish was out in the hallway with the others, so my mother and I helped Grandmère get changed, and soon we knew her room better than she did. She looked around quickly, and Claire pointed out a large stash of books to read, plus their e-readers. At least boredom didn't threaten!

At last, with that done, at one o'clock in the morning, Hamish and I went into our room and changed our clothes. My mother followed us in and helped hang up our formal outfits, and she showed us where she had put our clothing, nightwear and all. I chose a pink, medium-length nightgown, a robe, and my black flip-flops. Hamish put on his lounge pants and a tee shirt, which was what he usually wore to bed.

He petted our cat for a couple of minutes while I looked around. My e-reader was here, and so was a radio, an intercom in the wall, and many of my books. A copy of each of the ones I had written and published was included in the mix, plus lots of my old favorites. "Wow! You watch me more than I could tell until we went on the run!" I said to him, amazed and impressed.

My husband just grinned. But after a moment, he said, "We're going to be at sea for a while. I don't want you to be bored."

I hopped onto the bed for a hug. "This is really pretty. Did you plan the pinks and blues too?" Our bedding looked like a pastel flower garden, sort of like a Monet painting, with iris blossoms in pinks, blues, lavender, white…I could read in here for hours, I thought to myself.

"Aye, I did."

"I love you Hamish! You're taken my whole family away from the evil culling machine that our country had morphed into, and made it pleasant in the process. We even have our cats safe. It's perfect. I feel spoiled…utterly spoiled, spoiled absolutely rotten. And I don't want to be seen acting too happy and content about this outside this room, so I'm going to get all of the thank-yous done now, before Edgar or Claire see me like this."

"I understand." Hamish stopped looking so pleased at those words.

There was a knock at the door.

Hamish got up and answered it.

Dad was there. "Everyone wants to know the plan now that our getaway is a fait accompli," he said. "We've waited long enough, and no one wants to go to sleep without hearing it."

"Fair enough," Hamish said. "Let's all go upstairs to sit and talk."

It was like a march in a slow-moving, calm parade up the stairs. The boys were all staying in pairs down below us, on the same level as Ed and Aaron who, for now, had their own rooms. Hamish told me this as we tromped up the stairs, and added that he didn't expect that to change.

Once settled into the big living room, we all stared at each other like startled fools for a moment or two. This was a very strange situation to be in. The Woodward parents looked the most ill at ease, and I didn't blame them. What had they left home for, they must have been wondering, and was it really as dire as Jason had led them to expect?

It was, Hamish assured them. Then he laid out the plan, using a map of the world on the wall behind him, which included longitudinal and latitudinal lines. This wall abutted the dining room; we faced forward. It felt like we were delivering a university lecture, with Hamish leading the class. The map was on a huge flatscreen TV, and I realized that Jason had wired it into a computer for Hamish. We were looking at Google Earth Maps, so that Hamish could show us our projected route.

We were to head north, just off the coast of North America, as far as St. John's on the Island of Newfoundland. We might or might not stop there, depending upon the news reports. As far as anyone conducting surveillance on us, we were going to be back in Connecticut, so it might be better to keep a low profile. Besides, we had enough supplies to complete our trek across the ocean, Hamish added.

From St. John's, whether or not we actually went ashore, we would move across the North Atlantic toward the British Isles. When we got to them, we would turn farther north and head for Scotland. With that, I understood what was next: we were going to pick up Fiona and William.

Fiona Danae MacDonall was a couple of years older than Hamish. She was a retired professor from Edinburgh University, where she had taught Gaelic lore and Scottish literature. She had moved to a rural area that overlooked the North Sea. Her fiancé, William Wallace MacTavish, a website developer, lived with her now. They had a small stone cottage on the edge of town; we had seen it on Facebook.

"Will we be getting them out with the helicopter?" I asked at that point.

"Aye. My sister, her fiancé, her cat, their bags, and all."

"It will be nice to see her again, and to meet William," I remarked. She and William had met during Fiona's last year of teaching, four years ago, and recently gotten engaged. "So they are the ones who will be in that other cabin across from Anne and Peter?"

"You got it," Hamish replied.

"You've got it all planned out. You must have been plotting this with Jason every Saturday and every other day for months," I told him. "Not that it feels like a surprise, but wow. It just feels impressive."

"That I was. Fiona's freaked out. She wanted to enjoy reading books and writing novels in her retirement, but now she's too nervous to do much of anything. She's scared out of her wits, because unlike most people, she understands what's happening. I've got to get her out of there."

Uncle Charlie spoke up at this point. "How will we know what is happening elsewhere in the world? How will we know whether or not this was all necessary? It seems so extreme, even after seeing what you showed us back in Connecticut. I mean, we really appreciate all this, and it's been a fun vacation and adventure on *Lifestyles of the Rich and Covert*, but I have to wonder about all this. We're really curious as to how necessary this was."

Edgar couldn't believe it, and said so. "After what happened to Ellie and to Claire's parents, you need further assurance that this was necessary?!"

Grandmère was sitting next to him. She gave him a hug when he said that, but was silent.

Aunt Zoe glared at Uncle Charlie, and he sat back in his seat, quiet.

"I realize how bizarre everything feels," Hamish said. "It feels that way to me, too or I wouldn't have arranged all this. I grew up with just the basics and had no money for years. Spending it like this feels insane, but it's not to be frivolous. We are going somewhere with a purpose and with something to do once we get there. The idea is to wait out this monstrous cull of the human population of most of the planet someplace reasonably safe."

"And where is that?" Grandmère wanted to know.

"Switzerland. Switzerland has always been neutral, and successfully so because it is armed to the teeth. It is not overpopulated because it has always been very careful with its human, its financial, and its other resources, including food, clothing, shelter, and basic necessities. That nation won't let any but the wealthiest of the world in – those who can afford to stock up on a year's supply of all that. We can do that."

"We can't," Peter Woodward said. "We appreciate being included, but why us?"

"There's your son, who works with me, and you have useful skills that will fit in nicely. Why you in particular is because we want anyone who escapes with us to have their family safe, not frantic about who they left behind."

"Thank you, Dr. MacDonall." Anne Woodward spoke. "Thank you very much for fitting us in. It means a great deal to us. I'm starting to see that you've saved our lives."

"Please call me Hamish, and you're quite welcome."

She smiled politely. "Okay, thank you Hamish."

"So…is everyone comfortable?"

Nods all around.

Fabian spoke up next. "Can we really go all the way to Switzerland on this yacht?"

"We can," Hamish replied. "We will go all the way up the Rhône River into Lake Geneva on this thing, no need for any airplanes or other nonsense. We're going to head south after we get Fiona and William, around to the Mediterranean Sea. From there, we will go up to Port-Saint-Louis-du-Rhône and on up through southern France, then east to Switzerland."

"Won't we be stopped by customs agents?" I asked.

"Most likely, yes, but not to worry: I have documentation from the clinic in Lausanne, Switzerland, proving that we are all expected there and explaining what work several of us will be doing there. All younger passengers on this yacht have documented positions in my clinic. If you choose to do something else that you like better once we're settled, that's fine, but for now, we need you to play along."

Claire, Fabian, Edgar, Jacques, and Jason all nodded, agreeing to do just that.

"Grandmère will be our celebrity Regenics patient," Hamish added.

"Excéllent!" she responded, grinning and lapsing into a French accent.

Hamish and I laughed. Still grinning, Hamish continued, "Daily updates on the situation in the United States and elsewhere will be gathered and shared. Jason and I will take care of that. In fact, since you have all been through my vaccination regimen and had your Regenics shots, I have little else to do now. It's going to feel very strange to be on an enforced vacation."

Dad laughed. "You'll find a way to work non-stop and you know it."

"I suppose I will," Hamish agreed.

"It's after 2 o'clock in the morning," I said. "Let's go to bed and sleep late. We can have a brunch party when we get up."

With that, we adjourned.

Hamish and I went to check on Ed and Aaron before going below. They were drinking coffee and sitting on the bridge, with Ed at the huge, round, metal steering wheel. "How do you like the *Shadowcat*?" I asked them.

"It's great," Aaron said. "I've always wanted to do something like this."

Ed grinned and said he was having a good time, too. "I'm your captive eater now, Avril. I have no choice but to eat healthy foods."

"Poor you," I teased. "You'll learn after a while that healthy foods can taste very enticing. I don't feel sorry for you at all. But what about sleep for you guys? Will we be putting the anchor down so you can rest at all?"

They glanced at Hamish, who said, "Surprise, Avril! I can steer the ship and spell them a bit if we decide we have to keep running, but for now, we're going to high-tail it north, and see what the situation is. We'll likely take a rest tomorrow, though, and let them sleep."

"We're going to have to make food and set meals aside for you both, then," I said.

Aaron and Ed smiled and said thanks.

"Let's go below now," Hamish said to me. "There's one more thing I want to show you."

We went all the way down to the level where the boys were staying, and found another 6 cabins, plus an engine room. Hamish opened that door for a moment, and pointed out the engine, and a water desalination machine. "If you and Grandmère are conservative about baths, it should be possible to still have them, even in the smaller tubs on board."

"Oh! She'll be glad to hear that. Even with Regenics, I doubt that a person would never benefit from a nice, relaxing, warm soak in a tub of scented water again."

"No, people still need such things. Now come on in here," he said, and led me toward the room to the left. It was across from where Jason and Edgar's cabin. When he opened it, he did so with a keypad and a code. I watched: the code was our cat's birth date, 482012, for April 8, 2012. Thanks, Eowyn, and good luck, hackers.

As we entered, Jason came out of his cabin. He and Edgar were still up, tinkering with their electronic devices. I waved to Edgar. Jason walked over and came into this other cabin with us. It had a small bathroom with a shower stall, no tub (those were only upstairs, in each cabin), and a bed. "I couldn't do anything about that bed," Hamish said, "but if we absolutely had to accommodate more people, Jason and Edgar could be trusted to use this room."

After a second glance around it, I realized what was familiar. It was almost a replica of Hamish's basement lab at our house in Connecticut, right down to his medical equipment, nanobotic tools, and a safe. I was quite sure that when opened, it would contain 2 wiped laptops which would be used to provide those updates on world news.

Sure enough, that was what Hamish and Jason showed me.

With that, the tour was over. We locked up, went upstairs to our beautifully appointed cabin, and climbed into bed. It had padded railings! Oh, and there was even a safe for my jewelry, which I had put away when we first got changed.

Eowyn, suspicious of the motion of the yacht on the ocean, went over to her ring pillow bed and curled up in it. I had moved it to a spot on the floor between the poufy chairs under the portholes, and she liked being surrounded by the large shapes on either side. She looked up at me, cooed once, and closed her eyes.

I gave her a slitted-eyed cat smile in return, rolled over to face my husband, and fell asleep.

The next day, we did all sleep late, and I found out that Ed and Aaron were quite sensibly sleeping in 4-hour shifts rather than trying to both stay up non-stop until we got to the vicinity of St. John's. Good! They had been making me nervous with that suggestion. My mother suggested that they might have been joking with me.

"Oh great – joke with the boss's wife. Hilarious."

Hamish said that they really had changed their minds on their own.

"Thank you for backing me up," I said.

We were all in the kitchen, cooking a huge breakfast. Claire had mixed up whole wheat cardamom waffles, and Fabian was cooking them. "Is that our heart-shaped waffle-iron from home?" I asked Hamish.

"It is," he said.

Cool! It was hard to leave home, no matter how dangerous the place was to stay in. These little touches of it were nice. I tried not to be scared about…everything…and just looked around the kitchen…er, galley…at what was going on.

Uncle Charlie had found a melon baller and a cantaloupe and was making a big bowl-full of shapes. I cracked up when I saw that. Aunt Zoe was adding cut strawberries, red grapes, and blueberries in an effort to use up fresh foods before they could go bad. Good move.

Dad was cooking up 2 packages of bacon, and my mother had a mixing bowl of beaten eggs and a bowl of shredded cheddar cheese. She had shredded it herself; the pre-shredded kind had bits of plastic in it to keep it separated once the factory had shredded it. These disturbing tidbits of food preparation data had caught her interest at home. While she had watched the Food Network, I had slipped articles under her nose about such things.

Anne had found the coffee and 2 coffee machines and loaded them both. We had toasted praline coffee and Mandheling Sumatra coffee. Peter was out on the bridge with Aaron, looking around at the steering apparatus.

I looked around for something to do, but the boys had set the table already.

The cats appeared, winding around my ankles, so I found their food and fed them. Spock had a litter box, dry food, and a water dish in my parents' bathroom, and Eowyn had her own set of all that in our bathroom, but canned food was to be in the kitchen, just like at home. They already appeared to know the yacht from prow to stern, and everyone was careful not to let them outside.

Grandmère was standing by a window in the dining room, staring out what she said was the coast, but we couldn't see it. "Your husband tells me that we are staying out of the sight of other ships, and of the coast. I guess we won't see much, but that sounds safer," she said to me.

"It does. I'm glad everyone's passport was current, and that we showed them all around last night. We have to keep those accounted for, even though we won't be going ashore at least until we get to France, I think."

We had all gotten dressed in comfortable clothing and flat shoes, and the novelty of our situation hadn't yet worn off. I went into the big living room, and all of the other boys were in there. Jason was tinkering with the television set, looking for news.

"Jason, we haven't eaten yet. Shouldn't we wait and have brunch first before we see what awful things there are to know about today?" Jason paused and looked nonplussed.

Grandmère was right behind me. "Yes, please wait. There's plenty of time later to get upset."

He stopped what he was doing. "Yes, you're right. Awful news will be there later, whether we stare at it and obsess over it every second or not."

Edgar chimed in. "Let's not make the Farmers happy by letting them upset us constantly."

It was nice to hear him say that. I was still worried about him, but he sounded better.

The food was ready, so we went to load our plates in the kitchen. I poured some toasted praline coffee, added milk, and took it to the table. I would wait to get my food, I thought. That would look polite, and give me a chance to claim a favorite seat. I didn't like having no choice about a seat. It was a silly quirk, but I couldn't let go of it. With a seat claimed, I was less anxious in any situation.

I chose one in the corner by the end opposite the kitchen. The table was a long, wide oval shape, made of cherry wood. It was beautiful. It also had a brass lip over its edge in case the yacht got tossed around on the waves during a meal. These details were quite intriguing; the kitchen cabinets, also made of wood – oak, I thought – had catches inside them, stronger than any I was used to finding on land for the same reason.

Grandmère put her coffee cup down next to mine. "Oh, good!" I said. I was hoping you would claim a seat next to me." I smiled at her. Hamish sat down on my other side, at the end. Grandmère smiled and sat down. "Hamish, is any of the coffee half-regular, half-decaf?"

"Aye. She got that kind. I showed it to Anne when she was brewing it up."

"Thanks!"

"You two are spoiling this old lady," Grandmère said with an appreciative smile.

I just grinned at her. Yes, that was the idea. Grandmère's personality was getting sunnier and sunnier as time wore on since her Regenics shot, and I liked it. We all did. Before that, the aging process had been making her uncomfortable and terminally morose. She hadn't been happy or much fun. This was much better.

"Where's your food?" I asked, suddenly realizing that she had also come to the table with just her coffee.

"I can't carry a plate, a cup of juice, and the coffee, so I thought I would go back after the rush. I had the same idea you did. Hamish, are you just being polite, waiting until the end? Why aren't you in there getting food, a big guy like you?" she teased him.

He stood up. "Let's go get ours, then. I'm hungry now that you made me think about it."

We went in and got our feasts and returned in time to eat with the others. There was plenty of food. Did I mention the bathroom near the kitchen? We didn't need to go below. If I didn't think about the fact that all that was visible out the windows was open sea, and that this was intentional, I found myself enjoying this meal with my family and friends.

The Woodwards did feel like friends now. We were getting used to each other, and they were nice people. They adapted to Aspie quirkiness well, and didn't expect me or Hamish to emote more, or get the wrong idea from our deadpan facial expression. Of course, Anne was a nurse, like my mother. That was an added dividend: they had that in common and were becoming fast friends, too.

When we were finished eating, I went into the kitchen and peered around, suddenly worried about leftovers. Had 2 portions been put aside for Ed and Aaron? My mother walked in and asked what I was looking for, and I told her. "I made up 2 plates for them before letting anyone load their plates," she told me.

"You're so smart," I said. "I would feel really guilty if they didn't get what we got."

"You can take it out to them if you want; Aaron just went up to the bridge. I'll carry their coffee." So I microwaved both plates of food, grabbed flatware, napkins, and started walking. Jacques walked in and I remembered the juice; I pressed him into service pouring and carrying two small glasses of that.

Up on the bridge, Ed was still steering while Aaron sat on the long bench up against the wall behind him. "Brunch service!" I called out, and we laid each meal out on little shelves, built for the purpose of feeding captains. Wow…the more time I spent on this yacht, the more clever details I noticed. We were traveling at 15 knots.

We all stared ahead for a moment or two, asked if everything was moving along as planned, were told it was, thanked them, and then left. What else would they have said? The information we sought as waiting downstairs anyway. Hamish and Jason would do that computer and flatscreen TV routine. My stomach leaped in nervous anticipation at that thought.

Damn. The last time I had felt like this was when I had to take exams in school. Papers were better than exams. Hmm…that thought was an avoidance tactic. Back to the present: as much as I didn't miss those exams, that was a better…well, less horrific…reason for fear than this. This was real life, and real life was showing what a lie it had been that going to school would make my future okay.

When we got back to the living room, my mother wouldn't hear of a news session just yet. Instead, she organized a clean-up brigade, recruiting the boys to collect everything and wash, dry, and put it all away. I walked around with a sponge and towel doing the finishing touches.

Hamish and Jason were starting to head below at that point. I rushed after them, and Hamish turned around to tell me that this time, the news would be covered in the lounge. That made sense; he and Jason wouldn't have to bring their laptops as far from their hiding place. My laptop was already in there, he added, in case I wanted to write.

"Thanks," I said. They were going to work for an hour before calling everyone, so I decided to explore again. I still didn't know the *Shadowcat* – our home for the foreseeable future – as well as I wanted to. Thus far, the most practical observation had been the laundry machines by the stairs on the level where our cabin was, so I was curious.

I started with the cabin intended for Fiona and William. It looked like Grandmère and Claire's cabin, but with a beautiful thistle pattern in the duvet, sheets, curtains, and other upholstery. Pretty…and it might make Fiona feel more at home after we spirited her away from Scotland. One could only hope so. Fiona and William would be next door to me and Hamish.

My mother came downstairs, and I asked to see the other cabins on this level, so she showed me hers and Dad's next. Pretty – Monet's irises in pastel blue was the theme here. Aunt Zoe and Uncle Charlie had more Monet décor: La Havre scenes. How had Hamish known what the family would like? Did Aunt Zoe like this? Her house hadn't been decorated like this, even if ours featured traditional French décor. Oh well. I loved it, and I could see that he had tried very hard to make it nice for us here. The room that Anne and Peter Woodward had was decorated with Van Gogh's Iris motif.

The lounge was another plain but beautiful, streamlined, wood-paneled room. I quickly located my laptop in its case, set it all up by a poufy chair with a seashell pattern on it, tested it, checked it, and then put it away. I was too keyed up right now to do much with it.

The winding staircase was in between the lounge and my parents' cabin, and I went down it to see the other rooms. There were 5 cabins, all decorated with navy blue upholstery, and shared bathrooms between the two pairs of rooms. Interesting; this must have been meant for staff, I thought, because the cabins upstairs each had their own bathrooms. Ed and Aaron were on the side next to the office-lab cabin, which was across from the stairs, and the boys opposite.

The engine room hummed at the stern, and the prow area was for supplies. I looked in there and saw life jackets. They were all down here?! No…I remembered seeing more than enough for everyone upstairs, on the level with the galley. These must be extra, for party guests that we didn't intend to have.

That concluded the tour, so I shut the supply room door and looked in on Hamish and Jason.

They showed me the population counts on the Dark Net.

U.S.: 240,000,000 or so. What?! How the hell did it drop so fast, by 60 million?! Never mind; I knew how. It was a good thing that brunch had been a little while ago and not a few minutes ago, I commented.

"It gets worse," Jason said. "They've revised the cull goal from a reduction to 1930 numbers to lower than that. "Now they plan to leave 80 million Americans when it's over."

I stared at him for a moment, then took a breath and looked at Hamish, who nodded to me.

"Okay then. I'll just go upstairs and wait for our meeting to start," I said, and left.

Wow. They had already killed off 80 million or so Americans and would-be immigrants, and they still have double that many to go. There was no stopping them, either, only observing them from a safe distance. We were very lucky to be able to stay alive and safe and do that.

I changed my mind. I did feel like looking up data online. I found a website that helped me to understand how fast we were traveling, a speed which I had observed when bringing brunch to our protectors and pilots (15 knots), our route, and how long it would take to go everywhere.

Time to St. John's, Newfoundland from off the coast of Montauk, Long Island: 2 days, 8 hours, and 30 minutes. Time to the North Sea, just north of Scotland from St. John's: 5 days and 20 minutes. Time south to a spot off the coast of Rosehearty, Scotland: 6 hours and 12 minutes.

Reverse course and go back around and out to sea, then south, down toward the Bay of Biscay...that would take the same time to get north, then a day or so going southwest until we were far enough that no one in Ireland would see us. Next, head south...3 days and 22 hours.

"So...you're figuring out our route in some detail in advance of the presentation, I see," Hamish said, coming into the library-lounge.

"Yeah...can't resist," I said, my eyes still glued to the screen. "3 days, 22 hours, and 22 minutes at 15 knots from the Atlantic Ocean through the Strait of Gibraltar and on to the middle of the Mediterranean Sea, south of France. Of course, that won't be exact. Some other variables from real life will change that equation. They always do."

"Indeed they do."

"At that same speed – and there's where the math is all wrong, because we would have to go at a slower speed when we get close to shore – it would take 17 hours to get to the mouth of the Rhône River. That's it. I've seen enough. We're looking at a trip that will take a little over 2 weeks, probably with twists and turns of various sorts."

Hamish grinned. "Please don't tell me you've already figured out the most perilous aspects of it. That's the worst part, and I haven't even started today's presentation."

"Oh, I know there's more, and that this just has to get worse – much worse. But don't talk like it's the most exciting college lecture ever, even if it is. This is a horror show unfolding."

"You're right. When I'm through telling everyone about the next awful truths, we'll all be really upset. I'm a bit worried about how anxious I'm making everyone, but I don't really see a practical way of concealing any of it."

"There isn't any way of not telling them, because if you don't, when we have to face any aspect of it, they won't be used to those awful ideas. If they're not even a tiny bit inured to them, they won't be able to manage their emotional responses to those truths, and that could get them or us or both killed. No – none of us can afford ignorance."

Jason walked in. "I see you're both on the same page as usual," he said with a wry grin.

"Indeed," Hamish and I said in unison.

The others began filing in and taking seats, and Hamish told me to move to a spot up front by the television screen, next to him. "I want you to figure things out as I go along – out loud. If we just run through this without that commentary, a lot will be unclear. That, and the emotional impact might be too much."

"It'll be too much for some people anyway," I said, moving as he requested.

"You're probably right."

They were all there, staring at us expectantly a couple of minutes later.

Hamish launched into it. "Avril is ahead me as usual. She found a website that enables a visitor to plot one's route, complete with the rate of speed, and see how long the trip will take. The upshot of that is that we will be at sea for a little over 2 weeks. That assumes, of course, that we won't have to deviate from our planned route much, which I suspect we may very well have to do. Let's plan on 3 weeks, and that doesn't include the trip up the Rhône."

With that, I thought of my first reason to interject something. "What might cause us to deviate from our route, and what do we do about fuel? You may have provided us with enough food to last the duration of the trip, but I doubt that the fuel tank will make that work without refueling. If we're going to stay offshore the whole time, how will that work?"

"Good news: Blackout Security has a refueling-at-sea service."

"That is good news. Now what about the other problem? Are we being chased, monitored, watched, pursued, whatever? Do we have to worry that our own government or another government or even an international entity might not wish us to travel this way, or at all? And what about when we get at least as far as the Mediterranean Sea? We can't avoid interacting with other people then, and I wonder about being able to continue at that point. What will convince them to let us continue on our way?"

"Good questions. We are not being chased per se, but we must avoid being seen from another ship. If another ship sees us, then it is presumed that we too can see them: what sort of ship they are, what they might be doing, and so on. They won't want that. If that happens, yes, we could very well be chased. So we must be vigilant about avoiding that. That's why Jason and I have brought along all this do-it-ourselves surveillance tech. As for the Mediterranean Sea, we have copies of our work invitation from the clinic in Lausanne, Switzerland."

"That would satisfy them? As in, any officials on any military ships in that sea?"

"It should. The Swiss in Lausanne, if contacted by those officials, will indeed say that they are waiting for us and expecting us, and confirm the reasons why. However, it is entirely up to us to get there safely."

"And we really couldn't have just flown there directly?" Uncle Charlie asked.

Hamish looked at him. "I am about to show you what's happening at home and around the world. No, we really couldn't." With that, he started by tuning into the major North American news stations, which had all been running a lead story from early this morning.

The newscaster was announcing a worldwide travel ban due to an Ebola outbreak. Several patients had managed to get through quarantines in West Africa, and they had flown to airports in Texas, Baltimore, Vancouver, Madrid, and Hong Kong. Actually, the newscaster corrected, the one that got to Baltimore might have Marburg, which was an even worse virus than Ebola.

All flights had been grounded around the globe until further notice as of this morning. Martial law had been declared for the whole of the United States, with habeas corpus suspended. Every major city was on lockdown, complete with curfews. Towns were being secured as well. Teams of MRAPs had become a common sight in suburbs all over the U.S. and Canada, and the scene cut to a view of East Hartford, Connecticut. This was shown in the background behind a young woman newscaster with a microphone. The group all gasped when that location was mentioned, but the story moved on abruptly.

The newscaster was saying, "The U.S.A.M.R.I.I.D. is moving through the area, combing the neighborhoods for any sign of illness. If any is found, the entire area – just as we have seen elsewhere all over the nation – will have to be evacuated. As this tragedy continues to unfold, our news team will keep you updated." End of sound-bite.

A map showed the spread of Ebola and its expected trajectory. Hamish flipped around to a few other networks, all of which were running the same story. "At this point, I should mention that the Châtelet and Rosier relatives in Paris flew to Lausanne 4 days ago. They'll stay in a hotel there and wait for us until we arrive."

Grandmère had been gaping in horror at the map of the world, and when I followed her gaze, it was obvious that it went to Paris. So had my mother. They broke off and looked at Hamish again. Moving on, he brought up another image, which was a satellite feed of a suburban area. It was the same thing that he and Jason and I had been looking at every Saturday for weeks.

It was West Hartford, Connecticut. "What I am about to show you all is recorded from a satellite. It happened 4 days ago." He hit the play button and it zoomed in. "Look familiar?" It was the neighborhood where Aunt Zoe and Uncle Charlie's house was.

As we watched, MRAPs moved into the neighborhood, and my family and Jason's watched a REX 84 exercise carried out. There was even sound. "How did you get audio on this?" I asked Hamish and Jason. "Did you get a group of nano-spybots to follow this unit around?"

He quietly told me that it was one of the same groups that he had deployed a few months ago, and that we had been watching REX 84s carried out through it repeatedly. This was just the one that happened to go to our town. I nodded, feeling winded even though I hadn't moved, and sat back to watch the rest of it.

The rest of it included being treated to a covert view of the forced evacuation of the friends and neighbors of our relatives. These were people we had seen coming and going for years – decades in some cases – in that area, and who had attended some parties at Aunt Zoe and Uncle Charlie's house. Others had bought McMansions on their street when Uncle Charlie's real estate development company had completed them.

Jacques gasped and said, "I just saw several of the people I went to high school with get taken away in their underwear and cavity searched!" We looked at him for a moment, then back at the screen. Gas grenades got lobbed into some of the homes, and more people got dragged outside, kicking and choking all the way. Each person was roughly clubbed and tossed into the back of a canvas-covered truck.

As they drove off, I recalled showing this to my family before, and it had induced them to come with us, but now that it was being done in their own area, they were staring at me and Hamish like we had saved them from a close call. Aunt Zoe and Claire started sobbing.

"I think it's about to get much worse," I warned. "You think you're upset now, just wait."

This elicited some shocked and appalled looks, and I turned back to the screen. It was hard to watch, but we had to watch. "This may be upsetting to watch, but your neighbors had it worse. They had to experience it. We're fine," I added.

The horror show continued with the militia entering each home and exiting with small valuables, such as jewelry that hung from their pockets, and…pets. Claire stared. "Oh, they're taking care of the pets! They're not leaving them to starve."

"Oh, they're taking care of them, all right," I said to her, looking steadily at her.

She looked at me, confused, then up at the screen as the militia broke the necks of the cats and dogs and tossed the corpses aside. Abruptly, she screamed, as did Aunt Zoe and Anne. My mother let out a slight yelp and gasped for air. I panted a bit myself, and then noticed Spock and Eowyn in the room. They hadn't been looking at the screen, but they suddenly jumped at the noise that we humans were making. Then they walked over to my mother and me and put their paws on our knees and stared into our eyes as if to say, "What? What's wrong?"

I picked Eowyn up and petted her in my lap, wide-eyed. "No matter how many of those reality horror shows I see, it doesn't get mundane," I commented. "I doubt it will, either."

"You're stimming," Anne observed.

"Huh – you know what that is," I said. I had not only been breathing hard, but I had also been rocking back and forth before I picked up the cat, and hadn't noticed it until she pointed it out.

"Nursing school includes that now," my mother commented. "It didn't when I went."

We looked back at the screen. There was more. Another military team moved in as soon as the first one moved out. It brought what I now thought of as, and described to the group as, deconstruction equipment.

"Deconstruction equipment?!" Uncle Charlie said. "Those machines are for building homes," he protested, not catching on until the first building was razed. "Oh…hey! They're tearing down the houses I built!" He was outraged.

"Yeah, they're doing that everywhere. Didn't you notice the suspicious absence of human dwelling and other buildings along the route to Manhattan when we drove?" Dad asked him.

He looked at us, open-mouthed, as that sunk in. He didn't drive around much, unlike Dad.

Grandmère just looked at him and shook her head. She had known what she was seeing.

The military crews gutted the homes for whatever materials could be reused, sorting them and tossing the materials into huge trucks to be driven out. Whatever couldn't be reused in its present form was sorted into other trucks, such as shingles and other wooden frames. Hamish said that that wood would be ground into pulp and used to make newspaper, magazines, books, and other such materials.

"Where?" asked Fabian.

"At American paper companies, so that it doesn't have to travel far."

When the job was done, landscaping crews came and ripped up lawns and dug around the now-emptied foundations of cellars and swimming pools and garages. They pushed the earth around until it was flat with no deep holes. Finally, they drove into the farthest reaches of each street and ground up the pavement, whereupon other crews showed up to remove the power lines and street lamps.

"What are they doing now," my mother wondered.

"It's called giving the land back to Nature," I told her. She looked at me, appalled.

That concluded the horror segment for that neighborhood. Hamish and Jason had a few more to show us, however. Jason's parents' neighborhood had been emptied and razed, as had Elmwood. All around town most new development since World War II had been removed – erased, really.

It was the same in surrounding towns. "I guess that newscaster was escorted back to wherever she came from before the MRAPs could do their worst in East Hartford," I remarked as the view showed us the lack of much of East Hartford.

"Probably," Jason said. "That's all for now of that aspect of the show."

"Hamish, how much more is there to see now?"

"Right now? Nothing. I think you've had enough of a shock. This concludes today's reality horror show. Just one other thing: there may in fact be a couple of real Ebola and Marburg patients, but they are being contained very carefully in isolation wards to either die of that or survive to live on. But those cases are just for show really, to keep people scared and under control. It's the MRAP teams with their cancer-induction shots and mobile crematoriums that are reducing American numbers."

More stares of shock.

"Tomorrow, we meet here again for the other half of the presentation. You're going to hate it, but it's after 4 o'clock now, and Jason and I have some work to do to get that ready for you."

With that, he shut it off and closed his laptop, and so did Jason.

We all sat there, stunned.

It was time to make dinner now, and no one felt very hungry. We were passing by Maine, I noticed as I went up to the galley in a daze. Did I mention the fact that each room had a small GPS screen, and that we could see where we were in our cabins, in the galley, in the library lounge, the galley, and on the bridge? Well, we could.

I looked around at our food supplies and found lots of frozen fish choices in the huge freezer, and almost took some out when I thought to check the huge fridge first. Sure enough, there was a lot of fresh fish in there that should be used first. Salad items, too. I took it out and got to work, and soon felt less anxious as I got involved in a wordless gourmet cooking job.

Basmati rice…in a huge pot with a little saffron – saffron had calming effects, which we all needed now. Giant bag of green beans…half went into a large pot of water. I would make a sauce of butter, olive oil, herbs and spices for it. Cod…did we have enough large frying pans to work on that? Huh…we did. Four big ones. I dredged the fillets in flour, salt, and cayenne, and cooked them in melted butter and olive oil.

My mother, Aunt Zoe, Anne, and Claire came in, followed by Grandmère, assessed what I was doing, and attacked the salad items without a word. None of us felt like chatting. I paused to get the flat-leaf parsley and chop it up, and Claire had already started doing that. We smiled politely at each other and then I realized I had run out of tasks. Damn. Well, I had to share. They wanted to take out their anxieties on the activity of food preparation too, I realized.

I cleaned up what I could and mixed up some chocolate chip almond cookie dough, deliberately choosing a recipe with a lot of steps. I didn't want to think much right now. Getting the food processor out to grind the oatmeal up with the dry ingredients and the mixer for the wet ones, plus combining it and washing everything, stretched that task out. Then I did it all again just to get a huge batch of cookies.

"Damn," I remarked, "that didn't take as long as I'd hoped. I don't want to sit and think, so I was trying to make work for myself," I said to Grandmère. Aunt Zoe and Anne had already put away everything I had used to mix up the cookies, and I was baking the last tray of them.

Grandmère sat on one of the galley stools, watching me. "You can't always avoid that."

"I know."

"And we have enough cookies now. Stop this face your thoughts. I'm going to tell the men to get up here and set the table. You girls stop working this instant, or they'll all start to expect you to wait on them hand and foot. It sets a terrible precedent. They are going to clean up after dinner," she said. With that, she went down the staircase and we heard her go into the lounge and start bossing the guys around, telling them to go upstairs and help.

We all looked around at each other and finally smiled for real. My mother said, "They're cleaning up tonight and we're not, and it can continue that way after every meal as far as I'm concerned."

"I heard that!" Dad said, coming out of the stairwell. He and Hamish started getting the plates and salad bowls out. Uncle Charlie and Peter were right behind them, getting the flatware. "The boys washed up this morning, so we'll set the table."

Grandmère gave him an impish grin. "You'll wash up this evening, too. I know you older males set the table this morning to avoid getting stuck washing, drying, and putting things away."

Uncle Charlie groaned but said nothing.

We knew what the guys had spent the past hour and a half doing. They had been going over the details of what was happening on the land that we left behind, over and over and over again.

Dinner was a subdued affair, and I went out to the bridge with Aaron's food before we all ate. Aaron asked if they could sit at the table with us, one at a time, instead, and I said yes. Ed sat with us first, then Aaron. They looked as though they were in fact managing to get a decent amount of sleep.

Ed ate his food quietly, pausing once to tell me that he was enjoying it and appreciating the taste of fresh food more lately. I said it was the taste of non-genetically modified organisms and smiled impishly for a moment. Then I asked, "Have you either read J.R.R. Tolkien's stories of Middle Earth, with the Hobbit, the Elves, and so on?"

"Yes…why?"

"Do you remember when the Dwarves ate as guests of the Elves at Rivendell and it was heavy on salads?" He nodded. "Well, that's the Regenics diet. The Elves are immortal, so of course their diet would feature lots of grains, fruits, vegetables, and other healthy choices."

"Ah." Ed got it. He grinned back, got a couple of cookies from the galley and went out to relieve Aaron, who soon came to table to eat his dinner. It was much easier this way than to drag everything up to the bridge over and over again. We had talked them into it today. It was also nice to have them sit with us, even though it was one at a time. I hoped they could rest and relax more when we got to Switzerland. This must be a very tiring and taxing trip for them.

Aaron came down to eat next, and said he had seen us when we were about halfway through watching the middle of the West Hartford MRAP video on his way up to the bridge. "I guess it feels real now," he added. "We weren't just playing some sick joke on you all. Home is ruined. Well, several of your homes."

That was true…our house had been left alone, as had our neighborhood, because those homes were within easy walking distance of the center of West Hartford. But Fairview Cemetery was dug up, and the less expensive homes that had sprawled outwards from West Hartford Center were gone. I wondered who lived near our house. Banksters relatives?

The men did wash the dishes, after which we stayed upstairs in the lounge. The view of the open ocean was the same, with no other ships on it. Curious about that, I went upstairs to the bridge and checked the GPS display there. Aaron turned around and pointed out a little dark blue dot. "That's us," he said. "The other dots, the red ones, are the ships that we are staying out of sight of – Coast Guard, Navy, freighter ships, whatever."

"What about the little yellow dots?"

"Those are other privately-owned boats, like this yacht. We don't want to encounter them either," he told me.

"And what about fishing boats?"

"Those would be purple dots, if they were out there, but they aren't being allowed out for the time being, which makes it easier for us to avoid detection."

"We don't have all those dots in the cabin GPS displays. It would be nice if they showed elsewhere, though, like in the living room, the galley, and the library lounge," I said.

Aaron glanced at me, touched a few keys on the controls in front of him, and said, "Done."

"Thanks."

I went back downstairs and explained the dots to everyone else. Soon they couldn't look at anything else. This went on until Grandmère said that it was unhealthy and we should watch a movie, so I suggested *The Hundred-Foot Journey* and passed the DVD box for it around. People said "Okay," and I started the movie up, but they kept glancing at the GPS screen nonetheless.

The next day, we all ate cereal and fruit for breakfast and sat in the living room again all morning, followed by an equally normal, no-frills lunch. Aaron and Ed went in and out to eat, and we liked being able to see them and talk to them. It was good to just interact with them and feel like they were part of our group.

But when we met in the library-lounge again, it felt different. Hamish passed out nanite guns to every person in the room, including Grandmère. "It's the law in Switzerland that every adult, both men and women, be armed, so get used to packing a weapon now. Wear clothing with pockets and keep your guns in the pockets, not in your purses," he added.

"Make sure that those are deep, useful pockets, not form-fitting, shallow, useless ones," I added, showing my own nanite gun.

My family and the Woodward parents took their nanite guns and looked shocked. "Is this secret technology?" they wanted to know.

"It is," I told them. "Hamish invented this back in 2013, told absolutely no one, and then ended up using it on the Rockefeller Institute campus when Jared Clyde showed up. Clyde had a gun and was trying to kill me; Hamish fired a stream of nanites into his nervous system and had him helplessly writhing in agony instantly. When the N.S.A. saw that, they co-opted the guns. That left Hamish in possession of his own set of nanite guns, and forbidden to share the technology with the rest of the world. But...we're not the rest of the world."

More stares. "You are all becoming the champions of giving stunned stares," I remarked. "Listen carefully: the guns are nonlethal, but they ensure that you won't be pursued once fired. They are disabling. The problem with that is that once emptied, you have to have a way to immobilize your opponent before retracting and thus rearming your gun. If you release all of your nanites – notice the rocker switch and the fact that it has multiple settings of release, 1, 2, 3, 4, 5, and 6 – you won't have any more to defend yourself with."

"So it's just like a lethal gun in practice," Fabian commented. "Those have 6 bullets. How many nanites are we releasing with these things?"

Hamish told him, "They go out in batches of 30, and induce itching, stinging, and other maddening sensations. You can summon them all back into your gun, and the target won't feel ready to pursue you for a few minutes."

With that, he and Jason announced the second part of the presentation.

I didn't know what this part would be about.

"In case you are wondering what we must avoid running into once we get near Europe, and especially in the Mediterranean Sea, that is what I'm about to show you. I've managed to send groups of nanites – spybots – around to other areas of the world. It took a while, because they had to hitch rides on airplanes and then rides on motor vehicles to shipyards – European navy shipyards – but it's done now."

"So there's another reality horror show that I haven't seen yet?" I asked.

"Aye. Sorry about that. There was only so much I could show you and get us ready to leave."

"That's okay," I said.

"Hold that thought," Hamish replied, and the video feed began. "We are just in time to see this in real time. This particular group of nano-spybots is catching up with a large, converted navy ship from France. It set off from the Bay of Biscay a few minutes ago."

As we watched, the scene resembled a movie, with a view moving fast over the ocean toward a huge ship. The nanobots flew up onto the deck, and we heard a deafening sound. Where was it coming from? The nanobots flew around the ship's upper decks, providing a view of the crew, all of whom had large assault rifles, and the officers, who had pistols in holsters on their belts.

Then the view moved inside the ship, and down. The first level was just more hallways, until the nanobots came to a little control room. A computer screen and panel stretched across a console, and a window looked out over a huge, cavernous area that stretched out below decks. It was the largest hold I had ever seen. It looked as though a navy ship had been gutted, leaving standing room only down below.

That area was filled with people. They weren't dressed.

We looked from the screen to Hamish and back again. "Watch," he said.

"Oh shit," I said. "It's a mobile Auschwitz!"

Hamish sighed. "You always figure things out so fast…but there's no Zyklon B."

At least lunch had been light. I doubted that the people in that hold had eaten for quite a while. I guessed we would find out what the earlier part of their journey had been like later on, once we knew the ending, and more about who they were.

I looked at their faces, and at their clothing, and noticed something else. "They don't look like native French people."

"Very observant," my husband said. "Most of them aren't. "Europe doesn't consider itself to be overpopulated per se. It's the people from elsewhere who have migrated north for the past few decades who are being culled first. They are from almost anywhere south of Europe, for the most part, Arab nations, Africa, etc., and largely Muslim. There may be a few Romany people in there also." Europe had never been very good to its own nomadic tribespeople.

We looked back at the screen, still up in that little computer console area. The ship's captain and a couple of other officers were in there. They started pressing buttons. There were lights beaming into that huge, cavernous area on the confused people below. They were jostling each other a bit, but treating each other politely. Damn...I had seen this scene before, in World War II movies, both historical fiction and documentaries.

The nanobots turned back to the officers in the console room, and I realized that Jason was panning the view around like a movie director. The method was just right. "I hope you guys are saving recordings of all this for historical purposes. If we survive all this and can ever tell, and ruin the reputations of the Farmers, that would be just fine," I told him and Hamish.

"Oh, we are, even if we haven't figured that part out as yet," Hamish replied.

The officers were pressing buttons now. "That one is a strong anesthesia," Hamish said. "It will put everyone to sleep. Notice that there is nothing to hang on to; the walls are smooth." We all looked back at the screen, wide-eyed. People could not stay awake, despite their best efforts. Minutes later, they had all fallen down, some on top of small children and the elderly.

The officers pressed another button, which was to the right of the first one. "That's poison," Hamish said. "It's the ship's exhaust fumes, blown into that chamber. Like a staged garage suicide on an exponential scale," he summed up.

As we watched, the ship's doctor er, coroner, studied the readings. "Ils sont tous mort," we heard him say.

"Now what?"

"Did you notice the walls?"

I looked at them. They looked...charred. "Oh...I get it."

No one else did.

That didn't matter. The officer at the computer console entered a code, and the upper sides of the cavernous room began to fold down over the bodies within, until they closed with a clang. The officer entered another code. The nanobots turned back to the newly folded-down roof halfway below, and it glowed in hues of bright orange tinged with yellow.

The convertible, mobile crematorium took hours to do its job, and Hamish said that the view would not change much. He shut that video-feed off and brought up a pre-recorded video instead. It showed the roof panels opening up onto nothing but gray ashes, which were vacuumed out of the chamber, through a filter, up to the water level, and out of the ship.

We all looked around at each other, appalled.

At last, I spoke again. "How did they all get to that cavernous hull of genocide? Do you have the earlier part of this European reality horror show for us? Is that the other half of yesterday's upset? Because we haven't been in here long enough to call this another half yet."

My mother gave me a sideways glance, swiveling her head slowly to look at me.

Hamish said, "Yes, unfortunately, we have the rest."

It was like another version of a REX 84. People were collected from wherever they were, weak from the combination vaccines, some already showing the obvious signs of cancer. Those signs included disorientation, sluggishness, a jowly appearance to their faces, and either ballooning weight or gauntness.

They were taken directly to the navy ports, to a huge warehouse, and ordered to strip down. Soldiers walked among everyone, and when anyone refused to strip – often women – they were clubbed with heavy night-sticks, just like we had seen in the U.S. Then the officers removed everything, stuffing it all into bags. Earrings were ripped out of earlobes and necklaces yanked off. Watches went into separate bags. Apparently, people weren't forced to give those things up before the long truck or bus ride in Europe.

When everyone was stripped and thoroughly helpless, they were marched through a long, raised tunnel that served as a gangplank. That took a while, but the soldiers managed it. Babies, toddlers, tweens, adolescents, young adults, middle-aged adults, and elderly people of both genders all went through. At the end of it was the stairwell that led to another ship's huge, cavern of death and evidence concealment. Some other group of nanobots had gathered this travesty of reality show video footage.

Hamish paused the presentation for a moment. "The rest is just the same appalling stuff, so the next thing to talk about is a quick review of what is being done elsewhere in the world. India and Africa don't have the resources to make ships of death, so they are using Ebola and Marburg viruses in Africa, and I'm not sure what in India. I have some guesses, but I don't know yet. China is shooting people, and Japan actually has honor hara-kiri rituals and voluntary beheadings of elderly people. Japan had more elderly people than young ones, and they hope to avoid dying alone, unnoticed for weeks in their homes until people wonder why no one has seen them lately."

Next, he showed us a computer display with dots like the ones on the GPS screens upstairs and in this room. I realized that he had simply accessed that system, displayed it on the large flatscreen, and was moving the view around to the Mediterranean Sea.

"Those other cavernous hulls of genocide can be seen here. Their dots are black, appropriately enough. We have to avoid them all the way." He zoomed outward, and we saw black dots surrounding Europe, the Middle East, Turkey, Russia, Scandinavia, and the British Isles. There was even one near Iceland.

"What was that filter part of the murder system that we just saw?" Claire asked.

I knew without asking. "It does an automated looting job on the corpses, collecting whatever of value didn't turn to ash, such as gold or gemstones, and any electronics. The U.S. mobile crematoria do that, too. When the Nazis murdered people in their Zyklon B chambers, they forced teams of captive Jews, called the Sonderkommandos, to do that by hand. Mostly, the Sonderkommando guys were removing gold fillings. These people still had some jewelry on."

She stared at me, and then closed her mouth. There was really nothing more to add to that. We didn't want dinner until much later that day. People sat weakly in the sofas and chairs for a while, then gradually vacated the room.

Hamish and Jason packed up, and I suddenly thought of something. Dad and his cameras were a potential liability. That hobby, if seen in play from a distance, could be a problem. "We must keep Dad from being seen out on the deck of the yacht with his camera…if he were seen photographing those cremation ships, we would instantly become a target for annihilation," I told my husband.

He looked up at me, stared for a moment, and then gave his equipment to Jason to lock up. Hamish headed for the stairs, going up to look for Dad, I realized. I followed. Dad and Uncle Charlie were outside, chatting on the back deck. There were cushioned seats out there. Hamish and I explained why we had come to find him.

Dad listened, did a double take, and promised not to point his camera at anything outside the ship at any time. Family photographs were okay, we told him, and Hamish said that it wouldn't matter in Lausanne. My mother had appeared, and she listened to all this too.

"Life as we know it is over," she said. We all nodded glumly.

"We're passing Newfoundland," Hamish told us over dinner. "We'll be taking on fuel tonight, at around eleven, so don't panic when you see company off the bow. We're going to avoid Iceland altogether."

It was a bizarre sight when the Blackout tanker arrived, but we were glad to be speeding across the North Atlantic with a full tank.

The ocean got a bit choppy the next day, tossing the yacht a bit, so Claire and I had to stop doing yoga and sit down. Too bad; Hamish had made sure that there were enough yoga mats for us all. Anne and my mother and Aunt Zoe had already tried it a couple of times. Grandmère wouldn't having anything to do with the stretches, of course. We didn't expect her to.

Claire and I got settled with books, but I realized I would get motion-sick if I read like this, so I soon stopped. For lunch, I served vegetarian items, fruit and bread. That was the best thing when dealing with motion-sickness, and several people had it.

Six days later, after navigating our way past the black dots, still seeing no one else, we got within sight of the Danish Faroe Islands, and then the Orkney Islands, which were off the northeastern coast of Scotland. The Shetland Islands were even farther out in that direction. We crossed in between the island groups in the early evening, which was as light as midday in late August, and moved south. The black dots were elsewhere, and we were just north of Rosehearty.

We ended up staying awake until 2 a.m., which wasn't bad. It was a fairly smooth extraction, as far as non-military extractions of willing relatives went. We were removing Fiona, William, and their cat, with a suitcase each, from their small stone house on the coast, well away from the center of town. It was pretty much on the outskirts of that tiny town.

Hamish said that the British cull plan was to convert Rosehearty back into a tiny village. It had been fairly small anyway (1,300 people), but people who had been frightened while living in big cities had moved back to villages, increasing their sizes. Rosehearty was no exception, having swelled to almost 2,000 and counting, and the government was chasing these cull refugees, hunting them mercilessly. We would get Fiona out of there before the cull could touch her. The place was slated to be scaled back (what a way to put it!) to around 450 people.

"Isn't there already some sign of a government op in Rosehearty?" I asked Hamish.

"Aye, there is, but I've checked with my sources, and we should get there a few days before the MRAPS and camps arrive. People who went there from Edinburgh and Glasgow and Inverness are already showing some signs of sickness, though, Fiona told me. She's nervous, but she knows we're coming to get her. She just doesn't know how we're going to do that. I told her to pack light and bring her cat, and that's all," Hamish said.

Fiona had a British shorthair cat named Mallory. Those cats were beautiful, white with black tiger-stripe patterns and no other colors. I had seen Mallory on Fiona's Facebook page, and she had e-mailed me some images to keep. This cat was very cuddly and sweet; it showed in the photographs. I hoped she would get along well with Spock and Eowyn.

Aaron took off in the helicopter to get them. All was going well until it was time to go, he later told us. The cat would not cooperate. She heard the rotors of the helicopter and Fiona could not get her into the carrier. William, a huge, barrel-chested guy with a mane of snowy white hair and a beard, had to go crouching outside to explain what was happening. He gave Aaron the luggage as he did so.

Aaron actually decided to shut down the helicopter. I didn't know he loved cats that much. Or maybe he just thought that it was the fastest solution, but it worked. He went inside with William, and just as they got in, Fiona managed to lock Mallory into her cage. She grabbed her handbag and followed the men out.

"Passports?" Aaron asked. They showed them. With that, Aaron turned on the helicopter, had them put on seatbelts and headphones, and took off into the night. Soon they were landing on top of the yacht, and walking down the outer staircase and into the galley.

Hamish and I ran from the living room area, where my parents and aunt and uncle had been sitting with us, into the galley. Fiona came down after William, who was helping her to maneuver the cat carrier in front of her on the stairs. She was in jeans and a sweater with sneakers – she called them trainers – and her snowy white hair was twisted up into a clip.

Fiona and Hamish looked like male and female versions of one another. I hadn't seen her in years; we had visited at our wedding, of course. She and Hamish hugged, and William shook hands with me and introduced himself. They were all taller than me…story of my life, but so what? I was excited. They were here with us, safe!

Fiona turned to me and smiled…no, grinned a wide grin like her brother's grin.

I grinned back and gave her a big hug. "You're safe! Well, safer, and with us."

"Aye," she said, sounding like a contralto version of her brother. "Thank you!"

"Mrrow!" That sound came from the cat carrier on the floor.

"Oh!" I said. "Let's get you to your cabin immediately so your cat can come out and get used to that room." I led her downstairs. My mother and the others had followed us into the kitchen, however. A brief delay ensued for more greetings, so I grabbed Mallory's carrier and went down there myself.

"Good cat!" I said, giving her a slitted-eyed smile through the cage door. "What a pretty kitty you are. It's nice to meet you in person. I hope you aren't too upset from the trip over here," I carried on, cooing to her all the way. Poor cat. I knew it didn't really matter what I said to her; the idea was just to calm her and soothe her and get to the cabin.

When I got there, I flicked on the lights, shut the door, and let the cat out. She walked out slowly, suspicious and cautious, looking around at everything. I closed the cage door and stowed it in the closet on a side shelf. Even those shelves had brass rails. Mallory found the litter box in the bathroom, then her food and water dishes. She tried to go under the bed, but found drawers in her way. Poor confused, stressed-out cat! I petted her and smiled, and she settled down.

Fiona came in, dragging her suitcase behind her. "That Aaron is a great bloke," she said. "He was so nice! He made sure I had my cat safely in her carrier before we took off. I had been afraid that she would be difficult at the last minute, and she was, and that your pilot would insist on leaving without her, but he didn't!"

"Hamish and I worried about that too, and told him so," I replied.

"Ah, I see." She grinned, petting Mallory, who had leaped onto the bed, purring. "Listen to this girl, she's calm and happy enough now."

"We should leave her locked in here for a day or so to get used to it," I suggested. "There are two other cats on this ship for her to meet after that."

"Aye, I've seen your beautiful boy and girl on Facebook. Spock and Eowyn, right?"

"Right. You seem really calm for someone who was abruptly plucked from home," I said.

"Well, I was getting scared at home. Hamish was telling me that he couldn't explain over the phone or over any digital medium, but with his military and technical background, I was thoroughly spooked by it all. Life in Scotland is eerie. Large groups of people have been going missing without a trace – who neighborhoods of Glasgow, Aberdeen, Edinburgh, and towns all over the place."

I looked at her, listening, and realized that neither of us was smiling now. "We'll tell you the whole thing tomorrow. Eat light before you see and hear it, and tell William that, too."

She listened to that, and then said, "That sounds ominous."

"It is very ominous. But…that's another story. Are you hungry? Would you like some carrot soup and bread? Tea? Herbal tea? A scone? I made some cinnamon-cardamom-almond ones."

The grin reappeared. "Aye, a scone and some herbal tea sound nice."

"Great, let's go back up." We turned around in time to see William drag in the other suitcase. When he heard the offer of a scone and tea, he turned right around and came back upstairs with us. I liked him already.

In the galley, we all got scones and took them out to the living room. Aunt Zoe and Uncle Charlie excused themselves and went to bed, but the rest of us stayed. We were hungry from waiting up anxiously.

As we ate, I looked at Fiona and said, "So, you have a nice fiancé, we can see. Show me your ring!" I could see glimpses of it from time to time, but I wanted a good look. "I'm sick of ominous thoughts. Show me something happy and pretty."

She grinned and put her left hand into my two hands. "T'is an aquamarine, round brilliant, with a small round diamond on either side, in white gold."

"It's beautiful," I said, and I really thought so. "Is it exactly what you wanted?"

"Yes, he asked me what I would like." William smiled across to us.

The next day, with his sister and her fiancé comfortably settled and unpacked, Hamish waited only until after breakfast to give them the crash course in reality horror show and genocidal mania around the world. Part One was before lunch, and Part Two after. I sat through it, leaving all meal preparations that day to others.

At last the deed was done, and there was nothing else to do but travel the rest of the way to Lausanne by way of horror at sea. By dinnertime, Mallory had bolted from her cabin and met the other cats, and we could hear little feet barreling around the yacht. Fiona and William readily agreed to abide by the rule of not letting any cats out on deck.

William was into cameras, and had brought a nice one with him. He and Dad hit it off immediately. Soon they were going over their equipment in the living room, and Hamish had to warn William the way he had warned Dad about the danger of using it where anyone on any other ship could see. He got the message.

We had a couple of close calls as we went around the Iberian Peninsula with the black dots, but then Ed realized that they were farther off than they appeared on the GPS displays. I think everyone was getting tired and antsy from the stress of the trip at that point.

When we went through the Strait of Gibraltar, we saw no one around. Security was lax there. The navies must have assumed that either not too many people would actually be out there, or they were letting yachts through. I say that because I saw other yacht-dots on the display.

Aaron avoided them anyway.

I felt a bit sorry for Ed and Aaron in the Mediterranean Sea. They hardly slept, it seemed. They were constantly alert, and Hamish was watching a lot too. His laptop was out all day, and when I didn't see him checking on things, Jason was sitting in for him. They were totally off kitchen patrol, and we all knew why.

I couldn't believe it when we came to the Côte D'Azur of France. It looked so…normal. Provence looked as enticing as it always had, both in reality and in movies. We did have to show our passports to customs agents at the mouth of the river, and Hamish did have to call the clinic in Lausanne, but it was midafternoon on a Tuesday, so we reached them easily. The douaniers (French customs officials) verified everything, and that was it.

We were going up the Rhône before we knew it. "Can Aaron and Ed rest any easier now?" I asked Hamish as we moved up the river at a reduced speed of 5 knots.

"I think so. The MRAPs aren't going to appear, and the French government is still doing publicity videos that have to look nice and calm."

Once, as we passed Arles, I began to believe and accept that no one was after us.

We all sat in the upper levels of the *Shadowcat*, some on the back deck and others in the living room, watching as we moved through the French river, admiring the view. It was strange to think that I had stayed in this area with Nana, my maternal grandmother, over a decade ago, and to be back doing this. The area seemed less busy this time, of course. We had a ways to go up the Rhône, and we slept overnight during this part of the trip.

The GPS display had no dots to worry about anymore. Instead, we looked at the land around us. Nothing seemed amiss, and although I suspected that more monstrous evacuations were going on out there somewhere, nothing was apparent from the vantage-point of the *Shadowcat*.

Up north we went, and up: Arles…Orange…Valence…and we turned northeast, onto the Isère River. It had risen along with the sea levels and it had been decided that, rather than fight it with another huge infrastructure project, bridges would be removed for boat traffic. We were traveling through Grenoble…Chambéry…Annecy…Geneva! We had made it. The Swiss douanier checked our documents, called the clinic in Lausanne, and waved us through.

Ed and Aaron looked at me and Hamish like, we did it! And with that, they smiled, walked back up to the bridge, and piloted the yacht across Lake Geneva to Lausanne, where a reserved spot at a marina awaited us. Hamish had thought of and planned for everything.

Chapter 37

Population Matters

"We can't help most of the people out there, and they all deserve to live their lives."

Hamish just looked at me.

I was flopped on our bed, staring up at our cabin's ceiling, wondering how to feel about that.

He came over and flopped next to me, and put his arm across my waist.

"You must have known that all along. We were never going to be able to make a huge dent in the Farmers' agenda. But you didn't do this, and neither did I. It's not our fault. And you didn't just sit back and let it all happen."

"Uh huh." I was still spacing out, staring at the cloth above us. "Plutocracy, here we come."

"Look at me, Avril. It's not your fault. Live your life with me and try to enjoy it."

I looked at him at last. "I know. I guess I'm just thinking about all of the people who were and are being expediently murdered. They deserve that much, plus some sulking over their lost chances, at the very, very least. The population of every area matters. Don't you think so?"

Then Hamish said, "Of course. But I'm worried about you. I want you to stay out of trouble. Just be careful in Switzerland. I won't be able to rip out every RFID device in our work areas or in any hotels we stay in. Don't be too stressed out, but we should say everything that's on our minds before we go there and have to be careful. We can talk at home on this yacht, though. We will all have to be careful what we say for a while."

"I realize that. I'm trying to think of everything. But can we have a fire in our fireplace?"

"Aye. Why do you ask?"

"Oh, I'm just thinking low-tech at this point. If we absolutely have to say anything secret, we can write it down on a piece of paper and then burn it in the fireplace, right?"

He grinned. "Right."

"Genius!" We said to each other simultaneously, half-teasing, half serious.

"I love you."

"I love you too. You're the best guy in the world. You keep fighting back."

He kissed me., and I kissed back, and we went to sleep.

Chapter 38

Sabbatical in Neutral Territory

So there we were, settled in Switzerland.

It was neutral, it wasn't overpopulated, and it was self-sufficient.

We had to show our nanite guns to the Swiss official who came to inspect our supplies and weapons, just to prove that we too were armed and self-sufficient. After he tested Hamish's gun on his own wrist and nearly collapsed before Hamish had to take it from him and retract the nerve-jamming torture-bots, he pronounced us suitably armed and left.

With heat in every building provided by wood pellets from trees harvested in the laxly regulated forests of the southern United States, we looked back at our nation via a closed news channel and watched the chaos. It wasn't pretty.

Of course, neither were the personalities we had for company.

It seemed that many of the banksters and hedge fundsters had chosen to come here at the same time we did, and now we saw wealthy, entitled Americans every time we went out on the streets of Geneva. I hoped I wasn't looking in the mirror as I observed them, but doubted that at least some of my reflection wasn't sipping café au laits at the next table.

Leo Uberfein was one of the banksters who followed us.

Dad wanted to know how Hamish and I could be so sure that Uberfein was in any way behind the carnage at home. To answer that, Hamish had Jason punch up the data gleaned from a Dark Net search on who was funding the mobile crematoria. There, near the bottom, was Uberfein's name, along with the other banksters and hedge fundsters whose bodies we had guided the monster nanobots into. Dad peered at the list, said, "Huh," and walked off with a nod.

I started visiting Hamish at his new Regenics clinic once I had gotten a sense of what Lausanne was like. The clinic was beautiful, all new, modern, with wood paneling, floral metal work in designs that resembled the still-life watercolor art that we had seen in the Musée et Jardins botanique et cantonaux (mostly an iris design of cut-outs), and brightened with real floral arrangements in vases. A huge brag-wall of donors graced the entrance, in granite and glass.

Throughout the offices and laboratories, there was a theme color: lavender. It was the same hue as the Regenics serum. At least it was a pretty color, I thought, but then anything that regenerates you and heals the damage of the aging process should be. All of the cushions and curtains were that color, or else their patterns depicted flowers in it. Hamish later admitted to me that he had chosen a color that I liked for the serum, and advised both Jeffrey Nurse and Thierry Chavannes to decorate the Regenics clinics with it, and why. Clever!

As soon as Hamish had inspected the premises of his lovely new clinic, he had contacted our French relatives. They were staying at the Hostellerie Les Chevreuils in Lausanne, a nice, three-star hotel that he had booked them rooms at. There were quite a few of them.

There were Tante Adrienne Châtelet Poincaré and her husband, Oncle Pierre, plus their three adult married children and spouses. On my mother's side of the family, there were Oncle André, from Provence, and Tante Lisanne, with whom he ran a spice shop, and Tante Chloe, my one maternal aunt. She ran a chocolaterie nearby. Oncle André and Tante Lisanne also had adult children, both of whom were married with no kids yet. That was fifteen people to see.

Hamish made short work of personally checking their bloodwork. No nanites! Interesting; that spoke volumes about France's agenda and cull policy. Without a word to them about the cull, nanites, or anything about vaccines, he gave them each a dose of Regenics, explained what it was and, after a few days of visiting, they returned home to France. They seemed quite delighted with it all, and were fascinated with the change it had wrought on Grandmère.

If Hamish had found monster nanites in their systems, it would have been a very different story. We would have had to wait while he fixed them, explain everything on board the *Shadowcat*, and then keep them in Lausanne for the next year. But no…better to disclose nothing if they weren't being targeted for the cull. They could go home.

Soon after they got home, Tante Lisanne and Oncle André sent us a lovely thank-you note – well, a "merci" note – and a care package from their store. It contained all of the spices and dried French lavender that we could want. There was plenty for cooking and baking, and for scenting our cabins and bathrooms. Claire and I were the most excited about it, and she enjoyed hearing about the time I had spent in Provence with my mother's side of my family, years ago.

Seeing who was coming to this clinic for treatments was something that I had been putting off. Granted, I would not have access to patients' records, nor did I want them, but the patients themselves were sitting in the waiting areas. I would go in to visit Hamish at random times of day, often to drag him out for lunch at a nearby café, and there they would be.

They were clearly from many different nations, but they all had something in common: they were the wealthy, ruling, banking, elite. All were richly dressed and projected an air of confidence, calm, education, sophistication, and entitlement. They were of varying ages, but many were my age and Hamish's age, hoping to extend their own lifespans. I wondered how involved they were in shortening…or ending…the lifespans of others.

That was another thing I had to keep in mind: they could not all be guilty of doing such a thing. Some of them were relatives of those criminals, kept in ignorance of those crimes. Others, however, were definitely those criminals.

And they all recognized me as I walked through the waiting areas!

Of course they did. I was a famous author, co-inventor of Nae-Née, and every bit as sophisticated as they were in my own way, plus more educated than they were, and with a wide range of experiences that were unique to someone of my background. But I was disgusted to realize that such an awesome treatment was seemingly reserved for the elites of the world. It didn't seem so cool when I thought of it that way. Other people led mundane lives with no access to Regenics. But, Hamish said that once he got it established, he would find a way around that.

Often, I would have to pause and chat with people before I could make it all the way through to see Hamish. When I was sure that I was conversing with a criminal, I would sometimes deliberately get boring, delivering the most detailed,

Aspiest monologues about the museums of the city. I was doing to bring the interaction to a swift end without letting on what I thought of whomever I was talking to. It usually worked. When Hamish asked me about this, I told him what I was up to, and he approved.

When I asked Hamish why he had sent our French relatives off so soon after we had met up with them, he told me that the shorter our encounter with them, the better. We didn't know them well enough to risk telling them everything that we knew about the cull…or any of it. Once he knew that they weren't being targeted, it seemed wise to send them home, back to work and back to their routines. Grandmère approved of his strategy, and my parents and Uncle Charlie had had three days to spend with their siblings. It was fine.

Which brought him to his next caveat: under no circumstances, should we actually end up making friends here, was anyone to bring any guests on board the *Shadowcat*. Hamish looked at Claire, Fabian, Edgar, Jacques, and Jason in particular as he said so. And why was that? Because it was a blatant security risk. With that secret, encrypted Swiss news channel, we couldn't have anyone else coming on board and channel surfing in either the living room or the lounge.

Everyone around the dinner table gave him a shocked look, nodded, and kept eating.

About that news channel: the Swiss had access to real news, not faked news, and they gave us the access code to it. The Swiss computer engineers had put it together by using satellite and computer signals, plus an algorithm that Jason said had to be the best ever written because he and Hamish couldn't figure it out. They tried, but they couldn't break it, and they decided that it was better that way. No sense in aggravating our hosts just for the sake of curiosity.

Each device – computer, flatscreen television, hand-held device, whatever – had to have that access code programmed into it to see the Swiss news channel. The Lausanne clinic directors had gotten authorization for us to see that channel through their government, which meant that we got a visit from a Swiss computer expert to link our televisions and laptops to it.

We decided to skip the cabin televisions, though, and just have movie channels and other recreational stuff there. Watching the world burn while trying to fall asleep just wouldn't work, we realized. So, we had the ones in the living room and the library-lounge done…only those.

Hotels did not have this channel.

When I thought about why not, I surmised the answer with my usual speed and shared it with Hamish: the Swiss cities of Geneva and Davos often hosted United Nations summits. Since it was the United Nations that was driving this world-wide human population cull, it would be unwise to let any of its delegates see that private citizens of any nation, even Switzerland, had access to the truth.

That truth was as we had learned by hacking the data before leaving home, and during our journey to neutral territory. To find out the intricacies of what was a betrayal of its citizens by our own government, we had committed multiple acts that that same government would deem to be federal crimes and even treason. Well, we said, the hell with our government's point of view, since they were the criminals!

The Swiss could see everything that was happening in the world.

Their citizens knew that the Americans and Canadians were poisoning their citizens with cancer-inducing nanites, delivered in deliberately tainted vaccines, and then rounding them up as they got sick. The Swiss knew about the mobile concentration camps and crematoria.

The same was happening all over Brazil, and in several other South and Central American nations. News commentators wryly noted that water supply shortages in places such as São Paulo, Rio de Janeiro, and Mexico City would soon go away, drought or no drought. It was simple, appalling arithmetic, the commentator summed up. With fewer people making demands on the water table, there would be enough for everyone left alive.

The Swiss citizens knew that the rest of Europe – the European Union that surrounded their nation – was rounding up those whom it considered to be "excess persons" and taking them out to sea to die on board cremation ships. We saw one example that dealt with immigrants to Malta, an island nation in the Mediterranean Sea.

For over a decade, there had been an area with cargo containers that served as housing to African immigrants. It got horridly hot in summertime for anyone dwelling there, and these people were stuck in immigration limbo for years on end, because Maltese society had no place for them. The Maltese solved this problem with a cremation ship, and it didn't take them very long. The reason was simple enough: no one was getting out of Africa anymore.

And why was that? Ebola and Marburg viruses, helped along by a deliberate carelessness on the part of the authorities in African nations, plus those same nanobot-toting vaccines. Those vaccines had been experimented with on African citizens in the name of charity organizations for over a decade. Now they were proclaimed ready for use, and "donated" to all. Reported numbers of people stricken with fatal, disfiguring, and horridly painful cancers were around 90 percent. There were no crematoria, and so no escape from a painful, drawn-out death.

India was the same, as was Indonesia. The difference in India was that the illnesses were solely cancer-related, and thus vaccine-induced. Cremation was used with regularity and efficiency, and the government managed to enforce it fairly well. The River Ganges was soon choked with corpses and ashes, despite pleas not to pollute it and warnings that the ecosystem could not absorb all that human death. Indian engineers were already at work dealing with that question, plotting water purification methods to remediate the damage.

In Indonesia, more damage was done by those "donated" vaccines that any tsunami.

The same was true of the Philippines, except that the damage was compared to typhoons.

As for the Middle East, Jason had discovered that there was a plan to divest oil interests just ahead of any announcement that fusion energy had been harnessed. Not only that, but fusion energy was not as far off as the world had been led to expect. The tainted vaccines had been dispensed throughout the Islamic world.

Thanks to the high consumption rates of trigger foods, it was only a matter of time before the population suffered huge die-offs. I remembered how much of the juices that people drank there contained high-fructose corn syrup, and sugar consumption was off the charts. Killing off the competition for resources wasn't a difficult proposition.

This was going to make the banksters of the United States and of other nations where the financial meltdown had led to buy-outs by Arab very, very happy. Arabs owned whole skyscrapers, hotels, parking garages, and other coveted properties in North America, and the American elites wanted a way to buy them back. The cull would help them a lot.

The incredible aspect of this, at least to us and to the Swiss, was that, all the while, the United Nations continued its urging to people everywhere to please, please get vaccinated and protect themselves from a litany of illnesses. Patients in economically depressed nations with little access to education and information just kept on lining up for the injections, hoping that they would prevent one virus or another when in fact it caused cancer.

And then there was China.

The Chinese seemed to have little regard not only for human life, but also for keeping up appearances. They were quite honest about what was going on inside their borders. It was a ghastly irony to realize that, due to a dictatorship form of government, China had never concerned itself with any veneer of legitimacy or humanity.

It had simply declared that its population was too large to accommodate with food, clothing, shelter, clean air, clean water, and education, and with that, it began with the injections. But these injections were of China's own making: formaldehyde. This was no soft-kill. It was a fast, hard-kill, with no vaccine to explain away what was being done. It was a straight-up cull.

Australia and New Zealand were terrifying their own rights. Their governments had not been sneaky enough with the vaccination cull campaign, and it was all-out chaos after the job was about half done. Soon there was personal security as a chaotic resource war took over. I swear, it felt like we were watching a *Mad Max* movie without Mel Gibson or Tina Turner in it. It was more like an early Russell Crowe skinhead flick I had seen bits and pieces of long ago, and it wasn't pretty.

Since nothing in our present reality was pretty, I left the *Shadowcat* to visit museums in Lausanne as often as to visit the clinic that Hamish was settling into. Whenever I had to adapt to new surroundings, this had always been my method: I would see the culture and cuisine of the area, walk around if possible, and quietly get used to the place while trying to enjoy it.

I was trying to love Lausanne, and it wasn't difficult. The place was attractive, the food was delectable, and the cultural attractions were fascinating. It would be quite a while before I had memorized the contents of the museums, and that was just fine.

Hamish knew what I was doing, so after a tour of the clinic, he sent Aaron off with me for most of my wanderings. Ed preferred to be at the clinic. Ed was a lost cause and a hopeless case; he just wasn't interested in reading or cultural experiences like Aaron was.

There was just one exception: it was, interestingly enough, an Olympic Museum. The very idea fascinated me, and I didn't even care much about sports. When I announced my intent to visit it, I suggested that Ed might like to accompany me instead of Aaron, and he actual seemed excited about that. The family all laughed at his reaction, because they had gotten to know him too over the past month.

The Olympic Museum was part art museum and part history museum. It had been set up in 1993, and it had 3 areas of focus: Olympic World, which was a history of the games going back to ancient Greece, plus Olympic torches, which was fun; Olympic Games, which interested Ed the most; and Olympic Spirit, which included examples of Olympic Villages as well as Olympic medals. The medals were newly designed for each set of games, so I had fun looking at them all.

By the time I had seen enough, Ed was getting antsy, and I teased him for that. Dinner was on the *Shadowcat* that evening, so Aaron teased him some more. The two of them ate meals with the rest of us now that we were moored in place. They were quiet a lot, but could be funny when they started teasing each other. They seemed just like any pair of cops, special agents, or other pairs in a cop show, bantering, complaining, and otherwise interacting with one another.

Other museums in the area included one that I was immediately drawn to: the Musée historique de Lausanne. Anything about history drew me in, Grandmère pointed out, but she wanted to come with me, Fiona, Claire, my mother, and Aunt Zoe. Anne was at her new job at the Lausanne Regenics Clinic, as was Peter, who was handling the electrical engineering of whatever equipment Hamish required. This museum was founded in 1918, and covered Lausanne's history, with particular focus on the 17th century to the present.

As often as not, Claire and my mother wanted to come with me to see the art museums, which included the Fondation de l'Hermitage, the Cantonal Museum of Fine Arts (Musée cantonal des beaux-arts), and the Musée de L'Élysée, which housed a collection of photography equipment and photographs of all kinds, such as lithographs, and Charlie Chaplin's entire collection.

The Fondation de l'Hermitage had a great restaurant, so all of us women went to that one, along with William, Fabian, Dad, and Uncle Charlie. Hamish insisted upon working, and said he would visit that museum with me another time. That was fine; there was plenty more to see that we could take in over the course of just one day.

When this wave of self-guided tourism and work began, it meant that no one was watching the *Shadowcat*. We would all be out of it for hours on end. Hamish was ready with more watchers from Blackout Security, which came as no great surprise. I hadn't seen Jack or Rick since visiting Hamish's lab in Avon, Connecticut, but suddenly, there they were.

They had gotten a flight out of the U.S. on a private, Blackout-owned jet just before the world-wide travel ban had gone into effect. I didn't know them like Ed and Aaron, of course, not having traveled with them, so they didn't feel almost like family, but they were friendly enough.

Sometimes they accompanied me and whatever other relatives on my whirlwind museum tour. I was working my way through a list of them, like it was an academic assignment, even though I did intend to revisit the ones I liked best in depth later. Fiona came with me to the Cantonal Museum of Archaeology and History (Musée cantonal d'archéologie and d'histoire), and we were quietly shadowed that time by Rick. He stood nearby, wearing a long, gray trench coat, keeping pace with us throughout the visit.

The Cantonal Museum of Money (Musée monétaire cantonal) intrigued me and Claire. We saw coins from all over the planet, from what seemed to be every civilization throughout human history, right up to the present. There were weights and measures, too, demonstrating how different currencies were checked against one another when travelers met bankers and merchants. Often, there had been questions as to whether or not a foreign coin was of equal value to a local one, which was the point of using the scales and weights.

Claire asked me early on about the term "canton" in many of the museums' names. I told her that the Swiss divided their nation into voting units called cantons, just like the United States had states, Canada had provinces, and France had départements. She got it and nodded, satisfied.

Claire and I were getting to know each other. She was very nice, and I could see why Fabian had fallen in love with her. She also had a lot of questions, some of which were, not surprisingly, about the family. For example, "Why aren't you close with your cousins from France, even though you and they are the same age, but you are close to their parents, who are older than you?" That was a good one.

"Well, it's partly an Aspie thing and partly a cultural thing," I told her. "They think they are far cooler than me and always have because they are all neurotypical and I am different from them. It bothers them when I know things – obscure facts – that they have to look up. I just remember them. As for the cultural aspect of it, you'll have to watch out for the exact same thing: we Americans have a sharp, nasal accent. French people love to hold their noses and mimic it. It's tedious. I mean, yes, all things French are tasteful and beautiful, and the food delectable, but that doesn't mean that they have the right to act like twits."

"Wow," Claire replied. "That was very…honest."

I laughed. "You're trustworthy, and you don't act like that to me, so I like you. You're going to become a formal and official part of this family at some point, so why not tell you things that will prepare you for dealing with that?"

She smiled, and it was sincere. I liked her. "Thank you," she said.

"You're welcome." We were out walking around Lausanne, looking randomly at shops. I paused at one of them. It offered duvets, sheets, curtains, and throw pillows, and customers could choose the pattern. The patterns were pretty, too. I opened the door and walked in, and Claire followed me, thinking we were just browsing.

But we weren't. I had been thinking about something for a while. "What sorts of things do you find attractive?" I asked her. "I just want to get a sense of your personal aesthetics."

She stared at me, nonplussed. "Why?"

"So I can get to know you better, of course. I'm not a telepath, I like you, and I'm curious."

"Okay…" She looked around. After a couple of minutes, she said that she liked a sample with pink tea roses and violets on a pale blue background. The floral pattern was well-defined, not that stupid, ugly cartoonish crap that had been the only floral pattern I could find for the past decade in the United States. Damn the fashion industry for that!

"That's beautiful!" I said. "I love that. Too bad this sort of thing isn't what's most available in the United States. It used to be, when I was a teenager, but then Laura Ashley got an idiot buyer who made everything like other companies' stuff, and the business failed. No pockets, no more cotton, and no more pretty floral patterns."

Claire agreed; she even talked on convincingly about how she wanted that stuff too. She wore a lot of vintage clothing with floral patterns, so I believed her. We looked around for a couple minutes more, admiring it all. I could tell she wasn't going to change her selection.

"Well, that was interesting. Want to go? I think I saw a chocolaterie down the street."

"Yes! That sounds great." We headed out, and I took a business card on the way.

I wanted to cheer Claire up. Her parents were most likely dead, gone with the MRAPs and mobile crematoria, and between her and Edgar, we were all worried. I kept taking her out with me to spoil her with beautiful sights, sounds, and treats. One thing that was a bit surreal to us as we wandered around Lausanne was the fact that we kept getting mistaken for sisters. She said it was the Regenics formula. "Do you realize that you now have no white hairs left? We really do look like we're both in our twenties now. And your husband looks like he's in his thirties!"

"Wow. Cool! I'll have to take another look in the mirror later," I said, grinning.

There was also something else on my mind about her. Edgar's situation may have been less amenable to cheering up, but I could actually think of something to do for Claire. I dragged Hamish into our cabin as soon as he got home that evening and said, "Is there any way you might be willing to let Jason sleep in the bed in the cabin that is also your ship's lab?"

He looked at me, puzzled. "I hadn't planned on that, but why do you ask?"

"Because we don't know how long we will all be here, and Fabian and Claire ought to be sharing a room if they want to. Jason is the one I would consider most likely to handle himself carefully enough in there, and Jacques and Edgar could double up. Also, I was out with Claire today, and we went into this shop that does custom duvets, curtains, the works, and I actually managed to subtly induce her to tell me which pattern she likes best."

He stared at me for a moment, then sat down and laughed. "You win. Call the shop with the measurements and order the stuff. I'll tell Jason to move."

"Thanks!" I kissed him. "But wait until I talk to Claire first. I'll do that next. I think she's in her room, so go out, say nothing to anyone about this, and I'll get her to come in here. If that goes well, I'll bring it up at dinnertime with everyone present. That would be the most efficient way of getting this done, anyway."

"Okay." He kissed me and left.

I went out into the hallway, knocked on Grandmère and Claire's cabin door, and found Claire in there, reading a novel on her e-reader. "Hi Claire. Can you come into my room and talk for a minute?" She looked worried, but got up and followed me back in.

When she heard what I had in mind, she shrieked with delight and hugged me. "Thank you!"

I hugged back and leaped up slightly because I was so pleased myself. Then I stood back, grinning from ear to ear. "I don't know how long we're here for, and I don't want you to feel like your life is stalled because of this getaway."

She looked at me like I shouldn't feel awkward at all, which was sweet. "Oh no – you're doing anything but that. It's not your fault that the world has gone crazy! Why would you feel that way?!"

"Because you are engaged and rooming with your future grandmother-in-law, that's why! I thought it would seem as though we were applying ageist, double standards to you and Fabian. I mean, from the start, Hamish plotted the cabins with you and Grandmère, and another for his sister to share with her fiancé…and they weren't even on the yacht yet when we left."

"I never thought that."

I was so relieved I hugged her, and she hugged back. Then I explained the game plan for the room switch. She agreed to go along with that method. But first…we went downstairs with pen, paper, and the measuring tape from my sewing kit to size up the curtains. Then it was back up to my cabin while I called that shop. They were still open! I explained what I wanted, and that I needed help converting American measurements to whatever system they used, and they were very nice – no making me feel like a dope for not knowing the conversions myself.

The woman who spoke with me said that the goods would arrive tomorrow evening.

Perfect! I said, "Merci beaucoup," and ended the call.

"Avril?" Claire said.

"Yes?"

"I don't want to give up my last name when I marry your cousin."

I turned around and gave her an elated grin. "Ooh…company in feminism – I love it! What did Fabian say when you told him? He does understand that he has no ownership rights over your surname, right?"

"I haven't mentioned it yet. It's just something I've been thinking about."

"Then get on with it so that he adjusts to the idea fast. Don't give him time on that. Accept no wishful nonsense from a guy. He'll do fine. And don't tell anyone else until you've dealt with that issue. Marriage negotiations should be a fait accompli before sharing them. Don't worry."

She nodded, and I was pleased to see that she didn't look worried about that conversation.

The dinnertime announcement went smoothly, and no one looked disapproving. Grandmère even spoke up to say that it was only fair, and that she would enjoy having that big cabin all to herself. She started to suggest a switch to the lower level, and Claire, my mother, Fabian, and I all roared, "No!" so she dropped that idea. Nice, but we didn't want her alone on yet more stairs. Sure, Regenics was making her seem like an eighty-year-old, but let's not get stupid over it, I admonished. She grinned impishly at me for that.

The next day, the good were delivered, and I tipped the representative from the shop and sent him off, insisting that we would install the curtains ourselves. We did, too. We did not allow any strangers on board the *Shadowcat*, as per Hamish's previous orders…for all we knew, it could be a hit man from the C.I.A. or N.S.A. or whatever. No thanks.

Claire and I had no trouble, and she was thrilled with the result. Fabian came in, said he loved it, and that was that. Yeah…he ought to do just fine being married, I thought to myself. Already, Claire was in charge of aesthetics and he was okay with that. I later told her that it was one of the most fun aspects of being married. She grinned. I knew it…she loved it too.

Once the move was complete and the goods installed, my relentless tour of museums resumed. On all of them, I found fabulous bookshops. Each time, I found that I could not resist first staring like a kid in a candy shop at the wares and then buying some to take home with me. Home was now the *Shadowcat*, but there was plenty of room in the bookshelves, both in the living room and in the library-lounge downstairs. Anyone who had skipped a museum soon found a book from it to peruse that evening.

Hamish couldn't skip them all however, even if he was getting settled into a new lab. I dragged him out of there a couple of times in the first few weeks, insisting that all work and no play was bad for him, and that he had to spend some time with me. Never mind that we were together nonstop just to get here, I added. Learning about a place was my work, and he had to participate in some of it! He agreed.

There was the Musée de la Main (Museum of the Hand), founded by a surgeon who pioneered procedures to repair injuries to the human hand from work-related accidents. Everything there was in French, but that was no obstacle to me. It was, however, an obstacle to Hamish, who was fascinated by the topic, so we spent a few days there, on several visits, until he had seen all that intrigued him.

I suspected that he would incorporate what he had learned there into his own work. Hmm…some date! When I realized that my first attempt to get him to have fun had led to more work, albeit fascination as well, I insisted that he accompany me to another place. This was one that could not possibly induce work or concentration. It was a romantic excursion.

"Hamish, the reason why I insisted that you do this now and not whenever you felt like taking a day off is that when fall starts, it will be too late to do this until next year. It's already late September."

He agreed; we had to go out together while the weather was warm.

What was this idea? It turned out that there was one nice garden to enjoy in Lausanne. It was called the Cantonal Botanical Museum and Gardens (Musée et Jardins botanique et cantonaux). Okay, it also had an indoor section, but we spent that part of the visit staring at the most beautiful watercolors of flowering and other plants that it felt like a date. Hamish held my hand and stood staring at many of the paintings with his arm around me also, so no wonder it did.

The museum dated back to the year 1824, and was filled with collections of seeds, dried and pressed samples of every plant ever gathered by is botanists, catalogues, and it all covered the natural history of the canton of Lausanne. I must admit that we bypassed most of this, walking rather quickly through it all to the garden.

The Jardins botanique were a lovely maze of curving winding paths in the middle of a busy city, and we went there on a sunny day. I had insisted that Hamish agree to go on a random day, depending upon the weather. He in turn had checked the forecast and arranged his schedule accordingly. I couldn't really blame him for that; patients would soon appear at his clinic. It relaxed him sufficiently that we enjoyed strolling among medicinal, alpine, herbal, and other plants, wandering through an arboretum and an orangery, and seeing carnivorous and aquatic plants. There were even some plants that we were allowed to touch and smell, so we did.

When we were done with all of that, we took a cab and went out to dinner at La Table d'Edgard. That place offered seating on 2 different terraces, with views of either the Swiss Alps or Lake Geneva. We chose Lake Geneva, and called the *Shadowcat* from our table. Dad walked out onto the balcony with the binoculars, spotted us, and waved. We waved back. After that, he went back inside, and we opened our menus to find an array of the most delectable fish entrées with truffles – real ones! – and a chocolate treat with a pear sorbet for dessert.

This was not a typical dinner. We usually ate at bistros and cafés with the family, and not at the most over-the-top, expensive places. However…we were in one of the most expensive places in the world. Geneva, which we could see from Lausanne, had been rated as the sixth most expensive city on the entire planet. Escape and a safe place to hide while watching the world burn did not come cheap.

We also had to get used to shopping for food in Switzerland. The Swiss didn't go to grocery stores like Americans did. I realized that after walked around for the first couple of days and seeing no grocery store chains in which one could do one-stop shopping. So, I thought of how it had been in France when I took care of Nana: we went to different places for produce, breads, pastries, coffee and tea, dairy products, fish, chicken, and so on.

It turned out to be fun to get to know all of the local places to buy fruits and vegetables, and the quality was excellent. Claire came with me and was a bit confused on the first shopping day until I explained how it worked. Then she caught on. Fiona came the next day, and said that she was used to one-stop shopping too, which came as no surprise. I had spent a college term in London, and had bought all my food at Sainsbury's grocery store. Regardless, we were in food heaven, buying fresh cherries, berries, herbs, breads, and whatever else caught our fancy.

Once we got the hang of it, we started amassing the required Swiss food ark of one year's supply of food, toilet paper, laundry detergent, soaps, and whatever else it occurred to us to stock the *Shadowcat* with. It was a huge production, but we had been warned that it was required of anyone who stayed in Switzerland for a long enough time that the law would apply.

We took a side trip to Geneva to see what the U.N. was up to there, and another to the Conseil Européen pour la Recherche Nucléaire (CERN) to see the Large Hadron Collider, the antimatter generator. As we toured it, I found myself thinking, 'Why couldn't they figure out nuclear fusion already?! We didn't need to warp into space just yet; we needed clean energy!'

Aaron and Jack came with us on both of them, while Ed and Rick stayed with the rest of the family at the *Shadowcat*. The United Nations was up to its usual tricks, holding talks and deciding the fate of the world to whatever extent it could. CERN was ever closer to making the world of *Star Trek* a reality…one that few humans would get to see.

But that was the game plan that the U.N. had in mind: get rid of most of us humans so that those who remained could live in comfort and security, with plenty of space, resources, and education for all. The end result was lovely; the path to it was monstrous.

The jury was still out on whether or not this truth would be reflected in the history books. That it might not be was galling. After chastising the Japanese for sanitizing their own history to schoolchildren, hiding the dishonor of wartime rapes and other atrocities, all the while hiding our own internment camps and disenfranchisement of Japanese-Americans, it was happening again. We Americans had not been told about the coup that ousted Dr. Mohammad Mossadegh from the presidency of Iran in 1953 until the year 2000.

Now the same thing threatened yet again, but this time the crime was of epic and gargantuan proportions. It was global in scale, this potential deception of future generations. I said to Hamish one night, as we lay in the safety of our cabin, that if we could only truly see the whole story of what was happening all over the world from here, now, then wasn't it likely that governments all over the planet intended to cover up their crimes in the history books?

He agreed – that was their plan.

As I mentioned earlier, Leo Uberfein showed up not long after our arrival in Lausanne. He had chartered a plane, and the fact that he did so after the travel ban went into effect was an ominous and disturbing confirmation that he was, in fact, a Farmer. There was no doubt about the timing; we had eaten dinner with him the night before that ban went into effect, and left before it did, yet he had done so after that.

Hamish and I were both upset at the idea of Regenics being used only for the benefit of the planet's elite and wealthy. Everyone ought to have access to this! But we knew that as long as the world was on fire – literally and figuratively – we would have to bide our time with that. For the time being, we would have to present Regenics as something available to the wealthy few who could come to this clinic, and to the sister one in Manhattan.

Naturally, no one questioned the idea that Hamish had to spend time at each branch of the operation, starting with this one. The one in Manhattan wasn't built yet, and Hamish had deliberately signed on with the Swiss for a full year in Lausanne. We figured that the scourge of humanity would be complete by then.

But it was particularly galling to have to give Regenics to Leo Uberfein. (At least the Coke boys hadn't shown up yet; lots of other corporatists who owned big-box store franchises had already populated the clinic.) Was there any way to avoid it? I asked Hamish this question when we were at home on the *Shadowcat*.

"Well…I should tell you that I have spent most of my consultations covertly confirming a suspicion of mine. That suspicion is that the elites of the world – the Farmers – were each injected with a supply of vaccine that was NOT tainted with P53-neutralizing nanites."

"That's no surprise at all," I said. "I could have told you that, but of course you would have to check it. They're all in cahoots with the pharmaceutical corporations. With only four of them having cornered the worldwide market in the biggest antitrust violation of all time, I would expect nothing less. The Farmers are also Pharmers – with a 'Ph' instead of an 'F'."

"Aye." Hamish gave a rueful grin at that. "Good pun."

"Thanks. So…the question remains: how do we ensure that Leo Uberfein eats trigger foods? Where will we even get any for him to eat? How would we confirm that he ingests them? I mean, the guy probably eats exclusively at gourmet restaurants. I'll be damned if I'll have that Farmer-bankster on the *Shadowcat*! This suggests that we would need an op worthy of the C.I.A....and I don't mean the Culinary Institute of America. I mean the other C.I.A…the Company, as they like to call it."

"And when we toured that place, we were told that the Culinary Institute of America IS the other C.I.A.," Hamish replied with a grin. "Okay, I get your drift. This is a job for Blackout."

"How long is little Leo going to be in town?"

"Oh, long enough. But I should add that he is already doomed to die of cancer. No dose of Regenics will prevent that. His DNA profile was never that strong to begin with. He had hoped to avert what is considered an early death and a painful one with Regenics, but it would not have worked. He just wasn't coded for ninety or so years to begin with."

"So?" I said, asking the obvious, leading question, "What wouldn't Regenics have done for him?"

"It wouldn't have boosted his lifespan as much as it will ours. You and I simply have stronger DNA profiles than he does. Of course, anyone's profile can be destroyed with those monster nanobots, but we have a little head start, plus control of Regenics, plus full knowledge of the cull plan."

"So…what's going to happen to Leo Uberfein?" I still wanted to know.

"His system is going to feel much like a car that has both the accelerator and the brake pedals being depressed at once until the brakes win out." Hamish waited at this point, watching that sink into me.

A moment later I said, "You mean he will live a little past seventy or so, then get cancer?"

"Aye – maybe only sixty, though – and it will be a nasty, painful sort, as they all are, but those nanobots, combined with Regenics and his determination to beat it, will just spread it throughout his body, making it all worse. He'll have many different kinds."

"Wow. No court of law could have done better than that," I said.

"Indeed."

Chapter 39

To Survive…and Tell the Tale

About a month after our arrival in Lausanne, which was nearly two months after we had called Bethany and practically chased her and her family out of her home, we contacted them in Amsterdam. She was fine, her husband and her kids were fine, and her aunt and uncle were fine. They had plenty of room in her aunt and uncle's huge, old, stone house on the wealthy, historic canals of Amsterdam, and were in no hurry to see their niece leave.

Why was that, I wondered?

Jason did some checking on her uncle, Jan van der Waals. It turned out that he was a politically connected bankster. Her aunt seemed to have no idea what her husband was involved in, but Hamish and I realized what this meant as soon as we read the guy's profile. Apparently, it was her Aunt Annika, a younger sister of Bethany's mother, who she was close to. The uncle was just there, in the background. He made no objection to his niece and her family suddenly showing up, however. It was as if he knew why, and wasn't about to implicate himself by saying anything but "Welcome and enjoy our city" to them.

Fine; Hamish and I knew that he and Annika had no monster nanobots in their bloodstreams. We reserved a suite of rooms at the Hostellerie les Chevreuils for the Andersons – that was Phil's last name, and Bethany had adopted it. She didn't like her Dutch name, which was De Wit. Oh well…she and Phil arrived with their kids a couple of days later.

The travel ban had been lifted a week earlier, and panicked people from all over the planet had immediately started using airplanes again. Everyone was desperate to get elsewhere immediately, mostly to check on relatives, many of whom would be gone without a trace.

That was the appalling part of this. Many people did in fact get home to find that home had been wiped off the map. If they then got sick, the health management authorities of whatever nation they lived in scooped them up with alacrity. It was disturbing to see the news reports, whether on the secret Swiss channel or another.

The news reports on this were so similar that the only difference was the commentary added by the Swiss. That little editorial remark at the end that drew the inference about the cull being completed and loose ends dealt with was the difference.

We were determined that Bethany and her family would not become loose ends.

Hamish saw them in his clinic in short order. Edgar did some quick schedule juggling and had them in the next day after their arrival. Sure enough, there were killer nanobots in their systems – all four of them. Out with those, in with the healing nanites that Hamish kept at the ready, and the damage of the vaccine campaign was mitigated.

Next, he checked the kids', focusing on their immune systems. Angelica was 9 years old, and Matt was 12. Hitting kids with 40-plus vaccines at a time in one shot was insane behavior by the medical profession, and Bethany and Phil had been appalled when the policy was enacted into law. Fortunately, thanks to the gourmet, organic diet that Bethany had always enforced, the kids and she and her husband were all okay. But Hamish said that it was a close call.

He gave them each a dose of the Regenics serum, and that was that.

We persuaded them to stick around for a week, though. We hadn't seen them much for years, and now we weren't about to waste a chance for a real visit. They couldn't go back to their regular lives yet anyway. Jan had arranged for Phil to work as a computer software engineer at his office, but that could easily wait another week.

We had a lovely visit, showing them museums and chatting. Bethany and Phil told us that there were new roads constructed with plastic in the Netherlands now.

"Really?" I said. "I wonder how they hold up in extreme temperatures, going from intensely cold winters to very hot summers, plus with mud in the low-lying Dutch countryside."

"We'll find out soon enough," Phil said. "I've been hired to do some computer modeling of that. It looks as though these roads are convenient for their hollow design, with pipes running through them, but that they provide continuous employment opportunities by needing constant rebuilding."

"Maybe the idea is to keep using up old plastic, recycling it over and over again," I guessed.

"Most likely," was Phil's response.

Ed and Jack took the kids out to a science museum that first afternoon, which Hamish took the unusual step of inviting Bethany and Phil to the *Shadowcat*. He had Jason meet us there, and together we three showed them both the North American segment of the reality horror show that was the vaccine cull. Bethany and Phil understood what a huge secret this was.

The next afternoon, Ed and Jack were ready with another museum outing for Angelica and Matt so that we adults could finish the presentation. Europe and the rest of the planet constituted the second half of it, and when it was about finished, Fiona and William walked in and sat down.

Bethany and Phil were in shock by then. Jason had edited this version to include a satellite view of their former home in Massachusetts, and it had been erased. They now knew why they had needed to run.

Fiona said, "That's how we felt when we saw Rosehearty. It has been transformed from a large town to a tiny village. It's like that all over our area of Scotland, and it's happening elsewhere…everywhere."

"When this cull is over, and yes, it's a cull of humans," Hamish said, "We will help you figure out where you can live. Maybe you can choose a spot near us, who knows. Or maybe you will stay in Amsterdam. It's up to you. But whatever you do, wait until the coast is clear."

They nodded, wide-eyed. They also promised to keep what they knew to themselves. I think they were scared into secrecy, as well they should have been. Just saying openly what they knew was too dangerous.

With that disclosure complete, we left the ship, taking Fiona and William with us, plus Jason. Edgar met us at their hotel's restaurant, and Ed and Jack brought the kids. We all ate a nice meal, made plans for the remainder of their week-long visit, and did our best to relax.

And then…we enjoyed the rest of our week with them. I showed Bethany the art museums, and we reminisced about visiting each other's homes while in college and just after graduation. She had taken me to the Isabella Stewart Gardner Museum and the Boston Museum of Fine Arts, and I had taken her to the Mark Twain and Harriet Beecher Stowe Houses, and to the Wadsworth Atheneum. We ate in the museum restaurant of the Fondation de L'Hermitage and it felt like old times…sort of. At least we were doing something that we enjoyed.

All too soon, the week was up and they were going to the airport. "Thank you for everything," Bethany said to us. Phil echoed that sentiment. We hugged them and saw them off, and waited for them to call when they got to her aunt's place.

The call came without a problem, and Bethany said that her uncle seemed almost relieved about what Hamish had done for them. It was like he knew that his tracks had been covered somehow. Hamish immediately met with Jason to see why. What did Jan know?

As far as Jason could determine, Jan knew nothing specific about Hamish's capabilities. It was simply a matter of him understanding what Regenics was about, and knowing generally what Hamish's professional background was.

We thought this over and decided that because Hamish had entered a description of Bethany's family's bloodwork into the U.S. database, plus their connection to Jan van der Waals, the cross-listing in the Netherlands' database might be helping. There was that, and the fact that Jan had added them to his family in that database. We realized that Bethany, Phil, Matt, and Angelica would not be hunted for the cull anymore.

Well, good! It was a small way of fighting the cull, but it was something.

As we spent our time away from the chaos and control of home, to return who knew when, I slept in our cabin on the *Shadowcat* and dreamed dreams spawned by the weird situation that we found ourselves in. All that we had warned against and mobilized the family to prepare against swirled in my mind as I dozed off, with the result that my mind played some very odd movies.

Hamish was to give a speech before a United Nations group in Switzerland. The venue was some huge, sprawling, modern resort hotel, the time was night (after dark), and the complex was so complex that I got lost.

I looked all over the place for him, concerned that I was missing the speech. I knew what he was going to talk about – more on preparations and coping mechanisms for the coming chaos – and imagined him delivering the speech to a crowded room. Or was he doing so already, with it broadcast over the public address system of the resort, and I could hear it as I walked? No…

He wasn't doing the speech yet. I wandered up escalator after staircase after escalator. Huge windows wrapped around each curving-to-oval shaped room and balcony that overlooked the lower floors until my acrophobia kicked in and I had to lie down on the floor at the top level. It was carpeted with some pattern that reminded me of a movie theater in the United States, but all new. It even smelled new. There were some people up there, but they left me alone.

When the vertigo faded enough for me to sit up, I crawled to the escalator, stood up, and went down at least three flights, maybe four, until I was calm and on level ground. I could see one more level over one more balcony, but that didn't bother me. I went into a shop.

The shop was the resort gift shop and, consistent with the design of the rest of the resort, it was huge, oval, and took up two levels. Hamish was in there with a colleague, and glad I had arrived, because he needed help with his wardrobe.

His wardrobe was something that neither of us would ever have chosen for him had we been awake, but suddenly we both very determined that he should wear this outfit. It was a white business suit with the most bizarre pattern on it: swirling music staffs in red with a huge blue G-clef on each on, and musical notes that looked like miniature watermelon slices. The cuffs needed to be hemmed, and the moment I noticed that, I started fretting over that.

But Hamish wanted something else before he would let me get out my sewing scissors, needle, and thread (things that were in my handbag in this dream, and which I don't carry there when I am awake!). He was wearing a white dress shirt with the suit, open at the top, and he wanted me to buy him a tie. Not just any tie: a dark blue tied with an embroidered pattern of little watermelon slices on it. We immediately began a determined search of the gift shop inventory.

Before I could find what we were quite certain was available in this shop, Hamish and the colleague starting discussing a diversion for the people who were to hear his speech: they would go to our suite upstairs (just one level up) and stage a rip-roaring fight.

But wait – I wasn't finished shopping yet! I wanted to find and buy that tie first.

Hamish and his friend ignored me and went up to the suite, where I heard lots of yelling from both sides. After a couple of minutes of that, I heard him punch the guy (I knew it was faked), who fell with a loud thud to the carpeted floor. Meanwhile, I thought of his unhemmed pant cuffs, which needed trimming as well as stitching.

I continued to search for the watermelon tie until I woke up, confused and frustrated.

"Good morning, my dear!" Hamish said, kissing me on the cheek and pulling me close.

I looked at him and sat up on the bed.

He looked at me and grinned. "What did you dream?" Hamish always knew when I had dreamed something interesting.

"Oh, I had the sort of dream that makes me wish for a psychiatrist and a psychic to decode it," I replied, and told him the entire tale.

He was suitably fascinated, neither of us was sure of the interpretation, and both of us were convinced that it was all about the upheaval that our lives and circumstances had seen in the past few months. Terrific, I thought.

We got dressed and went to eat breakfast. At least the food was good on the *Shadowcat*. Grocery stores were expensive in Lausanne, but there were no shortages of anything, and we were finding plenty of new things to try, plus old favorites that we had forgotten about while away from Europe.

At dinner that evening, Claire was full of news. She and Fabian and Edgar had run into Leo Uberfein's son, Jacob, who had been a friend and classmate of Ellie's. When they had asked him about Ellie, things had gotten awkward. Edgar listened stonily as she related the story. He had seemed to want to observe the encounter with Jacob, watching him for any slip-ups, and Claire got him to admit as much.

Hamish and I exchanged glances and listened in shock and horror as the encounter was described. We knew what had happened, as did Edgar, thanks to the flying nanites. Also, new reports had initially shown the entire group of protestors with Ellie – including Jacob. Then, not mysteriously to us at all, they had been digitally scrubbed of his presence. But we knew he had been with her on the second-to-last day of her life.

Try as they might, Jacob revealed nothing in that conversation that gave away direct knowledge on his part about the protest, nor of his presence in Georgia at that time. Instead, he kept insisting that he had been back in Manhattan with his parents. He was now working closely with his father, learning the mechanics of managing their hedge fund. What a shock.

Fabian said, disgusted, "Jacob didn't even look scared. I think he looked…relieved."

"Of course he did. He escaped, and he knows it," Edgar remarked. Edgar was okay. He hadn't been in love with Ellie, he said, but she was his friend and he was outraged by her murder.

"We all are," Aunt Zoe said. "All of the murders in this cull are an outrage, but when we know the people, it seems…different," she concluded. "That seems selfish, but there it is."

"What that is, is personal," I said.

"Exactly," Grandmère agreed.

Peter Woodward, in an attempt to make pleasant conversation, asked Claire if she was planning her wedding yet, and if she was excited about becoming Mrs. Fabian Châtelet. I stopped eating and looked at him, revolted, but waited for Claire to handle this.

She did, with ease. "I'm excited about being married to Fabian, but I will never change my name and identity. My name is tied to my identity. I'm going to be Ms. Claire Charbonneau."

I breathed a sigh of satisfaction, grinned (which everyone saw), and said, "Good for you. There is plenty of herstorical precedent to back you up on that. No one owns our names, and they are very much our identities. The courtesy title of 'Ms.' dates back to the 1940s, and the first woman in the western world to get married and not change her name was Lucy Stone, in 1850. She married a really nice guy: Henry Blackwell. His sister was Dr. Elizabeth Blackwell, the first woman to get a medical degree. He walked her down the aisle to get her diploma the year before he and Lucy Stone got married."

Claire gave me a grateful smile, Hamish backed me up on the concept of men having no right to any say over what women do with our names, and Peter said, "I see. Well, if I had a daughter, I would be ready with acceptance on that point."

Anne looked at him and smiled. "So if Jason gets married, you won't ask her that question?"

Peter looked at her and said, "No. I've just learned my lesson."

There was laughter all around the table.

Anne had another question for Claire. "What made you want to keep your name?"

"Part of it is annoyance at the idea that any woman who gets married, especially if she is in her twenties, would automatically be expected to change her name. It's like there is an assumption that she might as well do so, because she has not yet distinguished herself professionally. She's too young, usually, to have done so as yet."

"I love that you're challenging that idea," Fiona said. "I won't be changing my name either, but I can't say the same, since I'm a retired professor. Oh well. I just don't want to."

Anne asked, "What is the other part?"

"My parents are most likely dead, and I'll be the last Charbonneau that I know."

With that, a pall of gloom spread over the gathering. Claire would not be having her parents at her wedding, which would spoil it. It seemed too early to press her for wedding details. I wasn't going to do it. After all, Hamish and I had gotten engaged six months before our own wedding, and known each other for years. Claire and Fabian's story was the same, except for the six months part. It had only been two and a half months.

Claire looked around the table at us all, observed that we all looked horrified and upset, and seemed to want to end that mood herself. She asked me, "Avril, when was it that you decided not to change your name when you got married?"

Fine. We would move on to more cheerful topics than murdered parents and genocide.

"I was eight years old," I replied. "The idea of changing my name and being called Mrs. HisFirstName HisLastName just galled me from the start. All of my mother's friends were Mrs. Hims, and although I wanted a girly wedding someday with lots of pink and then a marriage to a best friend, that name thing was spoiling the fantasy. Then I saw 'Ms.' in my third-grade textbook, asked the teacher what it meant, and she answered me honestly. Problem solved!"

"And that was it?" Claire asked. "It was that easy?"

"No, it wasn't. I didn't give it much more thought for a few years, because kids don't get married, at least not in the western world, but then I went to college and I had to get my parents used to writing 'Ms.' on letters and packages. They resisted for a few months, then gave up. After that, I was so into herstory and women's studies that they seem to have seen no point in making any further fuss."

"I never did that!" my mother protested.

"Yes, you did," Dad said. "You said, 'I would never do that to my husband, not take his name' on the phone to Avril." He grinned.

Hamish laughed. "You're a troublemaker, Henri!"

Dad laughed, and my mother looked annoyed at being busted. Then she said, "It's fine. There is nothing wrong with Avril's choice. She's really an easy kid to have raised. Studied hard, played her violin, learned to cook and bake beautifully, cleans things up, and took care of her grandmother. Other parents should be so lucky."

"Thanks, Mommy!" I said, smiling. She had accepted my choices quickly enough. "Now I have a question for you, Aunt Zoe, and Anne: why did you go with the traditional name-change after marriage? If you can question feminists, you traditionalists must take the question in turn. What is the thinking behind your choice, and how did you feel about it?"

My mother went first. "I didn't question tradition. I was just…satisfied to go along with it."

"You didn't miss Rosier for a last name at all, or have trouble adjusting to the change?"

"I did have to remind myself a couple of time, but the newness of being married and the fun of it made me adjust quickly, and since I wasn't questioning anything, I never thought about it being something to feel negatively about. But after all that you have told me about women's history – herstory – I now understand the benefit of leaving one's original name alone."

"Aunt Zoe? What about you?"

"What your mother said," she replied. "My experience was pretty similar."

"Anne?"

Anne nodded. "It felt the same to me too."

"What was your original last name?"

Anne replied, "Brewster."

"That's a nice one. Aunt Zoe's was Rosenthal, which was also nice. It probably meant a field of roses, or something pleasant."

Aunt Zoe grinned at me. "I think it did."

"Okay, Grandmère," I said with a grin, "we can't leave you out. Say something about this."

"In France, few women thought to challenge tradition unless they were Simone de Beauvoir, so I wasn't a likely suspect," she said. "After all, I was just marrying a bank attorney – an avocat, we call them in French – and I would just be his wife, raising the children, cooking with a housemaid, and then shopping and visiting friends, so I had no need of my own surname. I had attended the Sorbonne only briefly, and stopped after my marriage, so I felt no pull to it."

That was very interesting. Fiona even said so aloud. Then Claire said, "I'm glad we ended up talking about this. We've just said a lot. Since I'm going to marry into this family, I like the idea of having a chance to learn about everyone. Men are quicker to learn about than women, thanks to their public careers. Many women have had more private ones."

"I was a nurse," my mother pointed out. "I worked in a hospital, and that was after being married. Then I stopped after a while, but I'm glad I did it."

"You still read nursing journals, too," I chimed in. My mother smiled.

Aunt Zoe said, "I helped my husband run his business. I was well-prepared for that after getting a business degree at the University of Hartford, plus my father ran his own business. He was a yacht salesman, of all things."

"Really?" Peter said. "How ironic, considering our current residence."

"Indeed," Aunt Zoe replied with a rueful smile. None of us felt like this was a party, no matter how beautiful the *Shadowcat* was, or how great it was to be staying in Lausanne. Every conversation felt like a strained effort at not thinking too much about the world outside.

I did have one thing to contribute to it, though: "Land-lubber that I am, I never thought I would become accustomed to living on any sort of boat. This one is quite comfortable. Of course, it is berthed in a marina, not on the storm-tossed or choppy seas, but it is a boat nonetheless. I'm used to the motions of it, and can go from it to land and back again without difficulty now."

Claire and my mother and Anne agreed. It was just something that we were now used to.

Odd how life worked…one could get used to a lot of things.

Jason had wired the GPS monitors on the *Shadowcat* to show world population counters. We could switch back and forth, but this meant that we were now able to stay acutely aware of just how fast our species' numbers were dropping. It was scary. It freaked us all out just to contemplate, yet we felt that we had no moral right to not pay attention to it, so we left that display on. We didn't need to look at the GPS map anyway; we were moored in place.

I hadn't looked at those numbers since our trip over here. Now, just knowing that I was looking at unsafe territory – France, where the cull continued – by looking south, across Lake Geneva, I looked again. The United States had lost…culled…over 84 million people as of my last check-in. That had put us at 240 million people. Now we were down to 210 million.

The story was similar elsewhere. Oh wow…only 130 million more people to murder, I thought bitterly. And meanwhile, the murderers were likely among the patients lining up for Hamish's Regenics formula. It was a travesty to think that those who were removing the competition for space and resources were simultaneously arranging to get not only that but more time in which to enjoy it all.

It was one thing to get Regenics if you were among the lucky minority who was not being culled, but if you were actually one of those who engineering that cull, it was monstrous. It was the present version of Nazism. It was adding insult to injury.

There was one comfort, though: Leo Uberfein was not going to benefit.

Leo Uberfein got his dose of Regenics formula, but it was over Hamish's professional objections. Hamish just couldn't guarantee Uberfein a clean bill of health. He wanted to, he said, but he saw some signs of pre-cancerous cells in Leo's bloodstream, and the formula required a clean bill of health to work.

Now, Hamish realized, the monster nanites and Regenics would fight a constant battle in Leo's body. He would get cancer, but he would not die a quick death like the people who had been culled. It would be a long, painful, drawn out one, and he would have plenty of time and money to travel the world to the most elite clinics for eclectic treatments that would not work.

Justice! Where the law would fail, science – mad science – would prevail.

The trick was to preserve Hamish's professional reputation and to leave the impression that this failure was about something that Hamish could not have controlled. He never claimed to be able to cure cancer, after all. The fact that we both knew that he could prevent falsely-induced cancer due to his technical and medical expertise was our secret. It had to be a secret, because the fact that the vaccines falsely induced cancer was also a secret, and one that we were not supposed to know about.

Hmm…insert maniacal laughter here as we thwarted at least part of the cull.

The trick here was to live and to fight another day.

That meant keeping a low profile while remaining healthy, and patiently, quietly waiting out the scourge of this cull in a safe place, no matter how long that took. Some of that effort meant that Hamish would have to forego saving any more monster nanobots to infest any more Farmers with. Instead, he would take them back to the Shadowcat, and Jason and I would watch as he cannibalized them for spare parts.

No part of those things would be reused in any biological effort. Hamish didn't trust the things one bit, even after ripping them apart. He could recycle, though, which would do just as effective a job of concealing the evidence of clearing Bethany and her family of those cull-bots. Damn…with every thought about those evil nanobots, I thought of another name to call them.

Hamish was preparing a nanobotic security system for the *Shadowcat* in his spare time. The nanites would, once turned loose in the yacht, repeatedly check every square inch of it for any kind of outside surveillance of our activities, and inform us of any security breach. What he hoped to create next, provided he could glean more monster nanobots, was another facet of this system, one that could monitor for a human intruder and attack his or her nervous system.

"How will you make sure that it doesn't attack one of us, or lock us out?"

"It will be programmed to recognize each of us. What I want is a way to attack some hit man or hit woman. I'm still not convinced that we're safe here. Maybe we are, but just because you're paranoid, it doesn't mean that they're not out to get you."

"I know. I almost said that in unison with you, but then I decided not to be annoying."

He grinned, and Jason laughed. Soon we were all laughing, and it was a classic Aspie snort-laugh. "Listen to us…we're like the Aspies that get mocked in sitcoms," I said.

"Who cares?" they both replied.

"Oh, I don't care, I'm just noticing it. I think it's cool that we snort-laugh. Aspies and proud of it…and we are the ones better able to see a threat coming and avoid it, so there."

"So, how's the new security system coming? You've been working on it for a couple of weeks since you got that crap out of Bethany and Phil and their kids.

I thought that since you have been successfully creating nanotech systems for a while now, you might have something interesting to report on this latest project."

Hamish grinned without looking up. He was still peering through his magnifying glasses into his microscope and manipulating the nano-tools. "It is a bit slower from inside a yacht," he explained. "I had to get used to doing this while accepting the slow back-and-forth rocking by the lake's waves. But I know what I want to do, so it will probably be ready to go online in four more days. We'll see."

"I knew it. Genius!" I said. Jason laughed.

"Jason, how is it working out staying in a ship's secret laboratory?" I asked.

"Fine. I don't touch anything, I get to sit here and watch the mad scientist at work, and if I want to play computer games or read, I can go elsewhere. Your father and uncle and future brother-in-law seem to like the living room upstairs better than the library-lounge, so the other guys and I are getting plenty of game time. Claire likes to play sometimes, too."

I grinned. "Claire likes to do a variety of things. She may be more neurotypical than anything else, but she's a bit unconventional. She never sees anything wrong with liking science fiction or computer gaming. People like whatever they like, and that's that with her. She's cool."

"Aye, she is," Hamish said, still tinkering. He sat up. "Okay – got that phase of the construction done. Let's go eat." He put his tools away. He had disabled the monsters immediately after bringing them home, so now he was just working with the parts. Safe!

If only the world felt safe. Not only had our species nearly killed the planet's ecosystems, but we were a constant threat to one another over what remained of it all.

I asked whether or not I could dare to e-mail Sophia and Ginger in West Hartford, Connecticut, and Hamish said yes. He even said it was okay to say where we were, so I did, leaving out the harrowing details of our trip.

It seems worth mentioning that, as soon as I used the Internet outside of the United States, it was faster. I thought back to what Hamish had said to me about websites in the United States as I enjoyed Europe's lovely speed and efficiency: that it was a corporate agenda to eat up as much of citizens' time as possible, thus preventing us from using our voices as much.

That agenda hadn't counted on my determination to keep going, I thought, but it was still infuriating to think of all the time wasted on waiting for my commands to be carried out. Now, as I contacted my friends, I was amazed at how fast I could go through my e-mails. It wasn't just websites – it was the connections and carriers, too.

Sophia wrote back first. She and her daughter were fine, healthy, and still going about their business. But whole swathes of West Hartford had been depopulated and deconstructed, she told me. It was disturbing in the eeriest of senses to drive around.

Farms were being set up in every town where neighborhoods once stood.

The food was actually, legitimately organic, too. You name it, you could get it somewhere in town, in season. A lot less food was being trucked in from elsewhere, and much of it was coming by train when it did, to be offloaded onto trucks for the last leg of the journey. One could still buy a variety of foods, and nothing seemed to be lacking, despite the changes.

The only thing missing was orange juice. Sure, one could still buy that, but the price was a bit high due to climate change and the effect of moving the orange groves out of Florida. But Sophia was extremely knowledgeable about herbs and their medicinal uses, and she started a fascinating new project, one that Hamish and I were happy to assist with the launch of from afar.

We helped to fund the harvest and marketing effort of rose hips from the famous Elizabeth Park rose garden in Hartford, Connecticut. This place was just a short drive from where Sophia lived, and it was somehow still the most beautiful one in the area, despite all of the changes in temperatures. The roses were holding up wonderfully well, as gorgeous and fragrant as ever.

This rose hip project was a great idea that Sophia had come up with. The way it worked was natural and simple: a rose will bloom, producing a wonderful sight and scent, and when its petals have all fallen away, what remains on the end of a stem is the rose hip. This can be plucked off and dried, and then used to make a tea that is high in Vitamin C, a decent substitute for one's daily cup of orange juice. The marketing campaign suggested nightly cups of rose hip tea.

It was going rather well, and Hamish and I were excited that we had found a continuous source of income for Sophia…very excited. At last, Sophia had more than sufficient funds with which to educate her daughter, a diligent and brilliant student who loved to study. Catriona wanted to study marine biology and underwater biomes, and now she could. They were planning to transfer her to a private college as soon as it seemed safe…but not just yet.

No…not yet. Things were still in a state of flux, and Sophia wasn't about to send her daughter anywhere without knowing that it was stable, reasonably safe, and that Catriona could concentrate on her studies. Her attention should be solely on that, not on planning her patterns of movement around avoiding MRAPs.

Ginger wrote back later. She liked to drive to the library in Newington to use the Internet, so that was no surprise. She also wasn't the sort of person to keep current with the news, so she knew a lot less about what was happening all over the world. She wasn't living under a figurative rock, per se, but she didn't watch television and she mostly read in the genre that she wrote in – sexy romance novels – so really, she was confused by what was going on.

But she had noticed the silence and dramatically lowered traffic density on her almost daily trips to that library. She had also noticed that whole neighborhoods were gone now, and when she drove down the Berlin Turnpike, store after store was being razed. That route was notorious for having curb-cuts every twenty feet or so, and being so built up that no grass grew except between cracks in the pavement.

That was changing now. There was no need to have so many businesses. Actually, there never had been any such need. The middle-class lifestyle of Americans had driven the area into its condition of concrete, blacktop, and big-box stores. No one needed so much stuff so close by, but businesses and their owners wanted a middle-class income, and so the area had been developed to within an inch of its ecosystem's life.

After a few e-mails, we talked via Skype video phone calls.

They each said that they were fine, but that everything was changing around them with astonishing and, unfortunately, disturbing speed. They hardly recognized the town at this point. Again, they said that cooperative farms had sprung up here and there, and that many neighborhoods seemed to have disappeared overnight with no warning nor any explanation.

Police checkpoints and curfews will help with that illusion, I thought wryly, but refrained from sharing that with them.

Communitarian – er, community – gardens had sprung up, too, Sophia told me. She had always enjoyed buying into those and eating a share of fresh fruits and vegetables, but this was different. People who lived within a few miles of each of these gardens, within walking or biking distance, were expected to help out with them.

Bicycles had cargo containers on them now, really just large, deep, built-on baskets, with which to carry home the produce from the gardens. Now everyone from high school age to post-retirement age who was able-bodied was expected to hoe and weed and endure insects, heat, and more sunshine than they preferred to experience just to get seasonal foods. Wonderful.

Of course, beekeepers could opt out of this, as could anyone who grew and shared berries or peaches or whatever else they could grow. But that wasn't many people. Most found their time suddenly spoken for...by their local town governments! Thank you, ICLEI! There were some wealthy people who could simply buy their way out of the system and buy food, which was business as usual. It had been that way throughout history, and it was still true now.

I wondered how food shopping would be for us when we returned to the United States. Would it be enough to show up at the local farmers' market with my raspberries and honey, I wondered? Whole Foods and other grocery stores were still running strong; there were simply too many things that constituted a balanced diet which could not be grown in every town. Nice to see a tiny dose of realism in the mix, I thought.

Processed foods were, oddly, vanishing from shelves, no longer being produced or marketed. I wasn't about to cry over that, but it made me curious. Why were they gone? Had all of their market been culled? Probably. Only the organic eaters of the human population seemed to remain. Many of them had also been culled, I realized, but this remainder seemed to be by design. The corporations that had produced the GMO junk foods had diverted their efforts to organic foods, and to packaging without BPA (bisphenol A) and other contaminants.

Sure, now that there weren't too many humans in the ecosystem, NOW they do that...

It felt bizarre to be so far away as I imagined these changes to the area that had been my home for my entire life. The state and federal government had scrapped all plans to widen highways. Instead, they were now focused on maintaining smaller ones and fixing aging bridges and other infrastructure. Less was more at last. This was good, even if the way it had been made possible was unforgiveable.

Hamish and I had saved digital copies of everything that we had secretly observed. Someday, perhaps as Mark Twain had written near the end of his life, as if from the grave, we would reveal it all. Could we release the story over the Internet? We would have to prepare it neatly first, as a carefully crafted documentary first.

People would need something sufficiently succinct to take in, not a mess of data as it was. We could also offer that mess, as files to be view after first absorbing the general history of this genocide, for those who wanted to wade through it all.

I just had one thing to wonder idly about: would people condemn us for not pointlessly crying out about this crime during its commission, getting ourselves killed, and thus never managing to leak out its truth? Quite probably, they would. Well, too bad. If we had done that, would not have lived to tell the tale at all. The point was to survive and tell the tale.

Chapter 40

New World Order

Whether I tuned in to the Swiss news channel or another, official one, it was like watching a disaster movie, not the news. Floods, crowds of panicked people running, monsters, military personnel directing…military personnel directing?! All that was missing was a director's chair and a clap-board!

While all of this was happening, business as usual continued for those who were not sickened by the vaccines or murdered in the cull. As it was the fall season of an election year in the United States, that meant that it was time to vote again. The current President had served his two terms.

How we were actually going to do that presented a logistical dilemma.

It also presented another sort of dilemma, one that voters had had for as long as I could remember: what purpose did voting serve when there was nothing on the electoral menu but banksters and hedge fundsters – the very Farmers who were behind the Cull?!

It was beyond frustrating to watch the election campaign knowing that we were seeing lies worse than the ones we were used to. Banksters and lobbyists for banksters who had become politicians wanted the job, and they did their utmost to distract the voting public with nonsense about religion. On and on about which brand of Christianity they followed and how religious they were, when it fact they actually worshipped the God of Finance.

The United States was founded on principles of freedom of and freedom from religion, but you wouldn't know it watching the clown car of candidates. It was depressing and infuriating, and I ranted about it when we were on the Shadowcat. I ranted while cooking and baking in the kitchen, and I ranted when we had the television on, trying to save it for the ads so that people could at least hear and filter the lies on their own.

This question of what purpose voting served when the world was a mess could always be phrased to suit the conditions of each election, each situation. What answers to it could we give ourselves? One vote made the difference that let Hitler into power, one vote made Thomas Jefferson the U.S. President instead of Aaron Burr, who wanted to be its emperor and later killed Alexander Hamilton in a duel, one vote gave control of England to Oliver Cromwell…

…and how did we know what the winner would actually be like as President?

We never really knew that. The idea of not voting at all seemed like a cop-out. It was our last chance at free speech, too, because we could do a write-in vote. The two-party system made that option a protest vote. I decided to go for it. Why not? The world and its leaders were all tainted now – damaged goods. Fiona and William went through a similar process of reluctant, dutiful political participation followed by disgust through the British electoral system.

I ended up writing in the name of one of the few politicians who seemed like a decent person, a law professor from Yale, a woman with grandkids. She wasn't really ready for the presidency, but that wasn't the point. Even if I wrote in the name of someone who wasn't seasoned enough in politics, at least she kept fighting for consumers, bank customers, students with loans, and regular people. It was the regular people who made up a functioning country.

But first, we all had to get absentee ballots. We made phone calls to the West Hartford Town Hall one by one, a thing that I had to talk everyone into doing. Claire wasn't sure they would help her with this, but the town clerk agreed to send her the registration materials. Applications for absentee ballots were sent to the Lausanne clinic, filled out and sent back, and then ballots arrived a few weeks later.

A bankster from New York won, of course. It wasn't Leo Uberfein; he had not run for office. This bankster was a graduate of the Wharton School of Business, which now cost nearly $184,000 for a 2-year Master's in Business Administration. That put it out of reach for most people, no matter how qualified academically.

He was typical of the candidates who had run for office. In the primaries, all had been men with similar backgrounds. That was true of both parties. One from each survived that phase of the election, and this guy had won. It really seemed to make no major difference either way, which was a first. Both were in favor of Agenda 21, and with Nae-Née in use, access to abortion and birth control no longer distracted me. Politicians could no longer distract me with that.

Disgusted and depressed with the outlook for the future, we returned to whatever happy distractions we could find for ourselves. Claire and Fabian's wedding seemed to fit the bill, both to everyone else, and them. Despite the grim reality all around us, they wanted to have a wedding, so we started figuring it out with them. Claire took the lead, of course.

She wanted December 21, 2016 to be her wedding day – the Winter Solstice. It was a Wednesday, so that presented few logistical problems, we thought. We turned our attention to wedding dress shopping, and headed for Geneva to look around. She quickly found something chic and sophisticated that she wouldn't trip over, with thick, rich-looking white satin and rosettes. No veil – she didn't like those.

Flowers were to be from a shop in Lausanne, and Claire chose white peonies, pink tea roses, and French-tied with a wide, pink, satin ribbon. "I don't want any of the colors of fall," she said. "Fall represents death, and I don't want to be reminded of anything sad." I didn't blame her.

She was going for pink, and for a day that Wiccans noted for its length. "You chose the Winter Solstice, which is when the days start to lengthen, and I chose the Summer Solstice, the longest day of the year," I commented. "And we both like pink."

She smiled. "I like spring and summer best, but I don't want to wait any longer. Choosing a day that means longer days and more sunlight and warmth and cheerfulness is the next best thing," she told me.

Aunt Zoe and Uncle Charlie decided to get her something new. Claire had inherited her mother's white pearl stud earrings and a matching strand. They went to a jewelry shop in Geneva and (after wandering through several others) found something blue: a sapphire pin of an iris with the gold molded around in in a leaf design. Grandmère's pear-shaped diamond engagement ring was the "something old". Fabian and Claire went out and found white gold wedding bands; his was plain, and hers had an iris theme etched into it.

Hamish and I were putting on the wedding itself, with flowers, cake, dinner, and a night at a fancy hotel…with Ed and Rick nearby as unseen guards. We offered to make it a week, but Claire and Fabian wanted to come home after just one night. I didn't say anything, but I thought that she wasn't feeling like making a big celebration of her honeymoon with such a strange situation to come home to. Home was a floating, temporary place, in limbo, after all, and her parents were conspicuously absent.

Regardless, we all tried to make it as merry and festive as we could.

Fiona and William went next, and they did feel like spending a week away for a honeymoon. Fiona was a much happier bride, and also a first-time bride, as Claire had been. She chose a lavender hue for everything, a knee-length dress, and a bouquet that included Scottish thistles. "So Hamish was right about that choice for your cabin!" I said to her with a grin.

Fiona was a beautiful bride, and they were married on Valentine's Day of the next year. Hamish and I insisted upon throwing the wedding, and there were no objections, since we were technically the bride's family. It all went off perfectly, and William took Fiona to Geneva for a week, and to Berne and Zurich for a few days of the following week. That made a total of 14 days that Jack and Aaron had to tail them, but they made it out and back none the wiser, and safe and happy with their excursion.

But all the while, we kept staring at those population clocks on the little GPS screens. They were touch-screens, so it was possible to look around at the details of the counts, country by country, continent by continent, age demographic by age demographic, and see the numbers falling. It was amazing to see that any births were shown, but they were. I guess the Farmers didn't want to be any more obvious about what was happening than they seemed…at least to those of us who understood what we were seeing.

By New Year's Eve, the population of the United States had dropped to 140 million. The total population of humans on the entire planet was down to an incredible 3.5 billion. That just a few hundred million than what it had been when I was born! I tried to remember how crowded the world had felt around me when I was a toddler; as odd as that may sound, I could remember that, and being born. The world had still had traffic jams then, I knew that much.

My mother confirmed some memories I had of going out shopping with her in the car, and driving through long lines of cars in hot, humid summers just before a thundercloud burst. "It doesn't seem as though we spent much time idling in traffic, though," I said to her as I made Linzer Heart cookies for Valentine's Day. We were going to eat these after Fiona's wedding.

My thought back to those easy days, days when I had hated the seemingly endless trap of a clothes shopping excursion, the tiring boredom of it in which I scared her by hiding among the clothing racks, and said, "No, it doesn't. It was easier to get things done, time-wise."

"The price-tag is just completely unacceptable for returning to that ease," I went on. "What's even freakier is the fact that we will be going back even farther, to a sense of how it all felt when Grandmère was young. I can't help but plan to interview her about history, over and over again."

Claire said nothing, but she was obviously fascinated to hear about how life had looked and felt 20 years before she came into existence. She and my mother were just keeping me company as I baked. Keeping up with routine holiday foods was working out well as a coping mechanism during this bizarre transition to a new world order of fewer humans, fewer emissions, significantly less demand on the planet for resources, and much, much more surveillance.

Who would care if we ate raspberry-jam filled cookies, I wondered?!

That led me to yet more research. How would we shop for food in the United States when this was all over without our choices being tracked? What if we couldn't control that? Would we be denied access to foods that we wanted to buy over and above a certain amount within a particular time period?

I mentioned what I was curious about…and dreading…to Jason over dinner. Everyone looked up at that. We had been enjoying our time in Switzerland without having to worry about any of that. He promised to look that up and get back to me.

When he did, it was just a few hours later, while we all sat in the living room with our books. "It looks as though it may indeed be tracked. Everything we buy, when we buy it, how much, and the data will be crunched by government analysts. But I see no plan to control it – only to study it. Still, I wouldn't trust the government to leave us private citizens alone. They could always tack on more surveillance later on."

"Great. We're going to have a world-wide police state. Everything is going to be ruined for those of us who manage to survive the cull," I said bitterly. "I want to grow my own food, and to eat whatever I want whenever I want it. We all want that. I mean, I can understand that shipping certain goods from Point A to Point B might slow down access to some things somewhat, but it can't convincingly be cut off for logistical reasons. Clean energy is in the works, with electric cars and far fewer carbon emissions. We know how to do all this. This is about social control."

"All this and they may still ruin our lives," Claire said. "When does the control stop?! They kill off lots of us to make more room and clean up the planet, and to ease the strain on resources. They suspend democracy because they couldn't afford to provide it in overcrowded conditions. Then what? When will they finally be satisfied that all that is solved?!"

I looked at her and said, "You have summed up my constant thoughts and questions. Thus far, my conclusions have been: never. Once the Farmers have established social, economic, political, and surveillance control over society and made it a police state, the temptation to keep it that way will be too great for them to ever voluntarily restore it. It will be seen by them to be so much to their own advantage to just leave it that way that they will never restore democracy as we were raised to know it."

Dad agreed with that assessment, adding, "The Georgia Guidestones are coming true."

"Indeed." I looked at Hamish, who had been reading a book from the Museum of the Hand. He looked back at me unhappily. "We can't stay here forever. Sooner or later, we will have to return to the United States. Won't the Swiss expect us to do that after a while?"

"They will," he said. "We can come back and forth, but yes, we will have to experience the new world order in the United States at some point. I am curious to see what life in West Hartford, Connecticut and in Manhattan will be like under those conditions. How will it feel, how contrived or controlled it will seem, and how we might thwart surveillance devices. Each of those things presents another challenge."

"Maybe there will be a revolution of sorts. The United States has always refused to allow a court outside of its jurisdiction to dictate any of the terms of its existence. Now we have seen it allow them to sneak into our laws, first administratively, and then blatantly, thanks to an insidious treaty. It's like a computer virus took us over. A computer virus with nanites to carry it has taken us over, in fact. We have lost our security to a stealth takeover." I was bitter.

We ended up remaining in Lausanne for a full year, just as the contract stipulated. This ended up giving us the appearance of doing nothing odd, nothing that our government found objectionable, which rather amazed me. Didn't we seem like the most individualist, non-collectivist family? And what about Claire? She had lost her parents but escaped the cull and married into our family.

The cull was called a plague that ended of its own accord. Like any other plague, human immune systems must have coped with it by Darwin's theory of Survival of the Fittest. Those of us who were most physically fit to survive had, said those of the world's scientists who received government grants to study and assess the situation. "Always consider who is being paid by whom when assessing such assessments," I had remarked, with a strong note of sarcasm.

When we returned to the outside world, we brought Fiona and William home first, plus Mallory, and this time, we moored offshore, within sight of Rosehearty. We weren't hiding from anything anymore. The cremation ships had completed their ghastly missions and were gone.

Getting out of the Strait of Gibraltar had been interesting, because some dikes had been built to keep the Mediterranean Sea from consuming any more land. However, there were no fees, and no customs agents. The sensors simply detected our approach, communicated with the dikes, and we were allowed through. Human engineers watched the traffic constantly for safety reasons, however, and they did talk to Ed and Aaron as we passed through.

We found Rosehearty to be a beautiful, quaint village with lovely stone homes with slate roofs, and not many residents. Fiona and William found it to be a fraction of the town she had known, and many, many of the people she had known to be gone without a trace. Grim faces nodded when she asked about this or that person, shocked to hear that so many were gone. She had attended garden clubs with them, baked with them, and run a book club. It was going to be odd trying to reconstitute it.

When we pulled away from the coast of Scotland, this time we went south, down to the English Channel. We wanted to see how different the northern coast of France and the southern coast of England looked. They were different, all right. The mouth of the River Thames was being diked by another team of Dutch engineers. The coast of France was…farther inland. The Mont St. Michel was an even tinier island, with its human dwellings no longer peering down from such a great height at the water.

The trip across the Atlantic was done without the stealth of the previous year, though we were still careful to be aware of who else was out there with us. Nothing seemed amiss, and no one was following us. We moved across the ocean via Greenland, just to see what it looked like. The place was actually starting to show some green, and strawberries were growing wild on it.

Iceland's volcano was having another eruption – a mild one – so our return via the *Shadowcat* brought no notice. Boats could travel, but not planes. Airplanes were still in use for travel and trade, and there were no rules forbidding private citizens from using them. It was more a question of economics. Affordability was a great tool for limiting air travel. Fewer people could afford it thanks to the havoc that the cull had wreaked on economies everywhere.

With fewer people to power the economy, making goods and running services, there were fewer people to fill jobs, fewer people to need jobs, and fewer monetary units being earned to spend on extras. With less money, people could not afford the lifestyles that they had enjoyed before the cull, either. That, of course, fit in perfectly with Agenda 21's goals. The problem of developed nations as the devourers of the world had been dealt with.

China had decimated its own human population, and aided and abetted the United States in decimating that of the Philippines, Indonesia, Malaysia, much of the Middle East, and most of Africa. Now what remained of the people in those places had plenty of room and more than enough resources to survive on, thanks to the genocide of the cull.

The Chinese had done tremendous damage to their ecosystem before that, however. They had always trashed it with far more reckless and shocking abandon than even mid-twentieth century Americans had, and now they had to remediate the results. Good luck to them. They had turned the Yellow River red in some places, growing waterways thick with algae and choked with trash.

To that end, ships laden with Conex containers – those red, blue, and other-hued metal containers that good of all kinds were packed in for long-distance journeys – were sharply limited. The production of goods that were needed on each continent was now legally required to be conducted on that continent now. No sending things across the oceans, to be lost in the storm-tossed, high seas, or to burn fossil fuels just so that someone in another country could have their clothing mass produced elsewhere.

There were still a few luxuries and specialty items from afar, but their price and the reduced demand for those goods brought the consumption of resources back down to levels not seen since 1900…perhaps earlier. Less traffic, less to move around, less being ordered, wanted, used, and thrown away.

The governments of the world now met regularly at the United Nations headquarters in Manhattan to make such decisions. It was decided that some fossil fuel use would have to continue until nuclear fusion power was a reality, and money was actually funneled into that endeavor. The goal was within reach, getting closer and closer at last.

A massive plastic collection effort was instituted all over the planet as well. New jobs were created for that purpose. Heaps of it were gathered in the few spots that the governments had not seen fit to declare only for wildlife. After that, engineers developed a plan for recycling the stuff into housing, reusable bags (it was now illegal to use a "disposable" plastic one), and whatever else. Efforts were underway to break down plastic and return the formula to its separate ingredients. High school science projects everywhere competed to solve this problem.

Not all of the ideas of this New World Order were bad ones, but a police state with surveillance was unacceptable. Legal groups that fought for personal liberties were still around, including the American Civil Liberties Union, so there was some glimmer of hope to be seen.

But there not much hope. It was difficult to feel hope when we arrived home, moored the *Shadowcat*, and walked into Manhattan. We had detoured south a bit, to Philadelphia, so that Claire could see it from a slight distance. Philadelphia, the place where our nation's system democracy was first created, was not directly accessible to a yacht. Well, I suppose we could have gone up through the Delaware River to that city, but we didn't.

We anchored the *Shadowcat* near the mouth of the river and watched as Hamish sent a swarm of his solar-powered, nanite spybots out to do the looking. Back down in the library-lounge, we all stared at first an overhead view, and then a series of close-ups. Fabian sat next to Claire, gripping her hand tightly. She looked white as a sheet.

The view was actually a pretty one in terms of landscape and historic, pretty buildings. In fact, there was nothing other than either historic, pretty sights or new, mixed-use construction. We all recognized that style now: it had been dubbed Agenda 21esque by us the previous year, before we had left. The term was now in common use all over the United States thanks to a post I had made on my Facebook page as soon as I had learned about the idea.

With the Agenda 21 treaty making the idea common knowledge, that was no big deal. It was strange that it was just an easily accepted, matter-of-fact word to people now. I had played around with the satellite view of the United States as we approached, and Google Maps had updated the views. The buildings and streets shown really were up to date, and they really were in historic, colonial and Victorian styles with some early twentieth century looks, and this.

The part that Claire had been holding her breath over seeing soon came up: her hometown. Her neighborhood was wiped out, landscaped over, gone. Having been built in the 1980s, it had been slated for a travesty of eminent removal by the cull with everyone in it, as had the areas dating from the 5 prior decades and the 2 subsequent ones.

Pulling back from the area, moving straight up, the view showed very little urban development where once concrete and steel had dominated. It was pretty, but that prettiness had come at the expense of most of the people who had lived in those areas. It didn't inspire nice, warm feelings of admiration. It induced waves of nausea instead.

Claire told Hamish when she had seen enough and her curiosity was satisfied. He shut it down and recalled the nanite spybots immediately. This had been about closure for her, not morbid curiosity and voyeurism. We pulled up the anchor and headed north as soon and the nanobots were back aboard.

As we headed north, I glanced up at the GPS monitor, then reached out and touched the screen to view the population clock. The United States had 80.4 million humans in it, and the planet as a whole was at roughly 600 million. We were pretty much there now, at the New World Order that the Georgia Guidestones suggested.

Manhattan didn't look much different from the way it had the previous year, and the air smelled very clean, but there was something chilling amiss with it. After a day or two walking around it, we understood what it was: far fewer people. The urban planner's dream of this city had been made a reality, with grass-topped roofs, beehives and small gardens, and bicycle paths.

Small gardens and beehives on roof-tops? Perhaps individual gardens could be possible and less monitoring of our food choices after all, I thought. I went up onto the firehouse's roof-top and looked around. The raspberry vines I had planted long ago were still bearing fruit.

We didn't have time for much gardening, however. It was late September, and we would not be staying here long. Dr. Nurse showed me and Hamish around the new Regenics clinic at the Rockefeller Institute, but he knew that we would go to Connecticut to look around as soon as possible. "It's a lot different there now; good luck!" was all he said.

Our cars were still in good, running order. Hamish inquired about having them all converted to electricity, a service that was being offered all over the developed world now. Soon it would be common in the developing world, too, and done to cheap, ancient cars. A car didn't have to be sleek and pretty to be converted. The government offered subsidies to anyone who needed financial assistance with this, showing an eagerness that no doubt reflected business interests.

Lobbyists had gotten onto the business bandwagon of enabling this effort at eco-friendly everything everywhere it could be implemented. If anyone, any individual, wanted to make their cars or homes more eco-friendly and needed any financial help, it was there for them. They still had to pay something, but the act was encouraged and the help was offered with no visible strings attached.

The invisible strings were those abominable RFID chips. At least Hamish knew how to remove them. I looked about for laws against removing them, and found none. How odd. Perhaps the Farmers were banking on the idea that most citizens would not know how to do this, or even think to do so.

There was a place in Manhattan that would convert our family's cars to electricity, and there were now recharging stations everywhere. Getting stuck along a long route through the countryside was not an issue, but government credit cards were issued to pay at the charging stations. There it was; there was the tracking technology that would catalogue our movements.

The cars were ready in a little over 2 weeks. By then we had seen Manhattan, studying it from the shrewd point of view of people who knew what we were seeing. One thing that stood out to me was the fact that the cull had not targeted any particular race, culture, or other group. I saw people of all colors and ethnicities walking around, including Sikhs, African-Americans, whites, Jews, you name it. Just no homeless people; everyone looked like they had access to a living income. They were all well-fed, healthy, calm people.

The majority of the people around us were sad with a tinge of acceptance about having lost so many people. They thought it was just a plague that had killed them, not a cull. I don't know how Claire kept herself from screaming corrections at them, but she didn't.

I asked her about that, and she said that it was enough for now just to be one of the ones who both knew and who, thanks to her new family, had thwarted it. She would bide her time and see how she might fight later on. She was even considering attending law school. So was Fabian. They were angry, they were neurotypical, they had learned stealth from me and Hamish, and they were looking for a fight.

We all wanted our original U.S. Constitution and the life that it described restored. How we might act to bring that back was a question for our future, seeing as we would have one. Meanwhile, we would be no one's slaves, no one's peons, and no one's sheeple.

With the cars ready, we all drove back to Connecticut.

It took us the same amount of time that it had to get south a year earlier. Electricity-powered cars weren't the slow-moving disappointments we had expected them to be. I recalled that the queen of England had ordered her cars converted to electricity in the 1990s, and they had run efficiently also. Now it was a standard, everyday technology for everyone else. Cool!

Well, it hadn't been cool until Hamish and his team of Blackout buddies had retrieved the cars, parked them one by one in our firehouse garage, and extracted the RFID chips from them, but now they were cool. Now they were eco-friendly minus the invasive surveillance devices. Hamish and his colleagues knew how to keep the airbags intact as they removed the chips from behind steering wheel assemblies. I felt a smug satisfaction at his thwarting of the Farmers, and told Claire about it. She felt it too; I could see it spreading over her.

We really did look like twenty-somethings now. Hamish looked like he was in his early thirties. Hamish had no more white hairs, and his skin was flushed with a rosy hue that Fiona's had taken on while we were in Lausanne. Her hair had returned to its former dark, dark brown, gradually, over the course of a year. William's hair had turned red, at an equal pace.

My parents looked…wow. They looked much as they had when I was a teenager. The thick mane of white hair on my father had returned to black, and my mother and Aunt Zoe had gone to a salon to get the color rinsed out of theirs. Now they were growing their stripped hair out, and the new growth was a rich brown. My mother's had coppery highlights, like mine. In the light, they showed, and out of the brightness, my hair looked like Dad's.

Grandmère seemed to have regenerated to her former self as an eighty-year-old. She still looked pretty much the same, with snowy white hair, but it was thicker and more lustrous, and she was stronger and slept more comfortably and deeply. She was impish again, something that she had been losing for the decade or so before Hamish had given her Regenics.

We felt ready to go back to West Hartford and face whatever it looked and felt like, so we made the drive on a sunny Tuesday in early October. It was like driving through one beautiful farm and meadow after another. Occasionally, we saw a mansion or a historic home.

The rural roads were bumpy and had potholes, so we didn't drive too fast. That was part of the idea behind U.N. Agenda 21 for the United States: keep the country road infrastructure in a decrepit state so that most people would opt to live close together, in urban areas…and a few suburban ones, drastically reduced in population.

In contrast, the roads in the towns that we passed were in a great state of repair. They boasted carpet-like pavement, built to heat-and-cold resistant specifications that an engineer would be proud of, made of the layers that resisted cracking and upheaval over harsh winters.

But most intriguing was the paint on them: it was solar powered, a thing I had previously read about online. It was common in places like the Netherlands, and now we had it…complete with green bike paths along the curbs. Those paths were more like special lanes.

That wasn't all that we saw. There were wind turbine farms dotting the landscape where cityscapes used to be, and miles and miles of farms of all sorts. It was late in the growing season, so we saw crops that were almost ready to be harvested every which way we looked.

Cute little town centers remained, but we knew exactly what was missing. It all came back to us as we drove along – the memories of the towns and cities that used to be there – and we drove somewhat slowly so as to be able to look at it all. After four hours, we found ourselves in West Hartford. We had avoided the highways, so we hadn't yet had to see that much of that highway had been removed, rebuilt, and reshaped.

We all drove around, first to West Hartford Center, as if afraid to look around at home. It was still there, as was Blue Back Square, but that part was to be expected. It was Agenda 21esque construction. But much of the ugly, mid-twentieth century construction around it was gone. Grass and fields stretched around us. It was clear that a lot of land had been converted to farmland, and there were signs all around about 4-H Club events and training for adults and teenagers to participate it. Adults in 4-H! That was a new twist on an old institution.

We drove with Jason through Elmwood, letting him lead the way. His childhood home was gone, as was the neighborhood it had been in. We quickly reversed course and followed him to his house near the Center, which was still there. He pulled into the driveway, got out, and waved to us to go on. His mother got out of the car, stunned and teary. His father looked angry, but he gave us a stiff smile. We sat by the curb, motors still running, and Peter and Anne came up to us for a moment.

Anne leaned into my window to kiss me good-bye. "Thank you for saving us," she said.

I got out and hugged her. "You and Peter can keep working for Hamish. You're going to be okay," I said, "Right, Hamish?" He had gotten out too, and he nodded. He hugged Anne and shook hands with Peter, and then we got back into our car. We drove off with them in our rearview mirror, entering Jason's house. They would live with him now, obviously.

Our little caravan went up to Mountain Road and headed north, to visit the spot where Aunt Zoe and Uncle Charlie's neighborhood had been. When we got there, it was just more fields. We couldn't even drive up to the spot where we had so many memories. Aunt Zoe started to cry a little, but Grandmère just sighed and said we should go, and consider ourselves lucky.

Back down Mountain Road we went, all four vehicles, with Ed an Aaron behind us. Our house, if it really was still there for us, had 6 bedrooms in it – plenty of room for us all. Ed and Aaron had the small outbuilding that Hamish had had built just after sea levels began to rise a few years ago – had it been just a few years? It blended in aesthetically with the bigger house.

Our house was still there. We pulled into the garage, and Dad pulled in next to us. Uncle Charlie parked his car in the turnaround of the driveway. We got out in a daze, and started hauling in food first. The kitchen looked the same. Everything looked the same. We really were lucky…so lucky!

Hamish paused to run a nanobotic security check of the house. It was okay. The cull and the government had not messed with the house…or with Blackout Security. We were home, back to see what else was different and who was left.

But seeing the new world order and answering that question was for another day.

Chapter XXVII: Climate Change

Title 10:
The Convention on Global Sustainability and Communitarian Government
21 June 2016

INTRODUCTION
Content and Significance of the Convention

PREAMBLE

The United Nations Convention on Global Sustainability and Communitarian Government

Full text of the Convention in English

INTRODUCTION

On 21 June 2016, the Convention on Global Sustainability and Communitarian Government was adopted by the United Nations General Assembly. It entered into force as an international treaty on 22 June 2016 after the twentieth country had ratified it.

The Convention was the culmination of nearly 24 years of work by the United Nations Division for Sustainable Development, a body established in 1992 to monitor the situation of human health and quality of life. The Division's work has focused attention on the results of human overpopulation on overall quality of life, highlighting the need for sustainable policies, communitarian living, and restraints on development, building on the Agenda for the 21st Century as laid out in the Rio Declaration on Environment and Development.

The full text of the Convention is set out herein:

CONVENTION ON GLOBAL SUSTAINABILITY AND COMMUNITARIAN GOVERNMENT

The States' Parties to the present Convention,

PREAMBLE

Noting that the Charter of the United Nations reaffirms faith in fundamental human rights, in the dignity and worth of the human person and in the equal rights of men and women,

Noting that the United Nations Conference on Environment and Development affirms the principle of the inadmissibility of discrimination and proclaims that all human beings are born free and equal in dignity and rights and that everyone is entitled to all the rights and freedoms set forth therein, without distinction of any kind,

Noting that humanity stands at a defining moment in history, confronted with a perpetuation of disparities between and within nations, a worsening of poverty, hunger, ill health, and illiteracy, and the continuing deterioration of the ecosystems on which we depend for our well-being,

Noting that integration of environment and development concerns and greater attention to them will lead to the fulfilment of basic needs, improved living standards for all, better protected and managed ecosystems and a safer, more prosperous future and that no nation can achieve this on its own, but that together we can – in a global partnership for sustainable development,

Recalling that Agenda 21 addresses the overuse and careless use of resources threatens the principles of equality of rights and respect for human dignity, is an obstacle to the participation of future generations in the political, social, economic and cultural life of their countries, and hampers the growth of the prosperity of society,

Reflecting that a global consensus and political commitment at the highest level on development and environment cooperation, with its successful implementation is first and foremost the responsibility of Governments and national strategies, plans, policies and processes are crucial in achieving this and international cooperation required to support and supplement such national efforts,

Concerned that resource and land depletion lead to ever-increasing strains on access to food, health, education, training, and opportunities for employment and other needs,

Convinced that the developmental and environmental objectives of Agenda 21 will require a substantial flow of new and additional financial resources to developing countries, in order to cover the incremental costs for the actions necessary to deal with global environmental problems and to accelerate sustainable development establishment,

Realizing that Agenda 21 will best be achieved by implementing a new international economic order and one world government based on community, equity, and justice will contribute significantly towards the promotion of equality,

Determined to implement the principles set forth in the United Nations Conference on Environment and Development, and, for that purpose, to adopt the measures required for sustainability, communitarian living, and its benefits to quality of life,

Determined that the human species shall not become a mere failed biological experiment, or an endangered species among the many wonderful and already endangered species on this planet,

Determined that a global vaccination policy is necessary to preserve and protect the human species from itself being a casualty of species depletion,

Concluding that the implementation of a policy and practice of sustainable resource use and living will address the problem of land, species, and resource depletion,

Have agreed on the following:

PART I

Article 1

For the purposes of the present Convention, the term "sustainability" shall mean any practice which prevents the contamination, depletion, or inequitable use or allocation or any natural resource, be it plant, animal, land, water, or air.

Where the term "Governments" is used, it will be deemed to include the New World Economic Community. Throughout this Convention, the term "environmentally sound" means "environmentally safe and sound", in particular when applied to the terms "energy sources", "energy supplies", "energy systems", and "technology" or "technologies".

Article 2

States Parties wish to improve overall quality of life for humans and the other species with whom human share this planet, and therefore agree to implement by all appropriate means and without delay a new world government and financial system and so, to this end, undertake:

(a) To pursue a policy of unity in their national constitutions or other appropriate legislation if not yet incorporated therein and to ensure, through law and other appropriate means, the practical realization of this principle;

(b) To adopt appropriate legislative and other measures, including sanctions where appropriate, implementation of wealth redistribution, incorporating all currencies into one currency, to be called the Byte-Coin;

(c) To conduct periodic studies of needs and costs of providing clean energy, development of sustainable practices, and healthful environments to all;

(d) To allocate financial resources so as to make clean energy, sustainable living conditions, resources, medicine, food, housing, and education for all;

(e) To establish local and regional legal systems and to ensure through competent national tribunals and other public institutions the effective application of world governmental laws;

(f) To refrain from engaging in any act or practice of unsustainable practices and to ensure that public authorities and institutions shall act in conformity with and to enforce this obligation;

Article 3

States Parties shall promote sustainable development policies and practices in all areas of social and economic life, including, but not limited to, farming, education, commerce, trade, land use, access to fresh water, technological development, energy use, communications, food, housing, travel, and any other aspect of human life so as to have an environmentally sound impact:

(a) To take all appropriate measures to maintain the viability of ecosystems, access to freshwater resources, energy, technology, food, and comfortable housing through environmentally sound practices;

(b) To take all appropriate measures, including legislation, to modify or abolish existing laws, regulations, customs and practices which allow for unsustainable resource and land use;

(c) To establish vaccination laws, manage human health, maintain viable supplies of vaccines, and protect the human species from extinction.

(d) To ensure that each ethnic, cultural, or other group shall receive a fair share of resources,

(e) To maintain constant and consistent communication of each individual's needs while ensuring that individual actions do not negatively impact the environment or use more than a fair share of resources.

Article 4

States Parties shall adopt and take all appropriate measures:

(a) To conserve land and to protect it from any further encroachment by humans;

(b) To waste no materials in the production of any goods, and to reclaim and recycle any materials that were wasted in the past;

(c) To adopt a policy of cremation for all human deaths so as to preserve the land for the living;

(d) To protect ecosystems from pollutants, depletion, and habitat loss.

Article 5

States Parties shall take all appropriate measures:

(a) To protect the Earth's oceans and waters and to prevent international trade from wasting resources and spreading pollutants in the world's oceans, waters, and ecosystems, and to develop dietary policies and practices for preserving those ecosystems;

(b) To ensure that fisheries are not depleted, poisoned, contaminated, or otherwise destroyed, technologies shall be developed to remove trash and sewage from the oceans, and policies of use of these technologies shall be required by all vessels on any body of water.

Article 6

1. States Parties shall take all appropriate measures, including legislation, to preserve all species and biodiversity, including the banning of hunting endangered species, practices involving the use of any part of endangered species, or careless and dirty energy use such as nuclear fission that releases harmful materials into any ecosystem.

2. Technologies shall be developed to clean and heal damaged ecosystems, with employment opportunities being generated as a result.

PART II

Article 7

States Parties shall take all appropriate measures to ensure that all women and men in developing areas are educated in the practices and policies of sustainability, communitarianism, global economics, local, regional and world government:

(a) That career and vocational guidance in sustainable farming, technology, energy, and governance be provided for educational establishments of all categories in rural as well as in urban areas; this equality shall be ensured in pre-school, general, technical, professional and higher technical education, as well as in all types of vocational training;

(b) Access to the same curricula, the same examinations, teaching staff with qualifications of the same standard and school premises and equipment of the same quality;

(c) The elimination of any stereotyped concept of the roles of men and women at all levels and in all forms of education by encouraging coeducation and other types of education which will help to achieve this aim and, in particular, by the revision of textbooks and school programs and the adaptation of teaching methods.

Article 8

1. States Parties shall take all appropriate measures to ensure that each person be guaranteed access to living income through employment in order to ensure fair access to resources:

(a) The right to the same employment opportunities, including the application of the same criteria for selection in matters of employment;

(b) The right to free choice of profession and employment, the right to promotion, job security and all benefits and conditions of service and the right to receive vocational training and retraining, including apprenticeships, advanced vocational training and recurrent training;

(c) The right to equal remuneration, including benefits, and to equal treatment in respect of work of equal value, as well as equality of treatment in the evaluation of the quality of work;

(d) The right to protection of health and to safety in working conditions.

2. In order to prevent international trade from wasting resources and spreading pollutants in the world's oceans, waters, and ecosystems:

(a) Local resources shall be used before foreign ones shall be made available;

(b) Corporations shall refrain from outsourcing the production of goods;

(c) Plastics and other non-biodegradable materials shall be required to be recycled rather than discarded, and a global policy of reclaiming those plastics that have previously been discarded for use in all manufacturing shall be instituted.

3. Protective legislation relating to matters covered in this article shall be reviewed periodically in the light of scientific and technological knowledge and shall be revised, repealed or extended as necessary.

Article 9

1. States Parties shall take all appropriate measures to restructure farming systems so as to ensure that a balanced diet of nutrients is available in each community without requiring foods to be transported over long distances. To this end, agricultural land trusts and re-zoning shall be instituted to increase the amount of farmland available for use to each community.

2. States Parties shall ensure that pollinators and soil biomes are protected and replenished with sustainable farming practices.

Article 10

States Parties shall take all appropriate measures to preserve and protect access to freshwater resources. Enforcement measures, rationing in times of drought, and blocking of any contaminants or pollutants shall be rigorously maintained at all times.

Article 11

States Parties shall adopt Smart Technology to monitor the safety, energy use, and resource use of each individual, dwelling, place of business, transportation, and public building, and to ensure that each uses only their fair share. Public transportation shall be encouraged to reduce overall emissions while clean energy is developed.

Article 12

States Parties shall take all appropriate measures to manage and protect the health of the public from infection, virus, disease, and to reduce risk of illness by promulgating a mandatory vaccination policy for each threat. No exception shall be made without medical proof of potential harm from any vaccine serum.

PART III

Article 13

States Parties shall accord to all individual human beings equality before the law.

Article 14

States Parties shall take all appropriate measures to provide sustainable housing to all. Communitarian planning and Smart Growth development shall be encouraged so as to consolidate human habitation on as little land as possible, with mixed use construction. In re-zoning, greenlining shall be implemented to reclaim land taken from indigenous wildlife due to encroaching human developments, to be replaced by mixed use construction.

Article 15

Respect for indigenous peoples planet-wide shall be made policy. No further encroachment into areas occupied by indigenous peoples shall be permitted, and the sustainable practices of indigenous peoples shall be studied and adopted by governments for the benefit of people living everywhere else.

PART IV

Article 16

1. States Parties undertake to submit to the Secretary-General of the United Nations, for consideration by the Committee, a report on the legislative, judicial, administrative or other measures which they have adopted to give effect to the provisions of the present Convention and on the progress made in this respect:

(a) Within one year after the entry into force for the State concerned;

(b) Thereafter at least every four years and further whenever the Committee so requests.

2. Reports may indicate factors and difficulties affecting the degree of fulfillment of obligations under the present Convention.

Article 17

1. The Committee shall adopt its own rules of procedure.

2. The Committee shall elect its officers for a term of two years.

Article 18

1. The Committee shall normally meet for a period of not more than two weeks annually in order to consider the reports submitted in accordance with article 17 of the present Convention.

2. The meetings of the Committee shall normally be held at United Nations Headquarters or at any other convenient place as determined by the Committee.

Article 19

1. The Committee shall, through the Economic and Social Council, report annually to the General Assembly of the United Nations on its activities and may make suggestions and general recommendations based on the examination of reports and information received from the States Parties. Such suggestions and general recommendations shall be included in the report of the Committee together with comments, if any, from States Parties.

2. The Secretary-General of the United Nations shall transmit the reports of the Committee to the Commission on the Status of Human Overpopulation for its information.

Article 20

The specialized agencies shall be entitled to be represented at the consideration of the implementation of such provisions of the present Convention as fall within the scope of their activities. The Committee may invite the specialized agencies to submit reports on the implementation of the Convention in areas falling within the scope of their activities.

PART V

Article 21

Nothing in the present Convention shall affect any provisions that are more conducive to the achievement of sustainability and communitarianism which may be contained:

(a) In the legislation of a State Party; or

(b) In any other international convention, treaty or agreement in force for that State.

Article 22

States Parties undertake to adopt all necessary measures at the national level aimed at achieving the full realization of the rights recognized in the present Convention.

Article 23

1. The present Convention shall be open for signature by all States.

2. The Secretary-General of the United Nations is designated as the depositary of the present Convention.

3. The present Convention is subject to ratification. Instruments of ratification shall be deposited with the Secretary-General of the United Nations.

4. The present Convention shall be open to accession by all States. Accession shall be effected by the deposit of an instrument of accession with the Secretary-General of the United Nations.

Article 24

1. A request for the revision of the present Convention may be made at any time by any State Party by means of a notification in writing addressed to the Secretary-General of the United Nations.

2. The General Assembly of the United Nations shall decide upon the steps, if any, to be taken in respect of such a request.

Article 25

1. The present Convention shall enter into force on the thirtieth day after the date of deposit with the Secretary-General of the United Nations of the twentieth instrument of ratification or accession.

2. For each State ratifying the present Convention or acceding to it after the deposit of the twentieth instrument of ratification or accession, the Convention shall enter into force on the thirtieth day after the date of the deposit of its own instrument of ratification or accession.

Article 26

1. The Secretary-General of the United Nations shall receive and circulate to all States the text of reservations made by States at the time of ratification or accession.

2. A reservation incompatible with the object and purpose of the present Convention shall not be permitted.

3. Reservations may be withdrawn at any time by notification to this effect addressed to the Secretary-General of the United Nations, who shall then inform all States thereof. Such notification shall take effect on the date on which it is received.

Article 27

1. Any dispute between two or more States Parties concerning the interpretation or application of the present Convention which is not settled by negotiation

shall, at the request of one of them, be submitted to arbitration. If within six months from the date of the request for arbitration the parties are unable to agree on the organization of the arbitration, any one of those parties may refer the dispute to the International Court of Justice by request in conformity with the Statute of the Court.

2. Each State Party may at the time of signature or ratification of the present Convention or accession thereto declare that it does not consider itself bound by paragraph I of this article. The other States Parties shall not be bound by that paragraph with respect to any State Party which has made such a reservation.

3. Any State Party which has made a reservation in accordance with paragraph 2 of this article may at any time withdraw that reservation by notification to the Secretary-General of the United Nations.

Article 28

The present Convention, the Arabic, Chinese, English, French, Russian, and Spanish texts of which are equally authentic, shall be deposited with the Secretary-General of the United Nations.

IN WITNESS WHEREOF the undersigned, duly authorized, have signed the present Convention.

Participant	Date of Issuance	Action
A		
Afghanistan	21/06/2016	Signature
Albania	22/06/2016	Ratification
Algeria	21/06/2016	Acceptance
Andorra	22/06/2016	Ratification
Angola	21/06/2016	Signature
Antigua and Barbuda	25/06/2016	Ratification
Argentina	24/06/2016	Ratification
Armenia	22/06/2016	Ratification
Australia	22/06/2016	Ratification
Austria	22/06/2016	Ratification
Azerbaijan	21/06/2016	Acceptance
B		
Bahamas	22/06/2016	Ratification
Bahrain	22/06/2016	Ratification
Bangladesh	22/06/2016	Acceptance
Barbados	22/06/2016	Acceptance
Belarus	22/06/2016	Ratification
Belgium	22/06/2016	Ratification
Belize	22/06/2016	Acceptance
Benin	21/06/2016	Signature
Bhutan	22/06/2016	Acceptance

Bolivia (Plurinational State of)	22/06/2016	Acceptance
Bosnia and Herzegovina	22/06/2016	Ratification
Botswana	21/06/2016	Signature
Brazil	22/06/2016	Acceptance
Brunei Darussalam	21/06/2016	Signature
Bulgaria	22/06/2016	Ratification
Burkina Faso	21/06/2016	Signature
Burundi	21/06/2016	Signature
C		
Cambodia	26/06/2016	Ratification
Cameroon	21/06/2016	Signature
Canada	22/06/2016	Ratification
Cape Verde	21/06/2016	Signature
Central African Republic	21/06/2016	Signature
Chad	21/06/2016	Signature
Chile	22/06/2016	Ratification
China	22/06/2016	Ratification
Colombia	22/06/2016	Acceptance
Comoros	21/06/2016	Signature
Congo	21/06/2016	Signature
Costa Rica	22/06/2016	Acceptance
Côte D'Ivoire	22/06/2016	Acceptance
Croatia	22/06/2016	Ratification

Cuba	22/06/2016	Acceptance
Cyprus	22/06/2016	Ratification
Czech Republic	22/06/2016	Ratification
D		
Democratic People's Republic of Korea	24/06/2016	Ratification
Democratic Republic of the Congo	21/06/2016	Signature
Denmark	22/06/2016	Ratification
Djibouti	21/06/2016	Signature
Dominica	22/06/2016	Ratification
Dominican Republic	22/06/2016	Ratification
E		
Ecuador	22/06/2016	Ratification
Egypt	25/06/2016	Ratification
El Salvador	22/06/2016	Ratification
Equatoral Guinea	21/06/2016	Signature
Eritrea	21/06/2016	Signature
Estonia	22/06/2016	Ratification
Ethiopia	21/06/2016	Signature
F		
Fiji	24/06/2016	Ratification
Finland	22/06/2016	Ratification
France	22/06/2016	Ratification
G		
Gabon	22/06/2016	Acceptance

Gambia	22/06/2016	Acceptance
Georgia	22/06/2016	Ratification
Germany	22/06/2016	Ratification
Ghana	22/06/2016	Acceptance
Greece	22/06/2016	Ratification
Grenada	22/06/2016	Ratification
Guatemala	22/06/2016	Acceptance
Guinea	22/06/2016	Acceptance
Guinea Bissau	22/06/2016	Acceptance
Guyana	22/06/2016	Acceptance
H		
Haiti	22/06/2016	Ratification
Honduras	25/06/2016	Acceptance
Hungary	22/06/2016	Ratification
I		
Iceland	22/06/2016	Ratification
India	24/06/2016	Ratification
Indonesia	25/06/2016	Ratification
Iran (Islamic Republic of)	21/06/2016	Signature
Iraq	21/06/2016	Signature
Ireland	24/06/2016	Ratification
Israel	22/06/2016	Ratification
Italy	25/06/2016	Ratification
J		

Jamaica	25/06/2016	Ratification
Japan	22/06/2016	Ratification
Jordan	22/06/2016	Ratification
K		
Kazakhstan	22/06/2016	Acceptance
Kenya	21/06/2016	Signature
Kiribati	22/06/2016	Acceptance
Kuwait	25/06/2016	Ratification
Kyrgyzstan	22/06/2016	Acceptance
L		
Lao People's Democratic Republic	25/06/2016	Acceptance
Latvia	22/06/2016	Ratification
Lebanon	22/06/2016	Ratification
Lesotho	21/06/2016	Signature
Liberia	22/06/2016	Acceptance
Libyan Arab Jamahiriya	22/06/2016	Acceptance
Liechtenstein	22/06/2016	Ratification
Lithuania	22/06/2016	Ratification
Luxembourg	22/06/2016	Ratification
M		
Madagascar	21/06/2016	Signature
Malawi	21/06/2016	Signature
Malaysia	22/06/2016	Ratification

Maldives	21/06/2016	Signature
Mali	21/06/2016	Signature
Malta	22/06/2016	Ratification
Marshall Islands	22/06/2016	Ratification
Mauritania	21/06/2016	Signature
Mauritius	21/06/2016	Signature
Mexico	22/06/2016	Ratification
Micronesia, Federated States of	21/06/2016	Signature
Monaco	22/06/2016	Ratification
Mongolia	21/06/2016	Signature
Montenegro	22/06/2016	Ratification
Morocco	22/06/2016	Ratification
Mozambique	21/06/2016	Signature
Myanmar	22/06/2016	Ratification
N		
Namibia	21/06/2016	Signature
Nauru	22/06/2016	Ratification
Nepal	22/06/2016	Ratification
Netherlands	22/06/2016	Ratification
New Zealand	22/06/2016	Ratification
Nicaragua	22/06/2016	Acceptance
Niger	21/06/2016	Signature
Nigeria	21/06/2016	Signature

Norway	22/06/2016	Ratification
O		
Oman	22/06/2016	Ratification
P		
Pakistan	22/06/2016	Acceptance
Palau	22/06/2016	Acceptance
Panama	26/06/2016	Ratification
Papua New Guinea	30/06/2016	Ratification
Paraguay	24/06/2016	Acceptance
Peru	26/06/2016	Ratification
Philippines	26/06/2016	Ratification
Poland	22/06/2016	Ratification
Portugal	22/06/2016	Ratification
Q		
Qatar	22/06/2016	Ratification
R		
Republic of Korea	25/06/2016	Ratification
Republic of Moldova	22/06/2016	Ratification
Romania	22/06/2016	Ratification
Russian Federation	22/06/2016	Ratification
Rwanda	21/06/2016	Signature
S		
Saint Kitts and Nevis	22/06/2016	Ratification
Saint Lucia	22/06/2016	Ratification
	22/06/2016	Ratification

Saint Vincent and the Grenadines		
Samoa	22/06/2016	Ratification
San Marino	22/06/2016	Ratification
Sao Tome and Principe	22/06/2016	Ratification
Saudi Arabia	22/06/2016	Ratification
Senegal	22/06/2016	Acceptance
Serbia	22/06/2016	Ratification
Seychelles	22/06/2016	Ratification
Sierra Leone	22/06/2016	Acceptance
Singapore	22/06/2016	Ratification
Slovakia	22/06/2016	Ratification
Slovenia	22/06/2016	Ratification
Solomon Islands	22/06/2016	Ratification
Somalia	21/06/2016	Signature
Somaliland	21/06/2016	Signature
South Africa	22/06/2016	Ratification
South Ossetia	22/06/2016	Ratification
Spain	22/06/2016	Ratification
Sri Lanka	22/06/2016	Acceptance
Sudan	21/06/2016	Signature
Suriname	21/06/2016	Signature
Swaziland	21/06/2016	Signature

Sweden	22/06/2016	Ratification
Switzerland	22/06/2016	Ratification
Syrian Arab Republic	22/06/2016	Acceptance
T		
Taiwan	27/06/2016	Ratification
Tajikistan	22/06/2016	Acceptance
Thailand	22/06/2016	Ratification
The former Yugoslav Republic of Macedonia	22/06/2016	Ratification
Timor-Leste	21/06/2016	Signature
Togo	21/06/2016	Signature
Tonga	22/06/2016	Ratification
Trinidad and Tobago	22/06/2016	Ratification
Tunisia	21/06/2016	Signature
Turkey	22/06/2016	Ratification
Turkmenistan	21/06/2016	Signature
Tuvalu	22/06/2016	Ratification
U		
Uganda	21/06/2016	Signature
Ukraine	21/06/2016	Ratification
United Arab Emirates	21/06/2016	Signature
United Kingdom of Great Britain and Northern Ireland	22/06/2016	Ratification
United Republic of Tanzania	21/06/2016	Signature
United States of America	22/06/2016	Ratification

Uruguay	21/06/2016	Signature
Uzbekistan	24/06/2016	Ratification
V		
Vanuatu	22/06/2016	Signature
Vatican City	21/06/2016	Signature
Venezuela, Bolivarian Republic of	21/06/2016	Signature
Viet Nam	21/06/2016	Signature
Y		
Yemen	21/06/2016	Signature
Z		
Zambia	21/06/2016	Signature
Zimbabwe	21/06/2016	Signature

Copies of this document are available in English, French, Arabic, Hindi, Chinese, and Japanese.

Acknowledgements

There is a prominent and crucial acknowledgment to be made on the content of this novel.

It is to David D. Haines, Ph.D. in immunology. Without his expertise and constant willingness to engage in detailed discussions of the subject matter of this story, it would not have been possible to write it. Without him, I would never have known many of the details I needed in order to tell this story.

I must also thank my mother, Carole B.C. Fox, for looking up specifications on yachts for me.

That is not all that I must thank her for. She put up with me closeting myself away throughout the winter to draft this novel, ignoring most things until it was done. For that, I am very, very grateful. I could not focus on much else until this story was committed to software.

About the Author

Stephanie C. Fox, J.D. is a historian, lawyer, author, editor, and publisher. She is a graduate of William Smith College and of the University of Connecticut School of Law. She runs an editing service called *QueenBeeEdit*, found at www.queenbeeedit.com, which caters to politicians, scientists, and others.

Her imprint is *QueenBeeBooks*.

Stephanie lives in Connecticut, and has written about other topics, including Asperger's, the global financial meltdown, and travelogues of a trip to Kuwait and a trip to Hawai'i.

Her areas of interest include – but are not limited to –history, biographies, women's studies, science fiction, human overpopulation, ecosystems collapse, environmental law, international relations, Asperger's, and cats.

Stephanie has spent time in Manhattan, Hawai'i, France, England, and Venice. She loves cats and worries about the future of our planet.

About the Illustrator

Steve Palmerton is a graduate of the Art Institute of California in Orange County, where he studied Character Designs, Illustration, Background Designs, 2D-3D Concepts, and Concept Art. He specializes in science fiction art, and his portfolio may be viewed at https://www.artstation.com/artist/chelectonus.

He writes: "I excel at creating worlds and exciting places. Bringing interesting shapes to the canvas is what I am passionate about."

www.ingramcontent.com/pod-product-compliance
Lightning Source LLC
Chambersburg PA
CBHW070735120726
47910CB00001B/105